PASSION'S SURRENDER

"Joan, we are both young but let me show you a prince who knows how to please you."

"You speak not of love, my lord," she managed, her voice a shaky whisper. "I am certain you are used to merely commanding any lady you fancy and she is yours to do with as you will, but you cannot expect—you have no right—" She floundered.

He looked as though she had struck him. "I offer you the Prince of England's heart at your feet and you sit there like stone and will have none of it. The hell with reasoning words to a foolish woman I will have!"

His grip on her shoulders tightened, and he slid her to him across the tiny space of bench. Soft thigh pressed to his iron one as he wrapped his powerful arms around her and crushed her back. His mouth was warm, firm, demanding the response of open, soft lips she gave him mindlessly. His hands skimmed her back and hips, kneading, caressing. She slipped sideways so that he held her cradled across his chest while his lips traced icy fire down her throat to her collarbones and lower. She could not breathe, could not think and fascinating, violent colors jumped and reeled through her stunned mind.

"Jeannette, Jeannette, my sweet, you will yield to me, you must. Let me have you. . . ."

EXCITING BESTSELLERS FROM ZEBRA

PASSION'S REIGN   (1177, $3.95)
by Karen Harper
Golden-haired Mary Bullen was wealthy, lovely and refined—and
lusty King Henry VIII's prize gem! But her passion for the handsome Lord William Stafford put her at odds with the Royal
Court. Mary and Stafford lived by a lovers' vow: one day they
would be ruled by only the crown of PASSION'S REIGN.

STORM TIDE   (1230, $3.75)
by Patricia Rae
In a time when it was unladylike to desire one man, defiant,
flamehaired Elizabeth desired two! And while she longed to be
held in the strong arms of a handsome sea captain, she yearned
for the status and wealth that only the genteel doctor could provide—leaving her hopelessly torn amidst passion's raging
STORM TIDE . . . .

HEIRLOOM   (1200, $3.95)
by Eleanora Brownleigh
The surge of desire Thea felt for Charles was powerful enough to
convince her that, even though they were strangers and their marriage was a fake, fate was playing a most subtle trick on them
both: Were they on a mission for President Teddy Roosevelt—or
on a crusade to realize their own passionate desire?

LOVESTONE   (1202, $3.50)
by Deanna James
After just one night of torrid passion and tender need, the dark-
haired, rugged lord could not deny that Moira, with her precious
beaty, was born to be a princess. But how could he grant her
freedom when he himself was a prisoner of her love?

*Available wherever paperbacks are sold, or order direct from the
Publisher. Send cover price plus 50¢ per copy for mailing and
handling to Zebra Books, 475 Park Avenue South, New York,
N.Y. 10016. DO NOT SEND CASH.*

Sweet Passion's Pain

Karen Harper

ZEBRA BOOKS
KENSINGTON PUBLISHING CORP.

ZEBRA BOOKS

are published by

Kensington Publishing Corp.
475 Park Avenue South
New York, N.Y. 10016

First printing: May, 1984

Printed in the United States of America

Part One

Go, heart, hurt with adversity,
And let my lover thy wounds see;
And then say this, as I say thee:
Farewell my joy, and welcome pain,
'Til I see my love again.

Chapter One

On that rare and jeweled day, the great adventure of her life began. The lush blossoms and tender crops of fertile Kent gilded the May morning breeze with their mingled aromas, and nightingale songs floated from the nearby forest depths unutterably sweet. Her beloved home, the large, stone-walled house known in the English shire of Kent as Liddell Manor, reflected its gray stones and windows, beams, and brick chimneys in the encircling moat, but beyond the gardens and orchards, the great Kent Road to London beckoned eternally outward. At first in early dawn it seemed no one stirred, but soon enough the slender, blond girl knew, they would all be upon her: then she would go away to whatever lay out there and this gentle haven of peace and freedom would be hers no more.

It was not that she was afraid, she told herself determinedly as she stood barefooted at the window in a favorite short linen chemise she had long ago outgrown but still stubbornly slept in no matter how her maid railed at her about it. Joan of Kent, as the shire folk called her, had never been afraid of anything—not yet, at least. Besides, since she was granddaughter to the past King Edward I of all England, she had always known deep inside she should never be meek or afraid of anything, even if she were a woman. There had not been one thing yet, in all of her life here at Liddell, she had wanted to possess or to do that she had not had or done. That is, not until a fortnight ago when her eldest brother Edmund, lord of Liddell Manor ever since their father had died so long ago, had come riding home from king's service and told her she was leaving Liddell to be reared at court with the king's family.

Though the sun did not touch her recessed window yet, she pushed the casement open farther and leaned out on her elbows. Her flat stomach scraped a bit on the thick stone ledge and her bare feet swung free of the thin braided carpet on the floor of her little chamber, but this position gave her the full view of the fish pond and walled herb gardens below as she wanted.

Aye, the servants had just finished gathering breakfast from the well-stocked fish pond, and speckled bream or spike-nosed pike would soon enough fill the bellies of the travelers before they all set out for London.

"Poor silly fish," Joan murmured aloud as she wriggled back inside and her feet touched the floor. "Saints, you do not have one bit more say in where you are headed than I do! It is out of a quiet pool and into a seething pot for all of us, I warrant."

The scolding voice behind her was crisp and shrill, but so familiar in its rich Scottish burr that Joan did not even flinch. "Lady Joan! My own dear lassie, skittering about barelegged and mutterin' rebellions. Aye, I caught yer tone and know yer wayward heart about this honor that's befallen ye!"

Joan just rolled her eyes at the wiry, lively old woman, Marta, who had been so many things to her for as long as she could remember—nursemaid, companion, taleteller, playfriend, almost a mother even, since her own lady mother so seldom came out of her room. Joan gave her luxuriant, nearly hip-length hair a wild toss off her shoulder with one hand and shot Marta a sweet and tolerant smile as she sat down hard on the edge of her plump feather bed.

"Now, do not scold, Marta, please. It is our last day here together—my last day—and I could not sleep."

"Stuff and nonsense, lambie. Ye ha' slept like a soldier fresh out a battle sin' ye were a wee lass. The lord be right, ye know. A young woman grown and ye such a beauty to still be the task of plaiting her hair into two long braids to be coiled over each ear. Edmund said it was more in style to gather the hair in two huge netted cauls without braids, but her hair was so bountiful it would all bounce loose after one jog in the saddle and what would watchdog Edmund say then?

Marta bit back her tart reply at Joan's last flippant words. Aye, Edmund, Earl of Kent was right, much as it hurt Marta to admit it. The lass had been badly spoiled, allowed mayhap to run the grounds too freely since he was off to king's service and Joan's other older brother was being reared in the powerful Lord Salisbury's household far to the north. Only in the last year had Edmund married the Lady Anne and settled her at Liddell Manor, but Joan paid scant heed to Anne's meek pronouncement of proper demeanor for a lady.

And, then there was the dark shadow of Joan's mother, the long-widowed Lady Margaret. The tragic loss of two husbands had taken a grim toll on the once lovely, laughing, and strong-willed woman Marta remembered so vividly from her wedding day to the great Scottish Lord John Comyn whose family had always been full loyal to England in the terrible war between the last English king and the Scottish king, Robert the Bruce. The uniting of Margaret, English daughter of Lord Wake, to the Comyn clan was one political marriage that had been happy, and Marta fervently prayed at night on her bony knees that her Joan might have the same good fortune. Even when Lord Comyn died, the newly somber Margaret had found happiness a second time and it was only at her second husband's disgraceful and tragic death that the Lady Margaret had broken.

Marta surveyed her handiwork, the two huge coils of wheat-colored hair she had arranged at the sides of Joan's head. The old woman smiled fondly and her eyes misted. Surely, despite the polish and sophistication the lass lacked, here was a Plantagenet beauty indeed, one to rival King Edward's own fair daughters. It would be years before Joan's rose-and-cream skin would need any touch of court cosmetics like pomades or lead paste, or the eye colors

Marta had heard Edmund speak of to his wife Anne. Joan was fair of skin, with glowing cheeks and the full pouting lips men found desirable no matter what feminine look was supposed to be in style. Joan's head was a lovely oval shape, her cheekbones high, her brows beautifully arched with no need for plucking; her nose was straight and elegant with a slightly pert turn at the end, her lashes darkly fringed for such a fair blonde; and her eyes, the most haunting color of spring violets or of highland heather, seemed to darken when she was angered, which was a bit too often this last month since her lord brother had made clear his plans for her.

And the lass's body showed every promise of lush temptation that would attract many a man, Marta thought, as Joan helped her carefully settle a clean linen chemise, wool kirtle, and squirrel-lined *surcote* over her newly coiffed head. The kirtle, dark blue for riding, was made of perse, a fine light wool suited to this early May day named for the Feasts of St. Philip and St. James in the year of 1344. The kirtle was long-sleeved to ward off road dust; it buttoned from elbow to wrist with tiny, metal studs forged in the shape of rosebuds. As was the current Plantagenet style, the gown draped itself closely to Joan's slender form, accentuating the swell of her high, firm breasts. The oval collar was scalloped and embroidered with tendrils of entwined ivy leaves much like those which covered the outer walls of Liddell Manor and graced the family coat of arms, behind a white, antlered hart.

Low on Joan's waist, Marta helped her settle a narrow leather belt tooled in intricate designs and studded with metal ivy leaves. From the belt hung a lady's dagger. The lass was tall for a maid, long-waisted and leggy, and she wore the four new kirtles and *surcotes* Edmund had ordered for her well, Marta thought proudly. The sorts of garments Joan had been pleased to romp around the grounds in these last fourteen years, like this sort of chemise she insisted on sleeping in—well, all of that was over now, too.

"Marta, what are you doing with my sleeping chemise?

12

Give it to me."

"Foolish lass. Sit ye carefully on the bench an' we'll get on yer new riding boots."

"I will put the boots on. I will not have you kneeling on this floor, but give me my chemise, Marta!"

Joan made a grab for it, and the material ripped at the hem as she pulled it from the woman's grasp. "I *am* taking it, Marta! Oh, now look at it, and I hate to mend. Saints, just go finish the packing, and I shall put this in last. Dear brother Edmund hates for me to be late at midmorning meal and just to think I used to skip it entirely when I had half a notion to!"

Marta bent over the remaining open wood and leather coffer which would go by packhorse with the traveling party carrying Joan's worldly goods to court. "'Tis said at great Edward's court the fashion for bed be naught but bare skin, my lassie, an' I believe Lord Edmund told ye that clearly enough the other eve."

"I care not. This is what I sleep in. It is comfortable and warmer. There will probably be dreadful drafts in Windsor Castle or Westminster or Sheen or wherever they all live. I know I shan't have my own room and bed anymore— Edmund says three or four queen's ladies to one room—but I do not care a whit. I shall set my own styles, you will see, Marta."

Marta kept her eyes on her packing and her mouth shut as she heard Joan flop down on the bench at the end of her bed and struggle with her stiff new boots of imported Spanish leather. Aye, Edmund has spent a pretty penny on the new wardrobe for the lass; yet all his preaching, his veiled threats even, had not put a halt to the maid's willfulness. And if she ever caught wind of the scandal surrounding her father's death and the part the king and queen and even the handsome Edward, their beloved Prince of Wales, had played in it, there would be Satan's fee to pay then, and sure of it! If Joan of Kent, young though she be, were head of this family rather than her two elder brothers, the restful white hart on the family crest might well be a white, raging whirlwind.

Marta finished the packing and followed Joan down-stairs, careful to carry the child's cloak which would cover her *surcote* if it were rainy or chill on the way to London. The trip today would be short, commencing at late morn, Marta reflected, since they would only go as far as the great abbey at Rochester, seat of the shire, before sunset. With the nervous, reclusive Lady Margaret carried in a special covered litter Edmund had had built by carpenters here at Liddell, traveling farther in one day would be foolhardy.

Much to Marta's chagrin, she did not see Joan in the great hall where the meal was nearly spread. Glenda, who was watchmaid and servant to the Lady Margaret, had arranged a small wooden tray to take upstairs to her seclusive ward, and Morcar, the family's soothsayer, stood near a window apparently gazing out at nothing in particular. Marta's quick eyes scanned the large, lofty room again. No Joan. At least, praise St. Andrew, the lord and his seven retainers, who would guide the party to London and beyond to Windsor, were not down yet to slap their riding gloves impatiently on their palms or click their spurs or frown when they saw neither of the two ladies they would escort were ready.

Joan's brown traveling cape still over her arm, Marta hurried to the thin, old man who had been Joan's dead father's astrologer before Lord Edmund was caught in the dreadful mire of political upheaval that led to his bloody death. The practical Marta always thought that long white hair, pale skin, ice-blue eyes, and a slightly bowed back made Morcar appear to know much more than he could possibly foresee even with his charts and maps and stars.

"Morcar, ha' ye seen th' Lady Joan? She came down but a moment ahead a me."

The old man did not turn his head, but only lifted one blue-veined hand to the high window ledge. "Down in the walled gardens. Walking, Marta, just holding her lute."

Marta made a cluck-cluck with her tongue and whirled to

move away. But Morcar's other hand darted out to stay her as his pale blue eyes held Marta's troubled brown ones.

"Losing your chick is hard, I know, but leave her be. She needs some calm before the storm."

"What she needs, sir stargazer, be a firm hand to get her in here at her place—without her lute—so that her brother an' his comrades will not be out a sorts when he comes down all champin' at th' bit to be off and neither Joan nor her lady mother are about the hall."

"The Lady Margaret will be out only at the last minute, Glenda says, and we must hope there will be no pitiful scene. All those long years in that room—ah, she is a mere ghost of the lady we all remember. She is eaten by thoughts of revenge still, though she drifts in a fantasy world of her own making sometimes. This desire to take the vows of the Poor Clares of St. Francis and live cloistered in London for her last years—I pray it is for the best."

"But ye read th' stars, Morcar," Marta could not resist the gibe. "Can ye not truly read whether or not it be for th' best?"

He looked away, back out the window, and a wan smile lifted his thin lips and the white mustache that covered his mouth. "Ah, aye, of course. And that is my own special agony. It has been and will yet be."

Marta moved a step closer to the old man and lowered her voice. "Ye read th' planets for Lady Margaret last week, did ye not? And she asked if her taking th' vows a th' St. Clares would give her final peace?" Marta pursued.

"She asked that, aye."

"And Lord Edmund said ye assured her she'd be finding final peace there with the St. Clares in London."

"Aye, Mistress Marta, true enough."

"Then why do ye not show a little joy for them? Lady Margaret to the peace she ha' never found sin' her lord ha' been murdered and my Lady Joan to better things. Aye?"

Morcar nodded at the window but his eyes seemed to glaze over again. "But at the moment, she is so untouched, so free, so peaceful, Marta."

15

"Joan?" Marta's birdlike hand darted out from under the cloak to grasp Morcar's wrist. "My Lady Joan? Did ye read her signs, too? She said naught of it. What is it? What did ye see? She will come to no harm at th' court that slew her father?"

"Calm your feathers, Marta." Morcar's papery thin voice came to her ears. "I am old, I have seen much, the wheel revolves from fortune to fall to fortune again for all of us."

"Aye, but for Joan—"

With an amazing amount of strength for his frail appearance, the old man disengaged Marta's hand. "Leave off, Marta. I hear the lord's men on the stairs. I have given the Lady Margaret my word and I will not tell Joan what I have read until she is married."

"Married? When?"

"Leave off, I said. I am weary and the great journey has not even begun. I have no wish to leave Liddell, but like the Lady Joan, I am sent for. Remember, maids of Joan's age are marriageable at great Edward's court, as well you know, Marta. And surely, Joan will have time at court before she is wed."

Marta's eyes narrowed at Morcar's suddenly stern profile, and her heart beat very fast. "Wed high or low? The lass be so willful as ye know, Morcar, so passionate—to have things her way."

"Aye, but I will say no more." He turned to face the direction of the door through which issued the rumble of male conversation and laughter. "And, Marta, be not so foolish as to try to question the Lady Margaret herself. She is beset this day with fears for her journey out of her safe sanctuary in that room upstairs. And to tell true, I told her little of the Lady Joan's charts. What will be will be."

He moved away from the window, but ignoring propriety in front of the lord's men, Marta scurried after him.

"Please, Lord Morcar, by St. Andrew, the lass be all I ha' had to love these last long years sin' Lady Margaret turned against th' child."

He looked calmly at Marta, and his austere features softened as he gazed down on the wiry, petite Scotswoman. "Be calm in your heart, little Marta. Tell me truly, who would need the stars to read the Lady Joan's future? Will not she be well loved? Admired? And set her own ways and styles? Do you not remember the first chart we did for the Lord Edmund and Lady Margaret when the little Joan was born in the middle of July the summer her father died? Born under Cancer, eager for action, ruled by the moon, a romantic, moody, curious—an alluring woman. Hold to that, little Marta. I am sorry you shall not be with her there for she could have need of your sharp tongue and practical Scots brain, eh? I had hoped to live out my days here in quiet, green Kent, not back at the court of a Plantagenet king whose family had some part in my Lord Edmund's death. But the king has suddenly remembered my service to his dear uncle. The king speaks and we all—almost all—obey."

A strange smile lit his mouth again as he moved stiffly away. By St. Andrew, Marta thought, it was fortunate that the Lady Margaret in her litter would force their slow travel pace, because that frail, old man would never live to see London otherwise.

Lord Edmund, who looked as little like his father as Joan strongly resembled their sire, entered and stopped stock-still across the room. His eyes were violet, like poor Lady Margaret's, but other than that trait he shared with Joan, the twenty-three-year-old Edmund, Earl of Kent, and the Lady Joan looked nothing alike. Brown-haired and round-faced, Edmund resembled his mother's Wake family lineage; while, but for the eyes, Joan was as blond and fair a Plantagenet as her executed father.

"Marta? Joan is ready to eat with us, is she not?" Lord Edmund's clear voice interrupted the tumbling flow of her thoughts.

"Aye, milord. I shall fetch her direct. She but stepped out in th' garden for a wee breath a air."

He shook his head once and raised his hand as if to ward

her off. "No, Marta. I shall see to her. The Lady Anne will be down soon. You may help Glenda and the servants. They have orders to bring my lady mother down at the last minute before we set out."

He spun sharply on his heel and Marta's eyes followed his black- and red-garbed figure as he disappeared from the great hall into the corridor. "Aye, for th' love a St. Andrew," Marta murmured under her breath, feeling much better as she always did whenever she invoked the patron saint of Scotland. "No one ever said anyone with blue Plantagenet blood in their veins does not know how to give orders or insist their own will be done!"

Outside in the midmorning sun, Joan stood at the edge of a fish pond staring at the reflection of the manorhouse and sky. She cradled her precious lute against her like a child and let the sun on her back chase the chill of pending departure from her veins. On a whim, she bent to pick a little handful of violets, purple trilliums, and forget-me-nots at her feet.

"Take a care not to fall in, Joan. We hardly have time to fish you out and you are wetting the hems of that lovely new kirtle on the dew."

"Oh, my Lord Edmund. I did not hear you. But it cannot be time to go already."

Her brother gave her that quick, half-mouthed smile of his, and his eyes went approvingly over her appearance. At least he did not seem to be out of sorts this morning, Joan thought, much relieved. It just would not do to be arguing with him on this last morning here in who knew how long. Little butterflies of apprehension fluttered in her stomach, but she beat the feeling down.

Edmund looked ready for riding and very grand in his black tunic which had red piping over his powerful chest and shoulders. He sported a smart black beaver hat with a narrow brim jauntily turned up in back, and a short fur-lined travel cape swung from his shoulders. His gilt spurs clinked slightly as he approached.

"This is a lovely day, a special and great day for you, Joan. I want to be certain you understand that. Mother and I have decided this is best for you."

"As you say, my lord."

There was a moment's awkward silence between them while birds twittered from the cherry tree behind and the green earth, damp after last night's gentle rain, seemed to breathe out a heady freshness. She wished with a sudden stab of longing she knew Edmund better—knew and trusted him fully. He was some years older than she and had been reared, until his majority, at Lord Salisbury's grand household at Wark Castle far to the north, where her brother John, five years older than she, was now. She loved Edmund, of course, deep down, but they had never been a family, not since mother did not seem to love her anymore.

"The lute, Joan. You asked if you might take it, and I agreed despite the fact few court ladies play their own instruments. That is only a new trend and there are plenty of trained court musicians you will enjoy. It should be wrapped and packed if you are as worried about its safety today as you were last week."

"Aye, brother, I am. I told you it means a great deal to me."

"Aye, and your sweet voice with it is charming, I admit that." Edmund put an index finger on her arm as if to reassure her, but immediately moved two steps back toward the house. Then, as if to deliberately shatter the tenuous moment between them, he took up an old subject they had argued much over these past weeks.

"But I still do not approve of that glib-tongued French beggar, Roger Wakeley, wandering in like that when I was off to king's service and living here for over a year without my permission."

He held out both hands as if to ward off her protest. "Aye, you have told me, lady, he was a talented singer and musician, and I suppose it is quaint you learned so well, but you ought to have been busy enough with your tutor studying French, Latin, and numbers. It is an excellent lady's education without all the other fripperies you insist on, Joan. Your stubborn penchant for love songs and full-blown romances when your first responsibility is to learn chatelaine household duties is quite beyond me. You shall not be out riding free as the wind or playing lute songs in some forest glade at court, I assure you."

She ignored the slight to her own abilities to manage a household, but her pulse beat faster at his slurs on the poor, banished Roger Wakeley who had arrived with a fever and a broken leg and had stayed to have both mended by the manor leech. That she'd caught the fever he had and nearly died until the ugly swelling under her arm burst and drained, and that two servants caught the malady and died hardly mattered later. For Roger, in the year before he was asked to leave by a young Edmund, had taught her to play and sing and memorize a hundred *chansons* and troubadour and *jongleur* melodies—a whole world of beauty and joy to help fill the hours dear Marta and the servants could not. And now Roger Wakeley had been gone two long years anyway, so how dare Edmund bring it all up again now!

"I do not wish us to have this argument repeatedly, my lord," she said with a steady voice. "I shall try to please you, but you have no right to slander my dear friend and music teacher. You were gone, gone a whole year, and then you made him leave, and there was no one left but Marta since Mother even hates the sight of me—"

She stopped the rush of words, shocked that she had voiced the unspeakable thought. Tears crowded her thick lashes, threatening to spill down her cheeks. Her full lower lip pouted, then trembled. Edmund looked as surprised as she.

"My dear little sister—*chérie*—do not say so of our lady mother. Do not think so." He moved nearer, barely touching her elbows with his big hands. "She has been ill, ill and so unhappy since our dear father died. This, of course, you know."

20

She nodded mutely, her eyes as purple as the flowers crushed in her hand against the neck of the lute she held before her as if it could be a buffer against her brother's coldness.

Edmund's mind raced. Of course, she knew that much, but what else had she been told or had she guessed? She seemed so young and naïve to him still; yet she was very clever, and after all, she was the one who had been living here in this house with a half-demented, grief-crazed woman all these years.

"Joan, let me explain, and then we must go in for a quick meal before we set out. See, through the gate. I can hear the horses being brought around already."

"I am not the slightest bit hungry, my lord."

"I do not care. By the saints' precious blood, lady, you need some sustenance before you ride six hours to Rochester. Now, mark my words well. Our lady mother—it is not that she detests the sight of you, not at all. Rather, she loves your face too much and it hurts her.

Joan's voice sounded strangled in her throat. "Loves my face? It hurts—her!"

His hands reached to steady her at the elbows. "Our father. You did not know him, I know, *chérie*, as you were not yet born, but you resemble him greatly and you were the last child. You do see what I am trying to say, do you not? They were very, very much in love, our parents, and quite simply, you bring back all the agony of her departed happiness and the tragedy of losing him."

"But that is all wrong, Edmund! If that is what she feels, it is so wrong. If that were me, I would cherish that child, hold her close, a gift and memorial of the lost love," she protested, her voice quivering.

"Hush, Joan. We cannot judge other people, nor be other people. I am telling you she loves you, but it is just too hard for her."

"Let me go, my lord. That is fine, just fine. I understand, really; it is all right. She has always tolerated a short visit from me on saints' days, several times during Yule. I am the one who could not bear it after a while with her, and I would make excuses to leave that little inviolate sanctuary she keeps up there." She gestured wildly toward the small window above, from which the Lady Margaret could view the vast beauty of Kent if she were so moved. Was there a face, a wan, sad face, pressed to the glazed panes of glass and lead even now? No, of course not. This whole nightmare of Mother, this whole day she was leaving home, was one hideous dream.

Joan skirted the frustrated Edmund and strode headlong for the house before he caught her and swung her around to face him again.

"Look, Joan, I know it cannot have been easy, but she has been ill and more and more terrified to go out of that little room as the years have passed. She is almost fifty-two now, she senses death over the horizon, and she wants to make amends. She has been sick and hateful and she knows it."

"Now! There, you have said it. She has hated me!"

"No, no, that is not it. Hates that she lost one husband, then a second. Hates what life has done to her and hates those who murdered our father."

Joan's sharp mind halted, then spun back through all the whispers and half-bits of knowledge about her father's death, things she had heard over the years and buried in her mind: beheaded for treason; an innocent, gentle man beheaded for treason against the crown when all he had tried to do was inquire into the murder of the present king's father, a foul murder committed by an inhuman demon usurper named Roger Mortimer.

Her breath caught in her throat at her next words. "But, my lord, our dear King Edward had the murderer of both our father and his own arrested and executed as soon as he could seize his right to rule back from Mortimer. Was Mortimer not hanged, drawn, and quartered? Who then is there left for mother to hate all these years?"

Edmund hesitated. By the rood, this wisp of a girl argued

like a cleric from the Inns of Court in London. He had decided long ago she must never know the entire story; indeed, he knew he was taking a gamble with life's dice to take her to court where she might hear the whispers someday, but Queen Philippa had asked for Joan, to rear, and it did the family no good for her to be a cloistered nun here at moated Liddell. It was true, it was pertinent, and it would obscure the more devastating truth it cloaked.

"No, Joan, there is one other left, an accomplice to Mortimer, who carried out his orders to kill the king and no doubt helped to arrange for our father's death."

"Who? Will not the king execute him now?"

"No. You see, he escaped to Flanders and still lives there. Only, there are occasional rumors he may try to come back. Maltravers, Sir John de Maltravers, is his name—from a rich Dorsetshire family."

"Not so rich anymore, I warrant, now the king surely holds his lands," Joan said, and the trembling against his hands ceased.

He had indeed played that move well, Edmund thought, suddenly proud of himself for outwitting this shrewd, little hoyden when he had to. Just so she never learned the rest of it, the rumors that de Maltravers might return with full pardon and restitution to England—and that it was King Edward and Queen Philippa themselves who might pardon the man. It was even claimed by some that de Maltravers's fine position in Flanders was due to the good will of the king. At least Joan's quick mind was on de Maltravers now, a villain she could hate without ever meeting. And in the process, she had, perhaps, believed that their mother's insane bitterness was focused on the faceless de Maltravers and not herself. He certainly had no plans to tell Joan that de Maltravers's wife still lived on a farm in Dorsetshire which the Plantagenets held in his name.

"You will eat with me, Joan, and then we shall be on our way, fair maid," he ventured boldly. "Anne and I will want you back for visits when it is allowed, of course. Come on in now."

She followed him through the arched doorway crested with the white, antlered hart, the coat of arms of their dead father that was Edmund's heritage now with the house and title. "Of course," Joan repeated low, "when it is allowed." She held the wilted purple flowers on her lap while she ate and kept her lute by her side, too.

An hour later as the bell in the little chapel across the cobbled inner courtyard tolled its monotonous farewell, Edmund's men mounted fifteen strong to accompany them to Rochester, and tomorrow beyond. Joan's lute was wrapped in linen strips and, with a down pillow on either side of it, stuffed in the hemp sack on her palfrey's sleek brown flank. Although Edmund tried to insist she wait, mounted, with the others until the servants and he brought Lady Margaret down from her haven above, Joan refused and stood instead clutching a tiny bunch of blue forget-me-nots from the walled garden. All of them stared at the covered litter—with its four poles, canopy, and curtain— awaiting the Lady Margaret.

Joan stood on one foot, then the other trying not to panic or to weep. The vast gray, stone walls, covered by their tapestry of ivy, suddenly never looked more foreboding. A horse snorted; someone's spurs clinked while the bell tolled on.

Then, for the first time in these sad, slow revolving years, Margaret of Liddell stood on the front steps of her dead husband's ancestral home. Edmund held her by one gray-swathed arm, and her faithful Glenda by the other while Marta appeared behind. Everything seemed to stop, to totter for one instant on that threshold. The Lady Margaret, her head covered with a pleated veil, her neck hidden by a vast wimple that flowed over her shoulders, paused, and her violet eyes blinked wildly in the sun. Her gaze jumped across the courtyard to the waiting men and horses and then fastened on Joan. It seemed as if she might speak, but

Edmund nodded to Glenda and they hurried her down the few broad stairs. Then Edmund loosed her arm to bend and lift her into the litter. Before she could stop herself, Joan moved toward the little clustered trio.

"My lady Mother, I am so glad you are here and it is such a beautiful day for you. Here, from the gardens, flowers—forget-me-nots, Mother."

The desperate violet eyes darted, focused, widened. Her mother's voice sounded strange, for Joan could never recall it however hard she tried. "Oh, aye, dear Joan and going to be reared at their court. I am so sorry, Joan."

Sorry for my going away, that I have to be brought up at court, or that you never really loved me, Joan wanted to ask.

"Aye. Thank you, Mother. Here." She pried apart her mother's fingers tightly balled into a fist. Lady Margaret took the bunch of flowers. Joan had meant to give them to Marta when she came down, but Marta would understand.

Violet eyes met violet eyes. "Forget-me-nots," her mother said, but her eyes closed and she never looked at the flowers.

"Joan, get back now," Edmund whispered. "You can talk tonight. It will be dark before we see the walls and spires of Rochester if we do not set out." He lifted his mother, and his shoulders and head hid her slight, gray-cloaked form from view as he bent to place her in the litter and drew the curtains closed. It was immediately silent inside.

Fighting back tears, Joan hugged Marta good-bye again and let Edmund give her a boost onto her favorite fine black palfrey, Sable, which he was letting her keep at court. They clattered out across the cobbled courtyard and past the walled flower and herb gardens. They rode under the rusty, spike-teethed portcullis and funneled across the wooden drawbridge down the lane between the white-blossomed cherry, pear, and apple orchards. The gray, ivy-clad walls and Norman-built towers seemed to collapse slowly behind them under the clear cup of blue porcelain sky; then Liddell Manor was swallowed by the thickening forest beyond the little hamlet where their thirty tenant farmers and serfs in the lord's demesne resided. When they turned northwest toward Rochester, the noon sun beat warm on their heads and hands.

The pace was ploddingly slow because of Lady Margaret's litter, but Joan did not mind. The day was precious and Mother had taken the flowers. Maybe if it were allowed, as Edmund said, she could leave the court for a little while when they were at Westminster Palace to visit Mother at the Poor Clares down the Thames a way. It would be a little while, no doubt, before a novice took her final vows, and after all, Mother being cloistered was nothing new.

As the motion of Sable's bouncing back became hypnotic, Joan began to daydream. She would meet the wonderful Plantagenets and, despite whatever Edmund would say, play a French song for the queen and king. After all, they were claiming half of France through the king's French mother and there were rumors of war between the English and French over that, Edmund had said. Perhaps all the knights at court would rush off to war as Edmund always had, and she would have free rein over whatever vast royal forests or wildernesses were out there somewhere. If only the Plantagenet princes and princesses would like her, maybe they could be like the friends or family she had never had. And then, Morcar was along, though she knew he loathed leaving Liddell only a little less than she. But it was all a great adventure and on such a lovely day. She would look back on this journey as the beginning of her new life, she decided, and without realizing it, she began to hum, then sing low in her sweet, clear voice.

Several of Edmund's men turned to grin at her or winked and whispered to each other, and one who had carefully flirted with her all week, Lyle Wingfield, dropped back to eye her thoroughly as he always did. He was charming enough, she supposed, as she felt his gaze and blushed to see him stare, but she defiantly went on with one of the first songs her dear, lost friend Roger Wakeley had ever taught her:

"When the nightingale singeth,
  The woods wax green;
  Leaf and grass and blossoms
  Spring in May, I have seen."

Her voice trailed off, and she sent Lyle Wingfield her coldest glance, but he was not to be put off so easily.

"I know the words to that French *chanson, demoiselle*," he said and grinned broadly to melt the frost of her stare. "You will be very welcome at court, I assure you, *chérie*, for your brother will not always be so close about, eh?"

To her dismay, he proceeded to taunt her with the next two lines of the stanza which she knew all too well but had just decided not to sing:

"And love is to my heart
  Gone with a spear so keen,
  Night and day my blood it drinketh
  My heart in suffering."

She surprised herself by laughing in delight at the tease. "Not I, sir. Speak and sing for yourself. I will have none of foolish love's entanglements on me."

Why, it is easy and such fun to set a man back on his heels like this, she thought. Her laughter danced again on the forest breeze as she darted one quick glance through her thick-fringed lashes at the young man's beaming face before she looked back to the road ahead.

Chapter Two

At the great Priory of the St. Clares in bustling London town, the party of Liddell travelers spent the second night away from home. The prestigious sister house of the sprawling Abbey of the Holy Order of St. Francis just north of St. Paul's Cathedral, the St. Clares' was the frequent last refuge of pious noble ladies who, hearing the approach of death's steady footfalls, took their vows and donned coarse gray habits to escape any possibility of hell's fires. With full reliance that the purity of the holy, long-dead St. Francis, and their huge monetary contributions to the already wealthy abbey would assure them entrance into heaven, they remained within the gray walls cloistered with their memories and their continual prayers.

Joan and her mother were housed by the nuns in their dormer while the men stayed next door at the huge abbey. Yet Joan saw little of her mother until she was ready to set out for the rest of the journey with Edmund and his men the next morn. Deep inside, Joan had expected no less; she had only hoped for some last night of trust; of conversation, acceptance, or revelation—of what, she did not know. Joan slept little and her pounding thoughts reverberated within her like the steady clanging of the distant chapel bell at compline: London, London. She was in London, and tomorrow, Windsor, the court. My new life. The royal court.

At dawn she and Edmund bid Lady Margaret farewell in a small Gothic chapel lit by wavering candlelight. Already the St. Clares' newest novice had clad herself in the order's gray, shapeless robe with its small, attached hood, a cord belt around her slender form. Her feet, despite the chill of the smooth flagstones underfoot, were bare.

Edmund and Joan both knelt briefly, awkwardly, as if to receive her blessing.

"Do not worry ever for John or Joan, Mother," Edmund whispered as he rose, his round face suddenly gaunt and drawn. "I will see that John gets on with the Salisburys and Joan, of course, will be fine at court."

Lady Margaret's eyes darted to Joan's bent head before the girl stood.

"Aye, Joan," her voice came, a wavering wisp of a sound in the wan candle glow. "Joan, at court with them. I will send for you when it is time, my dear Joan. When it is my time."

The words echoed in Joan's jumbled mind: dear Joan . . . when it is my time, she had said. She called me her dear Joan.

"My lady Mother, you must not speak of your time," Joan heard herself say. "You will be fine, too. You shall see, but I—I will come if you wish."

"Aye. And then we shall speak of everything." Her mother faltered, but just as Joan raised her head to ask what things she meant, Edmund took Joan's arm and pulled her to her feet.

"We shall be off then. The court is yet twenty miles away, you know, Joan."

His firm grip on her arm tugged his sister a step back, and the girl nearly tripped over her skirts as she rose.

"Aye, so far away," Lady Margaret echoed. She raised one pale palm. "God bless you, my children."

"God bless, dear Mother."

"The saints keep you safe."

Joan and Edmund backed away from the unreal, stilted little scene, then turned through the low arched door of the small chapel.

"She seems quite good this morn, more steady," Edmund said, without turning his head as he hurried Joan down the corridor.

"You did not need to make our farewell so sudden," Joan

29

shot back, not breaking her long strides to keep up. "She seemed to want to say something, and I do not like the way she spoke of 'her time coming.' She will live a long time yet. She must, Edmund."

A Poor Clare nun accompanied them now, scurrying along, evidently to bid them farewell in the courtyard, so Edmund lowered his voice.

"Nonsense. It is only she is relieved to be here and safe, but I will feel better when we get you safely into the queen's charge at Windsor. Yesterday you chattered all the way about the excitement of busy London. Just wait until you catch sight of beautiful, vast Windsor. It will lift your spirits from this silent place."

The petite nun bobbed her head as if to agree with Edmund's judgment of the cloisters and swung open the narrow oaken door into the cobbled courtyard where their men and horses awaited. Joan and Edmund blinked in the blatant shaft of early morning sunlight.

"I am excited about London, Edmund, Windsor too, the court. But Mother seems to fear it so. She always calls the king and queen 'them,' and looks so odd when she says it."

"Nonsense," he repeated more sharply and gave her arm a quick shake as if she were a linen doll. He boosted her up on Sable's waiting back and Joan fell belligerently silent while the little nun at the door waved and trilled, "*Benedicite!*" over and over.

The avid-eyed Lyle Wingfield grinned to bid Joan a good morrow. And soon, though she meant it not to be so easy, her heart did lift again as their party departed the stony embrace of the sequestered priory in the middle of the busy city. Excitedly, Joan fingered the new little brass St. Christopher medal depicting the infant Jesus carried on the shoulder of the patron saint of travelers. The prioress had given it to her after vespers last night. They turned west on crowded Fleet Street amidst the screams of hawkers and vendors who sold from pushcarts or open shops guarded by huge hanging signs that advertised their trade.

"There are over fifty goldsmiths' shops on the next street, the Strand," Lyle Wingfield called to her, and she shot him a smile. After all, Edmund had turned silent and sullen late yesterday as they got closer to leaving Mother at the St. Clares', and she needed someone to pump for answers to her myriad questions.

"Are we nearly to the king's palace at Westminster yet?" she shouted back to Lyle. "I wish to see it even though the court is elsewhere now."

"Wait until we clear this street, my Lady Joan. When you see the fair sight of any of great Edward's palaces, you will know it for a fact!"

And Lyle was right. When their little entourage cleared the press of narrow daub and wooden houses leaning inward above them, each succeeding story overhead shouldering out the sky, the vista of the western suburbs along the Strand opened up before their view: the beautiful stone homes of the rich swept down immaculate lawns to the sparkling Thames dotted by marble piers at which floated tethered, painted barges. Then Joan's eyes lifted higher to the distant spires of the great abbey and palace of Westminster that lay ahead.

Even Edmund roused himself from his brooding at the sight of the Gothic arches, carved statues, and turreted rooftops of Westminster. His horse nosed Lyle Wingfield's big chestnut roan away from Sable's glistening black flanks. With an eager finger Edmund pointed out the wings of the palace which nearly touched the church, erected in the form of a huge cross, wherein were laid to rest the past Plantagenet kings and queens including their own grandfather, King Edward I.

"I shall visit there as soon as I can," Joan assured Edmund. "I wish Father were buried there, too."

"So do I, Joan, but we have spoken quite enough of that tragedy already today," he returned grimly, and she wondered how he could think they had spoken of that when their talk had been only of their farewell to Mother.

The palace and the city dropped behind them as they

31

followed the Old Richmond Road toward Windsor. It led through open meadows and forests, providing an occasional glint of river on their left. Only old Morcar remained stonily silent as the travelers chatted and bantered despite gathering rain clouds. At midday they halted to water the horses and devour the cheese, wine, and cold partridge pies the nuns had given them; then they pushed on again under a newly leaden-hued sky.

Traffic on the road around them swelled as they passed the palace at Richmond and pushed on: litters, drovers' carts, painted ladies' chairs, and important-looking men on sleek horses jostled, crowded, and cursed in French or English. Joan wanted to ask Edmund or Lyle the questions which had crowded to her lips in the last two days—the entire last fortnight since she had known she would come here to live with *them*, as mother said. What were they really like, these distant, lofty, glowing, royal Plantagenets to whom she was related and somehow linked? Like stars, like the glistening crown diamonds set in the fathomless velvet heavens, she thought, answering her own question. But something, some feeling held her back from the inquiry, as if in asking, she would know too much to still be safe and in control of her life as she had always been before this last month.

"Look there, on that hill above the timbered valley," she bubbled to Lyle the instant a new horizon rose to view. "Is not that Windsor, my lord?"

Lyle Wingfield grinned from ear to ear and dared to wink at her even as Edmund watched. "Aye, *demoiselle*. I told you that you would know her on sight. Only a blind, old fool could miss Windsor flaunting herself like a blowsy hussy upon the hill for all to see."

She thought the knave's choice of words despicable, but she was too excited to break the moment to tell him so. Above the wooded Thames Valley, like an imposing queen, rose huge, gray Windsor in rugged, solid grandeur: a massive protective wall studded with watchtowers encircled a lofty, round tower anchored in the central keep with a little town huddled at its stony skirts. But even as they rode down into the valley, raindrops from the bulging clouds overhead splattered them, and Joan quickly pulled up her hooded cloak to keep her head and shoulders dry.

The rain seemed to do little to dampen the brash market crowd in the narrow streets of Windsor town. The brief cloudburst merely settled the drifting dust which Joan had come to ignore despite the fact that they were thoroughly coated with it, but it wet everyone's hair including her own heavy, side plaits, which had managed to pull loose since she was hardly as good at braiding them as dear Marta had been. She would die, simply die, if anyone who ever knew Queen Philippa would glimpse her like this, so dirty and wet and road-worn. But then Edmund would surely never allow that. Why, she could even smell the woolen dampness of her once-clean and pressed deep blue perse dress.

Amidst cries and shouts for hot pies or fresh strawberries, they clattered down to the very foot of tall Windsor Castle, wending their way carefully, and passed through the portcullis gate into the Lower Ward. Everywhere above them, suddenly, in the freshening breeze and dwindling raindrops, flew the gold and azure flags and pennants of the Plantagenet kings.

Joan's wide eyes darted to and fro as Edmund stepped forward to head off Lyle Wingfield's quick move to help her down. Her legs and backside ached, her stomach rumbled with hunger, she felt muddy and wet and bedraggled, but the hubbub in the vast stretch of cobbled courtyard and the grassy Lower Ward was wonderful! In the glazed cobbles, now that the shower had ended, there were bumpy mirror images of every fine horse and hurrying person. Pages in liveries of various colors dashed by; important-looking church people and messengers strode here and there in no apparent pattern; and drovers with carts of animals, vegetables, and fruits lumbered past to two large entry ways beyond.

"Oh, it is marvelous—so busy, just like a day at the shire

fair. Do you see anyone—you know—important?" she asked, but Edmund merely motioned her over to the left as if she had not spoken. Old Morcar had been helped from his horse, and he fell into a slow, weaving step behind them as they entered through a small, low door in the foot of what Edmund said was Curfew Tower.

"Sit here, Joan. Morcar, over here. The men will probably scatter with the horses, but just rest a few minutes, and I shall be back directly to tell you where you are both to go."

"But, my Lord Edmund," Joan interrupted, "I thought surely you would know where we are to stay. You said I would be with two or three other ladies in the queen's wing."

"Just hush, Joan. I am as wet and tired as you are. I cannot merely drag you in all unannounced and wander through the queen's apartments looking for Euphemia de Heselaston to find where you are to bed, you know. Sit here with Morcar, I said, and I shall inquire about both of you."

She sank uncertainly down by the weary-looking old man in the little entry room where others were waiting, and a fat, oily man who appeared to be some sort of gatekeeper eyed her now and again. She and Morcar sat quietly, exhausted, on the hard bench for a quarter of an hour while Joan boldly stared down the impolite eyes. Her awe at being in such a wonderful place ebbed, and impatience flooded in.

Morcar shifted next to her on the bench, and before she realized he was asleep, she spoke. "I need to stretch a bit, Morcar. I am sure Edmund will not mind. Oh, I did not mean to startle you. However can you sleep and we just arrived?"

The old soothsayer's long, damp hair looked stringy, and she wondered why he had not covered it with the hood of his black cape in the shower. Strange, but she had hardly given poor, decrepit Morcar a thought, and he had been there at the back of the traveling party all the time, silent and watchful like this.

"Not sleeping, Lady Joan, not really sleeping. Too tired to sleep, but not you, eh? You are here, and now it begins."

"A new life, you mean?"

"Aye, lady. All of it. And you are too excited to just sit here in this dim little tower room when all that life awaits out there, eh?"

"It is taking Edmund a terribly long time, I think."

"It is all vast, Lady Joan, vast and busy out there. Step out a moment if you wish. All will be as it will be, one way or the other, whatever you do."

Joan turned to him to deny those words even though she knew the old man always talked in riddles about the stars and the future. Someday, though she hardly believed in all those readings of the heavens like Edmund and Mother did, she might ask him to tell her own future.

He seemed to doze again, and despite the continual stares of those who came and went in the tower room, Joan stood and shook out her damp cloak. She folded it, placed it next to the motionless Morcar on the bench and went to the door. Stepping out, she moved a little way along the stone wall to more inconspicuously survey the scene. The rain had completely ended and a fresh May breeze caressed her face and heavy, damp hair. The plait over her left ear hung so bedraggled that she loosed it and shook it free, then the other. Her damp, wheat-hued hair cascaded freely down her back.

Keeping an eye on the Curfew Tower door in case Edmund should come stalking back from wherever he had gone so abruptly, she skirted a cluster of horses several hooded pages held and stepped back into a little, recessed wooden doorway in the stone wall. Despite her fascination with the continually shifting courtyard scene, she heard and felt a distant clattering and clanging through the door behind her. Intrigued, she turned and pressed her ear to it. As her shoulder leaned into the door, it creaked slowly open.

Down a little flight of stone steps, a narrow courtyard met her startled eyes. A lone horseman on a huge, ebony destrier charged at a post attached to a rotating wooden arm which was mounted with a shield. He charged and wheeled and charged again madly slashing a big, two-sided sword at the swinging post and shield. The warrior was all in black, even his partial armor; a gauntlet on his sword arm, greaves on his shins, and a narrow-visored helmet on his head. His relentless path had churned the damp earth to mud; under his horse's hoofs was a deepening black mire.

Without thinking, Joan stepped inside the door and closed it on the busy courtyard behind her. Here, within these narrow, private walls, the knight wheeled and clattered to the post again. It was only the sort of quintain practice all knights like to use to prepare for battle, Joan realized, only somehow this was different. The rider seemed in deadly earnest as though a whole battlefield of war lay before his horse's charging hoofs. The quintain spun wildly, and when the knight rode away to turn again, Joan moved farther down the steps.

The man, even in proportion to the massive size of the black war-horse he rode, looked huge. As he bent forward for the next charge, Joan noted how his muscular chest, shoulders, and arms stretched his black, leather gambeson taut under the fine hauberk of dark chain mail molded to his body. The dull silver glint of armor over his brawny shins and left forearm and the conical helmet with narrow eyeslit echoed the slickness of his garments and the lathered gleam of the horse's flanks. Only then did she note the rider's right arm was tied closely to his broad chest in a sort of makeshift sling.

Intrigued and certain the rider would not see her, as he never turned his head to glance her way through the narrow slit of his visor, she edged along the narrow stretch of wall to watch his next mad charge. She bit back a giggle; the scene was ludicrous as he rushed, hellbent on the metal swinging shield in a path of new-churned mud. But as the quintain clanged and swung and scraped to a stop again, the knight changed his violent tactic. A blurred black wall of horse and glint of furious rider came directly at her. She squealed and darted, slipping in the mud and hitting her head hard against the stone wall as they thundered past only inches away.

When she glanced up, they had turned again and towered over her. She could feel the horse's snorting breath, see each single link of chain mail as it shaped itself to the man's powerful muscles.

"By St. George, woman! No one is allowed here now! Damn you! You might have been killed!"

Joan pressed her back and shoulders against the wall so close behind her and bravely flounced out her muddy, damp skirts.

"The door to the Upper Ward above was unlocked, sir, and it is hardly my doing that both of you beasts changed your blood-crazed, muddy path all of a sudden. You should get a better helmet and watch where you are riding, I dare say."

She could feel the eyes within the visor lock with her defiant gaze though she could not see them. There stretched between these two a tottering pause charged with some sort of unspoken astonishment. Just when she thought she had set him prettily back on his spurred heels, he leaned the elbow of his good arm casually across the pommel of his huge saddle built to hold a man in full armor. His long legs held so stiffly in the big stirrups seemed to relax, and he held his dented, two-handed sword more easily. He flexed his legs, and his greaves and foot armor clinked.

"You know, *demoiselle charmante*, your tongue is as sharp as my long, belt dagger here, and I have a good mind to take you on as an opponent in this foul temper I am in. Shall we say ten passes each at the quintain? You do have a war-horse somewhere about, do you not? 'Twould be a fair enough contest as this bloody, damn broken sword arm of mine does as much good as a maid's. You can ride?"

"Aye, of course, but I resent your making a jest at my expense. Saints, no woman is trained as a fighter."

"Ah," the man said, his voice low and shadowy within the helmet he had made no effort to remove. "Somehow, with those lavender velvet eyes and that shrill tone, I

37

thought otherwise."

He wedged his sword under his injured arm and, with his good hand, reached up and unlatched the leather straps which loosed his visored helmet. The square-jawed face, the tawny lionlike mane that shook itself free and emerged was—was magnificent. Joan sucked in her breath so hard he glanced down to see if he had accidentally kicked her.

Crystalline blue eyes set under full brows ringed by damp, tawny curls bored into hers. His nose was long, but slightly bowed as though it had been broken once; his cheekbones high, almost prominent; the mouth firm with a propensity to pride or maybe even cruelty in the set of the elegant lips. In Joan a sweet, warm, pulling tide mingled with the distinct feeling that she was balancing on the edge of a windy cliff and she nearly toppled into the mud at his feet. He seemed young, almost as young as she, but his gaze was so direct, so devouring, he seemed also very wise and very much in charge. It made her suddenly annoyed at how terrible she must look—all wet, muddy, and road-stained, her damp hair loose in a riot of curls and tangles.

"I believe you are no true and gentle knight, sir," she finally managed, remembering such an insult from a romance she had heard somewhere. "You must needs climb down off that mountain of a horse and not put me at such a disadvantage!"

He relaxed again, visibly, and grinned down at her with a flash of white teeth for one brief instant before his handsome, if arrogant, face went mock serious again. "I really cannot picture, *ma chérie*, anyone having you at a disadvantage under any conditions. That blown and windswept, damp look—quite entrancing."

"Saints!" she sputtered while her quick mind darted about for an insult that would do. Did he dare think she always went about like this and at the king's court? Could not the stupid simpleton tell she had just arrived and suffered untimely drenching in the rain?

"You dare to speak of how I look? Look at you, sir. Do

they dub you 'Sir Mud and Mire' here about?"

Her voice ended in a near shriek and, horrified, she watched him throw back his big head on his strong neck and roar with laughter. She started away, edging carefully sideways past the patiently standing horse, but the man easily lifted one half-armored leg over his pommel and dropped just behind her. A metal-encased hand held her arm above the elbow before she had gone four steps.

"Hold, *demoiselle, s'il vous plaît*! Stop the fussing. I am very weary of women's fuming and fussing. But you are not usually such a scold, I think. Stay but a moment. I meant not to tease. I find your wet and windy look entirely to my liking, and I can tell you must be new-come to court."

She paused and turned back to him, struck nearly mute again by the crystalline blue of his eyes, lighter than a pond on a clear day, more like those precious forget-me-nots she had picked for Mother when they had gone away.

"Aye. You could tell from my traveling garb and that I came down from the courtyard above?"

"No—well, aye. That, too. I meant not to seem angry but I thought I was alone here."

"You are angry, my lord, angry at more than that poor chopped-up quintain on this rainy day, I wager. Must you take it all out on this hot, lathered horse and that dented shield?"

He bit his lower lip looking suddenly like a scolded boy, and his eyes seemed to ice over, glinting blue for one moment. "Aye, *demoiselle*. 'Tis this damn, bloody broken wrist on my sword arm. I lose my temper at myself because I cannot handle the sword and lance so well with my left."

"But no one could do that, sir."

"By the rood, I shall! I shall do it if I will it so!"

She faced him faintly amazed at the outburst and intrigued by the vein that throbbed at the base of his bronze throat now so close to her.

"I see, my lord. I—I too have had things I have wanted every whit as badly as that."

His mouth and brow softened. "Have you, *chérie*? Aye, I wager you have—and shall. You must go back now, and we shall meet again without all this mud and anger, *oui*?"

His intimate tone, his use of gentle French, his clear eyes seemed to mesmerize her. She was close enough to him to see each separate gold eyelash that fringed the piercing eyes, and she went quite weak from her all-day ride on Sable's bouncing saddle.

"*Oui, certainement.* If you do not mind my asking, my lord, do you know the king and his family very well? I am to be Queen Philippa's ward as—as soon as my brother comes back to the Curfew Tower to fetch me."

"The queen? Fine. She will like you immediately, if you do not let her hear that quick tongue of yours."

"Oh—no, I would not to the queen, of course. If you had not been so rude—"

"And the king, *charmante*, will like you very, very much also."

"You really think so? I mean to prosper here."

"I promise you, sweet lady, you will prosper famously." He motioned her up the narrow steps which it seemed she had descended ages ago—before she had met him.

She hesitated two stairs up where she was at eye level with him. The impact of his nearness nearly overwhelmed her. Desperate not to show her feelings, she said, "And shall we part without introduction, sir? What if we do not even recognize each other without all this mud and damp hair and rain-drenched garments?"

He gave a low, short laugh deep in his throat and his eyes skimmed her face before returning to her eyes. How at ease he seemed to her again, how sure and worldly-wise. Suddenly she could not bear to let him go though he made her feel so very little even eye to eye like this, and she had never liked that helpless feeling before now.

"Fear not—ever—my lady. Just flash those deep violet eyes and wish for your Sir Mud and Mire, and he shall be there."

With his armored arm, he dared to touch her hip through her full skirts to send her up the steps. She went as gracefully as she could without deigning to look back. She heard the clink of metal and the stomp and snort of his great beast as he mounted from the steps. At the wooden door when she dared to cast a glimpse back, he had spun the quintain crazily and trotted off down the narrow enclosure. Dreamy-eyed, she pulled open the door to the courtyard and nearly hit the furious, red-faced Edmund who had just put his hand to the metal latch to seek her from the other side.

It was late morning on the morrow when Joan finally met one of the royal Plantagenets. Rested, bathed, and garbed in a gold-linked girdle and a willow green kirtle of the finest, shiny sendal which whispered when she walked, Joan followed her new guardian, the Lady Euphemia de Heselaston, a close friend of the queen and watch guard of her fifty ladies, down the long, oak-lined corridor. Torches in wall sconces set at intervals lit their way, for this inner hall was dim despite the clear day outside.

Lady Euphemia appeared to be at least thirty years of age, and quite strict, though pleasant-faced when she did not frown. A heavy set of keys, scissors, a pomander, and thimble dangled and clinked from her engraved leather girdle. The lady's chestnut hair was nearly hidden by an embroidered and fashionably pleated wimple, but Joan had been pleased to see none of the maids her own age went about in such constricting things. It was bad enough to be expected to set these netted cauls to hold back her bounteous weight of hair without Marta's skillful hands.

"I am so sorry, *Demoiselle* Joan, that our dear Queen Philippa is indisposed and unable to greet you herself for several days. Milk fever, now and again, from the eighth royal child, Princess Mary, you see, although the royal wet nurses and others rear the children after the *relevailles* where the child is first christened, of course." Lady Euphemia was quite petite despite the fact that she seemed terribly

41

imposing, and she tilted her pointed chin sideways to view Joan when she addressed her.

"I understand, my lady. I shall pray Her Gracious Majesty soon is well. But it is very kind of the Princess Isabella to see me now. We are cousins of sorts, you may know, as my father was her father's—our king, I mean—he's Father's uncle."

Lady Euphemia's rich coppery-colored silk kirtle changed hues in the torchlight each time they passed a wall sconce, and the treasures on her girdle clinked rhythmically. "Aye, your father. Most everyone knows of that, *demoiselle*."

Joan walked faster by the side of the bustling woman, her heart thudding harder, but the lady's tone kept her from a spate of other comments concerning her dreams of actually finding a sort of family as well as hoped-for friendship with these wonderful Plantagenets. Of a certainty, she knew her place compared to their royal status. Surely, the Lady Euphemia, whose good will she coveted, too, would not think otherwise of her.

"Here, *demoiselle*, in here," Lady Euphemia intoned and halted by a tall, carved oak door. From within came the intriguing sound of a deep male voice reading to the accompaniment of a single, fine lute. "Now, do not let Her Royal Highness Isabella and her butterfly *mignonnes* overwhelm you. They are all about your age and the princess herself quite favors having young and pretty maids like you about, my dear. Come, you shall see. Butterflies all."

The scene within was breathtaking. A cluster of exquisitely gowned ladies in rainbow silks and sendals sat on stools, like floating lily flowers on a pond of sky-blue carpet in a large and airy room. Gold and green tapestries of unicorns and winged griffins graced the walls, and a massive bed, covered and canopied in glittering silver silk, sailed like a tall boat near the living, silken lilies. A long-robed man, black-haired and sharp-faced, read deep-voiced in French from a book as all the lovely ladies inclined their heads and listened politely while their embroidery and tapestry frames stood temporarily idle. A young lutenist in the brightest yellow-striped tunic played a muted *chanson* to match the serious tenor of the reader's voice. Two deep-set windows with crystal panes flooded the scene with golden light.

"The princess," Lady Euphemia whispered and elbowed Joan gently. "Over by the window, the fairest of them all."

Her heart pounding, Joan's eyes sought the princess, eldest of the three daughters of the English Edward and his Flemish Queen Philippa. The lady was indeed the fairest, light-skinned and blond as herself. Her kirtle and armless *surcote* were silvery sendal, almost like her bed, and were edged with the finest white- and black-spotted ermine. She alone did not seem intent on the instructive reading. Her eyes darted about and she twisted the silver tasseled cords of her pearl-studded girdle. Her blue eyes snagged on Joan and then jumped to Lady Euphemia as a quick smile lifted her pouting red lips to a grin.

"Master Robert, a pause, only a pause for a moment's respite," the princess chirped, her voice dancing like little bells on a winter sleigh. "Euphemia, *mon amie*. Look, *mes belles*! Euphemia has brought us my distant cousin Joan of Kent, a fair maid indeed to grace our bowers and our halls. Come, come, Joan. Come to meet your new friends."

Joan's uneasy heart flowed out in gratitude to the lovely, young princess at this effusive welcome, more wonderful and charming than she had dared to hope for. With Lady Euphemia pushing her ahead and clucking something about "butterflies" again, Joan self-consciously wended her way past the ladies who hastened to rise in a rustle of skirts when the princess did. Lady Euphemia went out and quietly closed the door.

Isabella's dainty hands grasped her own and held them wide to look at her. Then she moved closer in a rush of crushing silver silk and jasmine scent for a hug so quick and light Joan had no time to return it. "My dearest, dearest Joan. How we shall all delight in having you with us, will we not, *mes amies*? Here, let me introduce you to everyone before we go back to the lesson for the day. Her dearest grace, the queen, insists my sister Joanna and I hear instruction from Master Robert every day, you know. Joanna is eleven and she has gone to visit the queen for a bit and escaped this reading today, it seems. You shall take her place then."

She winked slyly at Joan as though there were some unspoken message there and tugged her hand so that Joan faced the curious circle of pretty faces. "Constantia Bourchier, Mary Boherne, Nichola de Veres," the names began and rushed by as Joan nodded and smiled at each new face. Yet the fluttering eyes were more than merely polite or simply curious, Joan thought—nervous perhaps, resentful, even critical. She was much relieved when the petite and charming princess indicated a velvet-tufted stool near her own, and everyone rustled to her seat again so that the queen's Master Robert and his lutenist might finish.

The reading, Joan soon realized, was from a manual of virtuous conduct for women by someone named Ménagier of Paris. She tried to focus her mind on the words but she was too excited to listen. Besides, it was obvious from the princess' fidgeting that she scarcely took in the ominous warnings to ladies to always be obedient to their dear lords and on and on—that the man's pleasure in all things must come before the lady's. A lady must never nag whatever her lord's follies—here to Joan's surprise and dismay, the princess nudged her foot with her slippered one and surreptitiously rolled her light blue eyes—and again, Master Robert intoned, let your lord's pleasure be before your own in all good things. At the shared innuendo of that repeated line from the serious, black-gowned Master Robert, Joan, too, bit her lip to keep from giggling. Her heart soared; this lovely, young princess was not at all grand and austere. Here, with her, mayhap there could be friends and fun and freedom!

Master Robert and the little canary-garbed lutenist were

no sooner out the door than the room erupted in giggles and murmurs and darting females.

"Oh, I cannot *believe* what Her Grace chose for us to hear today," the princess squealed, holding her sides. Tears of laughter streamed down Mary Boherne's pretty face and the red-haired girl in green whose name had slipped by Joan was holding her sides in quivering laughter.

"The next reading tomorrow, *demoiselles*," Princess Isabella went on, her girlish voice deepened ludicrously to imitate the stern tones of Master Robert, "will be about how all you young, sweet, and quiet little things must fall at your master's feet if he but gazes on you with one grim glance, fall and kiss his muddy boots—"

"Aye, or kiss wherever he will have you," Mary Boherne shrieked, and they all fell into gales of hysterical laughter again.

Joan laughed too, but the jest seemed hardly palpable. Did they hate Master Robert or such pious instruction so much they had to mock it so? All Mary Boherne's words about kissing a lord's muddy boots made Joan think of was her "Sir Mud and Mire," the man she had watched at the quintain yesterday, and how he had made her feel she wanted to kiss him—or maybe scream at him and so—

"Oh, Lady Joan, forgive us," Princess Isabella got out between her attempts to catch her breath. "You see, we here have all taken a vow—and you, too, simply must join us, must she not?" the girl plunged on, not waiting for the assent which never came from her clustered ladies. "A vow to do all we can to seek our own pleasure and to have as many men in continual whirls as possible. If you will agree to keep it all secret, especially from all men, we shall tell you straightaway, will we not, *mes chéries*?"

"Aye, of course," the red-haired Constantia Bourchier said, and several other voices chimed in.

"It is tremendous fun, of course, and we all pick out someone new at least twice a fortnight to—well, to entrance, to make our obedient and eternal slave in love forever. We tell each other all our secrets and even"—here the titters began again as if all sensed a marvelous jest was about to be reiterated—"well, we even entice the same gallant knights sometimes, compare our tactics and the men never know. *Touché*! We fight our own battles *d'amour* our own way."

They all seemed to turn and stare at Joan. She hoped she did not register surprise—only, at most, interest and, hopefully, delight. "Oh, I see. A marvelous secret. Of course, no one would know, and I shall never tell. Only, I have never had a *beau*, you see, for there were no young men but a few pages and squires at Liddell until my brother Edmund came home with his retinue a fortnight ago to bring me here."

The lovely, young maids looked taken aback, dismayed. "No swains, no *beaux*, no romance?" someone asked.

"Romance? Saints, I did not say that. I have read them all, Tristain and Isolt, Lancelot and Guinevere, and I can play romances on the lute and many French *chansons* about love."

"But your home—your castle at Liddell," Mary Boherne ventured. "Such a small household there were no *galants*?"

"Leave her be, all of you," Princess Isabella swept to Joan's rescue. "Just think, not a one of you plays the lute. Will that not be a novelty to attract the knights like little flies, *oui*? Why, even my pompous brothers shall be swept off their feet by that, and where will their rude teasings of our dear secret society be then, eh? Shoo, shoo, all of you now and let me talk with our *chére amie* Joan, and if anyone protests someone as lovely as Fair Joan of Kent being our new and dear friend, let not Joanna or me hear of it! Be off now. Oh, if only my eldest brother Edward had not gone off to his lodge at Berkhamstead now, I swear by St. Peter's bones we would try your wiles out on him, dear Joan. He teases me unmercifully, though of course we adore each other. My dear Edward was never a quick catch like the other fools who snap at pretty bait and female cleverness."

"The Prince Edward," Joan asked, her mind reeling from the mere suggestion her dear new friend could mean she

should tempt such a one as the next king of all England.
"Our sovereign Prince Edward, the Prince of Wales?" Joan
faltered.

Isabella tugged Joan back down to their stools as the
remainder of the ladies trailed out the door with a mixture of
fond or dart-eyed glances the princess seemed not to note.
"Aye, the same. The stern, the grim, the most wonderful and
terrible brother a maid ever had. And when you meet him
upon his return, show him not the slightest trembling or
deference like the silly ninnies all do, or he will chew you up
and spit you out. I always speak up to him—when their
graces are not about—and so we get on famously."

"But, Princess Isabella, he is your brother. I could
never—"

"Oh, a pox on it all—on him! He gets all the fun things to
do, the wild days and nights. I wish I were a man. Would it
not be wonderful?"

"Aye. I had thought on that more than once. Freedom—"

"But, dearest, that is just why we have our secret society.
It is our way to freedom and a great deal of fun. Just wait and
see. Let them preach fond obedience and meek compliance
and marry us off to lords we have never seen and care not
for!"

"Oh," Joan sat up straight, her hands nervously smooth-
ing the green, shimmery sendal over her knees. "Then you
are to marry?"

"Of course. His Grace, my father, has eternal plans for me,
for Joanna, probably for Mary, too, already, and she is but
newborn. And your blood is blue Plantagenet, too, through
our grandsire, of course. They will have you promised in
marriage somewhere soon enough, so take your freedoms
while you can, *ma chérie*."

"But they could not possibly have plans for me. I have just
arrived. I have met no one, that is, only one man, and I do
not even know his name."

"Indeed?" Isabella swung her petite foot jerkily and her
silk slipper bounced and swayed where it clung tenaciously

to her toes. "If you favor him, flirt with him. I tell you true, mistress, it is best to take your pleasures as you find them. We all do, though, of course, we are careful to never, never be caught at it. You must describe this one to me and mayhap I can guess who he is. And if he is someone else's knight, oh, will that not be a delightful start for you?"

The description of the wonderful, angry, and muddy man crowded to Joan's lips along with a hundred questions, but she read well by the princess' fidgeting that her inquiries would have to wait. Surely, even if she joined the princess' secret little clique, she could still keep her own heart intact and do things her own way. She had no intention of being forced to be sweet and charming to anyone she did not favor. Perhaps if her brother Edmund's quick-eyed friend Lyle Wingfield were about, she could practice a bit on him to suit her new acquaintances. Certainly she had no plans of ever letting anyone know how the fascinating man on the big black horse yesterday had sent her heart fluttering clear down to the pit of her stomach!

"Joan. Joan! I said, *ma chérie*, do you promise? Will you keep it secret—the society and the motto?"

"Oh, aye, forgive me, Your Grace. Aye, of course. I would so much like to be your friend."

"And the others?"

"Aye."

"Then, here it is. We bend like this and whisper in the ear of any of our dearest friends, '*Suis-je belle*?'—Am I not fair?"

"'*Suis-je belle*?' Am I not fair?"

"*Oui*, Joan, for are we not all young and fair and in love with love? Is it not perfect? You especially are so fair—a perfect Plantagenet. Indeed, you favor my sister and me greatly, and wait until you see the rest of the Plantagenets. I tell you, dearest Joan, you could easily be one of us!"

Joan felt her cheeks flush at the astounding compliment, and a rush of affection for this sweet, charming girl flooded her. "*Suis-je belle*?" Indeed, why not? Fun, friends, freedom to help forget lost Liddell and Mother's strange parting words. As long as Isabella's predictions of some arranged marriage did not come true for a long time, surely she could be happy here. Mayhap she should just ask old Morcar about her future and settle Isabella's foolish predictions that way.

"Your Grace, is—are you—betrothed to be wed?" Joan ventured and saw she had earned the maid's immediate attention as well as a frown which furrowed her high, white brow above the pale blue eyes.

"Oh, aye, indeed. Eternally. When I was but three, they promised me to Pedro, son of the King of Castile, but that fell by the political wayside somehow. I did not even inquire how. Then to the Duke of Brabant and last year to the son of the Count of Flanders, Louis de Male. Flanders is where my dear mother came from, you know. I pay not the slightest heed to all their planning. Those men are all elsewhere and, remember, *charmante, 'Suis-je belle.'*"

The young, lovely princess's laughter echoed like brittle bells in the room and her clear blue eyes were strangely wild.

"Now I understand, Your Grace," Joan said and entwined that laughter with her own. "What is there to fear then? *'Suis-je belle?'*"

Chapter Three

Like a proud, young lion poised over his domain, England's tawny-haired Prince of Wales surveyed the broad Thames Valley below. Lofty spires of the three great London cathedrals, countless bell towers, and toylike, beflagged turrets and towers of the rich and royal; a stone and timber, daub and straw city of twenty thousand souls: the very heartbeat of the kingdom lay at his feet as his massive, black stallion stamped and snorted impatiently under him at the edge of Epping Forest.

"I know, Wilifred, I know. But someday their love too will be ours when we have earned it so. Even the most valiant heart must bide awhile until the hour is fully ripe. Our great day will come, good lad. You will see."

Edward Plantagenet, Duke of Cornwall, heir to the throne, Prince of Wales, loosed his taut, left-handed grip on Wilifred's reins, and the horse turned back onto the road southeast to their destination, the prince's big, stone London house on Fish Street. Though he did not glance back at his small entourage again, he knew full well what he would see if he did. Nine of his most select boon companions, themselves heirs to the greatest noble houses of the realm, followed their liege lord and future king closely with their small, private contingents of falconers, musicians, squires, pages, and packhorses. Indeed, they always traveled fairly light on these journeys to their prince's personal properties like Berkhamstead Castle, or to his manors at Sonning on the Thames near Reading Abbey, Bushey northwest of London, Newport Manor, Cheshire, or the others. Today, since dawn, this

50

traveling party hand-picked from his normal-size household of one hundred twenty men had made the journey of nearly thirty miles from Berkhamstead to London at a fast pace in just four hours.

He felt restless; he admitted it, more restless than usual. This spring—perhaps it was because his formal education with his tutors and his short sojourn at Oxford was over—he felt quite at odds with his life. He was poised, ready, waiting for something grand and wonderful, some sweep of circumstance to test his mettle and thrust him headlong into destiny. But to what, he knew not. And so, he bided his days in overseeing his vast and growing estates, in comradeship with those he would someday need to know to rule well, in observing his world, and in keeping in fighting trim in case this French thing ever came full circuit to a war, as he hoped it might. Damn, but this tenuous treaty with the French was only valid for two more years until 1346. He cursed quietly again and wished his broken arm from that bloody joust a month ago would heal and be done with!

As the horses clattered into the first narrow streets in the northwest suburbs of London, Hugh Calveley and Nickolas Dagworth, hands on swords, moved up to ride abreast with him, and Edward heard his faithful falconer's voice directly behind as the strung-out band tightened into a closer group. Indeed, there was no need for the added security here among the Londoners, Edward believed, but he accepted their concern. Though his sire, the Plantagenet monarch, had been riding a crest of relative popularity these fourteen years since he had seized the reins of his kingdom from his mother Isabella, sister of the king of France, and her lecherous, treasonous lover, Roger Mortimer—curse his soul—it was always wise to be prepared. The recent English claim on the crown of France through that same misguided Isabella, now living in luxurious exile at Castle Rising in Norfolk, meant French spies or sympathizers would be hostile and, in such a crowded place as London, hard to recognize.

"My lord, though you choose to wear the darker colors

like that forest green when you are absent from court, the people know you anyway," Nickolas Dagworth turned to say.

Edward nodded. The deep green tunic and hose with riding boots hardly disguised him, for he hated hats or hoods and went bareheaded. He also noted how the stares the London folk would give to any large, armed band turned to expressions of joy or awe as they recognized him at the front of his men. Occasionally cries of "God save Yer Grace" or "Long live our Prince o' Wales" floated after them until drowned out by the clatter of the horses' hoofs and raucous cheers.

He often wore the darker garments away from court festivities and frivolities, not because he meant to go unrecognized, for he seldom managed that, but because he truly favored them. The king always sported bright and riotous-hued velvets and silk but, by St. George, he had earned them in the Scottish Wars or in seizing the inheritance of his own throne from the damned Mortimer! But a prince-in-waiting—he felt like those ladies of the queen or of his lively sister Isabella, forever hovering, hanging on to someone else's words and awaiting some order or task or honor. And, damn, but when his moment came, he would seize it and use it! If he could only stand this blasted, bloody waiting!

They entered the walled city across Holbourne Bridge through Newgate and rode past the huge Cathedral of St. Paul's and down Old Fish Street to his three-storied stone house with the black slate roof. Unlike many of the older houses in the neighborhood, his London dwelling did not lean out over the street in each successive story. Rather, it stood straight and tall and boasted modern, large-paned windows and new-forged metal eaves and drainpipes.

Though it was the smallest of his properties, he greatly favored it over the other vast London dwellings of Westminster or Sheen which his family oftimes inhabited, and he often found himself imagining he was a rich, contented merchant, like Michael de la Pole or some such, just living here in peace and prosperity with a passel of strong children and a lovely, lively wife.

He shook his head to throw off the persistent, teasing fantasy as they reined in, scattering a children's game of Hare and Hounds. The crowd in front of the house grew; a few women shouted and waved from upper windows. Women in his life, ah, women. He felt almost an emptiness there. Many women: pretty, smiling, meek, willing, so willing—but none he truly favored. None who moved him in his heart one whit beyond slaking his occasional quick thirst for one under him. His mind darted to the wild, stunning maid who had stopped his furious attempt to joust with his damned left arm broken last week. He smiled broadly and the crowd cheered. She, for a certainty, would not be meek or willing. She, like his most prized destrier or precious female peregrine falcon, would take some handling and some taming.

Nickolas Dagworth's voice interrupted his reverie. "Your Grace, do you mean to sit in the street this fine May afternoon? The crowd will scatter if you go in, and the little ones whose game we ruined riding in like this are all peeking out and wanting to go back to play, I warrant."

Edward stared down at his tall, black-haired friend. "Aye, Nick. Just pondering. Give the little knaves some coins and have them play Hoodman's Blind. In truth, that is the way I feel half the time of late."

Prince Edward dismounted and went in through the door the huge giant of a man Hugh Calveley held open for him. He noted the look of puzzlement his two friends exchanged over his last comment. St. George, let them wonder what brought on his black moods in increasing frequency lately. Damn, but even his closest friends did not need to know his every thought and whim just because they served him so assiduously. He was their liege prince, not their private property!

He whacked his leather riding gloves on the narrow,

polished oak table in the slate entry hall and paused. He could hear the crowd dispersing and his horses being unpacked and led away around to the mews on the next street already, and soon the bustle of the carrying in and the voices of his entourage would be upon him again. He took his favorite hooded female peregrine, Greta, from the gauntleted arm of his falconer Philip Pipe, crooked his finger to his lutenist Hankin, and stomped up the stairs with the musician in his broad wake.

The house, which was frequently his retreat and his haven from all the demands of who he was and what he must become, welcomed him this warm spring day with cool, quite arms. Below ground, two huge cellars were stocked with food and choice wine for his closest friends, or for the rare occasions he chose to entertain here. On the ground floor were the oak-paneled hall and the parlor with its own fireplace, and the kitchen and larder at the back. The second floor above ground held his large combined solar and bedchamber with its own stone-lined fireplace and private privy and *garde-robe* rooms where his clothes were stored. Above, under the slanting eaves, were various chambers used almost exclusively by servants since, except during the day, only a few of his men stood guard and the rest stayed at their own London townhouses nearby.

The private solar he entered now was richly appointed with blue Persian carpets and green tapestry depicting forests of the hunt. A large table, cushioned heavy chairs, a massive red canopied feather bed, and huge storage chests were the only furniture in the vast room.

"My Lord Prince, you wished a song?" Hankin, his lutenist, was asking. The slender, brown-haired man stood ready, his full-blown, pear-shaped instrument in his hands. No qualms of insignificance held his servants back from their love of rich colorings in their garments, Edward noted grimly to himself, eying Hankin's fine tunic and hose of gold and scarlet, albeit covered with road dust. Saint George, what did it matter? He paid them well to keep them richly clothed. He cared for them well enough, too, whenever he had not fallen into the mire of one of these dark moods.

Mire—Sir Mud and Mire, the saucy, little blonde had dared to call him. He could not wait to see that pert look turn to surprise when she learned who it was she had rudely scolded. Damn, but he would like to be the one to tell her himself, and yet, would that not turn her meek and mild and simpering like the rest of them? He felt a slight, unbidden stirring in his strong loins. By the blessed saints, his mere thoughts of the little witch were breaking down his body's usual stony reserve.

He smiled again, the look lighting his grim face so that the waiting Hankin marveled at the change which came over his handsome, often austere, young lord's countenance. Hankin cleared his throat.

"Aye, Hankin. If you are not too tired from that jaunt, tell the steward to fetch me some food and hot water for a bath. And, except for Lord Dagworth, have the others go on home. I will have no need for them until the morrow early. Then come back in and play me something to lighten this foul mood!"

Hankin's eyes widened and he gripped the neck of his lute tightly. "Aye, Your Grace. At once."

The door was left ajar as he hurried out, for Edward could hear the voices of his men below. Always, always their voices just beyond some door. At times he wanted, needed them, but not today. He leaned his powerful shoulder against the recessed window sill and glanced down at his puffy right wrist. It had almost fully healed, although the swelling and stiffness was still with him. Next month at midsummer's tournament, he would be ready.

"My liege lord, Hankin said you wished to see me."

"Nick, aye, come in." The prince's shrewd eye appraised Nickolas Dagworth as he came across the wide stretch of solar to join him at the street window. A powerful man, a great fighter and irresistible to the ladies. But Nick was older, almost twenty and six, and had already earned his spurs both in skirmishes with the fierce Scots and in a crusade with the Teutonic knights in Poland. It was ludicrous, really, that he, Edward, who had never really proved himself to his father or his people in anything but in being born Prince of Wales, should dare to command all these proved fighters, these true knights. And now the king had seen fit to send men of proved mettle like Dagworth or Calveley or Sir Thomas Holland on foreign missions to Flanders, while the prince of the realm rode here and there and here again and waited!

"Nick, I have changed my mind about the backgammon and dicing tonight. I need time to be alone."

"Aye, Your Grace. Hankin said as much. But only until the morrow early, he said." A battle scar on Nick Dagworth's handsome face shone white against his brown cheek when he talked, as if flaunting itself, his scar of honor in battle.

"And then tomorrow, I have changed my mind about staying here for a few days," Prince Edward went on. "We are off for Windsor. When I went to see the queen a week ago she still was not well from childbed fever. I intend to visit her again, I know not for how long."

Nick Dagworth's expression was properly compliant. All the prince's men knew he favored visiting at his own castles and manors to the busy, demanding life on the fringes of his royal parents' labyrinthine household. Since the prince had been an infant, he had been reared in households of his own, as were his two royal brothers after him.

"Aye, Your Grace. I shall tell them," he said. "Windsor on the morrow. 'Twill be a lot of action there over the next few weeks with spring carryings-on and the summer jousting, eh?"

"Exactly. I mean to get this hand and arm back in perfect fighting trim to be ready when we need to teach the French their long-awaited lesson. Saint George, I pray it shall be soon."

"Soon enough, my lord prince. The peace treaty has but

two years left. And in the respite all England grows stronger, even like your broken arm."

"But did you mark the sports the commons played on the outskirts as we came in today? Stick ball, bladder ball—the king may have forbidden all sports but archery under pain of death in hopes of having a ready army or archers set to take the soil of France, but the people listen not. Damn, it does not matter. All that running out there will make them fit to charge forward and rout the French off true English soil when the time comes. I only hope it comes soon so those children in the street out there will not be grown soldiers then."

Nick Dagworth nodded his dark head. "Aye, Your Grace. Our king has rightly claimed the land of France through his mother's inheritance from her brother, the King of France. King Philip knows his claim—being merely first cousin—is not half so strong. And when we go to fight, my lord, I am certain, with your sire, you shall stand as our leader."

Edward's intense blue eyes sought Dagworth's brown, hooded ones. True, there was some intent to flatter there, his men's instinctive attempts to assuage these dark moods that plagued him. But they were full loyal and eagerly desired the chance for him to lead, to earn his spurs and thereby their undying loyalty through deed as well as birth.

"I will depart then, my lord. Pipe and Calveley will stay should you need aught else."

"There was one other thing, Nick. The Fletcher lass, Allison, you brought here once last winter. Fletcher, that was the name, was it not?"

Dagworth's face lit in a grin as though the mere mention of desire for a woman would clear all the unexplained moodiness from his prince. "Oh, aye, by the saints! The red-haired mercer's daughter from near the Fleet with green eyes and full breasts. The one who cries out 'more, more!' at her last moment." Dagworth's face broke into an even broader grin. "I did not know you even thought on her, my lord, as I recall you said she was a wild one and scratched your back all up."

"That is the one, Nick. But I am just in the mood for wildness, by St. George. These meek little maids my mother favors are enough to cool any knight's blood. The mood I am in—aye, see if you can get the sharp-nailed wench for me." For Dagworth he forced an answering smile he hardly felt. Let the knaves think a mere roll with one little hoyden would cure him. He would slake his thirst on this one, then send her away for good as he did the others.

Nick was nearly out the door when the house steward, John Macklyn, bustled in directing servants lugging a steaming tub of shallow water. Without waiting for their help, Edward stripped off his dust-laden garments and sat bent-legged in the small tub with water just over his hips while they poured more heated buckets in over him. A servant scrubbed him with lint dipped in essence of bergamot and toweled him dry when he stepped out. He donned a soft black robe while they scurried to set up his solitary table. All the while, Hankin played lively music from a chair in the corner.

Edward ate a hearty supper of stewed partridge with saffron on bread flavored by clove, mace, and pepper and sprinkled with chopped egg yolks—a favorite dish when he dined alone. And, at the thought of the outraged look he would see on the stunning maid's face at Windsor when she learned whom she had insulted at the quintain last week, he downed a pigeon pie and two nutmeg custards. Perhaps he could even entice some kisses from her in some sort of teasing retribution, he mused, as he polished off roast chestnuts, Brie cheese, plums imported from Syria, and liberal amounts of his favorite Bordeaux wine.

Daylight fled from the windows as Hankin played on. The children's voices from the street below finally faded, then ceased after they had last been heard shouting and playing follow the leader. Aye, that was indeed the great dynastic game he had his heart sore set on, Edward admitted to himself: he would be their leader and they must follow on,

eternally, to great glories to win back their rightful realm of
France and even, perhaps, beyond. Then he would wear
bright Plantagenet king's colors of gold and azure sprinkled
with the *fleurs-de-lis* of France and the three proud couchant
leopards of his own royal house. Then, he would feel content
and whole, and would choose some strong and worthy
woman to fill his heart with love and his palaces with
children, a woman wild and stunning like the blond one at
Windsor, young and strong with a sweet body—

"Hankin?" The man's fingers ceased their strumming and
the belly of the lute reechoed their last notes.

"Aye, Your Grace? Does the *chanson de geste* not please
you?"

"Do you recall that French song, Hankin, '*Li dous*' something or other about the lady's sweet body?"

"Oh, aye, milord. But you said lively tunes and that one is
full of love-longing which hardly suits the mood your
lordship has shown these last few days when—"

"I will be judge of that, Hankin. Just sing it, man, and I
shall be judge of my own moods."

"Aye, of course, Your Grace."

Hankin strummed a few running notes as if to recall the
beginning. A song of love-longing, he had said. Aye, that
would keep the glory-longing away, mayhap. A merry chase
after a new doe by a chivalrous hunter. That would arouse
the royal concern, no doubt, for his parents had even
bargained and hawked to find a suitable royal princess for
their beloved heir, though he cared naught for any of their
political matrimonial dealings or their choices so far.

He drank deeply of the rich, red Bordeaux wine again, and
the face of the hot-tempered, muddy, and wet maid at the
quintain drifted before his inner vision as his mind seized on
the words of Hankin's song:

> "That pleasant fever
> That love doth often bring,
> Lady, doth ever

59

Attune the songs I sing.
Where I endeavor
To catch again
Your chaste, sweet body's savor,
I crave but may not taste."

He seemed to float off as the words began again. Why, of all the maids or more experienced ladies he had been offered and of those few he had deigned to taste since he began to know the delights of a woman's body, did this one snag his eye and tempt his heart so for a week now? He had beheld her but a little while, a few brief teasing words, one quick touch of her rounded hip through her stained and damp traveling dress when he sent her away.

He had never been one for such foolish courtly love games or ensnarements of the heart and mind. There were too many other things to be accomplished, to be dared in order to earn his just approval from others and from himself. But now, while his fighting hand healed just a whit more, why not the chase for him to catch again her "chaste, sweet body's savor" he craved but did not taste?

A rapping at the door startled him, and he sat bolt upright, sloshing the last of his ruby wine from his goblet onto the table. Hankin's strumming stopped and the musician moved quickly to open the door. Nickolas Dagworth's grinning face appeared, and with a slight turn, he pulled the red-haired, wide-eyed wench Allison into view. Her eyes darted to the prince as he rose from the table across the solar, and her pink tongue wet her red lips.

"The, ah, lady you sent for, Your Grace," Nick Dagworth announced and winked at him over the maid's red head.

"Damn, I had almost forgot." Edward frowned without meaning to as the girl approached and Dagworth hovered near the door. "I suddenly feel out of sorts, Nick. I thank the lady for coming, but I shall just be giving her a bauble for her pains and asking you to deliver her back."

The girl's voice was rather shrill when she spoke. Why had

he not remembered that? "Oh, my dearest liege lord, I could make you feel better. I was so honored to be sent for—I thought you had quite forgot me. I could just stay quiet as a mouse and any desire you should have, I would be more than ready to fulfill."

Her ripe breasts pushed against the rose-hued bodice of her clinging kirtle as she leaned forward to plead. Even from several feet away, she emanated a musky aroma which tantalized his flared nostrils. But her coloring was too brazen, her voice too strident, her manner both meek and servile at the same time.

"I think not, Allison. I meant to be alone tonight and quite forgot myself. Nick—"

Nickolas Dagworth saw the lay of the land in one quick glint of the steely blue of his prince's eyes and he nearly swept the disappointed girl from the room while carefully masking the surprise on his own face. He would see to it, he thought, that this ripe, little hussy had a place to lay that lush body of hers this eve, for his wife was at Windsor with the court and his own townhouse but three streets away. Ambitious, changeable of mood and strong-willed though he was, the prince was one he would never feel loath to take the leavings from.

Dagworth hurried the still-protesting girl down the stairs, and Hankin, the fine lutenist the prince always kept in his entourage, quickly followed them down.

"What ails His Grace now, man?" Dagworth whispered to the lutenist at the bottom of the steps, careful the girl would overhear no tales to tell from her brief visit here.

"I hardly know, my lord," Hankin shrugged. "With anyone else, I would ha' said love-longing, but not our prince. Still, it is as though he wanted to be alone to think on some lady he cannot have."

"Holy St. Michael and his angels! Now that would be a change," Dagworth chortled as he darted the pouting, waiting girl across the hall a smile and a wink. "It cannot be, Hankin," he went on in a low voice. "I have been with him

61

for months with no such lady in sight, and besides, our prince only deals with females in one quick way if they are not members of his own family. He always gets anyone he has favored in a wink. Damn, but that would be rich!"

Nickolas Dagworth's laughter boomed through the house and then the front door slammed below where Edward lay on his feather bed staring up at the ceiling with his left hand behind his head.

His loins ached for release of their tension; his mind taunted him with thoughts and pictures of a beautiful, naked woman spread, vulnerable to his thrusts, under him. He could feel the building rush of desire, the hardness of his manhood paining for release in her. But, strangely, for the first time ever, he welcomed the sweet pain of this passion, this bittersweet longing of unfulfilled desire. It pulsated in his blood; it nearly overwhelmed him.

Damn her. Damn them all and life which did not give him the golden opportunities he wanted and richly deserved! He could, he would control his world, his mind, his rebellious body! And when he saw her, as indeed he must tomorrow at Windsor, she would get no soft words from him that she might enjoy his ensnarement. He would find her and she would know that he was master of her and himself and that she moved him not!

He groaned as he dragged himself off the bed and went to the door of his room to bellow for more wine and for Hankin to come back and play some brave, marching melodies of war.

The afternoon of Joan of Kent's eighth day at Windsor began much as the others had. Her brother Edmund had gone back to Liddell four days ago to oversee the early fruit harvest, and dear, old Morcar had disappeared into the depths of the king's vast array of servants at court. Queen Philippa was still abed recovering from birthing fever, so Joan had not yet been summoned to meet her royal legal guardian.

To suit the style at court, she had taken up embroidering on a standing frame, an occupation she detested. But all of Isabella's friends embroidered and it was a time in late morning when they met to gossip and exchange juicy tidbits, or *bonbons* as they termed any hint of scandal about love intrigues of the court. Much to her disappointment, Edmund had been entirely correct that ladies at court did not play the lute much and had their own musicians. Joan's dreams of singing and playing for Isabella or the rest of the royal family went entirely unfulfilled. She was so busy darting here and there with the others, and her time on her own was always with others about—in short, she grieved that her beloved lute went quite untouched while her detested, intricate embroidery scene of a hunter chasing a fleeing doe in the forest grew apace.

Today, however, would be different. She would escape them all for a little while to be free and alone and with her lute. Isabella would be called as she had been lately to spend time with her mother, the queen, and for once Joan was relieved that the queen felt too sickly to receive others besides her family.

The lovely, lively *demoiselles* of Isabella's entourage would surely be occupied with their own fickle worlds. Those ladies still did not favor Joan fully; she knew that for a certainty from their stares and whispers, but she was trying to win them over. Isabella had also introduced her to the king at dinner in the Great Hall two nights ago and to the young Prince John of Ghent, the second royal son who was visiting his ill lady mother. The king's eyes had gone over Joan with obvious approval more than once—more than twice—until Isabella had pulled her off to meet someone else. She was surprised the king had looked so young yet so vital. His handsome face was somehow vaguely familiar, and she later reasoned it must have been some sort of family resemblance to the portrait of her long-dead father which hung at Liddell.

Aye, today, she would escape them all for a forest respite

at the very edge of Windsor Forest beyond the walls, beyond the nearest private pleasure gardens. No people from the town could intrude there to bother its great herds of red, fallow, and roe deer. Lyle Wingfield, whom she had taken to flirting with to satisfy her new friends, had told her there was a little pond just a short distance beyond the postern gate where he would take her for a lover's tryst but, of course, she wanted no part of that. Alone, with her lute to remember the gentle forest pond at Liddell—alone in a self-made forest Eden—that was all she craved.

After Joan and the others left the princess's room in late morn, while the others primped and darted off to meet *beaux* and Nichola de Veres lay down to quiet her raging headache, which she said taunted her at the times of her monthly flow, Joan donned one of the new gowns Edmund had purchased, took her lute, and set out. She wore a close-clinging kirtle of Kendal green to hide stains in case she sat on the grass. The gown was very simple, embroidered with her favorite entwined ivy leaves as in her family crest; and a girdle of woven gold cord was slung low on her hips. From a gold filigree pomander suspended from her girdle wafted the delicate aroma of mingled rose petals and lilacs. The sleeveless green *surcote* she wore over her gown for warmth in the shade was edged with light gray squirrel. Even her fine cotton hose were green and gartered with green as was the headpiece she intended to discard the moment she escaped from Windsor's walls.

The cut of the sleeves of her kirtle was fashionably full at the wrists, and the neckline for this summer style, was a low oval so that the rounded tops of her breasts showed to full advantage. She was warm on that sunny May afternoon before she had even traversed the Upper Ward to go out the small garden door, so she leaned her lute against the wall and removed her furred *surcote* to carry it over one arm. If only she could dare to rid herself now of her angular headpiece with its trailing tippets of scarves Isabella had given her as one of several lavish presents she knew the other *demoiselles* resented. If only she could even be so bold as to let her heavy gathered curls free of their restraining cauls and go barefooted here as at home, she would feel free indeed.

She retrieved her lute and hurried across the northern edge of the Upper Ward annoyed at the pounding, clattering contingent of knights, servants, and packhorses that rode in and dismounted to bring noise and riot to the calm area directly beneath the windows of the royal apartments of the queen. All she needed was Isabella or Her Grace glancing out to see her leaving the premises of the castle.

There were at least ten men with the trailing company, but she quickly turned her head and hurried away under the Queen Tower to the postern door to the gardens Lyle Wingfield had told her about. Fortunately, he had gone home to Liddell with her brother and she might not see him again for weeks.

A fat, sleepy porter with a rusty sword and a patch over one eye grunted and opened the door for her without a word. Evidently, she thought, he was quite used to lords and ladies scurrying through like this for lovers' trysts. Mayhap, Isabella's butterflies, as the clucking tongue of Lady Euphemia called them, should interview this porter for some real tidbits and their precious, scandalous *bonbons*. It jabbed at her that she went along with their frivolities, which she thought quite silly, to earn their approval, to get on well here and prosper as Edmund always wanted. Would she not become like them eventually and not care for singing with her lute and riding free and forest glades? No, that could never be, she told herself, and that was why she was here today.

The gardens just outside the walls at the edge of the royal park were wilder than the perfectly tended pleasure gardens of clipped yew and boxwood and tinkling, sculptured fountains within the walls. Paths twisted naturally here, fruit trees looked untrimmed, and the greens were hardly rolled or swept. Wild hollyhock grew sporadically, and she stopped to harvest a few white blooms to tuck them in her low bodice and her hair cauls after she removed the constricting headpiece.

The forest began a little way beyond, its tall elms and hickories pierced by taller firs which definitely made the area look different from the forests of Liddell in Kent. She followed a crooked, splashing rill into the fringe of the forest thinking it might lead to the pond Lyle Wingfield had spoken of. There seemed to be a hint of a beaten path here, and she hoped no lovers had chosen to come out today. For now, this was all hers, and she meant not to entertain anyone else with her songs of longing for her own secret forest haunts of Liddell.

She thought of her mother then as the forest deepened, the slender Lady Margaret delicate and calm as she had seen her last when they had parted in London at the cloister of the St. Clares. "I will send for you when it is my time," she had said once and then again. Was it true what Edmund and even Morcar had said, that the Lady Margaret of Wake and Liddell felt the arms of death closing about her? Joan shuddered from the cool touch of the shade as she walked farther into the forest. If only mother had talked to her, loved her, they could have been such a comfort to each other.

Then, over there, the little quiet pool appeared, and even a broad, shifting shaft of sunlight filtering through the thick trees lit its calm, gray-green surface. The little rill she had followed seemed to feed it with a merry sound, but its shallowness seemed silent. A doe across the narrow expanse of water lifted its graceful head, glanced with its brown, liquid eyes and darted off. Two weeping willows trailed their slender branches on the pond's surface, and the banks looked soft and sedgy green.

Joan gave a heartfelt sigh of utter peace and contentment: she had escaped the bustle and all the eyes at mazelike Windsor. It was beautiful and simple here, and for now, it was all hers alone.

She explored the short shoreline and discovered a little stone castle with turrets and towers and wards—a miniature

Windsor—tumbled to ruins near the two weeping willows. A child's castle, an intricate toy close enough to the water to have once had its own encircling moat. She loved the enchantment of this place, a fairy castle, under the time-stopping spell of some cunning witch like Morgan la Fey of the King Arthur romances she loved to read or sing so dearly.

She lay her folded *surcote* and ornate headpiece carefully under a shagbark hickory tree and strummed her lute idly with a goose quill while her eyes drank in the peaceful scene. She loosed her heavy hair cauls and shook her long tresses free. On a whim, she removed her slippers, untied her garters, and peeled off her green cotton hose to dip her feet in the water. From the hickory tree, she harvested two bark boats and sent them wafting their lazy paths across the glassy surface. Her bare feet in the water, her green skirts hiked up to bare her knees, she sat on the grassy bank and reached for her quill and lute again. The melody was gentle, plaintive; her delicate, sweet voice sent the words that matched the music over the mirror of water to chase her two little makeshift bark boats. It was, she remembered, the same song about which Lyle Wingfield had teased her as they rode away from Liddell forever ago:

> "When the nightingale singeth,
> The woods wax green;
> Leaf and grass and blossoms
> Spring in May, I have seen.
>
> And love is to my heart
> Gone with a spear so keen,
> Night and day my blood it drinketh
> My heart in suffering."

Her voice hung suspended in the air; her heart lurched to a stop. A tall figure across the narrow pond took a step forward, and an errant shaft of sunlight struck thick, mussed tawny hair, a strong nose and chin, and broad shoulders. Still, the eyes were in shadow. His tunic, hose and shoes were all of deepest brown.

"Has your lover not come to meet you and that has pierced your heart then?" The deep voice floated to her. "Shame on the bloody fool. Had it been I, I would have been here long ago, but I see I did ride into Windsor just in time. And that sad song of a hurt heart—what sort of knave would do that to a maid as ravishing as you?"

From an absence of all but calm and peace, embarrassment and anger flooded in. It was the tall, blond man from the muddy quintain last week. Here—here, no doubt to meet someone and he had thought the same of her.

"You!" she managed and scrambled unsteadily to her feet on the slippery bank. One foot shot backward with a splash, and she balanced awkwardly to hold her lute carefully aloft. When she righted herself farther up on the bank and shook her skirts down to cover her bare, wet legs, he had come quickly much closer. His height, his stern handsome face— the mere impact of his nearness—hit her with stunning force. The little, unbidden fluttering low in her stomach began again like frightened butterflies' wings, and the bewildering thudding of her pulse astounded her.

He came past the willow, bending his tall body down to come through the leafy curtain of limbs, heedless that his boots splashed through the shallow edge of the pond.

"So—you have not forgotten me in these eight days since you came to Windsor, *demoiselle*? You look beautiful today, all in forest green, but then I found you entrancing in mud and wind-blown hair tangles, too."

"Do not make a jest of me, sir. And I had forgotten you. I have not seen you about, so I quite put you out of my mind."

"Alas," he said in a low voice, and she could not discern if his voice was teasing or not. "And here it was my fondest hope the lover in the song who had wounded your chaste heart might be me."

Head down, she darted him a quick look up through her

lashes before turning away. "No, of course not, sir. It is a mere song, a madrigal, or do you only know of such callous practices as charging furiously at the quintain all day and interrupting lady's private songs—"

His strong arms shot out an amazing length to grasp her gently but firmly above her elbows, and she noted his right arm looked much more healed than it had a week ago. "Is that insult meant to imply I know no tender mercies like charity or chivalry—or love, sweet lady? I must warn you, I delight in challenges so flippantly flung in my face and fear I must school you so you understand such gentle pursuits can be my deepest pleasure."

He bent forward, leaned close, his eyes a shattering blue like the clearest heavens on a windy day. His heavy mane of hair, tousled as if he had just ridden a great distance, fell loosely to just above his collar and hung over his broad forehead. His breath was of wine and cloves, his lips stern, then intent. His hands tightened on her arms as his lips claimed hers in a mere brief brush of firm mouth. He pulled back only slightly while his eyes studied her face; then he tipped his head to take her lips again, just a taste, before he settled closer and the kiss deepened.

Her head spun, her knees trembled as her mouth opened softly under the gentle demand of his lips. All thoughts, protests or pleadings screeched to a halt as his tongue darted over her lower lip to skim her even, lower teeth, then tease and plunder deeper within. A little sigh escaped from her throat as he pulled her, lute and all, one step closer until her soft breasts pressed against the iron muscles of his chest. His lips fluttered now across her cheek and into the loose tendrils of her hair. She turned her head away to try to break the spell and glimpsed the crushed white hollyhocks in the top of her bosom where she willingly pressed against him.

"Flowers, flowers everywhere," he breathed and touched her long, loose hair where she had stuck the other hollyhocks behind her ears. His warm, calloused, and scarred fingers trailed down her slanted cheek, across her chin, and down her throat while she stared up at him mesmerized. His tawny brows were thick, rakish over the deepset eyes. The nose was, like his cheeks, a bronze sun color, and there were tiny, crinkles at the sides of his eyes where he squinted against the sun. His thick eyelashes were brownish, but bleached nearly white at the tips, and his eyes—his eyes devoured her.

His roving fingers went lower down the alabaster column of her throat, across her delicate collarbones to skim the low-cut oval neckline where she had placed the flowers. Something hit her then, to awaken her like a thousand little slaps at once. He was smiling, his eyes low on the swell of her breasts while the curved, lightly haired backs of his fingers went lower than the neckline.

Suddenly, she knew fear; she wanted him to continue, to do all those other things Isabella's butterflies whispered about. He was enjoying this entirely and must know she wanted desperately to give him his way.

"No! No, do not! Loose me!" She yanked back so suddenly they nearly pitched off balance, but he steadied her at one elbow until she righted herself and backed away.

His face went instantly austere and hard, and he dropped her arm immediately. "A tease as well as a scold then? Saint George, I should have guessed it."

"You have no right—to insult me like this, sir!"

"Damn, but you can put on a good entertainment, *ma chérie*. I would have wagered my best falcon you were enjoying my insults, as you put it."

His eyes lit to see her cheeks so flushed and her full, heaving breasts straining hard against the green bodice. She caught his intense, hungry scrutiny and spun her back to him.

"You have no right to accost me like this—to come out here when I am wanting to be alone and bother me like this! You have no right to be here!"

He shouted a gruff laugh and, astounded at his reaction, she turned back to face him, her lute cradled like a barrier between them.

"I must admit I am relieved to hear there is no lover to come then—besides me, of course. And, I have every right to be here or anywhere else about, as you shall be convinced of soon enough, my teasing, little shrew."

"I resent your calling me all these pet names. You—you are enjoying all of this!"

"Immensely! And now since you have ruined this so lovely afternoon for the two of us with your ranting, let me tell you that you are never to come out here alone again. If someone else had stumbled upon you here, who is to know what might have befallen you?"

Her voice shook but in as icy a tone as possible, she managed, "What did befall me was quite awful enough. I hardly expected some rude, unchivalrous knave, who at least washed off the mud this time, to stumble on me, as you put it."

His square jaw set, and she could see the rapid beating of the pulse at his throat she had noted that first day. His hands clenched, then unclenched as though he would seize her, but he seemed frozen like a statue. "Damn, *petite femme*, but you have a lot to learn and need taming badly! I have every right to forbid you this forest and I do so now. Disobey and you shall answer to me." His eyes went roughly, almost possessively, over her from head to toe while she faced him defiantly. "And the queen shall hear of it," he bellowed as an afterthought. "Now get your slippers on because we are heading back immediately before I completely lose my hard-won temper!"

Energized to action by the look on his face and the volume of his voice, she bent to retrieve her stockings and shoes. He came at her again, but only took the lute from her hand. "No, not just the slippers. Don the stockings, garters, and the slippers, too, and then I will help you get all that hair up under this headpiece. Your *surcote*, too."

"It is too warm to wear today."

"Just do as I say. I will not have your reputation ruined or even enhanced should someone see you coming back with

71

me all disheveled and half-dressed."

"Half-dressed!"

"Gossips at court, *ma chèrie*, or have you not noticed yet? Let us at least guard your honor until we see the rewards not to are sweeter yet, eh?"

She moved away and, with her back to him, bent to awkwardly pull on one stocking and then the other. Saint George, the maid was as naïve as she must be chaste, he told himself, but he could not stem the flow of desire that made him go weak-kneed as he surveyed her rounded derrière while she stubbornly struggled to replace her stockings and slippers without sitting on the grass. The palms of his hands tingled to touch her again, to tame her, to force her, no matter how she ranted and struggled.

"Now the hairpiece, *demoiselle*."

"I can just coil my hair and push it up under this vile, old thing."

His eyes went over her champagne-colored hair loose to her slender waist. "That flowing bounty? Nonsense."

But she tugged it back and caught the wild ends in one of her discarded cauls, balancing it atop her head while she replaced the angular, two-tiered, green headpiece dangling its gauzy tippets. "I hate these, I hate head covers," she ground out low, and he felt his face break into a grin.

"I too, *chérie*, but the fashions at court must be obeyed, you know."

"Must they? Someday, I intend to set my own no matter what they all think."

"They? Their Graces?" The thought amused him mightily that she could hate Plantagenet fashions and orders, for did not he himself at times feel that same way?

"My lord, you would not tell the queen about today, would you?" she asked, making an attempt at contriteness.

"Not unless you carry on so foolishly again. As I was saying, certain ones must be obeyed. Would you not obey the king, for example?"

He carried her lute, but steeled himself not to touch her as they walked back out of the forest toward the castle walls.

"The king? Aye, we all obey the king?"

"The queen?"

"Of course. She is my legal guardian, and I owe her love and obedience in all things, sir."

Better and better, he thought, and his heart beat strangely faster.

"And Edward, Prince of Wales, our next king?"

She turned to face him in full sunlight as they emerged from the shadowy fringe of forest, and her eyes shimmered a violet velvet that smote his heart so deeply he almost stumbled. Her clear brow crinkled ever so slightly over her graceful, arched brows.

"Aye, as princes must be obeyed by us all. Is he a friend of yours, then?" she ventured.

"I have been most privy to our Prince Edward's desires since his birth," he answered feeling suddenly guilty that he had teased her so. Their exchange reminded him of a jousting match, the kind he knew from the very inception he would surely be able to win. But he was not certain how this vanquished girl would react.

He considered himself quite weak of a sudden, so weak that he desired to take her in his arms and tell her tenderly who he was and ask her name. But, Saint George, whoever she was, it did not matter now, for she would never escape him. Lavender eyes locked with crystalline blue ones as they hesitated at the little wooden postern door in the stone walls of Windsor. He sensed she must have guessed: the awed question or the sharp demand to know his identity would soon be on those rosy, pouting lips he longed to kiss again.

As if to decide it for them, he knocked on the wooden door which was immediately opened inward by the fat, one-eyed man who swept them a low bow. "My lord Prince Edward," he ground out in his guttural voice, "yer men were lookin' for ye but I told them what ye said an' they were not ta be disturbin' ye and they should just get unpacked an' do as they will."

"Aye, old Peter. Thank you then."

He could feel her wide eyes on him and heard the little intake of quick breath. Coward that he suddenly was, he did not look at her face as he indicated she should precede him through the door. They had just walked into a stone archway out of sight of old Peter when she halted and turned to face him. Her cheeks and throat had flushed scarlet, and her beautiful lavender eyes had gone wide. She reached for her lute and he let her take it. Damn, but he was not enjoying this victory half as much as he had imagined he would. He cleared his throat.

"Am I to assume you are your own best friend, Prince Edward of Wales, my lord?"

"Aye, *chérie*. And now you have me at a great disadvantage, for I do not know by what name to call you."

Tears filled her eyes, but did not spill, and she bit her lower lip for a moment. "I have you at a disadvantage?" she floundered. "You dare—"

She bit off the words and looked so appalled he yearned to touch her, just as in the song he had ordered Hankin to sing repeatedly last night.

"I should have known by your resemblance to His Majesty, the King," she said quietly. "And now you have let me insult you, and I am certain it was all a marvelous jest to you, Your Grace—my Lord Edward."

"My Lord Edward. I like that. Being with you has pleased me, lady. We were honest—just two people who liked each other at the start, but argued, too. No one dares to treat me honestly or argue either—but I dare to hope you still shall even now you know who I am."

She flushed again as his eyes met hers. Surprisingly, she dropped him a quick curtsy, then shot out, "Forgive me, Your Grace; but I must be going back. I pray you will not amuse yourself at my expense further by telling anyone—the Princess Isabella—of my foolishness with you."

"Cannot you see my pleasure is not the same as my amusement, sweet lady? Tell me your name now, and I shall

74

let you go."

"And if I refuse, Your Grace, as you refused to tell me when you should have? Would you chain me then in your deepest dungeon?"

She looked horrified at her words the moment they were out, and she jumped nervously when he threw back his head and roared in laughter. He must let her go without telling him; he saw that now. It mattered naught he would have her name from the queen or Isabella in a trice. Wide-eyed, she curtsied again and moved sideways away from where he had her nearly pinned against the wall. This time, today only, because he had feared he had hurt her spirit and lost the battle where he had meant to have such a victory, he forced himself to let her go.

"I will see you tomorrow then, *ma chérie*, and we shall begin over again with everyone knowing who everyone is then," he called softly after her. But what he wanted to say was, Chain you in a dungeon, love? Never. More like chain you to the foot of my bed when you are tamed and mine. Chain you to my heart, mayhap, whatever befalls.

The last flick of green kirtle and floating headscarf disappeared around the stone archway. He sighed and walked slowly the way she had gone hoping perhaps this wretched waiting for a war of any sort was now over.

Chapter Four

Not so much ashamed of the turn of events with Prince Edward as she was frightened by her devastating reaction to him, Joan kept herself closely confined for the next two days. After all, her stomach was a bit unsettled even if she did not feel so physically unwell as she let the other *demoiselles* of Queen Philippa believe, and besides, she needed the time alone. All this courtly banter among the ladies, the giggling, gossiping, and darting about took a toll on her inner, private self, and now that intimate world had been further breached by the clever and terrifying assault of a man who turned her quiet thoughts and very body all topsy-turvy. Even if she could manage to hold off Edward, Prince of Wales, the next time they met, it worried her that for the first time in her life, someone else could hold such sway over her emotions.

Even the pain over the mother love she had lost, if indeed the Lady Margaret of Liddell had ever loved her "dear, dear Joan," even the ever-present ache for a departed father whom she was said to resemble but had never known; even the bitter separation from Marta and her home to come here—all that had been walled up in a tiny, unfathomable inner recess where it touched her not. But this! This sweep of longing, this rush of weakness mingled with joy when she merely laid eyes on a man she had known but a little over a week and, of course, could never hope to keep—by the blessed saints, there were no thoughts, no words, no songs or music to even begin to delve into that unreachable realm!

She sat now alone in the chamber she shared with

Constantia and Mary, clothed to go out, full of a delicious meal from another tray the Princess Isabella had sent to her by her own servants with a cheery, little message in French begging her to eat and get well of whatever distemper had seized her and to come at midmorn before the others arrived. Whatever the bland, sweet dish Isabella had sent had been, it had warmed her as much as the note except for the tiny postscript in Isabella's flowing hand, which read, "And my dearest brother, our Prince Edward, has returned to us from one of his journeys to say he would like to meet his distant cousin, Joan of Kent."

That had moved her to get up and stop the cowardly sulking, to set aside her rushing fears more than all else. It was a challenge from him, albeit a gentle one, and she would not have him think he had bested her, even though—blast the royal, arrogant knave—he had for now.

She had dressed in the second finest of the four gowns Edmund had purchased for her. Though it was rather too fine for a day gown, she knew Isabella always dressed resplendently even during the day, and she intended to show her, and her vile tease of a brother, that she could array herself every whit as elegantly. Marta had claimed this kirtle and *surcote* were the most marvelous because they matched and set off her eyes that were the color of Marta's beloved Scottish heather. The kirtle was a lavender velvet which deepened to gentle purples in the soft folds of drapery clinging at the waist and bosom. As was fashionable, the material, soft as ducklings' down, molded itself to the swell of her breasts, then to her ribs and flat belly and tiny waist before falling gracefully over her hips. The sleeves were tight from shoulder to extended wrist and from her elbows dangled long, slender bannerets of matching fabric called liripipes.

The armless *surcote* over the kirtle was of a deeper purple banded with the fur of pure white miniver. If she were to walk outside in the spring sun, of course, the whole ensemble would be too warm, but she would stay in the cool rooms of

Isabella's lofty suite today, and besides, she had felt flashes of chill these last several days, so she could most truthfully say she had not been well.

Her lavender velvet was set off by her favorite silver belt slung low on her hips from which dangled a sweet-smelling pomander ball she had stuffed today with essence of dried lily petals that Lady Euphemia had given her. Her short, slender dagger for use at meals rode over her right hipbone. Beneath her gown, when she walked, white stockings and pointed purple slippers peeked out. She had spent over an hour on her own hair without using either of the two maids the three ladies of her chamber could summon to help. Besides, Constantia and Mary always had the two of them hopping about at their beck and call to fix this or fetch that, and Joan's toilet was so simple compared to the stylish complexities of the others.

She glanced quickly at herself in Constantia Bourchier's polished bronze mirror, a gift from some valiant admirer. Aye, her coif looked fine, if a bit unfashionable for the garments. She had parted it in the center, yet let some wayward, forward curls tumble over her white brow. But the heavy masses of hair were neatly plaited and coiled in two huge circlets over each ear, except for the foolish curls at the back of her head which tumbled down the nape of her slender neck. She pondered wearing the heavy gold locket which bore the engraved imprint of her father's crest, a white roebuck, one foot raised in stride, with the ivy leaf behind; but decided against it. Of her few jewelry pieces, this thin gold signet ring would have to do.

She half-wished Constantia and Mary could see how well she looked, but they would only dart each other secret looks or gaze down their pert noses at the new country girl who had come to court and taken the Princess Isabella's affections merely because she was some distant, long-lost relation and somewhat resembled the royal family in coloring and—she had heard them whisper—in her arrogant and self-important demeanor. How she would love to set them back on their silken heels by telling dear Isabella they had gossiped about that!

Joan walked slowly from the queen's wing to the northwest section near the Chester Tower where Isabella and her younger sister Princess Joanna and the new baby Mary had their rooms when the Plantagenets were all here at court. Fortunately, she thought, she did not need to traverse the even more distant honeycomb of chambers where *he* stayed with his closest retainers when he condescended to visit.

Relatively few courtiers were in the main halls this early, for since the king kept late hours sequestered with his advisors planning some sort of grand retribution on the French, people tended to keep his hours. Some sort of covert English plans would be unveiled as soon as this present peace treaty ended and the Plantagenets could fairly claim their French lands owed to the English King through his French mother Isabella, the grandmother for whom her dear friend Princess Isabella had been named.

At least the guards at the princess' door recognized her. No need to knock and have them call out her name today. When Edmund came back after fruit harvest at home to see how she got on in the vast court, she would perhaps have to tell him she was not prospering so well at all; other than Isabella and her eight ladies, who seemed not to favor her at all, she had only met the king once briefly, her royal guardian the queen not at all, and if Edmund asked about the Prince of Wales—oh, a pox on this whole mazelike place and all its busy, distant people!

"Joan, Joan, my dear friend, I am so delighted you feel put to rights at last!" The delicate Isabella bestowed one of her lightning-quick hugs and flounced back to her dressing table in a whirl of golden brocade robe. "Sit, *ma chère* Joan. I am a bit late this morn and just about to soak my hands in this warm goat cream. I detest the stuff if it cools. Tell me now, do you prefer goat or sheep cream for your soaks?"

Joan sat on the cushioned stool wishing Isabella had at

least noted her fine new kirtle and miniver *surcote*, but what was that to her when she had gowns ten times ten that were far better and when she was so used to worrying only about getting herself ready to be *trés chic*?

"I use neither, Your Grace, just wash water with sage and marjoram and essence of roses, since—"

"Oh, aye, that is what Constantia told me. How wonderful to have your natural beauty with none of this paint and art."

"But, forgive me, Your Grace, you are so fair and younger than I. The older maids, I know, but—are you certain you need all this?" Joan's hand swept in the direction of the clusters of perfume, paste, and unguent jars of fine, colored glass.

Isabella wiggled her fingers in the warm cream before she answered. "True, mayhap, dear Joan, for '*Suis-je belle*'—we are both fair, but it is the style, you know. Maud," she called over her elegant shoulder to her waiting, tiring woman, "dry my hands as I am ready for the rest."

While Joan sat beside her princess wishing she had not arrived so soon, the nimble-handed Maud scrubbed Isabella's teeth with green hazel twigs and polished them with a soft, woolen cloth. She rubbed sweet ambergris in the young woman's scalp and essence of gillyflower cream on her slender, white neck. Carefully, she plucked a few stray eyebrow hairs and smoothed the pale, white cochinal paste made from delicate seashells over her brow and nose before applying tinted hues to her eyelids, cheeks, and lips.

Discomfitted and slightly bored, since she had frequently observed Mary and Constantia perform the same ritual, Joan sat woodenly, her mind wandering, wondering just why Isabella had sent for her so early, before the others. Now will that not add to their whispered chagrin when they discover I have been summoned an hour before? she thought grimly.

But as soon as Maud had finished with Isabella's face and had begun to comb and plait her hair, the awkward silence was over. "Maud is a find, an absolute jewel among jewels,

Joan. We shall have to see about finding you a skilled handmaid. I shall speak to the queen on it now she is nearly recovered."

"But I have not even met Queen Philippa yet, Your Grace. I hardly think—"

"Oh, do not fuss so whenever anyone offers you a gift, Joan. It is done here all the time, I daresay. Besides, they give me whatever I ask, the king especially. That reminds me, I wanted to show you my new gowns but there is hardly time now. Did that porcupine seethed in almond milk I sent help to settle your stomach?"

"I believe it did help, though I did not know it was porcupine. I am so grateful for your gifts, please believe me, and I do not wish to seem otherwise."

"Aye, well, the queen loves seethed porcupine when she is under the weather so I thought you might, too. Maud, fetch the gown or he will be here while I am yet half naked."

Isabella rose so quickly from her little carved dressing table that all her cosmetic bottles jumped and shuddered.

"He, Your Grace? A man, some *beau* is coming here now?" Joan asked.

"My dearest silly goose"—Isabella's voice became muffled as an exquisite kirtle of white India silk embroidered with gold thread was slipped carefully over her coif—"it is only my brother Edward. Surely, you know a lady with any sort of reputation to guard does not receive *beaux* in her chambers."

Prince Edward, here, soon. That was why Isabella had summoned her early, of course. He had arranged it to force her out of her safe haven. He would amuse himself by teasing and taunting her in front of the others who would swarm in here like butterflies—no, more like buzzing bees or stinging wasps—in just a little time.

"Now, Joan, do not look so ponderous, if you please. I meant not to scold about *beaux charmants*. You have only been here a little while and you are so lovely, you will attract someone, you will see. And do not be nervous about meeting

81

my Edward," Isabella chattered on, alternately surveying the array of winking jeweled rings Maud offered her on a velvet-lined tray and popping one or another on her slender fingers to admire as it glittered in the light. "You may have heard somewhere that our Prince of Wales is stern and moody browed, but do not be afraid. With me he is always a mere puppy and we get on famously. He has only been here for two days now as he is always out riding circuit to his lands somewhere. He has visited me each day, and today he has said all my dear friends should be here and he especially wanted to meet you. It is such fun, dear Joan—all of the ladies go simply aghast and blush and stutter all over themselves when my dear Edward spends the little time with us he does. It is such a great jest how they act. I tease them for days after."

In the moment's respite while Maud and Isabella conferred about what gems should dangle from her jeweled girdle today, Joan tried desperately to regroup her senses. All the grand Plantagenets liked to torment and tease others, then. And the prince had no doubt arranged this trap for her in front of all the others to amuse himself at her expense just as he had the other times when he had goaded her to insult him, all the while knowing she would simply die of shame when she learned who he was in truth. By Saint George and all the blessed martyr's blood, she would find a way to pay him back if he meant to torment her again. And Isabella—had he told her and had they shared plans for that jest together?

Joan's eyes darted to Isabella's final primping. The princess bent her knees slightly while Maud placed a tall, pointed headdress that trailed tippets and scarves of whitest silk and then fastened the towering, unwieldy thing under Isabella's chin with a single white ribbon.

"Maud. Tell the guards to summon the others. I beat the prince's grand entrance at least so I shall not have to hear from him how I fuss entirely too much, the blackguard. '*Suis-je belle*?' dearest Joan?"

"*Oui, ma Princesse.* You are very fair," Joan assured the younger maid and paced over to glance out the window to steady her knees and make herself as inconspicuous as possible for whatever Isabella meant by "the prince's grand entrance." Mayhap he was bringing with him all his cronies who had clattered into the courtyard the other day to laugh at her too.

The princess' eight other maids trooped in, and they all stood about like vibrant silk and velvet flowers waiting for the sun to rise. It annoyed Joan mightily today that they spoke in hushed tones, trading *bonbons*, giggling, and most of all telling her how happy they were she was hearty and back among them, for she did not believe that from their red, pouting lips.

Just when Isabella had begun to flounce about and mutter something dire about showing even the great Prince of Wales he must not keep fair ladies waiting, the door of the hushed chamber seemed to explode inward, and—he was there.

His appearance, so close across the room, staggered Joan anew, and a nervous, chill foreboding of his magnetism crept up her legs and seized her very core. He seemed even taller and broader-shouldered than she had remembered him as she had reenacted their two brief meetings over and over in her mind. Resplendent in azure and gold tunic, he stopped just inside the door. His garments, arranged in alternating quarters, displayed the gold *fleur-de-lis* of French royalty on the azure background and the dark blue Plantagenet leopards on the golden sections. His hose were deepest blue and a low-slung gold-link belt set with winking jewels held a foot-long dagger encrusted with emeralds.

Across the span of the chamber and the nod of heads as Isabella's *mignonnes* swept him curtsies, their eyes met and held before she, too, bent deep in the obligatory sign of deference. When she arose, still holding her ground by the window, he had looked away and was greeting his younger sister with a kiss on her carefully hued and perfumed cheek.

"*Ma chérie*," his deep voice was saying, "before you give me one of your scoldings, let me assure you I was not tardy here on purpose. The king has had me sitting with him at emergency council all morn, and besides, I do not favor a scolding shrew. Just give me a sweet, compliant maid any day."

Isabella laughed in response and poked him in his gold and azure ribs while the ladies twittered. There, Joan thought grimly, he has made his first sally and he intends to do me in by bits and pieces.

He kissed and smiled and complimented his way through the cluster of Isabella's *belles femmes* toward where she stood. Of course, all the ladies and knights kissed for mere greetings, so she must steel herself to accept that taunt from him and show him no sign it meant a whit to her, she lectured herself desperately. Saints, but she wanted to reach out and slap that smug face which could make her feel all hot and cold and tilt-a-whirl like this!

"Joan, my dearest, do not hang back," Isabella's sweet tones floated to her. "My lord, our distant cousin you have inquired about and wanted to meet. My dearest new companion—and I hope our Lady Queen lets me keep her and does not spirit her off to her own household now she is almost better—Lady Joan, the Fair Maid of Kent."

He was next to her, towering over her in the expectant hush. He emanated the clean, masculine essence of rich, lemony bergamot this close, and she felt her nostrils flare at the sensual assault of it.

"My lord, Prince Edward," she said quietly and thrilled at how calm her voice sounded when her heart nearly pounded out of her chest. His blue eyes dropped to the soft folds over her bosom. Dearest saints, he could read her thoughts! She was to be entirely undone and taunted at his hands!

But his lips merely brushed her cheek in the most appropriate of brotherly greetings. "A fair maid from Kent, indeed, sweet Isabella, rather with Plantagenet coloring and carriage, I think."

"I said the same from the very moment I met her—was it just last week, dear Joan?"

"Ten days, Your Grace."

"And now two days you have been ill, I believe," the prince said solicitously and took her cold hand in his warm, big one. "Thank St. George, you are much recovered now."

She darted a quick look up at him, but he appeared sincere and his eyes held no hint of mockery. She breathed easier and gently tugged her hand from his grasp so no one would notice but he. He pulled his avid, if hooded, gaze away and swept the circle of others with a somewhat stiff smile. "My dear little sister, however do you manage to set yourself like a jewel in a lovely frame of the fairest, most enticing females in the kingdom?"

Joan kept her face serious as a palpable wave of excitement shuddered through the surrounding beauties. "I detest having to leave so soon but I will see everyone at the banquet this evening. The king says the queen may even appear at table, though I shall soon discover that for a certainty as I am set for to visit her—and to bring with me the Fair Maid of Kent, her new ward Joan, whom she regrets not being strong enough to greet these last ten days."

A murmur echoed in the room. "Am I to come along too, my lord?" Isabella asked, her pink lips in a near pout. "I have quite adopted Joan—I and my ladies—and Euphemia. She has a chamber with my Constantia and Mary. I believe I shall go with you to the queen, too."

Edward's big brown hands rested lightly on Isabella's India silk-clad shoulders. "Not today, *ma belle*. Do not fret but I shall accompany the lady to the Queen Tower, and we shall both attest to the fact you have taken excellent care of her and would like her to stay with you. Still, you know, Isabella, that may be unlikely as our queen is to be Joan's guardian even if you depart court with your own retinue."

He turned to Joan again. "We had best hurry, lady, as I was delayed in coming to fetch you by that other business."

That other business, the words echoed in Joan's mind. As

though she were some sort of business to be attended to and then put away or ignored. He nodded and his eyes told her to move behind him as he wended his way back out through the others with low words and continual kisses. She dared not balk or disobey, at least not in front of Isabella and her ladies, as well the knave knew! If he had tried to take her arm, to even touch her gently, she would have insisted his sister acompany them no matter what imperious orders he gave!

When they were out in the hall and the door had closed upon all the staring, annoyed faces, two blank-faced guards fell in behind them as the prince hurried her down the corridor. She walked obediently two steps back as was customary, but when he turned off into a side hall, she halted.

He spun back to face her, but before he could speak, she accused, "That is not the way to the queen's suite, Your Grace."

"Granted. I wanted a word with you in private before we face the queen."

"This hall looks very private."

One corner of his mouth crooked up. Aye, he admitted to himself, he should have known better than to try this with her so quickly, but she owed him some compliance for his exemplary behavior toward her the last two days and this morn in there with Isabella's sweet-faced, little harpies.

"Do not fight me and look at me that way, *ma chérie*. I intend to be your friend if you will let me."

He saw that confused her. So she had been expecting a rough, teasing tone. She stood there all serious-faced, expectant, so ravishingly, naturally beautiful in that clinging, draped velvet the color of her disturbing eyes. Her face was so elegant, so perfect in its oval shape; with its high cheekbones, pert nose, and pouting mouth. Saint George, he had never wanted another woman in this deep—this desperate—way, and this one had ties to the queen and his sister, the whole blessed family to cling to if she chose.

"You look lovely today, Lady Joan," he ventured, to follow his initial thrust when she did not parry. "The gown is exquisite and quite shows off your lavender eyes—the color of sweet lilacs, I think." She smiled and his heart flopped over.

"Thank you, my lord prince. I am pleased you noticed." Saints, she thought, and felt herself color. She had not meant to hint she had attired herself to please him; it was only that no one else had noticed her appearance.

"I told you we would begin over when we met again, and I meant it sincerely, *ma chérie*. I did not intend to hurt you the other times, but you were so full of fire and it was quite a temptation not to ruin that."

He stepped closer and his eyes sought her lips. From a distance, one of the guards coughed. "Thank you, my lord, for your kindness and restraint today, and for not calling me out on a point of honor for insulting the Plantagenet heir."

"But I am calling you out, sweet," he pursued despite the fact he saw her tense again. "The challenge is that—that we can be friends and you will let me get closer to you and should you need a protector, you may rely on me." He bit his lower lip and frowned as if he were dismayed by his rush of words.

Her heart pounded. Her eyes widened. Her gaze flowed out to meld with his intense stare. These two days hiding in her chamber, fretting, cursing him—this was not the tactic she had expected or the battle she had meant to enjoin. She needed time, time and distance to think, to stop this rush of desire to touch him and be as yielding as water, whatever he asked of her.

"The queen, Your Grace. I would like to meet the queen. Will she not be awaiting us?"

"Aye. But you know I had only one brief brotherly kiss back there from you and two from all the others. Shall we not seal our new-won truce with a little kiss? There is a small room just down this hall."

"Your Grace, I have been ill and I should never forgive

myself if you should catch the malady. I fear for your sake I must needs refuse."

His mouth set in a firm line at being gainsayed, but his eyes lit at her refusal. Aye, she asked for a battle, a jousting match, and he knew well how to win that sort of tournament.

"Then we shall straight to the queen, sweet Joan, with no more dire detours. Only, I fear I have already caught the same malady that has laid you low for these two days and with a vengeance."

She started away down the dim hall toward the guards before he could see his words had angered her. Then, furious again that he had made her forget herself so that she dared to precede him and walk away without being dismissed, she halted dead still in her tracks until he gallantly offered her his gold and azure arm and they went on together.

The last two weeks of May swept by in a blurry haze; then the first two sun-lit, crystal weeks of June tripped quickly after. Everyone knew her now and spoke her name or called her Joan, the Fair Maid of Kent. Everyone nodded gaily, and even Isabella's pouting *mignonnes* sought her out and if they whispered aught did so entirely out of her hearing.

The warmth of the Plantagenet sun—or was it son, she mused—shone full upon her. Queen Philippa, plump and soft-spoken with only a hint of a Flemish accent, was motherly, stern, but incessantly kind. She spoke fondly of the handsome, gentle Edmund of Kent, the father Joan had never known. The queen allowed her new ward to stay, for now, housed among Isabella's ladies because she felt Joan was a "sensible breath of fresh country air" to mayhap temper the frivolities of her own young, but sophisticated, daughter.

Joan tried with all her might to fulfill the queen's description of her as sensible. Though she was frequently in the circle of friends of Prince Edward, and it was greatly from his favor that her reputation at court grew, she fought to keep her head and to have other people about her.

Yet even with others in attendance, his lure for her was undeniable and there were no others she noted even in a very crowded room. They all faded into the hazy mist of background when Edward smiled or gazed on her. He talked her into playing her beloved lute and singing for him and the queen, and many praised her talents.

He taught her backgammon and regularly beat her at dice or chess; he took her and Isabella hawking and even arranged for her once to sit at the royal family's table in the Great Hall, but he had not repeated that since the king had monopolized her conversation all evening and had stared at her in front of Queen Philippa, too. However, Joan forgot that problem at once and the raised eyebrows it caused. The complicated world of Windsor had suddenly become very simple and very wonderful: Edward, Prince of Wales, evidently kept his place, and so, she, too, could be sensible and happy all at the same exciting time.

Tomorrow the court bustle would culminate in a fabulous Midsummer's Day Tournament before the court moved on to Westminster Palace in London and the prince and his household would be gone for a time. Joan's world bubbled and cascaded on despite that little worry of upheaval on the horizon out there. A new palace to learn, the city of London nearby, her charming prince gone off to his lands at Berkhamstead, which she would probably never see. Yet today, tomorrow, and the next day, it was fair Windsor at Midsummer Tournament time.

The entire castle and environs took on an expectant, different feeling. Knights and their retinues arrived from shires near and distant to set up their striped, beflagged tents outside the battlements on the greens near the tournament fields. Even over the tall tower walls wafted the scents of oxen turning on massive spits over cookfires; the smithies, farriers, and armorers sent up a merry din from their forges in the south precincts of the castle. Drovers' carts laden with mountains of piled food arrived daily; pyramids of barrels of ale, beer, and wine grew under archways near the lists and the newly erected and decorated galleries for ladies and guests to watch the jousting. Like filings to the great magnet of Windsor, musicians and entertainers, prostitutes and vendors flocked in with their lures of trestle stages, juggling bears, wares to sell, and fiery swords to swallow.

Caught up in the frivolity and excitement of the moment, Joan threw four weeks of caution to the winds. Though she had refused such suggestions or inquiries before, today she had decided to meet Prince Edward alone as he had asked—only for a moment—since this summer idyll he had made for her at Windsor was nearly over. He would be going off on a lengthy progress through the midland shires and she might not see him 'til Yule time, he had whispered. After all, he had been such a true, chivalrous gentleman these last weeks she had almost come to believe her initial assessment of him as arrogant, teasing, and demanding was quite wrong.

She crushed the little note he had sent her in her warm palm as she set out with a quick wave to Mary and Constantia. A tiny, walled private garden directly under the Brunswick Tower, the note said. Outdoors in a garden within the castle walls—indeed, that sounded safe enough, she had reasoned. It was hardly some private room in a deserted side hall of the labyrinth of the castle or some distant, forest pond.

She had chosen her garments more carefully lately than she would like to admit. This mauve-hued kirtle and *surcote* were one of five the queen had ordered made for her; the Plantagenets were generous to their own chosen few without a fault. The embroidery on the split-sided *surcote* depicted cavorting unicorns, and Joan loved it dearly. The enamel-and ivory-studded girdle low on her hips was another trinket from Isabella; yet in quiet moments, Joan had wondered if some of the bounty had been encouraged by Prince Edward. How pleased, how thrilled her dear brother Edmund would be to see how she'd gotten on here in the world of the great Plantagenets in the six weeks he had been gone. He was due here by today surely, for the tournament was tomorrow and both he and her younger brother's liege, Lord Salisbury, were entered in its extensive pageantry of the joust.

Easily enough, she found the little garden tucked into the northeast corner of the castle walls between two towers directly under the prince's suite of rooms. The two same impassive-faced guards who always trailed the prince about when he divested himself of his laughing, noble cronies stood outside the little wooden door. The wall of the garden was high, a very private place from all.

She was pleased with herself at feeling so calm of late whenever she faced him. Her pulse never failed to beat faster and the little butterfly wings fluttered when she looked directly into his crystalline, blue eyes; yet she was calm. It was as if lately they had been one happy and friendly family, not that the queen was quite like a mother, not like Marta had been, and she could never picture the avid-eyed King Edward as a father. Still, Isabella, young and flighty though she seemed, could mayhap be the sister she had never had and Edward—

He sat on a little stone bench under a quince-apple tree directly in the center of the garden when the guard swung wide the door for her. Leggy rose bushes in midsummer bloom above stark purple- and blue-fringed gentian edged the small, grassy space. The prince was garbed all in deepest, midnight blue with a huge linked-gold neckchain stretched across his shoulders and chest and a plain, wide leather belt low on his narrow hips.

"*Chérie*, you came this time!"

She returned his eager smile and let him take her hands. "I was not aware there were other times you were languishing in some garden and I did not come, Your Grace. The other times I told you clearly I could not come."

"Would not come," he corrected. "And will you not call me by my name, just when we are alone?"

"I—I do not think it a good idea. After all, we are so seldom alone."

"Not my fault, *chérie*. But agree to my wishes and I can

arrange it anytime you send for me."

"I send for you! My dear lord—"

"My dear Lord Edward, then. I will have it so, my little Joan. Jeannette."

The diminutive French sobriquet he had taken to using lately to address her when no one could hear hung there between them tender and affectionate.

"My Lord Edward, then," she breathed softly.

"Since we are soon to be parted, my Jeannette," he went on as if he had rehearsed some difficult speech, "and since I have taken the calculated risk of introducing you to many knaves about the court who may not be so restrained and circumspect when I am gone, I wish you to listen most carefully to the words I have to tell you."

His eyes skimmed her intent face and dipped once to the high, sweet breasts he had so often dreamed of touching, of possessing and tasting. "These last few lovely weeks when I have tarried here at Windsor, we have been almost family, have we not? Dear friends, at least. And I believe you trust me now."

Her quick smile wrenched his heart, and he felt the too-familiar cresting passion she always aroused in him though lately he had carefully cloaked his desires beneath the crushing armor plate of self-control to win her heart. "Just listen, Jeannette, *s'il vous plaît*," he managed.

"I do not wish you to be misled about my true feelings for you," he went on. "I have three sisters and they are quite enough. I do not wish another nor do I seek only a female confidante, though indeed you have become somewhat that to me with your firm, independent mind and tart, honest tongue."

"My Lord Edward, I think—"

"And so, if that clever little brain of yours can calculate half as well as I deem it can, you must conclude my need for your company is of quite some other sort."

She colored as she always did so tantalizingly when he teased her or gave her a direct, piercing look which unbeknownst to her shook him as completely as it did her. "This cannot be, Your Grace."

"Saint George, it is, and you know it, too! You are no simpleton, Jeannette, though an untutored country maid in the world's ways still. I flatter your intelligence and show you my total concern for your well-being by telling you plain in words before I claim what must be mine."

The old stunning impact, the flowing, desperate sweet rush of emotion she had first felt with him turned her limbs to jelly as their eyes held. "I must go, my dear lord. Please."

"No. Sit here and listen to me. You are not some coward to flee. Sit here. I am trying to just explain and not to touch you yet."

"We cannot—even should I consent. The queen. Isabella. We cannot."

"I will be gentle and tender. I will cherish you and protect you. These things can be accomplished in secret. You could have your own room and a discreet tiring maid."

"I would like to have my own room and my dear Marta from Liddell, but—"

"And would you not like to have me, *ma Jeannette*? I desire you very, very greatly and have since I first saw you that rainy day you just appeared. I have a townhouse in London. You could go to visit your mother once you are at Westminster. There are disguises, secret rooms, excuses to escape—"

His words pierced her, shattering her steely calm and shredding her little world of peace within. Images of a rapt kiss, his hands on her body the way the other *demoiselles* whispered about such things screamed at her from her deepest dreams and most buried, secret desires. How many times had she heard Mary or Constantia elaborate such things between a willing maid and a forceful man? But this was her, the queen's sensible Joan and the Prince of Wales!

His hands were gentle on her shoulders as he turned her firmly to him. "Jeannette, we are both young but let me show you a prince who knows how to please you."

"You speak not of love, my lord," she managed, her voice a shaky whisper. "I am certain you are used to merely commanding any lady you fancy and she is yours to do with as you will, but you cannot expect—you have no right—" She floundered. "After all, I am untutored, as you say, and well enough born so that the queen said I may expect a fine marriage and I will not bear someone's bastard children even if they be yours!"

He looked as though she had struck him. Had he been so certain of her, of his power and charms then? she wondered. She was afraid for the first time she could remember as she saw his square jaw set and his wide eyes grew ice-cold, glintingly blue.

"Saint George, Jeannette, I offer you the Prince of England's heart at your feet and you sit there like stone and will have none of it. The hell with reasoning words to a foolish woman I will have!"

His grip on her shoulders tightened, and he slid her to him across the tiny space of bench. Soft thigh pressed to his iron one as he wrapped his powerful arms around her and crushed her back. His mouth was warm, firm, demanding the response of open, soft lips she gave him mindlessly. His tongue invaded while his hands skimmed her back and hips, kneading, caressing. She slipped sideways so that he held her cradled across his chest while his lips traced icy fire down her throat to her collarbones and lower. She could not breathe, could not think and fascinating, violent colors jumped and reeled through her stunned mind.

"Jeannette, Jeannette, my sweet, you will yield to me, you must. Let me have you, fill you with my need." She felt him tugging at the low oval neckline of her kirtle, impatiently brushing the mauve brocade from her smooth shoulder. Dizzy, spinning wildly in the very center of the careening universe, she returned kiss for burning kiss until she gasped at a new sensation she could hardly fathom: her white breasts freed in the cool shade, he bent his mouth to kiss, to lick, and tease and flick back and forth at his will each shamelessly pointed, pink nipple.

Her hands grasped his back as the garden spun faster. Somehow she arched up toward him while he pulled and suckled one ripe peak of breast and then the other. Held across his lap, bared to his waist in front with her gown pulled halfway down her arms, she gasped at each wonderful new foray of his hands and mouth. Under her skirts, a big calloused palm stroked up her white hose past her knees which parted like water; he caressed the trembling inside of one warm thigh, then moved higher. He kissed her lips hard again as his eager fingers sought the sweet, warm spot at the very secret juncture of her long, writhing legs.

"Jeannette, you will come to me. You will let me," he gasped. She nodded wildly, clinging, moving to meet his stroking fingers. She could not think. She could not breathe!

From somewhere then, out there in the world of reality, a quick wooden knock resounded with the words, "My Prince, the queen!"

Edward cursed and hauled her roughly upright against him to hide her bare breasts. Flushed, disheveled, holding to each other, they faced an open wooden door filled terribly by the gaping Queen Philippa and Joan's livid brother Edmund.

The prince spun Joan away while she tugged up her sleeves and bodice, but she could hardly stand. A trembling racked her from deep inside. The queen's sharp tone hit them both like a whip.

"Edward! Joan, like this! My Lord Edmund, I had no idea, I swear to you—no idea!"

Joan's stomach nearly heaved in shame and agony, and the rose bushes and tall walls still cartwheeled crazily when she finally covered herself and turned to face them. To her dismay and surprise, the prince was in such a sputtering rage he could not speak.

"And is this why you condescend to remain about our court a whole fortnight when you could hardly abide an overnight visit lately, my son?" Queen Philippa demanded.

"For shame, and with my dear and once-trusted young ward whom Lord Edmund here has entrusted to our royal house for safekeeping. I thought you had always been above such foolish philanderings. Your royal father may be amused, but I assure you, I am not."

The prince's tone was fully as outraged as his mother's. "Leave off, Your Grace. I will not be whipped like some fond schoolboy. It just happened. You may believe it or not as you will, but it is the first time like this and honorable."

"Honorable?" Edmund of Kent roared, and Joan was thankful his foul temper was reined in by the fact the prince was the one he had caught with her. "Your Grace," Edmund shouted until he remembered he was addressing his queen and lowered his strident voice, "I did not rear the little chit to act like a wanton, I assure you. But she has been badly spoiled in my absence at Liddell over the years and her willfulness has gotten quite out of hand. Joan, come with me now and we shall deal with this."

"Calm, calmly now, my Lord Edmund," the queen intoned, her plump chin quivering in her restrained passion. "The Lady Joan has been entrusted to me here and I promise you I shall keep a closer eye on her. Besides, our dear son Edward leaves us for several months after the tourney tomorrow. Joan is quite lovely—naïve and tempting—and of marriageable age, of course. I see now I must give some time to thinking of that and soon."

"Lady Joan, you may go now to my rooms and await me there," the queen continued. "His Grace, the Prince Edward, will be quite busy now preparing for his part in the tournament tomorrow and then, unfortunately, departing from us until Yuletide. I assure you, my Lord Edmund, had I not been so indisposed after the birth of the Princess Mary, such foolishness never would have happened."

Joan pulled free of the prince's light steadying touch on her elbow. Never had she felt so humiliated or beaten. Ignoring Edward though she should have curtsied as she left him, she dropped a low curtsy only to the queen. "Forgive me, Your Majesty. It was great foolishness on my part, as you say, and I hope you may find it somewhere in your kind heart to forgive me for I shall never forgive myself or let some such occur again." Her voice was cold, haughty. Why did he not say something, she thought—curse her or blame her at least? It would be just like him!

Yet just as she walked stiffly around the queen and her still-furious brother, she heard an icy voice to match her own.

"Aye, forgive us both, my lady mother. It was but a moment's whim and got quite out of hand. Summer days and rosebuds, you know. The maid spoke aright—a mere moment's foolishness which shall not be repeated, and as you say, after the morrow, I shall be gone. Little Joan, I daresay, is a bit of an innocent, so I would not rush to marry her off to some poor scoundrel who just wants some good Plantagenet blood to breed his heirs, by St. George."

Fury and palpable hate pounding in her ears, Joan fled headlong up the curving tower steps toward the queen's apartments only to curse Edward Plantagenet, Prince of Wales, when she was halfway up and beat and kick the uncaring stone walls until the last shred of her strength was gone.

Chapter Five

The rest of that fateful day had been endless agony. The queen had been kind enough, especially when Joan had assured her there was no true feeling or ties between herself and the prince. Her utter hatred and contempt for him she dared not voice. And her brother Edmund had stayed away until he calmed down enough to be civil. He was pleased, he admitted, that she had found such favor with the king, queen, and Princess Isabella despite the one most grievous and dangerous error with His Grace, the Prince of Wales. And now, he assured her, Queen Philippa would be certain to make her a marvelous matrimonial match.

Joan knew her eyes were swollen from hours of silent crying into her pillow, and her face was pale and drawn from lack of sleep as dawn lit the window of her little room the next morn. Yesterday's shameful memories were further inflamed by the note the prince had dared to send her through his lutenist Hankin. She had read it again and again, memorized it, before she burned it as he had bidden, though she believed not a word it said:

Ma Jeannette,

Please understand my words to them were for your own protection since I must go away. My dearest wish was to wear your token before them all at the jousts tomorrow, but now for your sake I must not request it, nor may you offer it.

If they speak of marriage for you, do not resist; neither agree nor take any vows.

Please trust me in this, and we must surely meet again soon. Hold to that moment we both wanted to be as one, before the serpents crashed into our apple garden in Eden.

My deepest admiration and unalterable affection.

E.

Curse him, she thought for the hundredth time since yesterday. *He* was the serpent, the evil temptation, and she was well rid of him. Let him carry anyone's damned token to the lists—anyone who was foolish enough to believe he was an honorable knight. Let him lose at the joust and let him go off for months to his castles or palaces or fine houses in London. Meet him there at some private house in London! Submit to his treacherous caresses or fall victim to his words meant to trap and ensnare? Never! Love him? Saints, she *hated* him and always would. She could not wait until the morrow when this terrible charade they called a tournament of honor was over and he was gone.

Bitterness welled up inside at her own stupidity. What had suddenly become of all her vows to herself, to Marta, and even to Lyle Wingfield about never allowing any forbidden love—any love at all—to hurt her? It was not really love, of course, but here in just a little over one brief month she had managed to get her life into terrible tangles. If only she would not have had to face her brother Edmund and the queen. She wished she had been ordered back to Liddell Manor in quiet Kent forever!

She watched through prickly eyelids as gray turned to silver, then to gold at the window of her little chamber. She pulled herself off her mussed pallet, for Constantia and Mary shared the only real bed in the room and she would rather sleep alone anyway. She washed her face with last night's cool water, rather than calling one of the maids, and mechanically began to comb through her snarled hair.

She would get through this day and with a smile on her face, she vowed. She must. Her only consolation was that surely neither the queen nor Edmund would tell anyone what they had seen and surmised in the little walled garden, and the guards would not talk unless the prince did. Oh, saints! What if he boasted of his easy conquest to some of his sophisticated, laughing cronies? If he did, she would kill him—kill him and be beheaded for treason unjustly even as her poor father had been.

"Up so early, *petite* Joan?" Constantia's sleepy voice came to her. "Your first tournament, I know, and your prince is always so magnificent in them, is he not, Mary?"

"Um? Oh, aye, always *magnifique*."

"He is hardly my prince, Constantia. I need to be dressed early because I am to go to the queen's apartments to walk down with her."

"Oh, dear. Since when?" As Constantia sat up and stretched, the bounty of her russet hair spread like a rich cloak to cover her full, naked breasts where the sheet fell away. Joan averted her eyes not for modesty but because Constantia's pointed breasts recalled her own too much as the prince used them yesterday for his own amusement.

"Since last evening when I spoke with her in her rooms," Joan answered. "I forgot to tell you. I hope our dear Princess Isabella will not mind."

"Mind? By the Blessed Virgin, what can any of the royal brood say when the queen orders? I just wonder what it means."

"It means naught but she wishes me to sit near her, I warrant. I am her legal ward despite the fact my brother is here from Kent for the tournament now. I will just dress first and be gone out of your way."

"Fine, only call one of the maids which ladies are supposed to use, Joan. The Princess Isabella has nine though she only favors a few. You, at least today, could benefit from the use of one." Constantia snuggled back under the down-filled coverlet, and Joan quickly turned away before she could see she had been crying.

The remark about calling a maid to help her today—was

that an indirect remark about her lack of cosmetics or her hair style? Saints, what did it matter now? she thought. When the prince disappeared, they would probably all revert to their initial mistrust of her anyway. All she wanted was for this once-so-promising day to be over. She went wearily to the door to ask a linkboy to summon a maid.

A veritable parade of important-looking persons were filing from Queen Philippa's suite of rooms as a lady-in-waiting announced Joan, the Fair Maid of Kent, and Joan entered. Queen Philippa sat on a heavy, carved chair within a circle of courtiers, all gorgeously arrayed in their tournament finery of rich brocades, silks, and velvets. Then Joan realized the entourage was almost all women, and the few men standing about or talking quietly were quite elderly, save one reddish-brown-haired man leaning heavily on a walking stick and wearing a rakish-looking patch over one eye. By now, she thought, the celebrated young or middle-aged warriors of the realm were decking themselves in shiny metal armor as hard as Prince Edward's heart.

The queen caught Joan's eye and summoned her over with a flick of a plump finger. Beautifully attired in golden-figured brocade, the queen looked stiff and suddenly foreboding. A jeweled coronet was cleverly attached to her high, angular headpiece and a gauzy, gold-hued wimple framed her white face.

"*Ma belle*, Jeannette, here, over here, *ma chérie*," Her Grace called, and the woman's clever eyes noted well how the girl started at her use of the pet name by which she had been told her son, the prince was wont to call her of late. "As soon as the royal and very persistent Doctor John Gaddesden is finished peering at a perfectly recovered and healthy woman, we shall have a brief blessing for today's events and go out. Doctor John, *are* you quite through? Here, Joan, hold Duchie while I chase this dear old pest away."

Joan's hands were immediately filled by the queen's favorite white lapdog, and she tried to hold the squirming, little hound so he would not shed white hair on her golden gown. When she had him settled comfortably, she breathed a small sigh of relief. The queen today seemed friendly and normal despite her use of the little nickname the prince had dubbed on her. Then Joan noted that old Doctor Gaddesden stared not at his royal patient but at her. His voice was high pitched, like old leaves rustling.

"This is the maid from Kent then, I have heard spoken of. My friend Morcar from your home castle speaks well of you, *demoiselle*, and, I believe, reads grand things for you in the heavens as surely as I could read them on your face, I dare say."

"My lord doctor, I do of course know Morcar, for he was once my father's astrologer and now has come to court when I did to serve the king privately. Morcar has come for king's service, I mean, and not I, milord." She felt herself color slightly at the *faux pas*, realizing several of the queen's intimates standing about had hushed to hear the conversation.

"Ah, of course, lady."

"As for Morcar's prognostications, Doctor Gaddesden, I believe you are mistaken," Joan added, hoping their conversation was not annoying the queen whose avid eyes under her pleated wimple and jeweled headpiece seemed to take it all in. The little dog wriggled in Joan's arms giving her an excuse to look away while the doctor cleared his throat and shook his brown head which seemed sifted with a snow of white hairs.

"Ah, indeed, as you say, Lady Joan. Then perhaps I did not hear Morcar aright. I must tell you though, my dear, you look drawn and exhausted. Some sort of midsummer fever perhaps and, Your Grace, I would suggest for the *demoiselle* an herbal tea brewed of ash leaves and butterbur for—"

"Be off, my lord doctor," the queen's voice interrupted him, suddenly impatient. "The child is as well as I, nothing a good several days' recovery with rest alone after the excitement of today will not cure. Is that not right, Jeannette?"

Joan caught the intent, the cloaked warning even though the fumbling Doctor Gaddesden seemed not to as he continued to stand about in his distinctive doctor's gown of purple and red with its furred hood. But the queen, quick and pert despite her corpulence, bustled up and shifted the little lapdog Duchie to yet another's hands before her beringed hand gently took Joan's wrist.

"There, my dear little charge, do not look so dismayed," the queen whispered, bending close. "As I told you clearly yesterday, I shall not hold a foolish indiscretion against you and no one shall know of it. I have quite promised my son Edward that, stubborn tyrant that he can be at times. Besides, there will be no need for further ado."

A stubborn tyrant indeed, Joan mused. And had the knave then promised his mother he would never pay court to Joan again or some such? Saints, it would be just like the conceited, despicable wretch.

"And so, dearest little Joan, before our mass here for the success of our dear, royal family and the safety of all at the lists today," the queen was saying grandly, no longer whispering, "I should like to introduce you to your noble escort for the day, Thomas, Lord Holland from Lancashire, a dear, dear friend to me and my lord king."

From the cluster of staring folk stepped a man she had noted: tall, stocky, leaning slightly on a carved walking stick, and wearing a brown silk patch over his left eye. His other eye was an intense coppery hue that matched his reddish-brown hair; sun freckles dusted his ruddy skin. He seemed much older than Joan, yet perhaps not old—about her brother Edmund's age of thirty and four or five years, perhaps. His face was pleasant enough, bearing a wryly amused or merely curious expression. His velvet garments of deepest russet made him appear almost coppery-colored from head to toe.

Joan dipped in a slight curtsy, wide-eyed at the suddenness of the queen's unannounced and blatant matchmaking.

She steeled herself as the queen reached out and joined both Thomas Holland's and Joan's hands within her plump-fingered grasp.

"There now. I know you shall both enjoy the day, and fine things shall come of this new friendship. See to her, please, Lord Thomas."

The man nodded, but his eye followed the queen's bustling wake as she led them over to that part of her huge greeting chamber arrayed for a little chapel. An altar, tiers of wavering votive candles, and a large wooden gilded and painted statue of the Blessed Virgin lined one whole corner of the room.

Fine things shall come . . . this new friendship, the queen's last words echoed in Joan's tumbled thoughts. This man, Lord Thomas Holland of Lancashire, dear friend to the queen and her lord king, still held her hand possessively in his own large, warm one until, surprised they still touched, Joan tugged hers back.

"I fear that was a bit sudden, eh, Lady Joan? But perhaps some of life's best surprises are that way."

"What? Oh, aye, indeed, my lord."

He smiled at what he considered her quick recovery of poise and control. The maid was young, but so fair and, no doubt, clever too. Her blood line was nearly impeccable, flowing from the great King Edward I, grandfather of the maid as well as of the present sovereign. It was rumored about lately, of course, that the Prince of Wales had been quite enamored of her, but then he himself had lived long enough to see clearly why. The Hollands were never fools or rebels when the royal handwriting was on the castle wall, and he would be no fool in this fine snare. Her Grace, Queen Philippa, to whom he had always been particularly attached since he had been in the retinue sent to deliver her, safe from Hainaut as a blushing, lovely virgin bride seventeen years ago, had no doubt finally found for him the woman of his dreams—beautiful, young, and well attached. Granted, her father had died terribly under the foulest of questionable charges, but what was that to him if it did not bother the queen? People whispered of it less and less and any future Holland children need never inherit that cloud of shame any more than they would be born with one eye because their sire had lost his in battle.

"Shall we move over there and kneel for the brief prayers then, Lady Joan?" he said and indicated she should precede him. He saw her quick eyes dart to his legs to assess why he leaned on his stick.

"By St. Peter's chains, 'tis nothing *demoiselle*," he told her smoothly hoping to read some concern in her eyes and not disdain. Suddenly, he wanted to pull her aside and tell her of all his injuries earned in service to the king—in the Scots Wars, the crusade with the Teutonic knights in Poland where he had bravely distinguished himself—all his wounds, this healing, broken leg from the same joust in which Prince Edward had broken his arm—

"The leg looks worse than it is," he began again when she merely inclined her head. "I regret it does keep me out of the action today when I would rather be out there hacking away in the *grande mêlée* with the best of them. It will heal a bit more, fair lady, and then the limp will go, too, and I shall be back in king's service before we rout the French when this bloody treaty is up, eh?"

Her sweet mouth smiled graciously. "I am relieved to hear it is naught worse, of course, my Lord Thomas. And I will be appreciative of a guide today to tell me what to look for and expect out there."

She moved where he had indicated and knelt two rows back behind the queen on a silk-covered *prie-Dieu* in the area of the room the queen had ordered converted to a temporary chapel while she had been ill with birthing fever from her last child. This section of the chamber surrounding the delicate altar was exquisitely beautiful with Persian carpets, brocaded bed hangings, perfumed water in hand basins, cloth coverings, and rich tapestries on the walls over which jeweled light sparkled from panes of lead-glass, stained windows.

Joan felt and heard Thomas Holland kneel heavily beside her on his good knee despite the pain it must cause in his healing leg. Out there, her last words dangled still in her mind; tell me what to expect out there.

Aye, as the Prince had told her yesterday, she was not a simpleton, and now she was also quite undeceived about what to expect out here—anywhere, now. She would sit, this whole long, utterly endless day, beside this man the queen had chosen to watch her and to keep her mind occupied and for perhaps more, much more than that.

The voice of the queen's almoner droned on in Latin beseeching safekeeping and blessings on all the combatants today, especially the queen's own dearly beloved husband, Edward III, king of England, by Grace of God, and the heir to the throne—Edward, Earl of Chester, Duke of Cornwall, Prince of Wales.

It had been only six brief weeks she had known him, Joan told herself, as her own unbidden prayers for the prince's safety coursed through her brain. Pure, rank foolishness to fathom love in so short a span, so impossible a circumstance. Despite the powerful presence of the man kneeling next to her whose leg barely brushed her skirt folds, a vision of Edward rose up clearly in her mind's own treasure store: Edward muddy and huge battering at the quintain as relentlessly as he had at her walled-up heart. And now—now—

"Lady," the deep-voiced Thomas Holland whispered and offered her his muscular, velvet-covered arm. Amazed, she noted everyone was standing and filing out. She rose quickly and gently shook out her skirts to stall for time.

"Shall we join them then, my Lady Joan?" Thomas Holland asked, and his coppery eye under his reddish brow went most possessively over her.

"Aye, my Lord Thomas, of course," she said and managed a smile. Telling herself to feel nothing, she walked at his halting pace as they followed the others outside to the excitement of Midsummer's Day at Windsor.

The Prince of Wales rose from before the little altar in the corner of his huge gold- and azure-striped tent near the tournament fields. He had been hardly listening to the priest recite the prayers to the Virgin and his patron Saint Edward, the Confessor; his mind had been on the grand and glorious jousting to come—and on her. Although he had little time to dally since it took over a half-hour to be suited and mounted, and he could hear the blast of trumpets splitting the air outside already, he dismissed all his attendants but the little jeweler who had ridden in hard from London.

"I know the time was short, man," the prince said to the stubby, dark-eyed craftsman who had never been so honored before and still blessed his lucky signs he had somehow been selected from the fifty-two goldsmiths along the Strand in London. When the order had come with the ducal and privy seal and the gold coins had been offered across the counter just like they were pittance—praise the Blessed Virgin—he had had such a stone to set as he was bidden!

"Aye, Your Grace, and I pray it will earn your favor," the goldsmith Jonathan Quince spoke from his low bow. He extended the beryl ring set in an intricate mounting to the prince and watched as the tall man's big fingers plucked it out of its silk-lined, carved box and turned it over.

A lady's ring for slender fingers, delicate yet sturdy, the little goldsmith thought proudly. The royal instructions had been secret and most explicit: a small beryl ring set in gold with a filigree ivy leaf motif on each side of the clear blue-green stone to hold it to the ring. Beryl, the stone of faithfulness, victory, and protection in battle.

"Fine, a fine job," the words of praise were clipped, but pure delight to Quince's ears. "I shall remember your quick and excellent service to me," Prince Edward said. "I favor the way this green prism shifts to blue in the light—just so. My man has paid you?"

"Aye, most amply, Your Grace."

"He told you to say nothing. You know you must not boast of or advertise this?"

"I understand fully, my lord prince."

"Then my man will show you out."

His squires and pages were back through the tent flap instantly, but he sent them out again with a wave of his hand. "Hankin! Only my lutenist for a moment," he bellowed.

The brown-haired musician appeared immediately, lute in hand. "I have a special errand for you—a secret one on which I shall have your word," the prince began without preamble.

Hankin did not look in the slightest surprised. "Aye, Your Grace, and gladly."

"It means I leave you behind a day when I set out on the morrow and you will follow soon after." He extended the little box to the man although he seemed reluctant to let it go. "It is a beryl ring for Joan of Kent, Hankin, and you must give it to her in private with the words that beryl stands for faithfulness and protection in battle of all sorts."

"Aye, milord prince. No one shall see it but the lady."

"And then I want you to sing her the little song, 'Go, Heart.' Hide that box and sit here and sing it for me now. My men will be distracted if we do not get on with all this dressing for the tourney. There—sit over there and sing it for me as you will for her."

He shouted for his men and eight servants immediately crowded around him to clasp on his armor. Each of the approximately two hundred knights here today had at least two mounted squires, an armorer and five or six servants in livery to prepare him for and accompany him to the joust. But the prince, of course, had even more, including today his younger brother Lionel, Duke of Clarence, age six, who was here with two of his squires and a page just to watch. His four-year-old brother John of Ghent was still exiled to the ladies' galleries.

He tried to keep his mind on the words of Hankin's plaintive song played ludicrously against the clanking of his chain mail and twenty-three separate pieces of armor. Over a heavily padded tunic to soften the blows of metal against muscle, they placed his hauberk of chain mail, then strapped on his big molded and finely engraved breastplate. Buckles linked piece to piece as the full weight of sixty pounds of armor went on in fitted, silver parts: huge shoulder pauldrons, layered faulds to protect his hips and pelvis, clanking leg and arm pieces. Over that, a sleeveless silk jerkin in stunning gold and azure bearing the proud Plantagenet leopards and French *fleur-de-lis*, quartered. For a moment he held his dressers off from yet placing his padded hood, which would bear the weight of the ten-pound helmet, to hear the words to Hankin's song one more time:

> "Go, heart, hurt with adversity,
> And let my lover thy wounds see;
> And say her this, as I say thee:
> Farewell my joy, and welcome pain,
> 'Til I see my love again."

His gauntlets and rowel spurs clinked on last, and he slid his two-handed sword and eighteen-inch dagger in his belt. In the slightly gaited, rolling stride peculiar to warriors in full armor, he walked amidst his little retinue outside the tent. At over six feet tall, Edward, Prince of Wales, carried full armor better than most men and he knew it. But for him, mere skill and acumen in joust or *mêlée* did not make his reputation; he might wear his spurs, but he had hardly earned them. This stylized, grand mock battle was just that, and everyone realized it—as pretentious, he thought, as thinking he had earned the willful heart of the fair-haired Joan when she probably cursed him for his apparent desertion of her when they were discovered. But he would win today—and he would win her back however long it took, whatever he had to overcome.

In the blinding sun outside, he patted and spoke low to his huge destrier Calais. Like his rider, the horse carried molded plate armor and a decorative Plantagenet silk blazon. Chain mail draped itself over Calais' high arched neck and the wild, excited eyes were barely visible in the horse's head mask of decorative, etched metal.

At the last moment, they placed and lowered the helmet, and latched it down. His world narrowed, darkened, and his pulse beat faster as it always did when he became fully encased in this heavy, iron cocoon. For now, he kept his visor up to see and breathe more easily. Leonard, a squire, fastened to his shoulder plate a scarf of the queen's colors, by accident of necessity the one lady's token he would bear today.

The prince's squires and armorer held the destrier and helped him to mount. Some knights even needed winching up onto their horses, but he had never favored that. Hankin stood now in the open tent flap directly in his narrow view as two squires mounted to lead his destrier to the lists. Despite the thrill of combat, of performing here today before the adulation of the raucous crowd, he wished for one tiny moment to trade places with the lutenist who would see Jeannette alone and give her the ring and song. Her face, petulant, enticing, floated through his iron-encased skull as he was led outward from the clusters of tents and metal men and darting, screaming squires.

The backs of the loges for noble spectators went by; painted barriers loomed ahead as the combatants jogged forward in increasing numbers. Summer sun glinted on raised trumpets as their brassy blares silenced the excited crowds. Commoners who could not get a seat pushed and shoved to the barriers to be able to catch a glimpse of the show. The din of hawkers' cries as they peddled food to the crowd added to the cacophony of snorting horses, clinking plate and mail, and the shuffling of hundreds of hoofs on grassy turf. Over his head as he entered the field, he noted bunting swaying and bannerets flapping in the sudden squally breeze, and he wondered vaguely if the pageantry might be dampened under rain to turn them all to mud knights as on that first day he had seen Jeannette here at Windsor.

From her seat next to Thomas Holland at the side of Queen Philippa's sheltered pavilion, Joan's eyes scanned the rolling, jogging waves of shiny, iron knights entering with their squires and banners for the opening grand parade. Of course, she told herself, her excitement as she surveyed the various family crests was for her brother proudly mounted under their flapping family flag of the ever-alert white stag with ivy leaves behind. Anyone could see—everyone would expect—the king and the Prince of Wales to be easily visible since they were directly centered under the azure and gold leopards and French lilies.

"Marvelous, is it not, Lady Joan," Thomas Holland's deep voice invaded her thoughts. "Damn this leg, but my blood aches passionately to be out there."

Joan darted him a quick sideways glance. His blood ached passionately—aye, she could sympathize with that yearning for something one could not have, and she hoped fervently this joust was all he ached passionately for.

Swiftly, the entire field was jammed with knights astride their huge caparisoned destriers in complicated patterns. Armor clanked, leather creaked, men shouted, horses snorted in strange chorus. Despite her exhaustion and melancholy, a fluttering feeling stirred deep within her. Her cheeks colored slightly and she shifted forward on the cushioned bench and wet her lips. The king and prince were immediately before the royal pavilion now in the sea of silver surrounded by waves of colored shields and flowing flags emblazoned all with family coat of arms. In the first event, the king and prince would each lead half the warriors in a massive charge called the *grande mêlée*. As if drawn by a

111

magnetic force, her eyes sought the face of the prince, but his pointed visor was shut and cold steel was all she saw.

Although he was certain she did not know it, his thin-slitted line of vision took her in perfectly. She seemed to look directly at him; by St. George, surely she could pick him out easily. She had worn gold brocade. With her hair and gown in the sun, she looked all gold to him. And, as he had suspected, his lady mother had made good her subtle threat to have Jeannette—now of marriageable age, she kept repeating—meet some eligible knights of the court. Holland. Thomas Holland next to her there. It could have been worse, for Holland was older, no gay, charming gallant to go all misty-eyed; he was full loyal and very desirous of advancement. By the martyrs' blood, if the lucky bastard had not broken his leg in the same tournament that had ruined his own blasted right hand, he would take Holland on tour with him on the morrow and then see what the queen made of that!

The line the prince was in wheeled past the bevy of ladies who waved and applauded. The skirted horses ringed the field on two sides waiting for the marshals to signal the charge. He braced himself so that he was nearly standing in the long stirrups, relatively free to be able to deliver swift, swinging blows to either side. He fitted his lance carefully in his curved gauntlet as his squire Leonard ventured out in the press of horses and other squires to lift it to him. Muffled cries, "For heaven and St. George!" pierced his quilted hood and heavy helmet. He steadied his lance, spurred the horse, and shot forward.

The field churned with the onslaught. Ahead sword clanged on sword before he hit hard into the *mêlée*, unhorsing one surprised rider immediately. The shock of impact jarred him and his ears rang. He whirled the horse back, then charged further into the cloud of din and dust and silver bodies. "For heaven and St. George!" Wave after wave of armor seemed to swell and rise and crash.

The two jousting teams led by the king and the prince enjoined in mock battle, but real horses were down and real blood flowed. The dust and sweep of arms obscured all logic and any order in the struggle. Then the ruckus settled to single separate clangings as some riders were unhorsed and, burdened by their sixty pounds of armor, struggled like great, silver turtles to right themselves on the ground.

The scrambling scene, Joan thought, would have looked ludicrous had not she pictured the prince as she had met him first that day six weeks ago charging relentlessly yet purposefully at that quintain. And had not he told her of his heart's desire to someday lead the English knights and yeomen into battle against the flesh and blood French enemy? To him perhaps then, this was very real. He sat out there astride, in the *mêlée* still, over there, near her own brother, hacking at opponents with his two-edged sword, urged on by cheers and shouts of the crowd.

Behind her a lady's high-pitched voice she did not recognize whispered, "The Prince Edward is always exciting in tourney! I assume now that he has declared he is real flesh and blood at last by his little flirtation with Kentish Joan, he shall prove more exciting in other pursuits, too." Muffled giggles followed, and Joan longed to turn back and shout at the rude maids, but Thomas Holland's big hand moved to her knee in one quick touch before he took it back.

"Best to ignore that so they do not know you are flustered, Lady Joan. The queen would not like to think such remarks could possibly have a bearing on your feelings, of course, so I would advise just a calm and sweet demeanor while we view the tourney, eh? St. Peter's bones, I shall protect your honor myself if such continues, as long as you give me no cause to doubt that honor in the future."

Joan swiveled her elegant head to face him squarely, and the gold wispy scarves no knight of hers carried into battle trailed their delicate caress along the bare skin of her neck and throat. "My honor is intact and quite my own concern,

Sir Thomas. Pray, do not trouble yourself or the queen with wonderings or musings about what is only mine."

His coppery eye hardened at the icy rebuke, but it lit with admiration and titillation too. Such cleverness, so fiery a spirit in one so young and beautiful and—no doubt, with his dear patroness Philippa's help—so reachable. By the blessed saints, this period of rehabilitation for this damned leg might be more enjoyable than he had ever imagined. And now, the little violet-eyed vixen was annoyed again, for it seemed the prince had somehow singled out or found himself face to face in combat with her eldest brother Edmund. On both their torn tunics their distinctive family crests could clearly be discerned since only the best fighters remained ahorse this late in the *grande mêlée*. That battle went on and on as though it were a single *joust d'honneur*, and the petite Joan's hands grasped each other so tightly that her knuckles and fingers had gone stark white, he noted.

The two combatants' lances splintered to shreds under their horses' cavorting hooves, the men fought and balanced, wheeled, and turned whanging two-edged swords at each other. Joan was aghast—her dear Edmund in fierce attack on the prince; her dear Edward—blast the prince for singling out her brother as if to show her her place! Or was it in fierce retribution for Edmund's daring to embarrass him yesterday in the little walled garden?

Suddenly there as a horrendous smash that seemed to shake the very footers of the royal pavilion. Edmund, Earl of Kent, was down from a collision of the two plated horses and knights, his armor clashing piece on piece. Yet as the prince dismounted stiffly, Edmund rose and raised his sword again to continue the fray on foot.

Shouts of approval and wild applause filled Joan's ears when she stood, as did the others, the better to see these two continue their battle. Though their sword points were blunted with lead foils, the clash of their weapons on coats of armor sounded like a shop of brawny blacksmiths pounding.

By now, though, each showed signs of tiring in his weighty metal shell.

Joan stood transfixed, frozen, suddenly terrified for her brother. Was it not as if some horrible anger the prince felt at her was being hammered out upon her own dear Edmund?

"I cannot stand this! They will kill each other!"

"Hush, Joan, or you will have everyone staring and whispering again. And do not consider a dramatic departure or they will all wonder for whom you are concerned as I do," Thomas Holland hissed low, and his one visible russet eyebrow quirked up in some sort of warning.

"My concern is for my brother and the prince, since you seem to wish to be so very privy to my feelings, Sir Thomas," she shot back in a low voice. "Saints, my lord, my feelings are mine and no one else's as you and this court of whisperers shall learn, and tell that to the queen if you must!"

She sat down stonily and, without movement or expression, stared straight ahead while the others shouted and cheered. At last, the prince knocked Edmund's hacked-up sword across the turf and was victorious on a point of honor; yet Joan moved not a muscle. Let Thomas Holland fume and bluster and glare at her with that one sharp, intimidating eye. Let them all wonder if she were ill or speculate on what dire thing Sir Thomas had said.

Between events that long afternoon, spiced wine, figs, and apricots were served in the stands, but Joan politely refused to partake of any as she watched the endless parade of jousts without apparent emotion. The king jousted; both Edmund and the prince did so victoriously while the others applauded. Let the others wonder if she were ill; Sir Thomas would surely insist to the queen that he not ever have to partner such a sullen girl again. The walls of isolation which had protected her inner private world from a mother who did not love her served her well again that long, long day.

At last, when it was over and the gay company trooped off to a magnificent banquet in the Great Hall, she confounded them all again by relaxing, chatting, and apparently enjoying herself. Perhaps, she thought belligerently, they will think me mad, for was I not reared by a strange, demented mother who never came out of her house after her husband had deserted her in death?

After hours of feasting, upon being asked to attend the queen in her chambers with a few close friends including Sir Thomas and the Princess Isabella, Joan did so without protest. Too bad that Sir Thomas seemed all the more intrigued by such cryptic and moody behavior, she thought. She even smiled directly at him once when the giggling, tipsy Isabella insisted to the queen that Joan of Kent be asked to play the lute and sing.

Amidst promptings and smiles, no doubt from the very people who had whispered taunts earlier, she agreed, and selected a song her dear teacher and friend, Roger Wakeley, had taught her long ago. Let the words be a warning to them, she thought, as she plucked the four pairs of tuned strings and felt the light, beautiful instrument tremble slightly in her hands as a well-made lute must. And for certain, she had learned the honesty of the words of this song well enough in the short time she had been in this royal court:

> "The lady Fortune is both friend and foe:
> Of poor she maketh rich,
> Of rich poor also;
> She turneth woe all into well,
> And well all into woe.
> Trust no man to do well,
> The wheel it turneth so."

Amidst light applause and even a smile from the queen, Joan let the lute reverberate with the last tones. As though her deepest longings had conjured him up, the prince was there across the room, tall and grand—and very real. His eyes locked with hers before he looked away and she knew not how much of her song he had seen or heard.

He approached the queen and bowed. "Your Grace, a poor errant knight but come to bid you farewell until Yule," his low voice floated to Joan. Unbidden, a chill shot up her backbone and tingled along the nape of her neck. "I had no idea until I was out in the hall you would have others here about so late, my lady mother. I am pleased you have so fully recovered since the little Mary's birth."

Queen Philippa stretched on tiptoe to kiss his cheek and shooed the Princess Isabella and Joanna off as they hurried over to hug their brother good-bye. "Enough of farewells," the queen scolded in mock seriousness. "I will not have any of you sad on such a happy Midsummer's day. The king is in his suites late with his advisors, it seems. You will see him before you depart, our dear son?"

"We said our farewells and such at my tent earlier, after the tournament, Your Grace," he answered. "My retinue sets out at dawn and I meant but to stay here a moment."

Joan sat stiff-backed on a bench by Thomas Holland who had elevated his leg. Again she sealed off whatever could hurt her—or give her hope. It amused her mightily to notice how giddy with joy Lord Thomas seemed at finding her ignoring the prince once he had made his entrance and initial speech. But then, it seemed such mind-forged emotional armor was not enough to protect her from the next onslaught.

"*Ma chérie* Joan, our Edward is leaving for at least four months, 'til Yule," Isabella trilled suddenly close to her ear and tugging at her hand. "Your new gallant, Sir Thomas, will not mind a whit, will you, sir, if she bids him a farewell? My lord prince has been so much in company with both dear Joan and me this past month, you know."

"I believe I did hear some such talk about the court, Princess Isabella," Thomas responded drily as his wary eye sought Joan's face. "Of course, the lady may do as her heart bids."

KAREN HARPER

"Oh, of course," Isabella bubbled. "The song was lovely too, *ma chérie*. Come on now!"

"Dear Princess, I believe the prince came only to bid farewell to the queen—and Your Grace and the Princess Joanna, of course."

"Saints' bones, Joan! You are such a stick-in-the-mud at times!"

But the dilemma was entirely solved as Isabella whirled to find her brother and nearly bounced into him a mere two steps behind her.

"Did I hear you call me Sir Stick-in-the-Mud-and-Mire, sister?" his voice taunted, but his face was entirely serious, and no one but Joan took in the gibe.

"What? Oh, no, my lord, only I was trying to fetch Joan to bid you *adieu*," Isabella pouted.

"It is all right, sister. We can all say good-bye here. I am off to an early bed." He bent to kiss Isabella's rosy cheek, then took Joan's limp hand.

"Time goes fast at court, Lady Joan. You shall see," he said low while both Isabella and Thomas Holland leaned forward as if not to miss a whisper.

"Does it, Your Grace?" she heard herself reply.

"Aye. As quick as that wheel of fortune you sang of so prettily. Perhaps you will learn a new song tomorrow which will change your mind." He loosed her hand as though he was surprised he still held it. She was grateful he did not bend to kiss her.

"Farewell, Joan."

"Farewell, my lord prince." He stepped away and caught Thomas Holland's avid stare.

"Sir Thomas."

"Your Grace, forgive me for not rising."

"Does the leg pain you much now?"

"It heals rapidly as did your hand, my lord prince."

"Aye, it did, just when it pained me the most." He hesitated as if he would say more. "Isabella, you sweet *femme*, will you not see your brother to the door and wave

118

him off then?"

He turned away without another glance back. Just as well, Joan thought, and let a sigh escape before she could snatch it back. Soon Isabella flitted back in alone, and the day of the great tournament at Windsor stretched far into the summer night.

Chapter Six

Summer and autumn fled as had the prince; now, winter suited her more. Joan of Kent in the five months she had lived as part of the Plantagenet court soon enough fell into her place as one of many spokes on the massive feudal wheel which rotated around the king and his royal family. And so the increasingly familiar paths and repetitious patterns of her life came to suit her quite well enough.

The court lived at sprawling Westminster Palace on the Thames in London that autumn and early winter while the king held various council sessions and met with his lords and Parliament in the lofty room called the Painted Chamber because of its wall murals of bloody biblical wars. The council plotted war, too: everyone knew of it. Unless a new agreement or treaty could be established soon with the French, or some grand Anglo-French marriage alliance forged, war was a certainty.

Ever-changing rumors on quick running feet darted through the halls of Westminster and even the streets of London and the shires of the realm—there would be an English invasion of France soon; no, a new peace would be made. Prince Edward would marry the King of France's daughter or Margaret, daughter of the powerful French ally, John Duke of Brabant and Lorraine. Indeed, that tale is wrong; he shall marry no one and keeps with his retinue apart at his vast array of lands and castles. The Princess Isabella shall be wed to Louis de Male, son of the Count of Flanders. No—no, that cannot be, for the Princess Isabella is said to be headstrong and mightily spoiled by her fond royal parents, and she will only consent to marry an Englishman so she can stay home about the court.

Home about the court, Joan mused when she heard that last rumor whispered. Was it really home at last, away from Mother and Liddell and with the prince gone from her life for good? If it was home, it was for several reasons: the Princess Isabella's flighty but enduring favoritism for Joan; Queen Philippa's kindness in, albeit begrudgingly, not insisting Joan wed with anyone until she had been at court at least a year; and Thomas Holland's apparent unflagging patience, though she was secretly relieved he had gone home to Lancashire to tend to his demesne lands there since his leg was better healed. And, most of all, if the court was home to her now, it was because she had her dear Marta here with her. Or perhaps most of all, the vast palaces could be home because, though they were separated no doubt for good, Joan had seen three signs that Edward, Prince of Wales, still cared for her good will.

The beryl ring and the royal lutenist's sweet song of love and parting had, of course, been the first sign. Still, although touched by the song, one she had now memorized and often sang herself, and by the lovely ring so thoughtfully chosen for the ivy leaves of her family crest, she had at first put the ring away and refused to wear it. But then there had been the other two gifts, her fondest desires she had mentioned but once to the prince in the little walled garden the day they were discovered, and for those two signs, she cherished him still and wore the ring.

In early October, the queen had informed her that since her ties to the royal family, and especially the heritage of Edward I as her grandsire, placed her somewhat in a different position from the other maids in Isabella's or her own royal retinue, Joan was to have a little bedchamber of her own wherever the court traveled. Also, the queen had sent by messenger to Joan's brother Edmund to say that when he came next to court, he was to bring with him Joan's maid Marta, the Scotswoman who had reared her when her mother, widow to the deceased Earl, her father, had first retired from the world.

Dear Marta had come and now ruled Joan's little chamber, tended her growing wardrobe, scolded her for her willfulness, clapped for her songs, and loved her with a protective mother's love. Joan knew then that all this happiness had befallen her from the bounty of the prince, for she had told no other of her wishes for her own room and her own maid. But now and again she wondered if these preferments were a way of paying her off, or worse yet, a signal they were now well quit of each other forever.

Joan gazed about her familiar, little chamber in the river-front wing of Westminster Palace. The room spanned only a floor space the size of the Persian rug the princess had given her, but it was quite cosy here even in December with the river winds snarling outside her single lead window. From their mother's chambers at Liddell, Edmund had brought two tapestries that his wife the Lady Anne had said she could have to cover the stone walls, so now Diana at the hunt and a naked Venus rising from the sea graced the room on either side of her narrow blue canopied feather bed. Marta's little pallet with its soft coverlet was wedged in near the door by Joan's two coffers which barely held the bounty of her growing wardrobe of twelve kirtles, ten *surcotes*, and even many of the high headpieces she so heartily detested. The chamber had the advantage of a small hearth to chase away the winter chills, but she still had to go down the hall to share a *garde-robe* with other maids unless they used the little chamber pots in their rooms at night.

Her reverie halted as she heard Marta's quick footsteps in the hall. The wooden door to the chamber creaked open. The sprightly, little woman's familiar quick voice with its rich Scottish burr made Joan look up from where she had been staring into a dying fire.

"We'd best stir that up, lassie. Th' progress to Windsor for Yule be all called off. I just heard it for a fact from Lady Euphemia's maid. Th' court'll not be movin' on ta Windsor today or any day, not afore Yule th' word is."

"But Princess Isabella says they always go to Windsor for Yule. Is the Prince Lionel still ill then and that is why we stay on like this? There are still four days until Yule."

"Aye, th' princeling Lionel's sick wi' agues an' now th' little princeling John ha' caught it too. By the rood, we should be thankful we ha' a wee fire here ta keep off th' river's cold breath. An' all this two days a packin' to move for naught. Well, at least we'll not ha' to take down these chamber trappings an' beg th' princess for an extra packhorse ta cart it all. Next time ye see yer brother Lord Edmund, be certain ta ask him for another palfrey for yer household goods. An' best stoke up that wee fire, I said. Or were yer thoughts keepin' my lambie warm?"

"No, Marta. No warm thoughts, so do not tease. I really care not for any of the latest group of so called gallants—not for any of them, including Thomas Holland, so leave off."

Marta knelt to place folded linen and wool undergarments in a storage coffer across the room, and the sweet smell of dried winter packing herbs assailed Joan's nostrils. "I meant not ta tease, my lass. An' I spoke not a Lord Holland nor th' other little court flies that flit around my Lady Joan of Kent, by St. Andrew. Lord be willin', Morcar says ye shall marry better than that. I saw th' old goat yesterday, and—"

"Never mind, Marta. And if your old friend Morcar thought for one moment that you called him an old goat or that bogus stargazer in private, he would read you such a future you would never recover. Now come over here by the fire and put your feet up on this toasty iron rail and we shall roast a few chestnuts in this little iron grill the princess gave me. I will not have you getting sick with blains or agues even if I do wish your scolding tongue would ice over at times."

Marta's taut-skinned face split in a grin and she sat willingly by Joan at their tiny hearth while they wiled a wintry hour away chatting and popping warm chestnuts in their mouths as the best of old friends might. Each day, eventually, a page or squire would summon Joan to attend the queen or the princess, but today the summons was of another kind and spun the wheel of fortune crazily again.

"It be two a th' queen's guards at th' door, my Lady Joan," Marta called to her and shut the door momentarily upon their surprised faces. "We must get ye into a better gown an' then invite them in, I warrant."

Joan rose and the soft blue camlet material of her warm, squirrel-edged robe swirled in folds about her legs. "No, Marta. Two guards—this sounds different. I am fully covered. Bid them enter."

Marta swung the door wide and the two burly-looking men stepped in. The tall, square-shouldered one Joan recognized as yeoman guard to the queen when she went anywhere out of her suite. Had he not been the one who had accompanied Her Grace that day she had discovered her with the prince in the little garden? she wondered distractedly, and her heart beat harder. Both men were dressed in shapeless black capes and heavy boots for winter riding.

"Lady Joan, forgive the sudden intrusion. Her Grace, the Queen Philippa, wished to come to you herself, but her sons are ill."

"Aye, we know. I am so sorry."

"Lady, an' it please you, the queen sends the message to you that your lady mother lies grievous ill at the St. Clares and you are sent for," the guard went on. "She bids us escort you there as soon as you can travel out. She had also dispatched messengers to inform your brothers, but you, lady, are sent for with all due haste."

"If my mother is grievous ill, why was I not sent for sooner?" Joan demanded, but she herself knew an answer to that these poor guards could not, and she turned away to compose herself while the man babbled on about the nuns nursing the Lady Margaret faithfully.

Mother, her mother grievous ill. At St. Clares here in London, not too far. You could easily visit your mother when you are at Westminster, Prince Edward had once said, never realizing there were mothers who would not want to see a daughter. Marta's thin arm encircled her shoulders, and Joan's eyes again took in the nervous guards who looked at her warily as if expecting some further wild outburst.

"I am sent for," Joan said softly, hearing the crackle of the little fire behind almost drown her words. "Sent for by the queen."

"No, Lady Joan. Your mother, perhaps on her death bed even now, sent a request to see you to the queen. We ha' brought your palfrey from the stables and our horses await outside. Can you not be ready to ride soon? Four other guards go with us also."

While the men stood outside in the hall, a dazed Joan was dressed, hooded, and cloaked by a comforting Marta. "I shall throw on my cloak an' go wi' ye, my lassie. Ye shall need me there whatever ye find."

"No, Marta. I alone am sent for. She said when we parted she would send for me when it was her time and pehaps it is that—" Her voice wavered. She and the tiny Scotswoman embraced hard once. "I know you knew her long before I did, dear Marta, and loved her well the way she used to be— the way I never knew her. I must go now. All will be well. Stay here by the fire."

But Marta's slender fingers grabbed Joan's wrist at the door, and her brown eyes burned into Joan's fiercely. "My lass, go now along. It is right ye do, only listen well. Her mind be not so healthy now, an' it feeds too much on th' bitter past. If she say aught ta hurt ye, aught a yer father, keep a stout heart, my bonny lambie."

Joan pried Marta's grip loose suddenly astounded at the panic in the usually stern voice and steady eyes. "Aye, my Marta. That hurt is over long ago. Fear not for me."

In a swirl of heavy, warm wool cloak, Joan was quickly out the door and with her mounted escorts soon riding into the biting cold of the River Thames wind.

Prince Edward paced back and forth in the tiny receiving room in which the gray-eyed St. Clare prioress had told him he could wait. The snowflakes he'd acquired on his hurried ride from his London house had finally melted off the broad, black wool on his shoulders. Months ago he had had a promise from the prioress that if the Lady Joan of Kent should ever visit her mother here, he would be informed. Yet she had not visited once in four months, and now only, the prioress said, because the lady was dying.

His high leather boots made a lonely sound on the cold stones, and he fancied he could even see his breath in this chilly place. However much he admired, even envied, those who gave up such luxurious comforts of life as he was used to, he could never really grasp the duty of someone who would choose to join a cloister and leave the world out there completely behind. Why, indeed, had Joan's mother chosen to do so? And could not one love God and still love the world and the people in it He had made?

Yet he could understand a call to some sort of duty which overshadowed all other things; aye, he could grasp that. His call to duty must surely come soon and take all the dedication and the strength he could summon to face, to fight, to conquer the French in war. The Plantagenet claim to French Philip's throne was clear and honest. His lord father, King Edward III, had promised him a command of English noblemen and yeomen troops so that he might earn his knighthood which was only a polite title yet, a mere accident of royal birth. To prove himself—the idea filled him; it obsessed him making everything else seem small and unworthy except this one woman for whom he now waited, wondering what she would do and say when she saw that he was here.

He whirled to the door when the sharp knock came. To his utter disappointment, a tiny, gray-robed, barefooted nun he had not seen before entered with a nod and a steaming goblet on a wooden tray.

"Hot, spiced malmsey for Your Grace while you wait, the prioress says," her high-pitched voice told him.

He shifted uneasily from one warm booted foot to the

other, suddenly embarrassed by the tiny woman's bare feet on the stone floor. "My thanks, sister. Is the lady not arrived yet? The prioress promised I might have a word alone with her before she went in to her mother."

"I know not any of this business, Your Grace," the nun said as he took the warm metal goblet from her tray. The prioress' best wine, spiced and heated, the little nun thought, but then, this handsome, tall, and earnest young man was their next king. By the Blessed Virgin, if he knew only part of what sorts of terrible things the feverish Lady Margaret had said yesterday when she was helping to nurse her, he might not come tramping clear over here in the snow from wherever he had been to see the daughter of some lady who accused his family of the vilest of deeds. And then, to say he wished to comfort the bitter lady's daughter who would no doubt have her ear filled with those hateful ravings—if her mother still lived when she got here—well, thank the Blessed Virgin eternally she herself was a cloistered nun safe away from all such weavings of Fortune's snares in the cold, evil world. Then, as she turned to go, suddenly wishing to comfort the young man, the little nun said, "Do not fret for aught, Your Grace. If our dear prioress says the lady will see you, it shall be so. *Benedicite.*"

"Peace to you, little sister," he murmured before the door closed again on his thoughts. He had taken no mistress these past five months, but, of course, he could never just blurt that out to the maid with the champagne-colored hair the moment he saw her. He always felt right on the cutting edge of emotion when he thought of her like this, his Jeannette. He felt the desire to protect, but to possess; the will to give, and yet to seize; to drown her in pleasure, yet to take his own pleasure from her whatever protests came. She could be all wild fire and warm honey at once—in one glance was the softness of a woman and the brazenness of an untamed—

Another rap on the door sent his feverish musings crashing into a stone wall of fierce expectation. The gray-eyed prioress looked in, her mouth forming the words he had awaited for so long. "Your Grace, the Lady Joan has arrived, and I shall usher her in for one moment while I prepare her mother for the visit. Your time with her may be brief, you understand."

"Aye. My deepest thanks, my Lady Prioress."

He stood rooted suddenly to the center of the rough stone floor, he, Edward, Prince of Wales, feeling every bit the expectant little knave awaiting his first great gift of horse or hall—or battlefield—to call his own. There was only one narrow stone bench in the bare room and one little table. Why had he not told the prioress he needed two cushioned chairs, better lights than these fat tallow candles and wine to warm her from the cold?

The wooden door pivoted inward. She came in alone and the door closed on the watchful prioress' face he glimpsed behind Joan's brown-cloaked shoulder. Flecks of snow etched her head and shoulders in twinkling diamond dust before they melted into her woolen cloak. He meant to speak, to rush to her to take her hands, but they both stood their ground as though frozen to ice statues by the cold.

She curtsied shakily, her face still lifted, her eyes unbelieving. "No one told me you would be here, my Lord Edward. Did—did the queen send you?"

"No, Jeannette." He stepped forward and the weak light of the room made her eyes look deeper violet than he had remembered. Here among all these stones in late December, she smelled of cold, fresh air mingled with wild gillyflowers. "I only learned your lady mother is very ill after I arrived. I thought perhaps it was merely a Yuletide visit you planned to make here, and I wanted—I needed—to see you alone. I had thought you would have come to see her long ere this. It has been almost five months, Jeannette."

Her nostrils flared and her eyes widened in her beautiful, oval face. Her high cheekbones looked almost delicate in the wavering light; her full mouth set in the firm line of obstinacy he remembered only too well.

"After everything," she began, her sweet tones rising in

petulant stubbornness already, "you believed I might come to see her so that I might see you?"

"I had hoped, Jeannette, obviously in vain that you might think softly on me after these months apart—to want to spend some time with me—"

"Here? Here with the blessed nuns hovering and my mother ill to death in the next room?"

"Hush, love." He stepped closer and seized her gesticulating hands; yet he did not touch her otherwise. His heart soared when he noted the beryl ring on the little finger of her cold left hand. "Cease, Jeannette. The nuns do not need to hear all this, and I told you, I knew naught of your dear mother's illness until I came today. I hardly meant we would stay here in this little room together. I am sorry for your mother's illness. Perhaps, after all, I came to comfort—"

"Please, my lord prince, please let me go."

He dropped her hands and stepped back as though she had struck him. His eyes skimmed her light golden head from which her hood had fallen when she curtsied. "My timing is wrong, and for that I apologize, Jeannette." His voice barely reached her as she whirled away. Her heart beat so wildly at his mere presence she could not think, could not breathe. And now, like this, both hopeful and distraught, to have to go in to face her mother—suddenly, she wanted desperately to reach out to him—to make him understand.

"You have no right to wonder why I have not come before to visit her, Your Grace," she began, her voice on edge as she realized she had not meant to taunt him. "It had naught to do with wanting or not wanting to see you."

She could tell by his voice he had taken a step closer to her again. "I know full well that pious, noble ladies often take the vows of this order before—before they get too old, Jeannette. My own dear grandmother Isabella, once our queen, claims she will do the same before she dies to atone for her past sins."

She pivoted to face him, unshed tears she could not

explain clinging to her thick lashes. He stood so close her hems brushed his booted feet. How fine he looked, so strong and proud, leonine, a younger, taller image of his father—and so utterly out of her reach. "My mother atones for no sins, my lord prince," she bit off her words. "She has been quite the recluse for as long as I can remember, and in fact I have been hardly welcome in her presence since as far back as my memories go."

"But why, my Jeannette? Surely, *chérie*, you misinterpret."

"Saints, it does not matter! Not anymore. That is why I am certain she is dying and has some final farewell. Perhaps, now she will finally tell me why she could never love me."

He had reached for her before the quick knock on the door, so close it made them jump apart. The prioress' kindly eyes went uneasily from Joan to the prince and noted well the strain on both their young, handsome faces.

"The Lady Margaret will see you now, Lady Joan. She drifts in and out of fevered sleep, and you must understand she is very weak. Yet she is eager to see you and has been asking for you since the early hours of this morning."

"Aye. I am ready now."

"Jeannette," he said, so close to her yet. "I will wait here and we shall talk more."

"No, Your Grace. Do not wait on my account, please do not." Her eyes darted to the prioress. "And please thank Her Grace, the queen, for sending you."

She preceded the prioress out into the hall, realizing as she did that the ploy of mentioning the queen before the nun was probably laughable. The prioress herself must have been in on the plan to inform the prince anytime the Lady Joan of Kent came to visit the St. Clares. So the strength and wealth of royalty could reach anywhere, accomplish anything. She should have learned that by now. And the prioress probably thought her heartless and rude to gainsay the heir to the throne and turn her back on him without a curtsy. Saints, let them all think as they would! Her own mother had never loved her and how could anyone expect the prince of all England to sue for love from her?

"In here, child," the prioress murmured and opened an arched and pointed door. The room inside was dim. "I shall stay with you if you wish. The Lady Margaret is greatly troubled."

"No, it is all right. I just—I thank you for your care of her, and I shall call if she has need of aid, Holy Mother."

The prioress inclined her head and motioned the little nun sitting by the single, low wooden table and bedstead to follow her out. If only Edmund were closer than the long ride from Liddell, or even John could be here from Lord Salisbury's lands far to the north, she thought, as she stepped forward.

A pale cast of candle glow softly etched the sleeping face. So much change in so little time! The cheeks were drawn, gaunt, the body under the woolen gray coverlet slight and unmoving. A rosary and large wooden crucifix drooped from one limp hand. The skin looked waxen, the eyelids faintly bluish. But the small breasts moved. She breathed.

Joan bent over the delicate form. "Mother? My dear lady mother. It is I, Joan. I came when you wanted, Mother."

The wild violet eyes Joan had so clearly inherited shot open. The gaze jumped, darted, then focused on Joan's face so close. "My own Edmund's child. Dear, dear Edmund. He is dead, Joan," she whispered, her voice like dried parchment.

Joan's cold hand clasped her mother's even colder one. "Aye, dearest mother, I know. A long, long time ago."

"No. No!" The frail woman tried to pull herself up, but Joan pushed her gently back to her pillow. The silvery hair was spread wide across it like a pale, satin pillow of its own. "No, dearest Joan. He died but yesterday, again and again. Over and over!"

"Mother, please just rest. I am here now. You need your rest."

The thin, birdlike hands gripped Joan's wrist incredibly

hard, and the pale lips carefully formed each word as though it were painful to speak. "I sent for you. I have to tell you, Joan, Edmund's child, before it is too late." A terrible coughing rattled the frail frame while Joan cradled the bony shoulders with one arm. She awkwardly eased one hip onto the edge of the straw mattress to hold her mother closer.

"Tell me then, Mother. Tell me and then rest. Edmund and John have been sent for by the queen even as I was."

Lady Margaret's body went rigid as though racked by some unspeakable terror before she relaxed again. "The queen, curse her soul! The king, too, and their babe the damned Prince of Wales. Curse, curse them all for his death this morning, your father's cruel death."

They had warned her of this, of course, the feverish mind, the unreality. "Mother, it is all right. The king and queen have been kind to me—and the prince in his own way. You must hush now and quiet those awful thoughts."

"For years, for years—since they killed him yesterday, I have tried to forgive—to ask penance for my hatred. I have hidden myself away hoping, praying I could forgive. For that I never went out. For that I came here. For that loss of my Edmund, I could not bear to look on you, so much his dear face. He could not be here to rear you with me so it was not fair I do so alone."

Perspiration stood out in huge beads on Lady Margaret's white skin, and Joan reached for the sponge in the dish nearby to wipe her brow. "It is all right, dearest mother. Be calm, please, just rest. I am happy to be here with you now. Everything is all right now."

"No. I must tell you. Do not trust them. Do not love them. Your brother Edmund said the queen should be allowed to rear you, and all these days I tried not to tell you—but I must. I must!"

"Aye, aye. Tell me now. I am listening."

"This king—Philippa too—they let your father die. My dearest Edmund, the king's own uncle—they let him die."

Saints, she is so confused in her delirium, Joan reasoned.

132

Edmund had told her more than once that their father had been accused, trapped, and executed through the evil machinations of the vile Roger Mortimer, the lover of the king's mother, Isabella.

"Mother, the queen now is Philippa. Mortimer is long dead, his accomplice de Maltravers has fled to Flanders, and Queen Isabella is in exile at Castle Rising all these years. Edmund explained it all to me."

"Fool!" she hissed and the eyes went wildly piercing. "Listen to me! I have not forgiven though I have wearied myself with prayers and repentance and you must know. Listen. Mortimer had my dear husband arrested for trying to find if this present king's father, Edward II, had been indeed foully murdered, but this Edward who even now sits upon the tainted throne—he let it, he wanted it to be done!"

"Dearest mother—"

"Aye, let me tell you now how it was. Mortimer had the old king murdered at Berkeley Castle, aye, and de Maltravers is to blame also. But this King Edward gained the throne from that dreadful crime, and he hardly wanted my dear Lord Edmund to stir up questions on the murder." Sinews and veins stood out like cords on Lady Margaret's neck as she went rigid and tried to rise. Joan helped her to sit as she leaned clumsily into her.

"Listen, my Joan. Listen and remember all this as I will be gone tomorrow."

"Mother, you must not speak thus."

"I must go on so you will know what you must do. My Edmund, Earl of Kent—so decent a man to be so traitorously used. He only wanted what was right, but the young king did not want the truth. Murder, torture, hatred, and deceit—that is the royal Plantagenets. I have heard—heard they yet show favoritism to de Maltravers who lives richly in pretended exile in Flanders."

Joan bent forward cradling the raving woman. She no longer argued or tried to calm the feverish words. She listened, wide-eyed, hypnotized by the tale so terrible it had to be true.

"He was so good, his motives so pure, my Edmund—he saved my very life from deepest despair when my first husband died. So loving. But they tricked him into saying he believed the murdered King Edward II might still be alive—indeed there was word he had escaped. Aye, Mortimer and de Maltravers had him arrested and hauled before Parliament with trumped-up charges of treason, but the boy-king, Edward III, whom Mortimer and Isabella helped rule—he abandoned his Uncle Edmund in his hour of need—vacated himself from all our pleas and gave Mortimer the royal seal needed for the death warrant, too."

Joan's head pounded, and crashing reality loosed her rampant fears. The prince was here even now—perhaps to find out what Lady Margaret would divulge on her deathbed. The half-spoken rumors over the years about her father's death, Queen Philippa's pretended solicitations—Isabella's kindness—all a vast lie, a terrible bribe? No, oh, no, it could not be!

"They brought him before a mock session of Parliament hastily convened at Windsor where the young King Edward ruled with his regent mother Isabella and her lover Mortimer," Lady Margaret gasped, and Joan bent even closer to hear. "Treason was the charge. They dragged him in, protesting, with the rope already knotted around his neck to show his guilt. He was borne in in his shirt with a rope around his neck! I rode all day to Windsor from Liddell to see the king, to beg for my Edmund's life. All day on a horse to beg—ask Marta. Ask Edmund, or Morcar. They know the truth!"

A fit of coughing seized the wasted frame, and Joan held a little dish of water to her lips which she drank greedily. Marta and Morcar—Edmund. All knew this horrible tale and never told her aught of it!

"But the king was gone when I arrived exhausted at Windsor—gone to Woodstock to await the birth of his heir they said. And he had left the Great Seal behind him to doom my Lord Edmund. He could later claim his hands were clean. With the king's seal, Mortimer, even de Maltravers, would dare anything.

"They would not let me help my Edmund, not even see him. The very next day at dawn, they led him to a makeshift scaffold and block at Windsor off the Upper Ward in a little narrow place where there was a quintain practice yard."

"Oh, no, Mother. No!" Joan's mind pictured it instantly, the magic, private little place where she had first beheld her prince. Violent black and red colors cavorted, exploded in her brain.

"Aye, hush now, Joan. They sent me back to Liddell under guard while all day my Edmund stood waiting to die. Horror of the deed so obviously heinous gripped the castle and the countryside. The headsman fled and all day my dear Edmund was made to stand by the block while another axeman was sought. Long, long hours where he prayed—he knew—his dear nephew, the young king must surely intervene. But no word of salvation came, and I was de Maltravers's prisoner on the road back to Liddell. Finally, for promise of a pardon, a prisoner, under the sentence of death, from some foul hole agreed to do the deed. At nearly dusk, he died, betrayed and believing himself quite unloved by the king to whom he had vowed loyalty forever." The woman shuddered, gasped, and, as Joan was silent, plunged on.

"Some say it was his revulsion at this foul deed done by Mortimer that convinced young King Edward he must seize the throne from his mother and her lover shortly thereafter. But I say, the king let it happen to shock the realm into seeing why he must kill Mortimer and take his rightful throne. He left the Great Seal behind and abandoning all responsibility fled to Woodstock where on that very day his young queen delivered his heir, Prince Edward on June fifteenth. Guilty. Guilty as Judas kissing the Lord Christ that last night. The Plantagenets all have guilt blood on their hands. I did not want you to know any of it before, dear Joan, but your

135

coloring, the shape of your face and hair—all, all my dear Edmund's. I have tried to bear it all these years since they killed him—to forgive, but I cannot. I came here to pray for penance and then to die, but I can only die."

Again she fell into a fit of hacking coughs while Joan cradled her close like a child. Joan's stunned mind raced headlong down a dark passage, reeled into the blackness of despair and hatred. Her love for the fair and glorious Plantagenets withered and turned foul, and was smothered under the agony of truth—the terrible, awesome truth.

"Joan, forgive me."

"You should have told me sooner, Mother, years ago. We could have loved each other—could have shared this."

"No one could have shared this. It was too dangerous. Edmund said I must never tell you but now I have. You have gone to live among them. If you can forgive them, that is your concern, but I never have—I cannot—I never shall, God forgive me."

"God will forgive you, dearest mother. He must. Here, I swear to you I shall take it on myself against the king's family and de Maltravers, so you may be forgiven. Entrust it all to me. I am not afraid of them."

"My dearest little girl. When I saw you grow, for he left you as yet unborn when he died but yesterday, I saw his accusing eyes in you and I could not bear it."

"My eyes? But I loved you. I always wanted you to love me!"

"Accusing. Just that, my Joan."

Joan bent closer. The voice was raspy, fading, floating. "Aye, my Edmund's child, I shall leave it all to you. This long, long hatred, it has quite—worn me out. This huge, cold lump inside me will not go away. It grows and spreads. So cold."

"I am here, Mother, and I will not leave. Rest now and when you awaken, please let us talk of him—Father, as he was before—before they killed him."

"Aye. Before, so charming and so fair-haired, like a young

lion. My heart beat fast when he was even near. . . ."

The words trailed off and she seemed to doze instantly, her bluish eyelids closed, her pale lips slightly parted. Joan edged her mother back on the pillow and straightened her aching body. Those last words—how cruelly ironic, words she herself might have spoken of Prince Edward but this very afternoon before all hope of that was crushed in this inundation of knowledge. And now, somehow, some way, the great and mighty Plantagenets and a distant, faceless man named John de Maltravers would pay!

She sat rigid on the side of the narrow, straw mattress staring into a shadowy corner of the little room. Her mother's breathing became labored, and she knelt by her bed, then hurried to seek the nun who had nursed her. The tiny woman came instantly and touched Lady Margaret's forehead; then she felt the little pulse at the base of her neck.

"She but sleeps, lady, though her breathing is very weak. You know, dear child, you must not take to heart what words she whispers in this fevered sleep. Her agony has not been of the body but of her haunted mind."

Marta's parting, desperate words came back to Joan: "If she says aught of your father, aught to hurt you, keep a stout heart." It was all true, of course, not some feverish dream and Marta knew it well. They all had and for how long? All but dear, little Joan had known!

"Joan. Joan?"

"Aye, Mother, I am here."

"Ah, it is so dark now, I cannot see you. Tell Sister Alice to fetch a light."

Joan's desperate eyes met those of the little nun so clearly lit by the candle near the bed. "Just close your eyes, Mother. I am here."

They sent for a priest to perform the last rites, but the Lady Margaret did not respond as she was shriven. Then, at last, when it was nearly midnight, she gripped Joan's hand and smiled wanly. "My dearest Lord Edmund, how I have loved you so," she said. And died.

Joan sat by the bed, wide-eyed, uncrying, while the kindly nuns closed the eyes and reclothed the body. Then she went willingly with the prioress to her little study down the hall and sat wearily on the chair the gray-eyed woman indicated. She felt nothing now—stunned, bombarded, drained by too much in just a little span of hours. She bowed her head while the prioress prayed for her mother's restless soul, but her mind hardly grasped the words.

"Will you stay the night, Lady Joan?" the prioress was asking her. "Then in the morn your guards can take you back or you are welcome here until your brothers arrive and we bury Lady Margaret under the stone floor of our little chapel as she requested."

"Aye, I should like to stay here a few days. But are my escorts still here from the Palace?"

The gray-eyed Prioress nodded and looked as if she would say more. "Sit here, dear lady, sit for one moment, and I shall send someone to tell them they must go back to Westminster with the news at dawn tomorrow. We shall ask permission for you to stay with us a little while."

The prioress stood and moved away to the door. "Comfort will come, my daughter," she said, but Joan was too weary to turn her head or respond. "Comfort will surely come through prayer and the knowledge her troubled soul is now at rest—and through those who love you here."

The door opened but did not close. Joan stared down at her clasped hands which seemed to swim before her eyes. Those who loved her here—the kindly nuns, of course, and soon Edmund and John must arrive too late to bid Mother farewell just as poor mother had been too late to save or even to bid her beloved husband Edmund farewell so long ago.

She closed her eyes and leaned her head on the tall, wooden chair back. Her mind drifted, floated; a voice not of her own making inside her head chattered strangely in her ears. Footsteps on the floor. The prioress must have come back to kneel before her chair and take her cold hands in big, warm ones.

138

"Jeannette. *Ma chérie*, I am so sorry." The voice was velvet deep, and reality came screaming back. The prince kelt before her, touching her, his arm tenderly against her knee.

She heard herself shout something, and yanking her hands loose, she struck out at him catching him hard on his chin. Astounded, he lost his balance. She sprang to her feet, tripped by his heavy knee on the hem of her skirt. "No!" a woman's voice shrieked somewhere very close. "Get away. Never, never touch me again!"

His face a shocked mask, he stalked her to where she stood against the wall. "Jeannette, my sweet, I know it was a terrible thing to face alone. Please, love, let me help—let me comfort you."

She flailed out wildly against him as he reached for her, ducking her blows, and hauled her firmly against his chest, speaking comforting, pleading words. Sobs racked her body but there were no tears. He felt so unmovable, so strong against her. And he had dared to be born that very day the king had let her father be killed; he dared to be one of them—the murderers.

He pressed her close, one big hand awkwardly stroking her disheveled hair. Deceitful, all of them. So deceitful. Even Isabella with her gossiping butterflies—gifts, bribes, whispers, deceit. She could be that way, too, to defeat the great and glorious Plantagenets—so like themselves they would never know.

The man, crooning, stroking—he had waited all the hours it took her mother to tell her the awful truth and then to die. This great and powerful prince, their hope and future king—whether he was here to learn what the Lady Margaret divulged or because he truly cared and wanted still to possess her was quite inconsequential now. The well-being of this man was at the very center of Plantagenet happiness: through using him, she could pay them all back for the death of her father and the endless agony of her mother. She could be so clever at it she would escape unscathed, and no one would ever know. She must simply wall up her feelings for this big, blond man—close them off and never feel them and then do her work on them all. The little chanting voice in her head was icy, crystal clear, and when she realized it must be so, she finally relaxed against his muscular, wool- and leather-covered chest.

"*Ma chérie, ma demoiselle*," he comforted her in his gentle French. "Let me help. I know it must be shattering."

Her answer was muffled in his leather jerkin. "Aye, my lord prince, but I shall be better now, much stronger." She tried to move away but he seemed reluctant to release her.

"After this is all over, Jeannette, we must be very careful. I have asked the St. Clares not to divulge my presence here and the guards do not know."

"Fear not, Your Grace. I shall be very careful."

Surprised by her suddenly cold and quiet tone, he loosed his embrace and stepped back, merely touching her shoulders. She looked exhausted, haunted almost, he thought. He led her slowly to the high-backed chair she had been sitting on when he entered. She sat willingly, her strangely colored violet eyes on him but looking somehow past him or through him.

"Jeannette, the prioress tells me you have chosen to remain here for a few days, but she assures me the Lady Margaret will be buried before Yule. Your first Yule at court in mourning—well, it will hardly be a gay time as my two brothers are ill and the queen is consumed with seeing to their care. Will you—would you let me call on you here these several days before you go back to court?"

She shook her head slowly. "My brothers are coming. And what would the prioress and all the chaste nuns say?"

His blue eyes widened. Was she making a jest? "It is fit that someone from the royal family visit, and why not I?" he pursued.

Her eyes focused on his face as if she had summoned her thoughts from some distant sanctuary. Surely, if her mother had been such a recluse and cast the girl off for years, surely if she had not visited the mother once in the four months she had lived so close in London, the emotional ties could not keep her in mourning overlong. St. George, his time here in England might be so short before the French war, and the necessity to keep his family from knowing he was seeing her made such times doubly dear and dangerous.

"Jeannette, may I come to see you here?" he repeated when she only stared.

"Aye, Your Grace. Only, take a care not to expect more than I can give you."

He bent over her hand and his warm lips brushed the backs of her curled fingers. Astounded at her numbness of feeling for him now, she dared to smile. She felt a strange power over him suddenly when none of her own was relinquished—a firm grasp of what she must do.

This will be so easy, she mused, and closed her eyes to lean back in exhaustion as he rose and went to the door to summon the prioress. I shall do as I will and not care a whit for the consequences. I shall be clever and cold and conquer where poor mother had failed, she recited to herself.

Yet the Lady Margaret's words taunted her as, sitting upright in the high-backed chair, she drifted off: "So fair-haired, like a young lion—my heart beat fast when he was even near—my dearest lord, I have loved you so."

Part Two

Alas, parting is grounds of woe,
Other song I cannot sing.
But why part I my lady from,
Since love was cause of our meeting?
The bitter tears of her weeping
Mine heart has pierced so mortally,
That to the death it will me bring
If I but see her hastily.

Chapter Seven

It was a full six months after her mother died that Joan finally decided to risk seeing Prince Edward alone. She had made certain that his two visits at the St. Clares were well chaperoned by her brothers Edmund and John or by the nuns. It was easy enough to keep her distance at Yule for she was in mourning and court festivities were greatly truncated by the illness of the two youngest Plantagenet princes, both of whom had since recovered. And as winter melted into spring and the court finally returned to Windsor, the prince was often on progress to his lands which were being sowed for summer crops, and his mind was forever on the encroaching war.

Holding the prince at a good arm's length on the other side of the wall she had erected against his advances pleased and amused Joan: how easy he was to handle, this popular and powerful prince of the realm. Others cheered him in the streets, wrote ballads in his honor, and eternally fawned on his good will. But Joan dangled him on the woven, silken thread of twisted passion he felt for her. The ultimate result and where it would take her—the way she would use Prince Edward to bring them all down as they had her dear father and poor mother—she could not yet foresee.

Now, with war fever rampaging through court and kingdom, Prince Edward was back at Windsor. On the English Channel the king's navy awaited supplies, horses, bowmen, knights, and their armor. Men-at-arms and their retinues clustered at Windsor and London to set out together for Porchester from which the conquering fleet

145

would depart. The king, prince, and their advisors made speeches and plotted secret strategies for the subjection of France which the Plantagenets claimed as their own. Everyone waited and wished and whispered. Farewells were spoken daily. Sir Thomas Holland was due in from his lands in Lancashire on the morrow and the queen had told Joan she expected her young ward to bid that brave knight a fond farewell. But today, the prince's desperation to bid her *adieu* privately made her reckless and bold. She had consented at last to meet him for an hour at the pond beyond the orchards nearly at dusk the day before he and the king departed. Yet if he planned for this to be a lovers' parting tryst, the victory would be hers again: she had laid her own careful plans to set him sharply back on his spurred heels and to let him know she did not care for him, a small first step toward some great, shapeless revenge she sought.

The prince had gone out by another door to be waiting for and guarding her arrival as he had vowed he would. In the growing shadow of hickory and willows ahead, she saw him step forward and motion her farther around the gray-green pond.

He wore a leather jerkin belted closely across his flat stomach, and his hose and boots were dark as the greenery behind him; his tawny head was unfashionably uncovered and mussed; he looked as if he had been riding. She, in contrast, had dressed elegantly, flamboyantly almost, in a vibrant gown of the type she and her pliant compatriot Princess Isabella had taken to wearing in their increasingly mad and witty revels about the court. The kirtle was of orange-red sindon—a fine, expensive linen—and had a low, oval bodice, softly pleated, and a full soft skirt. The delicate silver-threaded roses embroidered on the narrow sleeves, full hem, and taut bodice were entwined gracefully. The *surcote* was sunset-hued and had a wide, golden fringe which the younger set at court had now made quite the style. Her heavy blond hair was bound up in two elaborate plaits with seed pearl ribbons at the side, and tiny ringlets spilled over her brow and nape in a fashion no one else, not even Isabella, accepted yet. Saints, but if the fickle courtiers could only know she had their beloved prince on such a taut leash—she grinned inwardly—such a coif would no doubt soon be all the rage, too.

He smiled and seized her hand to lead her a little way back from the pond to the far side of a single, massive oak the girth of at least four fat friars. Although it was hardly dark here yet, Prince Edward's eyes shone white as they went over her, and his teeth looked purest snow against the sun color of his face. One moment she hesitated to move away with him from the open area of the pond, for the snare she had set entailed their being readily seen. But, this was not back too far, not hidden really, and she would no doubt hear approaching voices and call out easily enough when it was time.

"Jeannette, *ma chérie*, here—over here." His voice was breathless and velvety deep. "I brought us a little wine and a coverlet so you will not muss that lovely gown. It is flame hued, Jeannette—the color of the French battle flag, the *oriflamme*, which means no quarter will be asked or given. Will it be so with us today, *ma* Jeannette?"

He tugged her down into the embracing curve of gnarled roots, where she sat comfortably on the woolen coverlet pressed against the massive, towering tree trunk. He sat quickly beside her, blocking her in but not touching her, one arm thrown casually across his raised knee.

"Always thoughts of the French and battle talk, Your Grace," she countered ignoring the tease which struck her almost as a physical caress. The little, wild-winged butterflies in her stomach which had been quiet for so long, fluttered, then went still.

"Thoughts not of that battle right now, Jeannette, but this other you have been waging so fiercely to keep me at bay. Since I leave on the morrow, I assume you decided to surrender just a little and, like the other sweet *demoiselles* of the realm, send your knight off with a kiss, at least."

The direct, quick ploy of the assault startled her. The few times she had been near him these past few months he had been so amenable, polite, and gentle. She beat back the desire to retreat and fervently hoped it would not be long before she heard the voices of the others she had summoned.

"No witty, gay reply, my laughing, flirtatious lady? I had feared lately Isabella's flighty fancies had changed you, but perhaps it is the other way around. Your silence I take for a truce, and I am here to stake my claim."

He moved quickly forward before she could turn away as she had meant to do. His hands held her head still while her grip went to his wrists. His eyes, nearly in shadow, studied her startled face, and just before his lips descended, her nostrils flared at the impact of his manly scent—leather, cloves, wine, and the touch of heady bergamot he often wore.

The assault was direct, firm, and it devastated her defenses. Thomas Holland's few but masterful kisses had never done this to her. And the others, like the fond, fawning Montacute, Lord Salisbury, she had held at bay entirely.

Her lips opened against the prince's and tingled at the onslaught of his wet, wild tongue. Her palms went flat against his leather-covered chest as if to push him away, but she had not the strength. How massive his body seemed so close to hers like this, how dangerous and overwhelming!

He deepened the kiss by slanting his mouth across hers and crushing her closer. She slid across the little span of woolen coverlet toward him, her hip through her gown pressed against his iron thigh. His tongue darted, demanded, and, mindlessly, she met the challenge in the deep, warm battlefield of his mouth.

His breath came ragged in her ears as he rained little kisses down her neck and throat. "My sweet, my sweet, it has been so long you have been forbidden me and on the morrow I am leaving. Please, Jeannette, yield to me, my precious."

He pressed her back on the coverlet, his arm tight under her back while the sweet offensive of his lips, mouth, and hands intensified. As so long ago in the little, walled garden, her limbs turned to warm water against him, and her thoughts darted wildly about as the net closed. Please—he was begging her please to yield—and then he would enjoy her, use her as she had vowed to use him. Even now his mouth burned her pointed nipples through the taut sindon gown and the gauzy chemise beneath; even now between her thighs his hand worked wicked magic that demanded she denounce her vow to her mother to hurt the vile Plantagenets!

"No, my lord, please. No, stop! I cannot!"

He raised his big, tawny head, and she saw doubt and pain flash in those deep eyes before he frowned. "No, Jeannette, I will not stop. It must be for us today and always. Be damned to them all. You are mine and will be mine today before I go."

"No. Loose me!" She pulled away, struggling in his arms. For one moment he crushed her down under him; then, he cursed and was off her in an instant.

"You wretched, little tease! All the smiles, the laughter—taking my gifts with sweet, low promises of later. St. George, vixen, later is now!" he roared.

She yanked back against the encircling tree roots. "You have no right to speak thusly to me, Your Grace! Oh, I am certain you are not used to being fought off but—"

His arms came hard on her shoulders and he gave her a single, rough shake. "Indeed I am not, *demoiselle*, that is, not by one whose eyes promise everything."

"That is not true. How unjust!"

"Aye, promise everything to others, too. I know. You and Isabella are the instigators of the rest of the silly, little flirts. Damn it, Jeannette, I thought you were different. You were different once!"

"Your hands are hurting me, Your Grace. I am not some Frenchman or enemy at the joust, I warrant."

"No, and so I shall conquer you entirely another way, but as completely and as thoroughly, wild little Jeannette of

Kent. I have watched you with the others—the amused Holland, besotted young Salisbury, and the rest. Indeed, I told myself they only get the same as I—precious damned little that—so why should I sport the green eyes of jealousy for your amusement? Then, I tell myself she only strings the others around her pretty little finger to cover up the feelings she bears her dear prince, but damn it, I have waited long enough and what is mine is mine!"

Her mouth dropped open at the anger and the arrogance: a roaring fire she could not quench, a conquest too powerful to thwart. Surely the French would feel this trapped and angry too when they faced this passionate warrior out to prove his fierce ambitions!

"I—I do care for you greatly, of course, my lord prince, but do not speak of me as though I were some prize falcon or palfrey you can break and own. I agreed to meet you here for a farewell, and now you grab me and accuse me—"

The Plantagenet temper she had only heard whispered of or caught brief glimpses of on Isabella's pert face or occasionally on the king's exploded at her like shattering lights. He pulled her fiercely to him, his hands wild on her back, waist, and hips. His mouth was branding burning kisses on her throat, across her fluted collarbones, and down to the slight swell of her breasts above the oriflamme gown. She twisted against him at first in rage and then in consuming, rampant desire.

Her blood pounded so hard it nearly drowned all quaking sanity. His knee pressed between her legs as he lifted her skirts. He moved even closer, his massive chest pushing her down under him, his knee riding higher until his hard muscled thigh moved intimately between her own soft ones. His big, calloused palm followed his leg up her thigh. To her utter panic, he was fumbling hard against her with the heavy lacings of his hose.

The world above of tree limbs, summer leaves, and dimming sky spun crazily around his shadowy head as he moved closer. He placed her hands around his neck; a second hard knee joined the other as he spread her legs wide on either side of him. Cool air crept up her bare thighs above her gartered, red cotton hose as, dazed by fascination and wonderment, she tried to shift away from under him.

He bent to take her lips again, then hesitated to whisper out of breath, "I did not mean for it to be this way or here our first time, *ma chérie*, but you are mine. After this war we fight in France, I swear it will be different, but I must have you now, so I go knowing you are mine."

His hard manhood grazed a silken thigh and nudged her vulnerable softness. No, a little voice screamed inside her. No! All the planning, all the strategy to hold him off until she could see the way clear to make them pay—

He kissed her hard. His passion ignited her. Pressed down, down into the soft, deep forest floor under him, she held to him to stop the sweeping whirl of trees and distant sky. A little push between her legs, a deep sliding as he thrust forward, a tearing hurt replaced by the dull ache of utter fullness. A little shriek, a woman's voice, her own, had rattled the placid calm.

"Ah—Jeannette, I am sorry for that pain, but no more for us, my love, never, never again. Relax now, *ma chérie*, relax and hold on and let me love you."

He had only moved within her once more engulfing her in a slow spreading tide of dazzling rapture she had never fathomed when he froze at the sound of a man's voice so close. It was followed by the high, silvery sound of a woman's laughter and then both voices calling Joan's name. His passion-glazed face so close over hers crashed from astonishment to disbelief to raw fury.

"Joan, my friend! Jo—an," the woman's voice trilled. "William says he cannot bear to be away from you so I brought him out. Jeanne-ette!"

The prince's big hand shot across Joan's mouth to silence her although she had no intention of answering Isabella and bringing them over to see her half-naked on the ground under him. She had planned their arrival to ensure his

151

proper behavior and to show him she did not favor him over the others, but she had never expected to have them walk in on this! His hard hand, the weight of his body hurt her now. Saints, he looked as if he would like to strangle her all of a sudden.

"Traitor!" he hissed, his mouth close to her ear. "I ought to let him find us coupling like peasants on the grass so Salisbury would call me out and I could kill him, only none of this is the poor bastard's fault, is it? And I will not have the queen marrying you off to some simpleton who cannot handle you before I have had my fill!"

He glowered at her and pulled out of her wet warmth, hastily turning away to cover himself. Horrified at the predicament and his anger, she scrambled to cover her bare legs and knelt on her haunches silent, disheveled and wild-eyed.

The calls were more distant now as Isabella and the slender, dark-haired William Montacute, the new Earl of Salisbury by his powerful father's death, traced the pond's grassy edge away from them.

"I have had enough of playing fond, country knave at your beck and whim, *demoiselle*," he shot out low at her, his voice cold and hard.

"You!" she dared, her temper rising at the unfulfilled ache between her thighs. "I dare say, you got what you came for, my lord prince!"

His eyes were icy blue splinters in the fading light. "You teasing, little witch, I hardly even got started, and I do not feel charitable or affectionate after your vile, childish trick of summoning those two or whoever else you planned to have parading out here to put me off. The way you have been stringing so many poor sots on lately, I am just surpised to know I had your maidenhead first."

Her hand shot out at his taunting face before she even realized the sharp crack was that she had struck him. Her eyes widened in shock as a red mark slowly suffused his lean cheek.

His mouth had gone chiseled, hard granite; his narrowed eyes were sculptured marble. His voice came low, controlled, when he spoke again. "I save you from my wrath now, little enemy, as I need my strength for the journey to France and great trials to come. But I shall take your challenge when we meet again, and you will see who is lord and conqueror then. Straighten your hair and go back to your silly friends. I tire with this child's play."

He stood gracefully, like the swift Plantagenet leopards he so often bore on his pennants and shields. His feet nearly silent, he turned his broad back and disappeared into the depth of green forest.

Isabella and William of Salisbury had stopped calling, although their voices seemed so near she could hear each word. Patting her coiled braids in place, she peered around the big tree trunk, amazed to see they were far across the pond and only their voices carried over. Her legs wobbled as she moved forward. But as Isabella and Salisbury drifted yet farther away, she merely leaned back against the tall tree.

Dusk descended. The voices were no more. She would give them some excuse; that hardly mattered now.

Caught in her own clever trap. A plague on the man! But she had not fully yielded, not given him the clinging adoration he no doubt expected was his due. How tantalizing it had all been—the sweep of passion she could not stem, the powerful need of his body for union with hers. Thank the blessed saints, he would be gone on the morrow to France to his precious, all-consuming war!

How it would set them all back to know: how Mother would have approved that she had dared to strike the proud Plantagenet prince on the eve of his glorious departure. Let the damned, bloody French fall at his feet! Saints, she never would!

Still unsteady in the silver hush of twilight, she picked her solitary way back to the little postern gate in the vast walls of Windsor.

*   *   *

Edward, Prince of Wales, stood in the open flap of the hastily erected tent where he had just eaten a quick, cold meal with his father and their closest councilors. Rain beat relentlessly in a sudden summer cloudburst to drench the scarlet, blue, and gold silk tent and turn the road and valley below to slick grass and cloying mud. For two days now, chased by a French horde rumored to be eight times the size of their forces, the vast army of King Edward III had been racing to reach safe haven north of Paris in their own duchy of Ponthieu. Now, realizing they could not easily escape to join their Flemish allies as they had planned and believing in the God-sanctioned right of their cause, the army of the English king and the prince had turned to face the fast-approaching enemy near a little French village called Crécy.

The mud would hinder the mounted French more than the English bowmen and men-at-arms who would all fight afoot, Prince Edward reasoned. Yet, awaiting the first real battle of his life, as the clouds suddenly lifted, his mind went back to that rainy day he had first seen Joan of Kent, wet, disheveled and quite muddy in the little quintain yard at Windsor. Over two months now since they had parted in hurt and anger after she led him on and tricked him in the forest trysting place—so much had happened already and the most important yet to come soon. Today.

Today was August twenty-sixth, 1346, and that made it—St. George, he realized, they had landed from England at St. Vast-la-Hogue in Normandy over six weeks ago. The king had knighted him and a small group of his young compatriots, including Joan's simpering beau, William Montacute, Earl of Salisbury, that very day in recognition of the great and certain deeds to come on the campaign. And the eager, ready group of young knights had not disappointed their king in their victorious sweep through hostile France. For the hundredth time, Edward prayed to the Virgin and his patron St. George that they would not disappoint him this day of days either.

He sensed someone behind him in the tent opening and

turned to face Thomas Holland, the man the queen had not only selected to squire the spoiled little Jeannette of Kent to official functions the last year but had also betrothed her to the night before the army had sailed for France. He would worry about that later. Betrothals were common, easily broken, and besides, after this campaign and the deeds he intended to perform today, surely neither his mother nor his father would gainsay him what he asked of them. Edward felt he and the fine, one-eyed warrior, Thomas Holland, had an unspoken truce over that betrothal. Holland evidently knew not to overstep his place, and the prince was loathe to let a woman affect the bonds between knights when they faced so great a common enemy.

"Thomas," the prince said only and turned back to his perusal of the waiting battlefield below.

"We are ready and calm, my lord prince," Holland replied, as if to read the prince's thoughts of battle and avoid the touchy subject of the willful woman he sensed still stood between them. "The place is ideal, the strategy is perfect. They will come into his narrow Valley aux Clercs below and we shall mow them down."

"The king will be angry if we do not capture the best of them for ransom, Thomas. An expensive two-month summer progress, this, even though we have taken spoils."

"And rightly so, Your Grace. St. Peter's bones, when we captured Caen and found that battle plan all made up for the second Norman invasion of the English realm, 'twas a wonder we could control our furious troops at all. If that damned pretender Philip had not had that large army hiding out at Paris, by the rood, we would have taken her too. We were but twelve blessed miles from the gates!"

"Save your strength and rancor for the French whenever they dare attack, Thomas," the prince said. "Everything awaits our victory—the army is loyal, disciplined and proud to a man. Shoulder to shoulder, bowmen with armored knight, we will face them well."

He turned and clapped the older man on his mailed

shoulder before turning back into the tent still addressing the serious knight. "At Caen you helped us save the ladies and children who might have been harmed but for English mercy, brave Thomas. See to it that out there today you do not confuse the Frenchies for the weaker sex, by St. George!"

Holland's copper eye widened at the surprising jest, and then he grinned and went out to gaze downward again, as did many others, at the roads south from which the lightning glint of French armor and the thunder of hoofbeats must surely come.

The prince's squires dressed him in his black chain mail and draped his silk scarlet and gold *surcote* over it to be belted. They all froze in one sharp instant as a screech and flapping noise punctuated by shouts of men shredded the air outside. He seized his big sword and dashed out to behold the sky above black with cawing crows.

"A sign! Another sign from heaven! But is it good or evil?" someone behind him muttered.

Dramatically, the prince lifted his unsheathed, two-edged sword aloft. Strength and flair and comfort at any cost, his sire had told him but two hours earlier when he'd set out to make a sweep of their positions—that is what a king and prince must give to their troops in war.

"Another propitious sign!" he called out to quiet the shouts and murmurings of his men around the tent and those of the waiting men-at-arms and Welsh spearmen on the spur of hill below. No matter—they would pass on his words and cling to them in their direst hour of need.

"A third sign—a holy number," his deep, youthful voice rang out. "First, the miraculous fording of the River Somme under fierce arrow fire when the French believed they had us ensnared. Second, this rain to mire them in their coming defeat. And now, French crows—the black harbingers of hell to warn Philip's foolish troops they cannot win against us here. Let them come on and learn the true, tempered courage of an Englishman!"

A cheer went up, echoed again and again farther down the line as his words were passed on. Beneath his tent, the battlement of which he was in charge—fifteen thousand noblemen at arms and four thousand yeomen archers in two divisions—rested after eating and drinking. Now that the rain had stopped, he could see the clever longbowmen taking out their carefully coiled, still-dry bowstrings from their conical metal hats and beginning to restring their weapons of stout English yew or ash. In earlier fierce battles with the French, the ruinous strength of the dreaded English longbows had saved the day, for the gray goose-feathered shafts pierced chain mail and armor alike as if they were mere velvet.

Below him, down a little slope of shiny grass and scrub brush, stood the wild Welsh spearmen who had driven pointed stakes into the ground to halt mounted French charges. In the valley below, the English had also dug square, knee-deep holes to send the armored horses and metal men crashing to the slippery turf.

As the prince and his men turned back to their tent to await the battle, Godfrey of Harcourt, the quick, wily Norman baron who was their chief advisor in this campaign, hurried up with a train of lightly armored men. It was partly for men like Godfrey that the English had invaded Normandy, because King Philip had confiscated the vast holdings of many such barons for their loyalty to the English king.

"My dear prince, stirring words. *Sacrebleu, magnifique*! Edward *le Roi*, too, he rouses the men, he comforts and urges them on!"

"Any word from our advance scouts, Godfrey?" the prince asked, cutting off any further flow of effusive praise. "There was word of their approach at three of the clock. The impetuous, conceited French probably deem they have daylight enough to attack, as it is but two hours later now."

"Word from the scouts, *oui*. The French approach apace, like dumb sheep to the slaughter, eh? Blessed Marie, this outlay is *grande*—the three battalions with your strength here and Arundel and Northampton's men to your left and the king behind should his reserved be needed. Let them come on! *C'est magnifique*! That escape path through the forest of Crécy to the sea—bah! Here, here on this vast plain our grand victory lies, eh?"

Prince Edward nodded, his heart beating wildly. Ordinarily such sweeping rhetoric from the clever, dark-eyed little man would seem foolish, overblown, but today—today! He could sense the moment despite the humid closeness of the air, feel the beginning of his new life out there where he would prove himself in heroic combat. For heaven and St. George! It must be his time to soar at last and nothing must stop him. Years of preparation, of dreaming, and desiring—such a flow of passion coursed through him that his mind tricked him by conjuring up a picture of the wild, alluring, yet unreachable Jeannette, just out of his final grasp and rough conquest.

"Your Grace, your father *le roi* at the tent," Godfrey of Harcourt interrupted his thoughts.

They gathered in a circle, shoulder to shoulder, the best flower of knighthood and bloom of Plantagenet royalty England could offer that day. The king's priest voiced a lengthy prayer while the men clanked greaves and swords by shifting anxiously from foot to foot. Yet even as they embraced stiff-armed and then disbanded to their final position, the low thunder of an approaching army seared the humid August air.

The king moved toward his son at the last, and they faced each other eye to eye, both tall, blond, and heavy-shouldered, so alike in appearance but for age and the king's golden, full beard.

"Today, my Edward, the chance at last to win your spurs," the king said, his voice gruff with emotion.

"I shall not fail your hopes for me, Your Grace. I have never been more certain, more ready."

"Aye. It was a sore plight to try to outrun the thieving

bastards further and so here we are. Your fine words when those blasted crows flew over were reported to me. Fine, fine words. By the rood, your mother and your family would be proud."

"They shall be proud of all of England's pride on the morrow when this is all over."

The king's gauntleted hand rested on the prince's metal shoulder. "Listen to me well, Edward. I have taught you thus, and you must not forget even in the shift and swirl of onslaught—war cannot be all rules and grandeur, knightly heroics and such. At the tourney, aye, speak chivalry to the ladies, aye. But war—war is real, my son. Use your wits, your cleverness. Planning, as we have done well here is one thing, but tactics under charge and fierce duress is quite another. By the rood, my son, keep your wits, that is all."

He turned away and was immediately swallowed by his protective horde of armored knights. Aye, the prince knew the story well of how his sire had learned to trust wiles and not only chivalrous strategies on that terrible night the wild Scotsman they called the Black Douglas had sneaked into his tent to slice him to ribbons. The young king had only escaped with his life because his little priest threw his body at the Scotsman's sword and died in his king's stead. Defeated, humiliated, tricked in the Scots Wars, the young King Edward had vowed never to be so trapped again, and the son had learned the truth of that war lesson well—aye, and in dealing with deceitful women, also, Prince Edward told himself grimly.

The English stood stalwartly in their positions upon the hill above the gentle valley hemmed in by forests. For over an hour, they watched the French approach and align themselves in perfectly balanced columns. By six of the clock, the enemy was assembled for a massive charge. Impatient, stamping French horses rimmed the southern entrance to the battlefield, and at the fore of Philip's massive army, the whole feudal levy of northern France swollen by many mercenaries from Genoa, Luxembourg, and Bohemia, stood the well-trained Genoese crossbowmen. The call to arms by the French king Philip had even attracted the elderly king of Bohemia, a hero of chivalry whose fine reputation studded with glorious deeds Prince Edward greatly envied. Despite John of Bohemia's blindness, no fiercer fighter was to be found.

Precisely at six when the French made the movement to advance, a fourth miraculous sign lifted the spirits of the waiting English: from behind the glowering line of sullen gray clouds, a sinking golden sun poured its rays to warm the backs of the Englishmen—and blind the eyes of the attacking French.

Too late, too late for everyone. With mingled shouts of *"Montjoye St. Denis!"* and the distant dip and tilt of banners and pennants dotted with the French *fleurs-de-lis*, the battle was enjoined.

Prince Edward watched, tense and wide-eyed, the visor of his helmet lifted to gauge the movement and force of the initial attack. Fifteen thousand Genoese bowmen advanced confidently, pausing on three occasions, in their traditional manner, to stamp and shriek their challenge. Yet, when they came in range and lifted their huge crossbows to fire, the prince's ensign fluttered a banner and the sky darkened, not with crows this time, but with English arrows from the stout yeomen's long bows. Few French bolts reached the English lines as the Genoese fell like shiny, wet, brown leaves mowed down by a breath of iron-tipped wind. Again, again, at five times the rate of fire of the hand-cranked French crossbows, the English hailed their deadly arrows upon the devastated front ranks of the enemy. As the bows did their bloody work, screams and shrieks of agony mingled with cries of panic and the Italian mercenaries began a fierce retreat.

The French knights beyond the fleeing bowmen hesitated, apparently astounded, and then moved forward in a huge, silver wall of horse and man with pennants flying and shields flaunted.

"By St. George, Holland," the prince yelled above the din,

"they are riding down their own bowmen! Insanity—and death to them all if they continue thus!"

The wave of French chivalry met the sweep of deadly English arrows; thudding bolts riveted shield to chest and fixed armor to thigh. Still, onward like a relentless sea they came, each breaker cresting over the fallen horses and fellow humans, trampling them in the slippery mud and mire.

Disdainfully ignoring the brave, common English yeomen and foot soldiers, the French took on only armored knights whether they were mounted or afoot. Again, yet again, the continually burgeoning French ranks encroached upon the prince's battalion's position only to be repulsed and shoved back. When the first French battalion had toppled into mud and writhing death below, the second massive attack surged forward and upward.

From his vantage point among the picked fighters—the earl of Oxford, Sir Reynold Cobham, Thomas Holland, and the fierce, indomitable John Chandos—the prince watched them come. He could read the designs on the battle flags and crested shields in this assault well enough now—the combined troops of the powerful Counts of Blois and Lorraine with a few distinctive knights surrounding the famous black armored King of Bohemia. Everywhere above the French ranks fluttered the blood-red flag, the *oriflamme*, about which he had once teased the willful Jeannette—no quarter asked and none given.

Prince Edward snapped his visor down and braced himself as the French knights surged at his position. He knew he was a prize they all desired second only to his royal sire. His blood pounded in his ears as if to ward off the battle din. He screamed aloud a challenge to heaven and St. George; his brain encased in the iron skull of his helmet echoed with it. He raised his huge sword at the first armored knight he saw and the battle he had waited for all his life was upon him.

Blows rained against his armor and shield as his opponent swung, parried, and hacked at him. He read the crested armor instantly—Duke of Lorraine, brother-in-law of the French king Philip. Perhaps the French wanted the English prince's death rather than his capture; they could read his gold and crimson leopards, and *fleurs-de-lis* well enough.

The prince dripped with sweat in his iron cocoon of black metal over heavy padding. He shifted weight, hit, charged. Lorraine went down, burdened by the sixty pounds of elaborately scripted armor, and a second man took his place immediately. Edward whirled and shoved, amazed as the next Frenchman fell at his feet, his back pierced by an English arrow from the darkening sky.

Another fighter screaming for "Mountjoye St. Denis!" took the place of the vanquished men—and yet another. A wild tip of a sword caught the side of the prince's neck where his helmet was beaten awry. He felt the searing fire of the cut where his neck joined his shoulder, then the hot stickiness of spreading blood. St. George, it was only his left side and not his sword arm, so he plunged on. Again a new, silver-plated man. As he fought, his strength slowly crumbled to exhaustion and then to the cold, mechanical, clanging performance of a spinning quintain dummy. Time turned, slowed, and stood still.

The enemy evaporated, beaten back, and two of his own knights were upon him to check his wound. "Your arm, Your Grace—much blood. Can you not use it?" Someone lifted his suffocating helmet off, and he drank great gulps of sultry, death-laden air. He was astounded to see it was nearly as dark outside as it had been in the helmet. His men were unbuckling his breastplate and divesting him of his ebony armor.

"Just blood—not bad. Back—we have beaten them back. How long?"

"How long was that charge, my lord prince? You have been taking them on for over two hours now—here, my lord, lie back and Oxford will fetch the royal surgeon."

"I saw the king of Bohemia go by just over there in one little respite. I killed Lorraine. By the rood, I would have liked to have him my prisoner!"

"Aye, Your Grace. We noted the king of Bohemia well in his all-black armor with his sable horse. Blind as he is, he had tied his bridle to four others and just charged in wanting to get a fix on you or the king."

"On me," Edward breathed and winced as his pauldron nipped into his wounded neck and shoulder when he sat in the mud on the ground. "John of Bohemia, the most chivalrous of all European kings excepting my father," he said softly and to no one in particular. "How I wanted to meet him—to take that king for ransom—to talk to him. I must get up—he was close about. I shall seek him yet."

He shoved Oxford's restraining hands away and had risen to his knees to stand when the king with a cheering retinue of armor-clanking knights appeared from the gloom. The father knelt by the son, his eyes wide, his face serious.

"My dear prince—they told me in the heat of the fray you needed my battalion for reinforcements and here I find you hale and resting on your bloody swords! St. George and England be praised, the day is ours and fairly won!"

He had clapped his heir on the shoulder before he realized the torn silk *surcote* bearing the Plantagenet arms was darkened by blood as well as mud. They rose close together, helping each other to stand.

"A wound—a badge of courage, my son. A surgeon! A surgeon to me at once!" King Edward shouted.

"A scratch—only a deep scratch. How many lost, my lord father?"

"Of the French, thousands. Their prideful, unbending charge drove them into the dragon's mouth of our arrows unceasingly. French Philip has yet to learn that wiles and not tournament chivalry will win the day. But you, my son, my mud-bespattered black prince—you have acquitted yourself well this day."

As soon as the surgeon appeared, the king went off with the joyous Godfrey de Harcourt and others to rally the men and warn them not to loot or slay the fallen French. A count would be taken at first dawn and many held for ransom to swell the dwindled English coffers. Yet out on the dark field of destruction, occasional cries and screams or clanging armor bespoke sporadic action where some of the enemy had not yet died or fled.

After they had removed his ruined *surcote* and the rest of his new sable armor, now baptized with the brazen blood of battle, the royal surgeon washed his bloodied cut with plantain water and doused it with winterbloom to seal the wound. The prince gulped the bitter ash leaf tea to ward off fever and downed a cool flask of Bordeaux wine the Earl of Warwick offered. The sure-handed surgeon wound a snowy bandage around his shoulder and ribs and immobilized his upper left arm to prevent the gash from being opened. Then, the surgeon and his assistants moved on to seek other noble English wounded about the area.

The prince stood somewhat unsteadily, whether from blood loss or physical exhaustion he knew not and cared less. All the wounded or dead Frenchmen out there—hostile, flaunting the *oriflamme*, stealing the duchies that were by right Plantagenet lands, aching to spill English blood—they were the enemy. But old, blind John, King of Bohemia, he was here today for some sort of honor in battle, for love of a fight. The prince not only forgave but honored that motive wholeheartedly.

He lifted a resin torch the surgeon's traveling band had left near him and moved down off the hill. If the king of Bohemia were injured or just trapped out here like so many, or mayhap wandering around in his blindness, he would find him. His black armor and black heraldric devices, his sable-hued destrier all meant he would be easily discernible among the other glinting silver-armored ones. He could not have gone too far riding that way; they had said he had charged by tied to four others.

His torch held high, the prince walked unsteadily down off the littered hill. He threaded his way slowly around mounds of horses crushing their shiny-plated masters underneath their huge forms. The reflection of his torchlight grinned at him from the muted mirrors of fallen helmets and breastplates. Somewhere out there in the distant darkness, a wavering voice called in French for a woman named Claudette.

Women. Jeannette and his mother and sisters—so distant in all this fierce confusion. But women were worth a different sort of war. Now, now that he had proved himself and really earned his spurs, Jeannette could be his—to conquer without quarter!

His torchlight seized upon something different then, beyond a pile of tangled bodies—black plumes aloft, moving gently in the slight evening breeze. He went closer and halted. Stone still, before him like a carved tableau, the black-armored John of Bohemia lay dead in the center of the circle of his comrades to whom his black horse's reins were still tied. One ebony-encased leg still thrown over the destrier as if he meant to remount, the body lay stretched out with sword in gauntleted hand. From his closed helmet fluttered the three distinctive ostrich plumes for which the heroic knight had been long known. From his dark shield the crest and German motto leapt up in the wavering torchlight: *Ich Dien*!

"I serve," the prince whispered. Awe suddenly overwhelmed his wearied heart, and he knelt stiffly to pray. All the things this dead black knight embodied, he himself wished to be—great knight, renowned hero, fierce fighter, Christian rescuer, beloved king. Today, out of all the hundreds and thousands on the field of battle only John, king of Bohemia, and Edward, prince of Wales, had worn black armor, and now they met like this—too late.

His hand stretched out to touch the soft, fluttering ostrich feathers. Gently, he removed the black, engraved helmet and gazed into the wide-eyed, silent face. Holding the helmet to him, he reached out with his left arm, despite the shooting pain it caused, and closed the staring, blind eyes.

He sat back on his heels and looked upward at the black

velvet sky where a sprinkle of stars shot out straight above between the sweeping clouds. He could hear his men now in the distance—Salisbury's voice—calling for him.

If he had met and talked with this warrior king and told him of his plans, his hopes, would they not have shared much? As a boy he had heard reports of his exploits—another Charlemagne or Arthur on a small, real-life scale.

The motto and the three tall ostrich plumes—he would adopt them for his own in honor of this fallen man. *Ich Dien*—"I serve" for him and for all Princes of Wales hereafter. Indeed, for his own son someday if he could only tame his wild Jeannette as he had these proud French.

Cradling the helmet and the shield with the motto, he stood and began to wend his way slowly toward his calling men. Behind him the low-burning resin torch at the head of the dead king was like a single beacon on the great black battlefield of Crécy.

Chapter Eight

It was the first foreign excursion Joan of Kent had ever made—a marvelous series of adventures with the greatest at journey's end. The prince awaited the royal travelers and their retinue at Bruges in Flanders. The trip was not only a domestic occasion for Queen Philippa to be reunited with her husband and son, now the celebrated victors of the glorious Battle of Crécy, but also a political occasion. To further bind England to her Flemish allies against the French, the Princess Isabella was to be joined in blessed, and necessary, matrimony to Louis de Male, the new Count of Flanders, through his father's death fighting for the French on the bloodied battlefield of Crécy.

Isabella had set out nervous, but full of hope and quite placated by her twenty coffers stuffed with sumptuous new gowns. The bridegroom, she had been promised, was handsome, proud, blueblooded, and amenable. Joan had been taken along in hopes she would divert her dear princess' flighty flutterings and serve as an English maid of honor at the nuptials. Isabella's own sister Joanna had been left at home to that girl's utter dismay and disdain.

The queen and her numerous retainers sailed from Dover to Calais in late February on wintry seas, but Joan and Isabella both weathered the rampant seasickness which laid low the queen, in the early stages of her tenth pregnancy, and most of the royal traveling party.

At Calais they were met elaborately by King Edward and his knights who for seven months had been waging a miserable siege war against the important, fortified French

town of Calais. After the sweeping victory of Crécy, the
royal Edwards had expected Calais to fall to them like a ripe
plum, but the starving townspeople had held out, no thanks
to the wretched cowardice of their impecunious and broken
King Philip. The royal English retinue stayed in the little
wooden town the Plantagenet rulers had built outside the
huge walls of the temporarily impregnable Calais. They
toured the fortifications, heard numerous tales of the French
wars, visited the English soldiers' market on market day, and
then set out northeast along the coast to Bruges.

Joan enjoyed the respite outside Calais immensely. Gulls
wheeled and shrieked overhead; the sea air was tangy and
fresh; many laughing *beaux* clustered about—and the Prince
of Wales had been sent on ahead before their arrival to
arrange for the festal gathering at Bruges, so he was not there
to ruin her fun. She dreaded their reunion after the bitter,
sudden parting ten months before. His anger, his cruel
words, and accusations paraded, piercing and poignant, in
the well-rehearsed scenes of her memory.

Besides, when she had lived near him last, she was certain
he cared for her—wanted her, at least—but, since she had
been betrothed to Thomas Holland at the queen's insistence,
whatever would the lionlike, arrogant prince say now?
Saints, he had had his precious victory at some little town
called Crécy, and she had no intention of feeding his
Plantagenet pride by letting him know she thought of him
entirely too much in an annoyingly tingling way anyhow, so
what did it really matter now?

To Joan, the passing countryside of Flanders near Bruges
looked like one of Queen Philippa's tiny paintings, depicting
her homeland of Hainaut, which hung in her bedchambers at
Windsor: painted windmills, canals, gabled houses, cobbled
streets, and tall Gothic churches. The warm, late March
breeze lifted Joan's heavy golden, side braids and brought
the fresh smell of plowed earth and new-budded flowers to
her flared nostrils.

When their mile-long royal retinue clattered into the

canal-etched, walled city of Bruges, which the queen proudly informed them was called the Venice of the North, Joan's heart beat faster. They rode among cheering, curious crowds past the Markt Square, then through the Burg Square under the massive Romanesque Basilica of the Holy Blood to the turreted palace on the Dijver Canal where the prince and his party awaited them.

The reunited Plantagenets exchanged embraces and numerous kisses while Joan was relieved to be helped from her horse by her constant companion since Calais, William Montacute, Earl of Salisbury. His previous gangly frame and jerky mannerisms appeared to be much tempered by the trials of war, the glories of Crécy, and the frustration of the siege at stubborn Calais. Perhaps, she prayed, such things had calmed and tempered the prince's fiery disposition, too.

Besides, as far as she could tell from this distance and in the glare of afternoon sun reflecting on the canal, the prince had hardly looked her way, nor could she see aught but the top of his tawny head from this far side of her palfrey. She cursed silently the weakness of her feelings for these Plantagenets who had so hurt her parents. Saints, she should be relieved the insulting, nasty-tempered man was ignoring her rather than paying her the slightest heed.

"We had best go up the steps with the others, Lady Joan," William said and shot her his white-toothed, ready grin. His green eyes drank her in and he nervously touched his dark hair always so smoothly combed under his fashionable beaver hat.

She smiled back willingly to settle her ruffled demeanor. It was fully evident to anyone who watched them that William was—what was that the prince had said of his young comrade-in-arms once?—besotted of her. It did not seem to bother William one whit that she was betrothed to Thomas Holland, so perhaps, when she finally had to face and pretend to be civil to Prince Edward, he would think nothing of it either and then mayhap—

As she rounded the little group of gaily caparisoned horses

on William's brown velvet arm, the Prince of Wales loomed ahead of them, towering over her, instantly close.

"Oh, my lord prince," she managed, sounding incredibly foolish to herself. She bobbed him a tipsy, quick curtsy and nearly tripped on her long, ermine-trimmed brocade riding cape which was nearly a match to the Princess Isabella's fine and costly one. The prince had somehow disengaged her leather-gloved hand from Salisbury who had quickly backed off several steps.

"Jeannette," Edward said, his voice deeper and much more controlled than she had remembered it. Pressed in the pages of her reminiscence as he had been these ten months, he now seemed taller, blonder, stronger.

"You look healthy and hearty," he went on, somehow stumbling on his words. "I would venture that sea air, or mayhap the joy of reaching here has put that rose bloom in your cheeks."

"It must be the sea air then, my lord prince; though, of course, I am excited to meet the Princess Isabella's fiancé."

"Of course. It must be that very prospect that stirs my blood so," he said, his voice dripping sarcasm. His eyes went quickly, completely over her. "No such hot blushes for your own fiancé, the level-headed, valorous Thomas Holland when he saw you after the long months, I warrant," he challenged, his voice still low although William had taken another awkward step away to give them privacy.

"You have not changed, I fear, Your Grace," she returned, her voice level. There, she thought, proud of herself. I am handling him with the haughty aplomb he deserves. Saints, but his sky-blue eyes are rude on me again as if his mere glance could caress my bare skin through this fine kirtle and cape.

"No tart-tongued comeback better than that?" he goaded. The sun nearly glittered off his brocade and satin *surcote* stretched taut across his massively muscled shoulders. "By the rood, Jeannette, I fancy I like the witty wildness better than these sullen stares." His mouth lifted wryly in a rakish challenge, a half-smile that made such similar attempts by William, Earl of Salisbury, pale by any comparison. "Aye, *ma chérie*, I understand." His voice lowered to a raspy whisper. "When I remember how fondly we parted and in what lovely circumstances, I, too, feel quite tongue-tied."

"You have no right to affront me here in the street the minute we arrive! There, on the steps, I warrant the queen is waiting for your fine hospitality."

"Lower your voice, Jeannette, and smile prettily or the queen and my curious little sister will take note of your— passion. And do be kind to poor Salisbury but not so kind that the queen betroths you to him, too, to keep me away from you. Until the banquet this evening then."

He turned heel on her abruptly and mounted the steps to rejoin his parents and sister. Isabella turned, waved, and motioned for Joan to join them as they entered the rambling palace which fronted directly on the square with no drawbridge or protective outer walls. Joan managed to smile and wave back, but each touch of the warm velvet on William's arm, each step up, she shot daggers at the back of the tallest man, the tawny head above her on the stairs. Saints, he had gloated over his victory on the trampled French, she told herself again, but he would not gloat over another one at her expense.

With the rest of the road-weary travelers, she toured the vast stone edifice that was to be their home until after the extravagant, festal wedding. But exhausted when she tried to nap in her room just down the hall from Isabella's fine suite, rest would not come and she only tossed and turned and punched her luxurious, goose-down pillow wishing she had found another way to avenge her parents besides taking on the vile and arrogant Prince of Wales.

At the great, ancient Basilica of the Holy Blood, the next afternoon, before the chapel of Christ's Holy Blood, Isabella, Princess of England, was formally betrothed to the sloe-eyed, shiny-haired Louis de Male, the new Count of

Flanders. He was twenty-one, but like the Prince of Wales, acted arrogant and a good deal older than that, Joan thought. Of course the bridal pair had been betrothed by both proxy and proclamation before the bride had ever left her homeland, but since all betrothals were easily broken, this one was completed with as much pomp and promptness as the Plantagenets could manage. Both Isabella and Louis were clothed in stunning gold satin trimmed in ermine and seed pearls—a perfectly matched and blessed pair, everyone said.

Of course, what everyone did not say was nearer to the truth: the reluctant, anti-English bridegroom had only been convinced of the wisdom of the marriage by being incarcerated for several months by the Flemish burghers who had no intention of ruffling the royal feathers of their economic ally King Edward. The fact that Louis had vowed eternal hatred of the English and the Plantagenets after his father died in his arms at Crécy bleeding from English swords was a moot point to the powerful Flemish burghers. And to the entranced and blushing Isabella, who obviously liked the appearance and polite demeanor of the dashing Louis, it was of no concern at all.

Hours later, as Joan spoke with the smiling affianced couple, she tried to push any such concerns she had about Louis de Male aside. Even when she tried to summon up the fervent wish that all the Plantagenets might suffer in revenge for her parents' tragedy, she could not include the laughing, dear Isabella. Blessed be the saints, *she* had no real traits in common with her insulting brother and dangerous parents!

"Are all the English *demoiselles* as beautiful as you blond Venuses, *ma chérie* Isabella and Jeannette of Kent?" the velvety-eyed Louis de Male inquired with a toss of his sleek head. His nose was rather pointed and his eyes a bit narrow, mayhap like a fox's, Joan mused, but he seemed regal and elegant enough to keep up with Isabella's whims of fashion or festivity.

"Oh, no, my dearest Louis," the princess' silvery voice replied. "When we go home to visit England, as surely we must do frequently when my parents are not here to visit their new-won lands, you will see that we have all sorts of English maids—just to look at from afar, my lord," she added and blushed prettily.

Louis de Male laughed loudly above the titters of the others pressing close, but to Joan his laughter seemed brittle and forced. When he listened to Isabella or Queen Philippa, his dark eyes seemed to glitter like shiny, fine-cut jewels, and a muscle moved erratically when he set his jaw hard as he did so often between his pleasant replies.

At last one of their numerous Flemish hosts, and an apparent watchdog of the handsome, mannerly bridegroom, bid them enter the great hall where the betrothal feast was prepared. They all trooped off in correct rank and seemly order with their velvets and brocades murmuring and rustling like an underlying current of whispers.

The lofty, hammer-beamed great hall was as bright as glorious daylight though it was dusk outside. Huge wax candles lit all the vast array of tables rather than the usual torches or smoky cresset lamps with pitch-soaked wicks. As Joan glanced across to the raised dais of the royal family and special guests, the room glowed golden like a thousand fireflies on a Kentish pond at night. The sweet aroma of mingled spring flowers wrapped the guests in a heady embrace.

"How lovely it all is," she remarked to William who had appeared suddenly at her side to escort her in. "Look—all over the brocade tablecloths someone has arranged fresh flowers and herbs."

"Aye," William smiled down at her. "Heart's balm to ease the bridegroom, for he likes not the flaunting of captured French banners mingled with the gold and azure Plantagenet bunting along these walls, I wager. But he is a wily one. He keeps all his resentful feelings against the Plantagenets hidden, and please do not tell the princess I said so. Louis de

Male just bears close watching until he and the princess are properly attached, that is all."

Joan wondered if she had so much in common with Louis de Male then—a man who had lost his father and now hated the Plantagenets for that loss. He smiled at them and was forced to hold his tongue against their power even as she did. She, too, smiled and picked up the thread of conversation as though nothing were amiss.

"Until they are properly attached, my lord? That rather sounds terribly cynical, rather like something the prince would say."

"Aye," he said and led her over to a table near the raised dais where the guests of honor would dine. "To tell truth, Lady Joan, that is who did say it first."

As if their speaking so had summoned him, the prince approached them from behind a carved screen near the dais. He looked resplendent in the royal colors of azure and startling gold, his elaborately belted *surcote* quartered to flaunt both the leopards of England and lilies of France. His brawny legs were encased in hose of darkest cobalt blue which fit like a second skin. A short *surcote* with side slashes lined with black dotted ermine made his massive shoulders look even broader. His low-slung belt displayed a jewel-encrusted dagger and on two of his fingers, ruby rings winked bloodily at her in rampant candlelight. She no longer wore the beryl ring he had given her so long ago with such pretty words and she saw by his quick glance at her hand he had noted that fact well.

"There you are, my lord prince," William said smoothly. "I had begun to wonder if I was to seat the lady and have her taken off my hands later."

"No—thank you, Will. The queen and I will see to her quite well enough from here on." The young Salisbury bowed stiffly, smiled his familiar smile that suddenly infuriated Joan, and backed adroitly away.

"Take me off his hands?" Joan sputtered. "Why did no one tell me of such seating arrangements, Your Grace?"

He took her velvet arm firmly and led her toward the raised dais where the Plantagenets, but for the king and queen, were gathering, still half-hidden from the other diners by the carved screen. "Now why should you be told ahead, sweet Jeannette?" he countered calmly. "So you could fuss like this or look grim like that or do something silly like refuse to come down to Isabella's feast at all? I suggest you act civil for her sake if not your own. Besides, I would wager the queen has agreed to my dining with Joan, the Fair Maid of Kent, betrothed to Thomas Holland, partly to reward me for the preparations for this whole extravaganza. Do you not approve of anything then?"

His big arm swept the room, the raised table, while his crystalline blue eyes went over her in obvious appreciation. She had worn a lilac-hued velvet and satin gown today, a gown that set off the color of her eyes. The kirtle was daringly tight-fitted both at bodice and waistline before draping to soft folds about her curved hips. Dangling from each elbow a fur-lined velvet piece called a liripipe nearly trailed on the floor. The *surcote* was a deeper violet trimmed in white, plunging low over the bodice to reaveal the taut thrust of her breasts against the velvet kirtle. A single, huge Majorca pearl the Princess Isabella had given her hung at her throat to match the knotted filigree belt studded with clustered pearls. From beneath her skirts peeked violet velvet, low-heeled slippers with the fashionable elongated toes she and the princess now favored. And though it was not her wedding week, in honor of Isabella's approaching nuptials, Joan had combed her flowing tresses straight back and bound them with a circlet of her own thick braid to let the golden abundance flow in ripples down the center of her back nearly to her hips. All this the prince's eyes took in just before the blare of trumpets announced the arrival of his royal parents. The Plantagenets, joined by Louis de Male and Joan of Kent, took their appointed places at the long, raised table.

The prince grinned inwardly that Jeannette was seated on

the end with only him to converse with easily. Let her lean over him and tease him with her sweet scent that put these strewn table flowers to shame if she wanted to talk to Isabella on his other side. Let her press close so he could drink in the intimate view of her elegant face with those beautifully chiseled features and that champagne riot of loose hair if she dared whisper to Isabella. She would spend the long evening of feasting, entertainment, and dancing with him whether she thought she wanted to or not. St. George, he would have some honeyed smiles from those sweet, red lips or else begin the first of his planned onslaughts and show the wild, little beauty no mercy even if they were right under his watchdog royal mother's nose!

The echoing room quieted somewhat as guests washed their hands at the gushing ewers at both sides of the room and sought their carefully selected seats. Fifty ushers arranged them by rank and quickly the vast chamber was awash with waves of liveried servants: the butlers rolled in carts of chilled wine bottles; sewers stacked the massive sideboards with covered dishes and began to taste the food to be certain it was not tainted or poisoned; the pantlers cut and tasted bread, delivering salt to the lower tables in hollowed out, day-old loaves like those most of the feasters would use as their plates. Here, at the head table and that of a few honored others, only the king's favorite, fresh white bread from Chailly was served, diners helped themselves to salt from the elaborate, tall, gilded and jeweled salt cellars, and the guests dined from gold plates. Perfumed, heated wash water was continually offered at the king's table.

It amused the prince mightily that the first of the fish and egg courses had even been served before Jeannette managed to reerect her pretended wall of indifference and undertake some conversation to ward off his silent stares. Her graceful hands took only a few jellied eggs on her plate and the slightest helpings of seethed pike in claret and salted herring in ginger.

"You made a disparaging comment upon our arrival

today, my lord prince, concerning my attitude toward my betrothed, Sir Thomas. I feel you must realize I was pleased to see him briefly in London before he left for his lands in the north. His wounds, though painful, will heal well enough given time."

"I know that, *ma chérie* Jeannette. I made certain he had the best surgeon's care on the night he was hurt. But stomach injuries can sap a man's strength. It is best you are apart for a while then."

She shot him a sideways look through her thick lashes, but his face was neither taunting nor bitter. "Do not believe I wish him any harm, Jeannette. He is a dear companion-in-arms, a brave warrior older than I who has taught me much. He told you, I suppose, that before he was hit by a damned French crossbow, he captured the Count d'Eu and Sire de Tarcarville on the field at Crécy and will ransom them for the hefty sum of seven thousand pounds? The money, no doubt, will go to formally furnish his new castle in Normandy with which the king has rewarded him for his bravery and loyalty. A moated castle called Châteaux Ruisseau near the River Risle at Pont-Audemer. He told you all this?"

There was a strange edge to his voice, a tenseness of expectancy his calm demeanor could not belie. He watched her carefully, his big, bronzed hand grasping, then ungrasping the stem of his gem-encrusted goblet.

"Aye, he told me all of it. The castle and farmlands do sound pretty. We are betrothed, so why should he not tell me of it?"

"Why not, indeed? You find the betrothal pleasing then? I would have to say your demeanor here with the ever-avid Salisbury suggests the whole thing does not mean a fig to you."

"Saints, Your Grace. You know how it goes at court with betrothals!"

"And with fidelity in general." He leaned closer to her as if to check to see if her wine goblet were filled. She had not touched her food but had managed to drink frequently from the goblet, perhaps to hide behind its fluted rim. His pulse thudded as his eyes dipped to the sweet, shadowy cleavage between her breasts pressing against the soft velvet and rich satin. There must be a way to be alone with her, to slake his perpetual thirst for her. He was a fool, and so was his temporarily amenable lady mother if either of them believed a little time with this blond Jeannette would ease his need for her. He motioned to one of the hovering butlers who filled Joan's goblet with the rich, burgundy wine.

"Not hungry tonight, *ma chérie*? I have heard that when one's heart is smitten, the appetite flees. In your case, in longing for the lucky Thomas Holland or someone closer, I know not. Perhaps you will play your lute and sing for me if you are too fond to eat all these delicious dishes for Isabella's joyous betrothal. How is it that little song about love goes now? Ah, I have it." He sang the words, low and raspy, his voice almost a sensual whisper that sent shivers along her spine to flutter little butterflies wildly in her stomach:

> "Alas, my love hath gone away
> And now no meat nor drink, I say,
> Shall ever please me more until
> He loves me of his own free will."

"Singing at table is forbid in mannerly company, Your Grace. I fear *you* have been away too long at war to remember that. And I care not for your reading of my light eating. Mayhap my kirtle is just fashionably tight-fitted enough or I do not wish to be overstuffed for the dancing. I promised several handsome lords a dance, you see."

He grinned wickedly at the ploy as though he believed it not. And then, she forced him to eat the words of his song as she tried to eat enough to match him helping for helping at the sumptuous feast. From the meat course she took generous portions of stag haunch, chicken boiled with ginger, and seethed partridge colored sky blue with mulberries. He eyed her hotly while she tried to best him with frosty stares and a large plate at the next course consisting of apricots from Armenia, pomegranates, dates, plum porridge, Brie cheese, and candied flower petals. They ate sometimes without speaking, annoyed that the unspoken challenge of their game was occasionally interrupted by Isabella's chatter or numerous healths drunk to the affianced couple. Even the king's boisterous asides to them hardly halted their gustatory battle. Joan almost bolted from the table when she licked her fingers in an intentionally annoying way only to have his strong knee and thigh thrust against her leg under the tablecloth. But when the sewers cut a huge, hollow pastry before the queen and twenty black pigeons flew out to circle to the lofty ceiling, Joan stopped long enough to realize she felt as stuffed as the roast peacocks with lighted tapers in their beaks had been.

The prince's eagle eye saw her waver, her lips tremble. "St. George, I favor a maid with a hearty appetite," he grinned at her. "Those other huge pastries in the shape of the leopards, mounted knight, and town of Calais will be cut soon and I shall summon us a big hunk of them. Some of that sweet orangeade from that castle moat too, I think, before you have to leave me for all that lively, bouncing dancing with your handsome knights."

She knew she had overstepped and badly. The room seemed to blur; the gay colors on the floating scarves of ladies' headpieces below merged and wavered. Too much wine, both ruby red and white and too much food, spices, and sweets. Saints, why had she let the devilish beast goad her into this display and on Isabella's betrothal eve? The queen would be furious. But if she sat here to gaze on the next course of sweets she would be sick before them all.

"I fear I must excuse myself for a few minutes," she heard herself tell him. She tried to force a smile. Never, never had she done something like this, never felt so full and floaty all at the same time. If it happened here in front of him, she would simply die of shame.

He leaned forward to pull back her heavy chair for her. Surely, she thought, people will think nothing of this as guests frequently made quick visits to *garde-robes* during a long banquet with much drinking. If only she could navigate that whole long room to the door—smiling, nodding—get upstairs, and find her room without being ill here, she would be eternally penitent.

He said something to Isabella and her smiling, handsome betrothed de Male, a word to the queen, too. He took her arm and she was glad. Others had risen to drink and chat, watch the dizzying jugglers, choose a first dance partner, or just stretch their stiff legs after the four-hour meal. She felt hot now, then cold, and her stomach twisted in a fierce knot.

They were nearly to the door where she would bid him good-night, then flee. She tried to be calm: thank the blessed saints, he did not jest or goad her now. People kept talking to the prince along the way, bowing and curtsying, crazily shouting out, "England and St. George!" or "*Vive Crécy*!" But they went on.

Near the doors a sturdy, square-looking man leaned a black velvet shoulder on the wall and peered over the edge of his wine cup grimly at her until he noted the prince and bowed stiffly. Her eyes snagged with his and despite her discomfort, she hesitated a moment. Black hair etched with silver fell nearly to shaggy brows to cover a wide forehead over deep-set, dark eyes. He looked to be about forty and five years of age. His long, aquiline nose seemed strangely in contrast to his square jaw, narrow eyes, and tiny mustache. He lifted both one disconcerting eyebrow and his cup to her as they went out.

"Can you make the stairs, *chérie*, or shall I carry you and let them all whisper about it later?" The two guards who must be with the prince fell in step behind them.

"No—I can walk. I am fine, really." They went up the endless, wide stone stairs.

"I am sorry I taunted you to this, Jeannette. You look grayish pale, and I believe I have foolishly lost you for the rest of the evening."

With great effort she arranged her thoughts and summoned her words: "That man back there—with grayish hair at the door. Is he a Flemish burgher? He looks—a villain. I thought I maybe should or might know him."

Prince Edward helped her up the last steps, his touch strong on her elbow. "The one all in black velvet? No—he lives here now though and is a fine ally to King Edward. I am certain you have not met him. Here, we are almost there. I will summon a maid for you and hurry back down before they all suspect the worst. The man you mentioned—his name is John de Maltravers."

She yanked her arm away and went wildly off balance at the top of the steps. The prince's quick hands shot out to seize her before she could tumble back, but her head hit the stone wall.

"Maltravers! Maltravers here!" she either shouted aloud or in the prison of her own shocked mind.

She struck out at the prince's encircling arms thinking she would scream or faint. But she did neither. He scooped her up, flying skirts and all, and deposited her in her little chamber as if he had known exactly which of the many strange doors in the long hall was hers.

The next day she was very, very grateful he had bid her a hasty good-night and beat a coward's retreat before he could see his Jeannette be very, very sick or curse him and his whole family for welcoming the traitor de Maltravers in their laughing midst.

Prince Edward stared at the seven hundred polished gold spurs stretching endlessly down the gray stone wall in the Basilica of the Holy Blood. Queen Philippa still knelt in prayer at his side but, unlike his pious mother, he neither closed his eyes nor sent his thoughts heavenward. At last she whispered an amen, crossed her ample bosom in reverence, and rose.

"The souls of three hundred and fifty knights all

slaughtered because they did not recognize the power of a mass of cornered peasants," Queen Philippa observed as they strolled slowly up the nave of the great church. "It is an omen we might all note well, especially in France where Philip taxes his serfs so cruelly. They can be a danger when inflamed and then show no proper respect for God-given authority."

"Aye. English rich and poor shoulder to shoulder at Crécy to face Philip's vainglorious knights who rode their bowmen down—that was our strength that day."

Philippa took her son's dark green velvet arm and her plump hand patted his wrist as she spoke. "And the blessings of God profited you, my dear Wales, and your own prowess to win your spurs that day. Soon Calais, which plagues you and your royal sire so and devours all our wealth to keep so many soldiers there, will fall, too. I was just thanking the Blessed Virgin that the spurs of my two dear Edwards are attached to their glorious heels and not hung like stag heads of victory in some foreign shrine."

He laughed as they emerged into the sunshine of the cobbled Burg Square to rejoin their retinue. But though smiling and waving pleasantly to the gathered crowd of Flemish citizens, Philippa spoke again to him out of the side of her mouth.

"My dear, dear son, I also prayed for a fine marriage for you, too, as well as that of Isabella. You simply cannot afford to pine after little Jeannette, you know. It is most foolhardy and must of necessity go nowhere."

People, standing two and three deep along the path they would take back to the palace across the square, shouted his praise for victory at Crécy, calling again and again, "Glory to Edward, the Black Prince!" in both Flemish and French. He recognized their adulation with a raised hand but his rakish, blond brows had crashed over the icy blue eyes and a chiseled frown etched his proud face in arrogant anger.

"I *like* her, Your Grace. She amuses me and I favor her greatly. She may bring no valued foreign lands or sought-for alliance as does Isabella's nervous Louis de Male, but she is different. Besides, she does not truly care for me and it pleases me to tease her, so just leave off, I beg you. Besides, she will marry your liege man Thomas Holland soon enough and be off all our hands in some moated castle in Normandy, so leave be, Your Grace."

No one but her two eldest, willful children, Edward and Isabella, even talked to her thusly, Philippa fumed, and she shot him an icy glare despite her last nod and smile to the crowd in the square as they returned to the shadowy arms of the palace. She did not wish for any sort of row with Edward now, for they had already argued bitterly twice over his attentions to Joan of Kent, and each altercation had ended in a stalemate of threats, moves, and countermoves that had resulted in both Joan's betrothal and Philippa's reluctant promise that the prince could be with her here, abroad, until her marriage to Holland this winter. Lately Philippa had actually begun to wish he would find someone else, anyone for a mistress, to forget the stubborn, if lovely, little Joan she had taken to rear because she felt such a responsibility that her dear husband Edward had not lifted his hand to save Joan's father, Edmund of Kent when, indeed, the court all knew he could have. At least now, she served as a fine companion to keep Isabella's frightful whims, tempers, and extravagances more in check.

Her lightning-tempered son disengaged her arm and for a moment, the queen believed he meant to stalk off and leave her before she could say more about his feeling for the wayward Joan. But he merely sprinted a short distance down the hall to join a rollicking group of courtiers coming toward them—no, mayhap, not rollicking with those grim, desperate looks. Blessed saints, that wily John de Maltravers was among them, and she never could abide him since that dreadful business with Joan's executed father and King Edward II's alleged murder years ago. That her dear husband Edward allowed the man to be a trusted, if exiled, ally was entirely too disturbing for thought in this blessed week of Isabella's wedding.

Her son was gesturing, shouting, giving a display of Plantagenet male temper she had seen often enough over these last several decades to recognize instantly. "My lord prince, what tidings are these?" she called to him even as she approached.

Edward's handsome face was furious, and he gripped her arms to steady her. "No, not the king ill?" she began.

"No. Your Grace, these men say Isabella's fine fiancé has ridden off and pursuit is futile."

"Ridden off to where, my son? Nonsense. He only went hawking with a small party. Ridden off unbidden to visit someone, perhaps."

The taut leash on the prince's temper snapped even as he shook his head to warn her hope was useless. "Damn his conniving French soul! To flee over the Flemish border to the French—to throw all this in our faces for Crécy! By the saints, I shall find the prancing, beady-eyed bastard and kill him for this!" he shouted.

"Oh, blessed Virgin! Your father! Isabella—no one has told her? I must go to them at once," Philippa cried. Her pale blue eyes swept the rapt, nervous men, a mixture of familiar English faces and the unknown ones of Flemish burghers. She turned away from her livid son still praying it was some terrible jest.

"You say he rode off, gentlemen? For good? Are you certain? He seemed to favor our dear princess well and was quite resigned. Oh, Blessed Virgin, this will crush Isabella and drive our lord king to further violence at Calais!" She felt flushed and suddenly very weary. Though she was but six months gone with this tenth pregnancy, her bulk was great. She tottered and felt her eyelids flutter.

Prince Edward helped her quickly to a bench and she leaned back against a secure stone wall. "Go to your sister, Edward. Tell her I am grief stricken and will see her as soon as I can manage. I shall find His Grace and tell him if he has not heard it on the winds already. With me, since I am with child, he must be calm. He will deny me nothing. And tell—tell Isabella"—she lowered her voice and gripped his green velvet wrist hard—"tell her that Louis de Male was not fit for a Plantagenet such as she! Tell her it is a coward who vows he only goes hawking and scurries away. She was desperately unhappy to leave her home at Windsor and now we will all be together again. Tell her."

"I shall, Your Grace. De Maltravers here can fetch the king since he is so privy to him lately." Edward turned and hurried up the grand staircase where he had helped the shaky Jeannette only last night. He had wanted to say something more to the watchful de Maltravers, but he really did not know why he disliked or distrusted the man so vehemently. His father had taken other favorites into his confidence quickly before, even the little French turncoat Godfrey de Harcourt who had helped them triumph at Crécy. If Jeannette herself had not reacted so strangely to de Maltravers whom she could not possibly have known, perhaps the man's presence would not bother him so.

In the nearly deserted hall upstairs, he paused to knock on Jeannette's door to take her along to help cushion the blow to Isabella. He had looked for her at morning meal, but like some of the other ladies, she had chosen to stay abed. No wonder, for the foolish baggage looked green about her pretty gills last night after that food and wine orgy. Her daring stubbornness always amused him at first but perpetually ended in upheaval, accusations, and general disaster.

He rapped once more, then raced down the hall to Isabella's suite. As he neared the door, it was as if his thoughts of upheaval, accusations, and general disaster had preceded him.

A woman's piercing shriek shredded the air, and as he shoved the heavy door inward, a crystal bowl of perfumed water exploded in flying shards just inches from his head. He jumped as a heavy, brass candlestick shattered a dangling chandelier and sent tinkling glass pieces raining to the deep

Persian carpet.

His eyes assessed the scene instantly. Isabella shouted curses, alternating them with blood-curdling screams of grief and rage. Jeannette, her champagne hair wild in a glorious tumble, stood behind the berserk princess, her loud voice mingled with Isabella's shrieks. Both women wore blue camlet robes and both looked almost pagan in their dishevelment and fury.

Jeannette's voice rose and broke as she sought to comfort his sister. "Your Grace, please dearest Isabella! Please! He was not worthy of you, dearest princess. A great affront, aye—he had no right, but—"

"Stop it! Stop it! Do not even speak of him!" Isabella pressed her hands to her ears, then darted to heave another crystal bowl at the wall, inadvertently sprinkling both women with water and glass fragments to add to the chaos. The prince held his ground, quite sure neither of them had seen him yet.

"But—the point is, Your Grace," Jeannette shouted back apparently undaunted, "a man who could act so cowardly is no true knight. Of course, you could never give your heart to such a one."

Another vase and a last candlestick shattered, thudded into the corner of the room. "A pox on him! I hope he rides straight to hell! Only hawking! Saints bones, I favored him, Jeannette, you know, and all the while he planned to—he—"

The shrieks dissolved into tear floods as Isabella crumpled to her knees amid the sodden ruins on the Persian carpet. Jeannette knelt by her immediately, and the prince gasped as her blue robe split up a smooth, white thigh. Her arms encircled Isabella's quaking shoulders while the girl sobbed wretchedly, then gasped for breath in panting hysteria.

He had taken a step closer when Jeannette noted him. Her eyes went wild in surprise, like a reflecting pool under wet lilacs in the rain. The picture she made for him there on the blue Persian carpet with her hair tumbled and her loose robe open made the blood behind his eyes pulse red, then white hot. He realized then both Jeannette and Isabella bore tiny red nicks on their hands and legs from the flying glass.

"You, my lord prince! If you came with the terrible news, it preceded you," Joan said.

Isabella looked up, pale-faced, her eye' cosmetics once carefully applied now a dark blur on her cheeks.

"Did they send you, Edward? Damn them! It is all their fault."

"The Flemish burghers? *Ma chérie*, perhaps they just could not hold that hawk in their cage anymore," he said low. "He is a damned, lily-livered bastard, and he will pay one way or the other, I swear it."

"No—not the Flemish burghers or his guards—be damned to them all. It is father's fault, mother's—yours too. His father died in his arms at your wretched, glorious Crécy, you know. Edward, whenever he looked at me, he must have seen his dead father and hated me for it all."

In four more long strides he stood over the two clinging women. He knelt with them. "*Ma* Isabella, listen. Your family—we love you more than anyone ever could. Now you are back with us all."

"Love me, oh aye, so I have been told. Loved me to bind me to that hateful, treacherous Louis de Male! It is all wrong—wrong for him to hate because of what happened to his father. It is not fair!"

Joan started at the words as Isabella dissolved into racked sobs again. Louis de Male had found his way to be revenged on the Plantagenets for the death of his father. In deserting, nearly at the altar, their dear and precious child, he had struck a blow at that same vile pride and power which had trampled her own father down. And here, before her, knelt the prince, their heir and son. If she were to lead him on and then do the same— Her wide eyes locked with his; she swam willingly in the blatant caress of the deep and dangerous blue sea of his gaze.

After a breathless minute, Isabella lifted her head again, and shook Joan's arms from her shoulders. Her lovely, young face looked twisted, ravaged.

"Leave us now, brother. Jeannette and I have much repair work here to do before they are all upon us whispering, wondering how the deserted bride is taking it. By St. Catherine, the virgin saint who died tortured on the spiked wheel, may I perish in like stead if they ever hear or see one whit of regret from me. Good riddance he is gone! Now Jeannette and I know full well not to trust a man and we shall bloody well do as we please and lead them all a merry dance! Aye, Jeannette? Jeannette!"

"Aye, Your Grace. Let us dress in our finest and outface the whole world by going hawking then!"

Isabella nodded wildly but her stiff, wet cheeks did not lift in a smile. "Aye, just the two of us then, and whatever gallants we can string along. I hope someone rides hellbent after the bastard rogue to tell him Isabella of the Plantagenets is just—just fine!"

Edward rose when they did but at the door he turned back. The room was a shambles and they would be hard-pressed to keep that quiet. Nor did he like Jeannette being a party to these half-hysterical plans to run rampant over any gallants in sight and trust no men. Still, he had no doubt he could handle the distractingly fascinating little tease if he could only get her off to himself.

His booted feet crunched over broken glass as he turned away, and the heady aroma of smashed perfume bowls haunted his thoughts for days after whenever he pictured Jeannette kneeling there with the blue camlet opening on her ivory thigh.

Chapter Nine

After the disgraceful loss of Isabella's bridegroom at
Bruges, the English royal party, three hundred strong,
remained in Flanders only two more days. The final flurry of
activities even kept Joan from seeking out the Englishman
John de Maltravers who lived so richly and smugly here in
his Flemish exile. Yet if she had been able to confront him,
she had no clever plan to seek the revenge she craved.

In those last two days, the servants packed hurriedly, their
task complicated by the wild shopping binge in which the
Plantagenet women indulged themselves. Bolts of the
famous Flemish cloth made from imported English wool
swelled coffers that staggered packhorses and broke down
baggage carts on the return jaunt to Calais. The quality of
the material was so excellent, the colors so varied and rich,
that tons of it had been exported as far as the Orient, and
King Edward remarked, it seemed at least that amount was
now destined for London.

The fashionable bounty the Flemish burghers boasted in
their own wardrobes was overwhelming, and their shops
which Queen Philippa, Princess Isabella, and Joan of Kent
plundered as an antidote to the grief and shame of Louis de
Male's great affront bespoke well of that bounty.

Joan and the princess had become especially enamored of
the wispy, diaphanous gowns the voluptuous women of the
Low Countries wore to their soft feather beds at night.
Despite the fact it was whispered that the enemy French
women of hostile Paris had made them quite the rage, too,
Isabella bought six and Joan four in a rainbow of soft hues.

It amused them to try to sway fashion at home despite what the staid, conservative court ladies far older than they thought, and Joan had always preferred to wear something to bed, ignoring the English custom of going stark naked. And in their increasingly wild plans to set all England back on its spurred heels to show that the desertion of Isabella's groom did not amount to a tinker's damn, this radical fashion of nearly transparent gowns seemed a fine beginning rabble-rouser.

Back at Calais, they lingered until the ships from Dover would return to take the women back to England, while the increasingly frustrated king and prince waited with their vast army for the siege of Calais to end. Blockade and starvation of those left in the town were the ultimate weapons, and the English played a waiting game: their huge siege engines proved useless in this area of marshes and sand dunes; however, it was that same weak footing that kept the French King Philip and his army of would-be rescuers at bay.

For the rest of the spring and the early part of summer, the court, during their stay here, had gone swiftly silent about this dark situation. Tonight, the prince, Jeannette, and their young friends had left his sister Isabella's suite over an hour ago after an evening of backgammon, laughing, and singing. Jeannette had played a new beribboned French lute he had given her, and she had sung her seductive songs. Soon, tonight, almost now, she would be his and then her supple, luscious, young body would be the lute which would quiver in his hands at his skill and bidding. If she protested, if the queen found out, or even if a child eventually resulted—St. George, he had waited too long and was full ready to throw caution to these balmy sea winds that blew intoxicatingly over the beaches tonight!

She slept alone as always in a little chamber three doors from Isabella. He grinned in the darkness and nervously stroked the vast black velvet cape he carried. That gift of her own room he had arranged for her over two years ago he would now collect on. Her old Scotswoman whom she valued so much had not been brought on this trip, so she was truly alone. Those light jesting kisses they had wagered at backgammon where he almost always won would be nothing to what she would give him tonight, willing or not.

He could hear his own breathing in the silence, feel his blood beat and course through his veins. His informant had told him that the last two nights she had dared to come out into this passage alone to foolishly, belligerently, disobediently stand at the grassy fringe of this sand dune before retiring. By the rood, if she did not come tonight soon, he would be desperate enough to go to her room to take her.

The moon had moved another inch through the wooden archway when he heard a light tread on the planks of the hall. He held his breath as she walked past him, her hair almost white in the moonlit dusk, her dark robe making her face and neck look transparent alabaster. He stood in awe for a moment at her almost ethereal beauty. A sea sprite, a moon maiden as chaste and cold as the goddess Diana, within his grasp at last for the mere taking!

She was clear to the edge of the sand dune before she sensed someone behind her and whirled around. She gasped in surprise and evidently did not recognize him at first. "There are guards nearby I can call for, sir! Who goes there?"

He strode closer, his eyes seemingly lit from within by reflected moonglow. "It seems you need a personal guard, a body guard, *ma femme.*"

"Oh! My lord prince, thank heavens, it is you."

"Aye, Jeannette. Thank heavens. It could have been some bloodthirsty Frenchman eager for a taste of an English maid, you know, or some vile barbarian hoping to—"

"And did you come to act as some vile barbarian, then?" she cut in, her voice suddenly wary. "I am carrying a dagger, you know."

He laughed deep in his throat and took another step closer until she fancied she could scent the masculine essence of him that always set her head spinning. But no, the sea wind was at her back, all tangy balm of free air and waves. It whipped her loose tresses over her robed shoulders so that his big, dark form seemed to dart and blur.

"Good night then, Your Grace. I must go in now."

"Too late, my sweet love. Much too late for both of us to ever retreat now."

He moved forward. Before she could cry out or struggle, a huge, black cape flapped around her like a shadowy, winged embrace. He lifted her and strode up over the powdery sand dune toward the sea where her cries would avail her nothing in the pounding of breakers and persistent roar of wind. They passed a first guard, then another who merely nodded and held their ground. He had brought his own men and she had walked like a dumb rabbit into his waiting trap!

Waves crested creamy white on slick sand almost at his feet. A horse whinnied close as he strode onward unspeaking. Threats, pleas darted through her stunned mind, but she discarded them as weak or foolish. Besides, his firm profile, etched by moonlight, was rock hard and she was suddenly afraid. She had meant for the trap to be hers, on her own territory, and now she would have to fight her own terrifying desires as well as his.

The huge saddle on his massive destrier Wilifred seemed a lofty seat far up into the moonlight sky when he lifted her. "Please, my lord prince. I want to go back," she said down at him as calmly as she could.

He mounted behind her in the wide saddle made for a man in full armor and held her sideways across his lap as they started off down the beach. Her cloaked shoulder and flushed cheek rubbed against the leather jerkin he wore over a dark tunic; his muscular thigh moved heavily against her in a rhythmic pattern.

"Then I demand to know where you are taking me," she brazened, her heart pounding in unison with the great beast's hoofs on the hard packed sand.

"Not far, *ma chérie*. A little place of our own away from everything where I shall just be your Edward until dawn. And then we shall see. I pray, my sweet, beautiful Jeannette for a very late, late dawn."

He reined in at a dim sand dune which looked like countless others. Two horses; two men standing about greeted the prince. He dismounted and helped her down. Though she would not have been foolish enough to make a scene before the two guards she did not recognize, he lifted her again and strode up over the dune. The sea below crashed, incredibly loud in her ears, but she welcomed the strength of it as she did the mastery of his unrelenting embrace.

He put her down and unwrapped the constricting cocoon of cape before a low-gabled, rough-shingled cottage. A cresset lamp glowed in its one small curtained window as if to challenge the more blatant overhanging golden moon. The door creaked open at the mere touch of his big hand, and his firm press against the small of her back moved her inward.

Her voice was faint, a mere ghostly echo but she fought to keep it steady. "It is a lovely fisherman's cottage, Your Grace."

"Edward, my love. For tonight, and many nights hereafter, saints willing, you will call me Edward."

"Edward, then—my lord."

He closed and latched the door noisily while she surveyed the tiny, sea-fragrant room: a fireplace unlighted, for the night was warm; a table and two upholstered chairs on a small Persian rug; a wooden bowl of fruit, two tall vases of heavy, blooming crimson roses and white lilies; a huge decanter and two goblets. And dominating the room, a large carved coffer and one of the biggest canopied beds she had ever seen.

"I believe, my sweet Jeannette, we are alone at long, long last. No fluttering Isabella or nervous guardians. No Salisbury to come stumbling upon us."

"And my betrothed, wounded in loyalty to you, is off on his northern English lands, of course. How convenient for you."

"And for you, petite vixen. I believe I quote you properly from Isabella's betrothal banquet, that time we spent so pleasantly together at Bruges, before you became rather indisposed and I had to rush you to your room—ah, aye, I have it now—'Saints, my lord Prince. You know how it goes at court with betrothals.'"

"You have no right to mock me! It is your court and not mine and I have been full loyal to Lord Holland!"

"Really? Then why does Salisbury think he has a chance, and—why do I?"

"He, my lord prince, is foolish and you are—quite mistaken."

His laughter rumbled in the room as he threw back his head and hit his chest for effect. "Ah, my Jeannette, so wild and daring. But I came not to argue or hear you sing or talk your way out of anything. Tell me now, under that deep blue camlet robe and those protectively crossed arms, is there one of those lovely invisible Flemish night chemises you and Isabella like to tell us poor bastards about so we can stand around with our tongues hanging out and take crazy risks like this to have a look? Well?"

He took a menacing step forward, his lips curved in an inviting grin. She felt the bare essence of the wispy material against her body even now and knew instantly the full impact it would have on him when he saw it—and then, on them both.

She stood rigid, her hips pressed to the table edge. For one shrieking moment she considered drawing her pitifully small dagger from the deep pocket of her robe; but then, this was the hero of Crécy. She thought of at least heaving a goblet at him for effect as Isabella, no doubt, would have done.

"I would like some wine, please, Edward."

A smile lit his face at her soft use of his name, but it did not sway his intent. "Later, sweetheart. After."

His big, warm hands went to her wrists to pull them gently to her side, then to the plush ties of the camlet robe. "The breeze is warm and sweet," he said gently. "I swear you will not be cold."

She did shiver with fierce anticipation as the robe left her warm body and slid down her gauze-clad shoulders to fall back on the table behind her. His bent fingers traced down her jaw to the elegant curve of her throat and lower over the upper swell of her high, firm breasts. As if mesmerized, she stood still and bit her lower lip in confusion as her nipples leapt erect beneath the merest brush of his hand.

"So exquisite, Jeannette. We have waited much, much too long. I have been too bloody damn patient, but there will be nothing to interrupt us this time."

He swept her up high in his iron arms, and the whole little room tilted and whirled. He lay her back in the puffy embrace of the velvet-covered featherbed and was beside her instantly. His free hand roved her body, stroking, pushing away the unresisting, diaphanous silk. Foolishly, she tried to rise, to stay his caress of her breast with both hands, but his strength was steel and stone.

His lips sought hers, a hard, demanding kiss that softened to the deep, persistent probing of a relentless tongue in the wet cavern of her mouth. A little, unbidden moan escaped her as she met his challenge with a frightening need of her own.

Eventually, breathing raggedly, he pulled away to rain kisses down the vulnerable sides of her throat, first under one soft earlobe and then the other. She meant to stop his hand along the curve of waist and hip but all desire to resist had long fled. At least, at least if this could bind him to her, later, when she could think and breathe and stop this spinning, she could hurt him when she told him she detested him. And then, and then—her thoughts ground to a halt as his mussed, tawny head bent low over her breasts to pull and kiss her taut, pink nipples through the transparent cloth.

The gauzy material became wet where he licked and tugged, and when he pulled away to devour her with passion-glazed eyes, icy shivers shot from her sweetly bruised lips and nipples clear down to her stomach and between her legs where his hand moved now. A warm languor spread through her making her limbs leaden with desire. The moonglow hem of chemise ruffled up around his big, bronze wrist as his hand crept up her smooth leg.

"At Bruges," he rasped, his voice like deep velvet, "the day Isabella went so wild and broke things, I was allowed a little glimpse of these bare thighs. It was not much for a starving man to live on, my sweetheart. You comforted Isabella then. Comfort your Edward now."

Her stunned mind told her to pull her knees together, but he was too quick. A stroking hand, a big knee separated her legs easily, then spread them wider while he knelt between to open her to the twin embrace of balmy air and his deliberately torturing fingers. His hands and mouth were everywhere, and she realized the gauzy material that had separated them like a mere mist was pushed up above her naked breasts. His hot mouth reveled in their fullness again as a hand and teasing, plundering mouth sought first one and then the other pink nipple endlessly until she thought she would scream from desire. She tossed her head back and forth at the sweet onslaught, her hair spread wild across the width of soft bed.

She clung to him, kissing him back, moaning, biting her lower lip to keep from crying out her need for him. She was supposed to hate him, to control him. She wanted to hate him!

His mouth was hot against her ear. "Shall I go on now, Jeannette? Remember how it was before when you first let me in? Do you want me now, my sweetheart?"

She nodded desperately, tears squeezing between her thick lashes. Her hands grasped his powerful shoulder muscles, her long nails digging into his leather jerkin as if to pin him to her.

"Say it then, my darling. Say 'I want you to love me.'"

When she hesitated and opened her eyes to stare up at his handsome face so close, his sure fingers sought again the warm, wet place between her legs so open to him on either side of his lean hips.

"Say it then, my Jeannette. 'Please love me.'"

"Aye, please—"

She almost cried out in fierce anger at his desertion as he moved swiftly away to discard his clothes. Boots thudded to the floor, and he yanked his leather jerkin and tunic over his head as if they were one garment. In the pale lamplight at the curtained window, his chest then his bare legs glowed faintly golden, dusted with curly blond hair. At the juncture of his muscular thighs she saw the blatant power of his desire for her.

As he knelt on the soft bed again, she sat up, wide-eyed and pressed handfuls of the ruffled chemise to her breasts. But he only gave a single, gruff laugh and lifted the cloud of material up over her tousled head. He reached for her bare shoulders and they were down again in the deep caress of velvet featherbed.

Her body quaked with the impact of his naked skin against hers. Jolted alive, each nerve felt bombarded with sensations etched in her memory forever: the velvet coverlet was soft, yet cool along her back and buttocks when he pressed her down; his big hand felt calloused from lance and sword as it traced a fierce brand along her satin skin. He smelled like leather and sea air, like forest and breezes and everything unutterably wonderful.

She reveled in the first probe of powerful masculinity at her very core. Last time, he had said he had barely begun but she could not fathom more splendor than this desperate need to submit, to conquer, to be one with him. He watched her face while he thrust hard and drove deep inside. The complete possession of the tactic stunned her: she belonged to him and wanted it so desperately, like this, forever.

His powerfully muscled arms kept his weight from her,

but his hips and legs set up a fierce rhythm wilder than the crashing waves on the waiting shores outside. She lost control of her thoughts, even her breathing. Only the two of them existed now in one wonderful union separate from all the world and anything that had ever been. The red silk canopy over his disheveled, tawny head tilted and spun while she clung to his thrusting body. And then, surprisingly, a deep, primitive something uncurled deep in her woman's core and crept upward, downward, even inward.

"Oh, my lord, I—oh, please, my Edward—" she gasped, unsure of what she was asking. She bent her knees along his ribs and her silken thighs pressed hard against his rocking body.

Everything built, whirled, exploded in a rush of color and sound. She climbed up, then threw herself over the edge and spiraled down, down into velvet exhaustion, moaning deep in her throat even as he made a final, fierce thrust against her quaking limbs.

She felt the bed again now under her; his huge body, damp with perspiration pressed her down. The weight of the man was incredible, yet she had not noticed before. He nuzzled her tousled hair along her throat, and shifted to lie close beside her. His voice was a raspy whisper.

"Content for now, my sweetheart?"

"Aye. Forever."

He chuckled silently, but she felt his ribs and flat stomach move against her. "Not forever, *ma* Jeannette. Only for a few minutes. I have much to teach you."

"Are you so skilled at this then?"

Now he laughed aloud and that annoyed her.

"Aye, my little innocent. Cannot you tell?"

"Then, my lord—Edward—you have no right to goad me concerning any *galants beaux* who may find me of interest."

He snuggled closer, his heavy left hand intimately on her waist and hip. "But all the others—that is over now, Jeannette."

She raised one blond eyebrow at him. If he thought his superior strength and admitted vast seductive powers would make her his willing slave, *he* had much to learn.

"I think not, Your Grace. One little bout—saints, that hardly makes an entire victory in war."

He was awake now when she thought but one moment ago he was content to take a nap pressed to her like this.

"One little bout, as you so foolishly put it, *chérie*, is not what this will be at all. Shall I demonstrate a second victory right now to prove my words?"

"A truce—you promised me some wine," she insisted.

His handsome brow furrowed in the hint of a frown; he moved one warm hand on her naked hip. Then he shrugged. "A little truce before the next battle, then. Shall we make our own plan of conquest, Jeannette?"

He rose, quite evidently unabashed at his nakedness which her eager eyes devoured as he moved to the table to pour the wine. His broad shoulders and cleanly delineated back muscles tapered to a narrow waist and firm buttocks before the powerful thighs began. When he turned, he caught her stare before she could look away.

"Intrigued again, Jeannette? I swear to you anytime you want me inside you I can be ready."

A fierce blush heated her neck and cheeks as she reached out to snatch her wine goblet. "Saints, no. I am only thirsty and then I want to go back."

Before she could drink, his big hand cupped her chin to make her look at him. His crystalline, blue eyes were narrowed and glittering. "Jeannette, never lie to me, ever, but especially not when we bed together. I could not bear it. I will not allow it. Do you understand?"

His hand tightened firmly and her goblet shook so in her hand a little cool liquid splashed on her warm, bare thigh. "I understand."

"They will try to keep us apart but if there is any need for subterfuge or deceit, it must not be between us. Say you understand," he pursued, his face completely serious.

"I did say it, my Lord Edward. Please. You are hurting me."

He loosed his hold and sipped his wine, his eyes still pinning her to the velvet where she sat, her knees pulled up and her golden tresses a veil to partly cover her nudity. His warm fingers lifted to stroke the slant of her cheek. He felt growing desire for her assault him again. For three years he had been watching her, wanting her. St. George, she drove thoughts of any other woman from his mind and turned his very insides to hot, molten lead when her violet eyes gazed wide on him like this. Yet her next words brought the outside world crashing in and he longed to silence her with a kiss.

"I guess it will not be too long now before Calais falls, Your Grace."

"Aye. This week, I judge."

"And then we will be sailing home for a victorious welcome for you. But those poor people starving in that city—"

"Look, *ma chérie*, they have had a standing offer to submit to our mercy at any time. It is their own choice to stay behind those walls."

"Submit to your mercy—a strange way to speak of it. And was it so with us today? I submitted to your mercy?"

"Save it for another time, Jeannette. I dislike a scolding woman in bed. I can get all the lawyers, strategists—or enemies—I need elsewhere."

"Oh, well—of course, I did not mean to be a scolding woman. Of course, I want to fall into line and any bed you choose anywhere, just like all your other women—"

To her dismay he grinned at her despite her shrewish tone. "*Ma chérie*, I cannot tell you how much it would please me to believe even for a moment you are one tiny whit jealous of what other women I may or may not have had. Now finish the wine you so desperately wanted. I have other plans for our evening—all of it."

She felt suddenly shy, then panicky. How dangerously close a few moments ago she had come to shouting out her love for him and yet—and yet she had vowed to her mother she would avenge their family cause on the royal Plantagenets. Isabella was foolish and innocent, the queen both kind and foreboding, the king so utterly unreachable. But this man, Edward, their dear son and heir, was close, vulnerable—so close that—

He took her half-emptied wine goblet from her unresisting fingers and drained it himself before dropping it to the carpet behind him as he had done his own. He reached for her waist, tangling his fingers in her long hair. He noted she was trembling barely perceptibly, but she faced him like a warrior with her shoulders back, her eyes steady, and her pert chin held proudly. She was a little warrior in her own way and one he did not quite understand. Other women, even noble or royal, he could have at his bidding yet he cared not. This one, all champagne and lilacs and wild spirit, he wanted to possess as desperately as he had ever wanted a victory of a more heroic sort. Yet she had put up some wall and however much he desired to scale it, it grew apace.

He leaned forward to take her lips which she yielded warily. "My beautiful, violet-eyed love," he said low and then he began his campaign of conquest that so often with this woman ended in his own surprising surrender.

Calais had capitulated; the lengthy siege against the apparently impregnable walls was over. Even the richest inside the city had finally been reduced to eating rats and dogs, and Jean de Vienne, the brave leader of the city's garrison, had at last asked for terms. King Edward of England gave a reply direct and simple. He had offered Calais mercy long ago before he had lost a year at siege and hundreds of soldiers to winter cold and disease camped outside these walls in rude, wooden structures. For long years, Calais had been a home port for pirates preying on

English ships in the Channel. Now the defiant citizens must surrender to either being killed or ransomed at his will—unconditional surrender. The famous Plantagenet temper Joan had seen in the king, Prince Edward, even Isabella, which was whispered of from the midland shires of England clear to the pope's palace at Avignon, had been fanned to fever heat.

But the king's advisors counseled against such severity. Philippa, near her time with her tenth child, pleaded for the Blessed Virgin's mercy. Even his warrior son, who amazed those closest to him by his calm and contented demeanor lately, suggested that power could best be served at times through gentleness—a true chivalric ideal most courtiers whispered the Prince of Wales had learned through reading about King Arthur but only Edward himself knew he had learned through his patient, secret conquest of the little Jeannette of Kent whom he was certain he had tamed now they had become lovers. They had spent a second long night together at their little sea cottage, though he had to risk going clear to her room down the hall near Isabella's suite and several other guards not in his employ had seen them leave. Still, the night had been beautiful: the whole world was beautiful despite his father's temper or the starving, wretched citizens of Calais on the other side of those high walls.

Finally, King Edward agreed to a compromise which would both bestow mercy and yet seek redress and justice—six of the richest city leaders must present themselves before him clothed only in their shirts with nooses around their necks ready to be hanged. They must present to him a naked sword, handle first to symbolize their utter defeat and bear the keys to the city and the castle within. The other conquered citizens left in the city would then benefit from the king's mercy.

The English court, which had gone to Bruges for the marriage that never happened, was all assembled that

Saturday, August 4, 1347 for another sort of festivity—the surrender of stubborn Calais. Joan sat next to Isabella on the dais behind the king, queen, and prince under a striped azure and gold silk awning which flapped gently in the sporadic, warm sea breeze. Everyone was richly attired; many had donned the expensive brocades and jewel-studded satins they had expected to wear at the Princess Isabella's wedding. Only Isabella herself and her dear friend Jeannette had vowed never to wear their pure white dresses once destined for that marriage day and never to mention it again to anyone.

Joan wore a clinging, peach-colored satin kirtle in which she was much too warm for the day. The long-skirted, tight-bodiced, and long-sleeved popular styles were uncomfortable in weather like this and someday, when she had enough power, she fully intended to change the fashion, she vowed. But today her gown stirred restlessly about her ankles and the traditional liripipes at the sleeves draped over the arm of her chair; even the wispy scarves fluttered from her high, pointed headpiece. Yet she had dressed as she knew she should, even to please the queen. If the king had not been in such a towering rage of late, she might have dared to talk Isabella into something far more frivolous to show them she did not care for their pious and proud Plantagenet ways. One of the slit *surcotes* she favored or a kirtle dripping with her favorite deep, swinging fringes would do. She would be bareheaded and laugh at their frowns or—saints, but one of those diaphanous night chemises they had brought from Flanders would suit this warm day! Then, the prince would be pleased at least.

She could not repress the little smile which lifted her cherry red lips as she squinted out into the sunlight at the small, approaching group of men from Calais. This town had fallen to the English, she told herself, just as the prince surely had fallen to her. He thought himself the aggressor, the conqueror, no doubt, but when he needed her as much as he seemed to the two nights they had spent at that lovely, little beach cottage—when he sought her kisses and caresses and lost himself in her body—she felt her control over him. That might have to be her eventual revenge on these Plantagenets. He would ask for her, need her beyond reason, and she would reject him and his parents—perhaps Isabella too, if need be—with him. She would tell them why. Everyone would know that Joan of Kent sought retribution for her murdered father and ruined mother. She would take Marta and go home to Liddell Manor in quiet Kent to live caring for the estate when her brother Edmund was away and playing sad songs on her lute. The picture of her poor father summoned before the assembled councilors at Windsor by Roger Mortimer and that oily-faced bastard de Maltravers drifted through her memory. And then, when she saw the present scene unfold before her, she nearly screamed out at its stunning impact.

With the wailing lamentations of grief from within the walls of nearby Calais as sad background music, six men approached the king's silken tent. A moment's swelling breeze lifted the awning and their garments, and flapped the leopard and lily banners smartly. The six burghers of Calais walked haltingly; gaunt-faced, ravaged, white-bearded, they halted before the colorful pavilion in linen shirts, barelegged with rope halters around their scrawny necks as they had been told.

They knelt down and held up their hands and once again said, "Gentle King, behold here we six, who were burgesses of Calais and great merchants. We have brought the keys of the town and of the castle, and we submit ourselves clearly into your will and pleasure, to save the residue of the people of Calais, who have suffered great pain."

Joan half rose out of her seat, her mouth open, her eyes wide. They had suffered great pain! The speaker was so frail and his voice creaked like an old oak door at home, not with fear but with utter exhaustion and desperation. He was so blue-eyed, so vital in his pitiful linen shirt with the knotted noose hanging forward on his sunken chest. Her father once, so blue-eyed, had pleaded in his shirt and rope, doomed, doomed before all who had stared, cold and haughty like this king. But then, this king had been off in cowardly flight instead of at Windsor where his uncle, Edmund of Kent, needed mercy!

Isabella's hand darted to Joan's arm and she pulled her back down into her seat. Suddenly, Joan was aware the prince had turned his head to glare, but she ignored him too.

"Sir, we beseech Your Grace to have mercy and pity on us through your high nobles," the old man of Calais concluded. The king took the keys and sword and handed them to Prince Edward but made no immediate answer. The scene blurred before Joan as her eyes filled with blinding tears. Her own blue-eyed father—his portrait at Liddell in the hall was so blue-eyed—he had pleaded like this, the terrible hangman's rope heavy on his neck and no one had listened.

King Edward's tawny, crowned head moved as he formed his terrible words. "Death to you all, rebels and enemies. My mercy you spurned earlier, and you may reap the harvest of my just vengeance now. Away with these Frenchmen!"

It took Joan a moment to grasp his meaning; then, she realized even if King Edward had been there for her father the result might have been the same.

She turned to the frowning Isabella beside her. "Your Grace, no. He cannot. He cannot have them beheaded or hanged. He cannot," Joan hissed to Isabella and grabbed her wrist.

"Sh! His Grace is so angry and rightly so," the princess whispered back at her. The surrounding crowd of nobles murmured, shifted, buzzed with whispers. Ahead of them, the queen's lofty headpiece tilted as she pivoted to stare at her daughter and her young, distraught ward. The king sat stone-still as if carved in marble. One clenched fist rested on his knee, his beard moved in a warm gust of wind, and his gold crown glinted dully in muted sunlight. English guards in leopard tunics were leading the men away. At last the king and prince moved down off the dais to confer in deep tones with their chief negotiator, Sir Walter Manny, newly arrived from the English victory over the Scots at the siege of Berwick.

Joan, her hands clasped tightly in her brocade lap, hunched further forward to speak to the queen. "Your Grace, please, cannot we plead for them? They are only old men brave enough to come out here for this. Cannot we convince the king to show mercy?"

"Cannot *we*?" the queen echoed, turning to face Joan more fully while a surprised Isabella looked on. "Who is *we* who would dare to beard His Grace when these enemies have finally capitulated and we may soon all go home to England?" Her face looked annoyed and stern. Joan had not talked to Her Grace for several days, and she had not seen such a hard look since that long-ago day when the queen had come upon her sprawled across the prince's lap in that walled garden at Windsor.

Joan clasped her hands together so tightly in her lap that she felt her fingers go numb. "Your Grace, I know the king would give you aught you ask of him. He bends to you only. I have seen it—you yourself have said it, and now you are so far with this tenth royal babe that he would deny you no—"

"And why are these old, foreign men anything to you, Joan? Did not your dear prince explain that at their glorious Crécy the French were vanquished? Is this not more of that glory? I begged my lord king for mercy for the women and children left in that miserable walled city and he hearkened to me. Why are these six lives so much to you then?"

Joan's teary, violet eyes locked with the queen's pale blue ones. Joan felt a battle enjoined there which was more than this issue of six old men's lives. Philippa's gaze wavered one moment in her plump face as if she remembered or realized something, but that face hardened again and Joan was suddenly afraid.

"Well, my Lady Joan, the king will not have them dispatched until they are shriven, so we have a few moments to speak further. Excuse us, my dear Isabella," the queen said and a strange half-smile parted her lips. "I have private business with our dearest Joan for a moment."

Isabella's eyes popped as if she had swallowed something huge, but she knew well that flat, direct tone her mother used but seldom and she reluctantly did as she was bid. All her wild vows of blaming her parents for her desertion by that pompous Louis de Male she had already forgotten. She much preferred being in their majesties' good graces even if her cousin Joan evidently did not see the wisdom in that.

Queen Philippa followed Joan a few steps beyond the farthest tent pole where they would be alone for a moment. The sun was stunningly bright and the sky arched porcelain-blue overhead outside the shelter of the silken awning where they stopped.

"Shall I fetch you a stool, Your Grace?" Joan began. She fully meant to plead again for the queen's intervention in these looming executions, but there was something else in this from the way the queen was acting now. Saints, if she had to, she would even dare to bring up her own father's cruel death though they had never spoken directly of that before.

"How badly do you wish for those lives, then, Jeannette?" The queen's use of the pet name the prince called her startled her, for she had reverted to calling her Joan for many months now.

"Badly, Your Grace. You see, I just feel—"

"And I want something from you badly, *ma demoiselle*, and will have your vow on it. You see, I know of your—liaison—with the prince at night—the little beach place, I know not how many nights, so do not bother to equivocate or deny it."

The tent pole behind the queen's floating head scarves

seemed to move; the distant castle walls of Calais seemed to jump closer, to quiver from their foundations.

"No, my dear, he did not tell me. He knows nothing of my knowledge of this, but that is not important, only that it must end now, completely, permanently," she went on in a rush. "I want your word you will go along with my arrangements that you wed William Montacute, Earl of Salisbury next week, here at Calais. The prince will be riding circuit to protect our beachhead, and the secret ceremony will be held after he is gone."

"Salisbury! But—what about Thomas Holland? You cannot ask this of me!"

"Keep your voice down, my dear. I do not ask, I demand. Our beloved heir is destined for a foreign dynastic marriage—a princess. Of course, you must realize that. And he had been so amenable on that point until you managed to—to quite unsettle his life. Oh, do not look so crestfallen, dear Joan. I do not blame you for the little seaside trysts or loving him, for who would not?"

"I—I do not love him. I truly do not love your son."

Philippa looked surprised, then doubtful and annoyed. "I do not believe you, but then, it really makes no difference. Fine, for there will be a ready smile for Lord Salisbury when we tell him of his good fortune after the prince has gone. And I expect you to take to your room with fever or some such until he is gone. I will not have all this upsetting him or his father until there is nothing he can do. And now, you will give me your word and I shall seal your vow by kneeling before my husband king and pleading for your poor burghers' lives. Salisbury is from a fine family and the marriage will suit you. I shall handle Thomas Holland and, eventually, my beloved son."

"Aye, I see." Joan felt as if she were sleepwalking through a nightmare, but the continual wailing of the defeated from behind the walls of Calais was all too real and she had to hurry to save the blue-eyed old man with the rope around his neck. At least there would be some pleasure in besting the prince, but just when she had fancied herself in control, the wheel of Fortune had spun to cast her downward in despair again.

"I shall have your vow on this and then you may go to your room until I send for you, Joan," the queen repeated, her words piercing Joan's thoughts until her eyes refocused on the pudgy, suddenly frightening face so close. She did not, could not love the prince despite how he took her to the heights of rapture, could she? When she bedded with him, he sailed her high above the sea. She could not ever imagine the fond, smiling Salisbury doing any such thing to her.

The queen's hand pinched her shoulder. "Swear it, Joan. All time for otherwise, but this choice has gone."

"I—aye, I swear it. Betrothals at court, mayhap marriages too—they are nothing."

"Go now. I promise I shall plead for the old men. Go now."

Dazedly, her mind racing faster than her feet, Joan hurried back to the one-floored wooden warren of rooms which had been her home near the prince these last four months. The mazelike edifice looked squat and ugly now. The sand dune where he had come to take her away on his horse last week seemed barren and cold.

The words of a song marched sullenly through her brain as she went along the hollow-sounding corridor to her chamber: "'Go heart, hurt with adversity . . . And let my lover thy wounds see. Farewell my joy, and welcome pain, 'Til I see my love again.'"

She sat listlessly on the edge of her narrow bed and stared at her lute with its gay silk ribbons resting in the dim corner. Damn the blackguard! She did not love him; she could not, but he had crept too far into her life. That lute he had given her, and how narrow this bed was after the vast one they had shared. How his massive frame had filled that little doorway there when he had come to seek her the second time. She heard his low voice in the screaming silence of her memory even now and felt his crystal blue eyes and the touch of his hands and mouth—

She threw herself across the bed gasping in silent sobs. Her shoulders heaved, her legs trembled. And in the midst of opulence and victory and a first step toward the revenge she had long sought, she felt only desolate, beaten, and utterly bereft.

Chapter Ten

The English autumn gilded the hunt park and woods of Windsor in russet and copper and bronze. The tang of crisp air and the excitement of tournament day blended to bring the vast labyrinth of castle and town alive with expectation. The royal family and their court had returned from France four weeks ago. The reception in London had been heartfelt but not grand, for the prisoners and loot had been dribbling home sporadically since the conquest of Crécy over a year ago. Today was the closest thing the court would see to a single, splendid celebration for the French victories: a full day of tournaments, parades, and feasts.

The hour was but six of the clock and dawn had barely crested above the gray towers and battlemented walls when Joan of Kent rose from her narrow bed in her bare feet to stare out through the casement window she thrust wide. Marta had just bustled out for warm water, but Joan could not even wait toasty in bed for that. Today, she and Princess Isabella had planned a blatant move to shock them all. It would be, Joan thought and her chin lifted defiantly, a statement to anyone who tried to rule and control her and Isabella's lives—especially the queen. It was a statement that young women could be keepers of their own fortunes no matter what orders were royally handed down. Isabella's betrothal to Louis de Male had proved an expensive, devastating fiasco and her own crazy, sudden marriage to William, Earl of Salisbury was mere farce and sham, though the queen had never yet deigned to explain why.

She heard Marta's sprightly tread in the hall and the door

creaked open. "My lassie ne'er learns, I see," the distinctive, heavily accented Scottish voice began a familiar and somehow comforting harangue. "Bare feet on these chill floors in October an' ye standin' about in one a those silly nothin' shifts ye spent good money on in Flanders. Get a robe on then, for old Marta'll not be nursin' ye through th' chills come winter tide."

"Now Marta, I never catch chills or agues. I am healthy as a horse and you know it. You did not by chance see my Lord Salisbury lurking down the hall as the other morn, did you?"

Marta began to pull a comb through her mistress' long, tangled tresses even as Joan bent over to wash her face and hands in the warm water scented with rosemary and laurel. "Not sin' th' queen must ha' set him back on his heel an' made him promise he would not claim marital rights until Lord Holland be arrivin' from Lancashire an' agrees his betrothal be forfeit." Marta clucked her tongue sharply as she always had to show disapproval. "'Tis th' strangest spider's web of a marriage I ha' ever heard, an' ta think it be th' queen's own makin'. Now why, for the love a St. Andrew, would th' queen betroth my bonny lass to one lord, then marry her ta a second but never let the marriage night take place? A veritable spider's web this whole court be, an' I ha' like ta tell them so!"

Joan vigorously rubbed her face with the linen towel Marta offered amidst further tongue clucking. "Saints, Marta, are you asking me to explain it? Aye, it is a puzzle, but I care not anyway. It is fine with me not to bed with William and not have him think he owns me somehow and order me about. This way I keep legally to myself except at meals and do as I will. I do not love either William or Thomas Holland, so I hope this bizarre arrangement never ends and the Princess Isabella and I can do whatever we wish eternally."

"Stuff an' nonsense," Marta snorted as her skillful, wizened hands began to deftly braid Joan's massive tumble of golden hair. "Who does my lass love then?" the old woman prodded after studying Joan's furrowed brow for a moment.

"Why, no one, of course, nor do I plan to."

"Ye canna' fool yer Marta, lambie. Sin' ye ha' been at court, especially sin' ye'r back from France, ye ha' changed."

"Of course, I have changed. Ouch, Marta, do not yank it back like that! Everyone thinks I am half daft for letting you bully me about and maybe they are right! No, it is just I have learned not to trust men and feel immensely better for it—not that I ever did trust any of them in the first place except usually my brothers and my old lute teacher, Roger Wakeley, before he left. But—well, saints, since mother told me what she did before she died and I saw my dear friend the princess deserted nearly at the high altar, I—just want to be more independent, that is all."

"Ye always did want to be that, lass. Ye know, I spoke wi' Morcar th' other day an' sin' Crécy, he ha' cast a new horoscope for th' Prince a Wales th' people be callin' the Black Prince now sin' he wore sable armor in that field a glory what made his name."

"He told me the sobriquet came from the fact he was all filthy mud at the end of the battle, but say on. I care naught for the prince's future, except that all English must care for our next king."

"Are ye really believin' ye can fool Marta, lambie? Now, never mind flyin' off in some contrary rage like a wee lass, only Morcar say he be castin' yer horoscope next. He did it once for yer lady mother afore ye left Liddell, but he says he took it further. He spoke to me a some a it."

"And I suppose I am to seek him out and beg to know it? I am still not sure I forgive any of you who knew why mother kept to her room all those years for not telling me, so why should I trust this all now—even you or Morcar? Besides, the princess and I have vowed to make of our own fortunes what we will, queen, kings, husbands, notwithstanding! I am going to spend the day with the princess now, so pray do not worry about me."

213

To Marta's obvious dismay that she had not dressed, Joan whirled her warm camlet robe about her and ran barefooted down the hall to the princess' vast chamber. It would never do to tell Marta of their daring plans for the tournament today; her scolding after she heard would be enough without listening to it before the deed was done too. The tall guard, Jaris, who often winked at her, opened the door as she approached and she hurried in.

Isabella sat in an ermine and jade velvet robe at her cosmetics table while two maids hovered over her hair. The familiar scent of the princess' favorite essence of gillyflowers hung heavy in the room already half-filled with giggling, primping *demoiselles*.

"Dearest Jeannette!" Isabella gushed and half-rose to encircle Joan's arms with a lightning quick hug. "I almost feared you had slept in but then with no *real* husband yet to bother you at night, I could not see why."

It annoyed Joan that several of the closest ladies giggled at that, but what did she care? The whole court, it seemed, knew of her strange, unconsummated marriage with William Montacute, Earl of Salisbury, if not all the details. Indeed, Thomas Holland had been sent for by the queen posthaste and could be arriving any day now.

"No real husband, Your Grace, thank the blessed saints, though I believe he hopes and pines eternally." Everyone tittered again, and Joan smiled broadly herself. At least if everyone was amused, she would pretend to be also. "And I did as you bid, dear princess, and have not put one bit of cosmetics to my face so that we all might look alike for our marvelous parade today. I hope no one has given out the slightest hint of it."

"If anyone did, I shall have her strung up by her hair or—or made to marry someone the queen bids," Isabella concluded with a grand flourish. All the maids giggled again, but Joan noted well the brittle voice and the sharp glint to Isabella's blue eyes. It took Joan aback a moment as she let the princess push her into her vacant place at the cosmetics table. "Hurry with her now, my maids, so we can all be dressed and down to our waiting horses before anyone discovers us and tries to interfere."

Joan darted quick glances in the gilded mirror as the talented Yvette and Annette, the princess' two favorite maids for cosmetics, worked over her. Since the return to London and Windsor from France, she had lost some weight despite the round of repetitive banquets and the myriad dishes of delicacies always available about the princess' rooms. Her cheekbones looked more prominent and tiny shadows hovered beneath her eyes to hint she had not slept well. What was that song he had taunted her with at Isabella's betrothal banquet? Oh, aye—

> Alas, my love hath gone away
> And now no meat nor drink, I say,
> Shall ever please me more until
> He loves me of his own free will.

Saints! Why did she think of him at all and ever at the strangest times? In the silence of her narrow bed at night, of course, with Marta's heavy breathing across the room, but also just walking or right in the middle of something her husband, who was not really a husband, said—and then he wondered why she was not listening! Oh, damn, damn this whole crazy Plantagenet court with all their intricate rules and customs, proprieties and strategems. Today, she and Isabella and the others would show them what they thought of it all!

"Lady Joan, please do not frown so or this pomade will go on uneven. Please, *madame*!"

Madame, a married lady now, Joan mused, but she did not feel married. The smiling, indulgent William of Salisbury touched her heart not a whit, and luckily so far, a few kisses and sighs had kept him somewhat mollified. Thank the Blessed Virgin, the prince with his accusing stares and nasty temper had been off at his lands in Berkhamstead since they had all been back home. At the tournament today, he, of course, would be much in evidence, but she had no intention of even speaking with him. St. George, she hoped this plan of theirs would make him fall in a tangled mass of precious black armor right in the dust at her feet!

She watched her reflection intently as Yvette and Annette bustled at their task. She scarcely ever wore any cosmetics but eye or lip color but today all Isabella's *demoiselles* would look alike as they dared to ride out in a parade of their own dressed and mounted like men. Let everyone gasp and whisper and wonder if the mockery meant the affront that indeed it did.

Over the rosewater pomade, they rouged her flawless skin a glowing pink above the high cheekbones. Her eye lids they painted a gentle violet to highlight her lavender eyes, and they smoothed her lips with a rosy-hued translucence which smelled and tasted faintly of cinnamon. They dusted glittering ambergris essence in her braided, wheat-colored tresses and powdered over her alabaster-and-roses complexion with a brush dipped in cochineal powder. They stared and squinted a moment, tipping their shapely heads together to confer, and then Yvette touched a slight hint of umber hue to her arched eyebrows.

"Ah, perfect," Yvette breathed and clasped her hands to admire her work. "Your long lashes are so sooty dark already, Lady Joan. Ah, perfect, no matter how you attire yourself like a man today, they will know you are a woman with that face and fullness of breasts, eh?"

"All right, all right, cease fussing over her and finish up with Clareene and Mary. Here, Jeannette. These tight hose, quilted jerkin and this tunic should do for you. By the rood, we have to be out of here and hidden in the stables or we shall surely be seen after the men complete their first tourney. Someone will try to stop us sure as rain! It has to be perfectly timed so we will be out onto the joust field in our own parade in the break between the two jousts. Oh, I feel ludicrous in these wretched, silly things, but will it not be a marvelous jest?"

They all laughed at each other and themselves as they poured their ripe female forms into the men's garments the princess had managed to borrow from her younger brother, John of Ghent's vast wardrobe without his knowledge. The tunics she insisted she and Joan don were both azure and gold, quartered, and sported the English leopards and French lilies Joan had so often seen the prince and king wear.

Joan, clad already in the tight blue hose which clung like wet silk to her legs and derrière and a dark blue boy's quilted jerkin tied closed in over her breasts, hesitated. "Your Grace, should we really wear these tunics? I mean, of course, you can, but I—"

"Nonsense. You are of royal Plantagenet lineage also, and besides, we do not have enough of the plain-colored ones to go around."

"But what about protocol? Should I not wear something with the Salisbury arms now, or maybe just carry a banner of my own house of Kent?"

Isabella stamped her foot and her blue eyes flashed in a hint of Plantagenet temper. "Jeannette, how can you preach pious protocol when we dare all this? Besides, this can hardly be great fun if you turn so difficult. We will be onto the field, around, and out to everyone's delight and amusement before anyone can stop us. Now hurry! All we need is my little sister Joanna running to tell the queen or John finding his wardrobe thoroughly ransacked—or the Prince of Wales catching us all in the hall!"

At that thought, Joan pulled the tunic over her head. If one was flaunting court etiquette, it should be done with a flourish! She chose a pair of dark blue velvet slippers from a heap on the floor and surveyed herself nervously in the mirror. She looked hardly a man: in this slender boy's garb her legs and derrière looked far too shapely and the tightly clenched belt for the swords they would attach after they mounted accentuated both her slender waist and rounded breasts and hips. Once they were safely out to the stables, they would all bind up their braids under silk turbans. Her face looked older, strangely not her own at all painted and powdered like this. And when the court saw them all astride huge destriers with swords held aloft in challenge—

"All right now, everyone down the back servants' stairs three at a time and keep covered with the cloaks. No one is to budge from the stable block until Jeannette and I arrive. All right, go on now and keep the cloaks closed, by the rood!"

Isabella's eyes glittered with an almost hysterical excitement that began to worry Joan. A little warning voice jabbered away at her confidence as if her conscience or maybe what she knew Marta would say were chanted in her brain. But when the fourteen maidens were not stopped on their circuitous route to their reconnoitering spot and the horses were all prepared, she began to relax. Indeed, this would be easy and highly amusing, too!

One of Isabella's numerous young pages darted in to tell them that the first series of knights' parades and jousts was nearly over. The ladies would not be missed in the galleries yet, for Isabella had thought to put out the story that after the first series of jousts some *demoiselles d'honneur* would present bouquets to the queen and her ladies in the stands. Indeed, four of the mounted maids were to carry fragrant nosegays close to their hearts as love-smitten court gallants often did; if worse came to worst, they could always give those to mollify the queen before cavorting back to these stables to laugh themselves silly over the row they were certain to have caused.

This stable block was very distant from the ones the knights frequented, so it was difficult to hear the shouts from the galleries, the blare of trumpets, and clash of armor from here. They mounted nervously, the giggles muted now, trusting the page boy's sense of timing to help them reach the jousting field at the correct moment between events. Joan noisily slid her unwieldy sword into its scabbard which also disconcertingly boasted the royal Plantagenet arms. It felt strange to ride astride, her legs spread on either side of the vast saddle without a skirt to cover her.

The coiled silk strips which constituted their turbans were multi-hued; she had chosen dark blue to match her tight, silk hose. To flaunt their legs like this even with the slit tunic draped nearly to the knees—saints, it was onward and outward now! Too late to draw back from what had seemed such marvelous sport only yesterday. Perhaps, she mused foolishly, as the now silent women rode out of the stable two abreast into the brilliant October late morn, with all these cosmetics, this turban, and this garb, no one could recognize who she was if they rode only one circuit about the field and dashed right off.

They made a real stir as they passed through the clusters of knights' tents and past the rows of farriers' and armorers' stalls with their smoking fires. Some men's gruff voices cheered them, some laughed, and a few shouted ribald insults:

"Ahey, little knight there on the end, I had like to joust with you, and winner takes all, eh?"

"I shall cuddle close as I can in my bed tonight if I share it with such a warrior, by St. Peter!"

"Damn, but those lucky steeds know what legs to ride between, what say!"

Joan looked neither right nor left and the boastful smile she had meant to sport crushed to a frown. Several had recognized the princess as she led their little parade toward the banner- and bunting-decorated arch to the field; Joan heard the princess' name and her own whispered, then shouted to spread like a wild Channel wind through the crowds of food vendors and peasants hanging on the guardrails of the tilt grounds. Ludicrously, the mingled smell of hot, pickled pigs' feet and yeasty ale was the last thing she remembered before she rode in last, to balance Isabella's lead of the fourteen knightly *demoiselles* come to do their own sort of joust with the crowd.

Their timing was perfect. The field had just been cleared of debris and broken lances, and newly powdered with sand where blood had been spilled; the second array of lesser knights had not yet ridden into view. Suddenly, Joan was very glad her brother Edmund had not yet come back to court from his duty in the northern Scottish wars that had brought the young Scots King David a prisoner to London to mingle with the noble French from Crécy and Calais who were yet to be ransomed. Now if only this could all be over without having to see Prince Edward or William's smiling stare, the day would be perfect indeed.

The crowded galleries gasped, then silenced. The fourteen riders pounded inward at a good gallop, swords raised in mock salute. The crowd roared with nervous laughter, then approval. A smile lifted Joan's firmly set lips, and she darted a glance toward the royal pavilion draped with massive Plantagenet banners to match her own tunic. People were standing, pointing, but neither the king nor prince had yet returned from his own earlier joust to watch the rest of the tournament. She relaxed and shouted, "For England and St. George!" as the other riders wildly followed her lead. The canter of the big horse felt good under her. The queen's face went by in a blur as they circled once more, brandishing, flourishing their swords in a final display. Isabella turned once in her saddle and shouted something Joan could not understand, but her face was flushed, her eyes wild. A blur of noise and colors, a cool breeze on their blushing faces, they wheeled and cantered toward the exit.

Joan could feel her heart pounding in her throat as they funneled slowly out of the field through the crowd of mounted, armored knights waiting to take the field. Shields glinted glaringly and proud family banners flapped overhead on squires' poles or raised lances. Joan recognized a few knights by their armor or crests but these were not the chief warriors of the kingdom who had jousted earlier. Masculine eyes, filled with surprise or dismay, glared from under visors ready to be snapped closed, but a few men cheered them on.

The fourteen *demoiselles* rode now in single file through the assembled press of knights and those who had run inward from the city of tents to see the brave sight of noble ladies astride in jesting mockery of their lords. Saints, Joan thought as the success of it all assailed her, next time we shall don full armor and joust in earnest!

She dropped back again, last in their group, and tried to sheath her sword as they neared the stable block where they would dismount. A big horse cut in ahead, pushing close from the opposite direction, but she did not glance up. Some poor rogue late for his chance at some conquest on the joust field no doubt.

She saw the single, mailed arm shoot out at her before she could react. Her sword had just scraped metallically back in its scabbard when the arm hit around her waist: she was seized, lifted bodily backward out of her saddle crushed to another horse and a man in a coat of chain mail from shoulder to knee. Her breath smashed out in a grunt; her stomach hurt as if she had been struck there.

She hung suspended against him while his horse rushed away down a side alley of crude stalls and tents. En route, the arm hauled her up, before him on his saddle, to lean back against a massive chest where a poised lance rest, still mounted, jabbed at her bruised hip with each bounce of the huge beast. When she saw a black onyx ring on the middle finger of the bronzed rider's left hand on the reins, she nearly dry-heaved in crashing fear. A mere moment had passed since he had grabbed her. They rode into the door of a stable far down the line of wooden buildings. She dared, at last, when they reined in to gaze up into the furious face of Edward, Prince of Wales.

Her own humiliation at being so roughly and rudely handled turned her initial fear to raving anger. As he shifted his leg to dismount, she shoved at him, and they both almost toppled from their awkward perch. He cursed low, seized both her flailing wrists in one big hand as if she were a mere child and jumped off hauling her into his arms in one purposeful movement. Stunned for one instant, she hung limply in his grasp as, stiff-armed, he held her in front of him. His blue eyes clouded stormy gray; the pulse at the base of his throat which she had seen beat erratically in another sort of passion, now pounded noticeably.

"You have no right to treat me like this!" she brazened, trying to pull his iron grip free of her shoulders. "I am not some vile squire to humiliate and—"

"*I* humiliate *you*? Bloody hell, vixen! What right do you have to be prancing about in public flaunting yourself like this—like some scarlet woman advertising her wares! I ought to beat you black and blue for this stupid trick, especially since your so-called husband is obviously not the one to control you!"

They both glowered at each other as a voice from the still-open door of the stable interrupted their mutual tirade. "Your Grace, forgive me, milord, but your men are askin' where you rode off to after we watched the maids, an' said that—"

The prince's voice was curt and cold, a harsh command of superior authority no dolt could mistake. "Tell them, Robert, only that I am delayed and not where. Keep your mouth shut about what you have seen or heard here. Go on back to send them off and then come back here and guard this door until I release you. Close the door and go now."

Robert's dark eyes widened as he surveyed the two tense figures ankle deep in fresh straw in the farthest stall of the little stables. His lord's voice angry and demanding, aye, he had heard that before, but he had not in his wildest dreams imagined anyone, any woman, with an angry voice and stance like that one facing the prince with her arms akimbo on her shapely hips despite the prince's hard hands on her shoulders.

"Damn it, I gave you an order, rogue! Go!"

Robert went, and the small stable dimmed as he slammed the broad door shut behind him. Joan pulled away from Prince Edward's grasp, and surprised he still held her, he let her take a step back. She moved into a corner of the huge stall probably meant for a poor knight's horse who had never made it to the tournament since this wooden hut was far to the edge of the jousting grounds and stalls were assigned by rank.

Jeannette's eyes looked luminous in the dimness, he thought erratically as his hard breathing quieted. The deep straw rustled around his feet as he took a menacing step toward her, and his horse Wilifred whinnied low across the way, evidently content to munch the untouched hay. His anger at her daring mockery, now and always, chewed at his self-control as he took in her defiance. To his amazement, he felt his palms tingle to spank her, yet his loins ached with a repressed need all blended with his fury.

"I am going to join my friends, Your Grace," she was saying and her full breasts heaved in her exasperation with him. "It was mere jest and the princess and I enjoyed it immensely and she is, no doubt, waiting for my return now. Before she sends for the queen to search for me, I will be going."

His mailed arm shot out to block her exit. "*You*, woman, are going nowhere until I give you leave. And perhaps, just perhaps, if I tell the queen I beat your beautiful little backside as you deserve, you will be spared some of her wrath for this silly farce."

"Get out of my way, please. She has punished me quite enough by marrying me to one of *your* friends. And you would not dare to touch me—that way. I should have known you would never see the humor in it."

"In what?" he roared. She jumped back startled at the sudden explosion of his temper. "At your mocking the tournament, or the Plantagenets in that tunic, or me?"

"It had nothing to do with you, my lord prince."

"By the gates of hell, it does! Isabella is wild with smothered grief over her desertion but nothing such has happened yet to you! Do you think the fact I went off to oversee my lands means I have forgotten you—or that the queen's marrying you to Salisbury means we shall not be together? I have sent for Holland and made the queen promise she would not bed you with Salisbury and—"

"You! You! Saints, it is your meddling in my life that has caused all this ruin in the first place! How dare you pretend to care—then—then treat me like some strumpet!"

"The way you act is exactly how I treat you—tight hose, your face all made up like some temptress, your hair in that wild silk whatever-it-is, that cinched-in tunic, which, by the way, clearly states you are a Plantagenet possession."

"Oh, you conceited—" She stopped, horrified at what she had almost called him, but his lusty, insulting stare and its thrilling impact on her senses infuriated her.

She flailed and kicked as he darted at her. Her foot caught his shin. He threw her back into the straw and dove at her as she tried to scramble away. He dragged her back into a sitting position between his splayed arms and legs, her back pressed to his chest and arms still covered with the molded links of his chain mail. She scratched at one wrist while his other hand roughly unwound her carefully wrapped silk turban until the golden bounty of her hair cascaded free to hinder both their wild movements.

"No, you cannot. No!" she ground out, but she said no more then in her growing panic, just concentrated on fighting him. He let her dart away only to flop her on her back in some quick wrestling move. She could tell his thoughts; for a moment he had considered binding her with the pile of dark blue silk turban strips. He was heavy on her, pressing her down in the sweet-smelling, prickly straw, a grin on his determined face. She read the inevitable and lay instantly still under him.

The tactic obviously confused him as she hoped, and she used her little respite to seek a chance to dart away. If she tried to struggle by mere strength, he would surely best her; the drowning sensations always swept over her when he touched her and they would doom her to be conquered for certain.

"My lord prince, please. The tunic the princess borrowed from your brother Lord John, and I meant not to ruin it today."

He studied her face assessing this new strategy, but his hands holding her waist lightened. Her face looked older to him, different, but awesomely beautiful, and he was not certain if it was the exquisite colors that lit her eyelids, lips, and cheeks, or some new strength or sadness from within. "If you do not want that tunic harmed, take it off for me then," he said, his voice a raspy whisper.

She had not planned on that turn of events, but she nodded and he released her to sit up. The gall of the arrogant blackguard, she fumed, as she watched him audaciously unbuckle his wide, leather sword belt and lift his own Plantagenet tunic over his broad shoulders and mussed head in one fluid motion.

She moved slightly away to kneel on her haunches and carefully tugged her silk tunic up through her own tight belt. She trembled in anticipation of her plan, but she had to get away. If he touched her, roughly or not, she was afraid of her own reaction much more than his. This would trick him, show him she did not favor him, however mindlessly she had responded to his seaside love-making in France two months ago. She had to do this to keep her vow to be revenged on all of the treacherous Plantagenets.

His eyes widened in blatant anticipation as he saw she wore naught but a quilted jerkin under the tunic tied tightly across her breasts. The boy's garment was entirely too small and the ties gapped to reveal a two-inch strip of flesh from her collarbone to navel.

But the sudden thought she had had to submit only to allay his anger with sweetness energized her to panic. She was on her feet instantly and nearly laughed at the shocked expression on his face as she noisily drew her sword.

"Damn it to hell, you teasing little tiger," he cursed softly, and to her horror, he drew his sword from the straw behind him and crouched to circle her. She had not meant for that to happen. She had meant only to surprise him so she could run out or brazen her way to freedom.

She held her sword with both hands, wide-eyed, facing him, shuffling carefully through the deep straw. To her utter dismay, she saw his eyes light. He grinned broadly. The vile demon was enjoying every bit of this!

"Come on, come on, little warrior," he taunted her between clenched teeth. "You have overstepped now, my Jeannette. St. George, but it is treason to draw a sword with such intent on the heir apparent, and I am going to revel in this special punishment just for you. Come on, little warrior. Lay to, then—and to the victor belongs the vanquished."

He feinted a little sweep at her raised weapon, a mere tap. She began to tremble. Damn him, he was playing with her. She hated him! All of this marriage mess—how mixed up she felt about him—this whole spider's web, as Marta put it—it was all his fault!

Furious, she lunged once at his sword and clanged it soundly. He parried, but retreated when he could have pursued her to the wall. He waited, grinning, his eyes going over her as if to size her up. He ran his wet tongue over his lips in obvious anticipation. It hit her with an impact which almost buckled her quaking knees that she had ludicrously raised a sword against the finest fighter in the land, the Black Prince, hero of Crécy.

He tired of the play, and advanced differently this time when he saw the look of awe and fear temper the anger on her face. She lifted her sword to ward off a blow, but he only swung once and whacked her heavy weapon over the rail into the deep straw of the next stall. He dropped his sword behind him and advanced farther.

"Have you a dagger to stick between my ribs, Jeannette? No? Then I shall take what is always mine before we go. We have both been away from the others too long already."

"I—my husband."

"As soon as Holland arrives, he will get *that* called off, and I know for a fact the marriage is in name only anyway."

226

"Then Holland will—"

"Will probably petition the pope to have your betrothal reinstated, a lengthy, tedious process, I hope. A sticky mess the queen has got us into, eh, but we shall weather it somehow."

His big hands lifted to undo the first tie of her quilted jerkin and dropped to the next one.

"No!"

"You are beaten, sweetheart. I have you now and you will submit. St. George, but you lead a man a merry chase, and there is only one I know who can and who will handle you. Relax now. Enjoy this as I shall."

The jerkin pulled open, gaped wide, and he held her tipped back in his arms. His free hand cupped and cradled first one firm breast and then the other. He bent his unruly, tawny head to sample her taut nipples while waves of devastating sensation turned her legs to jelly. Her lips longed for, pouted for the caress of his, but he pulled her down with him immediately into the straw. His hand was at the tied waistline of her hose and he peeled them easily down her legs despite her attempt to press her knees together.

The straw prickled under her bare hips and thighs, and when she tried to push him away, he merely lifted her arms over her head, tangled them in the twist of her jerkin, and went on with the delicious torture of hands and lips. He took his own hose and quilted riding breeches down far enough to bare his thighs and rampant manhood. His chest, still covered by his hauberk over a quilted garment, held her down under him.

When he spread her thighs, she was shamelessly ready for him, eager, moaning low, tossing her wild curls from side to side in the crisp straw. He pressed, slid into her so far she was certain she would die of the sweet stab of passion. He forced a quick, steady rhythm as though he rode her to master a fierce warrior's mount. He had loosed her arms now and tossed the jerkin free above them. She clung to him for the ride deep down and sailed high to the clouds to a final, utter collapse of wild ecstasy.

They lay pressed together for a moment and when he lifted his big head, still rasping for breath to kiss her lips, she realized the kiss was the first one for months. Reluctantly, he pulled away and helped her dress before he arranged his own clothes.

"Best not disrobe in front of your maid for a while, *chérie*," he said finally when his breathing had returned to normal. "There are clear imprints of chain mail with a royal crest pressed into those soft bosoms and straw marks along your thighs and sweet flanks."

"Oh. Aye," she managed, still stunned from the aftermath of their fierce coupling. She gathered her hair into a tight coil and he rewrapped her turban, cursing low under his breath at such feminine fussing.

She colored with a fierce blush when he kissed her a swift good-bye and handed her her retrieved sword. "Use it well on any other bastard who tries to lay a hand on you," he whispered with a wink, managing to destroy the hazy, pleasurable aura in which she still swam. But before she dared to start an argument again, he knocked once on the crude stable door and bid his wide-eyed man Robert take her home the back way to the castle. The stable door creaked, then thudded shut as she walked unsteadily away.

The summons to the queen's suite Joan was dreading came the next afternoon when she had begun to hope she might be spared. She dressed carefully in lilac velvet and violet brocade feeling she was girding herself for yet another battle: Her Grace must be furious about the mockery at the joust yesterday. Mayhap in punishment she now intended to hand her body as well as name over to her husband Lord Salisbury to chastise. Worse yet, saints forbid, someone had seen the prince abduct her and the queen's wrath would fall for that.

But as Joan entered the solar of the queen's rooms, she sensed immediately she had been mistaken. Indeed the queen was there, but so was the king in a most rare visit to his royal consort's chambers. And to her surprise, a nervous, seething Thomas Holland stood behind the monarch's two, big oak chairs.

She curtsied to their majesties, then angry with herself at her reaction, blushed to the roots of her hair at the steady perusal of the queen and her once-betrothed, Sir Thomas. The king's stare, she thought later, had been more of a devouring leer. How much Prince Edward looked like the king, even to the magnetic probe of icy blue eyes.

The queen cleared her throat in the awkward silence. "My dear Jeannette, as you can see, Lord Thomas has returned to us from Lancashire quite mended from his grievous wounds at Crécy."

"Aye, Your Grace. I am glad for it—both for the healing and his presence," she said politely, relieved that the queen's tone was not scolding and that Her Grace seemed more on edge than Joan herself.

"There, my lord king, you see it is as I have said," Thomas began but he cut his words short when King Edward raised his bejeweled right hand for silence. Despite that implied censure, Thomas stepped forward, bowed to Joan, and lifted her offered hand to his lips. He looked well, finely garbed in russet and sable, the black eye patch somehow strangely highlighting the fact he looked pale and thin, but then, of course, he had been ill a long time.

When the king spoke, Joan realized his sharp eyes had been studying the little reunion scene before him while his queen looked elsewhere.

"It seems your status, little Joan, is in somewhat of a legal tangle," King Edward began, "and several most important and influential sources are quite concerned."

The king looked as though he expected a reply but when she merely inclined her head to listen, he plunged on. "And so, Her Grace and I have hearkened to Lord Holland's plea that he be allowed to petition Pope Clement VI at Avignon to settle the matter."

"To settle it that she be married to me as was promised in the lawful betrothal here at Windsor chapel and before the queen," Thomas Holland inserted.

"Ah, by the rood—that is what you have declared, Sir Thomas, but the Salisbury thing, you know—" the king said, significantly raising his voice and one eyebrow.

"Aye, a marriage with my Lord Salisbury before the queen at the altar in Calais," Joan added, her heart beginning to pound beneath her velvet bodice. The heady feeling of deserved retribution swept through her like a warming wind. But the ultimate recipient of any revenge she might seek must be the king himself and not only his dear wife and precious son.

"As I have told my lord king," Her Grace said, her voice sounding pale and colorless next to the vibrancy of the three others, "I only acted in accordance with circumstances as I viewed them. It was obvious to me, my dear Jeannette, that you needed a steadying hand I could not always lend in lieu of my heavy burdens with my children, despite the fact our Isabella benefitted—it seemed—from your presence. And now, I am not certain that—"

"St. George, my dearest, I bid you pass over that silliness if you intend to bring that all up again," King Edward interrupted. "Mere frivolity in the joy of the moment in that little parade yesterday, eh, Lady Joan?"

Joan bathed her king in the most dazzling smile she could manage. It amused her mightily—a hero rescuer in the king himself to ward off the queen's meddling and, perhaps, even the blatantly rude and boorish behavior of the court's esteemed and adored Prince of Wales.

"Aye, my lord king," she said, the pouting smile still curving her lifted lips, "just a delightful jest to bespeak our joy for your wonderful French victories. I know proper *demoiselles* are never to admit such things, but in my heart, at times, I wish I had been there, a warrior to help. It must have been so exhilarating, so glorious to be there with you that day."

The queen's eyes narrowed ominously, but the king's gaze was riveted to Joan's and he neither observed his wife's icy expression nor Holland's frown. "Aye, Lady Jeannette, it was all that and more. They—your friends—do call you Jeannette, do they not? And has no one told you the tales of how we managed it all outnumbered at Crécy as we were? Holland, I know you were sore wounded, but have not you or Salisbury or the prince recounted the blessed victories the Lord in heaven saw fit to entrust to his servants to this fair lady?"

Joan chose to answer herself to ward off Holland's sputtering frustration. "Of course, many spoke of it, Your Grace," she said, remembering the long talks she and the prince had shared of his battle stories, but she could hardly tell the king of that—or of the warm bed near the seaside in Calais where they had loved and spoken far into the night. Indeed, had the wily prince gone to his royal sire himself to arrange this strange scene playing itself out here today?

"How wonderful it would be," she went on, "if you could spare those of us not frequently about your presence some time to tell us the real, heart view of those glories."

The king stroked his blond beard and mustache as if suddenly plunged in deep contemplation. "St. George, aye—a heart view of it all," he mused aloud. "A heart view."

Joan nearly smirked to think how easily such a snare had been cast. She had never fathomed this dangerous strategy in her fruitless longing for revenge against those who had doomed both her father and mother. This man was the center of the web, and through him, she could strike at them all—that loathsome de Maltravers hiding like a coiled serpent under a rock in Flanders even. She had seen the king so seldom from anything but a distance—and now, perhaps there was a way to choose this new path for her as yet formless retribution.

"By the rood, Sir Thomas, do not stand about gawking,

then," King Edward scolded as he clapped his big hands together once. The queen jumped but Holland still hesitated. "Be gone, man, petition His Eminence or what you will and the queen shall summon young Salisbury to explain it all to him. Meanwhile, the Lady Jeannette of Kent shall remain in Her Grace's and my royal protective custody as companion to our beloved daughter, the Princess Isabella, until such time as we untangle all the strings. Come along then, Lady Jeannette, you shall walk with me to council. By the rood, I am overdue, but tonight at high table I shall tell you a few battle tales to set your little heart aflutter, eh? Come along now."

"My lord king," Queen Philippa began, and rose to stand beside him. "I need to see you but one moment then—"

"Alas, my dearest, off to council, late already. I shall have someone send Salisbury up directly if we can track him down. You would not know his whereabouts, I take it, lady?"

"No, Your Grace, I am sorry, but the queen made me vow—"

"Aye, I quite understand. Follow me, then, Thomas. Lady Jeannette."

He is so big, magnificent in bearing, voice, and presence, Joan thought, as she curtsied to the queen without looking at her and swept out in the king's broad wake. She tried to ignore the meaningful, avid look Holland shot her in the hall. The king's guards and some courtiers waiting about fell in behind them as she walked properly several steps behind the king.

Power and victory assailed her: the king, doting on her, gazing fondly on her, yet unknowing of her true intents and purpose. She fought to keep from skipping from amusement at the fact that his strides were much too long, just like the prince's.

Saints, she realized, as the king began to speak about his army's flight through France to the village of Crécy where he met his enemy at last—perhaps now that she had really met the enemy, she could yet have a victory of her own. She had long heard of this king's reputation as a *roué*, but it had not concerned her before. Like sire, like son, she thought grimly, but then, mayhap there was something in that.

She smiled up at King Edward through her thick lashes as they turned down the long corridor with the whispering, wide-eyed courtiers at their heels.

Chapter Eleven

The glory and prestige of England and the Plantagenets flew as high that day as a flapping banner on the tallest tower at Windsor, as high as the prince's fine gerfalcon as it sought its prey. It was April twenty-third, 1348, the day King Edward III had ordained the celebration for his new Order of the Round Table. Twenty and five knights, heroes of the French campaign, were admitted as charter members of the honored group. Religious services, tournaments, and feasting had filled the three-day celebration. Tonight, the fête would end with a huge torch dance to honor the new embodiment of the legendary King Arthur's round table, resurrected centuries after its demise. The Princess Isabella teased Joan that most of the names of the regal, new Lancelots sworn in early that bright spring day read like a list of those who were attracted like little flies to the Fair Maid of Kent: Sir Thomas Holland of Lancashire; William Montacute, earl of Salisbury; Prince Edward of Wales; aye, Isabella had said—even the king himself.

Isabella had laughed at the jest but Joan knew she did not find it amusing. Anyway, Isabella laughed too wildly at everything these days. These last five months since King Edward had rescued Joan from a sure scolding by the queen after the fourteen *demoiselles* had paraded at the Crécy tournament, the king had greatly favored her, though Joan had managed to keep him at arm's length even as she had her stoic betrothed and her fond husband. She sometimes wondered if her aloofness with them was not her allure, but what did that matter. . . .

The prince was much about the kingdom and she seldom saw him; though she told herself his absence suited her, she had begun to realize things were only truly exciting when he was at court. How long it was since they had been alone together! Always now, something or someone was in the way—saints, not that she ever wanted to be alone with the royal rogue ever again. For once Marta was so right: her whole life had become a terrible, tangled web.

Relationships at court, she had finally come to realize, were always in flux. She and Isabella spent much time in each other's company planning wild pranks, but they were no longer as close. Joan's legal guardian Queen Philippa nearly shunned her, letting her do as she pleased without reproach as if Joan were now protected by some invisible barrier. And tantalizing rumors of the prince drifted through the court from time to time: some whispered he had a mistress kept at Sonning or Berkhamstead—perhaps there was even an illegitimate child. Or, maybe he would marry a daughter of the old, dead Count of Flanders, a sister to Isabella's vanished bridegroom, Louis de Male.

Like Joan, the Princess Isabella usually let the continual rumble of the rumor mill go on with the blur of beaux, fashions, and giddy games. But *that* last rumor Isabella almost choked on.

"Can you even conceive of such a thing, Jeannette?" she screeched half between indignation and contempt at the thought. "My dear brother Edward vowed to me when that coward Louis de Male fled Bruges that day he would make him pay. You remember, Jeannette. You were there. By the blessed saints, the Prince of Wales taking Louis's sister to wife to be our next queen would hardly be making him pay! I swear to heaven, I shall ask Edward of it at the torch dance tonight the first time I see him!"

"Dearest princess, you know court rumors. Just ask your lord father and he will explain away this foolish story."

"A pox on it. I care not. Besides, the king would tell you if you asked him before he would tell me, I warrant."

235

Half-dressed for the evening's festivities, they perched on opposite sides of Isabella's huge feather bed, a hundred jeweled garters spread like a rainbow between them on the coverlet. Garters, multi-hued on everything, were the coming rage at court. Of course, the lovely things had long served their purpose to hold up and shape hose to both masculine and feminine legs, but now they cavorted everywhere that Isabella, Jeannette, and their young butterfly friends could wear them: kirtles, headpieces, *surcotes*, gowns, their infamous, diaphanous night chemises, cloaks, and robes—everywhere. Garters lent an aura of scandal, or naughtiness at the very least, Jeannette thought bemusedly. It was like coercing the whole court to admit they were a double-minded bunch: aye, why hide their scandalous behavior like their garters when it was much more amusing for everyone to admire their colorful glitter?

"Perhaps you should wear all those blue ones and I shall stay with red just peppered across our gowns tonight," Isabella interrupted Joan's thoughts. "We need something— well, arresting—to set off these white dresses for the dancing. I warrant they will not take either of us for brides, though we be garbed in white. Do you think they believe we are as wicked as we like them to think? And here we both are, celibate as nuns in a cloister," Isabella sighed.

She stood beside the bed and summoned her maids to lower her elaborate white and gold India silk gown over her head and her voice came all muffled. "I have not worn white since that farce at Bruges last year, you know, Jeannette. Hurry to get yours on and let's go down early to parade around a bit. Besides, I swear, it will take a good hour to have all these garters attached and tied. I am so relieved my lord father has a special garter maker at the Tower to manufacture these. They say he works day and night, you know."

Isabella's voice went on like incessant chimes, but as was increasingly true these days, Joan only heard and did not listen. She stood stock-still like a quintain dummy while her soft silk dress of gleaming ivory was dropped into place. She lifted her arms as they buttoned her long wrist slits closed and adjusted her white figured brocade *surcote* with the delicate raised embroidery of lilies-of-the-valley lacing the long liripipes dangling from the elbows, the low bodice, and sculptured hemline. A delicate edging of ermine lined the liripipes and bordered the brocade *surcote*.

Four of Isabella's nine maids darted about both young women, draping garters, arranging coifs, and balancing their tall headdresses which trailed diaphanous silk scarves. As a last touch to their coifs and cosmetics, Yvette dusted essence of gillyflower on their hair, necks, and bosoms. A sneeze stopped Isabella's ceaseless, wandering commentary at last.

"Oh, dear," she managed and sneezed twice more. "I do not think men are worth this, really I do not, Jeannette. Let us go meet the others, and I do not mean to carp on last year's journey so. I know I was not the only one annoyed by a vile man when we were on that trip."

No, indeed, you were not, Joan thought, but she kept silent. It was not even her forced marriage to Salisbury which gave her terrible nightmares on that trip, though she would surely never tell Isabella or anyone else. It was two very different men, yet both rogues and villains who haunted her thoughts: the traitor de Maltravers and, of course, the Prince of Wales with all his deceitful, seductive tricks. At least de Maltravers looked a villain on the outside, too! Then, also, the trip Isabella still talked of entirely too much annoyed Joan for another reason she could not share with anyone but old Marta: when word of Queen Philippa's pleading for mercy for the six old burghers of Calais had spread across England, the people had hailed her as a new heroine of saintliness. Saintliness, indeed, Joan fumed for the hundredth time. She would never have pleaded for the old burghers' lives at all had I not begged her and had she not seen a perfect way to coerce me to obey her will and marry someone I care not a whit for! If only the fond people of England knew that, what would they say?

Joan followed Isabella out into the hall to join her gathered ladies so they might descend the staircase to the Great Hall together. The other *demoiselles* were awed at their daring display of garters, and that mollified Joan's ruffled demeanor somewhat.

"Any word from the pope yet, Jeannette?" Mary Boherne whispered, her wide eyes counting the number of gracefully draped garters on Joan's skirts and obviously comparing that reckoning to the princess' red ones.

"Nary a Latin syllable from the pope, Mary," Joan told her and rolled her eyes for effect. "It is such a sticky tangle it could be another five months. Mayhap, my Lord Holland and my Lord Salisbury will get bored with waiting for the flower to open and just buzz away back to their hives."

Mary laughed musically. "Jeannette, you are so wry about it all. I daresay about just everything. How clever and breezy you always are in the face of adversity."

Clever and breezy in a pig's eye, Joan thought, but she smiled to acknowledge the compliment. She never deceived herself that if the king did not find her so amusing, Mary Boherne and the rest would just as soon shred her fashionable dresses and her intriguing reputation to tatters.

Courtiers already stood about in the dimly lighted hall tapping their curl-toed, slippered feet to the melody lilting from the musicians gallery overhead, but of course, no one dared dance until the king and queen arrived. The *demoiselles* were no more out into the Great Hall with Isabella cutting a laughing, gartered wake through the pressing crowd than William Montacute, Lord Salisbury, appeared at Joan's elbow.

"Joan, my dearest, may I speak with you before all this begins? I have hardly seen you except for a tiny glimpse at the morning service. Here, dearest, step over here by the wall. Most other knights of the Order had their ladies in the first rows today, and I think despite all Holland's fuss with the pope, the queen should have let you sit there, too."

She walked reluctantly away from her friends with

William, hoping none of them overheard all this. "It was not the queen's bidding one way or the other, Will. I merely sat where the king suggested—"

"By the rood, I should have known that," he interrupted and his broad mouth turned sullen. "I warn you, Joan, he can be a hawk after an unsuspecting little dove, but then, I hardly picture you as that."

"I do not wish to have this entire discussion again, my lord. You have made yourself plain on it. Look, smile a bit. I am proud of your investiture to the Order of the Table, and you look absolutely resplendent tonight."

His eyes lit at the compliment, but he still looked more like a peevish, scolded pageboy than an honored knight. "You, too, as always, my dearest Joan. Dazzling in that gown of bridal hue but all those garters—have not you and the princess overstepped a bit? Everyone started buzzing the minute you two fashionmongers sailed into the room. I have not seen such a stir since that ludicrous parade of women in men's garb you staged at the tournament last autumn." He lowered his voice as an increasingly bitter tone crept in. "By the Virgin, woman, you will have the king and prince so starry-eyed they will not be able to lead off this snake dance."

"It is a torch dance, Will, as well you know, and I am excited to see it. I have never been to one so I shall let my good mood this evening allay my retort to your silly remarks about the king and prince."

"Listen, dearest wife." He glowered at her and dared to seize one silk wrist in a tight grip. "I have some rights in all this royal mess, for I fully hope and pray Lord Holland's pleas to the pope will go awry. The pope, no doubt, has more to occupy his ear, with the plague in Europe and all these rampant Anglo-French hatreds, than settling some petty dispute over which knight has the right to some lovely, willful maid from Kent."

"Let me go, my lord. You are hurting me and pulling this sleeve so—"

"I said listen to me," he hissed, but released her, blocking her in against the dim wall. "You avoid me. You are always too busy, so you will listen now. I must tell you something before you glide off with one of your other men in this dark hall—before the queen links you up with someone else."

"Tell me quickly then. I see Lord Holland over there and he appears to be looking for me."

"My mother, bless her, was once almost taken in by this king's wiles even as you, Joan. You must arm yourself if it is not already too late. By the Virgin, I have seen how he looks at you!"

"Keep your voice down if you insist on scolding me. And I do not see how your mother relates to all this, because she is never at court."

"No, but over two years ago, the king went to her. During the Scottish wars, King David's Scottish warriors besieged our home, Wark Castle. My lord father was prisoner in France, so my mother led the castle defense against the Scots from inside the walls. King Edward's forces arrived in the nick of time to chase the barbarians off well enough, but when she offered him a conqueror's hospitality and vacated her own rooms so he might have a soft bed, he demanded much, much more."

Joan's lilac-hued eyes widened and her mind raced. "But I heard your lord father was one of His Grace's beloved friends, a most trusted knight."

William snorted deep in his throat. "Listen to the lesson then, my foolish Joan. Do not you see it? He desired a beautiful woman, so her ties to whomever mattered not a whit to him. And the fact that she was wed—by the rood, we all know how that flimsy ploy is handled at court."

"I am sorry for this with your own mother, my lord, but you must not let it make you bitter—nor dare to imply that her situation could compare to mine."

"Damn, Holland has seen us," he groused with a quick turn of his head. "Now, hear me, Joan—I do not compare you to my mother and that is my torment. She had a husband she loved and she managed to turn the king's demands down. His Grace, King Edward, left the next morn at dawn without having enjoyed her favors, and he no doubt admired her for it later as he immediately ransomed home my father. You, however—I fear you have no lord you love and so when the king's demand comes, as surely it must—" He bit his lower lip and glared at the floor as Thomas Holland joined them.

"Good evening, my dear. Lord Salisbury."

"My Lord Thomas," William managed, his impassioned eyes raised jerkily to Joan's carefully composed face. "I thought you would be somewhere lurking about in this dim cavern."

"I rather like the dim halls for torch dance, Salisbury, and this is Joan's first one at court, is it not, my dear? You look exquisite. I fear my Lord Salisbury does not appreciate the charming, romantic lure of the dark for dancing with a lady."

"And you do, I suppose," William shot back. "Aye, you are *such* a romantic, of course, Holland, and that is why you never married all these years until the queen bid you—"

"Stop it, both of you," Joan cut in and placed a palm of each hand on their arms. "The jousting was the last two days and tonight is charming and romantic as Lord Thomas says. I do not wish to see either of you if you cannot act like the king's Round Table knights for one evening without this bickering. Excuse me, please, as I am supposed to be attending the princess."

She walked calmly away, but despite her chatter and laughter with others as she wended her way toward Isabella and her ladies across the dim room, the two men had quite unsettled her. They ought to be banished rather than honored this evening, she fumed, while she thanked Euphemia de Heselaston for her compliments on her garter-studded skirt. Saints, Euphemia probably hated the showy display, but soon enough she would no doubt be wearing them herself.

That story about William's mother and the king—and

then his daring to use it to warn her! Still, it did show she was not alone in having parents wronged by this king, so if ever she were forced to remain married to William, perhaps he would understand her own plans for retribution. And then that unfortunate mention of the plague in southern Europe! Tonight was supposed to be all fun and delight, and he dared to haul the specter of that in here.

Isabella was easy to locate since her silvery, perpetual laughter was like a beacon in the dimness of the high, vaulted hall. Joan noticed couples pairing for the dance already, and servants who would act as linkboys to distribute the newly lighted torches to each male dancer had entered the hall. The music from overhead quickened as fydels, lutes, and sackbuts romped through song after popular song. The lyrics of this one told of a blond maid who lost her virtue to an errant knave—oh, damn, why did she have to think of that—of him—right now? In the darkness along the walls lit by few torches, couples embraced and kissed. One quite tipsy man whose face she could not discern dared to put a hand down the bodice of his giggling lady's gown. She had not thought of that sort of thing here with the king and queen overdue!

Trumpets blared just as she reached Isabella's side and the room rippled with anticipation like the waves of a velvet and silk sea. Ladies' tall headdresses dipped, men bowed as the king and queen entered, both garbed in magnificent gold velvet, brocade, and purest ermine. The royal Plantagenets blazed with jewels when they caught the reflected flare of torchlight. Applause welled up before it was drowned by the renewal of the music far above the crowded scene.

Despite her attempt to appear nonchalant, Joan stood on tiptoe and scanned those who had entered with the king. Their sons, John of Ghent and the tall, gangly Lionel, Duke of Clarence, were in evidence. Even seven-year-old Edward, Duke of York was in tow, though the others of the royal brood were no doubt too young. And poor Princess Joanna, so beloved of Isabella, had died of disease last January on her way to marry Pedro, heir to the throne of Castile. Suddenly a shiver raced along Joan's spine as an unbidden foreboding racked her. Tall shadows darted up the lofty stone walls as the servants began to light the pitch-pine torches and pass them to each male dancer as the couples lined up. Joan's mouth dropped open in surprise as she caught sight of old, feeble Morcar standing along the wall behind the king. The gray-haired astrologer, once such a familiar figure about her dear home of Liddell, stared directly at her.

Isabella had drifted off with one of Prince Edward's closest friends, Sir John Chandos, and Joan slowly followed. Suddenly there was no one close by she knew. She should not have dismissed both Thomas and William like that; saints, but she would not stand about like some scare-the-crow in an empty Kentish field while they all danced. She caught Morcar's glance; his gaze glinted like a cat's eyes in the shifting torches.

She jumped when a warm arm encircled her waist, and she turned expecting to find Thomas or William. But where a face should be she stared at a man's powerful blue velvet chest. Wide shoulders and a tawny head towered toward the ceiling.

"Oh, my lord prince. You—startled me. Must you always be popping up to surprise me?" She felt herself blush but, thank heavens, it was too dim for him to tell. He had grown a full, clipped blond mustache in this last two months' absence, and it made him look older and somehow austere.

"You look ravishing, my sweet Jeannette, even if that rash of garters you and Isabella flaunt are a little too much. Now, do not get all shrewish and flustered, for I have not been able to breathe your sweet air for a long time, and we must not waste our few hours arguing before I leave again. I have missed you, too."

He took her arm firmly, and they joined the line awaiting to claim the torches. Her heart beat a wild tattoo to match apace the lively music from the balcony. "I do not recall ever saying I missed you, Your Grace," she returned as icily as she could manage.

He laughed low and she turned to study him for the first time. Like most of the fashionable men, he sported a jaunty, flat velvet cap perched sideways on his head, though she knew he detested that style as much as she hated these heavy, tipsy headdresses. Velvet, the hue of a deep Persian blue, stretched across his broad shoulders decorated with a massive, draped gold and jeweled chest chain. The *surcote* over his jerkin was edged with ermine as if to match her own, and when he smiled, it almost seemed as though his teeth reflected the glow of the dazzling, white ermine in the dimness. Each time she was away from him for so long, he looked taller, his eyes bluer, his shoulders broader. But now with the mustache, he looked somehow forbidding, too.

A feeling of unease spread through her like numbing cold as she glanced past the prince to see Morcar's continued, unwavering stare. But to her complete surprise, the old man also nodded in approval and his bewhiskered mouth moved in some sort of weird smile as if he were talking to himself.

"What ails you, *chérie*?" the prince's voice interrupted her thoughts. "Another giddy knight I shall have to ward off to have this dance?" He turned to follow her line of vision. "The wizard Morcar? Aye, it is strange to see that old falcon down here among all the twittering nightingales. Shall we bid him good evening then, before we get our torch?"

"I—we could talk to him another day. Besides, I have not promised to dance with you, and I am certain, from what I have heard of late, you have other ladies to see."

One rakish blond brow shot up and his mouth quirked in amusement. He lowered his voice but she felt herself blush at the gibe anyway. "Nonsense, sweet Jeannette. I believe you promised me this first dance and any other I would have when you were flat on your beautiful backside in the straw last October."

She tried to yank her arm free of his grasp, but his fingers tightened to iron. "You most vile rogue, you knave—" she sputtered as low as she could, desperate to keep her face composed whatever insults she threw at him. She was not such a fool to think everyone was not staring and that the prince's attentions to her would not cause a stir however dim this vast room was. He had pulled them up next to Morcar along the wall before she settled her ruffled feathers.

"Good evening to the king's most trusted soothsayer, Lord Morcar," Prince Edward said. "The Lady Jeannette thought perhaps you wished a word with us."

Morcar nodded almost imperceptibly. He was enswathed in a black velvet robe, and against the shadowy wall, he seemed invisible but for his parchment face and white head. His narrow eyes studied Joan's face, then returned to the prince's before his voice, creaky like an old door, answered.

"My lord prince, I have long wished to speak with the lady over several things, but she is so busy here and there she has no time for an old man from Kent. I understand that well enough."

"Marta keeps me well informed how you fare, Morcar, and I have no desire to know my future. The reading of stars and planets—saints, that is for kings and nations, mayhap princes, too. I intend to control my own future, that is all."

She could not decide if Morcar's look was disappointed or merely tolerant. "And have you done such so far here at great Edward's court, Lady Joan? You know the stars never rule our futures, for what will be will be. They only inform, not cause."

Prince Edward felt her stiffen beside him. He regretted already bringing her over to this old astrologer, for the last thing he wanted tonight when the whole court was here was a foolish scene from this willful, little vixen. He should have stayed with his original strategy to pretend to ignore her, or at least treat her like one of the other *demoiselles*, and then attempt to see her alone after. But she had forced him off his battle tactics again: the moment he had seen her he had been pulled by her allure like a fox to an all too obvious snare.

"Morcar cast a chart for me several months ago after our

return from Calais, *ma* Jeannette," he cut in before she could respond to Morcar's incisive challenge, but she was not to be put off.

"Morcar, I know the king values your wisdom greatly and it appears the prince also, but—" she began.

"And your father, Edmund of Kent, dear lady," Morcar dared to interject, "and I know you have not forgotten him."

Joan's chin jerked up and the scarves and tippets on her tall headdress danced and swayed. "Of course, I never forget him, Morcar, though some of those like you and Marta who knew everything of the old days would have me be ignorant of all that, I warrant. Saints, since you chose not to tell me the past before when I needed to know, I choose now not to hear the future from you either."

To the prince's astonishment at her bitter, cryptic words, she whirled away and took several steps before she was hemmed in by the line of couples awaiting their torches.

"I apologize for the lady, old Morcar," Prince Edward said quietly. "I should like to see the chart you cast for her even if she does not, and to hear more about what frets her so about her father. Until then."

"My lord prince, forgive, but I must not share the lady's chart with aught but her. I swore it to her lady mother once, before we all left Kent. I vowed that only Lady Joan or her old woman Marta could know. What puzzles me is that I believed that once she was married, she would desire to know the truth herself, but perhaps I misread that. She has been wed to young Salisbury now for ten months and yet she obviously cares not a fig to know her future."

"Aye—well, women, you know, Morcar. St. George, all the planets in the heavens could not keep up with this one!"

The prince forced himself to a slow pace as he walked after Jeannette to where she stood taping her slippered foot and chatting amiably with Princess Isabella and Sir John Chandos as though she were merely passing the time of day. He knew he dared not scold her or try to pick up the threads of their conversation again so close to ready ears, so he merely guided her back into line and took his newly lighted torch from the link boy without a word.

The lofty Great Hall was ablaze with lifted torches as the long line of couples followed the king and queen in the intricate procession of the torch dance. Each tall, pointed lead-and-glass window lining the other wall reflected rows of torches within torches. The music swelled, deliberate, grand, majestic at first as the lines wove and curved inward to make a great coil of couples. It was awesome, almost solemn, and Jeannette's hand was warm and quiet in his at last.

He was unbearably curious about the casting of her future from the stars which Morcar had mentioned; yet he did not put much stock in such and really did believe, as Jeannette had so stubbornly insisted, that people must make their own fortunes and futures. But his own chart, which Morcar had completed for the king, bespoke of the victory battle of Crécy clearly enough—Venus adverse to Mars that very month of the glorious French victory when he had finally earned his spurs.

And in the Seventh House touching on marital bliss after great trials, there had been the promise of great love and joy and he so hoped, aye—longed, for that. Like a floundering fool, he had clung to that one promise, for had not he and Jeannette been through enough grief and inharmoniousness already? St. George, he had not yet found the way for them to be together, but as soon as Salisbury got tired of waiting and the pope had ignored Holland's plea a little longer, he would seize some strategy to circumvent his mother's nervousness over the lady and his father's infatuation with her to claim her as his own! He would ask old Morcar to tell him more tomorrow or at least entice Jeannette to see how her future must surely link with his own. He smiled down at her beautiful face, his heart thoroughly ravished again by the sensual allure of both her lush body and vibrant spirit.

The king and queen had now reached the very core of the coiled links of the torchlit serpent's body. The stately rhythm of the music lightened, quickened, as the inward couples began to retrace their steps out, this time weaving among the others and changing partners at will, to stop and circle in place, then move farther outward. Soon, Joan knew, she would be partnering the prince no more, and it upset her to admit she felt not a bit relieved at the thought of that deliverance.

His eyes were intent upon her, lion's eyes glowing in the torchlight, devouring her under that tawny mane of Plantagenet hair. His deep blue velvet garments molded elegantly to his powerful, amazingly graceful body. Behind his huge silhouette, torches moved, cavorted, blurred. Massive dancing shadows shot up the stone walls and hammerbeam ceiling overhead. She quickened her steps to match the dashing rhythm swelling in the room. The twisting line of dancers snaked by, enclosing, encroaching on them. Everything whirled and tilted, except his glowing eyes and his hand, there to steady her.

People near her stopped and applauded as she tore her gaze away. The prince had suddenly halted. His torch, held high, illumined the king and queen. The prince reluctantly loosed Joan's hand, and she felt for a moment she would fall. Queen Philippa, plump, white-faced, seemed quite out of breath, but the king looked fit and hale as ever. Queen Philippa had turned away to be partnered with Isabella's gallant, Sir John Chandos, before Joan realized what was intended. The prince disappeared from her line of vision and she dared not turn to see whom he had chosen in this exchange of ladies. She heard Isabella's laughter nearby and fell back into step, this time partnered by King Edward.

Now she was at the head of the writhing, weaving line facing all those heading in, and she tried desperately to concentrate on the little running steps. The king's strides were fully as long as the prince's, only he took the floor at a faster pace since they had no one to run into directly ahead.

"Ravishing tonight, *ma petite*," he whispered, apparently not a whit out of breath. "Ravishing. My son cannot seem to resist seeking you out, by the rood, and frankly, sweet

Jeannette, neither can I."

"Your Grace is as smooth with words as with his feet," she said breathily. Surely, it was time for them to stop so they could all shift partners again on their outward pattern. She was too warm with all this bounding and hurrying, and the rampant glow of all these torches on them at the very center of everyone's attention made her feel as if she were in a furnace furiously fueled by burning eyes.

To her dismay, she felt a garter on her thigh loosen and slip. Her white stockings were tied by four garters each to mold them to her legs, but she missed a step and almost stumbled as she tried to keep this one from sliding down. The king's eyes were hot on her; yet he looked somehow amused as they turned in place, their hands held high. In the blazing torchlight she saw the blue silk garter with its single winking jewel under the king's slippered feet the moment he did. He halted. The surrounding dancers hushed at once believing another exchange of partners was imminent. Two couples back, Joan's eye caught Prince Edward's as he stood there holding hands with the flame-haired Constantia Bourchier.

Joan prayed no one else would notice the garter, but the king bent and retrieved the dark blue ribbon of embroidered silk to the surprise, then amusement, of the surrounding courtiers.

"By the Virgin, Jeannette," Isabella's musical voice called out, "mayhap to establish this new fashion we wore just one too many. I shall send my partner Sir John back to scour the floor for one of mine."

"And if I can lay my hands on one stray garter anywhere I deserve a least a kiss—or mayhap to put it back on the pretty thigh where it belongs," Sir John laughed, and everyone roared with laughter.

The musicians in the gallery overhead had stopped at the sight of the dancing coil dissolving into one swelling circle around the king.

"There must be more where that sweet garter came from!" a deep male voice in the growing crowd called out.

"Shall we deem that another trophy from a well-waged battle, our warrior king?" some other voice added, and the pressing audience shouted their approval again.

Joan blushed scarlet and did not even pretend to laugh now. Under the ornate curls of her coif her earlobes burned with embarrassment, and she could feel the blood course through her veins. Other titters and murmurs rose and fell in those few suspended moments the King of England stood there with her jeweled blue garter dripping through his raised fingers.

How dare they all smirk and jest, they and their king who had let her father die, she fumed silently. Now was the time to scream out her challenge, her accusations at him while she stood rooted to this little square of floor like an entrapped coward. She had opened her mouth to shout something when the king quieted them all with his booming words.

"Cease! Cease, all of you," His Grace ordered, his voice commanding despite his guilty smile at Joan. "Evil to him who evil thinks," he warned holding the blue garter aloft as if it were a sword or chalice. "The time shall shortly come when you shall attribute much honor unto such a garter! Our order of chivalry shall be a new fashion, so 'tis apropos it be named for the court's other fine new fashion. Chivalry and glory and the blue garter. The Order of the Garter! God wills it! For England and St. George!"

"For England and St. George!" the room echoed, drowning all thoughts of Joan's protest. "For England and St. George!"

Dazedly, Joan extended her fingers for the garter. "No, my sweet lady," the king's voice said almost roughly, "'tis the king's and history's now. But," he added more quietly as his eyes swept over her, "I shall make it all up to you and soon. A reward—you shall see."

As the music began again and the lines reformed, the king placed Joan's hand in that of a hovering Lord Salisbury and returned to the queen for the rest of the dance. A dark form moving along the wall near where Joan and William completed the dance caught her eye: the feeble, old astrologer Morcar was slowly making his way out of the Great Hall through the chattering, festive crowd. He reminded her suddenly of some dark-cloaked harbinger come up from the netherworld to chant his predictions of doom.

"Jeannette, are you quite all right? You know, you looked furious out there when the king displayed and proclaimed that garter before them all," William said, his voice as tense as his earnest, young face. "I thought, perhaps, you were thinking on what I told you about his attempt to seduce my lady mother, and you see him now in another light. If so, dearest, I am heartily glad for it."

"Your mother? Aye, Will, I do see His Grace in another light, but then I have for a long while—ever since my mother died."

"Your mother? Then he hurt her too and tried—"

"Please, I just do not want to speak of it now. This dreadful headdress is pulling on my hair coils and giving me a raging head pain. At least a fashion like garters seemed harmless enough until now. Look, Will, if you just wish to stand about and gawk, I shall seek out Thomas. I just want to dance, get rid of this vile thing on my head, and retire as soon as we can."

His green eyes lit as the broad familiar grin split his face. "*We*, lady? But whatever will Her Grace say? After all, I am merely your lawful husband whom fate has cursed to only look on his wife and not touch. Saints' blood, that is not even as much as some upstanding courtiers do with other men's wives around these hallowed halls!"

"So bitter, my lord, and on the festal day of your investiture as Round Table knight?" she teased, amused by his quicksilver mood changes. She realized suddenly that she knew this man, supposedly her husband, not at all. She knew no one of the court well, indeed, not anyone but the frivolous, flighty Isabella. Even the prince—saints, best not to ponder the entanglement of those feelings.

251

They danced, whirling and bowing, in the circle of couples on the floor. Joan concentrated on her steps, on balancing the headdress, even on William's avid face to shut everything else out. She knew people pointed and whispered, now because of the garter she did not have rather than the ones she did. Isabella wiggled her fingers in a funny little wave when their paths crossed once, so at least she thought it all still perpetually amusing. And Queen Philippa, sitting now on the dais and merely watching, was all smiles at last.

Despite herself, Joan craned her slender neck at the next turn to find out why. Directly in the queen's line of vision, very near William and herself, the Prince of Wales was still dancing with the ravishing, red-haired Constantia Bourchier.

Joan sucked in her breath and foolishly missed a side step. Constantia was in brightest green and dancing so close to the prince, gazing up bewitchingly into his eyes. Worse, Joan thought before she could catch herself to vow she did not care, his crystalline blue eyes had been avidly studying Constantia's catlike face and the lush white bosom swelling over the furred oval top of her low-cut neckline. All this in one glance: all the Plantagenets were happy tonight on a rolling crest of their glory and power. She had done—had gained—nothing on them; she had sullied and shamed the vow of vengeance she had given her mother on her deathbed.

"I wish to go upstairs now, my lord," she said and simply halted in the middle of an elaborate twirl. She felt suddenly wooden, ungainly, as she tugged her hand away from his.

"I shall escort you up then. The king has been gone a quarter-hour anyway and others have been starting to drift off to bed." He walked quickly at her side to keep up. "I wish it could be so for us, my dearest."

"Speaking of that, it is best you do not escort me up, my lord. Marta is waiting and the queen or Thomas or someone might misconstrue."

His face fell as though she had just beaten him at stick ball or backgammon. "We must play the game out to the end, you know, Will," she said. "Dancing with you tonight was very nice—really, and I shall see you on the morrow."

"Will you? And without Thomas Holland hanging about your skirts? By the rood, if his leg still did not pain him to dance, we would never have had a moment's respite tonight from his company, I warrant."

She stood on tiptoe a moment to brush her lips gently against his cheek. He was tall, but so much smaller than the prince, she thought erratically, before she silently cursed herself for allowing those haunting memories to crowd in on her again. Saints, let that snippy, big-breasted Constantia Bourchier have the prince if it pleased his dear mother so much!

Feeling more tender toward poor William than she had for a long while, she pivoted a little way up the broad central staircase to wave at him. Just as she turned the bend in the stairs, she noted the clever watchdog Thomas Holland had joined him, and she went up even faster. The two of them could compare comments or argue if they wished without her there to listen to their possessive, bothersome carping. She prayed the pope never answered them. No pope, nor queen, nor astrologer, nor husband would control her fortunes no matter what befell!

The hall connecting her little chamber to Isabella's rooms was quite well lighted, for the linkboys who had passed out the torches at the dance earlier had distributed the flambeaux throughout the castle after that ceremony had ended. A man stood a little way down the hall leaning back, just watching her approach now, a man she recognized but could not place. Marta would probably be asleep when she came in, but the minute she heard her, she would jump up to help her disrobe. By the rood, she could anticipate already how wonderful it would feel to be rid of this towering thing, to be rid of this whole night!

"Lady Joan of Kent."

She stopped, her hand to her door latch. The man down the hall had spoken her name so softly that—

"Milady, I mean not to startle or alarm you. His Grace requests—he beseeches you will join him for a brief interview."

His Grace! Then Prince Edward did mean to see her and that flaunting of Constantia had been for mere show. But if he thought she would bend to his will so easily at the mere snap of his royal fingers like a hunt dog—and then lie with him at his bidding in some pile of straw or little hut anytime he chose—he had a bloody fine lesson to learn!

"I am so sorry, sir. Tell His Grace I must decline. I am exhausted and my head hurts. Also, I have a great aversion to surprises."

The man moved closer and frowned. He had a rather square face, close-cropped hair about his ears and wide-set eyes. Her heart leapt. This man belonged not to the prince's retinue but was the king's chief falconer! The king—it was Edward the King who had sent for her at this late hour and unchaperoned.

"The king will be most griefstricken and most downcast, Lady Joan," he pursued. "I am certain he expected you to comply."

"Then I shall accompany you straightaway," she said levelly, pretending to ignore his obvious shock at her quick acquiescence. He nodded, lifted a torch from a wall sconce, and motioned for her to follow.

She grinned at his back as they went down the hall. Whatever His Grace said or did tonight, she would best him somehow, and he would feel her wrath for his cowardly deeds against her parents. Aye, now, after he had publicly linked her leg garter to his precious, new order of chivalry, was the ripe time to strike.

She was grateful the steps in the York Tower that connected this wing to the long walk to the king's section of Windsor were deserted. But to her surprise, they went up winding steps in the Tower instead of down.

Her guide's voice echoed hollowly to her as they wound up and around the old, uneven stone steps worn by generations of feet. "Only two more floors up here, milady. Our sovereign lord has not yet returned to his own suite this even, and this chamber is quite comfortable."

She lagged back as her guide put a hand to the latch of a narrow oak door with its threshold directly on the curve of stairs. His torch cast sharp, shifting shadows. Everything was silent. It could be a trap; no one knew where she had gone. For one second she almost longed to see the prince's face, taunting, arrogant, but familiarly so at the door.

"Do not fear, milady. I only serve His Grace here. He promises you no one will know. Here, within." He knocked once and pushed the door inward. A crooked shaft of light jumped out upon the stone steps at their feet. She moved up another stair while the man backed off evidently prepared to wait patiently.

She caught a quick glimpse of tapestry on a far wall, the end of a heavy oak table and a massive candle within.

"The Lady Joan of Kent as you requested, Your Grace," her guide announced in a hushed tone, but her insides leapt at his voice. Then the door creaked fully open to admit her, and she took one step in.

Chapter Twelve

King Edward of England rose on the far side of the narrow oak table. He wore a black velvet robe edged with royal ermine and was bareheaded. No fireplace lit the round-ceilinged, slant-walled little chamber, but the room glowed with candlelight. Joan's eyes darted past the king to examine it in one swift glance: two chairs at the big table, a deep gold carpet underfoot, the stone walls completely covered with crimson-backed tapestries of a dashing hunt scene, a narrow bed, and the only window set ajar to air the irregularly shaped chamber with an April evening breeze. Really, an exquisite little room dwarfed by the size and impact of the man coming around the polished table to greet her.

The door behind snapped quietly shut as King Edward took her hands in his big warm ones. "So—sweet Jeannette, just fresh come from dancing, I wager, breathless and blushing still. Your king is so grateful you would come, my sweet. Some wine? I wish to thank you personally and in private for your beauty and poise in all that excitement tonight. By the holy rood, I had thought long and hard of needing a symbol for the Order of Chivalry and then, thanks to petite Jeannette, there it was—a gift from heaven sparkling at my feet."

"More like a gift from the Princess Isabella to me, Your Grace. Your bow and garter maker housed at the Tower in London sells such fine ones—"

"Of course," he interrupted refusing to let her tug her hands free, "but time is precious and I meant not to speak of the garter itself, sweet. Here, sit. Have some wine, let me look at you and thank you more appropriately for all you do to cheer me even under some trying circumstances. I do realize that, of course."

She sat where he bid, relieved the two chairs were not close together and that he had to loose her hands to let her sit. "The most trying of circumstances, Your Grace, you cannot know," she agreed and leveled a steady gaze at him realizing he could not possibly guess what things she intended to accuse him of. It gave her a sharp sense of power he could not be forewarned or forearmed about her true opinion of him and his family. The way she had led him on these months, he must have no conception she knew of his cruel desertion of her parents in their hour of need.

She took a slow sip from her wine goblet staring at him over its fluted rim. Two can play at this cat-mouse game, she told herself, and fought to calm her pounding heart. She would listen for a time to see what he would say or ask of her; when the moment was ripe, she would declare her hatred, her contempt, and then—flee to her room or mayhap clear home to Liddell to let all of them rot in their vile stew of power and pride.

"Jeannette, my precious, are you listening? You looked all far away, so dreamy-eyed for a moment. Of course, I realize you must be ready for bed." He leaned far forward in his chair and his size and reach devoured the space between them as he covered the hand on her knee with his own jeweled fingers.

"I assure you, I am listening, Your Grace." His fingers curled possessively about hers and casually stroked her knee through the white silk of her kirtle. She felt herself tense but she did not flinch away.

"Well then, my lovely maid, allow your king to give you the first of my tokens of appreciation, a mere bauble." His blue eyes strong on her, he reached back on the table to grope behind one of the squat brass candlesticks for a flat, velvet-covered box. He scooted his chair much closer as he presented the gift to her, and when she did not take it, he

257

removed her goblet from her hand and placed the box on her lap far up her thighs. "Open it, my sweet, or shall I do it for you? So shy of a sudden? Here, Jeannette."

"Please, my lord king, no gift for the clever use of a lost garter," she protested. "We must talk. There is much I must say before this goes further. I will take no gifts from you!"

He frowned at her rising tone, and his big hands held her wrists firmly. "Nonsense, sweet. Relax and just listen. This is not so much for a mere garter, but a token of my great admiration for your beauty and charm here about my court."

He released her wrists and opened the flat box. Within, in a rippled bed of crimson silk, nestled a necklace of rectangular-cut emeralds and oval sapphires linked by diamonds set in gold. Despite her desire to coldly reject him and his ploys, she gasped.

"Lovely, like you, Jeannette. Here, let me fasten it for you."

"No, Your Grace, I could not possibly."

"You take gifts from Isabella, do you not? And, I wager, from the Prince of Wales. Perhaps you wished to speak with me on that."

She forced herself to sit back rather than rise to dart behind the chair as she wished. She met the flinty blue gaze of Plantagenet eyes. In the lean face with the golden beard and mustache, the king's eys glittered as coldly as these jewels.

"No, my lord king, I have no desire to discuss either the Princess Isabella nor Prince Edward unless you brought me here for that."

He chuckled at her reply. "Alas, no, my pet. Let me fasten this then. I thought perhaps you would appreciate other bestowments too—perhaps a title, some lands, since your brother Edmund holds your family's manor lands, other little things could come in time to you now that we are agreed to be dear friends."

He stood behind and lowered the necklace before her face

to fasten it. Despite her knowledge of this king's reputation, despite William's warning story tonight about his own mother, despite her long-tended distrust of the Plantagenets, the impact at the king's intent struck her fully, coldly, only now. He could not possibly know of her liaison with the prince; the queen must not have told him of their secret tryst in Calais. Because—because, he surely meant to make her his mistress, too—marriage, wardship, and pious chivalry vows be damned. The thought was perversely amusing, except in it she grasped a way at last to certain revenge.

He slyly slid the heavy necklace low, down beneath her neckline so that its gold links skimmed the tops of her firm breasts in a chill, metallic caress. Then he pulled it back up and his fingers lightly stroked the nape of her neck under the draped scarves of her tall headdress. The necklace settled in place. She realized then that the pain in her head had disappeared; her mind was cleared for this battle.

"Let me remove this vile, stylish headdress, Your Grace," she said quietly and rose to step away from his hands and untie the strands of ribbon beneath her hair coils which secured it. "There, the thing has given me a pain all evening. A fashion I detest, I fear."

He grinned broadly at her and held his ground at the back of her vacated chair obviously entranced by the swift change in her demeanor. If he sensed a trap, he looked every bit a man willing to step wide-eyed into it. "Such lovely curly hair," he began on a new tack. "But then you are so lovely— everywhere, I warrant. I thought—I had hoped for the little gift and others I have in mind, you might have a little trinket for me, sweet Jeannette."

She almost giggled in his face at that opening ploy, for she had seen far smoother tactics from even young Salisbury, but he needed to commit himself more before she could spring her trap. "Such as what, Your Grace?"

She thought he would beg a kiss, but she was wrong. "I thought, mayhap, sweet, you would let your king take one or two other blue garters from where the last one came—a token of all we can be to each other."

"But, my lord king, it did not just fall from among these on the kirtle skirt, you see," she parried. A mere child's game, she thought, to fence with this suddenly nervous man.

"I know full well from where it came, Jeannette." He moved around the chair so quickly, she could not dart back. He was almost as tall as the prince. Saints, she must never let the prince know all this, but she meant to shame this man so thoroughly he would never tell his son and she could work the same sort of revenge on him later.

King Edward's hands went to her waist; then he took a second step she had not forseen. He lifted her easily to sit on the long table between the two big candlesticks at either end. His face looked almost ruddy this close in the candle glow. His breath came quickly between parted lips. She needed a little more distance, now, before her counterattack began.

"Please, Your Grace, put me down."

"Just a garter or two, Jeannette." One quick hand ruffled her garter-studded skirt up over her knees. "Here, such slender ankles, how lovely, how fair you are, sweet maid. Let me just untie one or two for knight's tokens." A big hand clasped her knee and slid up her thigh to pull at the blue silk tie of a garter. It loosened easily and slid off.

"No, Your Grace. Stop, please. I have to talk to you."

As if she had not spoken, he tipped her farther back across the hard table top, one big black velvet arm around her shoulders, the other tugging a second garter free.

"No. Loose me," she cried and tried to shove him off, to kick out.

"Jeannette, my wild little maid, lie still," he ordered breathily and leaned his big upper torso harder into her. "All these months I have curried you and shown you royal favor, it was to woo you, sweet. All is well. No one will know and even if they did, 'tis great honor to be desired by your king."

His mouth rained kisses on her throat arched back over his arm, and his mustache and beard tickled. In blatant assault, his warm hand peeled one loosed white stocking down a smooth leg to her knee and returned to stroke her warm flesh. With great dexterity, a velvet-covered thigh separated her knees along the table edge. She squirmed and tried to shove him off, but his weight was tremendous. Saints, he meant to take her right here spread across this table like some waiting banquet! Her free hand groped for a candlestick to hit him with but she misjudged and it only slid heavily out of reach. She heard her headdress roll and fall to hit the floor. His eyes were closed and he breathed heavily against her as his tongue traced jagged patterns down her throat to the heavy necklace and lower. His hand darted to her neckline and she heard the silk rip. His tongue slid lower to wet the valley between her firm breasts. William's mother—her own mother on her deathbed—a table for a bed.

"Get off me! I deny you," she grated out.

"Your eyes, your sweet, young body, your hair—"

"My hair is the color of my beloved father's, my king. And my body came from his own loins and that of my wretched lady mother's. Do you never think on them when you look on me and wish you had not let them both be treated so vilely?"

He froze against her and lifted his face glazed with passion. From the single window a cool night breeze caressed her bare thigh. "Your parents?" he said, evidently floundering for words. His eyes focused on her calm features, her narrowed, glittering stare. "I spoke not of your parents, Jeannette. I ask you now, in all love and respect, only to please your king."

"And if I do not submit here, at your whim on this hard table top, will you allow some headsman to behead me too as you let them do to my father?"

"By hell's gates, woman, you have no right to speak of this—and now!" The fierce lightning of Plantagenet temper flashed across his handsome, arrogant face but was swift gone like a summer storm. "Look here, my sweet, I meant not to let my ardor so get the best of me like this, but I find you totally unresistible. Let us move to the little bed here and then—"

"I have every right to speak of my father, Your Grace. The miracle is, you never said aught of him who was your loyal uncle, loyal to your father, our second King Edward, and whom you allowed—aye abetted, I do now know—that whoreson Mortimer and his lackey de Maltravers to murder while you were off just—"

The king uttered a low, guttural cry and yanked her by her shoulders up off the table to her unsteady feet. He shook her once, hard like a linen doll, then merely stared aghast at her a moment before he spoke. "You had best watch that pretty little mouth, Jeannette, for you bespeak treason. I do not know who has poisoned your mind against me or put those wretched lies in your head, but you had best listen well to me and learn the truth you hear. You must have been so young when that all happened, of course, and you know not what you say."

"My mother told me the truth, all of it, on her very deathbed before she took the final rites of the holy church. She would not have lied for the peril to her immortal soul. All those years she shut herself up at Liddell when everyone said she was insane—a recluse trapped by a curse of lunacy. She was ruined by it all, mourning my father and that she failed to help him. You would not even see her when she sought to beg for Edmund of Kent's life here at Windsor. Oh no, you gave her to that beast de Maltravers and sent her away—de Maltravers, a man who even now does your work for you and profits from his Flemish exile! You cannot deny it! I saw him there!"

"Lower your voice, woman, or I swear I shall tie and gag you until you do listen. All of this is vile lies and I am grieved to see a lovely maid so taken in by it all. I had no idea. My, my, how clever you have been, but since you have tipped your hand now, by the rood, we must deal with it."

He pushed her back into the chair where he had once sat

and perched on the edge of the other one, covering his golden, hair-flecked leg exposed when he sat. Contempt etched her face, he saw, at the certain knowledge he had been naked under the robe and had surely meant to have her. He beat back his rising wrath at the little chit who had surely led him on these last five months, then had thrown in his face at a most vulnerable moment this terrible mess from the past he had hoped was buried forever. Aye, he had misjudged the wild, little filly, and badly, in his foolish desire for her. He had to admit for once he should have listened to Philippa: the maid was willful, a potential troublemaker; and to protect the prince who obviously favored her, to protect them all, she should be given to one of her suitors and sent away. And that meant whoever ended up with her had to promise to live at his distant lands—Salisbury far to the north along the Scottish border at old Wark Castle or Holland at that moated Normandy mansion he had earned in the last French campaign.

"I am awaiting your words, Your Grace," she challenged. "But I know my mother spoke true and neither necklaces, lands, titles, or your own affections can ever change that."

"My mistake, alas, but you had best realize I seldom allow mistakes to see the light of day, so listen well and take all this to heart.

"At the age of seventeen, I forcibly seized my own rightful throne from the regency of my poor, misguided mother Queen Isabella and her—her favorite, Roger Mortimer," he began with a steady voice as if reciting a litany. "Those two often made great decisions without my knowledge, and the royal seal to certify their deeds was often in their possession. I knew naught of the charges Mortimer raised against your father, nor of your mother's evident attempts to see me to have the treasonous charges laid aside. The just punishment for treason is and has been beheading for a noble such as Edmund of Kent, you see."

"How could you not have known?" she threw at him. "The people knew, Parliament had passed on it with Mortimer and de Maltravers ramming it through. The lowest field hand in my lord father's home shire of Kent knew and brought the news to my poor mother at Liddell!"

"Lower your voice, Jeannette, or I shall have you locked away until you will listen rationally. I can, of course, understand how this shattered your mother. She broke under the grief and her mind never recovered. Such a pity you had to be reared in a home like that all those years. My dear queen had sent to rear you at court long ago but the poor Lady Margaret would not hear of it."

"Aye. She could not bear for me to be among those who let—some said arranged for—my father to die most despicably while he stood all day at the axeman's block praying his young king would help his uncle, hoping on hope you would not allow him to die!"

The king's hand smacked down flat on the oaken table, and both heavy candlesticks jumped and shuddered. "Enough of it, I say! I grieved for him too when I heard! I saw to it Edmund of Kent had a fine funeral and sent the body home to his parish church for burial. I paid seven Benedictine monks coin to pray seven years for his soul. And I executed Mortimer and banished de Maltravers, who was only, as you say, a lackey, anyway. I will not be accused of such vile deeds by a woman who owes the Plantagenets her very fortunate place in this kingdom and who finds herself even now decked in royal trappings."

She reached behind her neck to unclasp the heavy necklace while he glowered at her. The metal and stones rattled noisily into a little pile on the polished table. The king clasped his fists together to hide his mouth, as if he had to keep control of himself to keep from striking her.

"What a grand show, little Jeannette," he goaded. "Why not peel off the *surcote* and kirtle too and all those garters from my bowmaker at the Tower you and Isabella praised so highly? Why not the stockings and that flimsy chemise underneath I was allowed a taunting little glimpse of? You really must learn, little one, not to bite the royal hand that feeds you. I believe I could even forgive your rash and foolish words tonight if we merely trade sureties here in that little bed that no other words of like claim shall be heard again."

Her mouth dropped open despite her attempt at steely aplomb. "You—you still desire to—but I do not want you, I do not love you."

He chuckled low, but his mouth now showed amusement in its grim line. He leaned back in his chair, the tension that gripped him obviously uncoiling. He crossed his slippered feet very near her own as if to taunt her. "Want? Love? Whoever told you such frivolities existed beyond the melodious minstrel's *chansons* you yourself so sweetly sing? It is time you grew up, Jeannette—you are already married to one man, son of one of the greatest earls of the realm, God rest his soul. And now betrothed to yet another."

"But the queen arranged—"

"I know. She meddled. But it is entirely her right. And that brings us to the last poor betrodden male, other than this king himself, of course, eh?"

"I do not know what you mean, Your Grace. I will be going now. I wanted you to know why I cannot care for you—beyond my loyalty to you as our king—because of my father which—"

"Now you are frightened, eh? The little dove scents the hawk's shadow in the sky. I speak, as you no doubt know, of my son, my heir, Prince Edward. I realize your brother and the queen caught you skirts up on his lap when you first came to court, but that was mere child's play, I told the queen. And has there been more of such of late and perhaps child's play no more?"

The king's eyes narrowed to blue ice as he assessed her. She remained seated, posed tensely as if to run for the door. Her mind darted here and there for an answer to give, a way out—not to lie, not to anger—any way out of this new and looming trap.

265

"I do not love the Prince of Wales, Your Grace. The day my father died, you had ridden away from Windsor to be with him, you see, when you should have been there to help my poor father."

"By the gates of hell, woman, you try a man's patience!" His face livid, he leapt forward at her, his hands gripping the arms of her chair to pin her in. "I went to Woodstock the day he was born—that is where I was the day Mortimer had him beheaded—that is God's truth! And I swear to you, if you haul any of these claims and half-corrupted accusations out into public domain around here, you shall rue the day you did! All the whisperings over Edmund of Kent's death lead directly to the wretched nightmare of my father's brutal, tortured murder at Mortimer's hands so I could have the throne. Aye, go ahead and look at me all terrified and stupid, then. Did your mother not spit that out with her lies when she died? I did not know they would slay your sire and sanction it with the king's seal! Nor did I ever plot or rejoice that they slew my own sire at Berkeley Castle so that I could assume his throne. I buried both dead Plantagenets most royally and I am guiltless of their blood."

His eyes looked blank; his mouth moved close to her own as he continued. "I vow to you, if whispers of any of this begin again after all these years when I have earned the right to have them buried under my victories, my glories, my good and Christian deeds, I swear to you, Jeannette, you shall be the first to pay. Ah, by the rood, I could design some delicious fate for you—all tied down awaiting my whims in some tower room like this or, aye, across my dining table!"

Apparently surprised by his own tirade, he straightened almost wearily, stood, and moved away. Instantly, she rose and darted behind her chair. "You woke a sleeping leopard, Jeannette," he said softly and shook his head. "I swear to you, if anyone else had broached me with such treasonous claims, however dear, that person would be cooling shackled heels in a dungeon tonight and worse in the days to come."

"Another beheading of kin at Windsor?" she brazened before she could snatch her words back.

"Exile at the least, like your villain de Maltravers, Jeannette," he said, "but then, that will be your fate with Holland soon enough. Aye, Holland, I have decided just now. You need a firm hand like his and that little moated place in Normandy would suit your sense of adventure well. It is quite surrounded by hostile French, you know."

"I am used to such, Your Grace, only the hostile ones have been English of late."

"Spitfire!" he said only, but when he motioned her to leave, his eyes swept over her disheveled appearance in obvious reluctance. "Wait," he said and moved to place his heavy hand against the door even as she lifted the latch.

"I warn you not to overstep again, Jeannette. I grieve for the loss of your father, my uncle, and of his dear wife, the Lady Margaret. I had not thought on them for some time but the hidden wounds are raw and painful. Keep your tongue—and your head—and thus avoid my wrath again."

He paused, his eyes studying her stony face before continuing. "And I tell you, little Jeannette, you either lie about your feelings for my son or are greatly misguided. He plays a good game and even sports a mistress and a child at Sonning, so 'tis said, and he at last admitted such to me, but he does desire you, Jeannette."

She tried the door again but he held it firm. "Your face fell just then, sweet, to hear of his mistress and child, so never lie to me you do not love him in return. But many young knaves have a woman, bastards here or there—mere playful indiscretions and ones that will have utterly no effect when he marries well for England, as indeed he must. You, too, shall have utterly no effect on his future either. Now I agree with my Philippa, though for new reasons she cannot know, that you are very dangerous for the prince. Morcar's astrological charts on the prince suggested such a disturbance and I did not believe it could be merely a woman.

Now, perhaps I do."

He stepped back from the door and removed his hand. "You may go. I told my falconer Adam not to wait but there is a guard outside you may have accompany you back if you wish. Best straighten your coif and hold together that neckline where it is torn. We shall never speak again of this night, but I tell you, Jeannette, if I decide there is to be another such and my summons comes, see that you are sweet-faced and willing wherever you are bidden."

He even opened the door for her, and she swept past him ignoring the loutish-looking guard who jumped to attention. She wanted to turn and scream her denial at that last order, to shout her continued contempt and hatred, but she was suddenly exhausted beyond anger. She motioned the guard to stay where he was, and at the first turn of tower steps, she lifted a low-burning torch from its wall sconce. Holding her skirts carefully in her other hand, she descended the curving, uneven stairs of the York Tower.

Her shoulder brushed the rough stone of the wall, dirtying the white material, but she did not care. One of the wretched, crazy garters which had helped to cause all this mess snagged, but she just yanked her skirt free and went on. Her arm quivered from holding the pine torch aloft and ghostly lights and cavorting shadows grinned from each turn of the stairwell. Twice she thought she heard someone down below her on the stairs, but when she froze to listen, there was nothing but her own pounding pulse and breathless rasp.

The door of the Tower grated open on the hall running toward her room. How long and lonely it looked stretching out into darkness before her; many of the gay dance torches placed along the walls had burned down and gutted out. Her own light flickered so low she could feel the heat on her fingers; the pitchy smell of resin bit deep into her empty stomach. Had she been so long with the king that everyone had gone to bed? An hour, mayhap two. Saints, she hoped Marta slept fast so she would not have to explain the ruined gown and missing headdress she had left in the king's tower room.

As she neared her door, something stirred in the deep-set stone window well in the side hall leading toward Isabella's rooms. Joan jumped; her stomach cartwheeled over. A tall form, a black-cloaked demon materialized from the void of the window beyond. She darted back as he came at her. Her sputtering torch revealed Prince Edward's grim face, a mask of fury and contempt. He knocked the torch from her hand. It smacked to the stone floor and gutted out in a flurry of sparks to plunge the hall into violet gloom. His hands were hard as he lifted her in a crushing embrace and strode away without a word.

For the first time this evening, in all she had dared and undergone, she knew the icy hand of numbing fear. She tried to master the feeling, desperate to regain control. But where this powerful man was concerned, she had never yet managed to stem the sweeping tide of her terrible passion for him. The king, the ghosts of the past, the whole realm of England come to watch her death would be mere whisperings next to her fathomless desire for this one man.

His footsteps, swift along the stones were nearly silent. Her ear pressed to his velvet chest reverberated with the racing thud of his heart. Cradled in his iron arms like this, she welcomed the rush into dark oblivion, whatever befell was of a making outside herself. Old Morcar had said it— what will be, will be.

Somewhere down an endless small maze of twisting corridors, he lifted a leg to kick a door inward. She almost laughed at the ludicrous fate of it: all royal Edwards of Plantagenet blood must have rooms about the labyrinth of Windsor in which to devour little maidens. His arms hurt her at the last moment; she could barely draw a breath. Behind him, he shoved the door shut in the hunched-ceilinged, dimly lighted room, then moved to drop her hard on a clump of soft sacks piled deep on the stone floor. She bounced once as, in little puffs about her, feathers flew.

She scrambled to right herself on the sacks when he strode away to slide a heavy coffer across the door. She knelt on her haunches, her hair tumbled wildly loose. Her eyes luminous in the low lamplight, she waited.

Now that he had her to himself, even cornered in this deserted wing of rooms where her cries could avail her nothing, he hesitated. Whatever he did to her she remained somehow, awesomely, just barely out of his control. That elusive spirit, that wildness, at moments like this quite tamed him when he wished only to do that very thing to her.

The curse was that other women bored him with their willingness, their properness, even the ravishing, available Constantia Bourchier or the sweet maid Katharine who had recently borne his child. He did not love the woman, but for the innocent life of an illegitimate son, he had established her at Sonning for the time being. But if only he could ever really possess this exquisite one, this Jeannette he so adored, even poor Katherine could leave the boy and be sent to live in some distant manor house he never saw.

When he spoke low at last, his voice was not his own. He meant not for it to be so fierce, biting like a whip, but she had obviously been with Holland or Salisbury while he'd waited over an hour for her in that chill, dark hall, and she looked tousled enough to have come from a passionate lovers' clinch.

"Only sacks of feathers here, Jeannette. No straw, but it will do for what I intend. I ought to break your proud little neck for this trick, but I shall settle for a sweet taste of your body. Is there no end to this—Holland, Salisbury, even the king? I swear to you, little vixen, you will know for a certain the one who beds you is Edward, the conqueror, who is not any conquest of yours."

Like a conceited bully who knew he would win, she thought, he unbuckled his belt noisily and dropped it to the floor. He threw himself down beside her and rolled them over so she was partly pinned under him. Fear and desire hardened to cold fury as she went rigid and tried to pull away.

"I want his name, witch," he hissed in her ear, "the one you came from so late, so disheveled like this." At her icy demeanor he felt his temper snap and vault away, out of his control. "I will have his title, his head! Both Salisbury and Holland followed you out and did not return. I had it all arranged to keep you untouched and now you have ruined all my plans." He pushed her down, his big hands clasped in her hair to hold her still. She gazed up into his distraught face only inches from her own.

He does not know, her stunned mind screamed at her. The king, his own sire—he does not know where I have been or what has happened. She had assumed this fury was because he knew it all, had spied or followed her. If she told him who had sent for her and tried to possess her, would his curse hold true? "I will have his title, his head," he had said.

"Name him, Jeannette! Name him! Your stockings are even loose, ungartered! Who was it?"

"As you command, Your Grace. Perhaps it was even the king. Now take your hands off me. I am sick to death of being vilely abused by royal, rutting Plantagenets named Edward."

His high brow crushed his rakish, tawny eyebrows down over his eyes. "I want God's truth, Jeannette."

"Then let me go. You have no right—you, the supposed greatest chivalrous knight of all Christendom—to haul me about in straw or sacks or whatever—no right to threaten and rape me and—"

"Rape? St. George, madame, I cannot recall a time you were not as hot and as willing as I once we started. If you could only curb this wild desire to string all men along as though they were so many little wooden knights—"

"I? Get off me, get off!" She shoved him away and he chose to budge a bit to let her breathe. "How dare you grab me and threaten me! Everyone knows you bed with some unnamed town freewoman—maybe more than one from the way you eyed Constantia Bourchier tonight. And let that unnamed woman have your bastards!"

"Enough! We are not here to discuss me. My life away from here is none of your concern."

"You mistake my contempt as concern, Your Grace, for I care not what sluts you bed with and where!"

"Saints' blood! Then sacks and feathers will not doubt serve just fine here now!" He pressed her down again, pinning her arms to her side while she kicked and writhed. He held her head still and covered her mouth with his, but cursed and spun away as she bit his lip hard. His eyes were murderous. He stared aghast at her as she shrank back along the stone wall. He looked to her as shocked as she. Then, in his muted blue eyes, she read the lonely agony of heartfelt pain.

The interlocking patterns of their breathing raked the silence between them. Blood appeared on his lower lip where she had bitten him, but he only wiped it away on the back of his hand and stared.

His voice was rough velvet, barely discernible when he spoke. "I heard your words earlier, Jeannette. Tell me you lied. You cannot have been with the king."

"I was with the king, Your Grace."

"But your dress is torn, your hair all mussed—so late at night. You are lying. You detest me—what we shared—so much then?"

Her eyes widened in utter amazement. Aye, the great prince was hurt, afraid, lonely as she had often been. Now she could use the truth to best him as she had wished for so long. He might dare to accost his father—they might fight or hate each other for this—and when a parent turned away, such agony of heart followed. She opened her lips to speak but no words came. Now she could give him pain, and all she wished to do was comfort. Her heart melted, flowed out to him.

"I see," he whispered. "So I have been alone in this little *affaire du coeur* all the time and was gravely mistaken. You would even use my father. What reality does to dreams, by the rood," his voice trailed off.

"My lord prince, it was not the way you think."

"Really? All mussed like that, your hair, dress, stockings, late at night—not what I think?"

Her heart crashed so hard against her ribs in longing she could hardly hear her own words. "I will not be owned or possessed, my lord prince, by any man. That is all."

"Hell, Jeannette, we are all owned, possessed by something—rules or birth or duty."

"But not by someone."

He got slowly, heavily, to his feet. "My mistake exactly, it seems, Lady Joan. Do not cower like that. I mean not to force, to rape, or defile you as you so pointedly put it. I swear to you, Joan of Kent, I shall never do aught to so offend your delicate sense of virtue again until you can unlock that hardened little stone of a heart and learn to be a woman. Get up now and I shall deliver you safe and untouched to your own room."

She stood, her legs trembling, her feet crushing down the feather-filled sacks. He buckled on his belt, and as he stood to let her pass, she saw his big hands were shaking. He shoved the coffer away from the door and snuffed the two lamps to plunge the room into total blackness. It was not until she accidentally stumbled against his shoulder in the hall that she realized her eyes were blinded by a rush of tears.

She had to tell him how it had been with the king, since the raving fury she had expected for that had never quite come. His reaction was sullen, controlled. She suddenly longed to share her burden of revenge—but then, must he not be the object of such hatred? Surely, he knew she cared not for the other men and had just been swept along in Isabella's fun, the court games, the queen's commands. But was she not then owned and possessed by others even as she had vowed never to be? That nameless woman out there who shared the prince's bed and bore his child—he had neither defended her nor protected her. If only things had been different, not so ruined, so doomed from the very start.

"Your Grace," she managed outside the door of her room, "may we not speak on the morrow?"

"No. I have much business. Old Morcar read it well, too well. I shall be gone to Sonning tomorrow."

"I see. Then, please, only remember things are not always what they appear to be."

"Aye, Jeannette. Poor stupid dolt that I am under all the titles and trappings, I have only recently found that to be much true."

"I am sorry for it."

"Are you?" His voice was cold but sad. It was too dark to read his expression. She felt tears trace jagged paths down her flushed cheeks. "I am sure you will not let it bother you a whit come the morrow," he continued. "And I assure you—of me you shall be free unless you grow up someday to wish otherwise. Trample on whomever you will until the queen and king ship you off, and when some poor wretch lies legally between those enticing thighs—damn you, Jeannette—when it is much too late for us ever, think on me then!"

He turned and stalked off, his dark form swallowed instantly by blackness until just his footsteps whispered back to her. She felt numb, totally bereft, the way she had felt the night her mother had died. Laden with regret, smothered by remorse, she was terrified of crashing brutally into something in herself which she could never hope to fathom or control.

The iron door latch was cold to her touch. The room appeared a blend of grays, but she closed the door quietly and tiptoed past Marta's pallet and across the carpet until her knees struck her bed. Trembling as though the room were icy, she stripped and draped her garments across the foot of the bed, then climbed carefully under the coverlet—naked, for she could not bear to reach for the diaphanous gown laid out. She had worn it the night the prince had taken her to their little seaside cottage at Calais. She curled up, shivering, between the cold linen sheets.

Exhaustion drained her, made her feel bodiless, floating. Across the room dear, old Marta flopped over, then began to snore. Saints, what did it matter, any of it? She would never sleep tonight after all this anyway.

She could almost grasp now why mother had chosen to live all those years locked away. To hate from afar and not at intimate range where one could be hurt again; aye, mayhap that had been wise. Why did all this have to happen when she only wanted to be free and happy?

She felt as if she were spinning, or the room whirled wild around her. Like a wheel, the whole bed, the chamber and court revolved to make her dizzy. She heard her own words now in her head, the lyrics to the song she had oft sung on the lovely lute the prince had brought her:

> The lady Fortune is both friend and foe:
> Of poor she maketh rich,
> Of rich poor also;
> She turneth woe all into well,
> And well all into woe.
> Trust no man to do well,
> The wheel it turneth so.

The wheel blurred by inset with glittering faces like an emerald, sapphire, and diamond necklace she had seen somewhere. Its colors melded, sparkled. Philippa sullen, demanding; the king leering. Holland, Salisbury. The princess laughing. Mother—her mother was sad and dead. But in the center—at the very hub, his prideful, handsome, leonine face—my lord, my dear Prince Edward. The wheel

275

rushed faster as she reached out to him. The planets rotated by, vast diamond stars and golden suns—Morcar's wheel of fortune she would never grasp, never trust. The prince's face darkened and blurred away as the wheel whirled and threw her off into the utter void. Then she pulled her foot back from the abyss of the dream and cried no more.

Chapter Thirteen

Green spring brought more to England than festivals and a rebirth of chivalry: in one monstrous leap across the English Channel, the curse of virulent plague ravaged the land. From the squalid ports of the Mediterranean, it had swept Italy and devastated France—hitting the coasts of English Dorset in August of 1348. In Devon, Somerset, Oxford, the pestilence glutted its greedy maw on rich and poor alike until it crashed through the gates of teaming London on All Saints Day in November. Those in London's populous tenements, crowded monasteries, and busy merchants' halls prayed for deliverance, but stayed for death. The rich and noble fled the city for the sanctuary of their great country homes, out of reach of the grim-fisted devourer called in whispered tones simply—the Death.

King Edward, his queen, and youngest children took their retainers to the hunt lodge at wooded Eltham Manor in Kent, a small house, but evidently these last two months, a safe one. The Prince of Wales and his large retinue hunkered down at Sonning Manor for the duration, while the Princess Isabella and most of her ladies settled in at Woodstock in Oxfordshire. None of the places were large enough to house the whole court for a long stay, but fear was on the land as Yuletide approached, and so, they stayed. There would be no joyous reunion at Windsor for the court this dreadful year, for all but great Edward's most noble courtiers kept close to their own walled houses in distant shires. While most of Europe suffered and perished, England's elite waited and hoped the black hand of Death would condescend to pass them by.

But, despite such precautions, a few of those closest and dearest to the king's family were ravished away with one-third of England's folk. Favorite servants perished, too: old Morcar, the king's astrologer, died in his seventy-first year without ever having shown Joan of Kent the precious astrological chart he had cast for her. And at Sonning, Prince Edward's most beloved minstrel Hankin, who had once played messenger to the Lady Joan, collapsed and died in delirious agony after two days of fitful ravings. Also from the Prince of Wales's vast household two kitchen scullions and a falconer followed in swift succession, sending the prince and his retinue fleeing north to Berkhamstead only thirty-five miles from Woodstock. When, after a month it appeared the Black Pestilence had not pursued the prince there, he sent his sister Isabella a note by masked, sanctified, and purified courier that a small party consisting of six other men and himself would be joining her at Woodstock Manor for a few days' visit at Yuletide.

Bubbling over with plans, Isabella immediately showed the note to Joan where she stood at a glazed window looking out toward the wintry blue-green fir and oak of Wychwood Forest which stretched east and west to the borders of Gloucestershire as far as the eye could see.

"The prince," Joan echoed Isabella's shrill words in a much quieter tone. "Here on the morrow? I thought the plan was we had all best stay separated in these dangerous times when death leaps from house to house on the merest breath of air."

"By the rood, Jeannette, such vile, depressing talk. Aye, I know, I know, commoners, villeins, and serfs die by tens of tens, but it has been so dreary here these two months with all *demoiselles* like us simply packed in here and a stodgy old garrison of guards to protect us and not a single, young gallant in the lot! My dear lord father has been a veritable, nasty bear since summer and now to just exile all of us here at Woodstock while they at Eltham have all the fun—and have all the men—face it, Jeannette, it has all been absolutely dismal here."

Joan's heart beat a rapid tattoo as she pressed her hands to her breasts to steady herself. The prince, here in this intimate, little hunt lodge after so long. Of course, he would still hate her and act haughty and cold, but then, might that not make being near him even easier to bear? She had not seen this exile at Woodstock as dismal at all; rather it was a blessed escape from that other plague which had smitten her heart.

"Well, for heaven's sake, Jeannette," Isabella scolded, "you cannot just stand there misty eyed! I expect your help to get everything ready for them. We shall show that wretched black disease out there it cannot stop some fun and delights we cherish for Yuletide, I warrant."

"Of course I shall help. I suppose your ladies will all need to move in together to free some chambers for His Grace. I wish I could go home to Liddell until this is over, but I know that is foolish."

"Foolish? Impossible more like. How could you wish to leave when we are finally to have something to do around here? The king distinctly said you are to stay at Woodstock in my retinue until you are sent for to wed. At least this pestilence has shut down the Vatican and that will stop that annulment matter and leave you free as I am for a while."

"Aye. There is all that," Joan said slowly. The annulment, Holland, Salisbury. She hardly ever thought of all that here as if it did not matter, did not really touch her life. She either reminisced about the prince, or really thought on no one at all. Instead, here at wintry Woodstock, set like a rough jewel among three ponds in the embrace of deep forests, she remembered her maidenhood at Liddell before all the confusions of the court: she thought on Marta, whom she had been forced to leave at Windsor with most of the ladies' maids; and her poor, violet-eyed mother sequestered by choice in that silent chamber reliving a wretched past; of Morcar with his charts and signs and strange warnings, now all stilled by death; and of Roger Wakeley, her dear friend who had wandered in to Liddell to fill her quiet life with music and song and then had left at her brother Edmund's insistence over six years ago—another of several childhood desertions by a trusted loved one.

"Now come along and buck up," Isabella was saying again. "By the rood, His Grace had better ride in here with fresh venison or be prepared to go out to hunt at once for we have only enough on hand for one huge feast. They all eat like mowers at harvest day, you know. Jeannette," Isabella concluded in a rush with her hands on her shapely hips, "you quite simply must stop this moping. Plague or no plague, you have been a stick-in-the-mud since that day after the Garter Ceremony when all perdition broke loose."

"The day the king scolded you for being a spendthrift, you mean," Joan countered as they walked the length of the low-beamed central hall toward the comfortable solar where Isabella slept and the ladies congregated in the daytime to keep warm.

"Aye. At first, of course, I thought all the show of expensive garters had set him off at me, but that could hardly be since he had made such a fuss over yours and renamed the new Order of the Round Table the Order of the Garter after them. Truth is, I believe, I got caught in his foul mood because someone told him I borrowed coins from my grooms and ladies to pay his bowmaker and, then, too, that was the day of his vile row with dearest Edward."

"The king fought with the Prince of Wales that day?"

"Did I never tell you? Aye, the morn after all that lovely torch dancing. I guess it slipped my mind with the plague talk and all, and I was so out of my humor the king scolded me for riotous spending when he knows he wanted me dressed well. It was so strange—the prince has been known to argue with our lady mother in that stiff-necked way of his but never to take on the king. I swear that is why Edward rode off in a huff with his men, remember, even before we heard all these dire predictions of the pestilence and he had to go to Sonning? And if we are not ready to put on some sort of show for Yule, we might feel dear Edward's barbed tongue too, so we had best get our heads together for something wonderful."

By eventide the *demoiselles* had planned and arranged a joyous welcome and Yule celebration for the prince and his men. Plum pastries and mince and suet puddings were baked, rooms aired and cleaned, and the queen's silver hip bath scoured to convert it to a massive Wassail bowl. The ladies practiced singing traditional carols in Latin and French and rehearsed an intricate madrigal and mumming dance to "Good King Wenceslaus," a king suddenly of more importance than distant King Edward. Joan was well enough pleased to play her lute and lead the music rehearsals until she realized she would have to be on display at the Yule feast where the prince's rude, accusing gaze could ruin her temporary gay mood.

The stalwart men personally selected to guard Isabella and her *demoiselles* got into the game by hauling in great Yule logs for the hearth in the Great Hall, which was hardly great, Joan thought, compared to those of Windsor or Westminster. The second day, awaiting the uncertain arrival time of the prince's men, the ladies dressed prettily in winter greens and Yuletide reds and rehearsed again in their newly decorated, fragrant, pine-scented hall. Draped swags of evergreen, winter waxed-leaf ivy, and mistletoe dripped from walls, staircase, and balconies. Newly lit, scented candles poured their essence of bay and myrtle into the air as the brief winter afternoon began.

Joan sat near the crackling fire warming her green-slippered feet on the andiron next to the barrel of chestnuts everyone would roast later this evening. She idly strummed her lute and felt it quiver with tone and rhythm in her graceful hands. Its old ribbons had been frayed and soiled, so she had today finally replaced them with new ones of green and burgundy silk, but she had foolishly tucked the others away as if she could not part with them. The lute the prince had given her so long ago she still cherished despite—or because of—her feelings for him. She could certainly weather this brief visit of his. She had been through far worse before and, besides, they owed each other nothing after that last bitter parting. And the way Constantia Bourchier had decked herself out today and chattered incessantly about the prince since they had all heard he was coming, she need not think he would have a moment's time for her or her lute anyway.

Rooming with the beauteous, loquacious Constantia was the worst thing about these plans for the prince's arrival. "Please call me simply Tia—all my friends do—the prince does," the chatterbox had said as Joan had been ready to finally relax enough to drop off to sleep last night. And the woman's habit of flaunting her lush body and recounting vivid tales of her numerous amatory conquests, with the best yet to come, as she so crudely put it, was grating on Joan's already rattled nerves. One would think a few simple rounds with the prince on the dance floor the night of the Garter Ceremonies were enough to make that conceited, big-bosomed witch the next Queen of England, Joan groused silently as she strummed the lute even harder to feel it reverberate against her green velvet-covered thighs.

Here at cloistered Woodstock in plague times, Joan, Isabella, and the other *mignonnes* had not bothered with fashion as usual—until yesterday when they heard the men were coming. This green velvet kirtle which molded itself so softly to Joan's slender figure was a two-year-old gown Marta had packed for mere warmth without a thought of Yule. It was very plain with no embroidered edges or adornments, but today, with a *surcote* of crimson velvet and a golden filigree girdle decorated with burgundy ribbons to match the lute, it looked festive enough for Yule in exile. And only because it had matched and picked up the green of the velvet gown and mayhap even echoed the deep pine hue of the protective forest outside, Joan had worn the little green beryl ring the prince had sent her by his sweet-voiced, now-deceased minstrel Hankin that first year she had come to court.

"They are here! They are here! I heard the hunt horn I told old Peter to blow when he spotted them from the wall beyond the hedgerows!" Isabella shouted as she whirled through the hall. Joan put her lute down slowly, deliberately, arranging its streamers carefully on the bench along the wall. "Jeannette, Tia, everyone, get out in the entry hall, arranged as we planned. All right, I am going out now, to greet all of them sweetly. Oh, St. Peter's blood, Jeannette, I hope the rogue brought John Chandos for me!"

Sir John Chandos, Joan mused, as she took her place on the lowest step of the great staircase among the nervous flutter of primping ladies. Sir John was much older than Isabella, a tall, hawklike man of great reputation and prowess on the battlefield. He was a fast friend and advisor of the prince, and probably, Joan admitted to herself, a good enough influence compared to the other cronies like Dagworth or Calveley with whom he amused himself. Sir John Chandos liked women, that was obvious enough, and like the prince, he had never yet married. He seemed moral, strong, and stalwartly upstanding to Joan—somewhat, she hated to admit, like Thomas Holland. Aye, he had a good bit in common with that dour, straightforward knight: both had lost an eye, though Chandos' total lack of vanity kept him from wearing a patch; both had new-won lands in Normandy, though she was not sure if Chandos' holdings were close to Thomas's at Pont-Audemer; and both, though middle-aged, seemed to favor much younger *demoiselles* like Isabella and herself.

She could readily see why Isabella was worth such courting, but she was yet to see why Holland did not get his pride stuck full of lances waiting for the Pope's reply and just retreat from his strange quest of a landless, young maid from Kent. Perhaps it was merely stubbornness at this stage of the long, drawn-out struggle with Salisbury for her hand—that and a warrior's instinct to win which all these English knights displayed as vaingloriously as their family shields at a tournament.

Two guards opened the door for an ermine-cloaked Princess Isabella as she swept out into the small, cobbled courtyard to meet the prince and his party. Chill air swept in the open door to ruffle the ladies' carefully arranged tresses and creep up the stockinged legs under their warm skirts. Outside, hooves clattered on cobbles. Men's voices shouted and Isabella's high voice floated to them as she made her welcome speech.

Joan twisted her beryl ring nervously and leaned more toward the wall as Constantia Bourchier moved down a step to nearly elbow Joan aside. The woman was dressed in deep red which vibrantly echoed the darker hues of her flaming hair so carefully braided, coiled, and dusted with a lily essence which settled heavily in the pit of Joan's stomach whenever she took a breath. The woman's full breasts strained against the red silk bodice as she leaned forward, pouting lips parted for a first glimpse of the prince. Saints, Joan thought, and elbowed Constantia back a bit, does the chit plan to lie with him the moment he gets here?

Men's voices, closer now; tall shadows thrown across the entryway—Isabella on the prince's arm laughing up at him with her voice of ringing, jangling chimes. Joan leaned her right shoulder into the wall to steady herself. Prince Edward looked hale and hearty—magnificent with the dual flash of whitest teeth and eyes as he laughed deeply and swept off his snow-covered velvet cap. He was garbed entirely in black and gold.

"Not the plague, God save us, not the bloody French or the gates of hell could prevail on us to spend a Yule away from such fair beauty," his deep voice began while Isabella and those around Joan laughed and cheered.

The broad, arched doorway behind the prince filled with stamping hooded or hatted men, commenting, waving, grinning—but nothing seemed to register on Joan. The impact of his nearness, his voice, those huge shoulders, the tawny mane of hair—by the Virgin, she dare not gaze into his icy blue eyes or she was doomed. Her legs felt like water, the steps under her like the deck of a Channel ship in October. She despaired as she felt a steady blush creep up her neck, her fair cheeks, even the tips of her ears hidden under the wheat-hued, beribboned coils of heavy hair. No. No! She must not, could not, feel this way for him still!

In the press of ladies, she moved down the stairs directly behind Constantia, who had managed to step completely in front of her. In a curving line, the *demoiselles* mingled among the seven men, greeting the prince and his friends with kisses and fond embraces and the hooded servants with kind words and sweet smiles.

Joan crashed back to reality with a thud as her eyes swept the scene to fully assess it. Praise be, he had not brought Holland or Salisbury, but somehow, she had known he would not. No wonder Isabella was all giggles, for her Yuletide wish had come true: the tall, hawk-faced Sir John Chandos stood grinning at the prince's elbow. The other three knights he had brought were his more raucous cronies—in plague time, when everyone wanted to escape the grim specter of hovering death, she should have expected as much. Black-haired and handsome, Sir Nickolas Dagworth was kissing Constantia directly in front of her, and that giant of a man, the only one Joan had ever seen taller than the prince, Sir Hugh Calveley, bellowed a laugh. Sir Robert Grey, whose reputation both as a great hunter and joker always preceded him, bent even now to take her hand in his cold one and plant a firm kiss on her cheek.

To her amazement, Joan found her voice. "And the prince no doubt brought you to play the Lord of Misrule at the Yuletide feast this evening, Sir Robert."

"Aye. Do you always read his motives exactly, sweet Joan of Kent?" Sir Robert guffawed and gave her a significant wink she chose to ignore. "In these terrible plague times, we need all the jesting we can get, eh?"

"Robert Grey," Isabella's high voice interrupted, "I will

not have anyone mention that vile tragedy during your stay. Any other who says 'plague' or looks a moment sad will pay a forfeit!"

"Sweetest sister," the prince's deep voice broke in, and he took a step toward Joan and Sir Robert that seemed to bring him ever so much closer, "we will have feasting and fun, that is of a certain, but we shall also remember our English folk out there terrified and dying. I had thought before the celebration for Yuletide we would ask the parish priest here to say a mass for all the lost and suffering souls—out there in our realm."

"Oh, of course," Isabella agreed, her voice and wild eyes more muted. "I—well, of course, we had thought of that," she added, and Joan crossed herself both for the princess' little white lie and for the fact they had not thought of that at all.

Sobered to calmness by his voice and words, Joan gazed up directly into the prince's shattering, sky-blue stare.

"My lord prince. Welcome to Woodstock."

"Lady Jeannette." His voice was now somehow guarded, the fervent tone which had colored it as he spoke of his people's suffering had fled. She curtsied smoothly and accepted the brief brush of his warm mustached mouth on her smooth cheek. There, she thought. The greeting, the kiss, the sweep of feeling is gone, over. I am fine now.

She watched the affectionate welcome he readily accepted from Constantia. The maid simply leaned into him, pressing her full bosom to his black leather jerkin which smelled so deliciously of cold air and forest and freedom.

Joan turned away to greet the dark-eyed Nickolas Dagworth whose practiced glance appraised her quickly as always. Saints, she thought as he squeezed her against him in a deliberate bear hug, if I cared one whit for Prince Edward, it would be obvious whom to choose to try to make him jealous. But she was older and wiser now. She wanted no tangled ties of heartstrings ever again with anyone. Let him make a fool of himself with that cow-breasted Constantia.

She was above any sort of games to rile him or vie for his affections. They only led each time to anger and eventually separation and grief. If he had ever slightly touched her heart, he never would again. She would show him a protective armor of her own fashioning!

Before she took Hugh Calveley's proffered arm as they all went in to sit down to a warming drink of hot spiced wine, she twisted her beryl ring off her finger and hid it inside the little silk pomander pouch dangling from her girdle.

But at the feast that evening, after the men had rested and washed away the road dust, after an hour of solemn mass for the beset souls of the realm, Joan's assumed cloak of calm was shredded—not by the prince or Nickolas Dagworth or any man she had greeted at the entryway earlier, but by a new servant Prince Edward had brought to cheer them all at Woodstock. Joan had hardly noted the three hooded servants when his retinue first arrived. The prince had brought his head falconer, Philip Pipe to care for his precious, hooded peregrine Greta; a favored squire, Wilt Clinton; and a new talented French minstrel as a present to the ladies. But until they began to eat at table that evening with a full haunch of venison, plum puddings, rabbit stews, and wines littering the groaning tables before them, Joan had not closely noted the new minstrel with whom the prince had replaced his old friend Hankin.

Only a middle-sized, middle-aged, round-faced man with brownish hair and a charming French accent, she thought the musician at first. He strummed his lute magically, sitting across the narrow hall before the fire which gilded his silhouette with a blazing aureole of light. But his deft touch on the strings to woo from them such resonant tones, his soothing, achingly sweet voice was utterly, completely, astoundingly familiar.

Joan halted her goblet halfway to her lips and stared.

"Your Grace, wherever did you find that marvelous new minstrel?" Constantia Bourchier was asking as if to save

287

Joan the trial of addressing the prince where he sat halfway down the table between Isabella and Constantia.

"My little Yule gift to all Isabella's charming *demoiselles*, especially those with their own sweet voices and good ears for lovely melody," he replied smoothly. Joan's heart beat even faster, but if the prince gazed at her to be sure the compliment reached its mark, she was not looking his way. "My talented new lutenist Roger was these past six years with my dear grandmother in her exile at Castle Rising in Norfolk."

"With the deposed and exiled Queen Isabella," someone murmured. Whispers buzzed about the long table to lend a strangely sibilant counterpoint to the lute and the crackling blaze of Yule log.

"Roger!" Joan said and those around her turned to stare. She stood at her place barely aware she had sloshed burgundy wine on the white brocade tablecloth. Sir Nickolas Dagworth directly across the table narrowed his dark eyes at her pale face, then craned his neck to see what had made the beautiful Joan of Kent look as if she had seen a ghost. Oblivious to the numerous stares and dying whispers at the table as others watched and elbowed those next to them, Joan shoved her heavy chair back and walked quickly around the length of seated guests.

She stopped and squinted into the blaze of fireglow at the man. The massive Yule log on the flames roared and crackled as, distantly behind her, Joan heard Isabella's shrill voice call her name.

Five feet away, the man halted his quick fingers midway across the strings and stood while his last gay chord of music hung suspended between them. He did not look surprised as she knew he must before them all. For one moment her eager voice was the only sound in the room save the crackle of fire. "Roger Wakeley! Oh, Master Roger, it is you!"

He swept her a little bow and extended his free hand to steady her at the elbow. His straight brown hair cut low over his forehead, his long nose, and brown eyes looked so utterly familiar after all this time.

"*Oui, ma demoiselle* Joan of Kent, and you, grown so lovely, here with the king's family, a place I just never thought to find you."

The kindly, avid-eyed face was almost the same as when Roger Wakeley had lived at Liddell for two whole years to teach her the lute and bring some joy and music into her sheltered, lonely existence there. The intricate twists of fate, the agonies of complicated womanhood in the series of Plantagenet courts and castles dropped away as Joan stared steadily, tearfully, into his face.

"I thought to never see you again," she began in a rush, at first unaware the table behind her was astir with muffled voices again and that both Isabella and Prince Edward approached from behind. "I cried for days that Edmund had made you leave and I had not known that you were going."

She jumped at Isabella's voice at her side. "Jeannette, you mean you know the prince's new minstrel from somewhere? But he has been at Castle Rising with our grand'mère Isabella for years and years."

"Six years, I said, sister," the prince put in. Damn this touching, tearful little scene, Prince Edward cursed to himself, annoyed that Joan, as usual, had managed to upset his equanimity just when he thought he had himself under tight rein so as not to let her rile him. "Before that, you two obviously knew each other," he said, trying to sound lightly amused at the coincidence while his quick mind calculated Joan's age back compared to Roger Wakeley's six years ago. Surely she had been much too young then for any sort of *affaire du coeur*, and not with a French minstrel more than twice her age.

"My lord prince, and dear princess, Roger taught me to love music, so many songs, to play the lute at Liddell when I was only a child."

"To play the lute," the prince echoed, remembering how long it took him to even master the fundamentals of the damned, delicate thing before he decided his fingers were made only for horses' reins and weapons. "But how long were you in their household, Roger?"

"Two years, my lord prince," Roger Wakeley answered, but his gaze was still on Joan. "*Sacrebleu*, two wonderful years. The lady and her old maidservant Marta nursed me through a deadly disease and set a broken leg bone, and I repaid them in the only way I could—by teaching the Lady Joan to sing and play."

"And to love beautiful things, Roger," Joan echoed. Prince Edward frowned despite himself. He detested the way Jeannette pronounced the minstrel's name in that soft French way as much as how she gazed at him all dreamy-eyed as though the rogue were some conquering knight in full battle armor. He had only brought the man to cheer up the ladies—aye, because he knew his fine voice and lute would please Jeannette especially. And now this whole thing had been a disaster and she was making a fool of herself, with tears clinging to her lashes, because she was reunited with her maidenhood music teacher! Coincidence and fate, cursed fate, always throwing obstacles between them! But had not he long resolved to be done with her, especially since that bloody, damn row with the king over the little vixen? If only he had not wanted so desperately to be here to comfort her when she learned the tragic news he must soon tell her. Damn! He should never have come here at all.

"I suggest you sit down now, Jeannette, and finish the meal," the prince said. "Let your 'Ro-jer' sing and play. That is what I wheedled him away from my grandmother for." He turned back to the table with Isabella in tow and announced grandly to all the intent faces, "My new lutenist turns out by chance to have lived at the Lady Joan's childhood home in Kent. Music! Everyone eat now."

He turned back as if to wait for Joan to follow also, but instead she curtsied and smiled at him and Isabella. "My lord, shall I not sing and play also? I would love to entertain with Master Roger, for I intended to sing later after the meal anyway. The princess has arranged it all. We know so many of the same songs, you see, and such a wonderful occasion—"

"Fine," the prince's steely voice cut in from where he stood halfway back to the table. "Just do whatever pleases you, Lady Joan. Far be it from me in these tenuous times to interrupt a joyous reunion."

The table quieted until the prince had reseated himself. His squire jumped to refill his cup, and Constantia Bourchier smirked, cat-eyed, directly at Joan before she leaned close to the prince to smile up at him. He laughed at her whispered words and playfully tugged a stray crimson curl as though the interruption had not occurred. Joan could tell Roger Wakeley was on edge, yet watchful, too, and vaguely amused as his quick brown eyes took in the whole scene. A pox on all the revelers at the table, Joan thought, before she remembered the plague and prayed instantly to have that curse recalled.

Straight-backed, chin up, she fetched her lute and sat in the chair next to Roger Wakeley's while they sang, whispered of old times, and played on and on. To play and sing at all—but especially to play with Master Roger whom she revered and had thought of so fondly all these years— was pure joy. As if she had taken a heady drug, the worry of the prince's glowering stares slipped away. They sang of wassail and green woods and unrequited love. They romped through melodies Joan thought she had long forgot, and she followed his lead through new ones, her delicate voice blending with his full tenor. Their little audience became rapt, applauding at times, laughing at ribald lyrics or even singing along. Aye, finally now, the prince's new musician seemed to be completely at ease.

The skilled lutenist sitting beside the beautiful Lady Joan led her into yet another melody. His fingers and voice were true and sure but his mind wandered. She looked stunning, he thought, utterly exquisite and somehow completely unaware of her physical and personal attraction for the prince. An innocent she was not, no doubt with that face and slender, beguiling body, but he would have to assure the king that she hardly led the prince on as he had believed when he'd assigned the musician to watch them in this lucrative post the prince believed he only had arranged.

Ah, *sacrebleu*, this life among the young and lively was a blessing after those six years at that wretched castle set amidst the forsaken, barren land above the Wash in western England. Blessed Mother of God, he was grateful the deposed Queen Isabella had behaved herself and earned her way back into King Edward's trust or he might have been there until he rotted away singing her eternally grievous love songs.

What marvelous fate to be reunited with the little Joan whose moated manor at Liddell in Kent had been one of his pleasantest assignments except for the broken leg and that vile touch of plague he had unfortunately spread to the young Joan herself and two of the manor's servants. He wondered in these times of rampant pestilence if she realized she had been touched by its grim hand once and had survived. He ought to tell her, remind her, so she did not fear the Death as others not so blessed must. But, *sacrebleu*, if she ever knew his two-year stay at Liddell before her eldest brother threw him out was not mere chance but an assignment to be sure the little family of the executed Edmund of Kent would cause the king no more trouble, what would she think of her dear Master Roger then?

His eyes returned to scan the table of revelers. The prince tried to keep his face passive, his eyes from the Lady Joan, but he was trying much, much too hard, and to practiced eyes, that gave it all away. Some lovers' quarrel or a love the Lady Joan did not return perhaps. Roger Wakeley shook his head in wonder and led his charming, little lute partner into another song of unrequited love.

As the evening wore on, these two musicians swelled to a group of six as some of Isabella's guards played halting crumhorn, fydel, and gittern. The *demoiselles* sang their well-rehearsed Yuletide songs while the bay-scented candles melted lower. The Yule log burned down and a silver-crimson pile of ashes deepened on the broad, open hearth. Several of the prince's friends cavorted about springing jokes on others while the foaming wassail cups went round and round. Sir Robert Grey plucked a bough of mistletoe from off the swags of greenery and took to stealing ladies' kisses while everyone laughed and cheered.

Unaware her musical partner Roger Wakeley observed her and the prince closely, Joan struggled not to watch him with Constantia, but some of their antics were hard to miss. Really, she surmised, it was a case of the flame-haired beauty throwing herself at the prince, but he made no move to say her nay.

Late, sometime surely after midnight, when people were feeling their wine and starting to act either flippant or drowsy, Hugh Calveley dashed in from somewhere and announced—with a snowball smacked into the wassail bowl—that it was snowing heavily outside. In a screaming, cavorting hubbub, they all rushed for capes and cloaks to venture out. The prince, near the doorway, pointed to Roger Wakeley and motioned for him to follow with a quick nod and sharp glance. For one second Joan started, thinking he summoned her so peremptorily. Roger Wakeley noted well the alarm that froze her lovely features.

"*Sacrebleu*, whatever His Grace says to me, this night I treasure always, sweet Joan," he whispered to her as he cradled his lute and hurried after the prince up the stairs.

Joan sat alone, in the suddenly still Great Hall while, in the distant reaches of the manor, squeals and cries and pounding feet reverberated as the revelers seized garments and ran outside. She could feel Woodstock empty of sounds of life. No servants even stirred to clear away the final course of pastry dishes and wine goblets. The fire felt warm on her back, and she was suddenly drowsy. Aye, whatever the prince or anyone else said to her, she would treasure this night with dear Master Wakeley always too. How sad she had been that he had gone away years ago, how furious with

Edmund that he had ordered him to leave. On the morrow they would catch up on all the years between they had not already whispered about between songs. And wait until Marta heard the news! Whenever the prince's retinue was at Windsor, she would be certain to see Master Roger and then the old, lost days at Liddell could live again.

Joan jumped at the deep voice so close and her eyes flew open. "I do not doubt you are sleepy, Jeannette. I sent your 'Ro-jer' out to hold torches with the other servants, I am afraid. Do you no longer taste for adventure and will you sit here like a coward before a warm blaze while everyone else frolics outside?"

A swirl of black velvet cape enveloped the prince's tall form as he towered over where she sat. Low fireglow etched each proud, handsome feature as his eyes glittered over her. She rose to her feet in order not to feel at such a disadvantage.

"Everyone will ruin their finery if they get it all wet, Your Grace," she managed lamely. "Besides I am not in the mood to dash about in the cold and get pelted with snow."

"No? But not pining for Holland or Salisbury either, I warrant. You did note I brought neither of them with me?"

She smiled at him but did not let him rile her into making a flustered or angry answer. Saints, she did not intend to be teased or to fight with him and ruin this beautiful evening. She could tell her ignoring the taunt unsettled him as he shifted from one big foot to the other.

"Best you go out, Your Grace, or they will miss you. The little—or should I say, big—red-haired Tia, especially."

"Dearest, sword-tongued Jeannette, how I would still like to think it mattered to you, damn my stupid, foolish heart. How can I or you or any of us sit here like we have in these terrible times and be really happy? I have seen it on our land, Jeannette, the hand of the Black Death, the grim harvester of agonized people. If we have enough serfs and villeins left for next spring planting, enough soldiers to return to France for another victory, it will be a miracle. The people, rich and poor, serf and noble, are much like grains beneath the thresher's flail in this."

Her rancor at him, the tense expectation of his next tease or gibe, flowed out of her. "I see it grieves you sore, my lord prince. I did not realize—"

"How could it not? Someday, Jeannette, long years away, I pray, this realm will be mine and I would spend my blood not to only increase it, but to spare it."

They stood close together bathed in the champagne glow of the dying fire, staring calmly, deeply, into each other's eyes. An urge to comfort, to embrace and touch him nearly overwhelmed her in that perfect moment, but she fought to control whatever feeling it was. "I think I understand, and I admire you for that, my lord prince."

He looked touched. "Do you, Jeannette? Then that helps a bit, almost as though I had been able to play a skillful lute and sing to catch your smiles and fancy tonight. Here, put this cloak around your shoulders and come out with me to the little chapel outside the walls. I need to talk to you and the others will not miss us there. And if we sit here, I warrant, they would all come tramping back in. Come now."

She stiffened at his low-spoken, but unmistakable command. "To the chapel? But, of course, the others will miss you and wonder where you are. If you are going out, you will need your own cloak."

"Come with me now, Jeannette. Isabella and my men will care for the others." She sensed further floundering protests were useless as he wrapped her in his cloak and took her arm to lead her from the hall. She almost hesitated when she saw he meant to go out through the back kitchens but her inner resolve and peace at his side grew with each step. To the little chapel, he had said, and surely he would not hazard any angry or foolish moves in a sanctuary and with the others close about.

As they stood gazing out at the back door, she gasped to see the deep cover of pure snow upon the ground in so short a time. Huge, lacy snowflakes floated downward silently. The black velvet sky of chill air was pierced with excited shouts and shrieks from around the far side of the manor. She could almost envision the others playing ducks and geese by the summerhouse, throwing snowballs, or sliding across the iced surface of the three shallow fish ponds.

"I had best go up for my boots, Your Grace," she said as he lifted a glowing cresset lamp from a peg at the door.

"No," he said. "We must talk now and I have decided on the old chapel out by Fair Rosamonde's bower. Do you know the story, Jeannette? Here, trust me and do not kick the cloak into this lamp. I am going to carry you."

He lifted her and they were out into the snow before she could protest. Her mind spun and whirled like these snowflakes pelting his broad, dark shoulders and her own arms placed reluctantly—no, acceptingly—around his neck. His feet crunched, crunched as they went deeper into the swirling, snow-sprinkled night.

They must talk, he had said. Near Fair Rosamonde's bower—aye, Joan knew the story well, for the Princess Isabella deemed it a true romance and told it over and over with various embellishments.

"Fair Rosamonde's story is terribly sad, my lord prince," Joan said quietly in the hushed sweep of snow as the lighted manor was swallowed up behind them.

"Aye," he agreed and his voice rumbled in his chest to which he had her tightly gathered. "But, then, before Queen Eleanor found out her husband King Henry loved Rosamonde and dispensed with her, I warrant, Henry and his Rosamonde were passionately happy here, desperately in love. If their ghosts could tell us now, I believe they would say that, despite the later grief fate dealt them, their precious love was worth whatever happened after."

Something poignantly sweet twisted deep inside her, and she stirred in his arms to look at his profile. Those words so deeply felt were more beautiful to her ears and heart than any song of agonized love had ever been. She meant to ask him if it had ever been so for him, that sweet passion's pain of which he spoke, but she cowered instead behind a half-jesting question.

"Do you believe queens always control their ladies' lives at court, Your Grace?"

He turned his head to face her in the sweep of snow. His brow furrowed; his eyes fascinated her. She watched his mouth under his snow-touched mustache move as he answered. "Unlike Fair Rosamonde, you do not love your king, do you, Jeannette?"

"No, my lord prince."

"Nor the others you have been driven to—not Salisbury, not Holland?"

"No."

He let out a long, painful sigh as they stood still, dusted white with snow like two marble statues content to remain in frozen caress forever. "Then, for now, the rest must be left unsaid," he added brusquely and when she thought, hoped he would kiss her, he went stolidly on.

They were both wet with heavy snowflakes when they reached the tiny chapel near the small stone house called Rosamonde's Chamber. Reluctantly, he put her down inside the open door of the dimly lighted chapel.

"Oh, you sent someone on ahead. It is all lighted," she breathed, suddenly in awe at the quiet beauty of the place as well as at her own acquiescence to come so readily out here with him under such strange circumstances. It worried her to see he looked so serious. He was even frowning as he took her hand in his and pulled her up the short twenty-foot nave to the stone altar. He pulled her down beside him on a bare carved bench, then brushed the melted snow away from her hair and shoulders as if from some sudden urge to touch her.

"Dearest Jeannette, would to God I had brought you here for another purpose. Perhaps, somehow, someday, I had thought—"

She tensed at the urgency of his words, the frightening intensity of his handsome face. She let him seize her hands gently. Despite this comforting touch, she instinctively began to tremble at his lightning-quick shift of mood.

"It is so strange to fathom, *ma chérie*," he went on in a rush, "how events seem to cast us together as though we were meant to be, yet to pull us apart too. That first day you came to Windsor, there I was doing furious battle in the mud of the quintain yard. Even now when I would tell you far other than my burden of news, I—" He paused and frowned again. She marveled that his big, strong hands could be so warm when they had come through the snow.

"St. George, Jeannette, I rehearsed this all on the road between Berkhamstead and Woodstock over and over again. I was there the night your mother died at the St. Clares, remember, though you would not let me comfort you? The times are very bad, my sweetheart, hard on everyone, and you must let me comfort you now."

Her mind raced to delve his meaning. He looked grief-stricken and almost afraid. "Comfort me? What do you mean? Marta? Is Marta dead like Morcar—at Windsor?"

She tried to yank her hands away but he held fast. A low-burning candle reflected its glow in the blue pools of his eyes. "No, my sweet Jeannette, no. I am sorry, but it is your brother Edmund and his wife Anne at Liddell and many of their household. The pestilence has thoroughly ruined that whole area of Kent."

Her mind reeled, stopped, disbelieving. "Edmund? Anne, too? Both? No, it cannot—cannot be!"

He pulled her to him but she pushed hard against his damp, velvet chest. "Aye, Jeannette. I had word from the king and queen in a dispatch the day before I left to come here. I am so sorry."

"The king and queen? They hate me. They made it all up. They have always hated my father's family, all of us, and now that I told that king I know what he did—"

"Stop it, Jeannette. You are not making sense. Listen to me, *ma chérie*. Your brother John has been sent for from Salisbury's household in the north since the manor and lands at Liddell are his birthright now."

"But John is all right? John is not ill?"

"No, John is fine. They already buried Edmund and Anne there at Liddell, Jeannette. You understand. They died almost three weeks ago, but news is so slow in these times of pestilence that—"

"Three weeks dead?" She sat shaking, not crying the same way she had not cried the night her mother had died. "Three weeks? But why did you not tell me the very moment you came? Why? Three weeks already, both Edmund and poor Anne."

She tried to summon up their faces but they drifted, blurred. Edmund bringing her and mother to London, Edmund looking fine on his armored horse on tournament day at Windsor only last year. And Anne, pale, scolding. She should have behaved better for Anne, should have listened to her quiet voice instead of always going off with the lute to chase her own daydreams while Anne kept the manor going. Tears flooded her lilac-hued eyes.

The prince's hands grasped her shoulders to steady her. She looked past him, through him, seeing her mother's face now, hearing those wretched, agonized last words. Aye, the prince had been there that night too—death, he always was there for death. His whole family hated hers, sought their deaths.

"Let me go! Let me go!"

"Please, Jeannette, let me hold you. There is so little time. Here is comfort." One hand swept toward the barren little altar. "Here, Jeannette, blessed Jesu and the saints. Here, let me help."

"No!" Her shriek echoed madly in the silent church then faded to nothing. She collapsed hard against his chest at last; his arms went around her in a welcome, crushing embrace.

"I should have told you earlier today, I know, my sweetheart, but everything was so joyous, and I wanted you to have tonight. And then it turned out you knew Roger

Wakeley and sang and smiled all night—with him. I just could not ruin all that for you however much it pained me. To see you there near me in the firelight when our days together are over now."

She raised her dazed face to stare at him. "There is more to tell then," she faltered, and her tumbled mind fought to clear itself from debris so she could reason. "Am I to be sent back to Liddell? I swear to you, my lord prince, it has been my fondest wish, my only desire."

He gave her a little shake. "Stop it. No, though I wish that were the next blow. The king, it seems, Jeannette, after you did whatever you did to thoroughly rebuff him the night of the Garter ceremony, himself wrote the pope to urge on Thomas Holland's request for an annulment from Salisbury. I can only be thankful for your apparent spurning of my royal sire's intents that night, but it has sealed your fate with Holland as the pope has ruled in his behalf. I would guess that Holland will be here any day now to claim his betrothed and soon enough be off to Normandy, the apparent price for the king's help in winning you. So you are free of Salisbury's claim and Thomas Holland has won."

"Holland! After all this time. Holland."

"Aye. The thought does not grieve you then?"

She pulled free at last from his restraining grasp, and he let her go. She stood, closely wrapping his huge, inky cloak about her like darkest, thickest armor of black midnight.

"Of course, it grieves me. All I ever asked of being here at the great Plantagenet court was my freedom—the right to be alone sometimes if I so willed it, to choose my own path, but that is not the way things are done. Holland, Salisbury—it is all the same."

"Is it, my poor, little maid?" His resonant voice sounded very tired, listless. "Then why should a wretch like the Prince of Wales say any different?" He shook his tousled, damp head. "St. George, but what I would not give to have this battle be as easy as that which won my spurs at Crécy!"

She stared down at the floor not daring to comprehend his words. Edmund and Anne dead. Holland, victor at last. She grasped her hands very tightly together. This frightening, magnetic antagonism she had shared with Edward, Prince of Wales, Plantagenet, must be ended now. Now she must wall off the pain of loss and hurt so it could not devour her like this. Aye, she might marry Thomas Holland, but she would never belong to him or anyone else but herself. Saints, at this little stone altar where poor, beset Rosamonde had probably begged the Lord for help, she vowed it!

No tears fell, he marveled as he watched her. How he had rehearsed this scene where she would collapse in his arms, and he would comfort her and vow his undying love before this tiny, crude altar even at their parting. But when had Jeannette of Kent ever not surprised him? He was not sure he even dared to carry her back to the manor, for he was not convinced he could keep himself from wildly sprinting off with her into the black reach of forest to freeze in eternal embrace with her in the pure white of untouched snow. Staring at her like this, he felt utterly bereft as if he were the one separated from a loved one by the wide chasm of death.

"Shall we go back now, Your Grace?" she said quietly. "Does Isabella know?"

"No, but she and the others must be told."

She nodded and turned to walk slowly up the cold nave of the dim chapel. She shivered as though ghosts crowded in upon her warmth—not of poor love-smitten Rosamonde, but ghosts of memory she must keep close to her now she was losing them all: father, mother, Edmund, Anne, even Morcar—now everyone here she would leave behind in England would be mere ghosts of reminiscence too. Thomas Holland would take her away to some place called Pont-Audemer in Normandy, among the hostile French, the king had said. In her room tonight, smothered in her pillow where Constantia would not hear, she would cry for them all.

She was not even aware the prince had followed her to the

door and lifted her at first. He carried no lamp now. The snow had ceased. The whole world lay before them deep black and silent white. Despite her resolve to be bravely alone, she held tightly to his broad shoulders and rested her cheek against his beating heart all the way back in the cold, dark night.

Chapter Fourteen

Edward, Prince of Wales, trailing four friends, two falconers, six hunt hounds, three squires, and his exhausted minstrel Roger Wakeley at his muddy heels, slammed open the door to his private solar at his country palace of Kennington and stamped in from hours of hawking in the cold January air. The prince, Nickolas Dagworth, and Hugh Calveley threw themselves into chairs clustered around the table near the fire while servants hovered to pour them heated wine. The cold, wet dogs, which had been madly retrieving felled heron and partridges all afternoon, flopped panting near the hearth. The prince drained the wine and immediately extended his flagon for more.

"Saints' blood, my lord prince, but you have set us a hellfire pace these last few weeks," Nick Dagworth observed and then coughed into his leather sleeve. "Hunting at dawn, hawking immediately after, and jousting bouts."

"Can you not keep up anymore, my friend?" the prince countered, no tone of jest in his strident voice at all. "How in hell shall we beat the French again when we go back there next year if you cannot keep up with a little winter gaming? More wine here, squire."

While their servants scraped their boot soles, Dagworth and Calveley exchanged a quick, worried glance. Something was driving their prince hard and they were in turn driven to keep up with him. They had come to this little countryside castle outside London almost a month ago and there had not been a moment's respite since. Dagworth had caught a chest cold he could not shake and even though the weather was mild for late January and the snow had melted to ruts of frozen mud, he always felt chilled. This breakneck pace had them all yawning in corners and nodding over dinner in the early evening. And when everyone else faded, the prince amused himself to all hours of the night, his minstrel Roger had said, with the voluptuous new maid Bethany whose father was a small landowner in this area.

Only very recently had His Grace seemed to become a real womanizer, Nick Dagworth thought as he was wracked by another coughing fit. Really, it was from about the time of the Garter Ceremony last spring when he had started to sow his wild oats here and there at whim, apparently never really favoring one particular maid for long. There had been that one woman Katharine de Vere who had borne His Grace a bastard son and now lived at Berkhamstead in the prince's household there, but lately it was a new maid every fortnight. By the rood, Nick Dagworth liked a willing woman to warm his bed as well as anyone, but at this rate, he would just as soon pass by a little sweetmeat like the raven-haired Bethany St. Clair, who no doubt awaited her prince all hot and ready in the adjoining room. At that thought, the violent hacking seized Nick again; then he wheezed until his eyes watered.

Prince Edward was pacing in front of the fireplace, tossing scraps of meat to the tired hunt hounds when Nick got control of himself. "That sounds worse, Nick. Best hie yourself off to bed."

"Well, if you would not mind, Your Grace. I do not think I could stand another marathon tourney at backgammon 'til all hours, though I probably will not sleep a wink with this wretched chest and throat."

"Not sleep a wink—aye, my man, I know how that is," the prince observed, his voice more subdued than it had been of late. He leaned his hands on the marble mantel and put one booted foot up on an andiron. "Just drink a lot of wine, Nick—a lot, and then hope you drop off before you have to start jumping up to the chamber pot all night."

"I thought perhaps your secret remedy for sleepless nights

was a hearty roll with a lass like the black-haired Bethany in there," Hugh Calveley chuckled and nodded toward the door to the luxurious sleeping quarters. "By the Virgin, Your Grace, at least you have her trained well to not come traipsing out here to scold us for being gone all day and now making all this ruckus. What a lucky rogue to have her right where you want her waiting!"

Hugh and Prince Edward laughed while Nick coughed and then swigged enough wine to temporarily soothe his raw throat. To have her right where you want her waiting, the words echoed through the prince's frenzied thoughts. These last two weeks—since he had heard Jeannette was to be married on the last day of January, tomorrow—such a desire as that haunted him, tortured him on a rack of exquisite memory and desire. To have Jeannette right where he wanted her waiting for him, even as the voluptuous, clinging Bethany no doubt awaited him on the other side of that door.

He had tried everything to drive these thoughts of Jeannette away: hours of penance on his knees in the chapel while his friends thought he prayed for deliverance of England from the plague; hours, days of violent physical exertion to check the longing; mental exhaustion in reading, chess, backgammon; two weeks of nights of wallowing between Bethany St. Clair's soft, white thighs. But he could not shake the grip of panic he had never felt before, the stark fear that he, Edward, Prince of Wales, was losing something he wanted desperately and could not have. He would almost call this feeling for Jeannette hate, if he were not so afraid it was love.

Annoyed his thoughts might show on his face, he spun away and bid his entourage a curt good-night over his shoulder. At the door to the bedchamber he turned back to summon Roger Wakeley and his favorite squire Leonard with a flick of his wrist. Fully aware of the taut rein on their lord's temper, they hastened to follow him, nearly tripping over the hounds which evidently had the same idea. Roger

Wakeley and Leonard shoved the eager dogs back and closed the door behind themselves.

Once in the luxuriously decorated chamber, Leonard darted to help the prince divest himself of his garments, a task he had already begun by peeling off his *surcote*, jerkin, and shirt and tossing them back behind him on a chair as he stood at the hearth seemingly mesmerized by its flames. The prince's naked upper torso gleamed like polished marble in the firelight, a fact obviously of great interest to the woman who sat waiting in the canopied bed across the room, her ebony raven locks tumbling loose. All of the women the prince had taken as brief liaisons since last spring had had black or red or brown hair, Leonard mused, as he knelt near the hearth to pull off His Grace's boots. And here, he had been certain once His Grace had only favored the more blond and fair damsels.

"My lord prince, I am so happy you are not so very late tonight," Bethany St. Clair's smooth voice floated from the bed to the prince's distracted mind. "You have been gone, you know, since before dawn this morn."

The crooning tone suddenly annoyed him. Why must women cozen and wheedle? he fumed. Why could they never be like a man and just come out with it to say what they thought? "I know well enough what time I left, *demoiselle*," he returned curtly and stood rock-still, both fists on the mantel while Leonard scrubbed him with lint dipped in water of bergamot.

Roger Wakeley, without waiting to be instructed, had begun to strum a tune on his lute, a pensive melody to fit his master's mood. Let the others around this powerful prince who were supposedly so familiar with him fret and whisper as to what strange malady rode their lord so hard, Roger mused, as he shifted smoothly to another tune. He knew, he who had made his way in the world of the powerful these last ten years by supplying King Edward with whatever it was he would like to know. *Sacrebleu*, he knew more of what ailed this proud Plantagenet prince, perhaps, than the man himself would admit or even recognize. Tomorrow at eventide, on the last day of January, at Eltham Manor forty miles from here, Joan of Kent was to wed Sir Thomas Holland.

Roger's fingers rippled a smooth series of plaintive chords between songs. Aye, he would wager his best lute that was it, and on a sudden impulse, he decided to test his theory. When the prince was at his moodiest and alone, he had oft requested a sad lay of unrequited love, "*Li Dous Cossiere*." He would sing it for him now and watch the fine profile, etched by fireglow, he could observe so easily from here. Whether by tears or sorrowful sighs, Roger would know for certain what grieved the prince.

He began the lyrics low, nearly whispering, picturing in his own mind's eye how grief-stricken both the prince and Lady Joan had looked on their parting a month ago at Woodstock in the snow. She, of course, had only just learned two days before that her brother Edmund, who had ordered Roger to leave Liddell years ago, and his lady wife were dead of plague, so her suffering was understandable. But, *sacrebleu*, if those others had just watched the prince's face as closely as he had—

> "Alas, parting is grounds of woe,
> Other song I cannot sing.
> But why part I my lady from,
> Since love was cause of our meeting?
> The bitter tears of her weeping
> Mine heart has pierced so mortally,
> That to the death it will me bring
> If I not see her hastily."

The prince listened, frozen to a rigid stance before the flickering fire. Then, his big, tawny-maned head pivoted, and his eyes glittered coldly like cut aquamarine stones. "I asked not for that song now! I did not bid you sing that one. Get out, both of you, and leave me alone!"

He should have expected that sort of reaction, Roger scolded himself. The skilled game of reading royal moods he thought he played exceedingly well, but he had slightly misjudged here and was pleased enough to escape unscathed as he carried his instrument before him to beat a quick retreat with the worried Leonard on his heels.

"But, my lord prince, you are hardly alone," the beauteous Bethany's voice came to Roger Wakeley's ears as he shut the door behind him.

"I hardly meant you, pet," the prince said gruffly, but he did not look her way. He fought very hard to beat down the fluttering wings of agonized loss so new to him, this damned suffocating feeling that he had to see Jeannette, touch her again.

Bethany stirred on the bed behind him, and he slowly turned to see her pull the coverlet down to provocatively bare her nude, alabaster body to her knees. There, he assured himself—there was a way he could bury this strangling need again and get control of his thoughts and life.

He padded over to the deep bed, the warmth of firelight retreating from his naked body. His feet felt warmer standing on this deep pile Persian carpet, his knees braced along the silken bed sheets as he leaned over her. She smiled up at him and ran a pink tip of tongue over her lips. She moaned and separated her knees ever so slightly and ran the palms of her hands up her ribs to grasp her lush, pointed breasts as if to offer them to him.

He felt his loins tighten as he knelt on the bed over her. Her hair black as midnight fanned across the silk sheets white as snow. He closed his eyes as he leaned into her soft body. Midnight and snow and Jeannette in his arms at Woodstock. Jeannette anywhere. Here!

He could see now the sweeping rush of scenes. Jeannette in his arms in the snow. Jeannette moaning, writhing under him on the straw of the stables that day he meant to punish her, but now she always punished him. Jeannette's beautiful body beckoned as she stood in that moonlit diaphanous gown in the windswept cottage by the sea at Calais the first night he took her.

Jeannette stroked up his thighs to caress his rigid manhood while he moaned low. She guided him into her waiting warmth, moving up to meet him, her arms pulling him down to begin the wild, rocking motion of a horse galloping in battle, a ship storm-tossed on cresting waves. He wanted, he needed her like this, submitting, giving, yearning for him even as he did for her. His heart pounded in his chest as he conquered her only to collapse, panting for air and sanity along her glistening, satin flesh. His facial muscles relaxed as his lips lifted in a drowsy smile. His eyes opened slowly.

It was like a smack of cold water in his face. The waking dream shattered. He was off the woman Bethany St. Clair in an instant.

"By lord prince, what is it? What have I done? Please, my lord!"

He ignored her and shook his head to clear the cobwebs. He was too tired. He was ill like Nick to be caught by a mere trick of his brain's fantasy. He had taken this woman, coupled with her here just now, and told himself it was Jeannette. Hell's gates, but he was no court magician or dreaming troubador to believe such fantasies. His minstrel Roger Wakeley—aye, that would do for an excuse! He had to be somehow free of Jeannette or he would go mad!

He wrapped himself in a black velvet robe and thrust his feet in felt slippers while the woman cowered wide-eyed on the bed. In the last moment because he either took pity on her or wanted her silence, he turned to her and said, "It is nothing you did, Bethany. It is not you at all," and stalked from the room leaving the door ajar behind him.

His comrades had all gone to their own beds, and the solar fire burned low. His favorite hunt hound, Rook, stared up at him with luminous eyes but, when she recognized him, flopped back down. He yanked the door to the hall open, startling the two guards on duty and waking a dozing linkboy.

"Stay!" he ordered them all as though they were hunt dogs too. He strode down the corridor alone, grabbed a low-burning torch and hurried down the corkscrew staircase to the chambers beneath where the servants bedded. Another linkboy dozed, amazingly upright on his feet as they were so adept at doing.

"Knave, awake! Fetch me Roger Wakeley, my minstrel."

The boy jumped like a puppet on a string, shocked to see his lord prince in a robe in the servants' hall in the dead of night. "Aye! Aye, milord, Your Grace," he managed and scampered two doors down to disappear into a room.

Roger Wakeley came out instantly, alert, a quill in his hands. The prince wondered what he had been writing so late at night. "Composing new love songs, minstrel?" he asked gruffly.

"In a way, Your Grace," the man replied in his smooth French accent, hoping the prince would not sense his alarm. "*Sacrebleu*, thoughts of love in new-written songs or otherwise know no rest."

The two stared at each other, Wakeley short and soft-looking and the prince so tall and angularly lean. Wakeley's heart began to beat noticeably harder; he gripped the quill pen in his ink-stained hand until he felt the shaft bend. Perhaps he had overstepped here tonight. And if the prince ever guessed he had been penning his monthly report to King Edward on his observations of his beloved, supposedly trusted son, whatever would be his fate then?

"I am riding to Eltham at dawn on the morrow and you are going with me." The prince interrupted his nervous musings.

"Aye, Your Grace. And the others?"

"Just two other guards. I mean to travel fast and light."

"I see."

"You do not see at all, minstrel. Pack your things because we shall be attending a wedding there and you are my gift to the bride."

Roger Wakeley's mouth dropped open before he could cover his surprise.

"Well, man, do not just stand there like a simpleton. Aye, I am speaking of your little music student, Lady Joan of Kent. I will expect you to serve her well and honorably, or I swear I shall string you up by your own lute strings."

The musician cleared his throat. The king had told him he was to stay with the prince's household and had gone to a lot of trouble to have his mother, the deposed Queen Isabella, offer his services to the prince. But now, if he was to be off at some moated Norman castle with Joan of Kent—

"Well? Do not just gape at me, man. Is there a problem? I will have the lady know I wish her all happiness in her new endeavor, and she obviously has favored your sweet services for longer than I care to know."

"May I have leave to speak, Your Grace."

"Say on."

"You, of course, know that she was indeed my student, and I still regard her only as a young maid."

"She has obviously grown up, minstrel. That is why I stressed *honorable* service."

"That is my point, an' it please Your Grace," Wakeley floundered. "It would be entirely honorable. *Sacrebleu*, I vow this on my mother's soul."

"And I vow to you I shall kill you myself if that should not be true, so what is your point? I will see you are paid well. And if her new lord does not favor your presence, you will be protected because of me."

Roger Wakeley's brown eyes opened wider. Was he then to be a sort of distraction for her to keep her affections from her new husband? Did the prince, whether he realized it or not, desire such a service—aye, honorable, of course, but it had been obvious how the woman's affections had been stirred by his appearance at Woodstock during the Yuletide celebration. He was hardly prepared, however, for the twist of fate the prince's final words added.

"And, Wakeley, by St. George, I am glad to know you can

write, for if I ever wish it, I shall want communication from you concerning the events, the happenings, her safety, *et cetera*, in Normandy."

It was a moment before Roger Wakeley managed a reply. "An informant, my lord prince?" he whispered low, hoping he looked appropriately surprised. "You wish an informant?"

"By the rood, I hardly meant a spy," the prince answered, his voice raised to its normal resonant tone that anyone lurking about, including that doltish-looking linkboy, could hear. "It is only that there may be times when—letters may be welcomed, that is all. Be packed and set to ride at dawn then." The prince turned and strode away with the quick-footed linkboy lighting his steps.

Roger Wakeley looked down to see he had splintered his feather quill and splattered his whole hand with ink. He leaned his round shoulder on the wall. The prince was not inherently deceitful like his sire, but how ludicrous that they both expected him to spy and report on people they supposedly loved. *Sacrebleu*, the twists and tangles of it all fairly boggled one's mind. He hoped he could signal the king that the necessary transfer of his services was about to occur before he became a wedding gift for the first time in his rather checkered career. After all, one of the things he was supposed to report to His Majesty had concerned the prince's apparent entanglement with the willful and somehow dangerous little maid from Kent.

Ah, exile with that sweet, but unpredictable lady in the beautiful French Norman countryside of his birth, Roger mused. After all, what more joyous assignment could one poor minstrel-informer hope to fall heir to? He shook his head and chuckled as he went back into his room to pack.

The last day of January, 1350, the day of her wedding to Sir Thomas Holland, winged by like a dream which Joan observed but felt no part of. The festivities were to be limited and modest, for the wretched plague was still upon the land

and the little chapel at Eltham Manor in Kent where the king and queen resided would have to do for the ceremony, and the narrow, high-beamed hunt hall for the bridal banquet. Perhaps because of the dangerous times, or perhaps, Joan thought, to punish her further for her indiscretions, the Princess Isabella had not been allowed to accompany her from Woodstock, though Her Grace had ranted for two days to think she would miss the fun of a wedding to break the tedium of her cloistered life. But Joan's twenty-year-old brother John, now the new lord of Liddell Manor, had come and there was solace in that.

Thomas Holland was in a soaring mood at his victory in winning her hand over William Montacute, Lord Salisbury, who was, after all, from a much older, nobler family than the Hollands. Joan knew the affront Queen Philippa had given Thomas—marrying his betrothed to Salisbury while Thomas was recuperating at his castle in Lancashire—had been a blow to some sort of ties he secretly cherished to the queen's affections. Saints, what did such well-tended, secret passions matter anyway, Joan told herself with a shrug. If it would comfort Thomas later, she might even tell him that it was his bride's fault Philippa was angry enough to marry her to Salisbury and not his. No doubt, over the years in some little French walled castle when bygones were far gone, there would be time for such explanations. But in these past hurried three days leading to the wedding today, there was time for nothing but forced smiles, fabricated gratitude, and the discipline of rigid obedience.

At least, dear Marta would be going to live in France with her instead of some of these snide, clumsy maids who served the queen, Joan told herself, as she was dressed and coifed for the late afternoon ceremony in the chapel. Glenna seemed to knot tangles in her hair instead of combing them out, and Eleanora tended to wrinkle skirts and sleeves.

She would have liked to show them all, mayhap wear that flashy, beribboned garter dress the king had torn. Then, when the queen scolded her for her wild appearance, she would recite for them all the whole story right before the very altar in the chapel. She sighed as they adjusted the wreath of ivy she had insisted on wearing in her loose hair. There were no flowers to be had this time of year, and ivy did garnish the coat of arms of the house of the deceased Edmund of Kent and his wife the Lady Margaret. Someday, she vowed silently, as she turned slowly to let them adjust her veil and lead her downstairs, her sons would sport the deer and ivy family crest every bit as proudly as the arms of Thomas Holland!

The little crowd waiting at the foot of the newel staircase hushed at the sight of her. She looked breathtaking—calm, poised, endowed with an uncharacteristic serenity which today made her somehow ethereal, untouchable. Her ivory brocade kirtle with scalloped hem brushed her slippered feet when she glided forward and molded itself longingly to her slender waist and full breasts and hips. The sleeves, tightly buttoned with pearls from elbow to wrist, dripped delicate liripipes of ermine-edged white velvet. The bodice was a scalloped oval which accentuated her graceful shoulders, fluted collarbones, and the barely visible upper thrust of her breasts. The traditional gauzy veil swept back shoulder length from the crown of ivy, offsetting the full wavy abundance of her loosed maidenly hair that fell in a shimmering curtain to her hips.

Her brother John swallowed hard in a sudden stab of emotion and stepped forward to take her arm. His height continued to amaze her, for she had not been around him except these three days and then the week Mother had died ever so long ago. He had grown to be so tall—and a stranger. She curtsied to the gangly, ten-year-old Prince John of Ghent, suddenly grateful she would not have to face the Prince of Wales who was at Kennington near London. She smiled up at John, Lord of Liddell, as they wended their way through the admiring crowd to the outer courtyard. No, she could not have borne facing Edward, Prince of Wales, today.

The lengthy ceremony blurred by, parts in sonorous Latin, parts in delicate French. Not realizing she did so, she held Thomas Holland's hand very tightly during the ceremony until he squeezed her hand back happily and she noted what she did. Let him think she was joyous or nervous or whatever, she thought, for she felt none of those things, only, mayhap, impatience to have it all over and be rid of the Plantagenet court for good.

Sir Thomas Holland, garter knight, looked resplendent in his garments of buff satin with the velvet blue Order of the Garter robe draped over his broad shoulders. His one sharp bronze eye took her all in when she darted him a glance. His hair gleamed burnished copper in the glow of altar candles. He was placing the ring on her finger now, a filigreed gold band which echoed his larger, crested signet ring. The metal felt cold at first. She stared again at the white-robed priest as he offered them the communion cup. On the altar behind rested the sacred reliquary boxes the queen had brought here from Windsor hoping to stay the hand of plague with such holy treasures: a stone which had touched St. Stephen, a skull piece of St. Thomas, and, some even whispered, a piece of unicorn horn which was known to be a powerful antidote to poison.

Were the Plantagenets expecting her to try to poison them, Joan's mind taunted. "*Ave Maria, mater dei, gracia plena,*" the chanted words swirled around her. She stared into the altar candles, her thoughts drifting, seeing Prince Edward's face that last night she had been with him in the tiny stone chapel of the poor, love-lost Rosamonde. That was when he told her Edmund and Anne were dead, and now, he might as well be too.

When she started to cry soundlessly, her new husband was touched and the audience murmured approval. Then it was over and they rushed out through the courtiers into bleak January sunshine in the cobbled courtyard of the manor.

As everyone shouted congratulations, the king and queen approached to wish her well. Philippa, looking plump and tired, for Joan had heard her ladies whisper she had greatly suffered from dropsy lately, bent to kiss Joan's cheek and give her muted blessings.

"Thank you, Your Grace," Joan replied properly while Thomas Holland beamed and stammered an effusive reply which she hardly noted.

"This is all for the best, my dear child," Philippa said, turning to Joan again. "When next we see you and my Lord Thomas, I expect to greet a family of young Hollands, too."

"We shall do our utmost to comply, Your Grace," Thomas boasted as they walked in to dinner in the Great Hall. "And if there should be a maid child, we shall call her Philippa for the fairest queen in Christendom."

The king nodded, smiled, commented, his watchful eyes on Joan as they all entered the hall to muted, then swelling applause from the revelers. When Holland turned away a moment to tell the queen of his lands in Normandy he hoped she would come to visit someday, the king stepped forward and tapped Joan's arm with one big finger.

"You have been magnificent today, Lady Holland."

For a moment Joan was startled at the use of her new title. "My Lord Holland is very happy, my lord king, and I shall do my best to see that he is rightly so."

The tawny eyebrows raised and the distinctive Plantagenet mouth under the full mustache quirked up in surprise. "St. George, an obedient wife, a blessing to any man. Perhaps you shall find French exile suits you then."

There, he had said it, Joan thought, and took the challenge whether he had intended it as such or not. "I rather look forward to it, Your Grace, since I apparently am too outspoken to suit court etiquette here. And after all, sometimes exile can bring favor and profit as in the case of that villain de Maltravers living so splendidly in Bruges."

The king's brow furrowed and his cheeks went beet red. He turned away quickly rather than let his queen or the now-attentive Thomas Holland hear his reply. By the rood, that wild little hoyden was a thorn in his side! The maid's brazen courage quite boggled the mind, but then, that business with her father had been unfortunate—sad even. His fond fool of an uncle should never have stirred up trouble about an inquiry into his royal father's murder at the hands of Mortimer and de Maltravers, just as this troublesome female should never have riled the royal waters. But, by the rood, he had outfoxed her now. Years abroad with a stolid, loyal man like Holland and a passel of sons to rear would tame her for certain and take the tempting bloom off that lush face and sensual body. Unaware his suddenly bleak mood had unsettled the crowd, King Edward slumped, preoccupied, into his chair before even seating his queen. The wedding feast, such as it was, began.

Rainbow-hued, candied flower petals, traditional at bridal feasts, led off each course. Seethed pike in claret, venison, and roast forest boar were the mainstays of the meal while side dishes offered by hovering ushers included jellied eggs, custard flawns, and waffles with jellies. Much to Joan's relief, as the meal stretched on under Philippa's benign smile and the king's flowering glare, there were no colossal final pastries or ornate subtleties to stuff the feasters. Roast chestnuts, dates, cheeses, and more of the continual flow of candied flower petals and wines concluded the meal.

When, at last, the bridal couple rose for the first dance, Joan's spirits had revived a bit, and she was grateful to stretch her legs. She and Thomas held hands and sidestepped through an arch of hands and arms in the traditional bridal circle, going the whole circumference of it before the others, laughing and applauding, could join in. More torches were lighted in the hall. Joan danced with the guests and Thomas did too. She whirled faster, laughing giddily, now anxious to have time drag its feet by moving hers so quickly, resolutely shoving aside thoughts of the wedding night to come in the room they had given her and Thomas upstairs.

The musicians crowded into the entryway ceased their quick music. Shuffling feet and laughter died to utter silence. Everyone craned his head. A horn blared. Joan caught the annoyed face of her husband from across the way, but she saw no one in the entry at which everyone stared. The king could not be retiring already. On the dais near the door from which she watched, Queen Philippa rose unsteadily to her feet.

Then, across the room, towering above the sea of heads and shoulders, Prince Edward entered even as the guard-at-arms droned, "Edward, Duke of Cornwall, Prince of Wales, Plantagenet, comes into court."

There was a moment's hanging hush, then the high-timbered room resounded with cheers and clapping. As the king swaggered over to greet the prince, Joan noted Roger Wakeley stood wide-eyed at the entryway behind those tall Plantagenet men. Only then did she let out a breath, a sigh.

Suddenly, Thomas Holland appeared from somewhere to seize her arm. "This is a surprise, is it not, my love?" Thomas observed amid the din. "By the saints, Joan, your cheeks are abloom with blushes."

"No doubt, my lord," she brazened. "I have been dancing for at least an hour straight, you know." She moved a few steps back to her vacated place at the head table and drank from her wine goblet while Thomas followed to stand first on one foot and then the other.

"We must greet him, of course," he said. "And I am proud my liege lord prince would come, only I believe the king told him to stay put at Kennington or wherever he was. You, naturally, had no inkling he would just appear like this."

"Hardly, my lord. I have not seen or heard from him since the day he told me you had won the little contest at the Vatican to claim me." She sipped more cool wine and stood her ground. The prince had seen her, he was coming, and she felt all queasy, all floaty. Saints, just like that day Isabella had that banquet in Bruges. She feared she might be sick before them all and now on her wedding day! Why did he dare to come here! Could he not pity her even enough to stay away?

318

The prince was obviously in riding garments, leather jerkin, Spanish boots over warm black hose, a short heavy cape. His eyes, his smile, thank the saints, went first to Thomas whom he congratulated warmly. Then the blue eyes pivoted to devour her. She curtsied. He kissed her hand and both cheeks while he felt her tremble under his brief touch. The room sprouted hundreds of eager eyes.

"I meant to be here earlier for the ceremony, Thomas, but my man's horse threw a shoe and Wilifred, as big as he is, carries two more slowly than one."

"Whatever the circumstances, Your Grace, Lady Holland and I are delighted you came."

"Fine. Fine. Then, let the revel-making proceed while I rest and have some wine. I had a few items of business for His Grace so I just rode over and remembered the queen wrote your wedding would be today."

At that comment, the music and dancing began again while Thomas, Joan, and the prince sat at the head table to pretend to watch. Eventually, the prince's crystalline blue eyes linked with Joan's smoky violet gaze again; the impact nearly devastated them both. A deep, deep instantaneous agony of loneliness, of understanding met there and then dissolved as he frowned and looked away.

"St. George, you two, I almost forgot," he said in a rush. "Thomas, for you on this momentous day I have brought a new peregrine falcon bred from my own select stock, well-trained. I sent it up to your room. And for the lady—" He craned his tawny head around and motioned to someone in the crowded room with a flick of a wrist—in that arrogant way of his, Joan thought—that always brought some poor varlet running.

Her old friend, Master Roger Wakeley, beribboned lute in hand, appeared before the three of them and bowed low.

"A song, Your Grace?" she ventured, her voice surprisingly soft in her own ears. "I recall you sent me a song once before."

Thomas Holland's head snapped up. "A joyous wedding song, I am certain, my dear Joan," he added curtly.

"More than a song, Jeannette," the prince said as though Holland had not spoken, as though he did not even exist. "I give you hearty wishes of much joy and peace—and this master minstrel to cheer your hearth in Normandy where I trust my brave comrade in arms, Thomas Holland, will care well for you."

Joan rose half out of her chair. "But, my lord prince, your dear grandmother gave Master Roger's service to you."

"Things cannot always be as one would have them, Lady Holland, and so I bestow him on you as a comfort and a blessing."

"She will have all that indeed anyway, my lord prince," Holland cut in as if to shatter the tenuous moment of which he had no part. He liked this not at all—none of it suddenly. The noisy little pieces of a puzzle clicked together in his sharp mind: the rumors, the king's unease, the prince's devastated, haggard look, and even his new wife's obvious dismay under that high-walled demeanor she could erect at will. By the rood, he could live with it if there had once been something between these two long ago, but he would never consent to rear another man's bastard even if it was the babe of the Prince of Wales to whom he had taken an inviolate oath of allegiance before Crécy! Those two days at Woodstock last month before he had arrived to claim his bride—surely, since the marriage plans had been announced to her, they had not shamed him—not with her brother newly dead.

The prince rose to his feet, patted the minstrel's shoulder and moved quickly around to the other side of the table as if he suddenly sought a barrier to hide behind.

"You will not, I think, see me on the morrow before you set out," he was saying. "I will be closeted much with the king and farewells can be tedious."

The aloof mask, the controlled gaze were all intact now,

Joan marveled as she noted Thomas's doubts buckle under the prince's steely stare. "My Lord Thomas and I go to Liddell, my home in Kent, for a month before we set out for France, Your Grace," Joan replied calmly, but she knew her hands trembled.

"How lovely for you, Jeannette, for I believe you have longed to go home ever since you first came to court over five years ago."

She smiled wistfully at the prince, but both Holland and Roger Wakeley saw her lilac eyes had gone guarded.

"Her home now will be Château Ruisseau in Normandy, Your Grace," Thomas said.

"The name means Brook Castle," the prince went smoothly on, ignoring the intended reminder of Holland's new rights of possession. "It sounds lovely. I shall picture you both there over the years."

His voice had wavered, nearly halted at the last, Roger Wakeley observed, as the prince nodded and turned to walk stiffly away. Roger even felt a sharp, resounding pain within himself. He was sure of it now: the little Joan of Kent was beloved by the prince, a man whom—because of the past of which she had no making—she could never have, and yet, he was quite certain he would never write such to the king.

The evening unwound like a tired coil after that. The prince, never once looking back, left the hall with Queen Philippa. The bridal pair danced a few more dances and then departed, silent, hand in hand.

The little affair of Joan and Edward, star-crossed lovers, was over now, whatever it had been, the pensive minstrel thought. That she had attracted, mayhap won, the heart of the greatest prince in all Christendom should not surprise him, for had he not seen a unique promise in her much as had that old wizard Morcar from her maidenhood home at Liddell?

But, *sacrebleu*, her story as it stood was not unique, for many who loved were parted to wed with others. Still, he

321

thought, mayhap the Lady Joan's story was not yet ended with her prince, for did one not sense that the very ends of the earth could not avail to keep those two apart?

As the hall's torches were extinguished and the room stood empty, the minstrel sat, at last, in the prince's vacated chair and consoled his own melancholy musings with a hopeful song of unquenchable love.

Chapter Fifteen

Joan of Kent, Lady Holland, stretched her legs across the woolen blanket upon which her two copper-haired sons played happily. The late afternoon of this spring day was so beautiful, all bathed in gentle, warming sunshine and wafted by a delicate breeze fragrant with newly plowed fields, budded bushes, and fruit trees. Thomas, her eldest boy, born the first year of her marriage, chatted a singsong lyric to himself and, temporarily content, bounced his carved wooden knights and horses on the blanket. John, the babe born only three months ago, was content to lie on his back, gurgling and kicking his chubby legs as he watched his older brother. Joan sighed in a poignant rush of love. Hard work, dedication, two years already in this lovely area of Normandy, two sons, a busy, stalwart husband: aye, she was content enough.

Her violet eyes skimmed the Holland castle, Château Ruisseau, set in its surrounding moat, forests, and rolling farmlands. It was not a large castle by any means, but it was grander than her maidenhood home of Liddell, and somewhat finer, too, now that they had worked so hard to improve it in the short time they had lived here. The protective blue-green moat, fed by a brook which was an estuary of the River Risle, reflected the tall stone outer walls, drawbridge, and twin tall outer gate-houses. Inside the stone curtain, the outer ward was grassy and even shady from the few newly planted Linden trees so common in this province of France. Across that ward rose the inner walls of the castle itself guarded by the towering stone sentinels of the inner gatehouses. The southwest upper tower room boasted a ghost which wailed at night, so the guards said, but Joan had never wanted to pursue that nonsense. Besides, she thought grimly, she was haunted quite enough by her own memories at times and sought no other ghosts.

She flopped back on the grass and stretched her arms luxuriously wide. The perfect cup of sky seemed to be painted eggshell blue all feathered by wisps of delicate, lace clouds. Her back hurt from all the bending she had been doing all morning in the castle's huge undercroft where the spare, precious spices were locked away as well as extra plateware, jewels, and bolts of cloth. She had decided all of a sudden today to rearrange the heavy, locked spice boxes, and her skirts and hands smelled of a strange scrambled scent of ginger, cinnamon, mace, pepper, cloves, and saffron.

Then she had overseen the all-day task of sweeping out the winter rushes strewn about the seven bedrooms the household seldom used; looked in on the scullions scrubbing the work tables in the buttery, pantry, and bolting rooms; and supervised the new plantings of the herb and green gardens in the outer ward to the northeast. This hour at least, until her Lord Thomas rode in from riding circuit of the *demesne* as he was wont to do frequently in these tenuous times between England and France, was all hers with just the babes to worry about.

She pictured Château Ruisseau as she had first seen it when Thomas had brought her here as a bride only two years and a month ago—yet forever. The lofty battlemented walls softened by the fringe of grassy greens, the gemlike moat, and surrounding forests had quickened her heavy-laden heart on that morn she had first beheld it as nothing had for a long time—except one man, and she never thought on that when she could help it.

How vast the place had seemed to her and Marta then, though compared with mazelike Windsor or Westminster, it was but a shepherd's cottage. How grateful she had been for all the work it took to set it aright, to occupy her mind and body, and exhaust her so she slept at night when her amorous, possessive lord rolled off her and slumbered heavily at her side in the silence of their comfortable solar bedchamber.

Marta had lived only a year, long enough to see little Thomas born and get the wee bonny lass she had long been a mother to started in her new life, and then, as if too old or tired to live on in a third country after her beloved Scotland and adopted England, she had simply, quietly died in her sleep one night.

Another sigh escaped Joan's parted lips, for she missed the old scolding woman so terribly at times she thought her heart would wrench awry. How quickly people came and went, just like those wisps of clouds up there. Marta gone, old Morcar, mother, her brother Edmund and his Anne, a father she had never even known, others who might as well be dead like the Princess Isabella, and, of course, the prince.

She sat bolt upright and hugged her arms to herself as if she had felt a sudden chill. Surely, it was getting late and Thomas and his men would be clattering in across the drawbridge soon, having given a show of force to the French serfs who owed fealty to the Hollands since the English conquests the year of Crécy. It was rumored now there might be another English campaign into France to win more soil back for the rightful Plantagenet owners. She hoped an English army never came through here, but then, if it did, she would at least be able to hear some news from London and not be so out of touch.

Just as she knelt to gather up the babe and wrap little Thomas's toys in the blanket, she heard the rumble of horses. "Your sire is back, Thomas. See! See Papa on his horse!"

The toddler squealed and laughed as Thomas Holland reined in while his party of guards funneled noisily across the wooden bridge into the outer ward.

"Ho, *ma belle*!" Thomas greeted her. "Out here alone with the two little knaves? Not a good idea, Joan, I have told you that before."

"We are fine, my lord. Madeleine was here with us but I sent her back in and Master Roger has a spring cold. You did not find any trouble, I pray."

"Nary a hitch except for serfs' continual complaining, and the barleycorn plantings are in the south fields. Here, let me take the lad in on Midnight then. What is for supper?"

"Mackerel, frumenty with simnel biscuits, and your favorite custard flawns."

"By the rood, that sounds fine. I swear, love, I could eat a horse!"

"Horse, Papa, horse!" little Thomas echoed as his father lifted him up on the big saddle. The boy's wide copper eyes fixed on the hilt of his father's long sword which he tried to grab.

Thomas trotted his horse alongside Joan as she carried the babe and the sack of toys in over the drawbridge. Her Lord Thomas had been in a soaring mood of late since she had weaned the second babe and her time of tenderness after his birth had passed. Now her body was his again at night after a respite when it was quite untouched. She did not mind, of course. She was fully used to it now and accepted the fact that the sweeping ecstasy she had known with another man had only been a passionate dream, a bittersweet reminder of something haunting gone forever. She felt affection for Thomas Holland, and a warm glow of contentment that he desired her and found pleasure in her. For that—and the babes—she would be eternally content.

How dim and faded, she mused, seemed that violent, engulfing rapture that had once devoured her with a man. Like the muted, wavering reflections in the moat, such foolish longings merely rippled through her memory and passed away.

In the cobbled inner ward surrounded on three sides by the castle's living and working quarters, Thomas reined in and dismounted. A groom appeared from the stables beyond the chapel to lead Midnight away, and the little family

walked through the arched entryway emblazoned above
with both the Holland crest and the deer and ivy coat of arms
of Joan's family.

In their Great Hall they could already smell the mingled,
delicious odors of supper cooking from the adjoining
kitchen. Although supper in the great houses of the realms of
England or France usually lasted from four to six of an
afternoon, here at Château Ruisseau, they usually dined
upstairs at their solar table while Roger Wakeley played the
lute and sang. Only when there were holy days or infrequent
guests—English knights passing through with news, messengers from Joan's brother John at Liddell, or from
Thomas Holland's lands in Lancashire, or even the monthly
traveling troubadors who passed through to visit Roger
Wakeley and entertain for a night—only then did they sup at
the long table on the dais in the hall.

Madeleine, the children's plump, stolid nurse appeared to
take her babe off to his little bed and Vinette Brinay, the red-
haired, freckled village girl Joan had elevated to the position
of her head lady's maid since Marta had died, appeared to
drop a sprightly curtsy despite her arms being full of newly
folded linen towels.

"Milord Holland. Madame. I was almost done with the
Madame Joan's sewing and Lynette says supper's to table
soon," Vinette told them.

"By the rood, I hope so," Thomas groused. "I am starved.
And tell Lynette to see the men are all fed heartily after that
jaunt out all day. And I saw Pierre Foulke this morn, girl—
that one so sweet on you whom I had to send away last week
from all his lollygagging about the premises."

Vinette's brown eyes lit in her attractive, blushing face,
and she smiled gap-toothed. "*Oui*? And did he say aught of
me my lord?"

"A bit. I told him to cease his damned rabble-rousing
speeches about the workers demanding fewer taxes and to
hie himself back to his workshop. Good tanners are aplenty
in this region and if he does not increase his output, I swear I

shall replace him."

"My Lord Thomas," Joan interjected, "Vinette hardly is a part of your dealings with young Master Pierre, the tanner."

"No, lady, of course, only she ought to be a settling influence on him if she sees him or ever hopes to wed with him—*with* my permission."

"The maid is much too young, my lord. Go on now, Vinette, and we shall be up directly. And stop to tell Master Wakeley he need not play lute at table if he is not much recovered from his chill."

The girl opened her mouth to reply but decided against it, and holding her newly pressed towels too tightly to her small breasts, she curtsied again and hurried up the stairs which connected the corridor outside the Great Hall to the upper balcony joining the main upstairs bedrooms. They both watched the maid disappear around the curve of stone staircase while Thomas joggled their toddler in his arms.

"Much too young," Thomas repeated, picking up the thread of conversation as if there had been no interruption. "St. Peter's bones, madame, you were also much too young when you came to court at Windsor, and that did not stop you from involvements here and there with roving rogues."

"Including you, my lord, so let us say no more on that," she shot back, amused he had dared to refer to the Prince of Wales as a roving rogue. "I do not need scoldings about the past. That is all water over the mill dam now."

"I pray so, Joan, continually."

Little Thomas looked from one parent's face to the other as their voices became increasingly tense; yet he nestled quietly in his sire's arms. Joan patted the boy's back and started upstairs while her husband clumped up close behind. She had no desire to begin to discuss the past now or ever: it was a topic they assiduously avoided on both sides like the plague as if they had a truce on that potentially volatile Pandora's box. But once Thomas fastened on his chastising tone, he was not easily dissuaded.

"I think you coddle Wakeley, too," he said from behind

her as they reached the hall which connected their solar chamber and the five best bedrooms of the castle.

"I coddle anyone in my charge when they are ill, including you, Thomas," Joan replied, refusing to rise to the taunt. She knew Master Roger's attentive concern for her well-being and happiness puzzled and annoyed her husband, but there was never any need for concern. Sometimes, she almost thought Thomas wanted some excuse to throw the minstrel out, but the fact the prince had given the man's services to them as a gift always stayed his final surge of temper. Then, too, she sometimes suspected the occasional visitors who knew Master Roger might also know the prince's servants, but she had never dared to ask. If so, perhaps Thomas knew it and held to his silence for that.

While Thomas deposited their son on the hearth rug and went behind the heavy tapestried curtain to use the privy *garde-robe* chamber, Joan surveyed the dinner arrangements. The long, polished oak table was set with plateware for two and she would feed little Thomas after they had finished since he had eaten before they went outside. Budded forsythia on branches she and Vinette had cut added a touch of beauty and grace to the comfortable chamber. There was a tall sideboard laden with pewter and silver plate on the far wall near the table and four soft-cushioned chairs stood by the hearth. A sewing table and frames for her four French maids rested by the larger of the two windows which even now caught the setting sun to wash the room in golden light.

She had slowly, painstakingly surrounded herself with beauty in this room, her sanctuary and her refuge. The two deep-pile Persian carpets, one a wedding gift from the Princess Isabella, were deepest blue and four tapestries, each of a different season of the year, graced the stone walls. The big canopied and curtained feather bed far across the long room was covered in gold brocade to match the chair cushions and even the ribbons of Joan's precious lute which held a place of honor on the tall coffer in the corner. The ransom money Thomas had won from his captives at Crécy had allowed these lovely touches of luxury here and in a few other select rooms throughout their home.

They had merely sat to dinner, waited on by two sewers and a kitchen maid who oversaw the transport of food upstairs, when their butler entered unannounced. He carried on a silver tray the wine bottles with which he was entrusted and for which his position in the complicated feudal household had been titled.

"You are late, man, and I am damned thirsty after all that riding today," Lord Thomas began.

"My Lord Holland, *pardon, si'l vous plaît*," the dour French servant whom Joan never really trusted, intoned, "but there is a visitor, a sort of messenger passing through, from your country, I take it."

Joan's eyes darted up and her heart thudded as it always did, quite unbidden, when news of the world outside encroached upon her moated sanctuary here.

Thomas Holland's mouth was full of simnel biscuits dripping with thick honey. "Below? Another of Wakeley's singing friends?" he choked out.

"No, my lord, *pardon*, some sort of messenger *certainement*. And attached to the English court, I might wager, because—"

"Court? Messenger? Well, bring him up, man, and get some more food from the kitchens then!"

Joan calmly, deliberately spooned up a bite of custard flawn, but stopped with it halfway to her mouth. "My lord, this could not mean a summons to arms, could it? All the rumors about a new English war, even the peasant unrest hereabouts might indicate such."

Thomas shook his copper-hued head of hair and hastily wiped his mustached mouth with the small, damp linen cloth Joan always insisted he kept at table for spills and neatness. He glanced over at his eldest son playing happily before the low-burning hearth fire and rose to his feet to greet his guest. His single sharp eye conveyed his excitement, Joan thought, at the prospect of some sign he had not been forgotten by his beloved English Queen Philippa for whom he secretly tended some unspoken bond—and by her royal Plantagenet husband.

The wiry, black-haired visitor they greeted hardly looked a messenger, for they were usually strong and burly. Short, with a hooked nose and darting eyes, he was obviously famished, road-weary, and nervous.

"Milord, Milady Holland. Richard Sidwell, Esquire, at your service. My gracious thanks for receiving me so readily into your beautiful castle. I have been ahorse all day to make it here by dusk. I am sent to Alençon, but I came only two months ago from London bid by Her Gracious Grace, the Princess Isabella."

Joan's amusement at the little man's overabundant use of the fawning word "gracious" sobered to joy and astonishment. "You have seen the Princess Isabella—sent by her?" Joan stammered and came around the long table to join her husband. She saw the expectation go out of Thomas at that bit of knowledge. No doubt, this visitor had nothing to do with Queen Philippa, the king, or the resumption of the French Wars.

"Aye, my gracious lady," the sprightly little man gushed, "for the princess does send her love to you, her dear and gracious friend, and to your Lord Holland and bids me convey to you news of her great victory."

"Her victory?" Joan asked. "Is she to wed?"

"No, no, my gracious lady—just the opposite! She said to convey to you she has escaped another snare—I do have a letter writ by her own scribe to you in my things, gracious lady—and she has gainsaid her royal parents and refused to wed with Bérard d'Albret, son of the great lord, Sire d'Albret of Gascony. The princess said that the Lady Holland, her dearest friend from other adventures, must know of this triumph to share it with her."

"Triumph!" Thomas Holland snorted. "Rubbish, more like—insubordination and foolish headstrong deeds, Joan, of which I am glad to say you at least are well quit of."

Richard Sidwell's dark eyes darted back and forth to drink in the nuances of tension here, spoken or otherwise, between this Garter Knight lord and his so beauteous lady. He had heard of her comeliness of form and face, for rumors that the Fair Maid of Kent had ensnared the Prince of Wales's heart had circulated for several years before her marriage to this man and their departure to live in Normandy on lands newly won at Crécy. But Sidwell had never glimpsed her himself before today, and never dreamed such a thing as ephemeral rumors could be so true. Aye, the lady was fair indeed—breathtakingly awesome.

Her abundant hair which tended to wayward curliness was pulled back in a single braid as thick as a man's wrist, falling down her back to her shapely hips. Those tresses, he mused, were the color of wheat in noon sun or moonglow on clear, windless nights. Her face seemed perfection—a lovely oval with elegantly high cheekbones, a slender, pert nose, and a full, almost pouting mouth which had ever been the envied style at court. But the eyes were so rare—clear amethyst or the hue of fringed gentians within the thick, dark lashes. And wonder of wonders, the lady seemed so natural in stance and posture, as if she were quite unaware of her disarming beauty. Her loveliness, he mused still studying her through slitted eyes, was the more stunning for being unadorned. While his practiced eye was nearly jaded by the glut of rich fabrics and cosmetics, and the abundance of jewels in the Princess Isabella's household where he served, this woman wore the simplest blue wool kirtle, soft and clinging, with only her linked belt, from which dangled her heavy ring of keys, about her waist. It was impossible to believe that a woman with that body had borne two children in two years. The breasts were full, but the waist and belly so tiny and flat he could almost span them even with his small hands. On her, no jewelry detracted the eye. She wore only a gold wedding band and a small beryl ring on her other hand, all set with some fine gold work of filigreed ivy leaves.

"My Lord Thomas," the Lady Joan was protesting low,

"the princess was greatly devastated at her desertion by her betrothed Louis de Male at Bruges, you recall, so she perhaps only feels here she has her revenge for that."

"Nonsense," the copper-haired Thomas Holland persisted, while Richard Sidwell pulled his eyes away from the Lady Joan to assess her lord in this interesting exchange of tempers. "Getting back at this poor bastard d'Albret is hardly getting even with de Male. The king and the prince did that well enough for her last year in that sea battle off Winchelsea when they trounced the fleet of Castilian ships de Male encouraged to wreak havoc on England. The princess is just too damned headstrong and Her Grace should have handled her daughter with more force."

"As she did me, I assume you mean, my lord. Saints, I for one am all for the princess's happiness. And would you so criticize the dear Queen Philippa about her daughter if Her Grace were standing here instead of poor Richard Sidwell, who is no doubt tired and famished and is in need of our hospitality rather than our heated words about the princess? Please sit at our table, Master Sidwell. Partake and then tell us whatever you know of events in London. Exactly why did the princess say she changed her mind about the marriage or had she never agreed to it at all?"

Despite her usual fears of hearing news from the court, Joan plied their visitor with hot food and wine while Thomas looked on glumly over a wine goblet, his little son on his knee. Between bites of mackerel and biscuits drenched in Normandy honey, Richard Sidwell told them how five fully laden ships, heavy with goods for the princess and her retinue, had been prepared to set sail for Bordeaux when the bride defected. Sumptuous gifts for the groom, a massive bridal trousseau—one robe of which took twenty-nine skilled embroiderers nine days to complete—everything was prepared when Princess Isabella refused to embark. The bridegroom was so devastated, rumors said, that he had taken holy vows as a cloistered Franciscan friar and left his inheritance to a younger brother.

"Pure insanity," Thomas Holland's voice cut in on the marvelous tale while Joan hung on every word, trying to picture it all. "Let your minstrel make up some sad song to sing about it then, lady, so you can get all misty-eyed over it again. All I can see is the princess has made a mess of a necessary alliance with her groom's father. King Edward needs all the friends he can get in Bordeaux for this coming war and a woman upsets the whole damned apple cart!"

"Thus it has been since Eve, my gracious host," Richard Sidwell ventured and spooned up more custard, noting how the grim-faced Lord Holland just eyed his lady wife askance and did not find the jest a bit amusing. Poor lady, to have so serious and dour a knight for husband in this walled, moated manor so far from the excitement and gaiety of the Plantagenet court, Sidwell concluded, and washed the custard down with another gulp of wine.

"Any other, better news?" Lord Holland asked when he was done eating. "News of war? I long for it sometimes."

"Aye, so do the other knights, of course, I have heard, my gracious lord, but the new King John of Frances bides his time and so does our royal king. King John, 'tis said, in obvious jealousy and affront to England's Order of the Garter, has founded a so-called Order of the Star this January, despite his depleted finances from the ruinous wars ending at Crécy."

"Saint's blood!" Thomas swore low. "The Order of the Garter shall vanquish the Order of the Star when English knights next meet French on a battlefield. Say on."

"Well, my gracious lord, speaking of Crécy and all—His Grace, the Prince of Wales has not been affianced again since the last negotiations fell through and 'tis rumored he bides his time waiting for the next French war almost in self-imposed exile from London at his vast manor holdings. 'Tis rumored too he has a second son now by another lady different from the one named de Vere who bore his first."

Richard Sidwell, esquire, regretted that last bit of news the moment he spoke it, for the lovely Lady Joan's face clearly showed shock and dismay before she covered it by turning away to take her copper-haired little son into her arms from his father's lap.

"A raft of bastard sons will do His Grace no good," she heard her husband say, but the words did not stop her flow of memories. "The prince will have to marry and soon to get himself heirs for the royal line of succession someday. Quite simply, the man has no choice as some of us did."

While Thomas Holland and their wiry, little guest spoke of other things, Joan bounced her son on her blue-woolen knees, but his delighted smiles and squeals hardly permeated her thoughts. She, in perpetual, forced exile here with Thomas Holland, had two sons; Prince Edward, in temporary, chosen exile there, with different women had two sons. The wheel of fortune had spun and cast them off in far different directions where they had perhaps much the same lives, but each alone.

Her vision blurred with tears which she rapidly blinked back. Damn this rush of silly feelings. Saints, damn this little messenger from Isabella who dared to remind her of what once could have been! She glanced down at the beryl ring the prince had given her over seven years ago. She should not have worn it. She would take it off and never look on it again!

"Lady, I said I thought I would take our guest downstairs to his chamber now and I will be right back."

"Oh, aye, of course. A chamber newly aired with fresh spring rushes on the floor I hope you will enjoy." She managed a smile and a calm demeanor as she held her son to her to bid Sidwell good-night. "In the morn perhaps you would like to look around our lands here before you set out for Alençon," she added. "I would like the princess to be told how well we get on here when you return to her."

"Aye, Lady Joan. A gracious lord and lady in a most gracious French castle. Good even to you."

The room breathed silence after their footsteps died away and Madeleine came to take little Thomas off to the nursery down the hall where she slept on a trundle bed in earshot of the Holland sons. Soon, Joan thought, soon Thomas would need his own room and then a pony—then a little quintain and blunted weapons, schooling, his own life of knighthood, and wars, and daily agonies of heart.

She pressed her fingertips to her eyes, suddenly exhausted. It had been a long day. She twisted off the beryl ring decorated with her family's ivy leaf insignia and dropped it in her jewel coffer even as she heard her husband's tread outside the door.

"Saint Peter's bones, that little esquire can jabber—and eat and drink," he said immediately and sat at the cleared table to pour himself more wine. "Here—the missive from the princess," he added and scooted the small, ribboned and wax-sealed scroll down the length of table toward her.

She came closer, sitting across from him to open it. "Do you know, Joan, besides stopping here, what the man's task is for the princess—why he is traipsing around over here in hostile France?"

She looked up at him across the forsythia on the polished table. "No, of course not, unless I did not hear him tell us."

"The poor knave is over here fetching figured brocade for her from Alençon! Clear across the Channel and a two-hundred-blasted-mile ride through French territory for figured brocade! The woman is daft—it is the new fashion at court, he says. By the rood, Joan, you are well quit of Isabella and the rest."

"And are you well quit of them?" she parried.

"Your meaning?"

"Do you not miss being with the Plantagenets in their glittering realm? The queen, for instance?"

"I have been loyal to Her Grace ever since I was in the party of knights sent to fetch her from Flanders as a bride. I told you that. Are you implying something about our marriage, madame, that I owe her a debt for such? She let me down when she wed you with Salisbury, but I have long forgiven her for all that even if you have not. I have been well enough content to live here with you as wife because I took comfort in believing you were well content to get away from the Plantagenets. I should be most disturbed, madame, to believe one little word of His Grace, our prince's private doings at home, would change any of that contentment."

She leveled a cool, violet stare at his one-eyed challenge. "Not a whit, my lord," she lied.

"Good. Then, it is off to bed for us. That damned brocade fetcher cost us a goodly part of a fine evening with such piddling news of trousseaus and bastard sons, fashions, and de Maltravers—"

Joan crunched the stiff parchment scroll in her hand. "What did you say? De Maltravers? I heard naught of de Maltravers. How—what did he say?"

"How the hell do you know aught of de Maltravers anyway, Joan? It is just more gossip Sidwell threw in when I took him to his room."

"De Maltravers, the exile from Flanders? Tell me, Thomas!"

His mouth dropped open and he half rose out of his chair to lean toward her across the table. "Aye, *that* de Maltravers, John de Maltravers. But he has been gone from England for as many years as you are old surely. Now, what in the hell did you know of de Maltravers?"

"Saints, Thomas, do you know nothing of me? He is the man I despise most on the face of the earth now that Roger Mortimer is dead. He helped King Edward murder my father!"

Thomas Holland's face went white as the parchment and he fell back heavily in his chair. He stared aghast at Joan. "The king's Uncle Edmund, your father," he stammered. "I knew, of course, about your father and his execution under Mortimer. But King Edward? That is treason, lady, and I shall hear no more of that!"

"I would hardly expect you to hear of it at all, or especially to ever side with me in it. You wonder why I have held my tongue for two years about what matters to me most when you talk to me of treason the minute I try to share it with you?"

"And what does matter to you most that you have not spoken of finally, Joan? Poor sot that I am, I guess I thought it was this place and your sons if not their sire. I assure you that I have never been foolish enough to deceive myself on that!"

"Please do not scream at me, my lord. We do not need Vinette or Madeleine telling the villagers of this misunderstanding. I saw de Maltravers in Bruges just for one second and he looked at me and I knew he was vile. I wanted to meet him, to kill him—I do not know—but everything with the princess' marriage fell apart then and we left so quickly I never saw him again."

Thomas Holland lowered his voice, too, and came around the table to her as he talked. "This is pure foolishness, Joan. The man will not bother you here or when we do go back to England to visit my lands in Lancashire. We must do that soon if there is no French war forthcoming."

"In England? De Maltravers is going back to England? Is that what Sidwell said?"

Thomas pulled her up out of her chair and put his arms heavily around her shoulders to hold her tightly to him. "No, not exactly. He only mentioned there was talk that for his loyal foreign service to the king in Bruges, His Grace might restore his lands to him."

She tried to yank away, but Thomas's grasp was like a vise. "No! Hell's gates, my lord, loyalty in foreign service! The serpent is rewarded for helping rid this king of my father and any others who would dare to show concern for the old, murdered King Edward!"

"Stop it, Joan! It is all past, done, and no concern of yours. Your duty is to do everything you can for your family now, the boys and me, and not rile royal tempers over what is past. No wonder His Grace wanted you to be wed and live abroad."

"Aye," she gritted through clenched teeth and stopped

struggling. "Mayhap that is why you got me at half price on the marriage mart of the court, my lord."

He stiffened against her. "Well then, my Joan, since this seems to be truth time all around, let me tell you something. By the rood, aye, you were a bargain with your beauty and strain of royal blood to mix with a Holland's from mere Lancashire and to please the queen I have long vowed to defend at all cost to my own person—a purely chivalrous vow, I assure you."

"Treason enough in this family from my wildness, you mean," she returned, her voice dripping sarcasm.

"I shall ignore that, Joan, to merely conclude that I am not at all dismayed by this dangerous little turn of events as long as you keep your comments to this little room. You see, lady, I have worried for over two years now that I was called in to get you hastily out of the royal sight because the prince had declared he loved you to them or some such insanity and so the king wrote the pope to help me out. Now, I have hope I might have been mistaken and, unless you choose to tell me about all that Prince of Wales business yourself, we shall go at least two more years not speaking on that subject while I tell myself the king wanted to be rid of you for your being your father's daughter."

"There is nothing to say about the prince or anything else then, Thomas."

"And since neither the prince nor memories of him mean a whit to you, as you like to say, we are off to bed." He loosed her only to scoop her up in his embrace and stride to the bed with her where he stood her on a small carpet.

She steeled herself to accept, to respond appropriately, warmly, despite her aching body and heart. De Maltravers—his lands back for loyalty to the crown; the prince—two sons for bestowing his magnificent body on other women; she, Joan of Kent—this man, this bed, this life.

She allowed him to unclasp her keys and belt and pull her single, soft wool outer garment up over her head. He divested himself quickly of his own *surcote*, jerkin, slippers, and hose while she pulled down the coverlet and climbed in, wearing only her thin chemise. She stared upward at the underside of the gathered gold brocade of their bed canopy before Thomas Holland filled her view. In the dim light of two near cresset lamps, her eyes fixed on his stocky, broad chest and his shoulders lightly dusted with freckles and copper hair.

"We breed such beautiful sons together, sweet Joan," he was saying as she forced herself to meet his thorough, one-eyed perusal of her body. "Give me another son, Joan, with coppered Holland hair, or if he is towheaded, I will know while we live here in France the child has his mother's fair looks and that is all."

As his big, square hand stroked the hem of her thin chemise upward, she recalled another time he had voiced the deep-seated fear that he would be forced to rear the son of the Prince of Wales. It was their wedding night at Eltham then, so long ago, the last time she had ever heard Edward's deep voice or drowned in the fathomless pool of those aquamarine eyes. Edward—so he had asked her to call him on that first night in seaside Calais when their passion had swept them away all that long moonlit night, so long ago and yet she could remember it so clearly like a sweet dream of now-painful passion.

Thomas Holland bent over her, determined to arouse the lush, soft body of his wife, to make her moan for him before he entered her. But to his surprise, the woman he tried so assiduously to arouse most of the times he possessed her was trembling with passion. The budded pink nipples of her lush breasts had swollen to bursting as he bent to kiss them; her eyes were closed and her full lower lip quivered; her thighs separated easily at the mere brush of his fingertips; and her soft woman's nest was warm and ready instantly for him.

Joan clung to him, moaning, reaching out with a passion he had never had from her before, and as he lost himself in the overwhelming ecstasy that always hurtled him so quickly toward his goal, he wondered briefly if her own lust had been aroused by her hatred for de Maltravers, or her insane anger at the king, or her hopeless feelings for her prince.

A beautiful rush of colors blurred by Joan as she squeezed her eyes tightly shut and clung to Thomas Holland. At first, she tried to halt the onslaught of erotic memories of Edward, but then she simply surrendered to them. All this time she had controlled herself and thought that feelings like this were buried forever, but now she knew her brain and heart could conjure them up at will to torment her body. The driving, mindless response she had always felt for Edward, Prince of Wales, drowned her like a phantom lover in the embrace of this other man.

The pictures swept around her then, the music blared in her ears: she lay under him in the stable straw as he rode her hard, plunging, taking, giving and she reveled in it all. On the forest floor that first time by the pool at Windsor, while the leaves blurred overhead, she could smell the sea breeze of Calais and feel his huge hands move under her hips to lift her higher to him. His mouth demanded, yielded, then traced little wildfire kisses far down her throat to her pointed breasts and lower as she seized him to her and exploded in a shower of wild joy she had nearly forgotten.

His passion spent at her side, Thomas lay watching her groggily, one arm still thrown possessively over her damp body. "By the rood, *ma belle*," he said, his voice raspy, "what did I do to deserve all that? *That* has never happened before."

She felt her throat and cheeks blush hot, but it was too dim for him to see. Rather than anger him or lie to him, she kept silent.

His tone was sleepy, almost drugged a few seconds later when he spoke again, but his voice increased in pitch as he went on. "Look, Joan, if you promise to forget this de Maltravers vendetta, I will take you to Liddell to see your brother for the summer. The boys are old enough to travel and we have been gone two years. You could stay in Kent and I could ride north to the lands in Lancashire. Things

341

have gone well between us until this foolishness today and I know you would like to see your brother John and your old home. You must understand I would not want your carting the tots to London though. Agreed?"

Her heart leapt. Liddell, home! And a chance to make an attempt to do something about heading off de Maltravers's return to England as honored, loyal citizen!

"Joan?"

"Agreed, Thomas. I have no desire to see London, so you need not fret for that."

"And the de Maltravers thing?"

"I swear to you, my lord, you shall never hear aught of it from me again."

His arm across her relaxed and he fell instantly asleep as he so often did after his love-making. But sleep would not come to Joan. She lay there, unmoving, next to him, her mind racing, plotting. Home to Liddell and a chance to stop de Maltravers, but how? How? A letter to the princess sent back with Richard Sidwell would be to no avail, for Isabella must surely be out of favor with her royal parents after that ruined betrothal. Again, again, her formless plan kept returning to the one person who could possibly be of help to her in this, but in facing him again after these two years, she was terrified that in one cold glance he would read her smothered desires.

Stir crazy from lying so long rigidly on the bed, she rose and carefully covered her sleeping husband. She picked up her dress, discarded in a blue pool by the bed, and slipped it on over her chemise. Her feet pushed into slippers, she took one of the two still low-burning cresset lamps to the *garde-robe* where extra clothes and linens were stored. Beyond this tiny tiring room lay their privy separated by yet another heavy tapestry.

She sat on a storage chest not even certain why she had come in here except to escape Thomas's contented snores in the solar when she could not sleep a wink. Her brain still raced, but her body felt so spent and sluggish. She stared at the coffer filled with Thomas's best armor, stared at the low cresset lamp, and felt the walls close in as her mind drifted.

How assiduously dear old Marta had worked to set this dusty room aright when they had first come here, she remembered. Marta! If only her crotchety Marta were here she would have someone to talk to who would understand.

She knew then what she wanted to do. Marta was buried just outside the walls in a tiny grave plot on a slope near the forest, a place of her own choice, more like a Scottish glen, much preferable to lying until eternity under the cold stones of the chapel near others she had never known, she had insisted. If she were just out of the castle for a moment, near Marta, then she could come back and sleep.

At other times in daylight, she and Thomas had used the ancient siege exit which went from this room out under the walls and moat, clear into the forest. Thomas had said many French castles had such secret passages; they were as common as ghosts, he had teased her. But to venture through it at night, when he might wake and miss her was most foolhardy.

She pulled aside the tapestry which covered the small door's outline and lifted her lamp. To be so alone down there in the dark was crazy; yet, the idea drew her onward.

She pulled the long, metal bolt. The heavy door, deftly balanced, pivoted inward at a shove. She glanced down at the pitchy oil remaining in her lamp. Surely enough left to just pray a moment at Marta's grave and come right back. The spring night was balmy, the moon full. She stepped in and let the door close easily behind her.

The rubble of broken stone with which the downward slant of the passage was lined hurt her feet through the felt slippers, but she hurried on. The passage was dank from all the rains of late or else the moat over the ceiling at the far end was dripping through again. How many times in the nights of past years under enemy siege had secret messengers with pleas for aid and succor crept out this way? she wondered, but never just to visit a grave at the forest's edge or to escape one's own thoughts.

Her heart pounded as she went deeper in. The floor leveled out now and then slanted up. The passage was so narrow her skirts almost brushed each side where it was buttressed up by stout timbers under the heavy walls. A thick lacing of cobwebs etched her hair, her face, but her light caught the glint of metal latch on the door at the end of the tunnel which could only be opened from within.

When the reality of this foolish, adventurous whim hit her at the door, she almost turned to scurry back. Marta would have scolded her for days for this. Saints, she was so drained of all emotion she knew she could sleep now if she went back. If Thomas found out, he might be so furious he would never take her home to Liddell this summer!

Holding her breath, she slid the heavy, scraping lock open. The metallic, grating sound sent shrieking shivers up her spine. She leaned hard into the door and spilled hot oil on one wrist.

"Saints!" she shouted and her voice echoed in the corridor behind. The door protested with a low moan as it opened, and she breathed fresh, free air. How much fun the boys would have with this secret passage someday when they were older—and when it was broad noonday.

The passageway ended above her in a little mound screened by budded hollyhock and lilac on the forest fringe. She jammed a branch into the door so it would not close behind her and, lifting her lamp, stepped out. A slight breeze stirred the leaves, and the moon poured its pale glow down to make her lamp seem insignificant in this outer vastness. The turf was wet on her slippers and the hems of her skirts as she went quickly toward the little mound and arched stone that marked the grave. After harvest she would have one of the village stonecutters make a cross for it too. Aye, sweeter far to sleep beneath this fragrant, soft grass than any cold stones of the greatest cathedral, she mused, as she knelt at the very edge of the mound and touched the cool stone.

But once she was here, she felt nothing and was terrified

again by the sweep of memories over which she had no control. Marta's presence with her the last five years she had been at court was through his kindness—her Edward's. She had vowed to forget him, to never see him again; yet now she planned to plead with him for yet another favor to stop de Maltravers's run of good fortune and to help fulfill her promises to Mother on her deathbed.

The trees moaned and sighed in the burgeoning breeze. The cold castle walls loomed, waiting dark across the moat. She could feel her heart beating, struggling to keep calm and to forget.

"Goodnight, my Marta," she whispered aloud but the breeze snatched her words away. "I am going home to Liddell. I love you, and I am so afraid I love him too."

She stumbled to her feet and hurried away. At the entrance to the passageway, the wind extinguished her lamp, but she bravely plunged on, feeling her long way back in the dark. Mayhap it was a lesson to her, a warning not to do foolish things, she scolded herself, as she hurried along at a good clip in the black void, her dirty hands skimming either side of the tunnel. Mayhap it was like trying to find her way out of the wretched ruins she'd somehow made of things or of escaping from her own dark, secret longings.

When she emerged shaken and perspiring in the little *garde-robe* chamber again, she knelt to vow she would not be so headstrong in the future—unless it was the only way to do what she had to do.

Chapter Sixteen

For two heavenly weeks after they arrived for a visit at her maidenhood home of Liddell Manor in Kent, Joan reveled in the woods and fields as she had years ago. Barefoot, she waded in ponds and streams, showing little Thomas how to catch a fish. The family went on picnics in the forest; with her brother John she rode the entire small estate of Liddell from hedgerow fence to forest edge. Joan went berry and flower picking while Thomas and John hunted and the children took their long afternoon naps. She remembered, she enjoyed, and she planned.

She bid her Lord Thomas farewell on the first day of July. He rode north to his manor lands in Lancashire planning to return by mid-August. She had renewed her promise to him that she would not go to London despite the fact her brother John was going to take part in the king's Summer Eve tournament at Westminster and she could easily have accompanied him. But Thomas Holland knew her at least well enough to realize she had no desire to see the king or queen. Of her hatred for John de Maltravers, Thomas said not a word as if that subject were at rest forever. As relaxed, as joyous as Joan had been to be home at Liddell, he could not have guessed otherwise.

Unbeknownst to her Lord Thomas, Joan's quick mind had hatched a hundred schemes concerning John de Maltravers: she would write the prince; no, she must rather go to him in person to seek his aid. She would write to

346

London to the princess and in that letter request to know where the prince was now. But that would be entirely too obvious, and what if Isabella told someone who misunderstood? This plan must be very clever, very discreet, and not subject to the common tattle of court rumors. The last plan she had just discarded since her brother's retinue was preparing to journey to London for the tournament was to take him into her confidence, tell him mother's dying words, and ask him to share her vow to be somehow avenged on de Maltravers. But what if John later told Thomas Holland, whom he seemed to admire greatly, or what if John rushed off to challenge the vile de Maltravers to some sort of combat? John was all she had left of her family, and she must protect him by taking this on her own shoulders.

Then, after she had uncharacteristically prayed heartily to her favorite saints for help to know what to do, the pieces of her dilemma plopped into her lap, all beautifully meshed.

She sat barefooted between the two fish ponds at the south side of the manor in the late, lazy afternoon. She and Roger Wakeley, who had accompanied them from Normandy over her husband's hearty protests, played their lutes, sang, and gazed half-mesmerized into the green, sun-splotched water. Beneath the glassy surface dotted with white water lilies glided pike, bream, and sunfish. Roger's brown eyes studying her, he sang her a new song then, one she had never heard before, and with its plaintive melody and lyrics, the days of escape and rest here at Liddell jangled to a quick close:

> "O man unkind,
> Have thou in mind
> My passion sharp!
> Thou shalt me find
> To thee full kind:
> Lo, here my heart."

The tune and words danced upon the water and floated

away on the breeze, but her emotions so carefully tended for so long melted and flowed to painful reminiscence of Prince Edward.

"I have never heard that one before, Master Roger," she managed, though her voice quivered. "A new one from that minstrel friend of yours who stopped here yesterday?"

"Aye. Do you not like it?"

"Of course, though it is very sad and I have felt so happy lately."

"Ah." His brown eyes went over her before he looked off into the distance. He plucked the strings with his quill again as he spoke. "*Sacrebleu*, Lady Joan, it need not be a sad song at all. My memories of Liddell were mostly happy, though there was sadness too. Now in this song, the lady obviously has suffered sweet passion's pain and yet she vows kindness and ventures to give her heart to the man she loves."

"Mayhap a great gamble," she returned, almost wondering if Roger Wakeley's talents did not extend to mind reading. "'O man unkind,' the lady said. She would do best to guard her heart with a good deal of carefully forged armor before she offers it to such a one."

The minstrel chuckled as he began to repeat the melody, but Joan did not wish to hear the whole melancholy thing again.

"Your minstrel friend, Master Roger—however did he know to find you here? Saints, you have as many visitors at home in Normandy as my lord and I, but indeed, it is a wonder they found you here too."

She thought a moment's alarm registered in his clear, gentle eyes before he smiled. "Being a skilled minstrel makes one part of a secret sort of fraternity, my lady. It is so seldom many of us can be together unless we serve at court. However are we to share new music and our interests unless we try very hard when traveling about to see each other?"

"At least I hope this friend taught you a happier tune as well as this 'passion smart' song," she countered. Then she asked the question she had been carefully hoarding until it seemed the appropriate moment. "I suppose, of course, your traveling minstrel friends help to keep you up on news and such. Did that fellow come from London by any chance?"

"Aye, now that you ask, he did."

"I suppose all the Garter knights are swarming to court for the midsummer jousting. I know my Lord Thomas wished he could stop there on his way north, but he had far too many duties to attend to. I wager most of the other knights will be there though."

Roger Wakeley glanced at her sitting near him on the sedgy bank of the fish pond. She looked lovely, her kirtle the color of daffodils. But his instinct was surely right, for she looked tense and jittery of a sudden: now if ever, the time was ripe to discover if she would reveal she still cared for the prince, who had been secretly apprised that the Hollands were at Liddell for the summer. Whether or not His Grace would dare a visit the musician knew not, but he did know for certain that both King Edward and the Prince of Wales eagerly awaited the separate reports about the Hollands he forwarded to them every other month.

"My lady, Lord Holland should not have been so dismayed at missing the summer jousting," he said hoping his voice sounded both innocent and jaunty. "After all, the Prince of Wales himself will not be there as he is presently at Canterbury."

Her head jerked up so hard that the wayward blond curls across her forehead bounced. "The Prince at Canterbury? Who said?"

"My minstrel friend just come from London. Everyone at court knows it. He was staying at Leeds Castle but now he has gone into Canterbury to do yearly homage to the shrine there in the cathedral. He was educated in Canterbury by Prior Hathbrand for several years as a boy, you know, and he loves the city well. Then, too, next week is the anniversary date of the enshrining of the blessed martyr's bones there so it is a popular pilgrimage time. Have you never been?"

"I—no, I never went far with my lady mother staying so

close to home here and all. But, I would like to go now."

"A special trip for most pious reasons," Roger Wakeley
was saying, but his words hardly dented Joan's awareness.
Canterbury was barely twenty miles from here and with all
the pilgrims on the road, no one would notice one more
penitent—or two traveling minstrels—come to entertain the
benevolent pilgrims and worship at the holy shrine of the
martyred Saint Thomas à Becket. And neither her Lord
Thomas nor brother John would be here to say her nay if she
left tomorrow.

"Master Roger, I need your help."

"To learn the new song?" he asked, a tiny quirk of a smile
teasing his thin lips.

"No. I wish to go to Canterbury. I will go to Canterbury to
visit the shrine. And Roger, you must vow your silence on
something, something very important to me and to the
honor of my whole family."

Two brown eyebrows arched up over Roger Wakeley's
intent eyes as she plunged on. "You see, to ask a boon, a
favor I have secretly vowed to carry out, I must seek out the
prince, Master Roger."

He expelled a little rush of sigh between his pursed lips. "A
boon, my lady? And may I know the nature of this secret
vow?"

"I cannot tell you now. Will you go with me? I cannot risk
taking Madeleine or Vinette for I do not want my Lord
Thomas to know and the children need the maids here. My
quest is secret from my lord only because it concerns my
family's honor and not his. Will you not help me?"

"Of course. The holy city is but a morning's ride distant
from this part of the shire, and you could bed at the priory of
Christ Church where rich pilgrims stay. With so many on the
roads we would be safe enough in daylight."

"I intend not to be gawked at or questioned. I plan to hire
penitents' garb when we are quit of here so I will not be
recognized. I know that sounds unusual, but I hope you will
trust me and agree—and understand."

She rose with her lute and strode back toward the large stone manorhouse without another word or glance, as if she knew instinctively he would obey completely.

He grinned and shook his head hard enough in amazement to bounce his flat-combed, brown hair. *Sacrebleu*, what a strong-headed woman, but then she had been so the two maidenhood years he had known her. By the rood, he would not miss this little escapade for a year's wages! It was only unfortunate he had not known of this yesterday to be able to send word to the prince when his messenger left Liddell for Canterbury, but the prince surely knew well enough by now no one could predict this woman!

He tapped his foot faster and the melancholy melody of "O man unkind" he had just learned yesterday dashed faster. She had hoped he understood her; now *that* was worth a laugh. Whatever plan she had in that wily, little head of hers, Roger Wakeley understood only one thing. She may not have shown it the last two and a half years off with her dour Lord Thomas in Normandy, but she still loved the prince whether she knew it or not. A secret trip to fair Canterbury with a beautiful, wild lady who would worship at the shrine of the Prince of Wales's power and charisma; what poor lute player could ask for more?

Roger Wakeley's laugh echoed loudly over the pond again as he strummed the sad notes at an even faster clip.

The pace the two hooded minstrels set for Canterbury was of necessity forced to a crawl the closer they got. From each road or land they passed on The Pilgrim's Way connecting Rochester, the key city of the shire, to Canterbury, sundry folk swelled the traffic. Some ambled on horseback like Roger and Joan, who was well enough disguised as a hooded man, and the rich jolted along in their elaborately painted canvas and leather chars. From Tenterden, Cranbrook, and Woodchurch, from Old Wives Lees and Knockholt Green, the lines of pilgrims gorged the narrow way.

Like most other travelers, Joan clutched the pilgrim's

penny she had purchased for a good deal more than that at the roadside inn where they had stopped for ale and cheese. They had fully expected to be clear to Canterbury before suppertime, but now they would be fortunate to arrive by dusk. But whether things worked out well or not in the quest to ask the prince to halt the return of de Maltravers's English lands, she knew this plan was her only hope, so she clutched her pilgrim's penny and tried to remember to pray either to St. Catherine or St. George or the blessed martyr himself each hour.

At last the spires of Canterbury rose from the darkening meadows of eventide. The River Stour seemed a gentle, protecting arm about the town, and the still-open west gate gleamed red in the sinking sun. Above the crowded clusters of shops, inns, and houses stood the massive gray stone cathedral in all her austere Norman majesty, her sunlit gilded angel perched atop the highest steeple in the town.

Even Joan, despite the burden on her heart to find the prince and dare to face him after all this time, was awed at last. "Mother should have come here," she breathed, her violet eyes lifted to the towering angel of the spire. "So close all those years. No wonder His Grace loves it here. I wish we could see it all today."

"But your plan to have me seek him upon our arrival is best, my lady," Roger Wakeley urged. "I only hope he is staying here at the house he uses when in the area and is not still at Leeds. Come on, now. As you said, Christ Church Priory is hardly the place to stay when one wants to see the prince in private, so we must find a little room for you to wait in while I take him the beryl ring and the news you request an audience."

The hawkers' shops, which sold the ampullas of the saint's blood or the commemorative brooches of his head and bishop's miter, were closing along High Street and Mercery Lane. "I am sorry it is so late, but then perhaps he will have time on the morrow," Joan called to Roger as he turned his horse into a side street and her palfrey followed.

Roger could tell her resolve was wavering, but this little inn where he hoped to get her a room was but a block from the rich merchant's house the prince often used when he was in town. Saints preserve him, if the prince decided his little minstrel-spy had done anything to put Lady Joan in danger! But from this inn, he could be to the prince and back to fetch her in a quarter-hour before she really reconsidered her so-called honorable, secret quest.

At last they halted in a cul-de-sac near the old Saxon Church of St. Martin where, it was said, St. Augustine had baptized King Ethelbert. The tiny room above a merchant's narrow house where Roger was familiar with the people had slanted corners under the eaves, but it looked clean and newly whitewashed. The close space was crowded by fresh straw pallets in two of the corners, a tiny table with three chairs, and one carved coffer. When Roger saw that Joan and her travel sack were in, he grabbed two apples from the bowl on the table and darted off on his errand before she could halt him.

Left alone in the silent, strange room, Joan washed, combed, and coiled her hair; ate some fruit; and pondered how she had ever dared to pursue this scheme. For two and a half years she had not seen the prince; she had received no word from him, nor had she sent any. It was blatantly obvious their lives, once so intertwined, had gone divergent ways. Now, she dared, without protection of husband or brother, with only a minstrel, to come in secret and disguise to barge her way back into His Grace's busy, powerful life for a favor. It meant, she knew, she would have to tell him her side of the de Maltravers story, or he would surely be clever enough to seek it out himself, and the king might get all angered and vengeful again. She could hardly afford such risk now with two sons to protect. And when she told the prince, whether she directly accused his father King Edward or not, it was meddling at the least—treason at the worst— and she would have to be very careful and very convincing.

She hoped he still cared enough for her to help her—

mayhap for Isabella's sake, or mayhap even for his old minstrel Roger Wakeley, as he obviously used to favor him before he saw that she and Roger had once been fast friends. Perhaps she should don the blue kirtle she had brought in her side sack, but then it was no doubt terribly wrinkled and she could hardly convince a man like that with a mere pretty kirtle.

She absently fingered her lucky pilgrim's penny on the chain about her neck. She paced the little, irregular room around and around the central table, her stomach tied in terrible knots. Perhaps he was at Leeds, he was too busy, or he refused to see Roger Wakeley. She stopped to look out the one small, smoky-paned window as twilight descended across the thatched or slate rooftops she could see from here. The casement overlooked a crooked close where the entries to several tiny shops were marked by frayed wooden signs suspended below her view. Across the narrow close, at the same level, an old, old woman leaned pensively on her crooked window ledge. When she spied Joan, her face crinkled into a web of lines as she smiled gap-toothed. Hoofbeats on cobbles clattered below, and Joan leaned out farther to try to see the street, but no one was visible, as if ghosts had ridden in to haunt the tiny cul-de-sac.

She had only begun to pace again when a soft rap on the door jolted her. Her pulse pounded instantly; she felt chilled. But the face at the door was Roger's.

"Oh, I am so glad you are back! I was just starting to worry that he—"

"Lady Joan," he interrupted, "a visitor is here who will see you now."

She opened her lips to protest, but to no avail. No, she shrieked inside, no, it cannot be! It is too sudden, too soon! I cannot face him here.

Edward, Prince of Wales, filled the little doorway. He had to stoop to enter. He, too, like Roger and she, was garbed as a common pilgrim, but who would have not turned a head to follow his magnificent form and grace! His hood fell back from the tousled lion's mane of tawny hair. In the fading light of the room, his blue eyes glowed as if lit from within.

She had forgotten he was so tall, she thought, and she had forgotten this overwhelming rush of uncertainty all mingled with joy when she was near him.

He took two steps in and the door closed quietly behind him. The tiny room shrank even further, dwarfed by the impact of the man. His gaze went completely over her. He held out one hand to touch her shoulder and then withdrew it. His finely chiseled features looked austere, perhaps even angry.

"Jeannette," he said quietly, and that deep rasp of voice shook her to her toes.

She curtsied. "My lord prince. Please forgive this way I have sought you so strangely and in secret, but I have reasons."

"I could not believe it when Wakeley came," he began as though he had not heard her words. "I could not believe you were here. Last time, you may recall, when you dressed as a lad at the tournament, I was quite angered. And now, here you are again in jerkin and hose—" he went on hopefully until his words trailed off to silence.

She blushed to the very roots of her hair at the memory he recalled, and in her lower belly, little wild butterfly wings fluttered, fluttered.

"Your Grace, these are pilgrim's garments. I thought it safer. I—the favor—I came to ask a favor of you, for I am in dire need of your help."

He frowned and touched her elbow sending an icy, blazing jab through her arm at the mere pressure of his firm fingers. "Thomas Holland?" he stammered. "I heard—I assumed he is good to you!"

"Oh, indeed, Your Grace. This has naught to do with my Lord Thomas. In fact, I—well, the reason I am come in secret is partly so he will never hear of this."

The carved mouth under the full mustache lifted slightly; a wave of nostalgia at that familiar little quirk she had never forgotten washed over her.

"A secret plea without Sir Thomas knowing," he was saying in that resonant voice. "Let us sit and you can tell me then."

As soon as they were seated Roger knocked and entered with a thick tallow candle and wine. As if to encourage her, he winked at her over the prince's shoulder and left them alone again.

"This favor, Jeannette, tell me," he urged, leaning forward toward her, his form, his eyes devouring the space between them. He rested his hands on his knees to prop up his chin, and she saw he wore on the first joint of his little finger the beryl ring she had sent him with Roger.

"My lord prince, there is a man who greatly harmed my father years ago. He helped to—to have him executed most unjustly."

The prince's thick tawny brows crashed lower over his eyes while the sluggish candle flicked wan shadows across his features.

"Say on, lady. Name the man."

"When we were in Bruges for the Princess Isabella's betrothal feast five years ago, when I felt ill at the banquet, we walked out together. Do you remember?" Her heart thudded at his nearness, at the intense perusal of his stare more than at what she would divulge and ask.

"I remember much, Jeannette, much of that whole trip. To whom do you refer?"

"You pointed him out to me. You named him. John de Maltravers, my lord prince."

"De Maltravers? The king's ambassador to Flanders all these years?"

"Aye. The same. Saints, Your Grace, I heard tell the king intends to give the man back all his confiscated English lands—mayhap to welcome him home and pardon him with open arms also! It is all wrong, it is not fair! He cannot!"

She tried to rise to dart around the table away from his closeness, but he seized her wrist with one big hand and pulled her back firmly into her chair.

"Lower your voice, Jeannette. All the walls have ears though I came here well enough in disguise and Wakeley and my man are in the hall. Calmly, now. How little you have changed to be so willful—so impassioned."

"I can tell you all about my father's death, Your Grace, a terrible tale of betrayal. I swear I shall avenge myself on de Maltravers whether you will help me or not!"

"I know the tale, Jeannette, and St. George, I sympathize with your loss and your bitterness."

She interlocked the slender fingers of her hands to keep from trembling at her eagerness. "You do? Then you will help me?"

He leaned back in his tall-backed chair at last and expelled a rush of air through his flared nostrils. "Jeannette, cannot the past be dead with the dead? By the rood, you tread quicksand to pursue this. St. George, woman, if I went after anyone who had ever wished ill of my sire, the fields of England would flow with blood like Crécy."

She jumped away, this time before he could reach for her. "I see. I mean, after all, de Maltravers is of use to the Plantagenets and then, too, such a halt to the heaped rewards the king plans for that villain would mean questions asked, rumors raised—"

The palm of one of the prince's big hands slammed down hard on the table top, and the wine decanter and goblets jumped and shuddered.

"Hell's gates, Jeannette, you never fail to rile me one way or the other! Now hush up and give me a chance to answer, or I swear I will stop that tempting mouth and you will listen then! For your own sake and well-being, you will absolutely cease whatever desperate schemes you are hatching in that wily brain of yours. I will look into this. I swear to you, I had not heard. If it is true and if I can dissuade His Majesty, I shall, but I will not argue against him if he is set and thus cause a permanent rift with you as the obvious cause of it all."

"Oh, I see," she dared, her voice laden with a sarcasm she knew full well was both dangerous and provocative.

He rose from his chair and the little room shrank again. Like a coward even before he moved toward her, she stepped back against the rough plaster wall behind her.

"I swear by all the saints, woman, you see nothing concerning me clearly. You never have. So I shall tell you a few things to set us straight for now." He advanced toward her. Her eyes went wide, and he saw her lower lip tremble. He fought back the urge to press her into the wall, to hurt her for all the agony she had caused him over the years only to use those same wiles now to tempt him again whether she was innocent or guilty of that intent. He stood two feet away from her, not touching her, but he leaned down to rest a palm on either side of her champagne-colored hair coils, to fix her with a steady, hungry gaze.

"First, aye, I will do what I can, Jeannette. You will trust that and should I fail, there will be insurmountable reasons for that failure and you will make no protest. No arguing! Just listen. Secondly, you will behave yourself as circumspectly as I assume you have been doing these past years so that the king's anger toward you which you brazenly aroused once will continue to fade so that you and your Lord Thomas may come home to court again. Are those two things understood and do you pledge to agree?"

"My lord prince, I have no desire to return to His Grace's court. In Normandy and at Liddell, I have been quite content."

The eagerness, the tenseness or expectancy of his face and stance fled. "So," he said, his voice gone cold and sharp like a sword's edge, "a virtuous, content woman these days—save, of course, for the desire for bloody revenge against de Maltravers. A dewy-eyed bride still. That is to be your shield and buckler with me now."

"Saints, Your Grace, what do you imply? I have two young sons, you know."

"Aye, madam, I am entirely aware of that."

"Are you? I hear you also have two sons, and are you not well content?"

A flame flared in each crystalline, blue eye. "Hell's gates, woman, of course I am content. Ecstatic! Jousting, signing papers eternally, moving around from manor to manor—from bed to bed—while waiting for the next damned French war to begin so I can command an army myself without His Grace watching every minute and waiting for a wrong move—ecstatic! And speaking of such delights, I left the prospect of a warm bed and a willing lady who knows her own heart to come here to see you, so I really must be heading back. But let me tell you, since you still seem so adept at your hard-hearted little wars, I only risk myself for what will profit me."

She tried to calm the rush of blood she felt at his tirade all spoken with such restrained, threatening control. "My lord prince, I do not mean to sound ungrateful. And I have known you to be very kind and charitable to those in need."

"Aye, Jeannette, to those in need, but *that* is obviously not your credential for help, is it? Never has little Jeannette been in need of what her prince could truly give her!"

"Please, do not say thus and with such bitterness."

"It does not matter. Only, I have just changed the rules of the game. What will you exchange for this help you ask me for—to halt the return of de Maltravers's lands—mayhap to stop his return home altogether?"

"Exchange?" she stammered. In her shock, her eyes strayed to the straw pallet so close, and she gulped audibly. "I cannot—just what do you mean?"

"St. George, Jeannette, there is obviously no tenderness here between us, so I am asking for a simple, mercantile bargain. I please you by helping head off de Maltravers, and in fair exchange, you please me."

Blood pounded in her ears so she could hardly hear her own answer. "You are insulting me, Your Grace."

"No, I am complimenting you. You evidently value this favor greatly enough to get all disguised in knave's garb and come traipsing clear to Canterbury to seek me out. Likewise, I value your sweet favors, your willing, sweet body in fair exchange."

Her knees went weak, and she pressed back harder against the rough wall to steady herself. Under her rough boy's jerkin and *surcote*, her nipples sprang erect at the mere thought of his big hands, his mouth on them. The butterflies in the pit of her stomach darted and feathered all velvety down her belly to her thighs and the very core of her womanhood.

Aye, aye, she wanted him, always had, a little voice inside her pounding head shrieked. Right now, anywhere, she would revel in being crushed under him, her legs spread, her body pierced and ridden hard at his whim and—and held— and loved by him alone.

Her voice when she spoke in the dim silence between them was a ghostly whisper. "I cannot, my prince."

"Can you not really, Jeannette?" he gibed and leaned down over her again. "You are thinking you have always put up with my unwanted attentions, are you not? Poor, little Jeannette."

"No, that is not it."

"Damn you, witch. I swear you will admit this feeling that pierces me! You shall!"

He leaned hard into her, his hands imprisoning her waist. She pulled back, but the wall was as unmovable as he. One big hand lifted to tilt her head back; the other cupped her *derrière* to bring her forward to him. Her hands rose to his chest but she did not push him away as she meant to. How powerful his chest muscles felt under her palms, how resilient and crisp his heavy chest hair beneath his linen jerkin.

"Oh, no, no," she moaned before his mouth took hers.

The kiss at first was harsh and demanding, but it softened, shifted and deepened with aching tenderness. Her breasts felt heavy, full; they tingled for his touch. Mindlessly she seized his hand at the side of her head and lowered it to her throbbing nipples. He stroked the taut peaks through the rough material, then in a lightning movement, yanked her jerkin up free of her belt to plunder her bare, quaking skin under the garment.

She moaned and darted her tongue into his mouth to answer his own challenge. One hand now seized, caressed, molded a full breast while the other dipped into her hose to cup and squeeze a bare, rounded buttock.

She wrapped her arms around his neck as he lifted her crushed to him. He bent to lay her back on the little straw bed, and when he lifted his lips from the bruising kisses and rough caresses in which she reveled, she heard herself plead, "Please, please, do not stop!"

His face, inches from hers, glazed with the fury of passion; yet it was dark in here, and the whole room spun wildly. He seized her wrists clasped behind his neck and pressed them to her heaving breasts. "Listen to me carefully, Jeannette. I love you, damn it. Aye, I have since I first saw you. And you, witch, have brought me joy only to be followed by anguish and pain."

"But, I—"

He shook her hard. "No, listen! I will do as I said about de Maltravers and you will go home under my guard early on the morrow. And we shall never meet again like this—not until you know you love me and have the courage to say so."

Dazedly, she gazed up at him, her lips tingling from his rough kisses, her whole body afire with aching desire. "Please, my lord—"

His big hand covered her mouth. "No excuses, no lies. Tonight, here when I touched you and you begged me not to stop, you were either a whore or a woman in love, Jeannette. Think on that dilemma the eons until we meet again."

His hand, the pressure of his chest, his warmth fled. Before she could rise up on one elbow to say whatever words she could find, he covered the little space of floor, opened, and then closed the door behind him so quietly she was sure he had not just touched her everywhere at all.

She held her breath as two pairs of heavy footsteps descended the stairs. Frozen, she heard two horses in the street below. After an eternity of staring at the flickering ghosts on the ceiling, she breathed out a great, rasping sob.

His cruel words, his touch she could still feel—see his eager face. Blessed Virgin, she wanted to scream his name and chase after him out into the dark, dark night!

Cold tears ran across her flushed cheeks to roll into her ears and down her throat. Her body ached, pained as though some integral, inner part of it had been wrenched away. Her mind crashed into a frantic emptiness where only his cold voice echoed in hollow repetition. Whore. Love. Eons. Meet. Again.

All night she heard his velvet voice and dreamed of horses' hoofs in the close below. She jolted wide awake whenever she thought there were men's footsteps in the hall. She believed she heard Roger's voice singing that sad song of bitter love again, again, but it must have been only echoes of her frenzied, futile dreams.

She was, no doubt, she told herself grimly over and over that next week, the only person who had ever gone on a pilgrimage to Canterbury and never seen the shrine. Guarded by three of the prince's plainly dressed men and accompanied by a glum-looking Roger Wakeley, she had returned to Liddell early the next morn. She had not protested the cold, efficient orders of the prince's men whom she did not know. She felt chastened, drained, shamed, and bereft. She held her head high and spoke to none of them. Yet they had bid her a polite farewell and turned their horses back to Canterbury even as the walls of Liddell first loomed in sight among the Kentish Weald.

The next week, she moved about Liddell at her duties and pastimes in a daze. Whatever she did, repeatedly her eyes glazed over with the veil of memory and she would stand stock-still as if frozen by a wizard's wand: her hands preparing spices or sewing, her arms full of her children, in half-stride on a brisk walk about the grounds, she would turn, listless, and hear his angry, impassioned words and see and feel his presence.

He had loved her from the first, he vowed. Loved, loved, from that first day she had seen him angered and muddy, with broken wrist tilting at the quintain in that lonely yard at Windsor. She had not then known who he was or what terrible thing that yard had seen—her father's murder, mayhap at the very will of the prince's father. How tangled the tentacles of passions had become—as dear, old Marta used to say, like a clinging spider's web that would never let one run to freedom again.

Freedom. How she had desired it once, fought for it, and how it had eluded her. Did she ever possess it? Did it end when she had first gone to court or when Mother died that night and the child had understood at last the woman's burden of lost love? Or had real freedom ceased to be when she had first gazed up into those deep blue eyes under that tawny mane of Plantagenet hair?

She shook her head hard to bring herself back to her surroundings. Vinette had just finished with her hair. She had dressed formally tonight for supper although Thomas would be gone for at least three more weeks and John had not yet arrived back from Midsummer Tournaments in London. She sighed as she stood to give herself a final, quick perusal in her polished mirror. She had donned a new emerald kirtle and white *surcote* edged with seed pearls to cheer herself. Besides, getting all dressed up like this for a lonely supper with only Vinette and Roger to speak to at least took time and attention and kept her from moping or brooding half the day. Then, too, last night she had dreamed again of running away down a long, black tunnel, chased by thudding footsteps. De Maltravers, mayhap, or even the king—but really, she feared it was something else there in the darkness which pursued her: something like her own desperate fear that she loved the prince and always had.

"No!"

"What? Madame Joan, you do not like the coiffure?" Vinette asked, her concerned face appearing in the mirror above Joan's shoulder. "But I did it just as you wished, Madame!"

"No, it is fine, Vinette. I was just thinking aloud, that is all."

The maid rolled her brown eyes as she had repeatedly this week at her mistress' jumpy behavior. Wherever Madame Joan had gone, whatever she had done this week had changed her, and Vinette did not believe for one minute that the lady and her narrow-eyed musician had gone off to Canterbury as they said. Had they not come home empty-handed with naught but one pilgrim's penny and was not there talk in the serfs' marketplace that she had ridden in with three strange men who had turned tail and fled at the sight of Liddell Manor? If only they had been home in France, her love, Pierre Foulke, would have known what to make of the fatuous doings of the nobility. Pierre said there would be a day of reckoning when the rich and noble would come tumbling down and then, he promised, there would be no more secret, haughty happenings among the smug nobility.

Vinette Brinay shrugged her slender shoulders. She did not really believe that day would ever come, but it did keep Pierre all astir with grand plans for heroic deeds every bit as secret and haughty as the doings of the nobles he said he hated. Besides, Madame Joan was a good enough young mistress, though she was entirely too moody of late. Then, too, the first two weeks Lord Thomas had been gone to his lands up north, the lady had chatted amiably with Vinette after dinner and given her much free time in the long, sweet afternoons.

"I said, thank you, Vinette. Why not see how Madeleine is doing rousing the little ones while I go on down? We shall all sit by the head table in the hall and sing after supper. At Liddell I cannot bear to eat here in the solar where my mother lived alone so long when I was little. The Great Hall is large, but it is better there."

"Aye, and so sweet-smelling on these summer eves, Madame. Mayhap your brother and his men be on their way home soon and you will not have to eat with just the little ones, all alone with your thoughts."

Joan pivoted to stare at the girl as she stood at the top of the newel staircase which led down to the front corridor. Vinette faced her guilelessly, a concerned look on her pretty, freckled face. Surely, this maid and the other servants, except Roger, could know nothing of what she had done and been through. "Do not fret for my thoughts, Vinette," she said and then to be certain the girl could never read her mind, she added, "My memories of my mother's days here are peaceful now. All that sadness is long past."

Partway down the curve of stairs, she heard the rattle of horses' hoofs outside. They must be close on the cobbles directly at the entrance to make all that noise. John was home or, perhaps, visitors had come from Canterbury on the road home to London!

She pressed her clasped fists to her pounding chest and hurried to the front door. The servants, including John's fourth squire Robert he had left at home, and two cooks, came darting from parts of the manor to see who it was. Squire Robert opened the big front door for her and she strode boldly out under the family crest before it even occurred to her it might be anyone else besides John returned or the prince come to apologize for his wretched behavior at Canterbury last week.

She halted on the top step of the entry and stared as her emerald skirts belled gently to a rest about her hips and legs. She faced six men in black, mounted on black horses. All

were liveried with the gold and azure leopard and lily crests
of the King of England.

"Lady Joan of Kent?" the silver-haired man at the head of
the impressive little band asked.

"Aye. Welcome to Liddell. I am Joan of Kent, Lady
Holland." Her heart began to thud wildly until it nearly
drowned out her thoughts and their crisp words to her. The
king was angered mayhap she had dared interfere with the
prince or de Maltravers and perhaps he had sent them to
arrest her!

The silver-haired man she felt she should recognize but
could not place had dismounted. "I beg your gracious leave
to speak direct to the point, Lady Joan of Kent," the man
said. Joan was aware Vinette, holding little Thomas, and
Madeleine, with the babe John, now flanked her on either
side, their eyes wide at the display of unfamiliar men black-
garbed, armed, and royally liveried.

"Speak, then," she answered.

"I am Sir Lyle Townsend, Lady Joan. His Grace, Edward,
King of England and France, bids me tell you most grievous
news. At the Midsummer's Eve Tournament there was a
grande mêlée which became quite bold and undisciplined,
lady."

Her voice sounded sharply piercing as it rang out. "John?
Has my Lord John been hurt?"

The man's eyes were lightest brown, and she saw him set
his jaw hard. "Aye, lady. The king sends his grievous regrets,
his most sad condolences. There were four knights accidentally trampled in the *mêlée*, lady, and your brother
John is dead. His body as well as gifts from the king follow
by a day or so in a funeral cortège which we—"

"No!" Her own shrieked denial shredded the spring air,
and her baby began to cry in frightened, rattled screams.

The man touched her arm, urging her inside, but she
shook him off and stood her ground.

"In the king's tournament?" she demanded. "He cannot be

366

dead! Men do not die in tournaments. Saints, I know they lose eyes or break bones, but not dead!"

"We are grief-stricken, Lady Joan. He was a fine knight of mettle yet fully untested, fine, young and brave."

"Young, aye. He was the last."

"The last of your family except for yourself, you mean," he said nearly shouting to be heard over the baby's cries. "The king at the urging of His Grace, the Prince of Wales, recognizes this too, lady, and bids you accept the lands of Lord John as your own duty and inheritance. His Grace declares you Duchess of Kent, with title rights to these demesne lands and hall."

The thought sank in slowly: Liddell—hers. She took little John away from teary-eyed Madeleine into her arms to comfort him and slumped back against the entryway for support.

Surely, this was all another waking dream, a black nightmare of pounding steps and rushing down an interminable, deep tunnel. John was only twenty with Liddell to care for and to love. The plague stole Edmund three years ago and now this!

Gifts from the king to foolishly try to compensate for John's death, she thought, as the other men dismounted and stood patiently at the bottom of the steps with loaded arms. "I will accept no gifts from the king," she announced to them. Her knees shook as did her voice, and she pressed back harder against the stone doorway to stop the spinning of the men and forest beyond.

"Please, Duchess, let us go in," Lyle Townsend was saying. "I know this is dreadful, dreadful news. We are bid to give you these gifts—to a member of the king's own family, His Grace said, and here, look, the king and the Prince of Wales, who has sent gifts also and a missive, bid you bear up under this sore trial and accept this with their love."

He motioned for another man to step forward. While she clutched her babe to her and Vinette and Madeleine and

John's poor, sniveling little squire Robert pressed close to her, the man unrolled a stiff parchment scroll. On it was painted exquisitely in luminous colors and gilded gold, the Kent family coat of arms with one vast difference: around the neck of the snow-white stag resting on the bed of ivy was now a ducal crown chained by golden fetters to a larger, grander royal crown.

Joan's eyes burning with tears stared unblinking at the beautiful crest.

"Your new coat of arms, fashioned at the desire of the king and prince, Duchess," the man was saying gently. "They bid you recognize your necessary ties to the crown as indeed your father and both brothers before you have done. They bid you accept this tragedy with peace in your heart and love for your distant cousins of Plantagenet blood, His Grace the King and the Prince of Wales."

Her eyes lifted to Lyle Townsend's intent face and she blinked the tears away to see him. She, beset by shock and grief and loss again, understood the new crest and the accompanying, warning words well enough. Aye, she could read this fair painting, these gifts, this wretched new turn of fortune's cruel wheel well enough. She was as captured as that deer there, chained to them whether she willed it or not, chained by circumstances and bitter hatred—and mayhap now, by love.

Blinded by tears, she held her babe to her and turned back inside into the vast silence of Liddell. She would survive this all. She must! She would bury John next to Edmund and Anne under the stone floor of the church and raise up a beautiful stone effigy to his young, vanquished knighthood. She would care for Liddell until her Lord Thomas returned. If the word of the tragedy had traveled north, surely he would come soon. But whether he did or not, she, Joan, Duchess of Kent, would be alone in grief for eons until she would see the prince again.

She turned to glance once more at the painted family crest she now assumed as her own due. The little golden chain linking ducal crown to royal—aye, that was the way she felt beneath all this bitterness. For the first time in her life, something terrifying seemed absolutely inevitable.

Tears streaming down her face, she bid the king's men enter the hall and sent the wailing cooks to prepare more food.

Part Three

O man unkind,
Have thou in mind
My passion sharp!
Thou shalt me find
To thee full kind:
Lo, here my heart.

Chapter Seventeen

Thrashing fitfully on the big feather bed, Joan awoke, but the dream pressed yet heavily upon her. A cresset lamp still burned low on the solar table. Her startled eyes widened, darted up to the underside of the satin bed canopy. Saints, she was home at the Château safe in bed! Alone.

Reality rushed back to shred the remnants of her nightmare: she had been in that tiny room in Canterbury again and the frightening footsteps were thudding up the steps, down the hall. The door of the chamber had opened, but before the cloaked figure could enter, she turned and ran into the dark, secret tunnel which led to freedom outside. She ran and ran until she could not think or breathe.

Joan pressed her hands to her temples and shoved back the masses of tangled blond hair. The coverlet and sheets wrapped around her perspiring body felt like a constricting cocoon. Damn, she thought, I have not had that dream for almost a year.

She shoved the covers off, rose, and wrapped herself in a warm perse robe. Although it was still comfortable this early September, the nights hinted at the tangy nip of autumn frost.

She sank into a chair at the solar table and poured herself a little Burgundy. She could not have been asleep too long before the dream began, she reasoned, for the lamp had not sputtered out. She would love to peek in on the children to assure herself all was well except that would rouse Madeleine, too, and then the servants would whisper that their Lady Holland, Duchess of Kent, paced the castle halls at all hours because her Lord Thomas had gone to war.

The tepid wine soothed her throat. Poor Thomas—happy enough like the rest of the English knights that war threatened France again, but not at all happy to be summoned into service of the Prince of Wales' younger brother John, newly created Duke of Lancaster. After all, Thomas Holland had bellowed when the orders had arrived via royal courier, he was a charter member of the Garter Knights who had seen service with the prince at Crécy. And to make matters worse, she knew it rankled him that she now outranked him as a duchess while he had not been elevated to a duke.

She had no way of knowing what it all meant—if it meant anything at all—and she refused to speculate. It had been more than four years now since she had seen the prince, and that one meeting was only a brief, impassioned half hour in Canterbury. Since then there had been naught from him but an annual written Yuletide greeting to her and her lord. The three other times she and Thomas had been back in England to oversee Liddell or the Holland lands in Lancashire, she had been near no one from the court, preferring to stay at Liddell while Thomas visited Windsor or Westminster only to report back that the prince had not been there anyway. He, like the other knights of the realm, had bided his time at his own pursuits until the long-awaited call to arms had come at last.

As she stared into the dark swirl of Burgundy in her goblet, she marveled that her life had been so relatively calm and content these five and a half years of her marriage to Thomas Holland. Except for that tumultuous week the summer she had gone to Canterbury and her dear brother John had been killed in Midsummer Eve tournament, really there had been nothing but memories to stir the blood, and memories oft burned low like this wavering cresset lamp. The adventure, the freedom, the desire to drink deeply of life that she had longed for as a maid—what had happened to *that* Joan of Kent?

Almost before she realized what she would do, she stood and hurried to the carved coffer which held her winter furred *surcotes*. Her hand burrowed down to the bottom of the chest through velvets and brocades and softest furs all smelling faintly of winter sachet herbs until she seized the flat, carved box which had once held her mother's few jewels. She opened the box almost reverently and stared in the dim light at the little beryl ring and the single parchment letter with the broken red wax seal. It had been a good long time since she had read the letter from the prince although she had once nearly worn it out with staring at the words until she had etched them in her memory. In the light of the lamp, his own firm, bold strokes of handwriting now leapt at her from the crinkled page:

My Lady Jeannette,

The inevitable separations—through death or otherwise—which we must face are indeed the cruelest blows life deals. Yet in this loss of your dear brother John as in that loss of your brother Edmund we shared two Yules ago, I pray you shall find solace.

Now let me speak this business clearly: the king is grieved for your past differences with him and the queen over the loss of your father years ago. He did love his uncle Edmund of Kent also and bids you accept from him two condolences for the loss of your family members as he sues for peace between you.

Firstly, he does create Joan, Lady Holland as Duchess of Kent and sole heiress of Liddell Manor House in the shire of Kent and all *demesne* lands attached thereto. Let your head and your heart accept this bestowal graciously for your father's sake, lady, for as you realize, with all male heirs of your family now deceased, Liddell would otherwise revert to the crown for bestowal elsewhere.

Secondly, His Grace, Edward, King of England and

France, bids me assure you that one Flemish ambassador of whom you and I have recently spoken, will not be returned to live in England, nor shall his vast land holdings once confiscated by the crown upon his exile be returned to him; however, he shall no longer be forfeit of his manor house in Dorset wherein his wife resides. (I know you will accept this too with equanimity, Jeannette, as surely you have no quarrel with the man's wife any more than you might have with the wife of whatever poor axeman finally did the deed.)

Dear Duchess of Kent, these things must of force content you for now. Keep close your dear home of Liddell for your second son John who bears his young, deceased uncle's proud name. The elder lad, Thomas, will, no doubt, inherit the Holland estates to the north someday.

Until that day we meet again, remember me.

Edward, P.W.P.

Post Script. I hope that you, like I, will see the golden fetters binding the two crowns on your new Duchess coat of arms not as an imprisoning bondage but as a golden link of eternal affection.

She stared long at the brash signature: Edward, Prince of Wales, Plantagenet. How skillful this letter was, how impossible to argue with or disobey. That day the king's men had come to Liddell with news of John's death, she had not accepted His Grace's tendered gifts except for the two bestowals Edward had urged her to take in this letter. Saints, how much there was here brimming beneath the cleverly selected words, if one dared to let the imagination free. He had used mention of her sons to settle her contentious spirit at accepting gifts from the king she detested. And who had told him her son's names, for she never had. Then, here at the very end—where her fingertip even now stroked the words—

did the cryptic wording not hint that Thomas Holland's eventual death day might be the same as "that day we meet again"?

Lost in the glow of reminiscence, she put the little beryl ring on her finger and replaced the folded letter at the bottom of the coffer. She had never shown the letter to her Lord Thomas and told herself she kept it only so that her son John would be assured of his inheritance of Liddell someday.

Distraught she had let her thoughts wander so and afraid she would never manage to reclaim sleep now, she moved to a window over the gardens and pushed the leaden pane ajar. In muted melody through the brisk night air, the strains of two distant lutes wafted to her.

It was, of course, Master Roger and that traveling minstrel friend of his, Stephen Callender, who had been here and at Liddell several other times the past year. The song was one she did not recognize, and yet the stirring melody, however distant, beckoned to her.

She donned her felt slippers and, lifting the low-burning lamp, went out into the corridor. Master Roger's room was directly beneath this wing, as were Vinette's and the small chambers of the other household servants. She padded down the staircase to the corridor below, recalling the late night venture she had made down the black secret tunnel of the Château to visit Marta's grave. In the dim, narrow hall, lit only by one rush torch at the far end, the melody of the two entwined lutes was much more distinct. They were strumming rather than plucking the strings; the song had a martial beat, and words drifted to her now as the refrain began again:

> "The prince among the press of shields
> In ebony-hued armor
> Doth lead his men
> French strife to end
> Under white-feathered banner.

"Beside my prince amid the fray
There's no place to be rather.
See helmets split, lances shatter,
And blows exchanged in battle."

The melody ceased but a conversation began as Joan stood fascinated by the new war song on the other side of the door. How beautifully Roger's clear, unmistakable tenor had blended with Stephen Callender's baritone in that marching song, and how distinctly their words floated to her now.

"That will please the prince, Stephen, though, by the rood, I know what little gift would please him more in these treacherous times while he raids France up and down from Bordeaux and tries his tricky damnedest to avoid the French king's growing army."

"What would please him more, Wakeley—a victory over the French or the beauteous Lady Joan of Kent in his bed?"

They both chuckled. Joan jumped at her own sharp intake of breath, and she nearly dropped her lamp. She could not have heard aright! That man could not have said those words, nor her old friend Master Roger have laughed with him like that!

Her first impulse was to pound on the door and accuse them, but she froze listening intently as Stephen Callender's voice went on. "By the saints, Wakeley, what shall I tell him new this trip when I get to reconnoiter with our forces at Tours? That the lady is lordless now that Holland is off to help Lancaster chase Frenchies? A hell of a lot of good that will do him as he has an eight-thousand-man army to protect and answer to."

Hell's gates, her mind shrieked, this man is off for the prince's camp at Tours, wherever that is, and to report on me! All those other traveling musician friends of Roger's— this man himself here before back and forth—a spy! And, worst of all, her own long-time confidant, Master Roger, a gift from the prince when she had married Thomas—all

378

these years, sent to spy on her!

Her shoulder pressed hard into the rough stone wall outside the door while fury wracked her. But then, that passion turned to overwhelming curiosity. If Roger Wakeley was a royal informer as well as a skilled musician, when had it begun? Those years at Liddell when she first knew him—oh, saints, sent to spy on them then too, mayhap on her poor, shattered mother to be certain she caused no upheaval over her husband's unjust murder: a serpent nurtured in the very bosom of her family all these years!

The welling anger, buried for all this time since the royal Plantagenets had given her Liddell and she had compromised on de Maltravers's lands, rose up in huge, overwhelming waves to assault her. A spy she had loved all these years; then, surely, the Plantagenets were guilty of her father's death as mother had claimed! The prince had only done what his royal sire had demanded of him. He had wooed her, guarded her, watched her at his king's command, and she had almost been snared by it all to fall in line like another poor warrior knight to do whatever he bid! Never. Never! How she longed to throw what she knew in his wretched, handsome face in front of his whole army!

She forced herself to listen to their voices again, and when she heard Stephen Callender's next words, the plan came to her full blown, perfect, and so thrilling, she curled her toes in her soft felt slippers to keep from screaming her joy.

"I will bid you a good-night then, Wakeley, with one more roll through this new song so you can teach it to His Grace's lively Kentish lass. At dawn's first light, man, I am off to report to the prince and I hope to hell for my sake he is further north than when I left him."

She turned away and ran down the corridor as they began strumming the pompous martial song again. Saints, if the prince loved a good battle, so be it, for he was about to face one that would make the French foe seem like mere tilting at the quintain. At dawn's first light, that wretch Stephen Callender had said. She had a lot to do in these few hours, notes to write, a saddle sack to pack with clothes and food. Settling the score with Roger Wakeley would have to wait until her return, and he would have to cooperate with her plan and help cover her departure or she would threaten to expose him and insist he leave forever. The knowledge that he had cared for her only because of his need to know what she did pierced her like a sharp pain, but she hurried on. By dawn's first light, she would have a horse and be awaiting Spy Stephen at the bend in the forest road and then she would tell him a thing or two she had gleaned from spying!

Her heart beat faster and she smiled despite herself at the prospect of meeting the prince in her own lance-shattering battle.

The next morn Joan let Stephen Callender ride past her in the damp forest mists of dawn and followed him, careful to keep her horse Windsong on the soft turf along the road so he would not look back. She had no intention of stopping him to reveal herself where any early-rising manor serf could see her or to be so close to the Château yet that the man might consider dragging her back. But he set a good pace south, and the one time he did glance over his shoulder that first hour of foggy daylight, he evidently saw naught amiss in the cloaked and hooded boy on a horse behind him as he plunged on, skirting the sleepy little village of Le Bec Hellouin about five miles from the Château. He looked back the second time as the road opened up through fields of barley and oats awaiting the harvesters' sickles in the weeks to come. The crops grew in tiny, random patches as they were divided or merged haphazardly over the centuries by serfs' deaths or marriages, reminding Joan of a brightly hued, irregular chess board. The time, she realized, for her next chess move was now. Sweeping her arm in a wide arc that Stephen Callender could not misinterpret since he'd turned around in his saddle again, she summoned him to her.

He halted and swung his chestnut-colored horse around to trot back cautiously toward her. She knew he would need to be close before he recognized her, for she had dressed in garments borrowed from Thomas's squire last night, and her thick tresses were tightly braided and coiled under a heavy brown hood. Her black palfrey bore no signs of rank or person.

"State your business with me, my man," Stephen Callender demanded, his eyes dark slits under his straight, black hair as he squinted to see the face within the deep hood. His right hand rested easily upon his sword hilt. He halted his horse about twelve feet away and simply stared.

With a flourish, Joan threw her hood off and stared back, reveling in the man's obvious shock and dismay. His long face dropped even longer as he swore a string of curses in French as if he could make her disappear or flee. "By the death of the Blessed Virgin!" he managed at last in English. "Duchess—are you alone? Am I sent for to return?"

"Of course you are sent for to return, Master Callender— to return to the prince to report on all my doings like a good little lackey," she spit out at the astounded man and relished the panic which rioted across his usually well-guarded features.

"My lady, please, I do not know what someone has told you, but—"

"But nothing, Master Spy-Musician! And, pray, do not look so alarmed. Since His Grace, the Prince of Wales, is evidently so eager to keep watch on my thoughts, my family, and my actions, I am merely doing you a service as well as he. Will he not be much pleased to reward you richly when you not only give him the little tattletales and rumors you and Master Roger have so cleverly gleaned, but actually deliver me in person to give him a hearty dose of what he would know when we get to Tours?"

The man's eyes nearly popped from their sockets at that, and at first only a strangled, little sound came from his throat. "To Tours! Hell's bells, Duchess, Tours is a hundred miles from here through enemy-held territory!"

"I do not believe you. We have heard all week that the

prince's brother's army where my husband serves is here in Normandy marching south to meet the prince's forces."

"True, Duchess, but I know not where either English army is for certain and I plan a hard, three-day ride to Tours and His Grace's forces may not even be there when I arrive."

"When *we* arrive, Master Callender. I can keep the pace, though I had not reckoned on so far a jaunt."

"A jaunt? Holy Saints, Duchess, the prince would have my head on a pike to rot in the sun if he ever thought I took you for a ride outside your castle walls in these dangerous times, let alone over a hundred miles through enemy territory to Tours! My head on a pike!"

"I suggest you stop screeching, man, and we get under way. The prince will have your head on a pike indeed unless you do exactly as I say anyway. I have important business with the prince, thanks to his continual meddling in my life, and I cannot help it that he is running around France when I need to tell him such. I will see you are protected and my dear friend Roger Wakeley too, for I wish to deal with him myself—*if* you deliver me to His Grace and then back home again safely. I brought food. I can ride, so let us be off!"

She replaced her hood and jogged slowly past the man who scrambled to follow. From a swift side glance she read his face well. His sallow skin had gone livid with fury and panic.

"Please, Duchess, have mercy on a poor man—on Wakeley, too. When His Grace loses his temper, no one is safe."

"Really? And I assure you, Master Callender, when I lose mine, the prince is not safe either. I think we had best set a faster speed here if we hope to make good time."

"I insist you go back. For your children's sake—for all of us, I shall escort you back. In truth, I do not know where the prince's army is. I may have to search for days and when your husband hears—"

"He shall not hear, for I left word I have retreated to the cloisters at the Church of St. Ouen in Pont-Audemer for a few days, and no French army will bother two swift-riding men on the road when they are desperately searching for a whole, vast English army."

She urged her horse to a gallop and Callender followed, pounding along beside her and shouting warnings she blithely ignored. It felt so wonderful to be out in the late summer air, free of constricting walls, servants' eyes, and whispers. The saddle, the horse's rhythmic movement were exhilarating beneath her.

When, in final desperation, the man beside her dared to reach out for her horse's bridle to halt her, she smacked his wrist sharply with her reins and settled him in his place for good. "You will escort me quickly and carefully to the prince and then home again and never tell a living soul, Spy Stephen. If you do this, I shall assure His Grace you saved my life on the road or some such and that I forced you to bring me. However, if you do not cease this foolish, wasteful foot-dragging, I swear to you by St. George's blood, I will tell the prince you sought to lie where you so jestingly told Master Roger the Prince of Wales himself would revel—in my bed. Do I make my serious intent quite clear by this promise, prince's spy?"

The man's mouth set hard, but his angry, intense eyes gazed straight ahead at last. "Aye, Duchess of Kent. Quite clear. I will tell you only, I expect no complaining then; for with wench bait even garbed like a boy, I have no intent to be seen or stopped. From now until we sight the banners of azure and gold and the three ostrich plumes of the prince, we halt only to rest the horses."

She turned her face back to the road south and smiled as she refastened her hood carefully forward over her curls. A victory over the prince already and she had not yet even given him a hint of the battle to come! She bent lower over Windsong's rippling mane, reveling in the intoxicating glow of freedom, adventure, and power she only last night thought had been lost forever.

*   *   *

383

Soon enough the thrill dulled to pounding hoofs on dusty roads or grassy fields as they skirted the French villages of L'Aigle, Mortagne, and Bêlleme. Joan got soaked to her skin when they forded the River Risle to avoid a bridge crowded with drovers' carts. Soon enough, her muscles ached and her teeth and head pained with every rough jolt. She walked stiffly bowlegged when they dismounted to rest or water the horses and, even as they sat to share simnel biscuits and cheese, she still felt the pounding rhythm of Windsong's powerful flanks. They slept a few hours one night burrowed into a haystack and the next in a damp rye field. They stole apples from orchards for themselves and the horses, and plunged on again, crossing the Loire on a tiny, unfortified bridge near Couture in the middle of the night.

Forced to hide in the thicket of the road the next day as a French contingent of soldiers passed so close that they overheard their every word, Joan turned spy herself. She and Stephen learned that King John II had brought his French army down from Chartres to Blois from which he hoped to cut off Prince John of Lancaster and his English battalions which had been raiding through Normandy. The thought that English troops and her husband might be somewhere in the vicinity heartened Joan until she realized that Thomas Holland, if he knew of this scheme, would definitely stop her. Nothing, nothing, she vowed silently again, would halt her from her own battle with Prince Edward. Aye, she and these dangerous French had one thing in common, at least, for she meant to win a victory once and for all over Edward, Prince of Wales, Plantagenet.

On their third day on the road, the calm weather turned blustery. Leaves rattled, trees sighed and swayed, and the skirts of a young woman ahead of them on the road whipped wildly around her ankles. They would have passed by the maid quickly, but her words nearly carried away by the wind stopped them.

"Good sirs, a little ride into the village, *si'l vous plaît*? I hate to walk against the wind, and I fear the whoreson damned English may be near."

Stephen said something to Joan about information and turned back to lift the girl up behind him. She was buxom, black-haired with rather swarthy skin and dark eyes, but Joan was careful not to stare too closely.

"Where are these terrible English forces, then, *ma belle*?" Stephen asked her in his smoothest French as they jogged on.

"I can tell you not far enough away. Wish't they were all roasting in hell, I do. The Black Prince of Crécy been raiding northward from Bordeaux all summer, the bastards. But Tours shall never be taken. The French hold it firmly, and our blessed king's army outnumbers the English over two to one. Gerard told me the whoreson damned English will be cut off at Tours and squashed like a beetle under a rock, the bastards."

"You are so very well informed, *ma belle*," Stephen flattered her. Joan noted the girl's dark eyes were trying to peer beneath her hood even while she spoke to Stephen, so she rode a bit farther ahead.

"Of course I am well informed," the maid's voice floated to Joan's alert ears. "The Comte de Poitiers's troops only yesterday were garrisoned in our village up ahead and hold it yet. I slept, fine sir, with Gerard, the Comte's first squire, who told me all those things after he enjoyed my charms. I pleased him greatly, you see. Wish't you or your handsome friend with the fine legs might want the same loving, eh? I have a room behind the inn and for a coin, I could show you both what the Comte's squire enjoyed and why he told me all his thoughts after he enjoyed my charms, eh?"

"The coin I shall give you as a token of thanks, but I must put you down as my friend and I need to go on our way and not through your little village, alas."

Despite her surprise and protest, Stephen swung her down and flipped her a coin. She did not dart after it but stood arms akimbo in the road staring up at them. "It shan't do you no good to avoid the French soldiers if that be what ye're thinking," she said. "The troops of our blessed King Jean le Bon—they are everywhere here. And say, sir, is your friend there a boy or a maid? And why does he never say a word then?"

Joan and Stephen wheeled away off the road and left her shouting her questions at them until the wind swallowed up her words.

"Have we miscalculated where he should be?" Joan asked Stephen as they followed a little streambed across a meadow southward. "Do you think the French could really hold Tours and be ready to cut off His Grace's outnumbered army?"

"Men only tell lies before they sleep with a maid, not after," Stephen said brusquely and spurred his horse to a faster clip.

On the hunch that the maid spoke the truth about the French army's position, Stephen and Joan skirted an extra half-day southeast around Tours. Between Langeais and Villandry they finally found a small unguarded bridge on which to cross the wide, Loire River, as Prince John of Lancaster was no doubt trying to do to reinforce and rescue Prince Edward's badly outnumbered forces. South of the Loire and of Tours, they rode east on the fourth afternoon, praying the first troops they saw would speak French only as a conquered language.

An hour before sunset, just as they had dismounted to discuss how they could best avoid the little village of Monbazon ahead, Stephen and Joan stiffened in shock. Horsemen exploded noisily from the bush. Joan's horse bolted in panic. Stephen thrust her between his mount and his back as he drew his sword. Three big horsemen instantly towered over them all with swords and pikes which glittered bloodily in the low western sun.

"One little move with that blade, rogue, and you two are vulture's meat," a gruff voice shouted down at them in French, and Stephen pressed Joan back farther behind him as he threw down his sword.

Another tall rider loomed over them, his clopping horse's hoofs drowning out Joan's pounding heart. This man wore a helmet with no visor, and with huge broadsword drawn, he leaned down to flick Joan's hood off her head. Her fingers tightened around the single, small dagger she wore thrust in her leather belt. The sun blazed behind the man's big head as his sword point caught both hood and hidden hair coil to yank her head back hard against the flanks of Stephen's skittish horse.

Instantaneously, Joan recognized their captor with the broadsword. Even as the man's huge gloved hand caught Stephen's chin to shove him away from where he hovered panicked in front of Joan, the skies thundered and Joan shrieked his name.

"Captal de Buch! Stop! Do not harm him. I am Lady Holland, Duchess of Kent, and we have come to see the prince!"

De Buch, one of the king's Gascon advisors on the French wars, halted with his sword in midair as though he still considered hacking Stephen apart.

"Saints' souls!" the Captal cursed. "Here? The Fair Maid of Kent? And think, we were looking for spies of the French king and we find a *belle demoiselle* out for a ride with a *beau*, eh?"

A low rumble of nervous laughter welled up to match the next roll of thunder, and Joan felt her dirty cheeks go hot at their eager-eyed perusal.

"His Grace, the prince is not exactly holding parties on the lawn while waiting for the French, Duchess, but I know he will be pleased to entertain so enterprising a lady, eh?" His words rolled off his tongue roughly with a strange accent, and his deep laughter bubbled up again as Stephen moved closer to stand guard over her and someone brought her bolted horse back.

"Then, Captal, we have ridden a long way today and would appreciate an escort to His Grace's castle," she brazened, feeling both relieved and nervous.

Huge guffaws punctuated by the rumble of even closer thunder erupted and, to her chagrin, Joan noted even Stephen, grim-faced as he was, dared to join in. "Saints' bones, pardon my bluntness, Duchess, but this is war you have come to see! Still I know with this storm on that French army we have been fleeing from, the prince, *certainement*, will be glad to see you. Let us be off then, before this coming rain drowns us all. Back to Monbarzon men, onward!" de Buch shouted grandly.

Under the Captal de Buch's annoyingly amused gaze, Stephen helped her remount. The rain had washed much of the road dust away in a great driving deluge by the time they sighted the English sentries lining the crenelated battlements of the little village of Monbarzon.

Edward, Prince of Wales, had become increasingly more ill-tempered as the calm September day turned more humid and a violent thunderstorm approached to rend the peaceful French landscape. He had sent his Gascon ally and advisor, the raucous but wily Captal de Buch, out to reconnoiter the area around the little village of Monbarzon which they had just captured and fortified several miles south of Tours. As soon as de Buch returned from his survey of the area, Prince Edward would summon his advisors to decide what to do next about their increasingly perilous predicament.

King Jean with his French army twice the size of the English forces was temporarily resting at Blois a mere twenty-five miles up the Loire, and his own troops, tired of marching and laden with heavy goods and booty from their two-month raid on hostile French territory, would be no match for size or vigor at this point. A rest, if they could afford one, was desperately needed. Now, with this sudden devastating change in the weather, he was beginning to worry whether they would make it back to safe haven south in English-held Aquitaine. And worse, he feared his brother John's forces would not manage to get across the Loire from Normandy to help in time—especially in this hellish weather that would probably trap them here!

A sharp rap rattled the door of the rich merchant's house the prince had made his temporary headquarters here in the heart of the little, high-walled village of Monbarzon. He looked up, annoyed, from where he had been studying a finely detailed map of the terrain to the south around Poitiers where he hoped to make a stand if retreat were impossible. It angered him that his mind continually wandered and he had planned little strategy in the hour he had been left alone at his request to do so. Another knock sounded.

"Enter!"

The young, slender, William Montacute, Lord Salisbury, whom the prince appreciated for his good brain in battle tactics despite the fact Jeannette had once been technically wed to the man, entered. Salisbury looked tired, but the sun color on his often pale face made him look healthier than most of the men.

"Is de Buch back, Will?"

"No, Your Grace, but the rain we feared has started like Noah's deluge out there. At least it will bottle up the bloody French at Blois just as well."

"Aye, but they are rested and not so heavy burdened nor short on supplies after all this marching and fighting. Then what is the news?"

"The French pretender—the French king, my lord prince—"

"Aye, John the Good, as he so pompously dubs himself. Well, say on."

"Our own envoy back from Blois is at the gate to say that Pope Innocent IV is sending two holy cardinals as envoys to sue for peace between King John and Your Grace, and that the French believe we are so ripe for the picking, they will no doubt demand ludicrously insulting terms."

The prince's handsome face barely changed, but his aquamarine eyes shifted back to the map. "St. George, Will, I can see one blessing in disguise in that. The Pope's elaborate negotiations always take a good deal of time, you know, and time to rest and plan is more a gift to us than to King John's forces at this rather tenuous point in our campaign."

"Aye, my lord prince. There is that."

Prince Edward, garbed casually as he often was on campaign in dark blue tunic and hose under an embossed leather jerkin, regarded Salisbury through slitted eyes. The look of intense perusal used to set Salisbury's teeth on edge, for once he knew he had been greatly out of favor with this prince on whom they all so desperately depended and admired. But now Salisbury had come to know such a look of glittering blue ice came anytime the prince was deep in serious thought, and his increasingly sharp temper stemmed from the fact he drove himself hard in this effort to please both his royal father and his own high standards. At least since Salisbury had lost Joan of Kent over six years ago and now had married well himself, he had evidently been returned to his prince's favor. Joan of Kent—he had not thought about her for days now—flashed across Salisbury's memory and he knew she must sometimes haunt the prince too.

Salisbury wondered again if it was due to the fact that Joan of Kent lived in Normandy that the prince had been sent to Aquitaine by the king and Prince John had been sent north to Normandy. After all, each prince knew the other area more thoroughly, but the king had been adamant as to assignments. Hell's gates, the ironies of life, Salisbury mused, that he and the prince might actually have been sent to Normandy to march shoulder to shoulder past Joan of Kent's present home. But that would have been too rare, too fatalistic for the three of them to be thrust back together after all this time.

"I said, Salisbury, when this rain lets up, our best move is to hie ourselves, baggage trains and all, down these mud-slogged roads south to Poitiers to make a stand. We will retreat from there if we can. That is all for now. I will send for you when de Buch returns if he has not been drowned in this downpour. If we are to have several days of this, these walls and roofs are God's blessing compared to those sodden tents."

"Aye, Your Grace. I shall just be about then until there is news from de Buch."

When Salisbury went out, there was a commotion at the door and Prince Edward heard the Captal de Buch's unmistakably distinctive southern French accent in the hall. He rose from his maps and strode to the door. Salisbury had halted halfway out and looked as if he had seen a ghost, or at least a bloody Frenchman with a raised sword. The Captal muttered something to Salisbury that sounded like a threat to hold his silence, and he shoved by the startled man with a sopping wet, hooded boy in tow.

"De Buch!" the prince protested as the Captal nearly pushed past him into the room and slammed the door in Salisbury's very white face. "Who in hell's hot borders is this wretch and what did you learn out there?"

De Buch was soaked to the skin: his leather jerkin actually squeaked to punctuate the water he dripped into a growing pool on the carpet. "This wretch, my lord prince," de Buch gasped out as if he had run for miles, "is—saints' bones, my prince, all I can say is the fishing is damn fine out there, and this is what I caught for you!"

The wet knave with de Buch lifted two slender-wristed, graceful hands to slide back his hood. The small green beryl ring set in ivory filigree that rested on the finger shocked the prince, and he grunted as though he had been struck in the stomach. He stared astounded, entranced, as the wet, rough hood dropped back to reveal a flawless forehead and straight nose tilted up at the end—and shattering lilac eyes flashing a fire appropriately accompanied by the crackle of lightning and roar of thunder overhead.

"Jeannette!"

"Aye. Did you think I would never find out your tricks or just ignore them if I did, Your Grace?"

The taunting way she drawled his title, the cryptic words stunned him, but he was so amazed at the vision of her, he had trouble thinking, trouble forming his words. He was aware the Captal de Buch looked all smug and greedy-eyed from Jeannette to him and then back again. He was astounded when he finally spoke that his voice was as cold and sharp as steel.

"Wait outside, Captal, and tell no one of this visitor."

"Salisbury knows, Your Grace, and my men. Also, that minstrel once in your employ was captured with her—ah, Stephen Callender, Your Grace."

"Then get out and tell them all to hold their tongues, man. I will take care of this guest—this prisoner, for now."

"Aye, my lord prince," de Buch managed gruffly, and sorry he could not stay to see the obvious battle brewing, he nearly stumbled over his feet on the way out.

Joan of Kent faced the prince squarely, her fists on hips accented by the tight boy's hose and her cinched leather belt which sported a pitifully small lady's table dagger. Her heavy champagne-hued curls and coiled braids dripped water forlornly on her face and shoulders, but her chin was held high in defiance. The pouting lips and elegant, high cheekbones were streaked with road dust and rain, but the eyes flashed a spirit within that made his stomach cartwheel over and his loins ache to bury himself deep within her. Fragmented visions of her in boy's garb that day they loved in the straw at Windsor and on that little bed in the room at Canterbury made him go hot all over as if he had been doused in the sweat of furious, blood-pounding battle.

"I suggest you explain this mule-headed, stupid action of yours before I lose my temper entirely, woman. You could have been killed out there, or worse, you know!"

"I am not your prisoner. You told the Captal I was your prisoner."

"St. George, Jeannette, it is either that we find sneaking

about our camp or a spy—or mayhap you are a camp trull. They are the only women foolish enough to trespass near armies where they can be paid for their services and so used at anyone's whim and—"

"You would say something like that! Oh, I am sure that is the only sort of women *you* consort with, but I only came here from home to tell you I know of your vile deceit and treachery and I will have no more of it!"

"Lower your voice or the whole army will know the Duchess of Kent rides about the enemy countryside with musicians chasing the Prince of Wales. First to Canterbury all intimate with Wakeley, now here with Callender! I tire of this passion for musicians!"

"Musicians—no. I have a great longing for spies paid for by the royal purse, since you ask, my lord prince."

"You have needed taming for years, Jeannette. I knew—*I knew* no one else could handle you. And I swear I will kill Callender for this!"

"Your eternal pomposity boggles my mind, Your Grace. I do not care what anyone thinks. Let them all know you hire spies and buy people off with lands and titles to keep them silent."

The tension which had held him rigid only six feet from her across the barrier of astonishment snapped, and he charged at her to clamp one iron arm around her waist and one big hand over her mouth. He bent her head back against his left shoulder forcing her to look up into his ice-cold, crystalline blue eyes. Beneath the sudden onslaught of his fury and his strength, she went momentarily limp against him. His hard mouth under the full blond mustache seemed carved from marble, and a frantic pulse beat at the base of his throat.

"Aye, I will have your silence and anything else I want from you, vixen. You could have been killed or captured, prancing in here like this through enemy territory, clear from Normandy, I take it. This is war here and not the kind you

393

and I always wage. I have no intention of sanctioning such female willfulness and stupidity—nor insubordination as you have shown today, and always. You will go with the Captal now, and you will hold your tongue until I come to you later. And if you value that beautiful little hide of yours, you had best find a sweet smile and soft voice before I come, or so help me, I will—"

He bit his lower lip as if to silence his tirade forcibly, and his distraught gaze softened barely perceptibly as his heavily fringed eyes glittered greedily over her. He loosed her mouth and stood her upright. "De Buch!" he gripped her elbow tightly, holding her at arm's length. His eyes devoured her again before he tore his gaze away almost guiltily as the Captal snapped open the door across the room.

"Aye, my lord prince?"

"I want this woman escorted by you and guarded by my private yeoman across the street at that little inn where I left my things. Get that old woman we found cowering in the cellar to help the lady bathe and find some dry, suitable garments."

"Aye, Your Grace. Suitable."

"If this woman gives anyone a moment's strife, just have them bind her until I have time to interrogate her later."

"Interrogate," de Buch repeated slowly.

"Hell's gates, de Buch, you sound like some simpering parrot the queen used to keep about on a velvet perch! Just do it, then get yourself back in here for a council meeting. I have too much to worry about here to be—be—bothered by some adventurous female's tricks. And send that bastard Callender in on your way out."

The Captal de Buch led her firmly away, and she went. Aye, she agreed it would not do to squabble in public when there was a war to run, but when she faced him later, alone, he would see she would not cower as all the rest did when he flashed the royal Plantagenet temper like that.

But at the door, her eyes snagged with those of the ashen-faced, wide-eyed Stephen Callender and, at his obvious trembling, she nearly crumpled in the hall despite de Buch's firm grip on her arm.

When she faced the prince later alone—saints, why had she not let her reason override her own fierce temper? The driving rain outside soaked her to the bone again, and when she stumbled, the massive de Buch picked her up as if she were a child to carry her across the cobbled street running with rivulets of water. Only then did she go temporarily light-headed at the thought she might have trod this long and dangerous path only for that precious moment she would face Edward truly alone after all these calm but lonely years.

Chapter Eighteen

The heavy rain brought an early, damp dusk to the captured French town of Monbarzon. In a sprawling, crooked-floored chamber of the inn across the street from the house the prince had requisitioned as headquarters for his closest advisors, Joan waited. An old French woman arrived and with her came five buckets of hot, fresh rainwater in which Joan bathed and washed her hair. After she had gratefully donned a warm, green wool robe the old woman produced, a boy came in to light the fire on the hearth and set a place at table for her. Joan toweled her waist-length tresses dry before the fire and motioned for the old woman to leave her; when she watched her shuffle out, she realized the prince's guards still stood in the hall.

As if she would try to escape from the first comfortable place she had seen in days, Joan sniffed, but her heart beat fast at the thought he had provided such protection and comfort for her here despite how she had so obviously infuriated him. The clumsy, nervous servant woman was hardly a substitute for dear, departed Marta, but the private room, bath, and fire were heaven.

Then, as if her next wish had been magically anticipated, the boy came back with a tray of hot chicken and vegetable stew with rye bread, Brie cheese, peaches, and wine. Joan stuffed herself the moment she was alone again. Never had food tasted so succulent, and though she had been a picky eater these last few years, she devoured every crumb and even wiped the wooden bowl with scraps of bread as she had seen serfs do.

She soon found herself nodding, her eyes heavy, half-asleep in her chair: the caress of a warm hearth, the marvelous sense of well-being from the hot food and fine wine, the feel of the soft woolen robe on her naked, glowing flesh all combined to make her drift in drowsy contentment. The thunder and lightning fought a war of their own above the thatched roof outside, and stray splatters of rain hissed on the hearth stones, but she could face anything now. In the morning, of course, she would demand that Prince Edward release both her and Stephen. Maybe he could spare them a guard to head back north since he evidently had assigned two men to just stand about in a damp, dark hall outside this room here.

Her eyes lazily roamed the room. It was no doubt the finest accommodation in this little place, for it sprawled across the entire third story under the eaves, whereas the common rooms and other chambers below were small rooms she had glimpsed on her ignominious ride up in the Captal's burly arms. The furniture here was all dark oak and quite plain compared to what she was used to. A long sideboard with a few dented pewter and wood plates stood under the single, tawdry tapestry of a hunt scene. The long dining table and four hard-backed chairs rested near the hearth on some sort of large, braided rug. The only imposing piece of furniture in the entire hump-floored room was the large featherbed with its burgundy velvet curtains to screen the occupants from drafts or intrusion. In the corner, however, were piled four ornately carved, stacked coffers which made the rest of the room's dark furniture and woodwork look plain and crude.

She sat bolt upright in her chair at the next thought. There was really nothing here of course to suggest it, except those coffers were entirely too fine for this plain room. She got up and padded across the oak floorboards to stand over the four stacked coffers. The carved design on the top one leapt up at her: in scripted, engraved letters it read, H. R. H. P. W.

"Saints!" she cursed aloud, her reverie broken. She had sat

here all warm and sated and so pleased with herself like a rabbit in a trap—the coffers, and no doubt, the exclusive use of the room, belonged to His Royal Highness, the Prince of Wales! What was wrong with her lulled brain? Had he not said something of the sort to de Buch which she had been too stunned to note?

She fingered the intricate metal catch on the top coffer, and, to be ludicrously certain, lifted it open. A fine jerkin of softest Spanish leather and a silk *surcote* with the unmistakable quartered Plantagenet leopards and lilies lay perfectly folded, and from them emanated the rich, heady scent of bergamot he so favored. Rooted to the floor, she snapped the lid closed. Aye, all this luxury after four terrible, bone-wracking days in the saddle had addled her brains— she had been sent to await his pleasure in his private room just as these yet unpacked coffers of clothing!

The awful fluttering in her stomach began as she paced on the braid rug around and around the table. Mayhap he was too busy, too angry, too proud to come here tonight. Indeed, he might mean for her to have this room and he would sleep in his quarters across the rain-swept, cobbled *rue*. After all, he must have tens on tens of coffers holding the precious clothing or armor he carried with him on campaign. These four might be mere overflow.

She considered redressing in the clothes she had draped across a chair before the hearth and demanding of her guards to be freed, or at worst, to be taken back across the street to face the prince among his men. Stephen Callender must be released; they must head back at dawn to once again skirt far around the French forces. She had a husband, sons, duchy lands to care for. She had only come to tell him she knew of his treachery and would allow no more, and she had not believed Stephen Callender when he'd said that Tours was so damn far until the evening of the first day out, and then it was entirely too late to turn back.

She halted her wild pacing and spun to face the door across the width of firelit room as it snapped open. The massive form, the tawny head gilded by distant firelight were unmistakable. He came in alone, shook wild, flying drops of water from a soaking cloak, then dropped it. He covered the space of creaking floorboards between them in six strides. She stood her ground mutely, stiffly, holding her robe to her body with both arms.

"St. George, it seems this rain brings two gifts from heaven at any rate, Jeannette, even if it might bog us down in a bloody French mire."

She stared amazed as he dared to shoot her a quick grin. How swiftly his terrible wrath had dissipated, she marveled, but if he thought this charming, hail-fellow approach would get him aught with her, he was sadly mistaken.

"Two gifts from heaven, Your Grace? I believe I must thank you for the food and fire, but to what else could you possibly refer?"

He plopped in the chair nearest her and yanked off his squeaky, wet boots. In the fireglow she could see the droplets of rain plastering his thick hair to his forehead and smell the damp odor of his dark woolen *surcote*. "Aye, those too, of course. I am pleased you ate because I did not know how long that council meeting would run. But I, *ma chérie*, referred to the respite here to rest the men while it rains and the delight of having you here to fulfill my every whim while we wait."

Her heart thudded at his blatant implications, and her hand gripped the chairback so hard, her fingers went numb. "I came here, my lord prince, as I told you over there in your other confiscated house, only to tell you I knew of your treacherous spies and I will have no more of them. I am certainly not here to fulfill your every whim as you so callously put it!"

"Of all the things we may do tonight, bitter arguing is surely not one, Jeannette, so do not start. Now, would you be so kind as to go to the door and bid my squire come in with the food and bath water? I am famished for more than you, sweet—tired, wet and eternally on the edge of a jagged streak of temper lately, as my men could tell you. Do as I say, or I fear if I have to administer my first lesson in obedience, I will get you all wet, as well as that bed I want to have dry and warm later."

She stared at him astounded at the brazen ploy. She entertained a score of tart replies as they stared at each other like wary adversaries, then froze him with an icy glare and walked slowly to the door.

The squire sat close outside, dicing for coins with the two other guards on the narrow third-story landing they had lit with one cresset lamp. "Your prince bids you bring food and bath, squire," she said as tonelessly as she could manage and closed the door quietly. She sat on one of his heavy coffers near the door, not even deigning to look back his way even when he began to speak again.

"Thank you, Jeannette. How pleasant—even delightful— this time will be now we are together. I keep you warm, fed, and happy, and you return the favor."

"I feel no desire whatsoever to please anyone who has had me spied on for years—years!"

"I only wanted to see that you were well cared for and protected and I am sorry you interpret that otherwise, but we shall not speak of that tonight. If you wish and I have time in the morn, we shall discuss it then."

"I will not be put off!" she ventured from her perch on the coffer, and made the mistake of darting a quick glance his way. Her blood pounded. Standing before the hearth, he had stripped off his garments and stood naked but for the woolen *surcote* he had tied by its long arms around his narrow hips. The fireglow seemed to highlight each molded alabaster muscle of the powerful shoulders, back, and the flat belly when he turned to meet her gaze across the table and the space of the chamber. Boldly she stared back, her gaze drinking in the angular planes of that body, the shadows and gold-dusted, curly hair on the swelling chest. She beat down the rampant desire to walk to him across that little space and touch him, but the treacherous butterflies fluttering within her loins would not be stilled. She breathed a silent prayer of thanks to heaven when his squire and another man knocked on the door behind her and entered with a parade of buckets of steaming water and aromatic trays of food.

She fought to still her panic as the bath water sloshed in the same hip tub she had used across the room. She moved away from the door until the men went out, darting a quick, curious glance at her. The door closed.

When she looked again, the prince had climbed into the tub and was sluicing his shoulders with the hot water. "Bolt the door, please, Jeannette, and come over here near the fire. I cannot spare a surgeon to nurse you through chills or fever when I shall need every medical man I have for the coming battle."

She knew it would be weak and foolish to protest. She would mayhap cooperate while it was possible; then when she denied him, he would know she meant it. Her hand trembled slightly as she shot the bolt and walked slowly down to the far end of the table where she intended to seat herself with her back to his noisy, sloshing display in the bath.

"A goblet of wine, please, *chérie*."

Despite herself, she glanced warily at him down the length of table. His eyes slitted, he had settled back in the little tub to cover as much of his big body with the water as he could. His knees and shins protruded nearly obscuring his arms, shoulders, and head from where she stood. She bit back a sharp retort that she was not his servant, but then obeyed. This mask of jovial calm was far preferable to his aroused temper or passion.

She poured him an almost full goblet of wine and walked near enough to him to extend it stiff-armed. She kept her eyes carefully lifted to avoid the golden expanse of muscled, wet skin.

"Thank you. Peek and see what is under those delicious-smelling dishes, will you, sweet? I am starved."

She was glad to move away and turn her back. "I thought I

overheard something about foodstuffs being low," she said, hoping she sounded calmly conversational and not a whit distressed by his nearness or the situation.

"They are, and on the morrow, it is back to rationing for all of us. Tonight—well, Jeannette, tonight is special and everyone needs his spirits lifted in this rain. We have been marching for days hoping to unite with my brother John's forces and avoid the French. A good roof, fire, and food will do all the men good."

She breathed in a warm, pungent aroma from the first lid she lifted. "Stewed partridge with saffron eggs, Your Grace, and this other one looks like new-baked nutmeg custards with molasses sauce."

"Delicious, but then, tonight, everything is," his deep voice teased. "Bring me a little piece of the partridge then, please."

"It will get cold."

"Just do it, Jeannette, or I shall come over there to get it myself. I have not eaten since midmorn and that was cold pastry and some damned smoked fish."

How easily the tired, ill-tempered edge came back to his voice, she thought. She picked up a piece of partridge breast dripping hot saffron sauce and edged around the table toward his hearth tub. She stood behind him, thankful the tub was so small he had drawn his knees up tightly to his chest to hide his strong thighs. His big hand gently covered her wrist to bring the food to his mouth. His thick mustache grazed her finger, and her entire arm began to quiver uncontrollably. He devoured the hot morsel, then licked and kissed her imprisoned fingertips, her moist palm, and inner wrist.

"Your Grace, please. Your precious food will all get cold if you do not get out of there to sup."

He loosed her the minute she tried to pull away. "Aye, sweet. I have forgotten in this war how to be a patient man, it seems—to woo opportunities and not just seize them."

Without warning, he heaved himself dripping out of the

402

tub, and behind him Joan got a good view of his lean, hard buttocks and muscular thighs before she darted back and turned away. She hated herself for the cowardice and wild flow of passion that flooded her. She ought to brazen it out, she told herself—to stare at him and pretend he moved her not one whit. But—oh, blessed saints, it was inevitable. *He* was inevitable, and it always had been so!

He dried himself quickly with the same huge piece of wool she had used on her hair earlier, and wrapped himself in a black velvet robe his squire had left. He sat at the table immediately to ladle huge portions of food onto his plate. "Come over here and try this, Jeannette. It is fabulous."

"As you said, I already ate."

He spoke with his mouth full. "Then have some wine or custard. Mmm—delicious."

She sat two chairs away to watch him devour three huge helpings of the food. She drank some wine and merely picked at a dish of custard, as marvelous as it was. Too soon he shoved his empty plate away and regarded her pensively over the rim of his goblet as he downed the rest of his wine. The next words he spoke terrified her. They made her feel she must run away down some long, secret, dark tunnel of fantasy to escape the painful truth: "We have wasted a lot of time, Jeannette. Days, weeks, years even. Morcar's charts were right—I know it."

"Morcar? I have not thought of him for years. His astrological casting of your horoscope, you mean?"

"And yours. I acquired his castings of your life from his goods after he died. You are destined for greatness, sweet, to bear a ruler of men."

"To bear—saints, I do have two sons, you know," she floundered.

"They are Holland's sons and not likely to be more than fine landowning king's men someday. Listen, Jeannette, I usually put little stock in magicians' words or foretellings of the stars—and mayhap I just want this to be true too much, only—St. George, love, our charts align perfectly with the sun in the seventh house as Morcar cast them. I have the damned charts with me. I will show you on the morrow. I brought them along hoping at first His Grace would send me through Normandy at the last minute and I might see you there."

Through Normandy. He had desired to come through Normandy to see me, a little, joyous voice echoed in her head. "You have the old man's chart of my life?" she said only. "You have it with you?"

He rose quickly and came to kneel beside her chair, and before she could rise, his big, warm hand covered her wrist. "Aye, Jeannette. I told you I care and that my spying, as you put it, was only concern for your continual well-being these years you were away from Plantagenet protection. You never have really believed or understood me, have you?"

"That is not true."

"We will not argue tonight, I said. We are destined in the stars, old Morcar said, and whether that is true or not, we are destined to be here tonight, alone together whatever storms of foul weather or foul warfare await outside."

The grasp of his hand slid smoothly up her arm ruffling the jade sleeve of robe in a big cuff around his wrist. He stood slowly, towering over her and then tugged gently to raise her. The top of her head came only to his broad shoulder as she stared stubbornly at the base of his throat where a little pulse beat visibly.

"We have tonight here in our grasp, sweet, sweet Jeannette," he breathed, and bent to take her lips.

She yielded her mouth while her mind darted about for a reply, a subtle twist away, a flat denial. His open hands dropped to span her waist, and his thumbs stroked her fluttering belly through the softness of the woolen robe. The kiss was gentle, beseeching at first, but then he moaned in his throat and slanted his lips eagerly across hers to taste deeply of her. His mustache grazed her upper lip; his tongue plundered, then retreated, then launched a delicious, little foray into the moist cavern of her mouth that left her breathless. Her arms lifted to clasp his powerful neck and she let him pull her full length against his hard body. His hands caressed her pliant buttocks and ran riot over her back as she arched up to return his kiss with a fiery fervor that consumed all desire to resist.

The fire crackled and a log settled lower on the hearth, bathing them in a warm glow without and within. His mouth pulled reluctantly away from hers and trailed a molten path of kisses down her throat to the top of her robe. He nuzzled her neck and breathed heavily of the scent of her rain-sweetened hair. Then, as she lifted her mouth to be kissed again, his hands rose to easily open her robe. In a smooth motion, he pulled her arms gently away from his neck to allow him to slide it down her shoulders.

She stood mesmerized, trembling, naked before him in the rampant fireglow which flicked golden shadows over the curves of her ivory skin. It stunned her reeling mind for one moment: she wanted him to do this, she wanted him with every aching fiber of her body.

"So beautiful, my Jeannette, so exquisite."

She felt the rough callouses of his hands hardened by reins and weapons as he caressed her gently—her shoulders, arms. She swam in the fathomless blue pools of his eyes as his fingers brushed a taut nipple until it swelled to bursting; then he lowered his tawny head to kiss and lick the pointed peak until she thought she would cry out his name to beg an end to the delicious torment. Unbidden, her hands, fastened in his mussed, thick hair as her back arched to meet the teasing demand of his hot lips and tongue on first one breast and then the other. Her legs, her entire body trembled so, she nearly collapsed against him.

He lifted her hands, she thought to steady her, but instead he placed her open palms on his muscular, lightly haired chest and untied his robe in obvious invitation. Moving slowly to not appear so eager, she followed his lead and opened the V of robe at the base of his neck farther. The black velvet split downward along his chest and belly to slide heavily off his broad shoulders. Seemingly impatient then, he shrugged the garment down his body so that it disappeared from her rapt gaze. Her naked arms still lifted to his chest looked purest alabaster against the bronze of his angular, lean body. Despite her fears, her eyes dipped down to behold his blatant, powerful desire.

"For you," he rasped. "For you. You have always done that to me."

He lifted her high in his arms and strode to the deep bed with her. Awkwardly, rushing now, he yanked back the velvet coverlet and sheet while still crushing her to his chest. They fell heavily into the bed together, their bodies touching everywhere.

The sensual assault of hands and kisses began again. He pressed her down, his hands skimming and stroking her flesh tenderly, then roughly. He moved a big knee between her thighs just to feel her spread vulnerable and ready beneath him and ravished her sweet mouth until she answered him with a primitive passion he knew she could no longer control. Nearly bursting with desire himself, he held off in sweet passion's pain, flicking her pink budded nipples until she cried out and stroking her soft thighs until she writhed under him.

"I love you, Jeannette. I love you. I want you now. Always."

"Aye, aye. I, too."

"Say it then. I have waited years to have you say it. I told you you would say it. 'I love you, my Edward.'"

His fingers stroked the very core of her womanhood, though in a final grasp at sanity she tried to pull her legs together.

"Oh. Oh, aye. Oh, please. I love you—my Edward."

She arched up to meet his deep, plunging thrust, and the jolt of their union blended perfectly with the wild tempo of the pounding storm outside. Deeper, fiercer, he rode her willing, quaking body until she locked her arms and legs around him in total abandon of all restraint. And when she began her own shifting motions, she dragged them both up and over the shattering cliff and down into the spiraling velvet tunnel of ecstasy.

When it was over, he lay carefully on top of her, like a warm shelter against the world outside. Their wild breathing slowed at last and her limbs went limp in sudden, floating exhaustion. He shifted his weight away and gathered her close to his warmth, her back to him, her body curled into his lap. The cocoon of covers made a warm little nest and, for one drifting moment, she thought she could simply die of utter peace and joy.

They lay unspeaking for a while and then his breath moved the hair at the nape of her neck as he spoke. "I pray you meant those words, Jeannette, that they were not just forced in the heat of the moment." His voice sounded drowsy but the tone was crisply urgent.

"Aye—my Edward."

"Then, for this one night I do not care what is outside this little bed of ours." He pulled her so possessively against him she could not breathe for a second. "Sleep, Jeannette. I have been so exhausted for days. Sleep here against me, my wild, little love."

He seemed to doze instantly on that last word, she thought. Love. Love with Edward whom she had ridden so far to hate, tried so hard to hurt ever since she had learned who he really was at Windsor that first summer. But who was he indeed, and who was this woman who turned to willing flame at his mere touch? All these years separated and the yearning between them had sprung alive full blown as if they had never been apart.

Sometime, hours later, in the drugged euphoria of dreams, she felt him move against her in the dark. One big hand lifted to cup a firm breast and the other rode intimately on a bare curve of her hip. She tried to pull her head away but her long tresses were caught somehow under him.

"I have slept enough," came the rough, warm whisper against the nape of her neck. "I could not bear it without you all wrapped around me again. It is like a waking dream, my sweetheart, being able to reach out and have you like this."

She opened her mouth to say something, but only provided him with an open-mouthed kiss when his lips imprisoned hers in the darkness. His big hands pulled her under him, settled her, positioned her.

"Your Grace, please—"

"My Edward," he scolded, the hint of a delighted laugh in his slow voice.

"My Edward."

"Please what, my sweet Jeannette? Please kiss me again? Caress me? Take me? Love me?"

"Saints, but you are maddening, my Edward."

"Maddened for you like this. Here, let me in."

"No, I—"

But her protest, which was a foolish sham anyway considering the way her softness welcomed his deep thrust, went unheeded. His body pressed tightly against hers; even as she ached for him to go on, he held momentarily still.

"Now, what was it you wanted to discuss, love? The weather? It is raining. Your status here? You are my prisoner in this room and this bed, this, ah, position, my lady, until I choose to release you."

"I say, Your Grace, but you are rather blithe and talkative for this hour of the night. Do you never sleep?"

"I am beset with joy—and utter greed—to use all our time together for best benefit." He moved once within her to punctuate his words, and her breath caught in her throat. When he chuckled low at her response and began to ravish her sanity with his hot kisses again, she fought to keep from turning eager wanton at the feel of him against her and in her. But it was another battle she lost, willingly yielding all to the powerful man who pushed her further, further with verbal and physical demands in which she reveled. But, when it was all dissolved to tumbled limbs and murmured endearments again, she knew she had conquered the conquerer too.

The next day at midmorn when she awoke all warm and drowsy in the big bed, he had dressed and gone. Rain still pounded on the roof overhead and spouted noisily in rivulets off the thatched eaves as she rubbed her heavy-lidded eyes to survey the room lit by pale daylight. She stretched, luxuriating in the feel of rested muscles although she felt slightly bruised and achy in places she had never felt before. At the thought of what he had done, what they had shared, her tender nipples sprang erect and the ravished butterflies of her lower stomach darted their velvet wings.

"Saints," she said aloud at the thought of his returning to find her waiting in bed for him in all too obvious invitation. She threw back the covers to be smacked with chill air on her warm flesh and darted to the hearth expecting to find her discarded robe. Instead, all laid out on chairs was a soft velvet kirtle of robin's-shell blue, matching velvet slippers, and a cream-hued *surcote* in ribbed velvet dusted with tiny seed pearls. She only stared aghast one moment before she slipped them on and tied her heavy hair back with a red ribbon draped on the arm of the chair. In the coals at one side of the broad hearth, she discovered an iron pot of delicious frumenty and a metal decanter of warm, spiced wine. She had barely completed a gobbled breakfast when the door opened and Prince Edward was back again, soaking wet.

"St. George, slug-a-bed, I thought perhaps you meant to sleep all day. Rainy nights can make one sleepy, eh?"

She smiled back at his broad grin despite the fact she had told herself she must not be so pliable, so eager. Then, as he came closer, she noted what he was unwrapping from under his wet cloak even as he stamped the water off his shiny boots.

"Oh, a lute, my lord prince."

"Aye, for my own private little musician. I need music to

soothe the savage beast." He grinned again looking like a naughty boy as he dared his next jest. "Since it appears you will be my guest here for several days, there really ought to be something you can do to amuse me."

"Saints," she shot back, her face serious but her heart dangerously exuberant, "a quick song or two it shall be, and then we shall be even for whatever you might have done to amuse me."

They laughed together and she took the lute from him to twist the tuning pegs until the eight strings resounded to her satisfaction. She felt strangely at home where she sat beside him along the hearth side of the table, and she looked up to note he had spread a parchment map on the table before him.

"I have been in meetings all morn with the pope's cardinals here to negotiate a peace, Jeannette."

She let the notes die away at his new, serious tone. "Then your army will not have to fight?"

"Hell's gates, but I have no doubt we will fight. The French terms are so despicably ludicrous, I cannot believe the French are serious to propose them."

"Such as?" she asked and noted the surprise that flashed in his eyes before he decided to answer.

"Such as, sweet, complete return of all prisoners and conquered territory, and total fealty and surrender of my own royal person and my one hundred most honored knights on our knees before King John the Good."

"The man is daft!"

"My thought exactly, my lovely, little advisor. Damn, but I ought to just put you on council. I am only pretending to listen to such doltish negotiations to give my men time to move ahead to dig in at Poitiers and light diversion fires in the suburbs of Tours."

"In all this rain?"

A new respect sobered his gaze and he said simply, "The rain is the problem, but we must try. Time negotiated is time for a rest—and for us to be together here which, may saints preserve me, I actually considered in my answer to the French when such personal concerns should play no part at all."

Touched, she lay the lute on the table before her and folded her hands in her lap to listen further.

"Jeannette, I have only thrashed your comrade in arms Callender with my tongue and not the whip he deserves. Now that you are here and safe with me, I find it nearly impossible to punish the man, and besides, he had best go back with you in one piece when I deem it safe to send you home."

"And when will that be?"

"As soon as the rain slackens and the pope's cardinals head back to the French at Blois. One day or two."

"Oh."

Their eyes held. She knew her grief that all this peaceful calm must be shattered by the outside reality of war and danger and lives lost was plainly written on her face.

"Jeannette, Callender claims much of the blame for your coming here. The man has simply fallen all over himself trying to excuse you. It seems—hell, love, it seems you have won him over as you have others and under the most dire of circumstances."

She felt her hackles rise at what would surely be his old scolding, argumentative tone about other men. "Saints, Your Grace, I cannot help what any of your little spies report to you!"

He seized her arm. "Sit, love, sit. I do not criticize. Quite the contrary, though you usually manage to madden me beyond control one way or the other. I understand the poor rogue's desire to protect you—his begrudging admiration. You may drive me to distraction, but I can hardly resent a man who falls for your charms—not that he is getting the same return from those charms as I, of course. And now, before those violet eyes pierce me like a lance, I have something else for you."

From a little leather pouch dangling at his belt, he drew

out a huge strand of pearls as large as spring cherries. Her eyes grew enormous at the bounty dripping from his fingers. "Oh, so lovely. And this gown, too. I meant to thank you."

In a single strand, the necklace fell over her breasts nearly to her waist, and wrapped around her head to hold her tresses back, it would surely go four widths. Her eyes glowed with pleasure. He rose and let the stiff parchment map roll itself back into a tight coil on the table top.

"I was going to have you show me," he said low, "the little bridge you and Callender finally got over the Loire on. I was hoping a messenger could go that way to locate my brother's forces, but I am afraid it will have to wait."

"It will?"

"It will." He reached for her waist and pulled her to him. Mesmerized by the clear aquamarine eyes, she moved forward as one who walks through a heavy-footed dream.

"I want to—I must see those white pearls against your bare, silken skin," he whispered. Their lips joined breathlessly as time stood still in their precious haven sealed by the driving storm.

On their third day together, the rain stopped, and the picturesque little village of Monbarzon came alive with myriad noisy preparations for an army on the move. The prince's love-making before dawn was possessively rough as if he could no longer bear to be tender or unhurried. Word had come from the Captal de Buch's spies that the French army was crossing the Loire at many points nearby and haste meant survival. After much equivocation in the pope's negotiations, the Black Prince, flower of all English chivalry, had thrown the harsh terms of surrender back in the French king's face, and everyone knew it. Joan, Stephen Callender, and three armed guards dressed as merchants were to set out to Normandy by a circuituous northwest route; the prince at the head of his greatly outnumbered battalions was to retreat south toward Aquitaine hoping to reach safety before the huge enemy army forced them to turn and fight.

Joan cast a long, last look at the sprawling, third-story chamber where they had spent three wonderful, stolen days they might never have again. What a different world it had been, a bittersweet fantasy, now turned cold by the reality of crushing dangers. She touched her pearls through the boy's jerkin and tunic she wore as her disguise. They felt warm and comforting under the rough garments against her bare flesh. Her eyes rested on the still mussed, red-curtained bed. She turned away and followed the scolding Stephen Callender down the stairs.

"A shame to leave that lovely lute behind," she remarked, desperate to say anything to halt the flow of grief. "But I suppose it started out in French hands so it might as well end up that way."

In the common hall of the inn where they were to await word from the prince to set out, Joan sank on a little bench before the low-burning hearth. "Wakeley says that other lute His Grace gave you years ago is a fine one, Duchess," Stephen said.

"Aye. Wakeley says," she mocked more bitterly than she had meant to. "I have him to deal with yet."

Stephen put one booted foot upon the bench and leaned an elbow on it. "I tell you, Duchess, Roger Wakeley has been on your side, wanting what is best for you these years, as well as for His Grace, whatever you think."

"I do not wish to discuss it now. I just want to have this wretched trip home over with."

The front door of the inn banged open, and the Captal de Buch with several others in partial riding armor crowded in. "Madame, men, we shall go out through the back where your mounts await," the imposing Gascon knight ordered, and everyone moved.

The Captal took her elbow as they went through the small pantry and larder and out into a narrow alley crowded with horses. Joan glanced from face to face searching for the prince, but of course, none of the men here were tall enough to be he. Surely, he did not mean to send her away without a final farewell after all this!

"You men, you Callender, may mount and hold your horses down there by the string of baggage wagons," de Buch shouted not even looking their way. While she stood by the Captal, twisting her little beryl ring nervously, Joan watched the men mount and trot off.

With only her horse Windsong standing by, Joan waited awkwardly with the wily Gascon advisor of Prince Edward. Shouts, sounds of clattering horses, clanking metal, and creaking wagons filled the air from nearby streets.

"My palfrey looks well cared for, Captal," she ventured. "The respite here has done him good."

"Saints' souls—it has been a boon for all of us, I warrant. His Grace included, lady. He was near the edge of his control with worry and tension but now—well, I believe his men have you to thank for the healing balm of his better temper and steadier mind now."

As if those words had announced him, Prince Edward galloped in on a huge white destrier. Clad in ebony-hued riding armor on arms, chest, and thighs, he wore no helmet and his tawny mane flowed free as he rode. Clanking piece on piece, he dismounted in an amazingly graceful movement as the Captal disappeared behind the two horses.

"I meant to be here sooner to send you off, Jeannette, but there was so much to see to." His vibrant blue eyes under the blond, rakish brows were serious and intent. His *surcote* was shiny black with his three Prince of Wales's ostrich feathers and his proud motto in German: "*Ich dien*"—I serve.

"I know you are busy and that your mind was elsewhere this morning, Your Grace. I am certain that everything will be well."

"I had thought, sweet, that my father's forces might make it here, but he is beset by troubles on the Scottish borders at home, and my brother's battalions are trapped somewhere north."

"But I know you can count on yourself and your men, my Edward."

A little wisp of smile lifted his firm, chiseled mouth upward. "Aye, my love. I intend to tell my men as we move out now that I shall count on nothing—nothing but victory. I pray it shall be so for us someday."

His face blurred, then doubled as she blinked back tears. "I do not see how, my lord prince, Morcar's elaborate star castings notwithstanding. All the other things too that we—"

With a metallic clanking, his big fingers lifted to still her lips. "God's safe journey home, my Jeannette. My guards will die to a man to protect you if need be. We must all be away now. No one will speak of this visit of yours here, they have sworn it."

He bent to kiss her, a mere brush of the lips, then lifted her to her saddle as if he could not bear to look upon her face again. She sat erect, gripping the reins he handed her so tightly that her fingernails bit painfully into her palms.

"May the saints keep you safe, my lord prince. For England and St. George," she managed, but her speaking of that battle cry was a mere whisper. Her face felt stiff, her wide eyes sought his. Suddenly, he looked austere, unknowable in his black armor and royal accouterments.

With a sharp smack on its rump, he sent her horse down the little alley toward the waiting men. She did not dare to look back.

Now just another mounted man in rough yeoman's garb, she held her hood tightly to her face as they melded with the throng pouring outward toward the narrow city gates. Yeomen with longbows and pikes walked afoot in well-ordered ranks; armored knights trailed by squires and personal baggage trains gleamed silver in the faint morning sun; horses and rumbling wagons lumbered along everywhere. Pennants and banners bobbed aloft like ship sails at sea.

Outside the city walls, Joan's little band parted from the swelling march of Prince Edward's army heading south to Poitiers where they were already digging in to cover their retreat. On a little hillock above the town, Joan turned stiffly in her saddle to look back at last.

Below, a moving silver river of armor flowed south and somewhere there, at the very vanguard, her prince would be leading them boldly on. Her own danger, the grueling ride back, even the future away from him faded to nothingness in that instant as she prayed fervently for his safe deliverance. How distant it all seemed already, how impossible that they had smiled and loved and bedded—and that she had dared to call that lofty, austere prince "my Edward." She smothered a little sob deep in her throat and turned her face to the muddy road north.

Chapter Nineteen

By midmorn the day after Joan and the prince parted, the pursuing French army had forced the outnumbered English battalions to dig in for a fight at a little plain called Maupertuis near the walled town of Poitiers. The disadvantaged Plantagenet forces, nevertheless, faced the massed, armored French fiercely, proudly and unafraid. Had not their hero-prince promised them victory despite the odds? Had not he carefully chosen this naturally protected stronghold and had it fortified despite the rain during their four days of rest at Monbarzon? The French leaders combined had not the brilliant tactical mind of their Black Prince, the English knights, bowmen, and baggage guards alike whispered; the French King John, his son Philip, and his brother the Duke of Orleans failed to recognize that the lay of the land at Poitiers did not seal the English fate, but rather their own.

Hunkered down within the natural barriers of thickly wooded hills to the east, marshy ground to the west, sloping vineyards and the shallow River Moisson to the south, and a broken thorn hedge to the northwest facing their enemy, the English awaited the inevitable. Only through two small roads in the thorn hedge could the massive onslaught of mounted French knights come, and on the defense of those two chinks in the English armor, the survival of Prince Edward's forces depended.

Wave after wave of mounted armored Frenchmen shouting *"Montjoie! St. Denis!"* threw themselves into the deadly storm of English longbow arrows. The prince and his

417

closest advisors waited behind their archers under the brazen flaunting of the Prince of Wales's banner with the three white plumes captured nine years before at Crécy.

"I can read those French *surcotes* and pennants, Your Grace," the one-eyed Sir John Chandos shouted to the prince over the ringing din of battle. "This huge first battalion must be under the king's son, the dauphin."

"Aye, John. Prince to prince, then, but I want the king himself as my prisoner before we leave this field behind as victors on this day!"

As the prince's eager eyes scanned the continual inundation of enemy horses carrying their armored, plumed men, he marveled, not so much at their awesome numbers, but at their immense stupidity. "It is Crécy all over again, John. Our stout English archers mow them down to stumble on the bodies of their fellows and yet they come on hardly breaking rank! Only when they reach our lines here we must fight dearly to keep their sheer might from trampling us into this mud."

"The men murmur at the unending host of French, Your Grace!" a bloodied Captal de Buch panted at the prince's side as if he had appeared from nowhere. "Your forces need something to lift their hearts, for their supply of arrows is dangerously low."

"Then we shall mount and charge—just long and hard enough to set the French back with our daring and cheer on our front line men. Meanwhile, de Buch, get a small contingent of clever Gascons like yourself who know this terrain as well as you—enough knights and archers to set up a goodly hue and cry. Go south, loop around the woods and hoist the St. George banner behind the French. Our numbers will be small but, saints willing, the bloody French may panic at the sight of us."

"Aye, Your Grace, and with pleasure! Any king who garbs nineteen other men in identical battle gear to avoid capture should fall for such a ploy. I swear by the holy rood, I shall fetch all twenty French kings to you and you shall have your choice of them!"

Prince Edward bellowed a short laugh despite the grimness of the situation. For a moment he watched the wily de Buch rattle off in full armor to collect his small force, then the prince's armored horse was brought up and his squire helped him mount. The huge plated destrier felt steady and good against his hips, the massive saddle weight a comfort under his muscular, armored thighs.

"Onward to the fray and victory!" he shouted and lifted an iron arm to urge on the others mounting behind him on the gentle slope of hill. He snapped his visor down with a clang, and his next words echoed in his brain: "For England and St. George!"

The cavalry led by the prince and Sir John Chandos pressed forward to cover their archers. They charged past the thorn hedge and around the edge of a gully to meet head on the closest French knights. Sword clanged to sword, armor on armor. Horses shied, reared, neighed. Heavy breathing and constricting visors muffled shouts and grunts of fierce exertion. The English soldiers in the front lines cheered to see their prince press on. The din was deafening.

When the French battalion of the dauphin reeled away at the brave counterattack, the prince pulled his big destrier around toward his own lines. Mounds of French dead stuck with arrows littered his path and, through the slits in his visor, he saw his archers stand almost suddenly stunned and mute. He shoved his visor up and gasped for air.

"Shoot, men. Shoot! Reload! Drive the next line back again!" he shouted to the little clusters of archers holding their longbows. Already with the hindsight of battle sense, he could feel the unending waves of French bearing down again.

"Your Grace—no arrows left, Your Grace, an' them French still acomin'!" someone screamed up at him.

"Look around you! Retrieve the arrows which have done their work already and fight on!"

One archer bent to the task, then another. All along the

English lines depleted of weapons, yeomen darted out to snatch arrows from turf or armor or bloody flesh. Again the prince and his cavalry charged to give them some cover. Finally, as they retreated behind the blessed thorn hedge, the sky went black again with English arrows.

Suddenly, while the prince watched breathless, sweating, and amazed, the edge of the first of three gigantic French battalions sucked inward, halted, then turned and moved away.

"They retreat, my lord prince!" the Earl of Oxford screamed in his ear. "A bloody, damn French retreat! Surely de Buch's men cannot have gotten behind them yet."

"Mayhap they wish to save their dauphin knowing we will yet capture their good King John," the prince mocked. He felt a jolt of heady energy surge through him at the thrill of beating back the first onslaught, much like that pure sensual rapture he had experienced when he had fully possessed his indomitable, untamable Jeannette.

And then, to his astonishment and the utter elation of all the beleaguered English fighters hemmed in within their little stronghold near Poitiers that day, the middle of the three cumbrous French battalions merely wheeled away to the northwest.

"By the rood, a full retreat!" Oxford crowed. "The damn fools in the Duc d'Orléans battalion must not know we are surely beaten by their overweening numbers if they but press on!"

"Beaten, never, no matter what their size or strength, Oxford," the prince corrected him sternly. "I bid you all expect nothing but victory and it shall be so. It must be so! They have disgraced their so-called Noble Order of the Star to retreat while we still hold French fields."

The prince's eagle eyes scanned the scene below him. Again his protective wall of archers, dug in behind the thorn hedge and a row of their own buried pikes, were nearly bereft of arrows; again another endless, swelling wave of the enemy rode forward through the funneled approaches to the Plain of Maupertuis.

"The king's own forces this time, Your Grace. But the yeomen have no time to forage out for arrows again, nor the protection of our cavalry to do so."

"Mayhap not, my man, but look. Look you over the enemy beyond. De Buch is there—see, the raised banners of St. George!" He swung around in his shiny shell of full black armor and lifted the hilt of his dented sword to catch the glint of sun.

"De Buch and our men are there behind!" he yelled over the battle din below. "To horse, to horse this final time for victory!"

They clattered down the hill amidst the rows of grapevines, past their own cheering archers and into the face of the enemy. Already the final battle line of the French churned and writhed in a chaotic mass of metal horse and men. But to panicked flight by the appearance of an English force behind, they halted, turned, and fled.

The hawk-faced John Chandos was pounding at the prince's side. "Push forward, forward! The day is yours, great prince! God has given this miracle into your hands!"

The day was theirs and swiftly ended as the English scurried to surround important noble prisoners and clear the area of all dangers. Under his proud standard, the Prince of Wales's red silk pavilion was raised and, as he sat there resting after wracking hours of marching, planning, and fighting, his men reported the final stages of the glorious English victory.

"We chased some clear to the gates of Poitiers, Your Grace, where the frightened townfolk have shut their doors. Shall we ferret them out?"

"No—enough of warfare for this day, unless we cannot find the French king among these forces here."

"Your Grace, all this glory without your royal sire even here to advise—without the help of your brother Lancaster's forces too. England will be wild with jubilee when we return to her!"

When we return to her, the prince's exhilarated brain echoed. When he returned to England, Jeannette must be there. Only a day they had been apart but what a day—an eternity of struggle. His head snapped up at the next shouted words.

"My lord prince—the French king! The king has surrendered and with his son and sues to be delivered to his cousin, Prince Edward!"

Throughout the clustering crowd of tired, sweating knights and archers, a cheering swell rumbled closer like a roar of seastorm. Metal helmets danced aloft in shattering blue sky; banners jumped wildly over heads as the captured king approached the prince's tent. Under the aegis of the Earl of Warwick, the tall, red-haired King John approached with his petulant, fourteen-year-old son Philip at his side.

"I yield to the better knight on this day," King John said in wearied, monotone French. His thick, red beard bobbed when he talked. He handed his sword and right gauntlet to Prince Edward as a token of surrender. The gauntlet the prince kept, but he magnanimously returned the sword hilt first.

"Welcome to our English-held ground, Your Grace of France," the now silent men heard their prince reply. "This victory feast shall mayhap not boast the rich fare you are used to, but I trust you will enjoy what we provide later for your stay in London well enough."

Those closest to their prince saw his square jaw set in smug pleasure; the aquamarine eyes glinted with scarcely contained joy. Behind the three royal men of two sovereign nations, the Captal de Buch edged his way into the tent to find his appointed seat. Aye, as the precisely honed code of fair chivalry dictated, the French would be treated in defeat as long-lost boon companions but for the necessary lack of their freedom and their pride.

Saints' bones, the Captal mused as he scanned the length of hastily set, silk-draped table, he could just imagine how the wild lilac eyes of the prince's secret ladylove would light when she heard of this second conquest of her Edward in one mere, bloody, battling week. The Captal bowed his bull neck for the victory prayer, but he wondered if in all this, the prince's excited thoughts, too, had strayed to conquest of a mere woman from this momentous victory over a king.

Joan, Lady Holland, Duchess of Kent, sat with her now silent lute in her lap in the warming autumn sun outside her Château in Normandy. Her children were both taking afternoon naps in their rooms, and her Lord Thomas, who had been here a week now as a result of having caught a flux and having been ordered by Prince John of Lancaster to go home to his lady wife's tender nursing, was still abed after his detested afternoon rest. She herself had been home three weeks now from that other world that never could really be, and the leaves were whispering all around her in their painted maroon, vermilion, and gold hues, rich as any illuminated prayer book.

No word. There had been no official word, for who could trust whisperings in the village of a great battle far to the south any more than one could ever trust the rumors at court? Had he escaped the powerful French army? Was he hurt or wounded or even heading home to England? How long again, how many years this time, until she would see his proud and handsome face?

Her slender fingers plucked the lute strings while the words of the tune rustled through her tumbled mind like falling leaves:

> O man unkind,
> Have thou in mind
> My passion sharp!
> Thou shalt me find
> To thee full kind:
> Lo, here my heart!

She pulled her slippered feet back under her woolen

surcote for, despite the sun, the October wind was chill. The rough tree trunk behind her back felt comfortingly steady and Marta's grave—a soothing place rather than a painful one as time went by—was near enough to see across the little growth of bittersweet vine from which the purplish flowers had long died and which now flaunted a display of their poison scarlet berries.

Bittersweet, she thought, my lord Prince Edward and I. Aye, bittersweet, but never poison. And yet in life, she knew such things happened. Her years of supposed friendship with Master Roger Wakeley had turned to bitterness and mistrust. Upon her return from Monbarzon, she had scolded him terribly and would have sent him away but for the fact her Lord Thomas would have asked a hundred questions and Roger Wakeley knew far too much. Better to keep him here so *she* could spy on him, she had decided. And so, she had made a truce in their little war, expecting promises from Roger that he would only send the prince messages she wished to go and none of his own.

She played the sad song's melody again almost without hearing it. Nursing Thomas at night when he called out, caring for the boys, worrying so about the English army, she was nearly exhausted. Her hand dropped to her lap and the shaft of sun on her face made her very drowsy. Surely they must hear soon how good this day felt—and bittersweet— over there, "o man unkind, lo, here my heart. . . ."

She jolted awake with a start, bumping her head on the rough hickory bark behind her. Aye, that was it—her maid Vinette shouting her name from a distance.

"I am down here, Vinette!" She stood unsteadily holding her lute and shook the leaves from her skirts. "I am coming!"

The red-haired maid rounded the corner of the château wall to motion to her as she hurried forward. "Is it my lord? Is he all right?" Joan called.

"*Oui*, Lord Thomas is awake now and sits by the fire in the solar, *madame*, but there is a messenger here to see you from the English Prince Edward."

Edward! Safe, alive, perhaps coming this way! Joan broke into a run along the tall castle wall.

"Where? Where is he? What did he say?"

Vinette Brinay's attractive, freckled face turned obviously bitter at her words. "He bids you hear yourself, *madame*, but the heart of the matter my man Pierre has heard in the village for days is the same. The French king is defeated as nine years ago at Crécy and now the taxes and griefs on the backs of the poor serfs will double again to buy their noble armor and fill the royal coffers. To see the king humbled, 'tis well and good, *certainement*, but not at the expense of our downtrodden folk! We shall not suffer it. They will see!"

Joan stopped and stared as though she had been doused with icy water. Vinette's light brown eyes glared wide into Joan's startled lilac ones before the girl lowered them evidently amazed at her outburst. "The man awaits—he is in the great hall, *madame*."

Joan touched the girl's shoulder in a comforting caress as she hurried past, but she felt the distinct shove of Vinette's shoulder as she shrugged her off. She must talk to the maid about such behavior and feelings, though mayhap if Thomas could merely stop that tanner Pierre Foulke from seeing her, it would halt the nasty bent of her tongue and temper of late. Vinette seldom went to her village home, so she was hardly being filled with such poison there.

The messenger awaiting her by the low-burning hearth of the great hall was Michael Brettin, one of the guards who had accompanied her on the grueling ride back from Monbarzon only three weeks ago. The knight wore no armor and she noted he was with only one squire who warmed his hands at the hearth and straightened to stand at attention when she entered.

"Sir Michael. You must have almost turned around to come straight back. Welcome! I have sent my maid to the kitchen to fetch food and wine."

"Truth is, my lady duchess, I had to go clear south to Chalais to find them, but I rested only two days before I headed back. By the rood, though I am proud to serve my prince in any capacity needed, Duchess, you made me miss the greatest English victory of the age!"

"Oh, I am sorry, my lord—sorry you missed it, I mean, but I never thought of that or I would have ridden back here all by myself. But a great victory—saints, that is what matters, my lord!"

The brown-haired, long-faced man smiled at the eternally stunning impact of the natural beauty of the woman. "I meant not to sound severe, Duchess. And the prince has rewarded me handsomely for my part in things, only—" Here he lowered his voice and winked at her conspiratorially, "I shall have to break my knightly code of honor and lie to my grandchildren someday about my assigned tasks during the battle, eh?"

"And you had best keep the truth silent here, my lord. The prince told you, did he not, that the nature of my visit to him was to bring sensitive material to his attention and so—" Her voice trailed off as she saw Sir Michael's long chin tremble as though he might dare to laugh in her face. Saints, had not the prince told his men that story and were they not bound to believe it as he was their sovereign liege lord? What if their secret three days of heavenly tryst at Monbarzon were common knowledge—with this man, this doltish-looking squire by the hearth, the whole damned English army!

"Follow me upstairs, if you please, Sir Michael," her voice now edged with steely aplomb cut the air. "My dear Lord Thomas is home from his duty with Prince John and he would hear of your message as eagerly as I."

That wiped the amused hint of smile from his pompous face, Joan mused, as she led him up the stairs. Bitter and sweet her memories of those three days might be, but she had no intention of letting such implications poison her reputation or her position here as chatelaine of Château Ruisseau!

Despite two weeks of the flux, weight loss, and the flare-up of his old pains in the leg he had broken years ago,

Thomas Holland, fully dressed, insisted on rising to meet the prince's messenger.

"My Lord Holland. I find your Crécy treasure castle a treasure indeed," Sir Michael Brettin began.

"Brettin, good to see you after these years. Crécy—fine memories, fine. But now you come with official word of another victory we have heard whispered of—or mayhap a summons for me?"

Sir Michael's amber eyes linked with Thomas Holland's probing stare before the knight looked away. "For you, Lord Thomas? Alas, no, not a summons, that is, at least not to battle or to join the prince's force. His Grace has gone far south back to Aquitaine with the royal prisoners, the French king and his young son, Prince Philip, to Bordeaux, and come early spring, they will be sailing home. For that day of glory, though, I do bring you summons—you and your Duchess of Kent—to join His Grace's force at Sandwich this spring and to proceed from there to London for triumphal entry."

"Us with him to London when we had no part of it?" Thomas demanded. "I was sent to serve with Prince John, you know, Brettin, and not with His Grace, Prince Edward, as I had ever been wont to do before this campaign."

"Aye, so I do recall, Lord Holland, but that was probably only because you could serve nearer to your precious lands here in Normandy while King Edward sent the Prince of Wales south to Aquitaine."

"St. Edward's holy blood, man, does His Grace think a little ride south to join with the prince would be some sort of hardship for me? I would have gone and gladly to meet him. I have a protective force I can leave here."

Sir Michael's sharp eyes lifted to catch the duchess' warning frown over her husband's shoulder. By the rood, but the humor, the irony of this pleased his jaded senses mightily, Sir Michael thought, fighting to stifle a grin. Lord Thomas here wished to do what his lady unbeknownst to him had willfully and fully accomplished, though saints

427

knew, her joining with the prince was of a far different nature.

Sir Michael cleared his throat awkwardly. He was tired from riding and needed time to compose himself. Whatever his mission, he never wanted his great prince to think he had not served him with utmost loyalty and sincerity, and riling this lady could be a very bad step.

"I have many details to convey to you about the battle, Lord Holland, and to the duchess, and I shall be pleased to tell them all whenever you so desire," he said smoothly as if tossing the matter in the lady's lap. As he had thought, she was as clever as she was lovely.

"My Lord Thomas, Sir Michael had only just now ridden in and there is food awaiting him and his squire in the hall. After he has supped, we may hear the rest. I shall take him down now and be right back."

"No, please, Duchess, sit here with your lord, and I shall be fine going just down the stairs." Sir Michael bowed curtly and moved away before she could follow, but she read his thought of escape well enough, and she let him go without a word. The man had almost grinned at Thomas's mention of riding south to join with Prince Edward, and none of this was a whit funny!

"I expected you to be elated at the news of an English victory, my lord," she began as soon as the door closed, hoping that by going on the offensive she could discourage that scolding tone Thomas often fell into of late.

"And I expected you to be all in whirls over the opportunity to go home in triumph with the prince—my duchess."

"Really? The victory parade will hardly be passing through Liddell and that is the only place I favor at home, as well you know."

"Let us not argue, Joan."

"Fine. I do not wish to."

"I know you have not seen the royal Plantagenets for years and care not to now for all those vile memories of your father and mother which you finally chose to share with me."

"Aye," she said only, as her mind skipped back over all the buried bitterness. Amazingly, except for her well-tended hatred of John de Maltravers, who was evidently still exiled in Flanders thanks to her support by Prince Edward, she hardly hated over that anymore. Except for de Maltravers's wily face in her dreams, it all seemed so very far away at times, even as did that little sprawling, third-story room in the inn where—

"What did you say, my lord?"

"Saints' blood, Joan, cannot you listen and not go about so dreamy-eyed all day? I said I only resented the man here because he was fortunate enough to be with the prince's army at the victory and I was not. Tonight, I intend to hear every detail of it while you worry about such things as proper fashions for our London return and whether the Plantagenets have forgiven you enough to let us both back to court from exile now and then."

She turned away and gazed out through the leaden-paned westward windows over the riotously painted forest trees stretching away to the blue ribbon of autumn sky. To London in the spring, to see him there, return with him in triumph, but to what? She felt no part of the court now; her laughing pranks with the gay Princess Isabella and all her *demoiselles* seemed but a pale memory.

To be with him as they had been at Monbarzon? But Thomas would be there, and the king, and a thousand staring eyes and whispering mouths, so that never could be again. Better not to go—to stay here watching this French woods of Pont-Audemer turn to gray-etched skeletons and then to yellow-green bud again.

But hiding here even in this room or down there underground in that dark tunnel of her old nightmares, she would never find escape any more than her poor mother had escaped reality hidden away at Liddell all those sad years. She, though her mother's daughter, had always chosen to go on, to face the world with a song that hid her heart if need be, and she would do so come this spring.

"Would it make you feel better to take a little crisp, fall air, Thomas?" she heard herself ask. "I was out before and it was lovely." She forced herself to turn around to face him squarely, and her lips lifted in a steady smile as she held out her hand to help him rise.

When autumn and the winter filled with long, long hours and days revolved at last to spring, Joan and Thomas Holland went to meet the prince's great victory retinue at Windsor. Prince Edward had landed, because of a change of plans and a vile storm on the Channel, far southwest at Plymouth. For three weeks, in a parade of royal captives, booty, and gaily bedecked heroes, he rode in triumph through the sweet May of England toward Windsor.

Joan, Thomas, and their little brood of sons and servants had come across the Channel to Sandwich with Prince John of Lancaster's Normandy forces and had made ready with the rest of the court to join the prince's cortège for the final, glorious jaunt into frenzied, rejoicing London.

Now, Joan's old friend the Princess Isabella swept into the Great Hall where everyone important awaited the prince's imminent arrival. The fair-haired, laughing princess was garbed in Plantagenet azure and gold brocade literally encrusted with swirls of gems. In the three days Joan had been back at court, she had seen little of her Lord Thomas but a great deal of Isabella. She found her continual chattering was beginning to fray her nerves, but because of the sadness in the princess' lovely blue eyes, Joan smiled and nodded and let her ramble on. She rose from a little curtsy to the princess and accepted one of her sweet-scented, lightning-quick embraces.

"You look absolutely stunning, Your Grace," Joan told her. "You will blind the eyes of the people in the sun and your brother-hero will be taxed with you for taking all the glory."

Isabella's musical voice chimed in laughter, and many gorgeously appareled courtiers craned their necks to see. "It will not be my dear brother Prince Edward taxed, *ma chérie*, but my father King Edward when he sees the gownmaker and goldsmith bills, I warrant, but then, as I have always vowed, *'Suis-je belle?'*"

"Aye, of course, Your Grace, it is important to be fair and you have always been far more than that."

Isabella leaned closer to Joan in a move that obviously annoyed her little bevy of ladies who could not overhear her next words. "Jeannette, I am so fond of you—so pleased you are back with us, if only for a little while. Stand here with me now, for I have a little gift for you and we shall then both face the king together, eh? Of all the things we shared before you went away, His Majesty's occasional anger was one amusement, you cannot deny it!"

"Please, Your Grace, you cannot mean to do something to rile His Grace, the king, today. I have not even seen him yet since I have been back and—"

"Oh, fifes and fiddles! Annette, where *is* that gift for the Duchess of Kent, and someone help her change her *surcote!*"

One of the princess' butterflies, a young and flawlessly complexioned maid Joan did not recognize, produced an azure and gold *surcote* studded with both the Plantagenet leopards of England and the gold *fleur-de-lis* of France—a perfect match to the princess' own, except that it flaunted far fewer jewels. Yet each leopard wore a jeweled collar which linked it to the center of a lily, making a design so delicate and intricate it dazzled the eye.

"See, Jeannette, my love gift to you for all the years we have been apart," Isabella's voice lilted while the growing crowd around them gasped and stared.

Joan felt herself blush hot. "It is too beautiful, too generous, Your Grace. I could not possibly accept."

"Blessed Virgin's veil—of course you can. Plantagenet blood flows through your veins as readily as mine or that of the hero of Poitiers who will be here at any moment, and you know he will not be decked in hopsacking. Do accept it, my dearest cousin Jeannette, and then we shall all go out to the

431

courtyard to greet them."

A lady removed the white brocade *surcote* with tiny seed pearls Joan had meant to wear over the lilac-hued brocade kirtle which accented the color of her eyes and clung just tightly enough not to reveal the slight swelling from her third pregnancy. How long she had planned her garments for this day over the winter weeks at Château Ruisseau thinking of the moment she would at last see him again. Thomas would be there too, of course, hundreds of courtiers, and thousands of cheering English folk along the way, but she had wanted to wear white for her skin and lilac for her eyes when she first looked, alone, into his blue, blue gaze.

The new *surcote* felt heavy on her shoulders and it glittered even here in the dim lighting of the hall. For one moment she felt so warm and dizzy that she thought she might topple over, but of course these were merely early bothersome signs of her new pregnancy and she had handled them before. She breathed deeply and her head cleared.

"I thank you for your continued generosity and love to me, Your Grace," Joan managed despite the sudden catch in her throat. "I hope your lovely gift will please them all—or," she teased as they went out into the press of the others to the courtyard, "at least His Grace, the king, will have two of us to bluster at just as that day we rode in our own Crécy tournament years ago."

The Princess Isabella's peals of laughter permeated the gentle air as both Isabella and Joan with a swarm of ladies behind them faced the waiting king and queen in the courtyard. The king, mounted on a white charger, dazzled all in his glittering white silk and full regalia of crown and massive neck chain. Jewels winked from his white-gloved fingers as he flexed his hands on his reins. Queen Philippa, also in white and blazing with jewels, sat in a chair someone had brought out for her. She looked older to Joan, plumper, paler—the only one who had evidently altered greatly over the years she had been away in Normandy. Both Isabella and Joan curtsied, but Isabella did it with her head up to observe her father's face.

"Joan, Duchess of Kent, you are welcome back to our court on this most glorious day," the king intoned grandly, evidently choosing to ignore the ostentatious show of fashion.

"Jeannette has been here with her family for three days, Your Grace," Isabella chimed in, "and we have been having the grandest fun recalling old times."

"Have you? Yet the duchess is much changed now of necessity, are you not, lady, with sons, ducal estates and a lord?" the king said, and Joan read the challenge of his tone and words almost as if he had tossed his gauntlet at her.

"Aye, my lord king, of course she is," Queen Philippa put in before Joan could answer. "She has been seven years away and has two fine sons and a third child on the way, so my Lord Thomas Holland told me only yesterday."

Joan's jaw dropped. So Thomas had been with the queen and had not mentioned a bit of it to her, but then he surely had been other places, too, as she had only seen him at supper and at night the three days they had been awaiting the prince at Windsor. It seemed he was on sword point their entire time back, and his temper had been foul, despite the fact he seemed genuinely pleased to have her with child again.

"Listen, my loyal friends and subjects, listen! They come!" King Edward bellowed and everyone ceased whispering and chattering. Like thunder on a distant horizon, a rumbling swelled the air outside the massive walls of Windsor—horses' pounding hoofs, cheers from a thousand throats. Isabella dragged Joan forward to stand behind the king and queen and their brood of children—John, Duke of Lancaster, tall and thin; Lionel, Duke of Clarence, at age twenty, over seven feet tall with the three-year-old youngest Plantagenet prince on his huge shoulders; Edward of Langley, Duke of York, and the little maids Mary and Margaret.

Joan felt herself go scarlet in the rush of emotion. Here—

she stood here at Windsor in the Lower Ward awaiting her prince with his family as though she were an accepted Plantagenet at last. Now—though she carried another man's babe beneath her heart—that heart itself was the prince's and mayhap it had always been so. The sweet, poignant pain of their years of mingled passions bit at her and made her head spin again.

It was here, just through that little door in the wall over there, that she had seen the prince her first day at Windsor while he tilted madly at the quintain, and now he had tilted with the whole army of France and won. Down through that little door—she had heard that the crowds screamed outside that day too—her poor father had died while waiting to be rescued by his nephew, this king.

Trumpets blew from the ramparts. The deafening cheers and cries outside drowned the noise within the walls as the mounted men under a thousand silk banners clattered into the cobbled courtyard. There—there on a white destrier was Prince Edward, smiling, waving to all, and his tawny hair shone like flared gold in the sun.

"By St. George, Jeannette, is that big red-haired man beside our Edward King John? He is as fiery-haired as we are flaxen," Isabella's shouted words floated to her.

"I suppose it is, Your Grace, and that sullen boy there the French Prince Philip, no doubt. Saints, he will be a difficult one to amuse until that mammoth ransom is paid!"

Now it was Joan and not Isabella who kept talking, talking. She was not certain what she said, but it kept her from screaming out her joy or her love while everyone else cavorted around in frenzied, futile motion. After the prince's men dismounted and he himself stood across the way between his two kings, the Captal de Buch appeared from somewhere in the crowd to bow to Isabella and give Joan a hearty kiss on her cheek.

"You know the Captal from Gascony?" Isabella queried as her quick eyes assessed the big, effusive man. "But he has only been about our court as the prince's advisor since you

434

have been away, *ma chérie* Jeannette. *Le* Captal, I always knew you were a rogue and a clever one," she laughed and darted off toward Prince Edward.

"Sorry, Duchess, only—hell's gates, what a wild three weeks since we landed, and I was not even thinking. Ah, is not Lord Holland here about? His Grace said he would be, I recall."

"He went out with the few Garter Knights not already in the procession to greet you all, so I am certain he rode in with you. He must be here somewhere. Did you wish to meet him?"

She noted over de Buch's big shoulder that the prince approached talking, laughing, kissing and hugging his family one by one and introducing them to the French king and prince whom he had in tow as if they were the best of boon companions. She felt terribly light-headed again. She knew de Buch was telling her something, but she had to concentrate on merely standing her ground unmoving. Prince Edward stopped a few feet away and his clear blue eyes all too obviously lighted at the sight of her. The Princess Isabella had draped herself on his left arm and was chattering in his ear. The French king's gaze went over Joan from floating lilac head scarves to velvet toes.

De Buch stepped behind her and bowed; Joan bent low to curtsy unsteadily. And then, the cobblestones with the prince's big, booted feet approaching rushed up to meet her.

"Jeannette!" she heard the prince shout.

Arms seized her, held her.

"Isabella, she is white as a sheet! What the hell is wrong?"

"St. Catharine, she was a little dizzy yesterday morning too!" Isabella's musical tones floated to her from afar.

"Here—lean her here. I have her."

"*Sacrebleu*—who is this beauty, Edward? And in Plantagenet trappings also," a new voice said in flowing French.

Embarrassed beyond reasoning, Joan flicked her eyes open. She was sitting on the ground in Prince Edward's arms, her back against his leg as he knelt on one knee, but her first glimpse was of the faces of both the kings of England and France pressing close.

"Give her a little air, my lord kings, *si'l vous plaît*," Isabella's high voice floated to her. "It is only that she is pregnant and nearly fainted in all this hubbub, I warrant." The princess gently pulled her father aside and bent over Joan, chafing her wrists.

"Pregnant!" Prince Edward's deep words rumbled close to her ear and she could feel his voice, too, where she leaned against his muscular thigh. "But how long? She looks fine."

When the impact of it all hit Joan with stunning force, she struggled to rise. The press of people, the eager eyes royal and noble was too terrible, as if the fondest fantasy she had cherished all these months of rushing to his arms before them all had been stripped naked for everyone to see.

The French king helped her stand, his green eyes burning holes in her. "I realize the times are hurried and most unusual, *mon* Prince Edward, but this lady, I take it, is not another princess of your fair family?" he asked in strangely monotone French.

The prince's strong grip still steadied her arm. "She is a distant cousin, Your Grace," the deep, haunting familiar voice came to her ears again. "She lived at our court before she married to settle in Normandy. Not a princess, though her grandfather was also a king. May I present Joan, Duchess of Kent, your Royal Highness."

The tall, flame-haired king lifted her trembling, white hand to his bearded lips and kissed it, something her own prince beside her did not or would not do. Saints, she thought, and straightened to stand clear of Prince Edward's arm at last, I could as easily have this foreign King of France as this Edward, hero of Poitiers! The Prince of Wales was as far out of her grasp as some cold, distant star Morcar might have consulted once.

The whirling in her ears stopped; the rush of emotions fell off into some endless void and left her very lonely amidst that large crowd of noisy people.

"I beg your forgiveness, Your Grace, for that foolish display or any other I might have given," she said quietly to the prince without quite looking at him. "As the Princess Isabella says, I am newly with child and we have traveled so far to get here, first at sea and then from the coast."

"I, too, Duchess, have traveled far from fair France and not of my own accord," the French king said, his eyes warm on her again. She returned his gaze in order to escape the magnetic pull of the prince so close, for if she even glanced into the fathomless depths of those blue eyes, her pretended strength would be mere dust and cobwebs in the strongest gale.

Blessedly, Queen Philippa's approach rescued her, for she walked on the proudly proffered arm of Thomas Holland and their cold, stern faces provided the final jolt Joan needed to get a grip on the ruin of her dreams.

"See, Lord Thomas, you must look to your lady better. With the new babe coming, she keeled right over at the Prince of Wales's feet and this fuss is holding us all up," the queen drawled, accenting the last words.

"Aye, Your Grace, but for another Holland child, any little problems are well worth the price, is it not so, my Lady Joan?" Thomas said pointedly. He bowed to the kings and prince and took his wife's hand in a possessive grip.

"Then to protect your unborn child," Prince Edward's voice cut in like the edge of a knife before Joan could summon up an answer, "I would suggest you take better care of the duchess and not let her be up and about if she is weak after travel. And most importantly, Holland, not even let her consider a jolting ride clear to London, whatever the occasion."

"I quite agree, my lord prince, but we were indeed summoned months ago as well you know."

Joan was astounded by the perceptible crackle of tension between the two men. The queen tried to hide a nervous smirk, King Edward glowered, and the curious King of France looked bemused at the whole, strange encounter.

437

Joan could have simply killed Thomas, and the prince she dared not look at.

"So, then it is decided that the Hollands will stay here until our return while the rest of us press on as soon as we have some wine," Prince Edward concluded and turned his back to speak low with his father.

While Thomas Holland looked shocked at their apparent dismissal, King John of France stepped forward once again and reclaimed Joan's hand. "My greatest pleasure in these weeks of dismay since I came to England is to meet you, Duchess. Disappointments in life, eh—frustrations? I have known many of late and mostly at the chivalric hands of this Prince of Wales and perhaps you sympathize with me, *oui*?"

Joan dared to tug her hand back. "Forgive me, Your Grace," she answered in smooth French, "but I do not follow your words."

"Ah, *c'est un grand dommage.* I only meant that I must ride an honored prisoner to London and now you must by turn of Fortune's cruel wheel remain here, eh? *Adieu*, Duchess, and her lord." King John's eyes went over her again in a studious, yet amused way. Then, he turned with his hovering retinue and rejoined King Edward and the prince.

Before Joan could even find Isabella to bid her farewell, Thomas had her in a firm grip on her upper arm and was guiding her away through the chatting crowd.

"St. Peter's bones, woman, but you do have a talent for getting us alternately sent for then exiled, do you not?"

"Let go of my arm, my lord. You are hurting me and I am still light-headed."

"Aye, light-headed near His Grace, the prince, as always. Do not think, dear wife, this one good eye I still have is not enough to see his face and your trembling. Queen Philippa warned me long ago and it is still true, though you have been a woman worth the having despite all that. And I know well enough, too, why I was not sent for to fight with His Grace at Poitiers where a Garter Knight belonged. He cannot bear to

438

be civil to me because of you!"

She pulled from his hold on the first step up inside the Garter Tower where they had gone in from the crowded Lower Ward. She pressed herself back against the curving, cold wall. "That is unfair, my lord!"

"Is it? And now the French king falls all over you with words of fond condolence for a fellow sufferer?"

"And where have you been these last few days? Falling all over Queen Philippa with whisperings of our private life? No one knew about this babe—no one until she announced it grandly a while ago out there just as you told her in private!"

He reached out to yank her to him, and his round face went livid with an anger she had seldom seen him display. "Aye, I went to her. St. Peter's bones, I am proud to serve her, and I serve her in the purest chivalric duties, *madame*. *She* looks to me for comfort unlike my steely, little wife who keeps all her warmth for her memories, her paltry lands at Liddell, her sons, and others."

"That is not true. I thought we had gotten along well this winter."

"Did you, Duchess of Kent? Did you? I tell you, you are just damned lucky you have been in my bed every night so I know this new child you carry is mine. We will rest here a day or two and then I shall take you to Liddell to join our sons. As soon as possible, we had best hie ourselves home, for this huge ransom the Plantagenets have put on your French king's red head will no doubt fall on our peasants and rile up rabble-rousers like Vinette Brinay's tanner even more. And I assure you, next time I come to court, you will stay at your blessed Liddell where you could not possibly cause such a spectacle!"

His copper eye was narrowed to a furious slit, and his chin quivered at his tirade. His pride, she thought numbly, his pride has been crushed, and if he ever found out about her time with the prince at Canterbury or Monbarzon, let alone before they were wed, he would be likely to explode and kill her for certain.

"I shall try not to cause you such distress henceforth, my lord," she managed calmly, "but you were hardly around to faint on since you were strolling with the queen who is evidently prouder of this babe I carry than you are. I will be going up to my bed now, so you may ride along clear to London with them all if you like."

She pushed past him up the curving stairs of the Garter Tower named in honor of that noble order and for her own garter lost so long ago. She heard him stamp down the steps and bang the door on his way out. She pressed her shoulder against the cool stones by a narrow slit meant for shooting arrows. The May breeze off the River Thames smelled clean and fresh up here, but it brought, too, the sounds of revelry below and of hundreds of people remounting for the festive victory jaunt to London. She peered out, but the depth of the embrasure was two feet, and she could not see the activity down in the Lower Ward.

This day she had awaited for seven long months was over now before it had hardly begun—a quick glimpse of her Edward among the staring crowd; the high walls separating them even as did the cold tower stones; rushed, public words that could never be personal or intimate again. Saints, she had been better off when the sweet passion's pain she felt for Edward, Prince of Wales, had been hatred and not this burning, bittersweet agony of love!

She sank down on the narrow steps and watched the tears plop onto the expensive, jeweled emblems of two royal nations on her *surcote*. She had to go on: the foolish dream was over. The prince belonged to all of them and to himself, never to her. In a day or two, before the court returned with all their happy tales of this triumphant day, she would be gone to sanctuary at Liddell and then home to Normandy even as her mother had once fled from painful memories hoping for escape. France might ransom her king for three million crowns of gold someday, but never, never would she let her heart be held hostage again for any fortune on this earth, she vowed. Never!

Chapter Twenty

"Vinette! Madeleine!" Joan called up the stairs, then decided to see what was keeping them. "Saints," she muttered under her breath as she lifted her dark green skirts and ran up the steps, "we shall be so late to the fair, everything decent will be already sold."

She strode down the quiet hall to the solar door and peeked in, fully prepared to dash on to look in the boys' room or the nursery where her four-month-old daughter Bella lay asleep. But, to her surprise, her maid Vinette; the nursemaid Madeleine, holding the startled blond babe Bella; and both sons were in the solar. The boys and Vinette scrambled on all fours peeping at the carpet while Madeleine scolded and Bella whined in her arms.

"What in the world!" Joan began as four guilty faces looked up in surprise. Her lilac eyes took in the whole little tableau and judged its import: huge pearls from the necklace Prince Edward had given her almost two years ago at Monbarzon lay scattered everywhere on the Brussels carpet.

"They just broke, Mother," eight-year-old Thomas protested in a voice that told her who was the culprit.

"My coffer! Why were you in my coffer and clear to the bottom, Thomas? And you, John," she scolded her second son who looked frightened enough to have been caught by a rampaging enemy knight. "That coffer is Mother's! Really, Vinette, what happened?"

Thomas stood up slowly, his fist full of fat pearls. His copper eyes widened at the anger he saw on his lady mother's lovely face. "Sorry, Mother. We were only digging for buried treasure."

"We found some with a whole bunch of old letters from a dragon," John piped up.

"My letters! All right, you have all been very, very bad to get in Mother's things. Give me the pearls—here, just put them in this basket and go wait in the hall. And, Madeleine and Vinette, you two are hardly ready to leave for the fair— and why is Bella up from her nap?"

"I heard a ruckus, I heard Vinette scream, Madame Joan—I heard it all and came running so fast with the babe to see what I heard," the plump-faced Madeleine blurted out in one of her typical long-winded answers.

"All right, I said. I realize accidents happen but, Thomas, I look to you now that your father is gone so much to be a good influence for little John and a help to me. No more digging for treasure or dragon's letters in my things—now, all of you get out until I clean this mess up."

She bent over to quickly examine the stiff parchment letters shuffled about the bottom of the coffer as the two chastised maids and grim-faced boys walked out and closed the door. Two letters—aye, they were all here, all she had left of the missives the prince had sent her this last year—all she had left of some faded, foolish memories of sweet passion's pain.

She touched the crinkly vellum, stroked the double wax ducal and royal seals, then stuffed them back under her winter clothes the boys had disturbed. Dragon's letters indeed! The official one she kept because it said her son John should have Liddell someday if the elder Thomas had the Holland lands in Lancashire. The only dragon it dealt with was that traitor to her family, John de Maltravers, but at least her pleas through the prince to King Edward had foiled the return of all the vile man's lands.

The other letter from the prince apologized for the terrible mess that had come of their reunion on his triumphal return to Windsor over a year ago. To the first letter, she had bound with a ribbon the old green beryl ring from so long ago and it still hung there forlornly now that she never wore it or even looked at it. Her eyes went again to her beautiful pearls she never dared to wear either.

"Damn!" she said to the silent room and knelt to gather the rest of the silky-hued gems. A broken chain—how perfect, she mused as the pearls rattled in clusters into her little basket. Broken links to Prince Edward, to the court, now even to her Lord Thomas, for since little Bella was born and her sire beheld her blond hair so unlike the copper locks of the two boys, he had ceased to treat her as a wife although he was civil enough to her when he was home. Even though he knew Bella was his child beyond a doubt, her Plantagenet fairness had somehow estranged him from both daughter and wife, and he had scarcely spent two nights in a row here since Joan had refused to name the child Philippa and they had settled instead for Isabella, after the Princess—Bella, for a sentimental sobriquet.

Her ties to Roger Wakeley too—broken after all these years, for the King of England, of all people, had sent for him, and she had let him go. Now, she played only occasional lullabies for the little ones on her lute and seldom sang. She drove herself to frenzied activity about the manor until she fell exhausted into bed at night.

This time, Thomas had evidently ridden off to try to join Prince John of Lancaster who, with King Edward, the Prince of Wales, and Prince Lionel, was rumored to be raiding to the south. She shoved the retrieved pearls in their basket down in the coffer under her garments and snapped the lid closed. Broken, all of it, just like the thread of her life, and—saints, she sometimes was not sure whether she cared to try to mend it all again or not.

She went to the door and yanked it open to see Vinette and Madeleine ready to leave for the fair at last. "The boys?"

"The babe asleep, the boys in their rooms playing dragons and treasure still, but not, madame, with your things," Vinette assured her.

"I should hope not. I had a good nerve in there to tell both

443

of them they could not go to the fair on the morrow with us, but then, one does not find buried treasure everyday. Come along then, and do not forget your market baskets."

Vinette winked at the portly nursemaid as they scurried downstairs trying in vain to keep up with Madame Holland's fast clip. The four-day market fair was just a mile away in a meadow between Pont-Audemer and Corneville-sur-Risle, and simply everyone would be there. Vinette never got much chance to see her old village friends now that she had been the Duchess of Kent's chief lady's maid. By holy Mary's veil, Pierre, Vinette's love who had oft scolded her for her loyal service to a noble family would no doubt be there in the tanner's booth and mayhap try to steal a kiss and mayhap even tell her again she must choose between loyalty to him and her own folk and loyalty to the fancy life she led at the Holland's high and mighty Château Ruisseau.

"Vinette, do not dawdle as we are late already and I want us to purchase many things today. St. George, I wish my Lord Thomas were here to help oversee the hired carriers, but we shall make do."

The three women mounted waiting palfreys and with their two armed guards from the household, clattered out of the castle. In these times when village serfs festered under the burdensome yoke of tremendous taxes to help pay for the French king's ransom and to reestablish the knightly army so decimated at Poitiers, armed guards went everywhere with the Lady Joan under her absent lord's orders. Sometimes, Vinette thought, as she smirked under the floppy straw bonnet the duchess had given her to keep the splatter of freckles from her pale skin, she almost thought Lord Holland had put the guards on his lady wife to be certain she did not run away.

"Vinette, when we have begun to purchase, you and one of the guards take the coins and look for bearers or carters to bring the goods back to the Château, and be certain you only give them half what they ask. I do not want them reselling our merchandise to someone else and keeping the coins to boot."

"*Oui*, madame, but Pierre says the carters from the village are honest and always underpaid."

"Aye, Pierre would say that. And remember that you promised me you would not go off lollygagging with him. I do not wish to have to hold our entire discussion about Monsieur Pierre, the silver-tongued tanner, all over again."

"No, madame, only—"

"Only what, *demoiselle*? I believe you told me you were happier living at the Château than you would be as wife to him in the village."

"And," the usually complacent Madeleine dared, "her ladyship did promise next time Lord Holland came home for a spell, a husband from the household or guards could be found for you, Vinette, a husband so you could live in the Château, girl!"

"*Oui*, Madeleine, so I have heard from madame once and from you repeatedly," Vinette replied, her full mouth drawn down in a pout, "only, I think people ought to be able to chose their own loves, and not have their betters putting others on them they cannot abide."

Joan held her tongue. The maid was a little snip at times, and badly needed to be chastised only—only, though she did not intend to admit it to her, the girl's little rebellion reminded her of her own frustrations at seeing the reins of her life wrested from her control by Queen Philippa who had married her to both Salisbury and Thomas at the whim and convenience of the lofty Plantagenets.

They joined the busy traffic through the little town of Pont-Audemer where the tanners, a few merchants, and twenty serf families in vasselage to Lord Holland lived. The serfs' cottages were out a ways, scattered amongst fields and copses; then began the clusters of wood and daub and thatch homes before one saw the few fine homes of stone and slate around the Norman Church of Saint-Ouen with its belfry towering forty feet over the town. The church was a lovely one for the area, Joan thought, with the local gentry or

nobles of two centuries in eternal sleep under the smooth
floorstones and impressive monumental brasses or occasional full-size effigies. The serfs rested under the turfy sod
in the little crowded graveyard at the skirts of the heavy
stone church.

Today the town marketplace with the adjoining stocks,
pillory, and ducking stool for scolding wives or merchant
cheats stood forlornly vacant by the duck pond—the only
creatures in view, Joan mused, who were not rushing to this
country fair.

On the other side of town, the market fair rose up in a
fallow, grassy field ahead of them, bright tents and banners
making a brilliant flash in the late morn sun. Saints, but it
looked very busy from here already and not at all tawdry or
shoddy as the shire fair had been last year up by Rouen. A
buzz of voices and the sounds of cattle and horses from the
livestock stalls assailed their ears as they dismounted and
paid a lad to watch their horses. Many people, both the great
and the serfs of the district, jostled and bustled in the cluster
of booths. Hawkers and itinerant peddlers shouted their
inducements to see, to buy.

With the wide-eyed Vinette and plump Madeleine in tow,
Joan began to stroll the first stalls heaped with displays of
dried fruit: raisins, dates, and figs from faraway Spain, and
quinces from Portugal, which Joan remembered had been a
favorite treat of the Plantagenets whose private rooms had
always boasted several flat, silver dishes of the delicious,
cooked fruit.

One booth sold naught but fine dyes—brilliant red from
Damascus and indigo from holy Jerusalem. They passed
shoemakers where Joan ordered boots for both sons,
coppersmiths, leather and fur makers. To Joan's relief and
Vinette's all too obvious dismay, the sly-faced Pierre Foulke
was not among the tanners at the leather stall which boasted
fine pouches, belts, and intricate scabbards. Joan fingered a
small scabbard for a lady's dagger. The leather was tooled
with little twining ivy leaves as in her family crest, but she

had many other purchases to make, so she put it back.

"Madame, should I not see to some bearers now so they are not all taken when we leave?" Vinette inquired and shot Joan a wistful smile.

"But we have bought very little yet, Vinette." Joan bit back the desire to warn the maid again about seeking out Pierre Foulke, but, after all, it was a public place and she was so seldom among her own people. Indeed, it was not fair to impose her own bitter moods on her servants, and the girl had been quite faithful even with the rumors on the wind concerning haughty serfs and peasant rebellions in the area. Joan counted out three coins from her squirrel pouch and pressed them into Vinette's dainty hand.

"There, then. Get some ribbons for yourself and little Bella's scant locks, but do not be gone long."

"Oh, no, madame, I shall not. *Merci*, madame." Vinette Brinay was gone in a whirl of brown skirts before Madeleine could remonstrate or her mistress change her mind.

A cloth hawker in a nearby stall had momentarily ceased his patter at the approach of Joan of Kent, an obviously wealthy lady, but the instant he caught her eye, he immediately resumed his recital extolling the virtues of each texture and shade. "Plush blue camlet for a winter robe, milady, most fine, soft as rabbit's fur. And here gentle sindon, ah, look, milady, brilliant cange for a Yuletide gown."

To his dismay she shook her head and strolled on. It was so difficult to care about fashion and next year's style here in Normandy with only Thomas's increasing absences for the future and evenings before the hearth with three small children and so little music now to look forward to. So difficult.

At the very hub of the fair where pie and tart makers plied their trade, Joan purchased for her guards, Madeleine, and herself hot meat pies pungent with pepper at one cart and custard flawns at another which they washed down with bowls of fresh ale. She gave them all coins then, with orders for buying, and sent them off into the next row of stalls while she drifted toward the entertainment area, ignoring beggars' cries and the scarlet-hooded whores who called out to every passing man. Her heart lifted as she followed the jumble of musical sounds: bardycoats and other itinerant musicians sang folk songs and even bawdy lyrics to the accompaniment of guiterns, shawms, and fydels. Acrobats in piebald costumes, dancing on balls, played cymbals. Jugglers and trick dogs cavorted on all sides. But when two minstrels nearby began to sing a lament of King Henry and his lost love the Fair Rosamonde, Joan's thoughts fled to that sad day at Woodstock in the snow near Rosamonde's bower when Prince Edward had told her her brother was dead of plague.

Now she turned away from where she had told her guards and Madeleine to meet her, and her eyes were entranced by heaps of lady's fineries—lady's fripperies, her Lord Thomas would deem them. She examined brooches of fine metals, splendid hair combs, belt buckles, and ribbons spread like a rainbow across vendors' carts. To lift her spirits, suddenly plunged so low despite the festivities about her, she bought several items and moved on.

At the next booth she purchased a lovely, polished steel mirror with an engraved handle of a lady gazing out of her castle window at her gentle knight-lover below. Joan lifted the fine mirror to gaze at her reflection: the woman who scrutinized herself in the polished, clear surface looked wan and very intense. I am almost thirty years old, she sighed as the heavily fringed, lilac-hued eyes looked away. Almost thirty and where was the adventure and where was the love, but for her three moppets?

At the next booth, she marveled at the strange eating instruments new-brought from Italy. They had handles and four barbs for spearing meat or fowl, and the barker said they were called forks. She had just decided to purchase two of the oddities when she felt a tap on her shoulder and turned slowly thinking Madeleine or Vinette had returned.

"Oh. You. Monsieur Pierre. Vinette is not here," she told the hawk-faced man whose flat, black hair looked almost greased down over his forehead. His narrow, dark eyes darted over her and he licked his lips nervously.

"I can tell Vinette be not here, madame duchess. There be something you had best see. Come wi' me."

Joan stood her ground. "I most certainly will not. My two guards will be here in a moment, and I have no intention of following you to some tanner's booth."

"Not that. Soon you wi' all follow where we bid well enough. Your guards gone already where I want you to—the money changers' booth, madame duchess. Vinette sayin' you would understand, but Vinette is wrong. Come see our power."

He took a step away, then looked back over his shoulder. Joan could hear a ruckus somewhere, shouts, and cries several stalls over. Her heart began to thud. "Saints, what is that?" she asked.

"The nobles' changing booth, I says. The beginning of the end hereabouts. Too late for any of you to stop it. Shame on him who holds back!" he shrieked at her in frenzied parting and dashed off toward the increasing racket.

Joan moved a bit closer to the next row of booths. The hubbub did indeed seem to be coming from the rim of the fair where the money changers were allowed to set up their narrow booths. She peered down one little grass-floored alley. Money and produce scales stood precariously on each rickety booth table. At one shed a small, raucous crowd of peasants argued with the changer.

She looked back to scan the crowd gathering behind her for her women or her guards, but that strange Pierre Foulke had distinctly said her guards were already here. That would make sense, for the nobles in the district of Pont-Audemer all profited from the changing booths and the guards might think they should protect Lord Holland's small interest in the fair.

She moved closer among the pressing peasants toward the

449

center of the confusion. For a moment, the increasing ruckus from one booth near which she stood seemed almost an echo of her own jumbled thoughts. Shouts and curses magnified; the booth rocked. Suddenly, the boards of the hastily constructed money changer's stall shuddered and crashed noisily upon each other. The angry, screeching crowd of peasants began pelting the cowering money changer with fruit or kicking him if they were close enough.

"No more taxes for the royal bastards!" a cry rang from hoarse throats all around. "Justice! Fairness! Damn them all! Shame on him who holds back! For glory, for the Jacquerie!"

The Jacquerie! Those rumors of peasant uprisings near Senlis on the River Oise and in the duchies of Valois and Coucy told of the Jacquerie. Surely, only rumors. A peasant rebellion could never happen here and at a mere, pleasant market fair.

Joan turned to hurry away from the burgeoning riot, but everyone else shoved inward gripping her in a human vise of screaming, taunting faces, crushing bodies, and raised fists. She saw her two guards wearing the Holland crest on their sleeves among the bailiffs trying to rescue the money changers and quell the crowd. Now, surely, all these foolish people would stop this screeching.

"Stand aside for the lord's men!" a bailiff she did not know shouted in her ear as he elbowed roughly past. Before her, the bailiff was struck with a shovel handle which materialized from the crowd. An arm swung a hatchet at the stunned man and blood spurted from his neck and shoulder. A pitchfork lifted ahead of her, spikes up to heaven in frenzied defiance. She heard fist on jaw behind her, the sharp grunts of a fight. The surge and swell of the screaming crowd suffocated her. Someone jabbed her in the stomach, and she would have doubled over in pain had not the vertical press been so great. She could see blood on distorted faces. One child's voice shrieked piteously for his mother. Joan tried to reach his arm to pull him to his feet, but she was shoved on.

She thought she would vomit or faint. Someone yanked at her green hood and her heavy blond braids, then spit on her from the back, for her garments and squirrel trim clearly marked her as a lady. A filthy hand grabbed her about the waist and fumbled roughly at her breasts. She screamed instinctively and hit back with all her strength. The odor of garlic-laden breath so close nearly gagged her.

The man did not loose her, but the desperate thrust of the crowd behind ceased suddenly. She hit out at her attacker again, and her elbow dug into ribs and soft belly. A horse neighed very close; a heavy stave swung from nowhere, whooshing by inches away from her face. The strangling arm freed her at last, and she spun around fighting to keep her feet. Her peasant attacker, a fat, dirty man, fell half against her legs with his head split.

She shrieked and darted back as her rescuer tossed the long wooden stave to the ground, moved his horse closer, and reached down to lift her. Half-stunned, still horrified, she grasped the black-sleeved arm and let herself be hauled up. Her eyes caught spurred riding boots heavy with road dust, a sword still sheathed. The horse bolted clear of the crowd while she clung precariously to her perch.

A bailiff? Not one of her own guards. She twisted her neck to glimpse the silent, brutal rescuer who had so neatly split her attacker's head like a soft melon. Sturdy chest and shoulder, black hair—

Her eyes stared in horror, and her mouth could only gasp. The whole screaming cup of blue sky above overturned and shattered. She was held aloft, half suspended, in the iron grasp of her sworn enemy, John de Maltravers!

"You! Here! No, no! Let me down!"

His deep-set, dark eyes glittered in preverse pleasure at her shock and dismay. He spurred his horse more quickly away from the noisy riot behind them on the now chaotic fair grounds.

"I am honored you recognize me, Joan of Kent, but then, it is obvious you are entirely too clever for your own good.

451

Cease this struggling now, or I swear by the Virgin, I shall break your pretty little head the way I did that peasant bastard's back there!"

His strong arm about her waist pressed into her soft belly like an iron band, and she sat momentarily still as they left the grounds behind. Her head pounded; her blood coursed so hard in fear and hatred that she saw flaming red waves of color dance before her eyes. The man's high forehead, large nose, thin lips, silver-etched hair, his shaggy brows, and deep-set eyes were imprinted as vividly in her frenzied mind as they had been that one other time she had seen him long ago in Flanders. All these years of loathing him—hating, scheming, wanting revenge for what he had done to her parents—smacked into her with sickening impact.

"So quiet now, lady?" the deep, rough voice behind her gibed. When he spoke, his voice seemed to have two resonant tones as in a nightmare, and she shuddered.

"Let me down," she managed. "My guards will have *your* head split for this!"

"Really? But, my dear, there is no one behind us on this road to town. Do not waste my time with threats for, Holy Virgin, I have suffered enough for those already."

"You cannot—" she began, only to have his cruel arm, holding her before him in the saddle, jab hard to crush the breath from her.

"I say, Joan of Kent, keep silence, unless, of course, you wish to thank me for rescuing you back there from the stupid predicament you were in. How much you do owe me for that back there, you know, as well as for the ruin you have made of my fortunes? The French serfs are up in arms in the neighboring regions I rode through to get here, and I am certain one more noble lady raped by a mob would be nothing to them. After that, I am certain you would greatly favor my tender mercies! But do realize, Joan of Kent, I rescued you back there only to have the intense pleasure of meting out your punishment myself."

Her skin crawled as if with unseen vermin while he

chuckled low in his double-throated voice. He was taking her into town, but the road was utterly deserted; everyone must have gone to see the riot. Why he was here, how he even found her at the fair—escape, help—spun through her whirling thoughts.

"As for this rebellion," she ventured, hoping her voice sounded calm, "my husband's forces will put it down, and he will be out looking for me. I demand you release me."

"A little liar as well as a traitress!" His voice struck her like the cutting flick of a whip. "I went to your precious Château Ruisseau to seek you, and they said you were at the market fair and—alas—that your Lord Holland was off to war games somewhere. And now, despite what you have done to me these years, by a mere twist of fortune's wheel, I have saved you—but only until we settle our own differences, and then I shall perhaps handle you myself as that fine fellow back there wanted—"

"No!" she screamed, going rigid to throw her weight back into him. He went off balance and grabbed for his horse's neck not to fall as her fingernails dug and pried at his wrist imprisoning her. Half off his horse, he was forced to loose her as she slid heavily into the roadway in the center of the little village.

She darted up even as he dismounted. The tall Norman Church of St. Ouen loomed over her, and surely some priests or monks would be inside unlike the villagers who had deserted the area. Behind her, de Maltravers noisily drew his sword.

She ran up the stone step and flew in the single, open door of the cool, dark church. "Help me! Help! Who is here?"

She tore down a vaulted side aisle even as she heard de Maltravers close the big church door behind him. The vast silence of hollow stone reverberated gloomily.

"Is anybody here?" she shouted and her own voice, dim and forlorn, echoed back "here, here, here" from somewhere high above.

De Maltravers stalked her down the aisle beside the rows

of effigies carved in continual, frozen prayer. Near the raised stone pulpit at the front of the church something moved, and Joan darted forward—an old man in hopsacking though not a monk.

"Help me, please! Get help! Get a priest!"

The man shook his head and pointed to his ears. "Nay. Sorry. Canna hear. Canna—I jus' sweep. Canna hear—"

She ran past toward the sacristy door where she could surely rouse someone. De Maltravers pounded closer, closer, and her skirts were such a heavy burden on her flying feet. Could not that old, deaf man see she needed help? Surely, he would get someone who had not gone to that damned peasant fair!

She rattled the lock on the sacristy door when it would not budge. She hit her shoulder into it once before she turned to face his drawn sword so close.

"Trapped, lady, trapped, just like your poor, meddling, stupid father before you. Your mother, too. That is what all this vile treachery has been about these years, is it not? Why have you tried so bloody hard to turn the king and prince against me?"

"Vile treachery—you ought to know of that! You and Roger Mortimer—a king's death, my father's then to cover up the first heinous crime. You did not really expect to escape your past, did you, murderer de Maltravers?"

A cold glint lit his deep-set eyes, and his thin lips pressed into an even firmer line. "So lovely to be so poisoned, but by the Holy Mother, I believe this jaunt of mine to find you even in these unsettled regions was well worth the trip. You know, Joan of Kent, I wanted badly, very badly, to deal with you myself, but I must tell you I let the peasants back there know that if they wanted to go raiding, burning, looting, or whatever, there was a very charming, nearly undefended Château just a mile away on the River Risle they could start with—"

Her jaw dropped and she gave a little, involuntary cry. Despite the sword point at her throat, she moved instinctively forward. "Stand, lady, just stand still until I am quite done with you."

"My children! My children are back there!"

"Really? And did you give one thought to *my* children when you coerced King Edward to keep my disinherited lands from being returned to me after all my years of slavish service? All I own now is the small parcel of land in Dorset where my wife lives and what is that for *my* children?"

Her eyes took in the distant approach of the old, deaf man behind. The fool! He should have gone for help, but if he could only distract de Maltravers, perhaps surprise him—

"How did you manage it?" de Maltravers's raspy, echoing voice went on. "I know you are a Plantagenet distant cousin, and I saw the prince's face in Flanders when he looked at you. Then, too, I heard the later court rumors even as far away as I was in exile. You stopped the return of my rightful lands I sweated for all those years in their foreign service by whoring for the prince, did you not? Whore! You opened your thighs for him and mayhap the king too, so my justice today will be doubly deserved and very appropriate. Another noble lady found brutally raped and murdered in this unfortunate French peasant rebellion they call the Jacquerie. What a terrible pity!"

His sword point held her back against the wooden door of the alcove as he stepped closer. His face a mask of controlled fury, his hand lifted to hook fingers in the oval neckline of her kirtle. The cloth tugged and ripped just as the deaf man reached out to touch de Maltravers's shoulder from behind.

"Please—not run wi' weapons in da holy church. Go now. No sanctuary."

De Maltravers wheeled around, catching the old man with his fist on the side of his bald head. Joan shoved at de Maltravers and tried to dart away, but his hand grabbed her elbow to yank her back. As if in one motion, he threw Joan hard against the wall, then ran the old, babbling deaf man through the chest neatly ith the point of his sword.

Cowering away from the next thrust, Joan pressed back to

the cold stone wall, her hands tight to her mouth. De Maltravers' face was livid, his features contorted in raging fury.

"You see what happens to those who defy me?" he hissed. He waited for no reply, but seized a wrist and dragged her at breakneck speed back along the aisle to the narrow steps to the belfry at the front of the church. Cruelly, he twisted her arm behind her and forced her to the steps.

"Up! Up, Plantagenet whore! Get up or I shall break your arm before I have you. Do as I say, and who knows but I might not spare you to run back to die in the peasants' fire with your so precious children. Up! I tire of revenge for mere amusement!"

Bent back against him, she started up the narrow, curving steps to the belfry which was visible for miles around. Her feet stumbled, her arm wrenched. On they went, on and up, around and up.

In the little wooden room above, the huge bell hung suspended over an open resonating space in the wooden flooring. Their footsteps sounded hollow on the planks edging the little room. He shoved her down in a corner, noisily sheathed his sword, and drew an eight-inch dagger from his belt.

"Now," he rasped, his double-edged voice broken by his long-drawn gasps for air, "let me set one thing straight before we end this. Let me tell you why—why you will suffer and die for your meddling. I have been home to see my family in Dorset. And I finally figured all this out. I should have been welcomed home by now, given all my lands and holdings. It amazed—astounded me at first, of course, that a mere woman could so ruin a lifetime of work."

Joan huddled like a coiled spring ready to flee, her back pressed hard against the wall. "A mere woman whose father you helped to murder most vilely—an innocent man, unlike yourself," she threw at him.

"Your daring and your stupidity does boggle the mind, Plantagenet whore. But as I was saying, while I was in

456

England—in secret, of course, as I am still exiled, thanks to you, I learned from a source that the king had said that Joan, the Fair Maid of Kent, was the one who had asked the prince not to allow the vast landholdings of the loyal, exiled John de Maltravers to be returned. I heard the other rumors of the prince's foolish infatuation for you—"

"That is not true!"

"—and so I put the whole wretched puzzle together. You are trying to punish me for your father's death and the king either besotted of you or guilty because he too wanted your father out of the way—"

"No! Oh, no, but I knew it!"

"Did you? Then you should have tried to ruin *his* life because you are going to pay dearly for ruining mine."

"Let me go," she brazened calmly, her mind on reaching the Château to be certain the children were safe. "You have made your point. I see your side of it now."

"You little liar! All those with blue Plantagenet blood in their veins are liars. Here, let me show you."

He squatted before her, his knife blade instantly pressed to her throat before she could shift away. "Your father, by the way, Plantagenet whore, deserved his wretched death and I only regret I was sent on a fool's errand by Mortimer to deliver your meddling mother back to Kent the day he died. Just like you, your parents were meddlers. Edmund of Kent—faugh! The fond fool tried to investigate the death of King Edward's royal sire, even to dare to whisper perhaps the old king was not truly dead at all. Obviously, that was treason against the rightful new King Edward III and it was clear he had to die. I hear your crazy mother is dead now and both your brothers too with no heirs. And so, I only have to settle this with you, the most treacherous of all the treacherous, arrogant fools with blue Plantagenet blood in their veins."

He pressed the edge of cold blade to her throat but she was not certain if he had cut her or not. This could not be happening—the peasants, this assault, the children in danger back at the Château.

"Get your skirts up for me and let us have this over," he hissed close to her face. She could feel his breath on her cheek and the knife surely must be cutting her throat. For the first time since he had torn the bodice of her kirtle downstairs she realized the tops of her breasts were exposed.

"Not in a church," she whispered.

He acted as if he had not heard her and yanked her skirts up to bare her legs. "It is almost a pity," he breathed heavily. "Holy Mary, I can see, of course, why the prince did what he did for the pure madness of possessing this tempting body. Such a pity it belongs to one so treacherous. How much I shall enjoy your dismay that one who indeed helped the king dispose of your father possesses you now."

She stared almost mesmerized into his deep-set, glittering eyes as he fumbled with his belt and breeches. His eyes like a cold snake's eyes: all her nightmares of her father's murder, all her promises to her dying mother of revenge, all that pinned down, devoured by this man's cold, glittering eyes. Then, instinctively, with all the strength of her agony and fury, she lifted both hands to claw at his eyes.

The sheer shock of her sharp movement threw him back and the pressure of his blade slackened. She hit at his face, shoved him back, surprised at a quick bite of pain along her arm. She shrieked, kicked, stunned at the sight of her bared legs smashing into his stomach. One hand over his eyes, he stumbled to his feet, the bloody knife held now to stab.

She scrambled, rolled away from the first thrust, amazed to see blood soaking the green cloth of her sleeve. The big bell silent over its cavern in the belfry floor framed John de Maltravers as he towered over her with dagger raised. As he moved toward her, she threw herself shrieking against his legs; he thudded, gasped, hit his skull back into the huge, iron bell which rang once dully. He stood stupified; his face contorted in pain, ran with blood from deep scratches near one eye. He frowned, shook his head as though the blow on the bell had utterly dazed him. He dropped the knife and grabbed at his chest gasping for air. His face turned livid, blue, then deathly pale. Against the bell, he slid heavily to his knees and collapsed on the edge of the void.

Amazed, she scrambled for the knife. Her arm throbbed with pain now, and her sleeve felt warm and sticky with her own blood. She threw the knife at the hole in the floor and it rang the bell once as it dropped away. Her legs trembling, she stood at last.

The man on the floor looked so small, so pitiful now, crumpled and unmoving. One little shove with her foot and he would fall over the edge forty feet to the floor below. But she knew he was dead and she could not bear to touch him.

She turned away, her hand on the stone ledge as she gasped for air, and saw the lovely reach of countryside and sky outside. Her children, her Château—she had to get home now to warn them. What if de Maltravers had meant it— had sent the peasant mob there?

Assailed by a wave of stomach-wrenching dizziness, she moved carefully around the body to stare in the direction of the Château. Although the view was blocked by the thick surrounding forest, there was still no one in the town below and the Château was but a mile away, the closest noble household if the peasants did go on a rampage after that riot at the fair.

At the top of the narrow steps down she glanced back at the man to be sure he would not leap up to pursue her—now, through her life, and haunted dreams. "Murderer!" she said and started down.

She leaned heavily against the wall for balance. Just a little cut surely, but the excitement and the shock— She could make it—find de Maltravers's horse and hurry home. In the fierce glare of sunlight outside, she spotted the waiting horse immediately and mounted it with some difficulty. She had only started out of the quiet town when she saw an old woman holding a goose on a settle before a cottage hemmed in by taller buildings.

"Back in the church," Joan called to her, amazed at the

faintness of her own voice when she thought she was shouting. "There is an old deaf man hurt in the church. Send someone to help him!"

"Ol' Tom?" the crone said. "None to help hardly. Merchants at the fair, serfs gone to rioting in the countryside—"

But the woman's words blended to nonsense as Joan had already forced the horse away at a faster clip, and she concentrated all her wasted strength on merely hanging on.

Chapter Twenty-One

The edge of town, orchards, ponds, the thickening trees of the countryside rolled by in a blur. Only a mile, only a mile, she told herself, but after the last bend in the country road before the Château, her worst fears began to take on a terrible reality. Ahead of her, down the road, with scythes, pitchforks, staves, or glinting hatchets on their shoulders straggled a line of field workers with a much larger crowd raising dust ahead.

"Oh, dearest saints, preserve us," she breathed. Her dizziness cleared instantly; the wracking pain in her arm ebbed. She pulled de Maltravers's horse off into the forest to skirt past the people on the narrow road.

Within the cool, silent woods she could hear their cries as she hurried on abreast of the ragged march. She would close the gates for siege if she got there before they did. How many guards? Thomas had four with him, two perhaps were trapped at the fair, only four at the Château and perhaps caught unawares on such a fine, fair market day with the mistress gone.

Or if the peasants had gone inside, she would brazen it out, mayhap buy them off. Or if they began looting, she would take the children and flee to the woods. The children!

She pushed the horse harder as the outer walls of Château Ruisseau loomed at her through the forest fringe. Branches whipped at her as if to seize her skirts and hold her back. The horse was lathered, exhausted, but who knew how far, how hard that fiend de Maltravers had already ridden it on this tragic day. Her last thought before she rode into the clearing

461

at the edge of the moat was that if worse came to worst, she would go in through the secret passage near Marta's grave to get the children out. They could hide in the forest, or all get on this horse to ride for help!

She slumped in her saddle when she took in the scene before her. The drawbridge was down, and there was no evidence of struggle. But worse, mounted on a skinny rake of a horse, clad in boiled, tooled leather for makeshift armor, the rabble-rouser, Pierre Foulke, motioned for the earliest marchers of the straggling peasant band to cross the drawbridge to enter the Château.

Her heart pounding, she assessed the dire situation, and rode boldly forward.

"Master Foulke!" she called out. Her voice sounded strong now, her own voice again. She sat erect in the big man's saddle and noticed for the first time that her long, blond tresses had pulled free in the fray with de Maltravers and rippled in the breeze over her shoulders. She remembered to close her torn bodice with her wounded arm and held the reins firmly in the other.

"Master Foulke! May I ask what you are doing here at the Château of the Holland family?"

The black-haired tanner turned toward her, and nearly fell off his horse in obvious dismay. "You, lady! But I saw you get hauled off back there. I thought—"

"I do not know what you thought, Master Foulke, but that was just a friend of my husband's who saved me from that—that trouble at the fair. He has gone to get a large force of armed men to join me here. Now, I ask you to take your men and go back to town. There has been enough trouble for one day."

She faced him on the narrow wooden drawbridge only a horse's length away. His wily brain obviously raced, and his heavy features seemed glazed over in barely controlled fury. For one tottering second this man's face blended to that of de Maltravers, and to stand for all she cherished she confronted that warped, contorted face again. Only, oh blessed saints, she knew this exploding danger of a violent peasant rebellion could hardly be taken away by heaven's gift of one man's sudden collapse into gasping pain in a belfry tower.

Joan's eye caught sight of her maid Vinette mounted behind one of the other two peasants she saw ahorse. She had to make Foulke back off quickly before the growing mob swelled to wild riot again.

"I see Vinette Brinay is here with you, Master Foulke. Thank you for bringing her back, for we were separated in the trouble at the fair. I will take her in now and, if you will just bid your people rest on the bank of the moat here, I will send out food to refresh you before you head back to Pont-Audemer."

Pierre Foulke' dark eyes over the hawklike nose showed a flash of indecision as they darted from her to the road, then shot up the open drawbridge toward the castle gatehouses.

"No," he yelled. "Vinette be going in all right, but with the Jacquerie as master. Your two men inside who fought are already dead, three locked up for later. Simon!" he bellowed to a burly mounted man clad in the same leather armor he himself sported. "This lady here be our prisoner, prisoner for the fair and just cause."

"My children," Joan interrupted him. "Give me my children then and I will go."

Foulke urged his horse closer and apparently noted her bloodied arm and torn gown for the first time. "This Château, this area, those bastard noble brats of yourn—even you if I says so—be all mine now, lady, for the Jacquerie and fair and just cause. And that so-called friend of your lord what you said rescued you at the fair and gone to get help—it looks you two had a knockups with blood and all. Hell, lady, he be the one told us this Château be waiting here for the taking like a ripe peach, and he was telling true. Simon, get her inside, I says!"

The big-shouldered, unshaven oaf seized her reins and dragged her horse at a good clip along the hollow-sounding drawbridge. She considered resisting only for one moment, but the children were inside, left in the care of two maids and who knew what had happened to them all if Foulke had already secured the castle and actually killed two of the Holland guards.

Her heart kept up its pounding as she saw the peasant rabble stream into the inner ward behind her. She dismounted unaided, flanked by Foulke and his loutish guard Simon.

Lynette, the castle's chief cook, appeared instantly on the doorstep with a peasant man Joan had never seen behind her. "Oh, milady, they kilt two men and says the Château is all theirs now. They says I am to cook them a fine banquet, milady." The woman wrung her floured hands on her apron, and it was obvious she had been sobbing.

"It is all right, Lynette. Aye, fix them a fine banquet. Where are the children?"

Pierre Foulke's voice cut in from close behind. "Hell's bells, she will fix a banquet for us and we gonna see to that wine cellar too, aye, rogues? As for your noble brats, lady, upstairs all three of 'em and likely all right as long as their mother behaves."

Joan lifted her head and fixed the hawk-faced man with a steady stare. "I will if you will, Master Foulke. I am sure you can control your men—I expect that of you as their leader. I would like to have Vinette come with me now as I go up to see my children. Please ask her to come to me."

With a steely aplomb she hardly felt, Joan turned her back and started away, a mistake, she soon realized, to stand up to the nervous Foulke before his men. He jerked her around by her wounded arm and a wave of pain crashed over her so she nearly toppled against his grimy, leather-covered chest.

"Not hearing too good, eh, high and mighty lady? Pierre and the Jacquerie do not care hellfire for what some foolish maid tells me of your kindness to her. I know you been warning her, you and the lord too, telling her keep clear of Pierre Foulke. You have. You have!"

He shook her like a rag doll until her head bobbed, then

thrust her back at the burly Simon whose hands grabbed her roughly. "Carry the new yaller-haired serf upstairs and lock her in 'til I see to the men, rogue. And if'n Pierre says he wants table cleaned, boots cleaned, my bed warmed later, lady—all our beds, eh?—Simon here will see you do it with a sweet smile on that pretty mouth. Now get her away!"

Simon half-dragged, half-carried her down the corridor outside the Great Hall and up the stairs. She did not fight him and she could see no dagger in his belt to seize. Already in the ward outside, she heard raucous cheers and chants much like those which had roused the serfs to unbridled violence at the fair today.

At the top of the steps by the solar door, the powerful man propped her up against the wall with one hand hard on her shoulder. His fat cheeks and crooked nose, broken repeatedly in forgotten brawls, his puffy lips came closer as he leered into her face.

"In the Jacquerie, noble ladies be not so high and powerful no more," his voice lisped obscenely low. "Be sweet to Simon now real quick an' maybe I can help, eh? Ladies learn to lift their pretty skirts and beg for favors from a man like Simon in the Jacquerie."

"Please let me just go in to my children. Have you children, Simon? Do you not worry about them?"

The ogling stare turned to a frown and she realized too late she had goaded him. "Children, a course. Children starvin' under taxes and new tithin' laws to keep the nobles livin' high like you, fancy, sweet-smelling lady!"

His avid brown eyes dropped to the torn bodice she held in place, and she saw his new plan clearly as though he had spoken it. A dirty hand lifted to yank her arm down and he peered lustily at the bared tops of her bosoms and even licked his puffy lips.

"Take your hands off me, Simon," she began low, but in one quick pull he had completed what de Maltravers had merely started: her dress tore down to the waist to expose her naked, full breasts. He leaned his bulk hard into her, crushing her back to the wall. The agony of her injured arm, pressed between them, flashed colored waves of pain before her eyes and she thought she would faint. His big, greasy head pressed under her chin to nearly strangle her as his hot mouth licked at her breasts.

"No! No!" she got out and managed to lift a quick knee between his legs where he tried to straddle her against the wall. He doubled over in pain, gasping—a second miracle today, her dazed mind shouted at her. She moved to the solar door and fumbled with the fastened lock while Simon moaned, apparently now oblivious to her existence. She shoved the door inward and her fearful eyes drank in the precious sight: both her sons sat fidgeting at the table and her maid Renée, who often helped Vinette, held Bella.

"Oh, my dearest loves!" Joan cried as the boys jumped up and cheered. They ran together and Joan shot the bolt on the door with the two of them clinging to her filthy skirts.

"It is all right, my loves. Everything will be fine now. Mother is here. Renée, is Bella all right? Oh, thank the saints, you stayed here with them! I can never thank you enough!"

"Aye, milady. That tanner friend of Vinette's, he told me to. He said a man would be up to watch us, but no one came."

Joan cuddled her daughter to her as her eyes skimmed the untouched room. Now, while Simon was temporarily locked out in the hall, she had to act. With this girl and the children, she could be down into the tunnel before they were missed.

The wooden door shuddered under the blows of a powerful fist. "It is your Master Foulke, Duchess! Open this damn door or it will get chopped down and Pierre will feed you and the brats to that crowd!"

She seized little John's hand to run to the tunnel entrance in the *garde-robe* even as the thwack of an axe shuddered the wood. "Now, lady, or I swear to you the nice handling is all over."

At Joan's nod, the trembling Renée scurried to unlock the door even as the second blow of an axe reverberated in the room. Foulke with a white-faced Simon behind him filled the doorway. He seized Renée's arm and shoved her past him out into the hall where she fled.

"No locked doors, milady duchess," he mocked, his voice dripping sarcasm at her title. "And no disobeying Pierre's orders, no more!"

"Your man Simon tried to attack me, Master Pierre."

Foulke's big head pivoted back to the sheepish Simon. "I told you, rogue—for later. Now get in here and tie this fancy bitch down."

Foulke swaggered in while Simon ransacked the nearest coffer and came up with a handful of silk scarves. "Please, Master Foulke. Take what you want, but do not harm the children."

"We are all right, my lady mother," little Thomas assured her. "I will be with you, and father will come soon."

"Ha! A brave little rogue," Foulke taunted. "Going to grow up a fine knight like your sire, eh, and run your serfs to death and raise their taxes higher and higher, little rogue, eh?"

Joan pulled the boy back against her, and in a wisdom far beyond his years, the child held his tongue.

Gloating at her, Simon tied the two little boys back to back in two chairs and turned to her while Pierre Foulke strutted around the room picking up cups to look at, examining the tapestries or bed hangings. When Simon reached for little Bella in Joan's arms, she moved quickly away to put the fussing babe in a blanket on the carpet.

"Just let her lie there. Leave her be, she is just a babe."

"Aye, true enough, but bred to be another arrogant, pure, little noble bitch like her mother!" Simon accused.

Foulke snickered while Simon shoved Joan back in a chair and tied her firmly to it. He bent over her a long while knotting the ropes terribly tight despite her tears from the pain they caused her injured arm. When he was done and saw Foulke was peeking behind the curtain to the *garde-robe* chamber, he deliberately plunged his hand into the torn gown and roughly fingered the breasts she had denied him earlier. Then, so Foulke would not know, he covered her again and stepped away.

"After the feast," he hissed low, "you will beg and beg and beg for Simon—I swear it."

"Simon! There's a good bit of armor back here, man! We will wear it down to our banquet, eh?" Foulke shouted from the little *garde-robe* chamber.

Simon lumbered behind the curtain, and Joan could hear them clinking about in Thomas's spare armor pieces he insisted on storing there. "Now, do not be afraid, boys," she whispered to her wide-eyed sons. "Someone will come soon. Do not be afraid."

Her heart wrenched at their stalwart little faces frozen in fear and bewilderment. How much they both looked like Thomas. No wonder he had been furious that the babe Bella was so fair and looked so much a Plantagenet.

Her mind raced as she heard them laughing and strapping armor on behind the curtain. From the Great Hall below the sounds of revelry floated to them and occasionally someone screamed or cursed. Her hands were going numb and Simon had thoroughly tied her to the chair. Their chance for quick escape had vanished like the security of their lives here— Thomas gone, that other dear love ruined, this Jacquerie like the iron fist of impending death, her life maybe over. No. No, not the children, too. There had to be a way.

The two peasants clanked out from behind the curtain in Thomas Holland's helmets and chest armor. "One wrong move from you, milady, and no second chance like I give you here," Foulke threatened, his black eyes staring out at her from under the raised visor of the helmet. He lifted his sword to point it at the boys and went out. At the door Simon looked back, laughed, then swung the ruined door closed so that it shuddered on its hinges.

"Mother, I am tied too tight. I cannot untie you!" Thomas cried.

"Hush, my darling. Let me think now. Someone will come."

While Bella fussed at her feet and began to cry to be picked up, Joan reasoned it all out. She must move her heavy chair over to the boys and somehow reach their bonds. If she could just untie one of Thomas's knots, surely he could untie hers.

"Hush, my pretty Bella. Mother's pretty Bella."

Terrified that the child's wails would summon or annoy someone, Joan began to sing. She had not sung much lately, less and less with Thomas gone, Master Roger gone—all her dreams of love for Prince Edward gone forever:

> "Lullay, lullay, thou little child,
> Why weepest thou so sore?"

she began the sweet lullaby, but then tried crazily to lift the children's spirits with happier songs of woods waxing green and even of Prince Edward at war "among the press of shields in ebony-hued armor." She sang as the baby quieted and the boys listened and as she scooted her chair bit by bit over to them praying no one came in.

She was panting hard from the singing and her physical exertion by the time her chair was near the boys. Each shift and lifting of her weight to move the chair wrenched her cut arm terribly and muted her brave lyrics until she recovered to move again. But when she had reached her goal the endless ten feet to the boys across the carpet, she could not grasp the knots by which either was tied however she struggled. Exhausted now, she sat silent for a moment as the horrible sounds of bawdy revelry floated up from the Great Hall below.

"Saints," she cursed aloud without meaning to. "They are all so drunk on our wine there will be no stopping the fools next time!"

Her head snapped around and she gasped as the solar door creaked ominously open on those foreboding words.

469

"Vinette!" six-year-old John shrieked before Joan could turn to see who was there.

Vinette Brinay, bleary-eyed, disheveled, looking almost like another girl from the cheeky, sprightly maid Joan knew, came in slowly. "Oh, Vinette, bless the saints, you are here. Untie me quickly. I must take the children and flee."

Vinette moved silently across the floor, and Joan saw she was barefooted and had a length of fine silk tablecloth wrapped around her almost like a shroud. "Vinette, please hurry. Are you all right?"

"He loves me, *madame*, he wants to wed with me."

"Pierre Foulke? Please, Vinette, you cannot approve of what happened today at the fair. They murdered people, and it is not likely to stop there. Please, for the children, untie me."

The girl stood stock-still as if she were in a stupor. "Vinette, have you been drinking? Here, untie these knots."

"They are all drinking your wine, *madame*, ripping things down and carrying them off. Dancing. Dancing. They broke your lute. They killed Stephen and Jeremy before I came back from the fair, Lynette says. He wants me to marry him and live here after all the nobles are killed in the area."

Joan's brain reeled at the awesome possibility that Vinette might not have come to rescue them at all. The girl looked dazed, exhausted; her brown eyes in her attractive face hardly focused on anything when she spoke. Even her voice was not her own.

"Vinette. Marry him if you will, and live here, only untie me so I may get the children away from here before something happens."

"Please, Vinette," little John chimed in almost wistfully. "Bella has been crying a lot and we gotta go for help."

"Sh, John," Joan chided gently. "Vinette will let us go so we can all get safely home to England."

"To England? To Liddell, Mother?" Thomas asked.

"Hush, now. Vinette, Pierre Foulke told me he intends to have me be his lady here after the banquet if I am still here

470

when he comes upstairs soon."

The girl's eyes focused on Joan's face at last. "No. He asked me to marry him and live here a fine lady. He is the leader of the fair and just Jacquerie for all of the Pont-Audemer region!"

"I am sorry, Vinette, but you see how my gown is ripped already. Only at the last minute did he decide to dine with his people first and join me here afterward. I told him I did not love him, I did not want to stay here with him, so he tied me here to await him. He said I must bear his son for he wanted one of Plantagenet blood—"

"No! Oh, no! *Madame* Joan, I think I hit my head today at the fair in the riot and it bled—see?" As if they were speaking of nothing else, Vinette lifted her long hair free of her forehead to reveal an ugly, blue-black bruise on her fair brow, but Joan thought the blood looked fresh.

"I feel so dizzy like things are blurring sometimes, *madame*," Vinette went on. "All their wine made me sick. I think they were all watching. He proved he loved me. He said he loved me."

"Untie me now, Vinette, and let me look at your head. Untie me so that I can flee Pierre Foulke's desire to keep me here. I will put you to bed over there and you alone shall wait for him—wait to marry him and be the lady here."

Vinette blinked bleary-eyed and bent to Joan's ties. She fumbled interminably while Joan held her breath and prayed, warning Thomas who could see her with a look and John who could not see her with the pressure of her knee to keep silent. Just as she felt a loosening of the bindings of her wrist, the babe started fussing again and Vinette looked up.

"I should bear him his children here in this house," the girl said low.

"Aye, of course, you will, Vinette. Untie me."

One scarf loosened, fell away and then the other. Joan flexed her numb hands ignoring the fierce ache in her arm injured by de Maltravers—all that seemed ages ago.

"I should have a babe like this one for him," Vinette was

471

saying as Joan bent to yank at the scarves binding her ankles to the chair legs.

"Mother, Vinette is taking Bella out!" Thomas cried.

Joan stood and nearly fell at her first step. Her right foot had gone to prickly numbness as though it were not ever there. She stumbled to the still-open door, took Vinette's arm firmly and led her back.

"Here, Vinette, my dear. Give me Bella and climb into that bed there to wait for Pierre. You have hurt your head somehow. Here, do as I say."

Joan lay the squirming babe on the floor by the boys' chairs, and dashed to the sideboard for a food knife. She sliced their bonds in four quick thrusts, then ran to her coffer to grab her two letters with John's birthright promise of Liddell.

"*Madame*, my head hurts and it is dark sometimes," Vinette called out loudly from across the solar where she stood gazing down at the big brocade-covered bed. There were raucous voices in the hall. Joan seized the babe in her arms.

"Lie down, I said, Vinette. Come on, boys, and do not be afraid. Remember when you were looking for buried treasure? Well, we are going to find some and you must help me. Come on now."

Her heart wrenched when she saw they were holding hands, but she hustled them immediately into the *garde-robe* room even as she heard boisterous voices so much closer in the hall outside. Armor pieces littered the floor and little John stumbled noisily over one.

Not daring to wait to see if they had been heard, Joan yanked aside the tapestry which covered the small, secret door's outline. She pulled the long metal bolt and, as she did, she heard Vinette's plaintive cry from the next room.

"*Madame*, he wants to marry me!"

The bolt scraped unbearably loud. "Mother, it is a door there. I never saw it before," Thomas whispered. He peered in behind her as she jostled Bella to quiet her. "Oh, it is so dark."

"Quiet. Now you must be very brave. I will hold John's hand and Thomas comes last." She pulled them immediately inward down the few dim steps she could see and shoved the pivoting door closed behind her to plunge them into utter blackness. Surely, the rebels would not find this right away and they would think they had escaped into the hall.

She took her youngest son's cold hand and pulled them on, but she could not stand the way he tugged on her injured arm, and Bella was too heavy in the other.

"John, listen to Mother. Here, hold my skirts." She heard a stifled sob and knew he was crying at last.

"Are there—well, if there is treasure down here, are there dragons, too?" he managed.

"No. No dragons, only bad men in our Château right now and we must run away. Thomas, hold on to him. I am depending on you."

They went slowly on, interminably down the slant of passageway covered with stony rubble until the floor evened out and they were in the dampest part under the moat. Her hand grew sticky-cold with the dank slime of the walls on which she felt their way along; they all sputtered sporadically as cobwebs laced across their sweating faces. As the tunnel slanted up, Joan hit her shoulder into a supporting plank and recalled her recurrent nightmare of fleeing desperately down such a tunnel chased by unknown horrors. Now that nightmare had become reality.

At the far door which was above them, she pressed her back to the wooden pillar, breathing hard, thanking the saints for their temporary safety from all the terrors of the day. Her fingers fumbled for the rusted lock above her. It grated metallically in the silence broken only by their breathing and little Bella's fussing. Slowly, carefully, she pushed the door to open it. It groaned but did not budge. The boys pressed tightly to her like little ducks, she thought erratically.

"What is it, Mother? Why does it not open up? It is so dark."

"You have both been wonderful, my brave boys. Come

here, Thomas and put your hands up on the door. Here, it is on a slant a little above us. When I tell you, we will push. One, two, three—push!"

The door creaked open a tiny space and a dim, gray line of light threw itself crookedly on the wooden steps. They had done it! The blackness was gone. So much time had passed since she had come back to the Château. It was already dusk outside, but that was good, for she had no intention of falling back into the filthy hands of those drunk, murderous peasants—fairness and justice of the Jacquerie be damned!

"Mother, are we going out? I am hungry," John whispered.

"Hush up, John," Thomas scolded in his best big-brother voice. "Mother is probably hungry, too, but we did not bring any food, did we, Mother?"

"No, my darlings, but we shall drink some water and eat some May apples or wild strawberries in the woods. You will have to help mother because we will have to hide in the woods all night and maybe walk a long way on the morrow. All right, now, Thomas, we have to push the door again. One, two, three . . ."

Cradling Bella to her, she heaved her weight against the slanted door above her. It lifted steadily as the tendrils and roots wrapped about its outline were stretched and snapped. New spring growth had covered it, nearly entombing them, she thought. It had been years since she had been down here, and she had just assumed someone would keep it open. She lifted the heavy door and peered out.

Darkness on the forest fringe comes soon, she realized, and blessed again her good fortune which had saved her all day. Prince Edward's words came back to her that she was destined for greatness. Saints, what foolishness old Morcar's star charts were, but on a day of safe deliverance like this one, it almost made her a believer in such a prophecy.

With Thomas' assistance and John's pinched fingers when he tried to help, Joan closed the tunnel entrance and they covered it with weeds. How forlorn and foreboding the walls of the Château looked now across the ribbon of dark moat. Voices, shrieks, sounds floated to them but no one was in view. For the first time she worried about the beautiful things for which she and Thomas had worked long years to adorn their home. The rioters had broken her lute, poor Vinette had said. Things—they mattered not at all now that she had the children safe.

Though a full moon shed cold, silver light on their retreat, all was black beyond old Marta's grave at the fringe of forest. Their eyes soon became accustomed to the darkness, but it was Joan's sure knowledge of the pathway toward the forest pond that made their flight possible.

"Where are we going, Mother?"

"I am so tired, I am not sure anymore, my Thomas. Just to the pond until it gets light, I guess. I used to love to go out in the forest when I was a maid, you know. This may be fun."

Thomas was obviously not taken in by her pretended enthusiasm. "In the dark?"

Her exhausted mind skipped back to that forest-pond trysting place where the prince had first made love to her at Windsor, the time she had arranged for Princess Isabella and Salisbury to come out and His Grace had stomped off in a fury before he had hardly begun. So many twists of fate to separate them, so many turns of Fortune's tormenting wheel.

They sat exhausted, tight together on the grassy bank of the pond which was fed by a spring from the River Risle that eventually became the moat about their Château. They washed their faces and hands, and Joan led them in a shaky, whispered *Ave Maria* and a prayer to the prince's patron, Saint George. They filled their empty bellies with only water, and Joan sang them a low lullaby as they huddled all together in a bed of soft leaves under a clump of bushes a little way back from the pond.

"Mother?"

475

"What, my John?"

"Thomas says there are no real dragons. Only they are in your head, he says."

"Thomas is right, my love, so do not be afraid of the dark."

"But they are in my head sometimes, so I guess they are real."

The child moved closer against her, and she could tell by his voice he was sucking his thumb, something she knew he had given up months ago.

"Bella is asleep, so the rest of you sleep, too, and in the morn we will get help. If anyone wakes up and is afraid, just wake me up and I will hold you," she told them.

The leaves rustled occasionally as they shifted closer. Bella was tight against her breasts and John lay between her and Thomas. She had been afraid to look at her cut arm, but on the morrow she must try to wash and tend it, mayhap find some plantain or figwort to ease the pain. In her sore back, legs, and arms she felt either gripping cramps or nothingness. When she closed her eyes, the whole forest careened around, whirling in the strange hum of her dizziness.

Faces floated to her from the dark places of her own brain: de Maltravers—he had been real at last, stepping from her nightmare of revenge, and she had beaten him. Pierre Foulke, poor distracted Vinette Brinay, so changed by something unspoken, something terrible beyond the blow to her head. Old Morcar's magic stars wheeled overhead in the vast heavens, and Prince Edward rode away in black armor, farther and farther away. Her mother's wasted face, beset by dragons of revenge and fear on her deathbed—Edmund and her brother John were dead, gone and dead. Sometime, she slept.

She awoke to the twitter of the predawn forest dusted with gray chill. Her body ached and she stretched stiff limbs, gathering the babe closer for warmth. John lay curled up, breathing with his mouth open. Thomas! She sat bolt upright jostling Bella awake. Thomas was gone!

"I am glad you are awake. I was guarding you," a voice behind her whispered.

She spun to see her eldest son sitting bent-legged a few yards away with a large stick across his knees.

"Oh! Thank heavens! I thought you were gone."

"No, but since Father is always gone to fight, I have to help," he explained patiently as though he were lecturing a foolish child. "Anyway, I heard horses and something like horns so I thought mayhap Father came back and brought some men."

"Horses! Horns. Are you sure? I do not hear anything."

She stood on wobbly legs and shook her filthy skirts out. Her head pulsed with a pain she could almost hear, and her cut arm was too stiff to move. Bella whined and John awoke with a look of bewilderment on his face as though he remembered nothing of the night before. And then, she, too, heard, or maybe felt, the rumble of horses' and the faint call of a man's voice.

She lifted Bella awkwardly with her good arm. "Get up, John. Up. They may have started looking for us. We should have gone deeper into the forest last night. We will have to hide. Thomas, bring your stick and come on."

They skirted around the far edge of the shallow forest pond. The voices now were more distinct as if the water brought them to her. Shaken by their quick pace and the way Joan held her with one arm, Bella began to cry.

"Mother, here—we can all prob'ly get in here," Thomas said and pointed to a huge, rotting tree with a nearly hollow base.

"Aye, all right. Get in, then. In."

So swiftly the voices and crashing of horses' hooves in the thicket came closer. They stood pressed in the tree, John in first, Thomas, then herself holding Bella. She prayed the child would not cry.

Saints! The male voices were calling her name, but it

sounded like so many horses and the peasants only had had three she had seen. No, no, of course—they had no doubt stolen all the prize horseflesh of the Château as well as everything else by now.

"Lady Holland! Lady Holland!" the mingled voices came closer.

"Mother, they know we are here."

"Be quiet. No one talks unless I say so."

"But, Mother," John whispered, "I can see one man through this hole in the tree, and he is not one of those bad serfs. He is a knight, just like father."

Her heart crashed against her ribs.

"Lady Holland! Hallo! All is well! Are you hereabout? Come forth in the Prince of Wales's name."

It was too wonderful—a trick, no doubt, but the accent of the voice was pure noble Plantagenet English. She moved out one step and peeked around the tree. The man was armored and wore the unmistakable azure and gold *surcote* of English royalty. She tried to cry out to him across the pond, but she had no voice. Tears of joy and relief coursed down her dirty face.

"Thomas," she choked out. "Run—call to the man—to tell him we are here."

The boy darted out shouting even as the tiny clearing around the pond exploded with Plantagenet knights, some even bearing the black and white trappings of the Prince of Wales.

While the boys jumped about shouting outside the hollow tree, she clung to her squirming daughter. Leaning in the embrace of the hollow trunk, she cried and cried while Bella, for once, did not. A tall red-haired man dismounted to speak words of comfort and take Bella from her quivering arm. And then, amidst shouts which hardly penetrated her stunned, exhausted brain, a tall, black horse loomed up behind the gathering crowd of concerned faces, a half-armored blond giant on its back.

His voice, his handsome, austere face lit with joy, then

blurred before her as his big form blocked out the world behind him. "My beloved Jeannette, you are all safe. I prayed God you would all be safe and came when I heard there was trouble."

She tried to nod, to speak. She collapsed instead into the protective embrace of the steel-covered arms of Prince Edward.

Part Four

Sweet passion's pain doth pierce mine heart,
For I have loved thee from the start,
But foolishly behind high walls
  I hid such proof
  Nor saw this truth.

Sweet passion's pain doth urge me plead
That I might be thy love indeed,
But blindingly and armored bright
  I hid such proof
  Nor saw this truth.

And now sweet passion's pain doth teach
That my last chance must be great reach,
For wildly doth Dame Fortune's wheel
  Spin by such proof
  Nor halt for truth.

Welcome, sweet passion's pain, until
My heart shall recognize its will.
Whatever prophecies proclaim,
  I know such proof,
  Accept this truth.

Chapter Twenty-Two

For two days, Joan lay suspended between the delirium of dreams and waking moments of pure joy. A man had cleansed and bound the deep slash on her arm. Marta had come back to her from Liddell so far away, and now nursed her mistress instead of little Bella. The prince, her own dear Edward, sat close by and held her hand when she begged him to untie the knots, to unbind the ties of her heart. Marta bathed her and brushed her hair as Joan floated in the security of knowing she was back in her familiar bed and no longer had to flee. Yet when she plunged into exhausted sleep, dark dragons with John de Maltravers's evil face pursued her as she carried the tremendous burden of the children down the tunnel of fevered flight.

Later, when everything stopped rushing at her, Joan opened her eyes and the room stood still at last. The silk brocade hangings of the bed had been stripped off, but she was covered with a warm, woolen blanket from one of the servants' rooms. Her heavy eyes skimmed the once lovely solar room where she lay. All bare, ruined, bereft of tapestries and coffers. She glanced down at her arm bound in strips of white linen; then her eyes lifted to Madeleine nodding in the chair by the low-burning hearth. But, of course—Madeleine had cared for her and she'd dreamed Marta had come back. The prince had been here, too, sitting by her bedside, holding her hand, and watching—surely, she had not imagined that.

"Madeleine." Her voice was a rough whisper drowned by

483

the crackle of the fire. "Madeleine?"

The plump woman's eyes popped open. "Oh, milady, milady. Blessed saints, His Grace will be happy to hear this!"

Madeleine bustled to the door and spoke to someone in the hall, then hurried back in.

"The children?"

Joan saw tears in the woman's round eyes. "Fine, all fine, milady, finer than fine. You are the only one took sick and that for the blood loss, His Grace's surgeon said. Renée been seeing to Bella and the boys been happy as little pups playing with His Grace's men and squires."

Joan tried to smile but her face felt stiff. "His Grace—how many men?"

"Just rest, Madame Joan. If she wakes up, he says, send for me by the guards and keep her quiet."

"Is everyone all right?"

"Aye, 'cept the prince's men been hanging the rebels right and left for two days—the men what took and looted this Château or killed bailiffs at the fair or our two men here. Women and the other serfs he told to get back to work immediately no matter what, at once!"

The long explanation seemed to roll right over Joan although she tried to listen. She drifted off again, and when she fought to climb from the heavy reach of slumber, she knew he indeed held her hand in his big, warm one. She opened her eyes in awe at the sight of him.

"My lord prince."

He leaned so close she could see each long eyelash fringing his crystalline blue eyes, smell the tart scent of masculine bergamot he always wore. Surely he would not dare to kiss her, but he was so close and she longed for him to.

"My beloved Jeannette, over and over again I have thanked St. George and any other saint who listened to my prayers to keep you safe."

"Thanks to you, too, my lord. However did you know to come?"

"Rumors of peasant uprisings in the Risle area of Normandy reached us, and I had only just heard from my brother Lancaster that your Lord Thomas was with his forces. Hence, I came."

"Oh." She stared dreamily up at him afraid to ask if his "hence" was for the peasant uprising or the fact her lord had been away. Whichever, she was so glad to see him that for one precious moment nothing else mattered. But then, memories of the day the serf rebellion had started crept back in.

"My lord prince, on the day the Jacquerie spread here—the day I went to the fair—"

"Aye, I know all, my Jeannette. Do not think on it now. Your spunky little boys are safe and your babe Isabella, too, so all is well."

"But I must tell you, Your Grace. At the fair, at the church—he told the serfs to come here to take the Château—de Maltravers was here."

He sat gently on the edge of the big bed but she nearly spilled against him. "Listen, my love, you have been very ill for over two days with a blood fever caused by that cut on your arm. You called Madeleine Marta and called me by your father's name on that first long day, so you probably thought—"

"No! My lord prince, John de Maltravers came here! You must believe me. Ask the servants. Then he came to the fair. He wanted to kill me because I kept his lands from him. He did this to me!"

She tried to lift her bandaged arm but it was so heavy, and the room spun crazily as her voice echoed off the walls.

"Jeannette, my love, lie back now. Hush. Listen, sweet, my men have been through the village with a fine comb, shops, church, peasant cots, fields and all, and there was no de Maltravers."

"The Church of St. Ouen—he is dead up in the belfry

485

tower where he took me and he killed an old man who was deaf. He wanted to—to harm me. Then he just fell over and died."

"We will talk about this more on the morrow, Jeannette, but my men even chased several fleeing rebels clear up there in the belfry. One jumped to escape capture. There was no one, nothing up there."

"Maybe the old woman with the pet goose saw him. Ask her!"

"All right, we will. Lie back now and calm down or I will be forced to climb in there with you myself and hold you still."

Despite her agitation, she blushed at his words and lay back on her pillow. How wonderful he looked with that thick, tawny mane of unruly hair and the turned-down blond mustache. The dim light of the room shadowed in the angular hollows of his cheekbones and under his shaggy brows. His slightly parted lips looked so firm yet so—

Saints! She had to get hold of herself. She had so much to tell him, but she must never let happen again the sweet, treacherous flow of passion that had made her all wildness at his mere touch in Monbarzon. Enough of that exquisite torment when he left again or when he passed by her coldly in the world to which he really belonged.

"You are frowning, my sweet. Does the arm pain you?"

"No. I—thank you. No, I am just fine."

"Oh, of course, as always," he mocked gently. "No one need take care of wild, little Jeannette. She can ride all over enemy territory, save her children from the unholy terrors of the Jacquerie, and slay fond princes at a single glance."

Her eyes were so heavy, but she tried to meet his teasing blue gaze with her own.

"My little boys are afraid of dragons," she heard herself say. "The escape tunnel was so dark they were afraid of dragons, and they thought once your letters to me were dragon letters hidden with some treasure."

"Jeannette, you had two of my letters in the woods with you, but you never answered any I sent you. I thought mayhap you detested me now."

She dragged her eyelids open one more time. The Prince of Wales, bending over her looked every bit a frightened little boy at that moment.

"No, never that, whatever the sweet pain," she whispered and fell heavily asleep despite her desire to hear what wonders her Edward would say next.

The Château had been thoroughly looted but the rebels had been thoroughly punished, Joan learned the next day from her various visitors. Pierre Foulke and the brutal, loutish Simon had fled so drunk and laden with loot they had been easily captured and hanged on the town green for murder and riot. Other rebels had been tracked and captured; yet others had simply disappeared. Several of the possessions from the Château, which had not been ruined in the brawling, were recovered but most had apparently vanished. Vinette Brinay was missing as well as any sign of John de Maltravers except for a knife found on the lowest level of the belfry of St. Ouen which Joan claimed was indeed his. And so the mystery of the prince's fortuitous arrival was offset by the strange disappearance of the dragon de Maltravers and the tragic vanishing of poor Vinette Brinay.

Joan sat on a bench one of Prince Edward's men had set out for her in the May sunlight of the inner courtyard on the first day she felt well enough to be up. She watched her sons jog around her on ponies and swing wooden swords in the air. She felt much stronger today but not sure enough to venture outside the walls to the greens or forest fringe—not after all the peasant upheaval still rumored to be racking the distant countryside and not with the prince gone right now riding circuit in Pont-Audemer.

"Mother, look at me! Bet I could win a joust with this

horse if I had some armor. For England and St. George!"

Joan sighed and watched them ride around and around in endless circumference of the courtyard, charging imaginary enemies with their swooping wooden swords. How quickly time passed: soon they would need a quintain and a low tiltrail—and a father at home to teach them such knightly skills. Little Thomas was eight already, John six, and Bella growing, and she had no intention of rearing the three of them alone here in this French Château Ruisseau whatever Thomas Holland thought of her! And how strange it was now to see this home of theirs through different eyes after nine years—to see it as cold and lonely, even hostile, or at least it would be when her Edward was gone again, for his moments here were fleeting and she knew that well.

As if her thoughts had summoned him, the prince with four armed men and one standard bearer thundered through the inner gatehouses to the delighted shrieks of her little warriors. How strikingly the Prince of Wales's emblem—the three white feathers and the German motto "I serve"—shone against its black background. How comforting to sense his strength and know his power protected them all while he was here.

"Jeannette, you look wonderful out here in the light of day. I have been waiting for you to feel well enough to come out," Prince Edward beamed down at her. The sun, gilding his hair and shoulders, shone in her lavender eyes as she gazed up at him. With his steady perusal still on her, he handed down to a waiting squire his unvisored black helmet and unbuckled his ebony breastplate. Under it, he wore a dark brown, quilted tunic and leather breeks. His polished boots boasted silver rowel spurs to match the horse's trappings.

"Duchess of Kent," he began, with a wave of his hand to dismiss the hovering squire, "will you not ride out with me? I saw some luscious red cherries just for the picking in the east orchard beyond the copse."

Her heart pounded at the invitation. She would not fear to ride outside now, of course, with him, but she had both longed for and dreaded the moment which must come now that she was up and about and hardly weak anymore. Lying there in that bed upstairs all these days, thinking, dreaming, she knew it was no good; she could never become his lover again only to lose him in the agony of interminable, eternal separations.

"I was keeping an eye on my little rogues, Your Grace."

"Two of my men will watch the boys, Jeannette, and we will take the two other guards with us just for insurance."

"Insurance?"

"Aye. The area is as clean as I can get it of violent Jacques, but with you I take no chances. Did you, perchance, think I meant insurance for aught else?"

"No, of course not," she floundered, miffed by his amused smile at her blush. "Besides, I am anxious to know what else you found out about—well, you know, the things you said you would look into further."

"Aye. Then friend Hugh here will give you a hand up. Watch that arm."

The avid-eyed, red-haired squire darted back in view to link his hands to boost her up. Prince Edward's strong arm encircled her and settled her firmly before him in the big saddle built for a man in full battle armor. She waved to the boys and they trotted off.

"Did you learn aught of Vinette or de Maltravers, my lord prince?"

"Business, business, my Jeannette. Here we are almost alone in glorious spring and you start about business."

"The girl was dear to me, Your Grace, a faithful maid and evidently more unhappy than I ever guessed at the fact my lord and I tried to keep her from seeing that bastard Pierre Foulke. She must have thought she loved him and it grieved her so, she just got all hurt and broken by the rebellion. I am only grateful I could convince her to untie my bonds."

"Aye, sweetheart," he said, his deep voice much sobered as they jogged over the wooden drawbridge and down the narrow road where she had dared to face the peasant rabble a mere four days ago. "I am sorry, my Jeannette, but I have no real news of where she has gone. Only, perhaps, an explanation of why she is gone."

"To flee capture as a rebel when your men arrived?"

"No," he said slowly as if choosing his words very carefully. "I have had my men ask around and I myself spoke with your little maid Renée who had her foot broken in the mêlée when we stormed the castle. Renée says that Pierre Foulke got blazing drunk at that riotous banquet they forced your kitchen servants to prepare."

"Aye. You said every wine cask was split and drained. If it were not for your men being good hunters and the spring fruit and vegetable gardens being on, we would have starved for certain after all the victuals they robbed us of. Say on."

"I thought mayhap you know now what I have to say."

Joan turned in his arms in the saddle to read his face. "Saints, my lord prince, she is not dead?"

He shook his head to reassure her and reined the horse in at the cherry orchard closest to the Château. Over his broad shoulder as he dismounted and lifted her down, Joan saw that his two men following them had stopped far down the road. The prince tethered his black horse to a tree branch laden with crimson fruit. His big arm lightly around her shoulders, he led her back into the thick grove of trees.

"At the banquet, love, Pierre Foulke, in celebration of his heinous victory that day, violated Vinette Brinay—on the table in the Great Hall before the drunken crowd—and then offered her to one of his henchmen who did the same. I am sorry for the maid Vinette, my love, but I am also grateful he was too drunk to fetch you downstairs for his obscene celebration. Other noble ladies elsewhere about in this Jacquerie have not been so fortunate."

"No—oh, no. Poor Vinette! Then, when she came upstairs to me like that disheveled and all disoriented—but she said she loved him and only had a bump on her head from the riot at the fair. I should have taken her with us! I told her to lie down and wait for him!"

"You did what you had to do, my love. Renée says she later heard Vinette was there in the solar when Foulke staggered upstairs looking for you. She believes the girl fled when he began ripping the solar apart in his fury you were gone. She was obviously stunned and distraught. She may turn up someday or she may not. Until I send you some other maids—English maids—your loyal, plump Madeleine and hobbling Renée will have to do."

"My lord prince, I am grateful, so grateful for all you have done but I could not accept servants from you, nor the beautiful things you have promised to refurbish the Château. Thomas would never allow it. And wherever would you get English maids to send me while you are here raiding France, or should I not ask such an impertinent question?"

His eyes lit to see she was teasing despite her tears, so he decided to hazard the last piece of unsettling news he had for her—besides the fact he must needs depart soon, which he hoped desperately would grieve her more than anything.

He fingered one of her wayward curls the color of finest white wine and gazed avidly into her stunningly beautiful face made even more exquisite by the hint of suffering.

"Jeannette, about de Maltravers, I never meant to doubt you, only the chance of his daring to turn up, to seek you out like that was nearly unbelievable."

"Did you find the old woman with the pet goose then?"

"Aye. An old crone who lives in a hovel by a duckpond on the south side of Pont-Audemer. She—and the goose—found the deaf man you spoke of run through in the church by the sacristy door just as you said."

"There, I knew it. But of course, she never went up in the

491

belfry—I did not tell her to."

"No." He hesitated to tell her the rest—the truth, for he had seen her go all wild at Canterbury or at Bruges so long ago over de Maltravers's part in her parents' tragedy, and he even sensed, deep inside, that his own father, King Edward, was somehow guilty of blood on his hands in the whole terrible story. By St. George, she would just have to handle it; maybe it would get her home to England so he would not have to pursue her here again under any circumstance.

"Jeannette, I know you believed de Maltravers was dead, but he actually must have only had some sort of fit or seizure, or his heart stopped for a minute, I do not know."

"Perhaps someone only stole the body. He seemed to be alone. He must have had money on him."

"He was evidently not alone. A stranger stayed all day in the Deux Hommes Inn on the near side of town as if waiting for someone and then stormed out by himself when no one came to join him. The old, goose woman later saw that stranger carry another man out of town, riding slowly on his horse and holding that man upright before him in the saddle."

"But he was dead! His man wanted his body mayhap for burial."

"The old woman said the man looked ill, but he was definitely alive."

He watched the passions flit across the lovely face he had adored so many years. *All this time apart, he fumed, and our last day together before I set off back to camp before my sire sends men in search of me is taken with all these dreadful topics instead of the only one that matters.*

"Jeannette?"

"I am all right. I feel so drained of hatred or revenge in all this now. The children and I are blessed to be alive—to have you here."

He put his arms around her in a heady rush of joy and crushed her against him. "My dearest love, how I have longed to hear that! I have never, never loved, adored, and desired you more than I do this very moment. The world, obligations be damned when we are together. We have each other—this afternoon and night."

He lifted her chin to kiss her but her lips did not pout for the kiss; rather, her lower lip trembled and her violet eyes filled again with crystal tears. "And then, you leave again—my Edward?"

"Aye, I must on the morrow. But there is tonight and other days we shall find, other rooms and beds and moments—"

"No."

"I cannot help leaving, my love. The king and Lancaster will unite near Calais in two days and I must be there."

"Of course you must. You always *must* and I must do certain things, too."

She pulled gently back from his embrace and, stunned, he let her go. She turned to face him; a trembling green and red cherry bough was the only tenuous barrier between them. She grieved that already a little frown creased his proud brow, and she regretted that this inescapable moment had to come before their final moments of parting.

"Jeannette, I know how hard it is when we are apart."

"Do you? It is hard when we are together. I could have died from shame and longing at Windsor last time. There is no real time for us—it is always hurried good-byes and wretched pretending."

"Wretched? Was Monbarzon and what we shared there wretched? Or the other times you melted to sweet, wild honey at my touch?"

"I beg you do not torment me with that. Aye, I do not deny it anymore. I have never loved—will never love—anyone as I do you, but it is not enough!"

"Oh, really? To be loved, adored all these years by the Prince of Wales—"

"Saints, I know who you are. I wish you were not the Prince of Wales, you know, just the lowest peasant—I, too—miserable though they are. Then at least we might be together and not hide our few stolen days. I am wed to one of your Plantagenet knights, Your Grace; I have his three children."

"I see."

"I doubt if you do. It is not for love of Thomas Holland I say these things. I just die inside to say this, my dearest lord, but I cannot be your mistress ever, ever again."

"Mistress! The love of the Prince of Wales is no mistress! It was far beyond that, more precious all these years—at least to me. But do not think I came here to rescue and then to beg, Jeannette. I have sons and duties too."

She looked away at last as the sheltering embrace of leaves and ripe fruit they had not touched all blurred scarlet and green through her tears. "That is just my point, Your Grace. We are trapped whatever the old astrologer Morcar's star charts promised once. I will always, always love you, but that love is doomed by fate or who we are or the terrible things our parents have done or something we cannot control."

"If you love me, you will not turn me away like this."

"That is not true. It is because I love you."

"Saint George, you are just exhausted. We had best go back then. There is much to do before we ride out in the morn. I shall leave six men as I said and only take six back. Aye, Jeannette, I do have duties and there is one I have shirked long enough to coddle my foolish heart—and that of one I love."

She meant to only take a shallow breath, but an audible sob racked her. "Aye, for the throne if not your heart, Your Grace, the Prince of Wales must wed."

"So I have been repeatedly counseled, Jeannette, and I thank you for your kind, motherly advice on it." His voice had gone hard and cold like the honed edge of a sword, but somehow that helped her to regain her composure.

He grabbed a huge handful of cherries from the low branch between them, tearing leaves and bruising fruit in his sudden motion. He turned away and his words floated back to her over his shoulder. "Come on then, we will walk back if you are strong enough for all this. And I shall be sending your precious Thomas Holland back to you when I see my brother Lancaster. I will not have you accuse me someday of being David to Bathsheba's Uriah."

She did not know what he meant, but she dared not challenge him on it. They walked in proud silence back into the stony embrace of the Château walls.

The next week passed for Joan in as much of a fog as her feverish illness had. She berated herself one moment for sending the prince away so bitterly; the next moment she felt she had done the best she could to battle the agony of continued separation. In a whirl of frenzied activity, she supervised the skeletal servant staff that had not been killed or run off in the Jacquerie, and she kept the men the prince had left behind busy at needed repairs. Yet she learned too late that bravely sending the prince away after mere words was just as devastating as sending him away after the ecstasy of glorious love-making.

She had saved restoring the Great Hall for last, perhaps because she could not bear to think of what poor Vinette had suffered there at the brutal hands of Pierre Foulke during the drunken orgy of the Jacquerie. Joan's long blond tresses swept up and bound in a wide strip of linen, she supervised the hanging of the single long tapestry the prince's men had recovered from the village. She squinted at it to be sure it hung straight; her head pounded from an almost daily pain she was certain was caused as much by her heartache as that of her brain.

"No, Jensen. No, man. Hang it a little lower on the left side, I said."

"Mother! Mother!" her eldest son's voice shrieked from the hall. She put her hand to her head as both boys darted in. "Horses coming down the road! Maybe the prince is coming back and bringing us some armor like he promised! Come on! Come and see!" He wheeled around with a cavorting six-year-old brother at his heels and dashed back out before she could answer.

The prince! Surely not—not after that awful parting, she thought, jolted to panic as she realized how terrible she must look. With a twist of cloth and a shake of her aching head, she loosed her hair and tried to smooth the flurry of heavy tresses.

Outside, the May sky shone pearly gray unlike that golden, clear morn she had parted from him only last week. Horses—aye, she could hear them now, a small number, surely not the prince. And then, even as reality crushed the foolish fantasy of joyous reunion with her Edward, the boys' excited squeals told her what she already knew.

"It is Father! Father has come home! Father, Father, we can ride knights' horses now!"

Joan stood her ground in the cobbled courtyard waving her uninjured arm as Thomas Holland and two squires clattered in across the drawbridge and past the inner gatehouse. He looked so small suddenly, and she was not certain if separation had dwarfed him or if she only compared his size to the towering frame of the prince.

Lord Thomas Holland dismounted stiffly, his face wary until the boys swarmed him and he lifted both in his arms a moment before he set them back down. His copper head turned to Joan; his eye, of much the same hue as his hair, surveyed her before he bent to kiss her cheek brusquely.

"My lady. Thank heaven I find you all well. I had no knowledge the foolish peasant bastards would really rise up against proper and lawful authority, of course, or I would never have gone. Forgive me, Joan, I did not know until word came through His Grace Prince John of Lancaster. Of course—of necessity, I have thanked the Prince of Wales for what he and his men did here in my absence."

The speech was monotone, stilted as if he recited it from something he had been forced to memorize. His eye looked slightly past her and might just as well have been covered by a dark patch as the other.

"Come in, my Lord Thomas. The Château has missed its

496

lord and the boys have greatly missed their father."

"And the lady of the Château?" he asked so low she was not certain he expected an answer. He walked slowly in beside her with their sons at his heels.

"It was really something, Father! His Grace, the prince saved us, and his men gave John and me rides all the time and some swords, too."

"Swords? John, too?"

"Sure," John volunteered. "Everybody got swords, 'cept Mother and Bella, and they did not get anything."

Thomas Holland's eye swept Joan at his son's words, and he chose to turn immediately and go upstairs rather than survey the ground rooms as Joan had briefly indicated he should.

To increase her foreboding, in the upstairs hall he patted both boys on the head and sent them back down to play. She heard him sigh wearily as she followed him into the solar and closed the door behind them. Of course, she thought, he had been to horse for days and his old leg pains bothered him.

"You must be exhausted from the ride, my lord. Some wine?"

"Aye. Why not? The bastards did not ruin all of it then?"

"They did but we have since purchased more."

"Did we? And who, pray tell, is *we*?"

"His Grace's men when they were here," she said carefully. She caught the shift of the wind well enough, and dreaded his words to come.

"St. Peter's bones, lady, but His Grace is helpful, is he not? He saves my wife, my home, my sons—"

"Your daughter Isabella, too, my lord. You have a daughter and she is sleeping right over there, so please do not shout."

His eye sought the little cradle near the big canopied bed, and he walked over to peek in. "Aye, lady, I know well enough I have a daughter and a fair one at that."

"She resembles me even as the boys do you, Thomas."

He came back and slumped in a chair at the table as she poured him a goblet of ruby red burgundy.

"I was about to say, Joan, His Grace, the Prince of Wales rides in here like St. Michael's avenging angels and then to boot, tells Lancaster to send me home posthaste."

"I cannot pretend your arrival does not please me, and you look as if you need a respite. Your usual good ruddy color has gone waxen-hued."

"Hell's gates, do you not think I know it? There has been much sickness on the march—flux, grips, hints even of plague from Poland. Some of my old wounds have pained me again, but not, I tell you, not half so much as being bandied about from pillar to post again by His Royal Highness, the Prince of Wales. Damn, but I would have come home on my own the moment I heard about the horrendous Jacquerie. I need not him to tell me as he has before at his convenience where to go, or how damn high to jump."

"My lord, I assure you, he was only being kind and, no doubt, wishing to solidify this region further by your presence when he asked you be sent home."

"Saint Peter, is that it? He made you privy to his plans, did he?"

"No, Thomas, only he did tell me he intended to send you home to me."

"How touching, how terribly noble! The man never gave a tinker's damn for any women but his own—sending knights here or there into battle or not—we all just jump and obey like jack-on-strings, do we not, my duchess?"

"You have always been so loyal to the Plantagenets, my lord, and this sounds not like you at all. Her Grace, Queen Philippa—"

"Hold your tongue on that. My service to Her Grace is quite another thing, lady, and you had best remember that. A pure and chivalric duty. You would not even name the child after Her Grace, so do not lecture me on her."

"I was hardly lecturing you, Thomas. I see you are very tired and I believe you have not been well. To defend one's home, one's lands, is a completely honorable and necessary duty, so I do not see why you must fret and fume as if you have been punished or sent to exile in Flanders or wherever. The boys need their father, and I am glad you are here."

"Glad? Are you? Then I shall expect a hero's welcome, love. We have been parted so long, and you are glad to have me home, eh? Even after those days here with him? My sons obviously adore him—too."

"That is not fair. Aye, I am grateful to him for rescuing us. The boys need someone to look up to just now, a man to spend time with them and teach them, and they just turned their affections to him and his men."

"'Turned their affections?' St. Peter's bones, wife, a good phrase! And now my hero's welcome. Let's to bed."

Her eyes widened though she tried not to show surprise on her face. "Now, my lord? The boys are waiting. Bella sleeps. Are you not hungry, Thomas?"

He stood and cracked his goblet down smartly on the tabletop. "Fed up, more like than hungry, Lady Holland. I demand—I *will* have my affectionate welcome. Two so long separated, both having been in danger—did not our lengthy, wretched separation pain you enough to greet me with open arms and legs, too, lady?"

He moved woodenly a few steps to her and pulled her close in an embrace either rough or desperate. Slowly, she put her arms around his big waist.

"No more protests, Joan? I have road dust on me. It is the middle of the day. But when people in love have been separated as we, any chance, any excuse to bed will do."

"I do not need your mockery, Thomas. I have been through enough lately and do not deserve it. I need you here to comfort, not torment me."

He started toward the bed, drawing her along with him.

"Let me at least move Bella's cradle, my lord."

"And wake her up? Just come around this far side, my dear, and she will not see a thing. Of course, I would never want the children to see anything they should not."

His tone, laced with sarcasm, made her stiffen and draw back despite her silent vow to please him, to cooperate. At her balk, he pulled her toward him and tumbled them both heavily onto the bed, she on her back, he pressing her down and staring into her flushed face with his single, copper eye.

"In love, Thomas, or even in duty, I could welcome this, but not with your cruel innuendos. Say what you will, but do not take it out on both of us this way."

"This way?"

"Aye. Saints, you have not touched me in tenderness since before our fair, innocent Isabella was born, and I will not submit to coercion, punishment, or humiliation in this way. I escaped that in the Jacquerie, my lord, and have no desire to face such treatment again."

Deep red suffused his round face and crept down his neck above his leather riding jerkin. His jaw set, the coppery eye hardened to glittering topaz as he leaned into her with his powerful chest and arm and reached down to unhook his broad leather belt. It flopped heavily across her even as he pulled her skirts up. On the far side of the wide bed in her cradle on the floor, Bella stirred. Furious and hurt, Joan glared defiantly up into his blazing eye, unflinching.

He heaved one knee between her legs and pressed closer to her. She bit her lower lip to keep from cursing him and wadded great fists of brocade coverlet to keep from trying to shove him off. Then, as if her brain wanted to punish her as much as Thomas did, her mind flashed tormenting pictures of Edward at her: she was in his arms here in the solar—she had not sent him away but reveled in a last ecstatic night with him. Edward pressing close, entering her ready warmth on the beach at Calais, in the straw at Windsor, in Monbarzon—anywhere, everywhere. She was opening her silken thighs for him, her very inner being flowered and opened wanting his touch so desperately that the sweet pain of passion nearly overwhelmed her.

"Witch! Witch!" Thomas hissed at her and jolted her from the realm of reminiscence. He heaved himself off her, and her startled eyes took in his meaning. Though he obviously had meant to possess her, his weapon lay limp and useless. She tore her eyes away from recognizing his obvious inability to enter her, but too late.

"Witch!" he said again, his face a livid mask of fury. "What a fool you have made of me! What a fool I was from the beginning to take you on for your blue Plantagenet blood no matter what she said. He has always had your fickle, spoiled heart, and damn you, no doubt, your body, too!"

He half-rolled, half-scrambled off the bed and turned his back to her as he stood and refastened his garments. His belt still lay across her where he had dropped it, but he made no move to retrieve that. Without turning back, he said, "I leave you to your thoughts, your bed, your daughter, duchess. As for me, I had rather be in hell than here!"

He stopped at the table on his way out only long enough to slosh more wine in his goblet and drink it straight down. He strode out and banged the door behind him.

She shoved his belt on the floor and straightened her skirts, all the while staring up at the newly replaced underside of the brocade bed canopy. Somehow, sadly, it had come to this: Thomas detested her, the prince now, too. She was deserted, as alone as her poor mother had been years ago when she took to her solitary room as a recluse.

And here, Thomas Holland had been specifically saved from possible death with the Plantagenet army on raid in France. Whether from disease or battle, he could have been killed just like Bathsheba's husband Uriah in the Bible. Joan had asked a village priest about the story to understand the prince's cryptic comment to her.

King David, Father Herman had said, had desired to marry Bathsheba so much that he had her husband Uriah sent into the front line of battle to die. But now, of course, His Grace's odd comparison meant naught: she had sent him away ungratefully after all he had done for her over the years, and hurt his pride. Now, she must learn forever to be

501

without him, so why would Thomas's fury or any outside danger ever threaten her anymore?

Much later, when the boys' happy voices drifted to her through the windows and little Bella began to fuss again, Joan got up and drank the rest of the Burgundy before carrying the babe outside to join them.

Chapter Twenty-Three

Thomas Holland never went to war again—at least not with the French. Rather, he waged his own subtle, continual battle with his wife using for his weapons innuendo and bitterness. As the months passed, their two sons, spitting images of their father, learned to ride and joust at the quintain; pretty Bella grew golden curls and charmed everyone's heart—but her father's. And so, Joan and Thomas Holland lived one and a half years after the Jacquerie as lord and lady of Château Ruisseau, of Liddell Manor, and of his lands in Lancashire; yet they were husband and wife only in duty and appearance to the outside world.

With their brood of three healthy children, they did what would be well enough expected of them although they were invited no more to visit the royal Plantagenet court. King Edward and his three eldest sons were seldom at Windsor or Westminster in those times, for the continual need to control their vast if tenuous French territorial holdings rode them as hard as they rode their enemies. When further raids and expeditions failed, the Plantagenets negotiated the elaborate Treaty of Brétigny with the French, renouncing all claims to Normandy, but keeping rich Aquitaine to the south which the Prince of Wales would eventually govern.

And now, as Yuletide of 1360 approached, France was beset by another threat besides the English might: for the second time in eleven years the plague swept up rich and poor alike in its greedy grasp.

"I told you, my lord, you should not have gone into Pont-

503

Audemer with all the rumors of sickness about," Joan greeted Thomas Holland as he strode noisily into the sweet-scented solar where she was reading to the children the heroic story of King Charlemagne from a lovely, illuminated book she had purchased the year before. Bay candles burned on the hearth and pine boughs made the room smell like a fresh forest. "If the whole English army is safe at home in England you need not go out looking to see if the plague rumors are true," she scolded.

"Bah! Rumors tell it all. But for the usual winter agues and blains, there is not a soul out of sorts in Pont-Audemer. If it does get this far, we are sequestered well enough here. There were some traveling merchants in town and they say it is far to the south yet."

Joan could feel the children's eyes as they darted from her to their father. Though they tried not to let the children sense the contentiousness between them, she knew they perceived it and she grieved for that. Thomas was almost ten now, John nearly eight, and Bella over two. She remembered well how she as a child had sensed trouble in her own household—her recluse mother, a father taken away for something awful. She had decided long ago that when her three were old enough, whatever Thomas said, she would try to find the words to explain that the trouble they felt had naught to do with them. Soon mayhap, soon.

"St. Peter's bones, I said traveling merchants, you little ninnies," Thomas was bellowing at the children and poor, dainty Bella looked utterly startled at his booming voice. "Do not any of you want to know what I purchased for you as Yuletide gifts?"

The boys jumped up and exploded with shouts, and Bella soon caught the spirit of things, shrieking, jumping up and down, and clapping wildly.

"All right, all right. I see I have your attention at last," he teased. "No good sitting about listening to foolish romantic stories of dead heroes when one can practice to be live ones, eh? Thomas, lad, over here. You are the eldest, so you first. I put my hand in this gunnysack and just see what I brought you."

Tears of joy blurred Joan's vision as she watched the round-faced, copper-haired boy accept a silver pair of rowel riding spurs Thomas had produced from the deep sack. But the moment, like so many others which might have been so sweet, turned sour through pure mischance.

"Oh, they are fine, my lord father. Saints, Mother, look. These are just like a pair the prince wore, I warrant, just like them!"

The smile froze on Joan's face as she saw her husband's round jaw go hard and firm. "Our heir has a good memory, eh, Joan? Too damned good, like all of us. John, you are next, boy. I put my hand in here once more and then—"

Thomas's arm disappeared into the sack and emerged with a curved hunting knife that produced delighted exclamations. Thankfully, there were no more accidental mentions of Prince Edward, who was usually a forbidden subject at the Château unless she and Thomas traded bitter barbs over him in private. She had never yet admitted to Thomas she had loved—still loved—the prince, and sometimes she wondered if it might not have cleared the air if she had.

"And now, the little maid—our pretty Bella," Thomas Holland went on as the boys gloated over their gifts.

Joan smiled as she pushed Bella forward a step. She was thrilled that Thomas had included the child in this sudden burst of Yuletide good will, for he had often ignored Bella, who, luckily, had been too young to notice much yet. "For you, Bella. Go on, sweet," Joan urged. "Father has a present for you. Say 'please.'"

"Please," the tot echoed, and her angel face dimpled. Struck with a shaft of strange awe for the tiny maid he seldom heeded, Thomas Holland put his black velvet arm into the sack and pulled out a little tin horn. "Here, maid. Your mother loves music. Now you can play, too."

His voice gruff, he showed Bella how to lift it to her lips

and blow. At the high-pitched toot of the horn, Bella startled, then giggled. Instantly, she mastered the blaring, shiny instrument and darted off after the boys blowing it for all her little lungs could bear.

"That was wonderful of you, Thomas," Joan said, truly touched as he stood awkwardly before her.

"It is Yule after all, Joan. If our Thomas is to go to Warwick to be a squire to the Beauchamps next year, we have to enjoy him while we can, eh?"

"Aye. I cannot believe he is almost old enough to start that long path to knighthood, and John only two years away if we can obtain another fortunate placement. Bless the saints for little Bella being so much younger."

"Mm," he grunted and wiped his brow with his sleeve. "Damned hot in here with this room all shut up and this fire blazing, lady," he said as if to change the subject. "St. Peter's bones, that ride over and back today heated me up royally."

"It is winter, Thomas, and I think it is quite comfortable in here. Just sit down to rest and you will be fine."

"Mm," he repeated, and then, to her surprise, produced apparently from up his sleeve a silver brooch in the shape of a fleeing deer. "Here," he said gruffly. "For your winter cloak. The merchants claim it is from Spain. I thought of the hart on your family crest you favor so, and I just bought it."

"Oh, my lord, it is lovely, a lovely surprise!"

His avid copper eye swept her face as she rose to accept it. She smiled genuinely up at him and he felt his blood heat further with a long-smothered passion for his beautiful, willful wife. Ah, little Bella would be such a beauty to break hearts and ruin a man's calm in his later years with doubts and pain too, he mused.

He watched Joan's slender fingers fasten the brooch on her blue perse wool kirtle. "It is a fine piece, my Lord Thomas, and I shall wear it proudly, even as the children love their gifts."

"Love," he said low. "Aye, that would be nice. I will see you for dinner and mayhap talk of such things as love and gifts then. Now I am thirsty and need some cold wine and a good breath of fresh air."

His usual ruddy complexion did look especially florid, she thought, as he strode away to his own room down the hall where he had settled in after his return over a year and a half ago. He always pushed himself hard, too hard, for his old war wounds acted up at times and his digestion was never good anymore.

She lifted the discarded book on Charlemagne to put it away in its metal box, and glanced down at the lovely illuminated page of King Charlemagne with his heir Prince Pippin. Both the king and prince were suited in elaborate fourteenth century armor though they had lived and loved and fought two centuries ago; Prince Pippin's hair was gilded blond with a down-curled mustache and Joan realized with a start that the artist must have indeed patterned this heroic royal pair after the present English king and Prince Edward.

She sighed and closed the book carefully. Time had helped to mute the pain of losing him, of never seeing him, but occasionally he leapt at her, full-blown in her busy brain, to disarm her thoughts and stir her deepest passions. Here, on painted page; in minstrels' songs or her own tunes of unrequited love; in rumors of his victories; news of his illegitimate two sons being knighted; in the blessed, haunting fact he had not married yet—Edward, Prince of Wales, possessed her still.

She put her slippered feet up on the hearth andiron next to the little iron cage for roasting chestnuts and stared into the leaping flames. Thomas was dead wrong—the room was chill without this comforting blaze. She absent-mindedly fingered the little, silver brooch and, listening dazedly to the tinny toot of Bella's distant horn, she saw her heart's imaginings in the orange-red flames.

"Mother, no. No!" Bella shrieked as Joan pried the beloved horn from her little fingers two days later. "No, no! Mine!"

"Come here and amuse your sister, boys. Saints, I am glad to know you two are old enough to understand."

"But is Father very sick, my lady mother?" her son Thomas queried. "And, are you certain the disease could be on these gifts to make us sick, too? St. Peter's bones, we have already had them about us for two whole days so mayhap the damage is done."

"No, do not say that. I want to take all precautions. After all, the gifts came from traveling merchants from the south and that is where—well, I just want to be careful, that is all. I do not know how sick your father is, but sick enough I should pack you three off to Madeleine's family's croft for the day. And Thomas, I do not approve of your cursing by St. Peter or anyone else." She realized her voice was shrill, but she could not help it.

"But Father always says that and you say 'saints' whenever the littlest thing goes awry."

"Now, listen to me! I do not need your sharp tongue. You are in charge of these two and I expect your best behavior today when you are visiting! And please see to Bella's whining as I am going back in to your father now."

She hurried to Thomas's room wishing she had parted from the children with softer words, for she had planned to send them to their old nursemaid's family's croft on the edge of town until she was certain that Thomas Holland had not been smitten by the plague.

There—she had said the word to herself. Already, she was so on edge and exhausted after nursing him all last night, desperate to get his fever down. The signs—the early signs were perhaps there, but then it could be a more benevolent disease at this point too. If only his fever would break; it made him shriek such delirious, terrible words she could not bear the children to hear! If only the painful swellings on his neck and under his arm—which shot him wide awake in pain—would shrink. Saints, if it was the plague, all of them could be as good as dead already!

As the day wore on, the Château lay silent in a dusting of new snow outside. The children had been gone with Madeleine for hours; Joan had even ordered the front gate closed though she could not stand to have the drawbridge pulled up and certainly wanted no big red plague cross painted on the front door.

In fairness to the servants, she had told them all to stay downstairs and twice a day food and wine for her were brought to the top of the staircase. She was not hungry, not anything except desperate, scared, and regretful, but to keep the servants' spirits up, she threw the food down the *garde-robe* shaft so they would believe she was eating.

She kept the fire roaring day and night in his room where she nursed him. She burned the gunnysack he had evidently purchased from the traveling merchants from the south. But, on the second day, his fever was unabated and his neck and arm swellings had turned a putrid black.

She cried then in great, heaving gasps, crumpled exhausted at the side of his bed. The black death—aye, those black swellings were the final sign he was doomed, he and mayhap anyone else who came in contact with him. But she had no fever yet and no one had come to say the children were ill: she had ordered the guards to send for her the moment one of them showed the slightest hint of fever, and no one—thank heavens, no one—had come to break what was left of her heart with that.

She pulled herself up to kneel, leaning against the bed. Thomas' breathing was labored; he tossed heavily, alternately burning and quaking with chills. Last night he had been so violent as to rise and walk, to embrace her even, that in desperation she had ripped a linen sheet into strips and tied him loosely down. Only now, that made it nearly impossible to change his sweat-soaked sheets under the pile of blankets she had covered him with hoping beyond hope that he could sweat the poisons out. She had tried everything, everything! In wintertime there were no toadstools to hang about his neck, but she had sprinkled the room with dried borage flowers and placed in bed with him a bozoar stone that she had sent the kitchen lad Matt out to fetch.

She folded her hands and tears squeezed from between her heavily fringed eyelashes as she said again the familiar, desperate plague prayer which she remembered from the gentle days at Woodstock Manor ten years ago when she had hidden from the death there with the Princess Isabella: "Dear and most benevolent St. Roch, blessed protector of plague victims, guard this one from death's mighty hand. Amen."

Her mind drifted even as she recited the words again. How strange, another cruel twist of Dame Fortune's wheel that in bringing her and Bella the Yuletide gifts—the boys too, but then he had always favored them—Thomas had been stricken. Just when he had reached out to her a tiny step at last after these two terribly tense years, he had been stricken. "Dear and most benevolent St. Roch, blessed protector . . ." For that last kindness, for all the years she had hurt his pride without meaning to, she would see this through. Besides, if she was to be stricken too, except for leaving the children, she almost would not mind dying. No. No. She was only thirty years old and she had not meant that. "Dear St. Roch, guard this one from death's mighty hand. Amen."

When the low knock sounded on the chamber door, she was not certain she had heard it at first. "Aye? Is someone there?"

"Matt. Matt from the kitchen, milady."

Thomas's eyes flew wide open but closed again, and he mumbled low, undiscernible words, but that would not last long if he kept up as he had been all night alternately mumbling then screaming his terrible accusations. She rose and, as she went to the door, she marveled how she almost floated. Her head no longer spun but her feet hardly seemed to touch the floor.

"Matt, what is it?" she asked, her cheek pressed to the wooden door. "No one is to come up unless I call, I said."

"Aye, milady, only this be very important. Master Roger Wakeley, he come back, come in through the back kitchen door so Lynette say I come tell you at once, milady."

Roger Wakeley! He had been gone since before the Jacquerie and now to just dance back into her life as he had done before and at this time seemed much too much to bear all of a sudden. "Why did he come, Matt? Tell him no, I cannot see him. Tell him there is plague and send him away!"

"He say he knows that, milady, and that is why he say come talk to him now."

"The fool," she whispered to the door. "A spy, a fool, a deceiver." Her voice dissolved in a sob, and she bit her lower lip to halt the flood of tears which threatened.

"Matt. Tell him to come to the bottom of the stairs and I will talk to him. Tell him it cannot be long."

She heard the boy's flying feet in the hall. He was probably only too glad to get away. She smoothed back her wild, loose hair, and left the door ajar so she could hear Thomas when the raving began.

In the dim stretch of corridor, the air seemed fresh and calm in contrast to the inferno of the little room where she nursed him. The sulfur powder she threw into the fire and the borage hardly even fazed her anymore since she had grown almost numb to their penetrating odors.

She sat several steps down the curving flight of stairs where no one at the bottom could see her. She heard nothing below. Nervously, she smoothed the skirt of her green wool kirtle over her knees.

"Master Roger?" she ventured and her voice sounded almost ghostly in the aching silence of the Château.

"Lady Joan! Aye, I am here and I need to see you. Please, lady, I must come up."

"No, you cannot. Did they not tell you my Lord Thomas is hard smitten?"

"Aye. And with the plague. The fact I have come now is God's gift to you, Lady Joan, I am certain of it. I am sorry for Lord Thomas, but do not fear for your own safety."

511

The words seemed to roll right over her although she tried to grasp each one. He made no sense. It made no sense he had come back. Then she heard his quick, light tread on the stairs but before she could rise to flee, he rounded the curve of wall and seized her hands in his.

"Lady Joan, do not run. *Sacrebleu*, it is all right, I tell you."

"No! Are you crazy! It is plague, I said! Plague! I have sent the children away and—"

"And stayed here to die yourself?"

"Mayhap!"

"That is just it, lady. I believe you cannot die from it. I should have explained it long ago to you but there was never any threat or need."

"I cannot? What do you mean I cannot?" Her eyes darted over the kindly face which had been so familiar, yet so deceitful and so treasured over the years from her maidenhood days. A little glimmer of thought leapt out from her deepest buried memories then, even as Roger Wakeley, still grasping her hands in his, began to explain.

"When you were a child and I first came to Liddell years ago—"

"When the king sent you to spy on Edmund of Kent's traitorous wife, my lady mother, you mean!"

"Aye. We have had that conversation before. You and old Marta bound my broken leg then."

"I remember that."

"And do you remember then those who lived at Liddell also nursed me through a disease where I had a fever and swellings on my neck?"

Her lavender eyes lifted to lock with his intense, brown ones. "Aye, I do recall it."

"And I recovered."

"So you mean Thomas might recover?"

"That is not what I mean, lady. When I was sick, it spread to three others at Liddell. Two house servants died but you and I recovered."

512

"I was sick with it? And it was plague?"

"I believe so. Few recover but we both did and once you survive it, you are destined to never be smitten with it again."

"Destined," she breathed, her stunned mind darting not to that maidenhood illness of which the faintest memory persisted, but to Morcar's star charts she had in her possession in the solar now, and to Prince Edward's last departing words that he had once believed she was destined to be his. Destined, she marveled. Destined to escape de Maltravers's attempt to kill her, destined to escape the brutal Jacquerie—and now this.

"You do remember. You do believe me?" Roger Wakeley's smooth voice slid into her reverie.

"Aye. But why did you come back here? Why now? His Grace, King Edward, surely has not sent you on another fool's errand to report on me, for I am no worry to him anymore."

"Are you not? But indeed, I come of my own free will for the first time in so many years, I hate to admit it, my Lady Joan. His Grace has sent me once to your lady mother, once to you, once to his own poor, lonely mother, the deposed Queen Isabella, and once even to His Royal Highness, the Prince of Wales to spy, but I swear to you that is all behind me now."

He looked at her so earnestly that his lower lip trembled, and his forehead, hid by his long, straight brown hair, crashed down to nearly hide his intense, shadowed eyes.

"His own mother and the Prince of Wales too," she faltered. "Indeed, I have kept good company over the years. And now?"

"The old boy wanted me to travel clear to Castile to sing for and spy on Pedro, King of Castile. *Sacrebleu*, I am too weary of it all, too old, and besides, Pedro is rumored to be crazed and sadistic. And so, lady, I come to you a refugee, to one who also has disobeyed our great King Edward and likely will again. I only pray that you will trust me enough to take me in here."

Her weary eyes searched his earnest face. "Aye, my old friend Roger, when you put it so, I can hardly deny you. Saints, I have made enough of my own stupid mistakes in a life much shorter than yours not to recognize the need to escape and begin again. You may stay."

As if to protest her ready decision, Thomas Holland's voice shattered the silence from down the dim hall behind her.

"I must go to him. Thank you for your blessed news. Later, when you have rested—the children are at the weaver's croft on the south side of town. You could visit there and tell them I love them, see how they are."

"I shall, lady, and then I shall be back. When you take a rest next time, there is more to tell. You are exhausted and must have help in this. I shall be back soon." He loosed her hands as startled as she that he had held them all that time. Appalled at the words he heard the sick man shouting in the distance, he turned and ran down the steps to spare her the added shame.

"Joan! Joan!" the demented voice shrieked down the echoing hall. "I will kill him, kill him! Fetch the prince to me. Kill him. To keep you. Bastard! Royal bastard! Kill him to keep you."

Joan ran down the hall to his room and slammed the door. She bent over Thomas to sponge his face.

"Hush, my dearest lord, hush. You know not what you are saying."

"The queen. All her fault. I adored her. She only used me. I cannot kill her son. No one but kings dare to kill kings. Is he king yet, the prince?"

His wild copper eye darted, rolled. His eye patch had pulled free again and for one of the few times in their ten-year marriage, Joan beheld the poor, emptied eye socket.

"The queen. Queen Philippa," his frenzied words tumbled out much lower now. "She never sends for me anymore. The prince never wants me there—to fight with him anymore. Never."

"Here, Thomas, drink a little cool wine. It has winter-bloom in it to keep your sores from bleeding. Here, my lord."

She poured a little through his cracked lips, but most spilled out to run down his unshaven jaw and neck. He breathed heavily now, almost panting, and his breath smelled foul. His copper eye had somehow glazed over with a look of distant unreality, the coldness of death.

"Dear and most benevolent St. Roch, blessed protector of plague victims, guard this one from death's mighty hand. Amen."

She repeated the prayer again, staring helplessly down at him, waiting for she knew not what. She heard the creak of door behind her and turned expecting to see Roger Wakeley. But there, her gaunt, white face etched by cavorting firelight, her reddish hair all wild like blown straw about her staring eyes, stood Vinette Brinay.

"Saints! Vinette!"

The woman seemed to glide toward Joan. She came close and leaned slightly over the bed. Her long, disheveled hair fell over her face like flaming silk, and Joan took a step away in some unnamable horror.

"I knew Pierre must be here somewhere," Vinette said, and her voice sounded rough and crackled. "I am glad they did not catch him and he is not dead yet, *madame*."

"Vinette, where have you been? Two years. How did you get here?"

Vinette turned her head to answer but stared past into apparent vacancy. "Here? I belong here. You promised it to me when you fled with the children. Did you think I would forget? Pierre loves me, *madame*. He wants to wed with me."

"I do not know where you have been, Vinette, or how you came here now, but you must go away. This is my Lord Thomas, and he is very ill."

"I am so glad your prince did not kill him. Poor Pierre. I will take care of him now."

Vinette's hands, so thin Joan could almost see bones and blue veins beneath the papery skin, reached out to untie

515

Thomas's linen bindings. Joan pulled Vinette's hands back sharply.

"Vinette, you are not well. I am going to put you in another room as you cannot go back down to the servants now. Come on with me."

"No. No! You wanted to be untied, you begged. Do you not remember? Pierre is mine—*my* Château Ruisseau. You get away. He wants to marry me!"

In a frenzied move, her hands raised like claws, she threw herself at Joan and they hit hard into a carved oak post of the bedstead. Thomas jolted awake to shout his incoherent curses as wild colors danced before Joan's eyes at the blow to the back of her head. A sobbing, screaming, wild-faced Vinette scratched and kicked at Joan under her on the carpeted floor by the bed, but both women were hampered by their skirts and hair. Shocked for an instant, exhausted and furious, Joan at last struck out at the girl's contorted face. Then, even as Joan's wasted strength allowed her to subdue the maddened, thrashing woman, Roger Wakeley appeared to yank Vinette off her. Vinette writhed even in his arms, screaming and cursing as he dragged her away out into the hall where a door slammed and all fell to silence again.

On her knees, Joan hunched over, both palms flat on the carpet to stop the room from swaying. Shaking, stunned, she gasped for breath even as she heard Thomas do so on the bed above her. She shoved the great, golden curtain of her hair back from her face and stood unsteadily.

She prayed aloud to St. Roch to comfort herself as she tried to give Thomas more of the cool winterbloom-laced wine she realized would do him no good now. She heard Roger Wakeley come back in. Without glancing up, she knew he stood on the other side of the bed.

"Forgive me, Lady Joan, for letting that happen. I found her in the next village on my way here and barely recognized her. I thought she had gone mad or had simply run off and was playing daft to avoid being punished. She was living in the back room of a mill and served, I warrant, as not much else than the mill owner's poor, demented trollop."

Joan did not look away from Thomas's increasingly bluish face. "Poor Vinette," she whispered through sudden tears.

"When I heard from the servants here about what had happened, I told them to care for her downstairs, but she somehow drifted off and no one would come up here to seek her. I am sorry."

"It hardly matters now, Roger. It is judgment on me somehow, destined to be saved or not myself. You heard what Thomas has been yelling and what Vinette said, too. My husband who loathes me lies here screaming his hatred because I have loved the prince, and that poor, insane girl down the hall detests me since she thinks I take her dead Pierre whom the prince had hanged over two years ago! Saints, it is just too damn, awful much to bear sometimes!"

He came around the bed to comfort her, but she put a hand up to stop him. "No. I am all right. My husband is dying now and I must care for him. You go out in the hall and sing, Master Roger, not of anything that would distress him but of green woods and riding. No songs of glorious battle or love, only mayhap of sweet springtime coming soon."

He touched her trembling hands for one moment. "Aye, my Lady Joan. And gladly for you."

He went out and closed the door, and shortly after the soothing flow of lute and lyrics began. Between her increasingly frenzied prayers to St. Roch, she clung to the music to keep her sane as Thomas Holland gasped the remnants of his life away in the grinding grip of plague delirium.

Thomas Holland had been buried under the floorstones of the Château's chapel for an entire week before Joan felt the place was safe enough to summon the children back from Madeleine's family's crude little croft near town. None of the servants had been smitten and she herself felt no encroaching disease. She felt nothing. Absolutely nothing.

She ordered the servants to scrub every room he had been in since he'd returned from buying the Yule gifts in Pont-Audemer. All his garments, the bedclothes from his room, even the fine Persian carpet she had burned and the charred remains were buried outside the Château walls. She insisted his squires wash his horse twice with ash-leaf balm to cleanse it. She had the gifts he had brought them that last day he was himself soaked for three days in black willow-bark water to purify any of the vile contagion clinging to them. Even now, she could hear Bella somewhere downstairs tooting that ridiculous horn she so loved, her last—her only—gift from a father who could not love her.

Joan stared up at the too familiar underside of her brocade bed canopy in the solar. A widow at age thirty, her life all turned upside down again. Destined for what? To live on while those about her died over the years? To keep inheriting lands and titles until she was the only one left? To have truly loved only once and to be fated—destined—to never fulfill that love?

Roger Wakeley began to play again outside her door as he had each morn and afternoon while she slept or rested. It was a blessing he had come back. He amused the children and taught them songs, although the boys took much coaxing to sing and eleven-year-old Thomas had lectured Roger that since his lord father had not cared a whit for music, he did not either. Still, the fact that Roger had known both the king and Prince of Wales went a long way toward making Roger acceptable in young Thomas's copper eyes.

She must get up, she told herself, but after three days in bed she still felt listless and separate from the world outside. Had mother felt this way all those years in her solitary room at Liddell? she mused. For the first time she could almost grasp why she must have not wanted to be disturbed or made to feel, not even wanting her own child about to upset the sweet silence.

The children. Of course, she must care for the children.

But over the years the boys would be reared to knighthood in the great houses of the realm as was proper, and Bella would grow to a beauty and be married. And then, in her bed, just like this, Joan, Duchess of Kent, would be alone.

Thomas would inherit the birthright lands in Lancashire one day. In four years on his sixteenth saint's day, he could claim them legally now that his sire was dead. And when she died, John would have Liddell, of course, and this French Château and lands would—

She sat up in bed and pulled the down-filled coverlet up about her shoulders. Bella did not need this place and the boys would own English lands, mayhap even accrue more through favorable marriages if she could arrange it. She did not want this place, ten years of work to improve it notwithstanding. It was French and she was English and besides, now that the Treaty of Brétigny renounced English claims to Normandy, it would be much harder to hold over the years.

She would sell this Château and lands and walk away without another look back at the place where Thomas had died, the place where the Jacquerie had left its cruel mark, the place where dear Marta had died so long ago, and where she had parted from her prince forever. Surely there could be no protest from the Plantagenets that a bereaved widow sold her dead lord's Crécy landholdings and retired to her modest country manorhouse in Kent. She would bother them no more at court, and they would never even hear her name.

Her brain pulsing with excitement for the first time in weeks, in years, she wrapped herself in the huge coverlet and strode barefooted to open the door to the hall. Roger Wakeley looked up amazed from his chair, then a huge grin lit his face to see the look on hers.

"I see my lady, the Duchess Joan of Kent, is back again," he said as his fingers plucked a livelier melody than he had dared to play for days.

"Aye. Could you summon the children and then come back? And ask Renée to come up when she can. I need to bathe and get dressed."

"Your wish is my command, fair lady," he said and surprised her by handing her his lute before he hurried off down the hall.

Holding the lute by its neck, she darted a quick look in her polished mirror on the table. Terrible! Purplish circles under the huge, sad lavender eyes, the cheeks drawn and pale, the hair as wild as a Kentish haystack! She tugged a comb through her tresses and tried to pinch some color into her cheeks.

She sat in a chair by the hearth and wrapped herself more completely in the puffy coverlet, the lute resting in her lap. How long it had been since she had played and sung and meant it. Now, mayhap, at Liddell, she would sing again.

She strummed the four perfectly attuned strings and felt the light, pear-shaped body of the lute reverberate against her thighs. She smiled wistfully despite herself. Aye, for only the love of music and the love of one man had she ever felt her inner being tremble like that, and at least now, she would have one of those loves to cherish.

Almost hypnoticaliy her fingers began to pick out the pensive song which had tormented her these last days, and very low, she sang the words aloud unafraid:

"Sweet passion's pain doth pierce mine heart
  For I have loved thee from the start,
  But foolishly behind high walls
    I hid such proof
    Nor saw this truth.

"Sweet passion's pain doth urge me plead
  That I might be thy love indeed,
  But blindingly and armored bright
    I hid such proof
    Nor saw this truth.

"And now sweet passion's pain doth teach
  That my last chance must be great reach,

For wildly doth Dame Fortune's wheel
  Spin by such proof
  Nor halt for truth.

"Welcome, sweet passion's pain, until
My heart shall recognize its will.
Whatever prophecies proclaim,
  I know such proof,
  Accept this truth."

Although she knew Roger would bring the children in soon, she put the lute down and hurried to her coffer of treasures. Her broken pearls had never been recovered after the looting by the Jacquerie, but she still had the two letters, the dainty beryl ring, and now the two elaborately drawn zodiac birthcharts the old astrologer Morcar had cast for her and Prince Edward years ago. "Map of Joan of Kent of Liddell Manor" one was labeled and the other read, "Map of H. R. H., the Prince of Wales, Plantagenet."

She unrolled them side by side pressing elbows and hands awkwardly to their curling corners to hold them flat. The delicate drawing reminded her of a bull's-eye target for archery: four concentric circles, the two outer ones bearing the astrological symbols with occasional notes in Morcar's spider-web calligraphy.

Aye, just as the prince had said, perfectly aligned in the seventh house of matrimony. On her chart was the sun. That indicated, the prince had told her once at Monbarzon, that her marriage would assume considerable importance with a great widening of social status, surely not a wedding with Thomas Holland. And here, on the prince's chart the sun in good aspect with Mars: success through personal efforts, the prince had said it meant, and obstacles overcome by sheer will power. Ah, but she did not dare to dream!

She let the parchments roll closed noisily as the children came in with Roger Wakeley. As Joan sat back in her chair and rearranged her cocoon of coverlet, Bella climbed up in

521

her lap and Master Roger strummed his retrieved lute gently, playing nothing in particular. The boys stood as if at attention for some dire pronouncement.

"I have wonderful news for you all," she began eagerly. "As soon as we can, we are going to pack our things, sell the Château, and go home to live in Kent at mother's old home of Liddell!"

The boys exchanged silent glances and Bella's smile did not change as she cuddled to her mother.

"But Father is buried here," Thomas managed at last.

"Well, aye, my dear, but we are all English, and you are going to Warwick Castle as squire to Lord Beauchamp this summer anyway. I do not intend to rear you all here in France with no lord in the castle to protect us. We are going home, and I am certain you will all soon love Liddell as much as I do."

"It is nice to visit," John drawled, "but, I just thought this was our home."

It struck her then, harder than she wished to admit, that indeed Château Ruisseau was their Liddell, and brief summer visits to her beloved childhood home in Kent could hardly have changed that. The solid surety she was doing the right thing fled.

"My darlings, I know it is all very sudden, but I have to do what I believe is best for us all now that your father is gone."

"Father went to heaven," Bella piped up wide-eyed, while the boys stood first on one foot then the other.

"Aye, my Bella," Joan said. "I need all of your help now, very much. Thomas and John will carry on the proud Holland name and inherit their own lands someday. I love you all very, very much as your father did and I hope you will help me to do what I believe we need to do."

"I will," John said a little too loudly.

"And you, my dear Thomas?"

"St. Peter's bones, of course, I will, Mother," he answered, "and as you say, I am off to earn my own way this summer anyhow. Besides, in England, there will be more knights about to learn from and I intend to be the very best I can to make Father's name great through my deeds. In England, closer to the court, we might even get to see the king or the prince again, eh, John?"

"Oh, sure! Is the court far from Liddell, Mother?"

Joan's eyes darted behind her sons to Roger Wakeley's carefully composed face. Flustered by this turn of talk, she looked away guiltily but not, she knew, before Roger had seen and understood.

Chapter Twenty-Four

"Edward Plantagenet, Duke of Cornwall, Prince of Wales, now departs this hall!" the House crier's voice bellowed as, amidst blasts of horns and the rumble of lords rising from their seats in fealty, Prince Edward strode from his father's canopied throne on the dais in the great Painted Chamber of Westminster Palace. He often took his royal sire's place at Westminster of late—on the throne as well as in discussions, as the Houses of Parliament struggled to understand and deal with the complicated terms of the Treaty of Brétigny by which years of hostilities with the French were to be ended. The Treaty, signed by both kings last May, encompassed a labyrinth of negotiated territories, ransoms, hostages, and, of most important interest to the Prince of Wales, the future control of the huge southern French province of Aquitaine of which he would soon be proclaimed governor. He welcomed the duties, the challenge. He welcomed anything that gave him power over others in the hope it might help him assert power over himself.

Nickolas Dagworth and Hugh Calveley met Prince Edward in the outer hall already crowded with his retainers and companions. The prince handed his crown to one squire and his purple velvet and ermine cloak to another without breaking stride with his two boon companions close at his heels.

"A marvelous explanation of strategy," Dagworth said, hardly nonplused at all by the usually quick way the prince exited Westminster or anywhere else. When he was done with one task lately, the prince simply dropped it and plunged capably into the next, Dagworth marveled. No wonder the aging king had come to rely on this son as well as John of Lancaster so much these last few years.

"No flattery from you, Nick," His Grace was saying as he refused an offered cloak to cut the stiff January wind off the Thames and mounted his tall black destrier. "Explaining that scramble of clauses in the Treaty is as complicated as a woman's whims. Mount up, anyone who is coming. We are off for the house on Fish Street!"

His band of closest friends and advisors scurried to their mounts after hearing where they were headed this time. At first, in the scramble, only four guards and the two standard bearers kept a good pace with Nickolas Dagworth and his prince as they headed north past Whitehall toward the city. The chill breeze from the river flapped the prince's proud banners and mussed his tawny, uncovered head. Bold and reckless, he was, Dagworth thought, as if he dared the weather, Parliament, his royal sire—fate itself—to stand in his way. Yet the man was frenzied too, consumed by some inner drive that plagued him.

From Charing Cross, along the Strand and Fleet Street, the cheering crowds began. Some Londoners who spotted the prince's entourage leaned from windows; others turned in their tracks of daily duties to bellow their blessings, and Dagworth noted how the prince acknowledged his popularity, yet almost never accepted it. Word of their entourage, as usual, spread like the wind, and the crowds continued to swell.

"They love you, Your Grace," he shouted ahead to the waving, nodding prince.

"Aye, for now, Nick. They think times are good for their Black Prince of Crécy, Poitiers, and Brétigny. But, St. George, where is there to go in their hearts after all that but down?"

Cheers of "Long live the Prince of Wales" and "Poitiers! Poitiers!" nearly drowned out Dagworth's attempt to answer as they turned onto narrow Fish Street.

"There will be other great days yet, Your Grace! Aquitaine! Someday you will marry and then there is the throne—"

The prince's blue eyes glittered coldly as his retort cut off Dagworth in midthought. "I need not your predictions on my future, triumphant or otherwise, Nick. I used to think new glories awaited, but now, sometimes I tire of it all."

Unsmiling, but still nodding to acknowledge the yelling, running people, Prince Edward dismounted before his narrow, three-storied stone house and went immediately in. He saw Dagworth sit astride without dismounting for a moment. Hell's gates, let the man sulk if he could not abide being put in his place. Let him sit out there in the street like a sullen jackass and listen to the cries of capricious crowds. The man might as well plan his own coronation or wedding as dare to speak of those two events for the Prince of Wales!

The prince tossed his riding gloves where he always left them on the oak table in the slate entryhall. He went into the oak-paneled, first floor parlor where a low fire burned. He slammed the door, tossed a new log on—which shot a shower of sparks at him—and collapsed in a tall-backed leather chair.

As much as there was to do, he felt the oppression, once again, of having nothing to do. Duties here in London always beckoned, overseeing his vast land holdings too, seeing to the rearing of his two illegitimate sons, enjoying numerous women to slake his occasional lusts—nothing was enough. Even the vast remodeling of his favorite palace at Kennington across the river bored him now, and he had not checked on its progress for weeks. He missed his friend Sir John Chandos who had been sent to France as king's lieutenant to expedite land transfers from the Treaty, and he wished desperately he might have gone himself. At least then he would have had a reason to travel besides just visiting places. St. George, he might have even gone through Normandy!

Jeannette's face as he had seen her last over a year and a half ago, all teary-eyed, stubborn, ever exquisitely beautiful, teased his memory from the leaping flames of the fire into which he stared. She had claimed she loved him, only him, but she had sent him away without a caress, without letting him do what they had both surely longed for more than life itself. And so, he had sent her Lord Holland home and forced himself never to write to her or speak her name. Only once, last summer, when his sister Isabella had heard the Hollands were visiting in Kent and had mentioned inviting them to Windsor, had he made a fool of himself by furiously forbidding her to do so. And then, though Isabella's shocked face showed she knew the truth of his tormented heart at last, he had merely stalked off to come back here and buried himself under the welcome weight of his duties once again.

A sharp rap on the door startled him. "Aye? Enter. So you decided to come in, Nick. Back for more of my bitter moods?"

The tall, black-haired man entered with a parchment scroll in his hand. The old, jagged battle scar on his brown cheek looked especially white as his face suffused redder.

"No, Your Grace. I apologize for my hasty words out there. This missive is from Chandos in France. The messenger rode up with it even as I sat out there on your cheering front doorstoop."

The prince held out his hand for the parchment, and Dagworth stepped closer towering over him. "Sit, Nick. You would like to call me out for my vile temper of late, admit it. Mayhap that is what I need—a few cracked heads in a joust or some new voluptuous bedwarmer but, unlike the indefatigable Sir Nickolas Dagworth, I even tire of that. What the hell lasting good is a woman's body unless you love the woman inside? That is my real motto lately, you know—not 'I serve.'"

Dagworth grinned despite himself, nervous at how close that must come to the truth of his liege lord's heart—the heart that no one ever saw into, no one at all. He watched the prince's austere, handsome face as his eyes scanned the letter from John Chandos. The prince frowned, startled, stared closer. Dagworth sat up straighter on the bench. Anybody who knew Chandos realized his written hand was atrocious to decipher, but the prince must be good enough at it by now to not stare agape like that. This was surely something else.

Dagworth leapt to his feet when the prince did, but only stood stock-still like a wooden quintain dummy when His Grace began to pace back and forth before the hearth, muttering. He unrolled the parchment further and stared closely at it again, then cast it into the leaping flames at his feet.

"Bad tidings, my lord prince? The territory transfer of Aquitaine has gone awry?"

"What? That. No, I am certain it is fine. He says naught of that. Nick, have them fetch fresh horses. The plague has gone through France and Thomas Holland is dead of it a month ago. I will be right down. Have the horses and anyone who will ride waiting in the street. I knew it. I knew it! Old Morcar was right!"

The prince ran from the room and the door banged open into the oak-paneled wall as Nick Dagworth stared after him. "Old Morcar? Who is old Morcar? But Thomas Holland—that means Joan of Kent again! Damn, but I should have known," he said aloud as a new realization crashed in on him. "But then is she not in Normandy? Hell's gates, I do not relish a cold ride clear to Normandy!" he muttered and hurried out to call everyone together.

But it was not Normandy they headed for at a pounding pace that increasingly blustery, late January day—it was Windsor Castle where the queen and Princess Isabella had been in residence this winter while the Plantagenet men kept to business in London. By dusk, they had rattled stiff and saddlesore into the vast castle's gray stone embrace of walls and towers. And before the prince's arrival had even been announced to the queen, let alone the Princess Isabella whose chambers he now sought, he was striding still dressed in the same dusty garments he had worn to sessions in Parliament ages ago today.

His exhausted retinue fell away like flies either voluntarily or at his bequest as he approached Isabella's suite in the southeast stretch of towers and rooms. Strangely, no guards were at her door and no flighty butterfly ladies clustered about the hall. She probably was with the queen and had taken all her retainers there, but he had no intention of seeing his mother until this business with Isabella was done and could not be undone.

He knocked twice and lifted the doorlatch expecting to see a deserted room. But he heard a muffled noise, a voice and stepped inside the dimly lighted, large chamber.

"Isabella, *mignonne*, it is Edward."

A flutter of movement, a gasp, a shriek seized his attention from the distant corner of the room—no, in the bed. In a flurry of wild blond hair, his sister Isabella sat up in bed and a man's broad-shouldered, naked torso bent close to protect her nakedness.

"Isabella! What the hell! Who is *he*?"

"Oh, Blessed Mary's veil, my lord, how dare you just come in here!" she shrieked. "Oh, how could you, Edward?"

Incensed at first to see who the man was, the prince noisily drew his sword as he approached the bed only to see an ire matching his own cause Isabella to shake her fist nearly in his face. "Oh hell, my lord, you ruin everything! If it is not you, it is our beloved, overbearing father! Oh, dearest Ingelram, I am so ashamed, I could die!"

The man's nervous, dark eyes fixed on Edward's sword; he pulled Isabella's quaking shoulders closer into the protective crook of one arm.

"Ingleram?" Edward floundered. "Also known as Enguerrand de Coucy? So—one of England's most expensive hostages from the Treaty exchange and in bed with the princess royal!"

"Just stop it, my lord prince," Isabella scolded between

sniffles, and furiously tossed a little silk pillow his way. "Obviously, I invited the man here and obviously, I sent everyone away, even the bothersome guards. I am twenty-eight, you know, and sick to death of having no one to love. And I do love Ingelram de Coucy!"

"And I do love the princess, my lord prince, I swear it," the sloe-eyed, handsome youth declared.

Edward spit out a string of oaths, but his sword arm went slack, and he stalked away from the bed to sit slumped over staring at the fire. He ought to challenge the French bastard, to run him through or at least call him out. The king would have. Any chivalrous, protective knight, any elder brother worth his salt would have and yet his initial outrage had ebbed to—damn them, they had looked so happy, so glowing and defiant even caught like that, he felt only an aching jealousy he could not be that way with his Jeannette. Now. All these years. Always!

He heard them scrambling to rise and garb themselves behind him. Low firelight danced along the sword blade resting across his splayed knees and then he actually smiled. Now, at least, Isabella would have to be his ally, willing or not, for she needed his good will as desperately as he needed hers.

"Your Grace, my lord Prince of Wales," Ingelram de Coucy's aristocratic French voice addressed him.

Edward rose, turned, and fought to actually stifle a grin at the young man's obvious discomposure at being so caught—or mayhap, dismay at his slipshod, slovenly appearance at dressing so quickly or at vacating his obviously delightful resting place before the deed was fully done.

"I realize, my lord prince, I am here in England under the aegis of the Treaty as a hostage. However, should you wish to challenge me, to call me out, then *certainement*, I shall comply fully."

Isabella, wrapped in a silk robe with her hair disheveled, ran over to seize de Coucy's grandly gesturing arm. "No, no, my lord. Your Grace, Edward, no fighting or I swear you can fight me too!"

"No, my Isabella, no fighting over this. You see, I approve of love—and I need to talk to you alone."

"Oh, Edward, thank you, thank you! I knew you would understand. I love him so. And this is our first time, I swear it!"

"And do you swear, my dear little sister, that it will not happen again?" Edward said, his voice suddenly gone light.

Isabella's fawning flurry of words halted, and de Coucy asked quietly, "You do not jest with us, Your Grace? *Oui*, I love Her Grace, the princess and would wed with her *certainement*."

Isabella's sharp gasp told Edward they had discussed nothing of the sort. He turned to study the serious, limpid-eyed young man, heir to vast title holdings and a fine aristocratic lineage from just south of Paris.

"I do not jest with you, de Coucy, if you do not jest with my sister."

"Never, Your Grace!"

The man was arrogant from the tilt of his sleek eyebrows to his jeweled, clasped fists, Edward thought, but Isabella had been so gaily brittle, so hurt all these years since another Frenchman had jilted her at Bruges that this could do well enough. And from the glint in her blue eyes, he knew that it had better.

"How old are you then, Ingelram?" the prince pursued.

"Twenty, Your Grace."

"And unwed, unbetrothed?"

"*Oui*."

"And you would wed with the princess?"

"*Certainement*, Your Grace, I have sworn it, as soon as we can convince the great English king, the princess' royal sire, *certainement*, on my word as a de Coucy!"

"Then I apologize for the untoward interruption, but I have need of the princess' clever Plantagenet brain now for arrangements of my own. Matters of state."

"Of course, Your Grace. I am proud to know you, proud

to serve."

Suddenly embarrassed at his concluding *double entendre*, Ingelram de Coucy bowed to Isabella and with as stately a gait as he could manage, fled the room.

"I will kill you, kill you, if I lose him over this, my lord," Isabella's usually lilting voice threatened.

"Saint George, but that threat is a far cry from 'oh, thank you, thank you, dear brother' of a moment ago."

"Do not dare smirk at me! I do not give a tinker's damn if you are the Prince of Wales, the next Plantagenet king or lord of the whole universe, Edward! I love him and I want him."

"Believe me, I understand and sympathize. And I will help you get him if you settle down and stop hissing at me." He smiled again maddeningly, she thought, as he leaned his hips back on her polished dressing table. It struck her then for the first time that he was happy; he was enjoying this and somehow the too familiar pent-up tenseness was gone from his austerely handsome mouth.

"By the Virgin's Veil, my lord prince, we have not had such a *contretemps* since you used to always order me around years ago, you know. So then, I shall forgive you for this terrible blunder and you shall tell me what you are doing here all unannounced and unabashed. Damn, I know I just forgot to lock the stupid door. Do I have a promise?"

"You had best beware trying to force advantageous promises from one of the architects of the mazelike Treaty of Brétigny, Isabella, but, aye, it is a promise. Quite frankly, *ma chérie*, if I did not need your help tit for tat as you need mine, I might have bashed young Ingelram's elegant French brains out or hauled both of you before the king, but I know what it is to throw all caution to the winds, and so, I seek your help."

Isabella folded her arms across her full breasts. "Is it something about our Jeannette then?" she ventured. "Last time I brought up her name to say I would invite her here you almost *brained* me."

"Aye, it is Jeannette again, and I do want just that—for

you to bring her here. I received word only today from John Chandos in France that Lord Holland has died of plague in Normandy. I am asking—beseeching you—that whatever it takes, however long it takes, I need her here to have my chance."

"Here? Under the king and queen's noses to rile them all up again?"

"It must be done that way, openly, deliberately, honorably."

"Then you mean to marry her?"

"Hush. Do not screech so. What did you think I meant, dimwit—a little roll in the hay before she finds her next husband! Or mayhap I should send all my guards and retainers away and have her come to my palace chamber. I have loved her for years, Isabella, only her, and I will have no other. It is destined."

"Destined? Holy Virgin, I admit I have seen it over the years how you have felt about each other and how she has fought it. Do you believe she will fight it no more?"

"It will not matter in the end. I can convince her. Only, I must have her here, to court her properly. If she fusses about coming right away, I thought we could entice her somehow."

"Entice? Such as?"

"She has no close family and Holland left none. Her sons need sponsors, and you realize she has a blond daughter with a Plantagenet face named after you?"

"The child—she is not yours, my lord?"

"No, sister. Not mine, but the mother must be and then heirs of my own for the throne. I thought to get her here we could offer to be godparents to her fatherless children, you and I."

"Aye. The king and queen could hardly protest that since Jeannette has Plantagenet blood, too. But the king is likely to hold up the proclamation of you as Duke of Aquitaine if he catches wind of all this, is he not?"

"St. George, Isabella, I should not have teased de Coucy about needing your wily brain. Indeed the king might try that, but I know what I need to fill my life and it is not another title or duty however hard I have worked for every foot of precious French soil we now claim. And you, sister. If father threatened, let us say, to rescind the entire funding for your vast wardrobe, could you be extorted to give up your de Coucy?"

"Never!"

"Then we are agreed, and in league to the end on this. What help I need to get Jeannette here I shall have and whatever aid you need to keep de Coucy you shall have, parental or national strictures be damned."

Isabella's face broke into a beautiful smile, and she clasped her hands like a little girl who had just been given the most wonderful of presents. "Aye, Edward. And someday, we shall tell our children of this pact and they will laugh and wonder why we made such a heroic story of it. I only know I will never, never be hurt in love again."

"Nor I, Isabella. Whatever it takes—nor I."

They drank a toast of sweet wine Isabella had obviously meant for her de Coucy, and talked, and laid out their battle plans far past midnight.

Because of a thunderstorm, it had been far past midnight when Joan had finally gone to bed, but she tossed and turned fitfully in the solar bed at Liddell, her mind full of racing thoughts. On the morrow, the morrow, she would part from her eldest son, her dead husband's pride, as he went north to Warwickshire to begin to serve the great Beauchamp family—the first, traditional step toward knighthood. Parting from him—admitting he was old enough to go— would be difficult. She dreaded the farewell, but sleep eluded her for another reason too. Today, by royal messenger, had come a letter from Princess Isabella.

The poor, exhausted messenger had been clear to Normandy to seek her and their paths had somehow crossed at sea, so a necessary reply to the letter issued over two months ago was long overdue. It was mayhap the invitation, the sign, she had prayed for and yet its actual arrival with the silk ribbons and red royal seal terrified her. Come to visit as soon as you can, it had said. Princess Isabella had offered the Prince of Wales and herself as godparents to her now fatherless sons. And Isabella had closed with the reverberating words, "My dear brother and I desire both to see you and to renew our long and close relationships."

Saints, she thought, rolling over in bed again and punching her goose-down pillow repeatedly. "Desire to see you" and "our long and close relationships"—when it came to the prince, that could mean anything. How desperately she wanted—needed—to see him now that she was really able to love him with good conscience, but she would die before she ever consented to be his mistress again. And yet, she knew when she saw him, when she looked into those crystalline blue eyes or breathed in that heady scent of bergamot he always wore—before he even touched her, she would be utterly lost in love.

She flopped onto her back in the big bed and pressed her hands to her flat belly. When he looked at her—it had always been so—his gaze burned to her very core and set her most private fantasies ablaze. It was as though, in one raking glance, he stripped her garments from her and pulled her to his strong, hard body.

She moaned and shifted her legs tightly together. Oh, no, no, not this treacherous, pulling tide of passion. She felt her nipples leap taut against the diaphanous Flemish gown she had taken to wearing again at night because it felt so luxurious and somehow comforting. Only now, she recalled she had worn such a gown that night so long ago when he had taken her to the little fisherman's cottage near Calais and made love to her until dawn.

Tears of longing, of frustration trembled on her lashes. How forceful, how direct, yet tender he had always been when he had touched her, even from that first time he had pulled her on his lap in the private garden at Windsor. But then the queen and her own brother Edmund had discovered them and all the trouble with his parents had begun. And now—would not the king and queen be just as disapproving of their love as they had ever been?

The flow of feeling continued, rolling over her in caressing waves, throwing taunting pictures and teasing memories at her tired brain. Those stolen, precious days they had spent at Monbarzon after they had first come together the night she arrived, he had rained tender, velvet kisses all over her before he had moved to take her again: kisses down her throat, across her aching breasts to pull her nipples to hard peaks of desire, down her belly and between her thighs—

"Oh!" she moaned aloud and sat up in the soft bed with the coverlets pulled awry all around her. It was as if she could feel the actual touch of his lips, his warm, calloused hands, his plunging again and again to fill her desperate need for him.

She dragged the covers off and got out of bed. The cresset lamp had gutted out but there was moonlight by which to reread Isabella's letter if she went to the window. She took the parchment from the table and unrolled it slowly in the shaft of moonglow. Too dark to see the words but she knew what it said and that it meant a chance for them.

Aye, she would go back to Windsor despite the bad memories there which threatened the good thoughts. She had to try, to face the king and queen, to risk all to just know that it might be possible. In the morn, as soon as they had bid Thomas and his guard from Warwick a farewell, she would write to the princess and then, mayhap, it would be too late to ever venture back.

King Edward sat hunched over papers he was signing: Edward R III . . . Edward R III, while his scribe at his velvet elbow carefully sanded each official signature. When the door of the conference room at Windsor opened, and he heard his eldest son's distinctive, quick tread, he did not look up at first. He did not relish this interview or its dangerous implication, and his clever son would know it soon enough. He signed Edward R III on the next crinkly parchment page before he looked up.

"Good. You came. You have been off riding to the horn so much in the Great Park, I have hardly seen you unless I summon you. Sit, my son."

Edward sat stiffly in the chair across the big, littered conference table as though he knew something dire was coming. He watched one more careful Edward R III sprawl across an elaborately scripted page. His royal sire shoved the rest of the pile of letters to the side. "Enough for now, Will. Leave us," the king mumbled to his hovering scribe.

"Aye, Your Grace." The thin, young man bowed to both king and prince and went out on cat's feet. The king leaned back in his chair and sighed.

"Actually, Your Grace," Prince Edward began in the tense silence, "the hunting has not been good. I rather tire of it."

"Hunting. Oh, aye, that. I did mention that, did I not? And since the hunting at Great Park is disappointing, you have chosen to hunt elsewhere, is that it? Come, Edward, we shall not joust over this," he challenged his son when he saw a frown crush the proud brow so much the mirror of his own. "Do not pretend you do not catch my drift. Isabella let slip today she has invited the widowed Duchess of Kent to come to court—and the lady has accepted."

"Aye. Then you have heard the news too that Isabella and I have offered our services as godparents to the two Holland heirs. The elder has already gone off to Warwick to the Beauchamps a fortnight ago, so I hear."

"Really? So you hear! And are you not in contact more directly with the lady then, too?"

"No, Your Grace, but since you have reared me to be a warrior like yourself and since you do not wish to joust, I shall tell you flat out—I shall be in close contact soon with Jeannette if I have my way."

He watched his father's sharp, blue eyes widen at his

blatant admission. Years ago such a look of dismay on his royal sire's face would have sent him into paroxysms of activity to amend the fault, to fulfill any command. But now, for this, he just met steel gaze with steel gaze. He had waited for this attack to come, and he only hoped it might save Isabella or even Jeannette some of the brunt of the battle later.

"She is hardly suitable for you, Edward. A widow with three children by a knight of the northern, small-landed gentry who—"

"She is descended from the same royal grandsire as I, my lord father—indeed, your own father, King Edward II."

"Aye. Then there is that too. If you ever considered marriage, you would need papal dispensation for your ties to her by second and third degree."

"Permission is granted by His Holiness freely and frequently, Your Grace. All the simple complications aside, I have thought perhaps the biggest stumbling block is Joan of Kent's long-held conviction that you let Roger Mortimer and that slippery bastard de Maltravers dispose of her father."

The king stood and moved to stand behind his tall-backed chair, so Edward, who never sat in his presence, rose also. The king's hands gripped the chairback so hard his fingers went stark white, but his voice was deceptively low.

"That is all long, long past. The maid was deceived by that insane mother of hers who locked herself in some little room at their manor for years before she died. No one thinks on that now that de Maltravers disappeared over two years ago and no one needs to discuss it with him now. It is over—over and that woman need pursue such treason no longer!"

"She does not pursue the treason, Your Grace, although it almost killed her once."

"I never thought to harm her—never! I only told her to keep her foolish thoughts to herself or she could join de Maltravers in exile."

"I am sure you told her such—and more, but I meant not that you ever threatened her with death over it. She was certainly sent off to exile anyway, was she not? Married to Holland and exiled for a price, and so I have been without her for so many years—"

King Edward's mouth dropped open in surprise, the prince thought, a king who always hid his real feelings so cunningly. It was suddenly as if he were seeing his father for the first time.

"And for so many years, you have longed for this woman, separated from her, while she was married to another?" the king floundered as if some great illumination shone on him at last. "So long ago since she first came to court. You have been longing for one particular woman when you could have had any—have had many? This is why you never lifted a finger to help with marriage arrangements? This is why you choose now to coerce your sister and go behind my back to gainsay my wishes?"

"I will have Joan of Kent, my lord king—if she will have me."

"*If?* Saint George, boy," the king shouted in a half-laugh, "but would that not be just like the little vixen. Shall I pin my hopes on that then? There are French princesses who will gladly have you—and solidify the new alliance, too."

"One of the reasons I have been so zealous for the Treaty of Brétigny to be completed and ratified, Your Grace, is because it serves as far better Anglo-French binding than any bloodless political marriage ever could."

The sullen blush of controlled anger suffused the king's fair skin as he stared almost awestruck at his son and heir. "And Aquitaine?" he said low.

Again the tension of tugging wills nearly crackled with energy between the two tall blond men. "And Aquitaine?" the prince parried.

"Holy saints, Edward," the king shouted as if he would lose control of himself at last. "For the past few months I

539

have been right on the verge of announcing to the world I intend to name you Duke of Aquitaine, to send you there to rule the southern half of our long-coveted France until you shall rule here someday in my stead! I cannot allow the scandal of your marriage to a recent widow, a woman engaged to one man once, then wed with another—aye, petitions for her fair hand have nearly flooded the Pope's desk before—I simply cannot allow the announcement of that marriage to conflict with your becoming ruler of Aquitaine. Indeed, my son and proud heir, you will have to chose!"

Prince Edward fought to keep his own volatile Plantagenet temper in check. Often in the exhaustion of a fight on the battlefield he had seen the victor was the man who kept his head however hard his blood boiled. His voice, when he answered, was controlled but much too strident and too loud.

"I *have* chosen, my lord father. I cannot love Aquitaine, or need Aquitaine the way I love and need this woman. I cannot fill my soul with Aquitaine—or get sons by it for our family's throne."

"But all you have spent—years of work, battles, flaming victories for France—"

"That is just it. Hell's gates, Your Grace, I am thirty-one this June and I have done all that, but I will not ignore my destiny to love her! The people cheer me in the streets and I cannot make myself care anymore. I am contentious to my servants, bitter to my men, and have never been yet able to accept how the Plantagenets sold Jeannette to first Holland, then Salisbury, then Holland again. Isabella is like a mirror of me—she flits about and longs for love, rushing here and there to avoid being truly alone—"

"We do not speak of the Princess Isabella here!"

"No? Do we not? Then let us speak of that other one you mentioned but awhile ago and thought I would not heed. If de Maltravers disappeared over two years ago, then, of

540

course, no one may speak with him now, but that is not how you meant those words of him, is it, Your Grace?"

The wily, blue eyes in his father's face darted off, then refocused in slits of pure challenge. "St. George, my boy, state your meaning blunt."

"You spoke of de Maltravers as if you knew where he was. You implied he was quite well, my lord father."

"Quite well!" the king sputtered, his eyes shifting nervously again, so that the prince sensed he had the advantage in this dangerous skirmish now. "Holy saints, I shall explain your 'quite well' then and tell you why no one shall ever question de Maltravers again. Two years ago in the spring, he came back to England from Flanders to see his wife in Dorset. I knew he did from time to time, of course, but he stayed not long and it hardly mattered. But it seems he had a vile accident, fell down some stairs or had a seizure of some sort. I never did get all the sad details. At any rate, the poor wretch is greatly paralyzed, his entire left side, and his speech is dreadfully slurred. I sent a priest down to see him in Dorset and it is true."

"John de Maltravers is in Dorset?"

"Hell, would you begrudge him that, my son? He served me well enough once, and I choose to let him die at home in his own bed when and if God wills it."

"Served you once well enough? Not only those years as liaison in Flanders, you mean."

The king heaved a great sigh; his tawny, silvered head drooped; he reseated himself slowly in his chair as if he had capitulated. When his ice-blue eyes threatened tears, he hunched over his quill pen and slid the stack of unsigned papers before him once again.

"Kings, as you will learn all too soon, my self-righteous son, have much to do, too damn many things to take the time to worry about them. But for foreign enemies, this crown has not had to fear traitors for years. Not since I allowed my fond, dear uncle Edmund of Kent to be tried and beheaded."

541

His pen scratched out his name on the paper as the prince standing over the table held his breath.

"Aye, it was treason, my son, for Edmund of Kent would have even roused the populous and my fledgling advisors whose good will I needed desperately to move against Mortimer who had so bewitched my lady mother to become his—paramour. She was besotted with him, and I had to take the crown from them by force. I was only fourteen. In truth, my guilt over my uncle's sad death was not that he did not deserve it but that he had betrayed me and yet that I owed him much for what he did for me."

"Did for you? But you just said he was a traitor to you."

"Aye, but he was sadly misled—a fond, trusting man. And it was his defection which made me realize I must strike soon to seize my throne from Mortimer. When I heard how the man with his de Maltravers at his side had literally rammed the call for Edward of Kent's immediate execution down the throats of Parliament, then sitting here at Windsor, I knew I had to strike and soon. I have my uncle, your Joan's father, to thank for that precious lesson despite his treason."

"Then, Father, for that debt, will you not bless my love for her?"

The pen scraped erratically across another parchment which he shoved away. "Mayhap. I shall think on it. But do not deceive yourself about her. She is prideful, willful, and stubborn!"

"And are we not all so, Your Grace, and does not that as well as her fine royal bloodline make her the perfect choice for England's Princess of Wales? I will have sons by her, my lord father, or none to sit the throne at all. Declare my brother Lancaster Duke of Aquitaine if you will, let the people shout his name in the streets. If the lady will have me, I am hers alone."

When his father stared up at him almost vacantly without a word, Edward, Prince of Wales, bowed and left the room. The door closed solidly. The king stared down at the last parchment he had signed and the French words seemed to rise and blur before his eyes. Unheedful of the hard work it had taken his scribe to complete the order, he tore off a huge square corner of it and dipped his quill in the ink pot again.

"My dearest Philippa,

The princely walls were attacked, but hardly breeched. Your son is adamant. Despite it all, his almost desperate love for her touched my own tired heart. It seems our only hope lies with the lady herself, but who can predict the wild wind?

How my thoughts turned to the old days, my Philippa, when he spoke of his passion for her. Tonight after council, plan for me to visit you.

Your fond husband,
Edward R III

Chapter Twenty-Five

A sultry, mid-July threatened rain on the day the Prince of Wales had awaited for so long. Below his view across the twisting green ribbon of Thames lay Windsor Castle in all her haughty grandeur. From this distance, the watchtowers seemed to beckon like stony fingers; the vast sweep of walls circled the central keep like rings around an inner target. Aye, that was what it reminded him of. At last, he was an arrow shooting straight for the inevitable joining with the core of his desires, Jeannette, down there at Windsor waiting for him.

He knew by his messengers she had arrived from Liddell Manor at Windsor three days ago as she had promised in her last letter to Isabella. Meanwhile, for almost five weeks the king had managed to keep his heir apparent busy on important royal errands to remind him who he was. Only yesterday the prince had returned from Calais across the Channel where he had finally delivered the French King John back to his nation after another massive exchange of hostages and ransoms.

"But now let His Grace try it," he said aloud, oblivious to the stares his men exchanged whenever he talked aloud lately to no one in particular. "St. George, I am here to stay a good while and let him try to send me elsewhere then!"

He spurred his huge black mount Sable faster down the incline into the valley sheltering the town huddled about the castle's gray stone ramparts. His retainers, squires, standard bearers, and the ever-present Nick Dagworth soon left their train of packhorses and handlers behind in a fine trail of dust.

Amidst the usual cheers in the streets, they clattered into Windsor straight through the Lower Ward and past the Round Tower to the Upper Ward where they dismounted noisily. Prince Edward swung his sharp glance around the nearly deserted cobbled area; his blond hair prickled along the base of his scalp and at the back of his bronzed neck as though he could feel her eyes already on him. But no. At first perusal, at least, the windows fronting the ward looked blank and no lovely white face with hair the color of champagne gazed out the leaded panes set ajar to catch any breeze in this heavy heat.

After all, it was nearly evenmeal time and courtiers might already be gathering in the Great Hall. Damn, but he should have pushed his entourage harder; he did not intend to be reunited with Jeannette after all this time at a public gathering where everyone could gawk and whisper.

Although he knew fully well what a fine suite of rooms she had been given in the wing close to his sister's chambers as they had planned, he headed not for those, but to see his accomplice, Isabella. He did not have far to go, for the laughing princess rounded the first turn of stairs, draped on the elegant silk and jeweled arm of young Ingelram de Coucy.

"My Lord Edward," her musical voice chimed, "I knew you would be here today. I said so, did I not, my Ingelram, that no storm on the Channel like the one threatening here today would stop him once he got rid of that red-haired giant, your King John le Bon?" She gave her brother one of her lightning quick hugs, then stepped back to take de Coucy's arm again.

"*Certainement*, Your Grace, Prince Edward, that is what *ma demoiselle charmante* said—that and more."

Even his instinctive mistrust of this proud French peacock could not stop the prince from returning de Coucy's sly grin.

"St. George, my dear de Coucy, but you are learning, you are learning."

"And you, Your Grace, are a vile tease as usual," Isabella pouted, amused by her often stern brother's blatantly buoyant mood. "My Ingelram and I are off to evenmeal and then we had thought to stroll the ramparts if it does not rain. And you, my brother, do you expect to sit with anyone special in the hall tonight or would you like to join us? Our lord father has taken to giving us great signs and suspicious, sideways looks of late though he pretends he hardly cares a whit if we keep to our own end of the table, but we will soon have company enough on that, I warrant, when you find your Jeannette."

"Enough teasing of your own, my pet," the prince warned Isabella. "I know you can give out as well as receive when you have a mind to. Now, where is she?"

"*She*, Your Grace, went for a walk outside over half an hour ago. I am surprised you did not see her as you came in."

"Around the grounds? Such as where? Unguarded?"

"I believe so. I am certain she would not venture outside the grounds, my lord prince, truly, but she is so moody of late and takes it into her head to just go off alone sometimes, though I am certain your arrival will change all that. She was dressed for dinner in brightest green brocade so I am certain she has not gone far. A few drops of this threatening rain would simply ruin her gown and she used to be almost as fussy about fashions as I."

"I will be in to dinner later then, even though word will spread soon enough I am back from Calais." He nodded to de Coucy, dropped a fast kiss on Isabella's rouged and powdered cheek and spun to hurry back down the curving stairs ahead of them.

Isabella had looked absolutely glowing and that made him move faster despite the way the clattering of his spurs on the stairs must tell the couple above that he was nearly running. Love—this great shooting of hot passion through every vein, this livening of the senses—had come at last to Isabella, too.

It made him happy for her but even more desperate for himself.

A few folk hurried or strolled the Upper Ward, but no slender blonde in brightest green brocade. To random greetings or pointed stares, he strode the cobbled length of courtyard in his full riding regalia, despite the persistent, clinging heat. He could feel the leather jerkin over his tunic stick to his back muscles as he walked faster. Then, suddenly, the walls of Windsor reverberated from their very foundations with the low roll of thunder.

Under the circular, crenelated Round Tower, he stopped to scan the Inner Ward from the Norman Gate. Surely, she would not have come down this far toward the city gates, and yet, when had he ever predicted Jeannette aright?

He stopped to reason it out as the first big drop of rain plopped on his leather jerkin and deep thunder rolled again. If she had gone to walk alone, there were three places she might favor, but one of them was in view of the royal apartments and she would probably not go there. Besides, she might harbor bad memories of the little private garden where she had been caught once on his lap by the queen or of that little trysting place just outside the postern gate where he had first tried to take her and all hell had broken loose.

"St. George, but I should have asked Isabella what sort of humor she has been in since she has been here," he scolded himself, and despite the rain, hurried down into the Lower Ward to investigate the third spot.

The Curfew Tower loomed over his head as a band of knights waved and shouted to him. When they had passed, he turned his back on the ward almost furtively and stepped into the tiny alcove with the recessed wooden doorway which led to the irregular, narrow little area on the other side. The door creaked open. From the top of the flight of stone steps, he saw Jeannette instantly.

She stood in the middle of the little area in a green gown that shocked the gray encompassing walls to muteness. She leaned against his old wooden quintain post now stripped of the swinging arm against which he had often done furious battle. She leaned—and, in the pelting rain, she actually embraced—that rough, dirty wooden post as if it were a person.

Oblivious to the sprinkles, even as she, he moved down the stone steps. Her slender back was to him and her lifted arms accentuated the narrow waist and the swell of her rounded hips. His heart pounded in his ears to outdo the patter of rain on his leather jerkin. He hoped, he prayed, that her embrace of that stalwart quintain post was a reaching out for a memory of him!

"Jeannette."

She stiffened against the post only a mere six feet away now after all this time. "Jeannette, my sweetheart, it is raining and you cannot simply stand out here. This whole courtyard swims in wretched mud and mire when it rains. Do you not remember?"

She did not move toward him as he had hoped but clung tighter to the post and swiveled her elegantly coiffed, uncovered head to face him. Then she lowered her arms and curtsied, one now-mottled green brocade shoulder touching the post as if for support. He could not be certain in the rain, but he believed she had been crying. He wanted to embrace her, he wanted to say so much, but they both simply stood and stared as if awestruck in the rain.

"Aye, my Lord Edward, I do remember," she said at last when he could not recall when he had said to her.

He took her elbow and escorted her up the steps and under the narrow stone arch over the door. Sheltered there from the increasing deluge in the courtyard, they each leaned against opposite stone pillars and gazed into the other's eyes.

"So very long, Jeannette."

"Aye. Over two years this time."

"And so long since we first met here in this courtyard. You were holding for dear life onto that quintain post just now, my Jeannette. Were you remembering when you came here all those years ago and saw me charging hellbent against it?"

Her beautiful lavender eyes lowered, then rose to meet his steady gaze again. Saints, she thought, one mere touch on my elbow, those devouring eyes like that and I am undone already, but she said only the other truth so she did not make a fool of herself instantly at his booted and spurred feet.

"In truth, Your Grace, I came here for another reason. My mother told me once, you see, that in this little quintain yard, it was long ago that—it was here they built a scaffold and executed my lord father."

His heart fell to his feet at her ominous words and teary-eyed face. He had hoped for so much—smiles, laughter, a welcoming, clinging embrace. And here was a barrier again rising up before their love, their union he had planned so hard to attain.

He reached out both big hands to touch her trembling shoulders. "I am sorry, Jeannette. I did not know it had been here."

"I did not either—at first. It rained the first day we were here, too. Do not think, my lord prince, I carry only sad memories about in my foolish head. I wanted to be here to come to terms with not only my father's death, but I was thinking of us, too. I guess I always do, you know."

He pulled her to him and she rested her wet cheek against the middle of his chest where it fit so perfectly. Her arms encircled his strong waist, and she could feel his powerful thighs pressing against her trembling legs through the rustle of her damp green gown. He bent his big, tawny head to drop a single caressing kiss in her fragrant hair. Yet they stood still, quiet, together. The moment in the gathering dusk and whispering rain was nearly heaven.

"I am sorry about Thomas Holland's death, Jeannette," he said low at last, and held her at arm's length as if to study her. "I wanted you to know that before we go any further."

"Thank you, Your Grace. His death was terrible, but I warrant he thought his life with me was, too."

Prince Edward frowned and she thought for a moment he was angry. "Then he was a bigger fool than I took him for,

549

ma chérie, but we must talk of other things now too."

"Aye, I do thank you and the princess for godparenting the children."

"You are welcome. It is an honor, but I spoke not of that, though I would like to see all three so you must bring them next time you come. Young Thomas, you wrote is off to Warwick."

"Oh aye, you should have seen how proud and serious he was the day he set off from Liddell, my Edward—"

She gasped to realize she had called him by that most intimate of terms, his own given name, an honor forbidden and insolent unless he granted permission. But she had thought of him for years now deep inside as her own, dear Edward even when she knew she could never have him, and now—

He took both her hands in his big, warm ones and lifted them to his mustached mouth. She could feel his breath stroke her fingers. Slowly, lingeringly, with his piercing blue eyes steady on her, he kissed the backs of her fingers, then each palm.

"You do care for me, Jeannette, tell me you do," his deep voice rasped so quietly she almost lost his words in the rush of rain.

"Of course, I do. You know I do, Your Grace."

"My Edward. I want to hear that again, and I want to hear it all the time. I want you with me everywhere in my arms like this."

He gave her a little tug and she was against him, mindlessly lifting her mouth to meet his. The kiss began tenderly but swept them both away in a whirling vortex of repeated kisses and searching, caressing hands until a jagged bolt of lightning crashed and hissed nearby to shatter their trance.

"Oh!" she breathed and pressed her open hands flat on his leather jerkin to catch her breath and stop the shaking and the swaying of the world. "Did it hit the quintain or what?"

His breath was ragged, his voice broken. "Somewhere up

on the towers, I think. We had best start back or everyone will be scandalized, and they will have enough of that soon anyway when they hear my plans. You are soaked and trembling, and I will not have you catching a chill. We will walk back along the north walls where we are protected and try to spirit you upstairs to change this gown before anyone sees you."

"I am not so very soaked, Your Grace, nor am I trembling from a chill," she shot back but she did not ask what she wanted to know most. If the court would soon be scandalized by his plans, he must be hoping to openly make her his mistress, that very thing she had vowed repeatedly to herself she could never be again. She would tell him that; she would make that entirely clear. But, foolishly, she had already shown him how weak she was with him and how one little touch could send her reeling into his arms where he could do with her whatever he wanted.

"What is the matter?" he asked over his shoulder as they hurried along in the rain shelter of the thick, stone wall. "You are pulling back. Come on, it is dark and no one will see us in this drizzle."

"And what if they would?"

He turned back to face her and pressed her lightly between his big, dark form and the stone wall as if to protect her from the rain.

"As willful as always, my Jeannette, but then, I would have you no other way. You are the Duchess of Kent now and we will not go into my position here. You, my sweetheart, are rain-wet, your hair and mine look as if we have been cavorting in the forest pond. Your sweet lips are all bruised with my kisses of which I intend to give you more, and that low-necked emerald dress which drives me to distraction even now reveals the places where my lips and the stubble of my day-old beard have rubbed your fair skin rosy-hued. If we can help it, I intend for us to do this circumspectly, and I hope the Fair Maid of Kent will cooperate."

"I am hardly a maid anymore, Your Grace—"

"And if you will not cooperate, I will have no choice but to go down in history not as a warrior-conqueror of France, but rather of one blond beauty who did not realize it was time for her to surrender to the inevitable. Come on, now, I said, we are going back in."

He sent her up the back servants' stairs of the York Tower while he went in some other way. In their hurried parting, they had decided that he would put in an appearance at evenmeal but she would not go at all. Everyone would be expecting him, but she could hardly walk in late and damp-haired also under everyone's beady-eyed stares. He would order food sent up to her rooms, spend the evening reporting on his safe delivery of the French king to his royal parents. Then, early on the morrow, she had promised to ride with him to see the builders' progress at his Palace of Kennington on the Thames near London.

Her two new English maids she had brought with her from Liddell darted up from their game of dice and coins on the parlor table when she went in. The princess had allotted her a lovely suite of chambers very near her own: she had this paneled, tapestried parlor with two spacious windows overlooking the park to the south, a charming bedroom, and a little *garde-robe* chamber.

"Oh, duchess," the petite maid Gertrude gushed, "you got caught in the rain sure enough. The dress, your coiffure is a shambles! Oh, duchess!"

"Do not fuss. I am only glad you two are here to help. I have decided since I am such a sight not to go down to evenmeal. I would be late anyway, so I am having some food sent up."

She went on into her bedroom, the two maids trailing after, appalled at the sodden destruction of their mistress' appearance over which they had labored so carefully only a little while before. They had accepted well enough the fact their duchess often went barefooted in the ponds at Liddell or sometimes wore men's breeches to ride the fields and meadows, but this was the great Plantagenet court!

Sarah and Gertrude peeled off her soaked gown, and Sarah sponged the soiled hem while Gertrude rubbed her skin with a tingling towel and combed tangles from her long blond tresses.

"Ye've caught a little chill or rash here, Duchess, all along your neck and throat," the brown-haired maid observed and clucked her tongue.

Joan seized the silk robe from the girl's hands and covered herself. "Never mind. And stop that clucking like a hen. My dear old Marta used to do that too, and I will not have it from you, girl—not until you are at least sixty. Now, go on to the door and wait for the food. Suddenly, I am famished."

She sat at her lovely carved dressing table and combed her hair herself. Aye, she had a faint, pink glow where he had seized and kissed her like that again and again. Saints, she had loved it, cherished it, wanted it and more. Only, she must be very, very careful not to let it go further unless she had assurances he would not just love her only to leave her again. She had no intention of waiting breathlessly at Liddell or here for him to visit—especially not here!

The food came amidst delicious, wafting odors—a great deal of food, so she insisted Gertrude and Sarah take some too. Awed at the exotic dishes on fine plateware and being seated to eat at the same time their mistress was, the two picked at their portions until they saw the duchess attack her food with fervor, and then they, too, reveled in seethed pike in claret, slices of stag haunch, gooseberry pastries, Brie cheese, apricots, dates, and fine Bordeaux wine.

"Laws, my lady duchess, wisht you would eat everday in your chambers," the perky-faced Sarah giggled. "Never, never seen such fine victuals."

"Aye and so much," Joan murmured. "Does he think he is feeding his army?"

Both maids looked up wide-eyed and suddenly awestruck again at sitting so improperly while their mistress sat sharing her food. "*He*, my lady duchess?" Sarah breathed. "Is *he* come back then and you saw him out in the rain?"

Four shocked eyes darted to Joan's neck and throat where her silk robe revealed the muted rosy rash which now blended with her blush.

"Now, you listen here, you two," Joan said and was about to scold both of them when a knock at the door froze them all. Joan read the looks on their startled faces, no doubt a mirror image of her own. He would not dare to come up here like this! He had said they must be circumspect, careful of scandal.

A man's voice boomed through the door even as Joan rose. "Duchess of Kent! The queen awaits an interview. Are you within?"

"Saints!" Joan cursed low and instinctively pulled her silk robe tighter. "No, leave the dishes there and, Sarah, fetch me some scarves," she hissed at her maids. "And you, Gertrude, open the door slowly and say I will be right out." She shoved Gertrude toward the door and ran after Sarah's flying feet into the bedchamber.

She could hear Gertrude's shaking voice as she opened the hall door. Joan wrapped four silk scarves around her neck and draped their flowing ends down her back while she heard Gertrude say, "Please to enter an' your will, Your Grace. The duchess, she was only taking a little nap. I will fetch her direct, Your Grace."

Joan shot herself a quick look in the mirror. The queen had sought her out here far from her own chambers when surely they were all still in the Great Hall at evenmeal. Why was she not with the king or her son just returned? She had seen her briefly with the princess the day she had come to Windsor, but there was no reason she should break propriety to come here. Even as Joan steadied herself to go back to the parlor, she heard the queen's low voice which held only a hint of Isabella's lively tones.

"My guards may wait outside and the duchess' maids also are dismissed. I wish to speak to the Duchess of Kent quite alone."

Joan halted in the narrow, paneled entry, her heart thudding. She heard people shuffling out, the door closing quietly. Why had she drunk so much of that fine Bordeaux wine he had sent her?

"Your Grace, forgive me for I was resting. What an honor to have you visit these rooms the Princess Isabella was kind enough to grant me for my short stay." Joan curtsied low, nearly at the queen's feet. "And, Your Majesty, please forgive the cluttered table, for I supped earlier."

"Set for three? And not even going down to evenmeal?" Queen Philippa intoned as her blue eyes in the plump, white face scanned the table.

The queen was elegantly gowned and coifed as usual, and the massive pleated wimple under her headpiece hid all her hair but the two foremost coils. A heavy necklace encrusted with rubies was draped across her ample, gold-brocade bosom, and a sprinkle of jewels studded the massive rings on her fingers which looked like small, white sausages.

"There seemed to be quite a lot of food sent up, Your Grace, so I fed my young maids. They are wonderfully in awe to be here at court, of course."

"But how quaint, my dear Joan, eating with your servants. I cannot imagine anyone reared at this court and who lived through that vile, French peasant uprising doing that, but no matter. You may sit now, lady."

Joan sat straight-backed in the nearest chair while the queen's small eyes under the vast white forehead studied her. "Your maids are awed to be at court—and you these days, Joan?"

"I, Your Grace?"

"He is back, of course, and has been for almost three hours, but I have not seen him. I assume, my dear, that you have."

"Prince Edward, you mean," she floundered wondering, fearing what was coming. "Aye, I ran into him just after he arrived downstairs."

"Indeed. Perhaps, then, since he obviously is not here, I may have a chance to see him soon, but for now I only wish to see you. Let us not mince words here, dear Joan, for surely we do want the same thing for His Grace, the Prince of Wales—only the best for him and his happiness always."

"Agreed, Your Majesty."

"Then you also realize he must marry—for England, for the family, even for himself." The blue eyes glittered as coldly as the stones in her big rings, Joan thought.

"In that pursuit, I would certainly wish him all happiness, Your Grace, even as you."

"Let us not mince words, I said, Joan. I want your promise you will not let the prince believe you will be waiting for him anytime he wishes to seek you out, nor will you entice the prince to marry you."

"Entice him to marry me! Indeed, Your Grace, I shall not be so presumptuous if you will not!"

"I only came to be sure that you understood the import of this or—"

"Or what? Or I shall be married to someone convenient I hardly know to please others? I have already been through that, Your Grace. Or mayhap be sent away—exiled for misbehaving like the prince's grandmother, banished to Castle Rising all these years, or like John de Maltravers to Bruges? But, Your Grace, I have had all of that for so many years. I am Duchess of Kent with titles, lands, enough of wealth and with three children to love and rear. Ask your son if you want such promises, for despite the burden of his birth, his life is surely his. And my life, at long last, for the great price I have paid, Your Majesty—is mine!"

Joan realized she had risen half out of her seat in leaning forward, and she sat back. The queen's plump chin seemed to quiver; suddenly, she looked very much beaten. "I see," she whispered and stared down at her tightly clasped hands. "Parents, royal or not, can never really trust their children not to hurt them," she said low as if to herself. "This problem with Edward is Isabella all over again only it matters so much more. I only hope, Duchess, your little brood someday shall not cause you such grief as my children have me!"

The queen got to her feet ponderously. It seemed she had shrunk despite her increasing bulk over the years. Joan rose and curtsied.

"I thank you for your concern, Your Grace," Joan said quietly, "and I pray you will not judge those too harshly who only seek love."

At the door Queen Philippa turned slowly back. "Love," she repeated, her face suddenly gone girlishly soft before it turned to pale marble again. "Love fades, poor Joan, and then there is only duty and remembrance."

Joan heard the guards snap to in the hall when the queen opened the door herself and went out. Long after it closed again, she just stood and stared at it, her thoughts racing futilely to find escape from her own duty and remembrance which pressed in on her like the stony castle walls of Windsor.

Soon after dawn stretched her rosy fingers into a cloudless sky the next day, Joan and Prince Edward set off for Kennington Palace with a guard of four discreetly armed men who rode a ways back, so it almost seemed they were alone. They chatted and reminisced but there were no plans or proposals, Joan noted, beyond showing her the fine new London palace he had been expanding and remodeling. By midmorn, almost unrecognized because of their plain riding garb, small entourage, and lack of royal banners, they arrived at Westminster to take a barge across the Thames. It was shorter, the prince said, and they would not have to be slowed by crowds in busy London that way. Scandal, Joan thought, a scandal to be seen with me. And again, for the hundredth time even today, she vowed she would not be swept away by passion only to feel its reverberating pain thereafter.

The bargemen pulled hard to row them upstream past the barren Lambeth moors to finally tie up at the newly constructed Kennington pier. Through a screen of trees, Joan saw the clean stone walls of a large palace where already a flag with the three white ostrich feathers and the Prince of Wales's motto "*Ich Dien*" waved from a turret in the warm, river breeze.

"It is a lovely site, Your Grace," she told him as he lifted her from the barge onto the pier. His hands lingered on her waist when he need only have held her hand while she stepped out herself. She had worn a dark blue kirtle and matching *surcote* all embroidered with summer flowers and her riding boots made a hollow sound on the wooden pier even as his did. They had laughed that he wore almost the same hue of perse blue tunic today under his fine embossed leather jerkin.

"A lovely site, indeed, my Jeannette—near the city and yet definitely in the country. By autumn, this path up to the buildings will be all terraced and planted. And," he went on as he tucked her hand in the crook of his arm and held it tight against his ribs, "you did promise to call me Edward today."

"So I did, Edward—my only promise for the whole day mayhap. Oh, saints, it is huge!"

Before them rose up a newly constructed Great Hall and complex of adjoining rooms with glittering windows facing the Thames. At right angles to that wing of the palace lay the prince's private quarters with views of freshly planted gardens.

"The gardens are extensive already," she noted, her free hand resting on his arm too. "The herb and green gardens look marvelous, and what are those vines on poles among all those flower beds?"

"I wanted some sequestered and shady walks and nooks out here for scorching days like this one will soon be, my Jeannette. And then, when they are thick enough, they will keep the rain off strolling lovers, too. The gardens, I am afraid, are far ahead of the completion of the interior. I had once planned to be residing here by now, but I changed my mind. The gardens were already seeded, and you can hardly stop that. But for the final decisions on decorating the interiors—come along, and I will explain."

"But where are all the workers if it is not yet finished? And who will use all these vegetables and tended herbs if you are not ready to live here?"

"Questions, questions. Come into the Great Hall with me, Jeannette. The vegetables and herbs will go across to Westminster or to the abbeys of London until I need them. And I gave the masons, carpenters, and my mastermind architect, Henry Yevele, the day off so we would not have dust and clutter as we look the place over. In here. I hope you approve."

They moved into a cool stretch of corridor through an arched entrance crested with the prince's coat of arms. The walls inside were oak panels burnished golden by sunlight filtering through the clear, glass windows.

"It is so charming, so airy. Not like a stone, protective castle at all," she murmured, awestruck at its quiet, elegant beauty.

"It is stone like a castle, but I wanted Kennington to open up to the river and trees—to be more like Woodstock. Please God, we shall never have to wall up English homes anymore with moats and towers to keep out invaders. In here, *chérie*, the Great Hall."

She gasped at the expansive grandeur of the room. It was almost a hundred feet long and half as wide with high windows set with medallions of colored glass so that the sun splashed many hues upon the beige Reigate stone and statues of kings and queens which lined the walls. A lofty musicians' gallery big enough for at least twelve players hung over the end of the room where the dais for the head table rested.

Four huge fireplaces with carved acanthus leaves spilling across their mantels stood waiting patiently for future Yule logs and roasted chestnuts. The vast stretch of floor was covered with intricate tiles inlaid with the prince's coat of arms. Struck mute by the beauty of the room, she let him lead her to the nearest fireplace.

"You do like it, my sweet?"

"It is so wonderful, Edward. I can just picture it here with a dance or banquet."

"Or just a family at dinner, Jeannette."

Her eyes lowered from the fine hammerbeam roof to slam into the crystalline blue impact of his steady gaze.

"Aye, of course," she floundered, and her shaky voice seemed not her own. "I just—well, sometimes it is comfortable for a family to eat in their own solar when not entertaining."

His tawny brows lowered over his eyes. "St. George, I would not really know of that. There is a lovely State Chamber and adjoining solar through here. Right this way, my duchess."

"And should I not now address you as Duke of Aquitaine?" she returned hoping her voice sounded light. "When I first came back to Windsor, everyone was all agog at your new title and that you would be going to live at Bordeaux to rule that huge province. Is that why you have not wanted to finish Kennington then—that you would have to live away?"

"Partly," he admitted, and took her hand again as they strolled half-finished corridors and various suites, surrounded meanwhile by ladders, scaffolding, and the smell of fresh sawdust and paint. "But now I do plan to live here at Kennington for a time before I go to Aquitaine and this will be my London base whenever I am home."

His voice trailed off as he remembered how his father had threatened not to honor him with title and duty. He wanted to share that victory with Jeannette now, only he could not bear to break the mood of showing her around. By the morrow he should have that precious papal dispensation to marry her in hand. Then he would face his parents to tell them his decision once and for all and would ask Jeannette when she could not possibly have any reason to protest.

He pointed out the window of one hallway to a range of half-timbered buildings housing the big kitchens and sprawling servants' quarters, and beyond to a chapel he told her was barely completed inside. They turned down two more hallways where he paused at a carved double door.

"I could never trace my way back out of here, my Edward," she laughed, pleased her voice sounded so normal now.

"Then, my beautiful Jeannette, you will just have to trust me, guiding you every step of the way." He swung open the doors and stepped in behind her closing them.

It was the most lovely solar chamber she had ever seen, with large glass panes to let in the light and two recessed window seats. The huge fireplace was carved with leaves and flowers to echo the frieze along the edge of the painted ceiling. The floor was of finest azure- and gold-glazed tiles set with the Plantagenet leopard and French *fleurs-de-lis*.

Tears came to her eyes at this sunlit realm of peace and grace his workmen had created here, for even bare of hangings, furniture, and carpets at this moment, it was the most enticingly intimate haven she had ever beheld.

"It is exquisite! I love it, my Edward!"

She thought for one moment he would seize her but she must have been wrong, for his eyes only looked away to a recessed doorway past the mantel. He walked over to open the door, and she moved closer to see. As she peered into the next large chamber lit by warm sunglow, his voice behind her rasped dangerously low, "The State Chamber, but no bed quite yet, damn it."

She stepped into another wonder. This bedchamber was as elegant as the solar, but more charming for its mullioned windows, ornate mantel, and painted ceilings—a painting of an azure, cloud-studded sky. But most breathtaking was the lush pile of furs, brocades, silks, and velvets all on bolts or in huge swathes spilled across the tiled floor like a great, shimmering sea.

"Saints, Your Grace! They are beautiful! Which of these will go where?"

He clicked the door closed behind him and followed her in. "Now that you have seen the principal rooms, I thought mayhap you could help me decide, love," he said. "I would pay you for your help most royally."

She shot him a quick look and took in the grin on his suddenly devilish face. She smiled back but chose to ignore the veiled taunt and knelt at the edge of the rich array of materials, stroking, examining each she could touch. He came to sit cross-legged beside her, his eyes watching as she scrutinized the bounty.

From somewhere in the room he had magically produced a leather-covered flagon and poured two golden goblets of bubbly wine.

"Oh, thank you, my Edward. My throat is parched. Then there are servants here?"

He lifted one eyebrow as his gaze went thoroughly over her, almost causing her to spill her wine on the rose-hued swath of velvet across her lap. She pressed her legs tightly together and leveled as cool a look at him as she could manage over the rim of her goblet.

"No, sweetheart. I told you, no one is here but the guards we left down on the pier. I had this placed here for us. The leather bottle keeps it cool."

"Oh. It is delicious. Look at this velvet, Edward. I really would love it on chairs and bolsters in the solar."

"Done. What else? What would you like for bed coverlet and hangings in here? This is exactly where the big bed will go. I am too tall to abide short ones, you know."

She drained half of her wine and set the goblet back away so he could not see how her hands were trembling. "The bed.

A big bed here. This azure brocade over in this stack. Look, Edward, it is the same hue as Plantagenet crests and banners and it would perfectly fit the heavenly ceiling you have had painted."

She leaned forward on her knees and put one hand down in the riot of fabrics to reach for the azure brocade. Behind her he moved, as swift as a lion, crinkling satins, crushing velvets under his big knees as he reached for her. One hand snaked around her waist and the other touched, then turned her hips. Instantly, she found herself on her back amidst the downy pile of rich materials staring up at his intense, handsome face with the painted blue sky beyond.

"Edward, let me up. We will wrinkle all of this fabric," she began, but his hands and body pressed her softly down.

"Damn all this fabric and this whole place if I cannot have you," he said only before the sweet onslaught of hands and mouth began.

He entwined his fingers in her loosely curled coiffure to hold her head still when she tried to protest. She hated the few, feeble struggles she permitted herself before wrapping her arms around his neck to return his demanding, blazing kisses. But she was so afraid of her own sweeping reaction, of screaming out her love for him, of giving and promising him anything, that she even tried to say no once deep in her throat.

His lips took hers repeatedly, pressing, turning, pulling, slanting wildly sideways one way and then the other. His slick, demanding tongue invaded her mouth again, then again; later, when she could not breathe, he raised his passion-glazed face to rake her with a look that pierced her to her very core. She thought he would speak but he only pulled her up against him with one hand around her waist and one cupping her buttocks through her mussed skirts.

He rained bites and kisses down her neck while he tugged off her disheveled *surcote* and untied and peeled down her soft linen kirtle and chemise to her waist. Dizzily, she held to his broad shoulders to stop the whirling of the room as his head bent over her breasts and he leaned her back in his iron embrace.

"Oh, oh!" she breathed as his warm lips and tongue teased to tortured peaks each rosy nipple his free hand lifted, squeezed, and caressed. "Oh, Edward, my love. Mm. Oh!"

"I love those little deep moans you always make when you let me really love you, sweetheart. Hold me. Let me love you on and on today and always."

He leaned into her again and they went down amidst the clouds of silks and velvets. All her vows, her planning, her long-rehearsed denials drowned in a raging sea of helpless futility. He could never marry her, granted, she thought, not after how his parents felt, after everything. But she would be with him like this whenever he sent a letter to her, or raised one shaggy brow, or crooked one little finger. Anywhere. Always. Now.

His tongue and mustache grazed a rasping, molten trail across her silken skin and anywhere he touched her. He marveled that she was as yielding as water. He had not been wrong to wait all these years, he told himself through the rush of passion so powerful he could barely hold himself back from just spreading those elegantly tapered legs and taking her. He needed her to fill him as much as he must fill her even now. He would tell his parents tonight and on the morrow he would ask her formally. They could wait no longer and must be wed. A betrothal on the morrow. She would be his forever from the morrow on.

He was gasping for breath when he tore his mouth away from her lush breasts. Her hair had spilled wildly loose across the rainbow of rich colors under her; her ivory skin had taken on a rosy blush everywhere. He tore off his jerkin and tunic and tossed them somewhere behind him. Even as he fumbled with his belt, she sat up in a tumbled curtain of champagne hair and moved her hands and then her lips enticingly across his golden-haired chest and shoulders. And when he sat completely naked next to her, her eyes went possessively over him with a boldness that shook him to his very soul.

He pulled her to him, reveling in her curving softness against his hard, angular body. Her skirts, caught about her rounded hips, suddenly infuriated him, and he yanked them down her shapely legs in one good pull so that she lay completely nude beside him on their bed of colors, her alabaster skin washed in sweet July sunglow from the windows. His eyes drank in her beauty while, like a man who had never had any power over anything where this woman was concerned, he surrendered his love and body to the adoration of hers.

Again he kissed her everywhere, and her kisses and bites seared his skin. She kneaded and grasped his back muscles as he knelt between her legs and moved closer; her nails raked his lower back in wild, little circles of ecstasy.

He pressed closer to her, his intense gaze devouring her beautiful, impassioned face as she moved seductively against him. She bit her lower lip in the rapture of longing as he pressed against her moist warmth and drove slowly in.

He felt at a white-hot peak at their first joining as though he could not bear the agony of waiting any longer. She moved against him, clinging, wrapping her silken limbs around his powerful thighs and back. Deep, deep in her throat, she moaned his most intimate and frequently forbidden of names.

"Edward. Oh, my Edward. Love me. Love me, please."

"I do. I have and always will, my own Jeannette."

When he began the rhythmic rocking, driving into her as she had desperately dreamed and desired for so long, she thought she must surely die of pure joy. She feathered half-hysterical kisses down his muscular throat and across his powerful shoulders dusted with golden hair. She bit and licked at his earlobes to make his increasingly rapid motions in her even more frenzied.

And then, he swept her around and away so far up into that azure sky over his mussed head that she lost all control and could only cling to him while they sailed aloft together in a cerulean heaven of their own making. Finally, they spiraled back down to rest on the softest, coolest sea of shimmery silks the color of rarest rainbows.

Chapter Twenty-Six

All that night after she had been to Kennington with the prince, Joan paced her bedroom at Windsor in dizzying circles while her two maids slept in the outer chamber. Of course he loved her, wanted to have her, as he put it—she believed all that now. He had said all those things again at their parting this evening as well as assuring her they would be together from now on and that she was to trust him to care for her always. He had left written orders behind at Kennington for his workers, carefully describing the fabric samples she had chosen which must be used to complete each room. Saints, she saw the royal handwriting on the palace wall clearly enough—he had decided Kennington would be her home while she lived in elegant splendor as his acknowledged, well-beloved mistress.

She stopped her furious circling of the room to lean on the small, deeply recessed window ledge. Outside it was that tenuous silver-gray which hovered just before dawn. The whole night had passed; she had paced in circles and thought in circles and arrived absolutely nowhere.

He had said he must see his parents to explain things and then he would speak with her this afternoon about their strategies. Strategies! Did he think she was another town to be conquered or battle to be won? She had a name, a heritage, and family to worry about, and his strategies for her would just never do however much she loved him.

She began to dress hurriedly in the same riding outfit she had worn to Kennington as her frenzied thoughts rattled on. She could never be another Fair Rosamonde to be hidden away in a bower to be visited when he had time. Edward would no doubt ask her to go with him to Aquitaine next year, but bastard children born here or there would still be bastards.

It was her fault, she scolded herself again as she yanked on her riding boots. Her fault not only for loving him so desperately but for leading him on, aye, for letting him *have* her, as he put it, on their first full day back together after years of separation. His beguiling smile; his lean, manly body; a stunning new palace to decorate at her whim, and she had capitulated as completely as any French town he had ever conquered. Saints, there was only one thing to do to seize control of her life whatever the cost of passion's pain.

She opened the door to the outer chamber. "Gertrude, Sarah, get up. I need you."

They stumbled in bleary-eyed, and Gertrude stubbed her toe on the leg of the dressing table.

"Heavens, you ninnies, be careful. Now listen to me. Get your cloaks, take a wall sconce from the hall, and send a linkboy from downstairs to the stables. I want my horse saddled immediately and two of the guards and the squire I brought from Liddell found and roused. I am going home this morn. You two will pack and follow on the morrow with the other guard."

"Home? Already, milady?" Sarah protested. "But we only been at Windsor these four days an' you said—"

"Forget what I said. Gertrude, if your toe is all right, you two go on now."

She left a hurried note on the little table of her room for Edward, her dear Edward, and said a quick prayer over it he would love her enough not to curse her or follow her either:

My Dearest E.,

There is so much I would say, but let it be only this. I have loved you from the start and knew it not. I do know the truth—and full pain—of that love now.

Fortune's wheel has spun again to put us within reach, but now I see it must go no further.

Please understand and let me go though I shall always love you.

Bless you, my Edward, and your great destiny.

J.

She left another quick note for Princess Isabella, and in a half hour she was mounted with her startled little band of Liddell retainers although the squire could not be found; by dawn the walls and towers of Windsor were mere child's toys in the Thames Valley below. By late afternoon, she was home.

She stood on shaky legs still holding her horse's reins in cramped, gloved fingers and stared glumly about the familiar courtyard of her beloved fortified manor house. What was that he had said to her only yesterday? "Please God, we shall never have to wall up English homes anymore with moats and towers to keep out invaders." Aye, that was it. But now, eternally, her invader would be here within these walls, within her heart, for the invader was the love she would always carry for him. How different this place looked when she thought of it that way, as a sanctuary invaded by what she could never have, by what she had chosen to lose. Dear saints, how had it ever come so quickly to this, and yet she knew what she must do.

"Emmett! Jonathan!" she shouted to the old pair of guards who had watched over Liddell's gatehouse for years. The men who had ridden hard in with her from Windsor turned back to stare at her as they led their mounts off toward the stables. She knew they had glanced askance at her and whispered all the way home, but she did not have to explain a thing to them if she chose not to. Let them all think she had gone insane—become a recluse from the outside world even as her mother had years before.

"Aye, milady," Old Emmett called from the gatehouse

entrance. As always, the old man turned his cap nervously in his gnarled hands and shuffled his feet when he spoke to her.

"I want you, Jonathan, and whoever else it takes to pull up the drawbridge," she called to him and heard someone behind her gasp in surprise.

"Duchess," Thomas, one of her guards, put in as he ran across the courtyard from his horse. "Are we being pursued? Should we to arms?"

"No," she told him, told them all in a loud, commanding voice. She was exhausted, grieved, right on the knife's edge of a crying jag, and they dared to question her, to protest. "No," she said. "I just want it up for a while, that is all, so do it!"

Old Emmett shuffled across the cobbled courtyard toward her, his wrinkled face crumpled in a frown. "Doubt it even works, my lady duchess. Hain't been up fer years a course. No need here'bouts."

"There is a need. I say so. Oil it. Fix it or whatever, but get it closed. Is that understood?"

She did not wait for the bumbling answer nor to be subjected to their whispers or pitying glances as she spun on her booted heel and strode into the house. On the steps she nearly collided with Roger Wakeley, lute in hand.

"*Sacrebleu*, Duchess Joan! Back already? How was His Grace? What is all the yelling?"

She glared at the kindly, smiling face and charged on up the steps with him in her wake. In her own solar at last, she stripped off her gloves and threw them on the table, then collapsed in a chair. Roger stopped, looking precariously balanced across the table from her, his face all too obviously disappointed.

"I am really tired from the ride back, Master Roger, and wish to have some time alone. I will see the children as soon as I have composed myself, and I shall call for you later."

"You evidently left Windsor in some haste. And the children are not here. You did tell Madeleine they could go to the summer fair at Chatham, you know, and they went with Lord Wrothesby and his niece as you had said they might. Bella was thrilled. They cannot possibly be back before the morrow as they were to spend a night at Wrothesby Hall en route both ways. It was your suggestion, you know."

"Aye, fine, I hear you. I am not ranting or raving about it, am I? I told them well enough they could go, and you should have gone too. No better place to find a few new love songs of fair romance, eh, Roger? And close the door as you go out. And see if the old fools at the gatehouse have pulled up the drawbridge as I ordered them—please."

"The drawbridge—that rusted old thing? Duchess, have you—are you fleeing from someone?"

It disturbed her that she had seemed to lose control of her voice, of her words. "No! No, of course not, only mayhap from myself, though that is nothing new. Saints, Roger, just get out and leave me to myself. Now!"

She could tell he considered disobeying her, but after a hesitant moment, he turned away, went quietly out, and closed the door. She sat. She stared. She wept. She remembered. At last she fell on the bed and slept in great heaves of rolling dreams like a frightened little craft tossed by huge, weltering waves of agonized seas.

When she woke at dawn the next day, she was sprawled across her bed, stiff and sore under a coverlet someone had draped over her. She sat and stretched. Her stomach was cramped with hunger but she drank only wine left on the table and at last washed yesterday's road dust from her body and her long hair. She let her damp tresses dry and curl themselves in the growing heat of the July day. One window had been left wide ajar and out there somewhere on the slate roof, one stupid bird kept warbling his song as though nothing had happened. She lay back on her bed ignoring the slow spread of water from her damp hair across the linen pillowcase beneath her and stared at the shadowy underside of her bed canopy for endless minutes.

Sometime later she heard Roger's voice, then a sharp rap

on her door. "Go away, Master Roger. I do not want to see anyone."

"But I need to see you."

"Is Vinette all right?"

Brazenly, he opened the door without permission to enter and poked his head in. "Vinette is normal for Vinette," he said, his usually bland voice angry. "And how about you?"

"If Vinette is all right, go away. You might sing to her a little while. It always calms her to have you sing."

"My dear duchess, Vinette, as we both know, is well enough lost to this world since she believes her Pierre died of plague back in Normandy and you would not let her stay forever at his grave. She is not changed. She sits and stares at corners of her room, even as you evidently intend to do. You are not your poor, sad, helpless lady mother to handle losing him this way, dear duchess. I cannot bring myself to believe it, but is that what has happened?"

She saw he had come much closer as she sat up on the side of the bed and swung her feet down. Saints, but she was dizzy.

"I do not wish to discuss it, Roger, and I have asked you to leave me alone," she said low. Why did not the fond fool just go? Aye, she had thought of her mother closed up in this room for years after she lost the man she loved, but this was not like that at all. Or not like the demented, ruined girl downstairs who moaned and wept for her lost love. No, not like them at all!

"Did they—is the drawbridge secure?" she heard herself ask him.

"Aye, the damn rusty thing is up. I only hope you do not intend for all of us to starve walled up here as we are. I hope we can get it down when the children return. You do intend at least to let your children into this little fortress you are making, do you not? Castles today hardly need walls anymore with moats and towers since peace with the French, I dare say."

"Get out, get out! Go spy somewhere or sing somewhere!

572

Go play fond lovesongs elsewhere, but not here!"

The look he gave her was one of pity rather than concern or anger and for that she hit her fist on her bed after he went out and closed the door in maddening silence. Then, she sat frozen as he dared to sit right outside in the hall and strum the melody to a song she had made her favorite since Thomas had died and she had dared to hope the destiny hinted at in the old astrologer Morcar's charts might become reality:

> Sweet passion's pain doth pierce mine heart,
> For I have loved thee from the start,
> But foolishly behind high walls
>   I hid such proof
>   Nor saw this truth.
>
> Sweet passion's pain doth urge me plead
> That I might be thy love indeed,
> But blindingly and armored bright
>   I hid such proof
>   Nor saw this truth.
>
> And now sweet passion's pain doth teach
> That my last chance must be great reach,
> For wildly doth Dame Fortune's wheel
>   Spin by such proof
>   Nor halt for truth.
>
> Welcome sweet passion's pain until
> My heart shall recognize its will.
> Whatever prophecies proclaim,
>   I know such proof,
>   Accept this truth.

She wanted to scream at him to stop, but it was all too perfect, too ordained—even destined. When he sang the lyrics again from the other side of the closed door, it was as if she herself sang them accepting the truth of inescapable, inevitable reality. Saints, she could probably survive without Edward, Prince of Wales, but she could never really live without him. And she wanted to live, very, very much.

"Roger!"

He opened the door and nearly fell into the room. "Aye, my duchess?"

"I feel better now. I need some food. The children are not back, are they?"

"No, Duchess. And if they were, they would find your blessed drawbridge stuck."

"Oh, saints. I should never have done that. Gertrude and Sarah should be home today, too. I have been acting crazy, I know it, so you need not lecture me again."

"I? Never, milady. But, is there something else you have done you should not have? When you fled back so suddenly from Windsor like that after I was so certain—"

"Please do not start! Aye, I left him! I ran away like a coward because I could never be his wife, and I could not face more of these separations like we have had over the years."

"Not be his wife? Whyever not? What has happened then? I know for a fact he always intended it, dreamed of it."

"Hell's gates, so the master Plantagenet spy of all times speaks! Dreamed of it? Intended it? Well, so have I, but what does that matter to the king and queen? To duty and necessity? To England? I—betrothed, wed, unbetrothed, wed again—I, a widow of a minor knight with three children—I, a rabble-rouser over my father's execution to boot—it is utterly impossible, my dear fellow lutenist. Aye, mayhap I am crazy like Vinette. Do you know what he planned? To have me as an acknowledged mistress, aye, with a velvet cage—a whole palace—to await his visits, but a wife—impossible! Now just leave me alone and tell them I will be right out. St. George, dearest Roger, I have made such a mess of things, left him, insulted the queen too, and I shall never make things aright! Just go on now!"

He retreated swiftly without another word but left the

door wide open. She brushed away her tears instantly and tried to catch her breath from her tirade. She rose to stare at her blurred image in the mirror and dusted rice powder on her cheeks and nose to mute their shine. She seized a green ribbon to tie her masses of hair back, slipped on her comfortable old felt shoes, and walked out.

She went down by the servants' back staircase toward the end of the courtyard near the gatehouse. They would probably all laugh at her but she would make amends for yesterday's rampage by standing there to encourage them while they repaired the drawbridge and lowered it. Word would be all over the shire soon that the Duchess of Kent had gone daft.

She heard Vinette Brinay's plaintive voice down the lower hall where she had a small room in the servants' quarters. Joan was glad she had brought the poor wretch with them from Normandy despite the fact she took some watching and kept people awake by chattering to herself at the oddest times. Aye, having the girl here was a sad reminder of earlier, unhappy times, but then she had never really felt more desperately unhappy than she did now, so what did it matter?

She stopped at Vinette's door, pleased to see the chamber's window was open wide and Lynette the cook had taken a few minutes to visit. Lynette peeled peaches and Vinette merely stared at nothing, talking to herself in her singsong voice.

"Oh, milady duchess, you are up," Lynette cried and tried to gather her bowls to stand.

"No, sit, just sit. I only thought to look in on Vinette before I go out to help the men lower the drawbridge."

"Oh, aye, an' that is good. Drovers and carters be through soon enough mayhap an' they would not believe their eyes if it be closed after all these years."

"Well, aye, but we shall fix it right away. I really just wanted it tested in case we ever need it. And how are you, Vinette?"

The gaunt, eternal haggard look of grief never left the maid's face but her eyes lighted somewhat at Joan's voice or her own name. "I am fine, fine for such a sad day," the girl went on as Lynette's eyes popped to hear less than gibberish from her. "Is he here yet then? Has he come?"

Joan's heart leapt at the strange questions, but she beat down both her annoyance and surprise. "No, my dear. Not yet, but never give up hope."

"Oh, I do not, no, never. I used to, but now I know he will come back for me."

Joan's eyes filled with tears as she nodded to the startled Lynette and backed from the room. She leaned against the wall in the corridor and summoned back by sheer will her newly won self-control. She forced herself out into the warm July sunlight of the cobbled courtyard. The brightness nearly stunned her and even as she repeated Vinette's foolish words to herself—I know—he will—come back—for me— she heard her men's excited voices from the crenelated battlement above the drawbridge of the gatehouse.

She lifted her skirts and hurried up the steps. Four of her men were leaning through the stone elbow rests for archers which cut into the wall at regular intervals, and Roger Wakeley was with them already.

"Roger, what is it?" she demanded. "Did they get it to go back down?"

When he spun to face her, a huge grin transformed his features. "I just sent a squire to fetch you, Duchess Joan. No, the bridge is not fixed, but see for yourself—there is someone demanding entry and I only hope you are prepared to deal with it."

She pushed past the hovering man into the narrow embrasure. Below, on the part of the solid bridge left before the gap where the wooden drawbridge had lifted away, all alone on a tall black destrier, sat Edward, Prince of Wales. She gasped and only Roger's hand on her waist kept her from toppling dizzily backward.

"Saint George, Duchess Joan of Kent, it is about time you

576

dared to show your pretty face!" Prince Edward bellowed up at her.

And saints! Saints, one hand rested on his sword hilt—but he was smiling!

Her whirling mind and pounding heart almost kept her from grasping his next words: "If you, Jeannette, are not the most difficult, impossible, willful woman in the kingdom, I will give up Aquitaine! Have *your* men get this damned bridge down before I return with *my* men I left down the way at an inn, storm this little place, and take its mistress hostage!" He grinned up at her again in a blinding flash of white teeth under the tawny mustache.

"The mistress of this little place may be difficult and willful or what you say, Your Grace, but she is prepared to hold out until she hears yours terms!" Her own brazen words and tone of voice shocked her; several of her men gasped, and Roger Wakeley had the nerve to snicker behind her.

Despite her bravado, her men ran back into the upper room of the gatehouse off this small rampart and she could hear them hammering and cursing at the old rusted drawbridge chains within. Below, at the edge of the bridge, Prince Edward dismounted and gazed up at her, despite the July sun bright in his face.

"Terms, my sweetheart? All right, though I had planned for a more private place. I will have naught from you but unconditional surrender and yet I offer you the same. Saint George, my love, the Archbishop of Rochester should be here soon to hear us plight our troth and it will be spread throughout the kingdom that the Prince of Wales's princess-to-be makes a dolt of him by locking him out of her home! Now either get that damned bridge up or toss me a rope!"

Roger Wakeley cheered while Joan just stared. Her Edward looked so frustrated, so handsome, so in earnest as he stood below, shading his blue, blue eyes with one big hand to see her better. She tried to answer, to tell him she loved him, but tears coursed down her face and she could only nod wildly. In the tumble of thoughts and joyous emotions, she heard the grating creak of the old, iron chains lowering the bridge.

She wiped her wet cheeks on her sleeves, leaned out once more to be sure he was really there, then ran down the narrow steps to the courtyard. She stood waiting, trembling, while the grinding, creaking chains lowered the bridge and inched up the iron portcullis. Her legs shook beneath her as she stood rooted to the small piece of cobbled courtyard while the horse and man appeared bit by bit through the shaded archway. The drawbridge thudded into place and in that instant she darted toward him.

Either she jumped or he picked her up to swing her; she was never really certain. His kiss was demanding and possessive; his hands strong and sure as always.

"I ought to break your beautiful little neck for this stupid trick," he cursed low among the love words, but when she nodded tearfully, he added, "but instead I shall just tie you to my life and to my bed with every legal and religious chain I can find."

She spoke so incoherently through her smiles and tears that he finally just scooped her up in his arms and strode in out of the hot sunlight with her. Her arms held tightly to his neck and she did not budge even when she heard him order someone to ride for his men at an inn down the road or when Roger Wakeley called out to him the directions upstairs to the solar. She swayed in his embrace up the curve of stairs, pressing her cheek to his tunic, her senses overwhelmed by his nearness.

In the cool dimness of the room he strode to the bed with her, but evidently decided suddenly against putting her down on it. Instead, he stood her by the open window, leaning her back against the high sill and holding her steady with both strong hands on her waist.

"Are you all right, my love? It is essential you understand what I am saying—what I am asking of you."

He was so big, yet suddenly he looked more like a frightened little boy. She bit her lower lip to keep from bursting into tears of joyful hysteria and nodded.

"I would have you for my wife, to be Princess of Wales. All is arranged with the king and queen. All is agreed. My esquire has returned from Avignon with dispensations and a marriage license from the pope. I have hired chantry priests to pray for us, and as you have seen, Kennington awaits its lord and lady after their wedding this October. Say aye, my sweetheart. Say something. Saint George, my Jeannette, we have been through hell and back these many years we have known each other, but I have never doubted this moment. Tell me 'aye' or, so help me, I will force your compliance!"

Through a blinding veil of tears, she smiled and lifted three fingertips to his mustached lips. "I surrender, my dear love Edward. You do have my compliance. I love you so. Forgive me for fleeing Windsor, but I was so afraid and confused, so terrified of being parted again from you that I was crazy enough to cause that parting myself."

He curled her fingers around his and pressed them to his warm lips as she spoke. "If marriage is what you want, then nothing will stop me from facing it with you, only I do not want to be a scandal, Edward, a problem, or disappointment to you ever. The queen—"

"She told me what she said to you and that you claimed a right to rule your own life now, my love. I wish you had told me she had come to you. I was trying very hard to protect you from all that, but it is all behind us now. They do want me to marry, Jeannette. They know your beauty, your strength, and your fine blood—Plantagenet and pure English, and they do want an heir from their Prince of Wales."

She smiled and, to her own dismay as well as his obvious delight, blushed hot at the thought of unhurried nights in bed, nights no longer forbidden but sanctioned, and even hoped for.

"My exquisite little maid Jeannette," he murmured and pulled her gently full length against him. "My fiery little maid who blushes as fair at thirty-one as she did at sixteen. I always meant to have you, my sweetheart, even from the first look that day in the muddy quintain yard. You drove me out of my senses thereafter, and I could not fathom anything but having you to wife."

She snuggled closer. "I know, but I fought so hard at first because of what had happened between our fathers and my fear you could control me at your whim."

"Saint George, no worry for that," he said, his velvety low voice suddenly gone to that familiar, teasing tone she had grown to love. "Just try to get rid of me and I will follow you anywhere, storm any well-fortified castle single-handed, yank down an armored drawbridge with one blast from my royal nostrils—"

She giggled then despite the solemnity of the hour. Her laughter warmed him so, he laughed too until they clung together weakly, silent again.

They lifted their heads at noise in the courtyard, the clomping of many hoofs on cobbles. "Probably my men," he said and the spell was broken.

"Or my children with their nursemaid and the Wrothesbys."

"Or the Archbishop of Rochester with his entourage. I guess it will be like this for us from now on, my Jeannette, but I swear to you, we will have private moments too, even beyond those hours in our own curtained beds, wherever we may be."

She tilted her head to smile up at him. "Aye, my Edward. Big beds, I hope, for you are much too tall to abide a small one."

He smiled but she could tell his quick mind was dashing ahead. Gently he took her wrist and pulled her over to the table in the center of the room.

"Look, love, before we go out, we shall say the words—alone, before we say them for the archbishop and all the staring faces. In my fury to leave after I saw those notes of yours, I left the ring I had chosen and the other jewels at Windsor, so this big signet ring of mine will have to do for now."

"Wait, my lord. I have a ring that will do—one you gave me years ago and I have cherished always."

He watched her move away to open a little carved oak coffer. She knelt and shoved aside clothes and dried herbs, then her precious treasures she had hoarded over the years— his letters, Morcar's star charts which had foretold their mutual destinies, and then the little green beryl ring entwined with gold filigree of twisted ivy leaves.

"The beryl ring," he said in a hushed voice as she placed it in his big palm. "A beryl ring which gives victory in battle and protection. And it has done that for both of us. Aye, my love Jeannette, this ring will do for now."

It looked so delicate in his fingers as he slipped it on her hand. "I, Edward, plight thee, Joan, my troth, as God is my witness," he said low.

She stared down through dazzling tears at her hands in his. "I, Joan, plight thee, Edward, my troth, as God is my witness."

He bent eagerly to claim his betrothal kiss, a sweet caress of tenderness which then deepened swiftly to stun her with its sensual power. She swayed against him even as a man's voice coughed pointedly behind them. The kiss was ended; they both turned, still in their embrace, to face a beaming Roger Wakeley.

"Everyone is arriving, Your Grace," Roger managed. "His Eminence, the archbishop too. The kitchens are going mad to prepare a meal. And I believe the duchess has not eaten for going on two days now, so—"

"No food?" the prince glowered at her, but then he winked. "Saint George, my love, I have not eaten for too long either, but we shall see them all below and then make up for lost time—all the lost time over all the years, I swear it."

As they gazed raptly into each other's eyes, the watchful man, the room, duties all faded to nothingness. Then, someone yelled in the courtyard below; someone bellowed a distant laugh. The prince's head jerked up and he shot a grin at Roger Wakeley.

"Hell's gates, musician, do not just stand gawking. I do not intend to take you with us to Windsor, Kennington, or clear to Aquitaine to just gawk. Give us a tune—a good one of love conquering all—a good romance of love's sweet passion victorious at last."

Roger and the prince laughed loudly at some enormous unspoken jest, and tears of sheer joy clung to Joan's lashes as they went down together to greet their guests.

Afterword

Joan, Duchess of Kent, stood stock still on the morn of her wedding, October tenth, 1361, while her maids-in-waiting and the hovering Princess Isabella fussed over the final touches of her hair and crown. Outside, the courtyards of Windsor Castle echoed with the continued pealing of chapel and town bells which would be silenced today only during the actual marriage ceremony. In the St. George's Chapel, arrayed more magnificently than it ever had been for an Order of the Garter Ceremony, the Archbishop of Canterbury, Simon Islip, four bishops, and the abbot of Westminster awaited; in the Upper Ward of the castle the great and noble of the realm awaited; on the roads of England between Windsor and Kennington Palace in London, their honeymoon destination, thousands awaited; and most thrilling of all, downstairs, Edward, her beloved Prince of Wales, awaited.

"The perfect touch—all these jewels and this gold-threaded embroidery," the Princess Isabella was saying again. "Gorgeously exquisite, lovelier by far than that dress of mine I had at Bruges, do you remember, Jeannette? Oh, and this beautiful foliated princess crown Their Graces gave you! By the Virgin's Veil, I shall have some way to go to outdo this when I wed with my Ingelram!"

Joan smiled, nodded, and forced back tears of joy. She felt very calm and peaceful deep within, and yet all of the festivities of the last few days, the arrival of a papal blessing, the replighting of the troth four days ago, the excitement of her children—she felt utterly swept away by everyone else's

583

joy as well as her own. But she wanted to savor, to cherish every moment of this precious day.

Two maids tilted a big mirror for her so she could glimpse herself before they went down to join the prince. Aye, it was magic. How proud dear old Morcar would have been to see his predictions come true and how her precious, long-departed Marta would have scolded that she had told her so, and why did her bonny lassie never listen?

Saints, she was bonny on this day of days, she marveled. Two huge wheat-colored plaits of hair encircled the rest of her tresses as they tumbled down her back, and a gold princess crown set with rubies and emeralds graced her head. The ivory-hued kirtle of rich India silk draped to a four-foot train edged in gold embroidery to match the ribbing of her tight-fitting bodice and sleeves. Over her kirtle, a gold satin *surcote* lined in royal ermine fell away to reveal a graceful girdle of golden links set with rubies to match her crown.

Every time she breathed in she smelled sweet essence of roses from her body and hair, and tiny embroidered rosebuds even decorated her pointed ivory satin slippers. Her only jewels other than the crown were her big betrothal ring, an emerald circled with opals, and the delicate beryl ring she wore today on the small finger of her right hand.

It had taken fourteen seamstresses four weeks to embroider and create all of this, but Joan and Isabella had been careful to guard its view from the court. Soon enough though, this bridal array would be as public as her busy life these last few months of their betrothal, and soon all this exquisite grandeur would be public domain as their wedding procession rode from Windsor to Kennington through a wildly bedecked London.

"Are we ready to go down, Jeannette?" Isabella's musical voice lilted.

"Aye, of course, only I told the guards my lutenist, Roger Wakeley, was to be admitted up here before we joined the others. Has he not arrived? I just want to know what my Edward thought of the song I wrote for him."

"You can ask him soon enough yourself, Jeannette," Isabella scolded and shooed the clustered maids away with a quick flick of royal wrist. "Oh, for heaven's sake, here he is then. Aye, summon that man in! He is no spy, I warrant."

Joan caught Roger Wakeley's eyes at the princess' last, unintentioned words, and they laughed together in the awkward silence.

"Aye, not a spy, I warrant," Joan said low so only he could hear, "for the prince and I have decided to make an honest man of this rogue and spy."

"My dear duchess, about to be my dear princess," he returned jauntily, "I do at least thank you and His Grace for saving me from the king's wrath when he heard I had not gone to sing to sadistic, vile Pedro in Castile as he ordered me."

"Saints, my Roger, His Grace, the king, in the joy of the moment has pardoned even the worst offenders like the Princess Isabella—and me," Joan said and Isabella, too, joined in their laughter. In one fell swoop of benevolent scepter lately, it seemed the king had indeed forgiven one and all for previous rebellious behavior, including even Isabella who had publicly declared her love for the wealthy French hostage, Ingelram de Coucy.

"I must report that the prince, Duchess, loved your nuptial song and bid me come back to sing it to you before you come downstairs. His exact words, I believe were, 'Tell my princess it is long overdue time she realized she will not flee' and something to the effect that at Kennington tonight he will prove the truth of these sweet lyrics, or some such—"

Isabella gasped and giggled while Joan blushed hot despite the welcome truth of the prince's brazen reply.

"Well then, Master Roger, sing me the song once before we go down to face this day with joy and anticipation," Joan declared. "Sing on, my friend, and next time after you shall sing for the new and very happy Princess of Wales."

Isabella fluttered her hands and skirts, nervous to be off, but Joan just closed her eyes and concentrated on the song she had sent by Roger to the prince today, but would no doubt sing for him herself with her own voice and new ivory-inlaid lute over the years to come:

> That heart my heart has in such grace
> That of two hearts one heart we make;
> That heart has brought my heart in case
> To love that heart that loveth me.
>
> Which cause gives cause to me and mine
> To serve that heart of sovereignty
> And still to sing this latter line:
> To love that heart that loveth me.
>
> Whatever I say, whatever I sing,
> Whatever I do, that heart shall see
> That I shall serve with heart-loving
> That loving heart that loveth me.
>
> This knot thus knit who shall untwine,
> Since we that knit it do agree?
> It shall not slip, but both encline
> To love that heart that loveth me.

The sweet melody and lyrics mingled in her mind with the peal of bells in the clear autumn air, as Joan smiled at Roger, embraced Isabella, and floated downstairs. Maids appeared to lift the trains of her kirtle and *surcote*; trumpets blared as they rounded the sweep of staircase, and she saw her bridegroom below with all the glittering Plantagenets. His lean, tall brothers called out good wishes as Isabella chatted something in her ear all the way down. The prince's friend Nick Dagworth shouted a comment to her, but it was as if no one stood below waiting but her tall, blond Edward fully arrayed as Prince of Wales as she had never seen him.

His crystalline blue eyes captured her misty violet gaze as he smiled at her and took her hand. She marveled anew at his towering height and overpowering physical presence as though their love was beginning all new and tender again. Azure and gold silk stretched across his broad shoulders decorated with the royal English leopards and French lilies that would soon be her official coat of arms too; yet had not her Edward promised her that someday their son, the next Prince of Wales, would claim her own chained deer on a bed of ivy for his own royal insignia?

The prince's heavy, jewel-encrusted crown was a larger version of her own. His purple velvet and ermine cape split away at his side to reveal his wide gold belt with the big ceremonial sword emblazoned with the proud Garter Knight insignia.

"My dearest love Edward," she murmured, suddenly awed at his magnificence.

He bent close for one moment and his warm, fragrant breath stirred a curling tendril of hair along her temple. "Come with me now forever, my sweetheart. This moment has been awaiting much, much too long."

The ceremony began as a beautiful blur of colorful images and sweet sounds: rows of vibrant banners, the boys' chapel choir's dulcet tones, the drone of the Latin ceremony, the repeating of their vows in French and Latin. To the side where the royal family sat, Joan's eye caught that of King Edward; he nodded solemn-faced as if to encourage her as the ceremony went on, and she looked back toward the ornately accoutered altar.

Her attention wandered only one other time when the prince helped her arise from the silk *prie-dieu* after prayer and smiled that rakish, almost boyish smile of his under the clipped, tawny mustache. Her heart fluttered, her insides careened and cartwheeled wildly at the stunning impact of her love for this man who had pursued her fiercely through the varied perils and sweet pains of these turbulent years.

Peals of bells high above in stone-vaulted arches exploded as the old archbishop declared the final *pax vobiscum*. Courtiers smiled, laughed, but tears of raptured bliss sprang anew to Joan's eyes when she caught a quick glimpse of her little Bella's excited face as she and the prince walked out arm in arm into the sunny tang of autumn air.

The wedding banquet staggered the Great Hall with its opulent and varied fare. A thousand dishes, a thousand chattering, laughing courtiers, Joan thought. The entire crowded hall reverberated, "To the Prince and Princess of Wales!" A whirl of toasts, blessings, and farewells surrounded them as the prince and Joan led their mounted cortège of courtiers and guards slowly out of the gates of Windsor to progress triumphantly toward London.

All along the way through fields, hamlets, and towns, the people took their new Princess of Wales to their stout English hearts. Countryfolk hung from tree limbs, waving, shouting; little boys ran for miles along the roadways; milkmaids and harvesters on a day of rest threw flowers from roofs and windows.

By the time they entered London past Westminster and up the Strand, the shouts and clangings of London's church bells were so deafening, the Princess Joan could no longer hear the gay silver bells which decorated her own silken caparisoned white horse. Like the prince, she waved and smiled and nodded until she thought her arm would lift no more.

Crowded Fleet Street was awash with ribbons, banners, tapestries, and flowing bolts of cloth draped out windows to make a silken canopy above. Lovely maidens threw rose petals and silken *fleur-de-lis* until the horses were fetlock deep in them. The city conduits ran with fine French wines which the royal cortège sampled when they were met by the Lord Mayor of London and city aldermen before progressing into the city proper at Temple Bar.

Now their procession of courtiers and guards was swelled by Londoners in painted wagons decorated with captured French tapestries from the prince's great victories of Crécy and Poitiers, and, at one spot, the Prince and Princess of Wales gaped as girls in gilded cages suspended over the streets scattered gold and silver leaves to the crowds. Past

St. Pauls, over a wildly bedecked London Bridge, their entourage headed down the Southwark Road toward their waiting Kennington Palace.

The Prince and Princess of Wales paused under the Southwark entrygate newly carved with both their proud family crests as the setting October sun gilded the joyous, frenzied scene. Both blond and fair, so striking, so in love, the newly wedded couple turned and waved at the courtiers and townfolk who had followed them this far today.

"You got her now, sure 'nough, Yer Grace!" a rough male voice in the raucous, cavorting crowd bellowed, and the prince turned to his princess and took her hand to the cheers and whoops of all.

"Go on and kiss her, kiss her then!" the chant welled up to drown any solemn thought or memories of other, unhappy days. "Kiss her, kiss her then! Kiss her, kiss her then!"

As if there were nothing which could delight him more, the prince tipped up his princess' lovely face with just one big finger and kissed her then.

Author's Note

Joan and her prince resided both in England and in Aquitaine in southern France during the years to come. King Edward III, however, outlived Prince Edward and was eventually succeeded by one of Joan and Edward's two sons, who was crowned Richard II. As Prince Edward had promised his Jeannette, their son as king did adopt her own crest of a deer collared and chained with gold on a bed of Liddell Manor ivy.

Princess Isabella married her young French suitor Ingelram de Coucy and moved to France with him. Yet, despite a luxurious life there and the birth of two daughters, they were separated after twelve years of marriage when Isabella returned home to live the rest of her life in England.

John de Maltravers, whom the Princess of Wales evidently either forgave or forgot at last, died in his own bed in 1365, perhaps with as much guilt on his conscience for Joan's father's sad death as Joan's royal father-in-law took to his grave.

But for two lovers whose destinies entwined at last in "this knot thus knit," sweet passion's pleasure was theirs at last.